THE OTHER
AMERICA

THE OTHER AMERICA

LANA SANTORELLI

To order additional copies of this book, contact:
Xlibris Corporation
1-888-795-4274
www.Xlibris.com
Orders@Xlibris.com
16490-SANT

For Lenny
My Partner, My Lover, My Friend

Letter to the Reader

I have always been a person who has questioned and it has gotten me into trouble many a time, with my elders and with those who profess to know. There were times when I felt I was a wild horse and others were trying to break me. Thank God I had the sense to keep fighting.

It was not expected in my family that I would write. My parents were born at the turn of the century and life in our neighborhood in Italian Harlem was limited. Few received even a high school education. Our social circle was strictly limited to a small circle of friends and family who lived within a few square blocks. Strangers were treated with distrust and girls – especially unmarried ones – were watched over by uncles, aunts, friends and neighbors.

Although my mother, Anna DeGeorge, never imagined more for me than marriage and family, she was a true storyteller who set my soul aflame with tales of her early childhood and passionate adventures. I was a young girl when I left my mother's house for my husband's – and I had only a mile to walk to get there. Looking up, I saw a sky filled with shadows from clouds barely moving, as if the world was still. A voice inside whispered to me that no matter what others said or expected, my journey would take me far beyond these short blocks. For years, I had tried to be like the other girls. But on that moonlit night, windless and calm, my own power began to rise up in me. I began a life-long marriage of another kind, one with my own destiny and my own choices.

I now have a wonderful marriage, six children and three grandchildren. I have had a rich, fulfilling life, filled with travel and dreams coming true. Yet sometimes over the years, I have found myself longing for something more – missing something I could not name. I felt such guilt for this. "What kind of person am I, who has such an extraordinary life, not to be always grateful for it?" I asked myself. My husband would say such things as, "Don't you realize you have everything already, right here?" This made me feel worse and more ungrateful than ever.

How ironic, too, that he was right. Though not in the way he thought. I went through many periods of change. I retraced the moments of my life, digging up the past, shaking it up like so much hard dirt and sifting through it to find the good. I began writing seriously, collecting my poetry into books such as *Lessons of a Lifetime, Things that Make Me Happy, Essence of Cloistered Inspirations* and, this year, *Valley of Sighs* and *73rd Street*, an anthology of all my poems. I began sifting through the documents of my life, creating books of collage out of letters, poems and photographs. I created family histories of my mother, my father and my husband. I wrote short stories, personal essays, a travelogue *Dreams of Africa* about a safari I took with several friends a few years ago.

After my mother died in 1983, I began this novel, *The Other America,* wanting to collect the stories she had told me and to tell some more of my own. Since then, I have traveled to Sicily three times, researching the country and my father's hometown. I have reworked and rewritten the novel, polishing and refining it to tell the story of five generations of Italian Americans.

Beyond my writing, I learned photography and traveled throughout Europe, Africa, Israel, Egypt and the Caribbean. First a nurse, I later became a Eucharistic minister and a facilitator for children suffering from divorce or the loss of a parent. I also became an artist, working in sculpture, mixed media collage and encaustics. Besides writing, it is my art that occupies me most today. One of my works, "The Other America", is on the cover of the book. Through the use of images – some sacred in origin, some fueled by the kaleidoscope of modern life – I want to take the viewer on a voyage, serving as a channel to a realized truth, memory or question.

So much can happen when we dare to stretch our wings! While there is still life and breath within, we have the chance to do anything we want. Each day, I find myself restless with anticipation for what tomorrow will bring. There are times when I exhaust not only myself, but my husband as well. "Why can't she just be satisfied?" I can hear him thinking. But I can't. I hear that voice from the depths telling me to fly – and fly I must.

I see myself in my mind's eye, as far back as I can remember, lying in my baby carriage, watching and listening as others talked amongst themselves. Even then, I knew that I would have a great struggle – that I had chosen this struggle formerly and that this time my path would lead me to my higher self. Some said that I had a warrior's heart. Some said it was too bad that I was a girl (as if this was a curse) and others explained me away as a trouble-maker who wanted too much, whose opinions were too strong, whose dreams were too strange. Often I felt that I had no one to confide in. God was there, but my life was a solitary one. Not even my mother, who encouraged me so much, could help.

What a gift it was when I found my husband. Who knows what would have happened if I had married anyone else. He has let me grow, explore, be free. He has let me *be*. I feel more passion for him now than I ever have. When I was first married, I thought I knew everything. I thought it would never get any better. But passion is not what society would have us believe. Passion is not excessive and unpredictable. It is the quiet at the center of all things. It is the calm *after* the storm, the peace – almost like exhaustion – that is reward of a great effort. All this Lenny has shared with me, and it is to him that my I owe my greatest thanks.

I would also like to thank my father, Angelo DeGeorge, whose abiding sense of humor kept me on my toes, my mother Anna DeGeorge who taught me so much through her own dedication and passion, her own allegiance to a moral compass. I would like to thank my children: in my heart, there is a place that belongs solely to them, and to no one else. It is filled with all the love and hope I feel for them, and no one else can penetrate this place. It is because of my children that I have been able to express myself in so many ways. They have also brought me closer to my own siblings, the gift my mother left to me.

I thank my editor Louise Wareham who has been my mentor and teacher over the years. Like a true editor and friend, she helped me to push myself, to move always to the next level. She has given me confidence and a belief in my own stories, my own unique voice in the world.

It seems to me that I am not in this world just to survive. There is enough of that going on already. I want to be part of the engine that makes a difference. Searching for something more in each day allows me to transform myself, to continue to grow and embrace an ever-changing world. I am so glad that the young girl who walked from her mother's house to her husband's was not wrong to dream.

I hope you will look at my website LanaSantorelli.com, sign my Guest Book or send me your thoughts. Passion has shown me my true self, my true prayer, my joy and my desire. It gives me refuge so I can survive. I look forward to hearing of your journey.

Lana Santorelli

The Seasons of Sicily

I

The strong soul of Sicily warms and illuminates no matter what the season, even as it creates dark shadows. The mountains form an almost unbroken chain from the Straits of Messina west along the northern coast of Sicily, past Palermo, and around the Gulfo di Castellammare toward Capo San Vito, the western tip of the island.

II

The miracle of water repeats itself every autumn.
Gray storm clouds puff up against gray mountains, olive trees toss their silvery leaves to the wind, a bright blue sea breaks through the necklace of tunnels and caves strung out along the coast.

The sowing of wheat begins, smells of must and roasting chestnuts heralding a new season. October rains are the heaviest.
Flooding and damage to crops is followed by deadly drought.
Rains soften the soil before the peppers, eggplants, and tomato vines give way to winter, water-soaked earth congealing into clay.
For the farmer, the rain never comes at the right moment.
The sun is either too hot or too weak, the wind ill-timed.
After a long, dry summer only the most stubborn vines and citrus trees hold their color; grasses and weeds are scorched and withered.
Light and dust bleach the country.
Leaves turn yellow in the vineyards, dark red and orange in the orchards.

III

November is the season of All Soul's Day,

Commemoration of the Dead, known as *I Morti* when the dead rise up from the cemeteries, in procession through the town at night, leaving soul-cakes for the children who have remembered them in their prayers.

But these are gifts brought by souls in purgatory, not angels but demons come to haunt those who wronged them in life.

The *paladino*, a knight in shining armor, appears at puppet shows mounted on horseback and brandishing a sword, a snippet of ostrich plume cascading from his helmet.

Next to him stands a peasant girl balancing a basket of eggs on her hip.

The stalls of *torrone* vendors groan under the weight of almond trays and hazelnuts in caramelized sugar.

The *semenza* sellers spread their wares on painted carts in bright colors strung with paper garlands.

Flower sellers hold brushes of yellow, white, and purple chrysanthemums destined for tombs.

The women of the household visit graves, cleaning out dead flowers. A neglected tomb causes talk.

Walking arm in arm, families in their finest clothes crack semenza nuts, a trail of shells marking their path.

Afterward, they spread fresh lace on chapel altars.

Coffins journey in glass-sided carriages drawn by black horses with black plumes nodding from their harnesses.

The funeral procession, headed by the priest and two altar boys, is followed by wreaths of flowers, six feet high, bearing black ribbons.

The wearing of black for mourning is a message for the dead rather than the living, a disguise to escape the ghosts.

After a loved one has died, the lights are kept very low in the house.

If it is summer and you wish to sit outside, you can do so only in the dark; otherwise, someone might doubt the genuineness of your grief.

Once a young girl was severely beaten by her brothers for not crying hard enough at her father's funeral.

If a widow or mother of someone recently deceased wants to leave the house for some air or distraction, she has to exit by the back door.

She might be told not to clear the table of all its crumbs and to leave wine overnight for the spirits.

Some people address the dead directly; they say "Buon Giorno" in an empty house.

IV

For each year the olive bears fruit, it takes two years to rest.

Children stop and stroke the tree's old gnarled bark.

Moss grows up its trunk, soft after the rains, shriveled in summer.

The olive harvest is one of the few times when the women go to work beside the men in the fields.

Harvesters spread their nets under the olive trees, picking olives they can reach from ladders, beating down the rest with canes.

Old men, small and white-haired, are bent and prematurely aged by a lifetime working under a Sicilian sun.

Women with sacks slung over their shoulders gather wild greens along the hedgerows.

The sounds of conversation drift through the groves.

V

Olive oil is the soul of the Sicilian people—strong, harsh, and slightly bitter. The still-green olives are soaked in cold water, then stored in salty brine with fresh oregano and fennel seed. Layered in fruit crates, they are sprinkled with salt to make the bitter juice drain away. A week later, they are dried one by one and put into jars with oil, newly pressed. Baked Sicilian bread, soaked in olive oil and salted, is served hot from an oven fired with almond shells. It is used as a cure for squeaking hinges or, beaten with lemon juice, rubbed into chapped hands.

VI

In the wintry December landscape, the mulberries, pomegranates, pears, and plums have mostly shed their leaves.

The oleander bushes, tall as trees, are scraggly and lifeless.

Palms sprout as many fronds as they can squeeze into their circumference.

Every cypress has a character all its own— some tall, some thin, some fat and squat, some curled at the top like candles in the sun.

Wild capers grow over soft stones, cascading down limestone.

VII

Palermo is a maze of tiny streets, hovels leading past palaces in ruins, balconies brimming with greenery, corners blocked by heaps of uncollected garbage.

Even the darkest alleyway hides a treasure: a window, a flowering shrine. Look up and you'll behold a sea of faces.

Slung from balcony to balcony, laundry lines thread through the ironwork railings where wisteria blossoms drip like early grapes.

Markets spill over with fresh vegetables, sides of beef, entrails, heads of slaughtered animals hanging from meat hooks.

Fish stalls sell boiled octopus, raw mussels, inky sea urchins tasting of iodine.

Occasionally, an open window in a baroque facade reveals an aristocratic, moth-eaten splendor.
But most people wear threadbare clothes: you can see the almost invisible outline of an apron on a woman's shapeless, long-sleeved dress.
Long-fingered and graceful, Sicilian women measure out indulgence and sympathy with calm determination.
As young women, however, they can be quite naive, believing— even as they are going into labor— that the midwife has to cut a hole in their side in order to deliver the baby.

VIII

Winter storms leave the mountains white around Palermo. It is said that when snow fell in the city itself, the people once went mad.
Almond trees proffer up puffs of pale pink blossoms.
The roadsides are thick with wild calendula speckled orange.
Camomile spreads miniature daisies throughout the vineyards, while great swathes of brilliant lemon-yellow flowers and cushiony green leaves mark the advance of wood sorrel.

IX

The first daffodils rise in February, yellow petticoats tossing in a hard cold southern wind then falling in a shower of white petals.
Sowing links field and family in a prayer for fertility for new crops and new generations.
Dark clouds roll back and forth across the March sky, a battle between the hot *sirocco* wind blowing from the Sahara, and the *tramontana* whose gusts chilled by Alpine glaciers change abruptly in temperature at every swing.

The pace is furious, allowing clouds no pause to pour their precious burden of water.
Beneath gray skies, java beans are in bloom.

X

The Sicilian spring is like a christening, full of colors and smells
and heat waves that catch and hold onto you.
The mountains roll to one's feet.
The peach orchards are pink.
Tall pine forests sing in the wind; chestnuts and oaks turn golden
when the robenia let down their bloom.
Almond blossoms are joined by sorbapples bursting forth with
tiny bouquets of white flowers, bunches of little yellow fruit
growing rosy patches by October.

The shepherd's wife lives in a farmhouse, a one-room cottage with
a sloping roof and a small vegetable garden next to a pig pen.
In the garden is planted *finocchio* for success, camomile for courage, oranges for mountain joy, laurel bushes to shield the family from lightning, rosemary that grows to the height of Christ
in 33 years and mint, used as an aphrodisiac and for abortions.

The windows are dark and shuttered but the red tile roofs glow in
the late afternoon sun.
The Sicilian countryside dips behind the house so that, seen from
the sea, the sky is its only backdrop.
The wells are dug by hand.
The family donkey sleeps on hay under the house.
The shepherd's wife raises seven children without electric lights or
running water, sleeping in alcoves fashioned by curtains.
The flaking, white-washed walls are dotted with pots, coat hooks,
and pictures of saints.
The furniture is old and lopsided from multiple coats of paint; the
commode is stored under the bed.

April mornings are cold and damp.

The shepherd's wife is making *ricotta, pecorino*, from the morning milking. Her life is harsh, relentless.

In summer, she makes cheese twice a day.

The first lot of milk is boiled and separated.

The curds are packed in baskets, then taken to a shed where they are drained on wood trays.

The women take turns stirring the whey, heated together with more milk in an enormous copper cauldron propped over a blazing fire fed by four-foot logs.

XI

Sicily exhausts her riches each ebullient

Spring. Bursts of color give way to summer, sun burning through the haze, lighting up the sparkling sea, glistening white stucco, bright crimson and fuchsia bougainvillea, tropical green palms and banana plants.

The Sicilian landscape has changing shades of blue, purple, and emerald green.

The mountains are like painted forms of architecture, all with their own expression.

Mint and sage flower grow in various shades of pale purple mixed with rosemary white.

The quince, like the pomegranate, prefers to wait for foliage to frame its flowers, but will shortly blow away.

The pomegranates go on for weeks, new buds still opening when the first flowers are already swollen with fruit.

Wild grass grows outside the villas, a profuse, if shaggy, lawn.

XII

*To achieve the apotheosis of the artichoke, you must grasp it firmly
by the stem and pound it vigorously on a stone until the leaves
flatten and allow access to the heart. Poke in a clove of garlic,
chopped fine with mint, salt, pepper, and olive oil. The artichoke is then placed on ash-covered coals to roast gently until
the tough outer leaves have charred. The tender heart steams
in its own juices and absorbs the oil and other seasonings in
one of the world's happiest marriages.*

XIII

Summer is the time of the wheat harvest.
A long line of reapers rise their sickles in unison.
For every seven reapers, a gatherer walks behind them, scooping
the severed stalks into the fork of a stick by means of a blunt-
edged sickle, then tying them into a sheaf with a long plume
of tough ampelodisa grass.
The arms of the reapers move to the rhythm of work songs.
The farmer is thin, weathered, his eyes brilliant blue.
Stoic and inscrutable in the shadow of his cap, he has the look of a
Sicilian Buddha, one who knows how to defend his honor but
hold his tongue.

The flattest part of the field is a smooth threshing ground where a
pair of mules are driven round and round, trampling the ears
of wheat with their hooves, breaking off grains as the peasants
stir and toss the wheat with pitchforks.
Hymns are accompanied by endless circling, cries of encouragement to the mules, and prayers to the saints for a blessed harvest.

XIV

Cucuzza, or Sicilian squash, a long, smooth, pale-green cylinder, grows in a comma on a curlicue of vine, or straight as a ruler as much as five feet long when trained on a trellis. In the absence of its own flavor, it has the amazing capacity to absorb and neutralize any other taste.

XV

In July, heat and light seem to float on the land as on the surface of a giant cauldron. The harvests erupt with mounds of eggplant, green pepper, sweet red tomatoes, variegated crimson nectarines, watermelons and red table grapes.
The rich red winter earth has dried to old brick, dead grass on the roadside tussling with the wind.

Fruit is eaten straight from the tree – figs, the early ones, are dark purple sacks, yellow-green figs leaking golden honey.
Peruzzoli, tiny pears an inch in diameter, grow in bright yellow bunches on young trees whose thin yellow skins are stretched taut with juice.
Bright ovals of fuchsia, chartreuse, and yellow pulp are extracted from their spring skins and heaped upon a platter.
The first of the melons are already ripening.
Black mulberries are bursting with crimson juice, trickling down your arm when you reach up to pick them.
Golden peaches and apricots drop gently onto dried grass, waiting to be gathered and turned into jam.
String beans are pulled from the vines.
Parsley hides from sight in the flower beds until it grows to enormous heights.
Forkfuls of rust-brown dried java beans are tossed into the air so

that some slight breeze will carry off the pieces of sod and dried stalks as they fall heavily to earth.

Java beans are shelled by the children.

When cooked, they slide unawares into your mouth.

XVI

The storyteller illustrates his story with gestures—one hand held up with palm and fingers slightly inclined, the other darting back and forth from one side of the upright hand to the other.

On a street corner, a mother sweeps a little girl into her arms and kisses her, saying sangue mio—"my own blood."

XVII

It is 117 degrees Fahrenheit in the shade.

Candles are melting in their sconces and the elderly are dying.

Now the newborn fruit, once cradled in foliage, is exposed and defenseless.

August brings a slight cooling of air.

Wool from worn sweaters is unraveled and wound into balls.

The mountains fall abruptly to the sea, narrowly bordered by tiny fields and vineyards scrambling up the slopes of grass and bristling clumps of Sicilian palmetto.

In the gorges, eagles circle and waters teem with life.

The sun bakes the clear sea, now azure, now turquoise, now aquamarine.

After the sun eases itself down, thunder and lightning throw light against the windows and across the ceiling. The interval between flash and roll grows shorter and shorter as the voice of thunder deepens. Then the storm passes on, fades, and disappears leaving silence behind. A wind begins to rustle and soon, you can hear the familiar sound of raindrops.

PART ONE

turned away without a word and resumed her pace through the gradually lifting mist. To her horror, however, Luciano nudged his horse alongside her, smiling down as he rode.

"Bianca," he said, "I apologize for startling you. But you also startled Hades, darting out in front of us like that."

Bianca flinched at the sound of the horse's name and impulsively stopped in its path.

"Tell me, Luciano," she said, emboldened by her jumbled emotions, "are you always so at home riding creatures from hell?"

"Actually," he said, his smile undisturbed, "I would rather mount creatures from heaven, but I am not always so fortunate."

Unsure of how to react without acknowledging his innuendo, Bianca walked on silently, though he continued to follow her and, in another moment, spoke again.

"If you're worried that Pauletta might scold you for being late," he said, "there's more than enough room for both of us on this horse."

Pauletta Moresco was the formidable kitchen mistress in charge of all the young women who worked on the estate. Despite her harsh reputation, however, she was very fond of Bianca and sympathetic to the responsibilities that Bianca shared with her mother in supporting a fatherless family and farm.

"No thank you," she said, certain now that his smile was mocking her.

They made quiet progress for several minutes, until they reached an expanse of velvet green grass that stretched in the full morning sun to the horizon of the manor house. Women were never allowed to walk in the village alone. Even the village farmers made their trek to the working fields together. Yet there were always places to hide away, and Bianca often came to this meadow so she could lie in the deep grass on the quiet hillside above the village, and escape in her dreams far beyond the clouds above her.

"Since you won't share my horse," he said, "I'll thank you for allowing me to share your path and be on my way. Perhaps I'll have the chance to escort you again."

Luciano gave a low bow in the saddle, then turned his horse

and galloped across the meadow, storming the falcons and scattering the pheasants in the thunder of his passing. As he rode away from Bianca's dwindling figure, he smiled at the thought of her fragile form, the long, shimmering hair, the quiet intelligence in her slate-gray eyes, and her ethereal skin which lay out before him like the dawn. But then he remembered her outspokenness and realized that she might not be quite as easy to pluck as some of the other blossoms.

VAGUELY MOORISH IN design, the manor of Santa Pietro was built in the late seventeenth century, when the high walls and dark, cylindrical stone towers were an aberration in the countryside. Though it harmonized with the Arabic influences scattered throughout the island, the castle clashed with the graceful Greek villas lying in pieces on the landscape. Now, as the people willingly forgot a history that had never ennobled them, its menacing form had become just another antique in a country filled with ruins. Even Bianca's cottage, built by her father out of poor limestone, resembled the dwellings that existed on the island long before the Spaniards came to rule. An instant relic among all the others, it seemed to crumble into dust even as it was being erected.

Although the Santa Pietro estate might be destined for ruin as well, it was still magnificent with its haughty air of cold defiance. Behind the thick stone walls, the ideas of one century intruded upon another. Bianca walked under archways, up and down little staircases, past splendid tapestries, and down seemingly endless corridors to the manor's many rooms. The polished wood floors were covered in richly woven wool rugs. Portraits of family ancestors hung high on the walls in ornate frames, each figure dressed in regal clothes from vanished times; each face was severe and seemed to judge her suspiciously. Heavy drapes covered all the great windows, not so much to keep out the sunlight, but to hold in the heat.

Yet Bianca, whose rich imagination could not begin to encompass the scope of the manor's luxuries, was fascinated most by the plurality of doors. Her own humble cottage had but one narrow door and a single window too small for any but the smallest child to squeeze through, as confined as her own life would likely be. At the castle, she entered by way of the kitchen, or through an iron door set into one of the stone walls that opened onto a hallway leading to the upper chambers. It seemed magical to her that one house could have so many passageways to the inner and outer world. The greatest advantage of being rich, she thought, was the many opportunities it provided for escape. Once inside, she was unwilling to confront the suggestive calls of the men who worked in the stables, so she seldom ventured back out, content to stare at the courtyard from the kitchen window.

The courtyard was the entrance for family and guests, an area that had once been enclosed by a curved stone wall as a defense in the days when the Spaniards had flattered their Sicilian subjects by supposing they might rise in revolt. One of the Santa Pietros from an earlier generation had knocked down the wall so that his bride could have an expanse of earth in which to plant her formal gardens on the southern face of the estate. Had they been able to return, the Spaniards would have been appalled to see that even the land had managed to breach their defenses.

Bianca rushed into the kitchen. Fortunately, the other girls were too caught up in their gossiping to pay any more than passing attention to her flustered entrance. She walked straight to her worktable and began her needlework.

Loretta Bosca, a robust, olive-skinned woman who helped the cook (and herself to whatever the cook was preparing) was in the midst of saying how handsome Luciano had looked that morning when he left for his ride before dawn.

"And now that he's home for good," she said, "none of us will be safe from him."

"You have nothing to worry about," said Maria Roseli, giggling. "I'm the one he was noticing." At sixteen, Maria was the youngest of the household's bedroom maids – and the prettiest. She had the sun-lightened blonde hair and fine frame of a Grecian goddess, although her coarse manner betrayed any trace of the mythical beauty whose image had been hopelessly corrupted in the years since Olympus.

Bianca heard their chatter everyday, mixed with both stern disapproval and futile longing when they spoke of Luciano. But she rarely listened, content as she was to daydream about Massemo Manzino, her fiancé, a sweet and boyishly handsome young man who shared the running of a modest farm with seven brothers in Corleone, a village not far from the estate. For five years they'd had an ammucciuni, a "hidden engagement" that they planned to announce to their families as soon as he returned from military service.

In a world where poverty and family responsibilities often delayed marriage, and where a stringent moral code became an obsession with the appearance of being morally unblemished, extended contact between unmarried couples was forbidden, however chaste. Consequently, the tradition of ammucciuni had evolved from a medieval concept of courtship. A young couple would privately declare their love for one another, or their willingness to one day become lovers. Thereupon, they would enter into a secret engagement, and suddenly the deadening routine of an impoverished life was touched with an aura of promise. Each day was infused with a special glow of excitement. Though they would move through their lives exactly as before, their romance contained all the magic of myth and the passion of history. They would see each other only in the most innocent of scenes – passing on roads, at large social gatherings, or at Sunday mass as a member of the same congregation – but only they were aware of the link that existed between them, briefly finding expression in the glances they would now and then risk exchanging. The purpose of the arrangement was to allow the young people a relatively calm adolescence, secure in the knowledge that the trauma of choosing a mate had been resolved. No one could steal their love away as they struggled to prepare for the burden of raising a family, and the fact that they had never so much as touched one another somehow enhanced and deepened the thrill.

For Bianca, however, to accept an abstraction of love in place of the physical reality was purely a thing of the mind. She needed to feel it in her flesh. She had been engaged to Massemo Manzino since the age of fourteen, and crossing paths with Luciano had temporarily blotted out her thoughts of him. Their conversation was distracting her from her duties and amplifying her need for true affection. Still, she was determined that none of the other women would know that she and Luciano had spoken, nor that he had, in a very real sense, pursued her. She hadn't seen Luciano for nearly a year – he'd been attending school in England – and didn't realize until now that she barely knew him, even though she had worked for his mother for over eight years – ever since her father had fallen from a scaffold and died.

If it hadn't been for the Contessa, in fact, her family would be destitute. Bianca remembered how the sympathy of the neighbors had run out along with the last of the breads and cheeses that had been brought as condolence offerings. They had wanted to offer more, but their own supplies were too meager. Soon after, Bianca's mother, Brunella Stobina, began to weaken at the burden of supporting her family alone.

She was left with four growing children to feed and a small farm that was already a struggle when Bianca's father was alive. In fact, when she couldn't pay the usual tithe that her farm was expected to produce, the collector threatened to have Brunella and her children removed from the property. Bianca, who was the tallest among the young village women at thirteen, was willing, even desperate, to help but she was so slight of build that she couldn't meet the farm's crushing physical demands. Despairing, Brunella suddenly struck on an idea – perhaps Bianca could acquire work at the estate, doing housework and simple sewing. And so, Bianca was immediately sent to ask for a position. She explained their need without shame to Pauletta, the kitchen mistress, impressing upon her that she would do any work needed. Pauletta knew an eager worker when she saw one, and with the approval of the Contessa, hired her that very day. The money Bianca earned paid for assistance from one of the local boys a few mornings each week, and kept the farm from the brink of failure until Bianca's three brothers were old enough to take over the chores.

Then, the Contessa discovered Bianca's rare gift with the needle. Bianca had been working at the manor for three months when she arrived one morning wearing a patchwork shawl that she had stitched together from remnants of silk and other brightly-colored fabrics which she had collected over the years. Her mother called it her "coat of many moods" because Bianca had chosen the fabrics according to how she felt that day. The cloths were so randomly patched, however, that she usually wore it only as protection against bad weather.

When the Contessa came into the kitchen to ask for a compress to be taken upstairs to treat the Count's gout, she had seen the shawl drying before the fire and examined the strange creation, the intricate work. Bianca had stitched together so many unmatchable pieces into a pattern of such startling originality that the Contessa turned to the shy girl who was staring at her with wide, gray eyes and asked, "Where did you find such a garment?"

"I made it, Madame," Bianca said in a frightened voice, afraid that her eccentric handiwork was seen as somehow offensive. "Just for amusement," she continued, "something to keep me busy in the evenings. The little ones at home are so wild and noisy that it's sometimes difficult to sleep."

The Contessa studied the frail child, then abruptly departed the room, leaving Bianca in a state of confusion. In the next moment, she returned, carrying a silk dress with an elaborate lace collar and placed it in Bianca's hands. One section of the collar had been torn away, opening a gap in the emerald green silk, and a small section of lace was missing.

"This is from Paris," the Contessa said, her voice almost breathless with reverence as though she were speaking of the Blessed Virgin. "It is very precious to me. Do you think you could repair it?"

Bianca nodded solemnly, then quickly bowed her head, "May your Excellency bless me, Madame."

"Good," said the Contessa, who started to leave once more.

"But I will need finer thread and needles," said Bianca with sudden confidence, "and an assortment of lace in order to make the right match."

The Contessa stopped and nodded. "You will have all that you need," she said.

A short while later, baskets of sewing materials were brought to the kitchen by a puzzled maid from the mistress's chambers. By the end of the afternoon, the gown had been restored, and instructions were handed down that Bianca was not to be wasted on mundane tasks any longer. Only someone with a fine intelligence could create such artistry. Bianca was to undertake an apprenticeship with the Contessa's dressmaker at once. Soon she became so valuable that the Contessa increased her wages and Bianca's earnings enabled her mother to hire a second handyman. From that point on, Brunella was fond of saying, "My daughter, delicate as she is, does the work of two strong men." The farm, at least by local standards, prospered.

So began Bianca's favored place in the Santa Pietro household, a role that eventually allowed her to work with luxurious silks brought from exotic places throughout Europe and the Orient. The life wrought beneath her fingertips told of a brighter world beyond the dust and heartbreak of her sun-drenched home and gave shape to her childhood dreams. As each day ended, however, Bianca would put away the silks and walk home through the twilight, taking each step through the forest as if it were a ritual to cleanse herself of romance. If she brought home too many ideas of the world, life in her mother's house would become unbearable, she thought. And so, like scattering bread crumbs to mark her path, she surrendered her dreams willingly, one by one. On this day, however, seeing Luciano had imbued her with a strange flush of power. As the hours went by, she wondered how many stitches she would have to sew before she distanced the feelings that were stirring in her.

Going home through the forest that night did not quiet her, and her quickened heartbeat only made her more annoyed. She was acting like a silly manor girl, she thought. To the manor maids, and even Luciano, romance might be a game, but to Bianca, her honor and respect were all that she owned.

And yet, despite her proud thoughts, Bianca was dismayed to discover that when she woke the next morning, and stood brushing out her long black hair, a fugitive thought of Luciano's green eyes ran quickly through her mind. Hastily, she pushed it aside and left the cottage, only to hurry back a few minutes later to knot her hair into a braid; loose hair would look far too willing. Setting out once more, she took the proper road that circled the orchard instead of walking through it. And yet, as she passed beneath the trees, she became conscious of the way her hips moved under the fragile confines of her thin dress and imagined herself being watched. Instantly aware of her childish emotions, her embarrassment was about to blossom into shame when suddenly she heard a horse come up behind her.

"You're going a different way," Luciano called as he approached. "I almost missed you. We have to learn to coordinate directions if we expect to have any time together."

Stunned by his presence and the disarming intimacy of his words, she adopted the previous day's mask of composure. But this time, when he suggested that she ride the rest of the way on his saddle, she graced him with an almost whimsical smile before she said, "No thank you." Nothing else was exchanged between them that morning; however, for the rest of the day and night, Bianca felt as if she were drifting through clouds of smoke. She told herself to be sensible, yet she could not. Life held little more for her than routine, and she yearned for a dream, any dream, to come true.

On the third day, Luciano dismounted as soon as he approached her, meeting her long before she reached the orchard path. Together, they spoke freely as they walked through the expanding light, the only two figures visible on the land. Then, on the fourth day, when he wasn't waiting for her as usual, she decided to wait for him. He rushed up a few minutes later, mumbling about Hades' thrown shoe like a young husband apologizing to his bride for delaying dinner.

In the weeks that followed, the Contessa was busy preparing for a trip to Spain where Luciano had promised to meet her after his annual trip throughout the continent with his father, conducting business with distributors of the family's marasala. Everyday Bianca went to the estate to help her plan and pack her wardrobe, and on most afternoons, Luciano was there to greet her on her way home. Gradually they extended their moments together, and in the sun that danced in their eyes and the warmth that hovered between them, she could see that they were moving toward a union over which she had no control.

When his first kiss came at the end of their second week, it was gentle, then deepened and strengthened, awakening Bianca's body with a longing that turned to fire on her skin. A few days later he kissed her again, their lips barely touching in the comforting half-light of the orchard. She felt the lingering brush of his lips and the tips of his fingers pressing against her breast.

He moved away too soon to feel her shudder, but quietly said, "Come earlier tomorrow," before parting from the shelter of trees into the waning light. Her shuddering, Bianca realized, was not only delight in Luciano's touch, but a fear of what she would express. None of her daydreams had prepared her this; maybe, she thought, they had been too timid.

THROUGH THE PRE-DAWN darkness and chilled morning dew, she rushed through the fields toward the orchard grove. She had not slept. Her fevered restlessness was the product of pure desire. As soon as she reached him, Luciano wrapped her in a warm woolen blanket scented by cedar and held her. He said nothing until her trembling subsided. Then he spread the blanket on the damp soil and engulfed her in his embrace. He undressed her completely, discarding even the cotton chamois she wore next to her skin. Then he undressed himself, and as the heat of their mingling rose to meet the icy morning breeze, she surrendered to him. They made love in the illumination of the golden light, enveloped by the dew as they dissolved together in the steamy mist, capturing each ray as he entered her again and again, burgeoning to a shivering climax.

And yet, lying quietly together afterward, a sense of hopelessness set loose within her that seemed to embody all the blood and the pain and the secrets of Sicily that were buried in the meadow beneath them. Women had been murdered, and families had waged vendettas for sins far less than this.

"Soon," she said as he drew circles on her back and shoulder, "you will be lord of the manor. What will happen to us then, Luciano?"

"The day is too bright for such dark thoughts," he said. "Why can't we simply go on as we are, like everything else in nature?"

Bianca realized then that Luciano's nature was not hers. Safe in his castled wealth, Luciano slipped out of his world only to taste her innocence. He could never truly know the hardship of her life, its dangers or harshness. This is all he could ever give her, however intimate their words and deeds. He'd never speak of other women he had known, which she came to accept as part of his past as beyond her understanding as his future. No matter how deeply he may desire her now, he never intended to share his life with her. From the moment Luciano had touched her, she had known all along that the colossal accident which had brought them together would one day right itself and she would become a mere memory. Her only hold on him was the present.

She rolled over on her back and watched, as he did, the flawless Sicilian sky. Sunlight has a special quality here, she thought, a clarity that could banish any shadow – and she called to Luciano to come inside her once more. But the knowledge that this pleasure would end had distorted all sound – of birdsong above his impassioned voice, of her very heartbeat. But she was careful not to show her gathering sense of dread as they prepared themselves to leave the clearing. And if Luciano sensed any difference in her, it was blurred by the way they clung to each other before she smoothed her damp hair and said that she had to go.

From then on, they made love to each other everyday in the quiet corners of the countryside. Bianca thanked fate that she had no jealous older brothers or father to watch over her, and the manor girls were too wrapped up in their own talk to notice any change in her. In the early hours of the morning, or at dusk after all the workers had gone home, she and Luciano would ride deep into the orchards and over the meadows where no one could find them.

Although Bianca didn't know what form their ending would take, or when it would descend upon them, she knew they were drawing closer to the moment when the same forces that had brought them together would irrevocably tear them apart. On their final afternoon before his departure, Luciano took her on Hades to a wine cellar that was set into a natural cave just below the limestone cottage where the grapes were pressed. As they lay in the stone chamber on a bed of blankets and straw, his body deep within hers, Bianca stared at the walls encasing them like ghosts locked away in the catacombs. They wouldn't see each other now for almost a month. Reliving perhaps for the last time the only fate that seemed worth surviving, she knew at once that he had wrested the truest part of her, a love that could never be reclaimed. Had he any knowledge of the danger of this love? If someone had discovered them, would he have protected her from ruin? Though Bianca had no father, it was not past the village men to take it upon themselves to punish her. Bianca had seen a beating before, and a wife or daughter who was grateful to have survived it. The fact that Luciano was of such a high birth would provide even more fuel for their rage – as if the village men had become cuckolds by association. Then too, Bianca had given away a gift that she could give to no other again. Naked in the bare cave, Bianca felt a rush of anger in her veins. She could never lie with him as a respected woman. She could only be hidden away, like this, common and coarse. She could no longer bear it. His green eyes, she thought, were like the cave's shadows.

Even so, she had chosen him. And now she shared a knowledge of him that needed no explanation, no promise, but which held itself above all earthly concerns, like her meadow dreams. As she watched him, Bianca's luminous eyes seemed to absorb him completely, yet the wisp of her smile had disappeared with the light. In her hauntingly somber look was a farewell too permanent to utter.

Luciano's face clouded with troubled thought. Yet he said nothing more than her name and held her once more. Her body slackened, and she slipped from him, rising up to gather her clothes and dress as he followed her.

Bianca did not ride with Luciano that night, but told him that she would rather walk alone. As he lifted her face with his hand, and kissed her softly on the cheek, she felt for a moment that the smile in her had died forever. She drifted home numb and undone, as though she'd been ravaged from the inside out. Emerging from a stand of lime trees, her legs gave way without warning. With a sob, she stumbled to the ground in a slow fall, striking the earth and losing her breath with the impact. For some time, she knelt in the shadows of the trees, crying steadily, overwhelmed by all the feelings within her that were competing for ownership. Bianca was pregnant, she knew, the victim of love's oldest consequence. The shock of it put her in a state of suspension, as if her power of consciousness had been revoked. She had been so immersed in her fantasy that she had acted like any foolish girl frolicking in haylofts on hot afternoons. Though the farms of Sicily may be filled with such girls, Bianca had never thought of herself as being one of the empty-headed multitude who blundered into motherhood. Perhaps she was a heretic after all, she thought, one of those who believed that humanity was better off having lost Eden, that only after banishing childlike bliss did life gain its edge, its exhilarating blend of spirit and despair. Yet, she could not regret what she had done. She'd been given a rare opportunity to reach beyond the bars of her allotted life and seize a chance for something more. The thousands of joyless days without him would more than atone for her sin.

She thought through each of the options open to her, thought through them again and again. But as she sat there under the darkening sky, the fear of discovery, coupled with the even greater fear that someone might guess the identity of the father, filled her with the impulse to run away. But where would she go, and how would she survive if she did? She was penniless with no sense of life beyond the valley. Her blind desperation was like stepping into a black void. She was unable to provide even a vague outline of how she might proceed. Ending the pregnancy would mean risking her life. She'd heard stories of the witch-like women in the hills who used thin blades or caustic lye solutions to smother a fetus through some frightening power. Still, she knew – in the unshakable way one knows the important things – that she couldn't destroy this life without descending into madness, no matter that hers was a world where such a transgression would never be forgiven. The village was too aware of human weakness to allow sins of the flesh to go uncondemned. As their own desires kept reminding them, passion was always ready to burst forth and flood the land. Whenever it took some visible form among them, they struck it down, often brutally. Nonetheless, she couldn't help but think that to give birth in shame and destroy her family's honor might be worse.

Bianca stood up weakly and wiped her tears on the hem of her skirt, then started down the slope toward her mother's house. She was too exhausted to run the same terrible certainties through her mind once more. Tomorrow, she would walk to the village and tell the parish priest that one more of his daughters had brought sin into his community. If she was going to be cursed, she thought, let it begin with someone who might feel a sacred obligation to punish her as Jesus would – with more sorrow than fury.

FATHER COSTELLO WAS a man composed of two circles: a round body topped by a perfectly round head. His few strands of gray hair seemed randomly pasted on his pink scalp and looked faintly comical. All the children loved him. He had a bulbous nose that dominated his face and turned red in every season. His cassock was always wrinkled, as if he slept in it, and maybe he did; his Roman collar was always soiled.

He was available everyday for counseling, prayers for the sick, debates with village leaders about the state of the world – whatever his parishioners needed. The crystal light in his bright blue eyes would become a darker blue at the mere mention of some holy cause. On most days, however, no one came to church at all, and he would spend his time polishing the few brass surfaces and gold objects that the church could afford until it was late enough to join the old men pitching horseshoes. Sometimes the older women in the village would seek his advice on invented problems just to make him feel essential.

That morning, Father Costello was performing his chores as usual when he looked up and saw Bianca standing before him. She had entered the nave so quietly that she could have been a field mouse.

"What an unexpected joy!" he said, surprised but grinning broadly. "Welcome to my empty shrine. All is well at home, I hope – it's so rare to see you on a weekday."

"I have come to give confession, Father," Bianca said, subdued.

"Wonderful! I mean, I'd be happy to receive your confession. That's why I'm here, though I'm not sure the other villagers remember."

Slowly, he stood up from his task of polishing the altar rail and they walked to the confessional, side by side. He seemed so happy that she had come to confess, it was almost as if he was grateful to her for having taken the trouble to sin. Bianca watched him enter the dark, wooden booth, and was reminded once more of the magic cabinet that she had seen at a traveling circus from which a bouquet of flowers, a bird in a cage, and finally a pretty young woman appeared. Though there were many who spoke of the similarities between a coffin and the confessional, Bianca had never seen it as a symbol of death; to her, it was a midwife for change and salvation. But now, she found herself warding off unfamiliar fears with the safety of knowing that she was speaking to a priest she could trust. As soon as the musty curtain fell into place, Father Costello would cease to be the grandfatherly figure she had known growing up and become God's anonymous ear. Nothing she said would ever go beyond the ancient mahogany box, despite the enormity of her sin. He was a fair and sober man, unlike the previous priest, Father Simmino, who'd been too fond of wine and had often amused his fellow patrons at the tavern by recounting the confessed sins of their neighbors. Eventually the Bishop from Palermo had to be summoned and warned him that if his behavior did not change he would be removed. It might have been better for Father Simmino if he had listened. Instead, his tongue was as loose as ever, and only a month went by before his body was found at the bottom of a ravine. No one doubted the cause.

Father Costello, however, was of a different ilk. After the usual preamble of prayer, he listened in silence while Bianca said with surprisingly little hesitation that she had been "intimate" with a man on several occasions and was now carrying his child. She finished her confession as abruptly as she began, and wondered if the priest's continued silence meant he was so shocked that he had just quietly vanished. Suddenly he cleared his throat and said softly, "Bianca, are you sorry for this sin?"

"Father, if God is offended by what I have done . . . ."

"He is offended," boomed the priest in an uncharacteristically severe tone, then added. "Is the man married, Bianca?"

"No, Father," she said, praying he would not ask his name.

"Then he must marry you," said Father Costello, his voice strengthening as he arrived at what he considered to be a solution. "Your sin against God can be forgiven by God, but the child must be saved from being born into sin and contaminated by it. The man must marry you, even if it proves necessary for the leadership of the community to make him accept his responsibility, as your father would have done if he were alive."

The impossibility of the situation washed over Bianca with amusement. She imagined a group of little old men from the village marching in formation to the Santa Pietro estate, demanding that Luciano marry her like storybook dwarfs defending her honor. The image almost caused her to laugh out loud.

"Bianca, you must ask God for forgiveness so that I may give you absolution."

"Of course, Father," she answered in a barely audible voice. She repeated her act of contrition mechanically, the words meaningless to her ears, then left the confessional to repeat her prayers of penance.

That night, Bianca stared into the darkness and felt again the trembling in her knees and the drumming of her pulse. The aching in her body was now a part of a universe gradually crushing her beneath its weight.

Some time the next afternoon, Bianca was repairing the fence that rimmed the sheep pasture when her youngest brother, Paolo, ran up to her breathlessly.

"Bianca!" he said, taking in huge gulps of air. "Massemo has been granted an unexpected leave from his regiment. He sent word from his family's farm – he'll be here within the hour."

She stood staring at him for a moment, too stunned to react. She felt affection and a certain measure of joy, but her love for Luciano had dispelled all thoughts of Massemo. It was almost as if he had ceased to exist.

"That's wonderful news," she said finally. "We'll have to hurry and prepare a nice welcome."

Paolo smiled and then looked at her in the maddening way that little brothers have of making their sisters feel embarrassed about romance.

"Go on!" she said, and rushed forward to give him a soft slap on his dusty rear.

All at once, the events of her life were forming a pattern she did not recognize. She thought of Massemo's trust in her, his innate goodness, and felt a surge of guilt. She knew she had the power to make his life full and happy, and that if they were to wed, only good would follow. Though her conscience was expressing its outrage at the plan that was suggesting itself to her, for the first time since she realized she was pregnant, Bianca felt the faint stirring of hope. Massemo would be her salvation, she resolved, however unworthy she was to be saved. She rushed back to the house to wipe away the day's dirt and put on her only clean dress.

A short while later, Massemo was waiting outside the cracked walls and eroding facade of her mother's cottage, the white shutters on the windows spread open like arms to welcome the day. Awkward, as always, in the face of Bianca's beauty, he soon relaxed when he watched her run through the quince trees to give him a warm embrace. Struck by her apparent happiness at seeing him again, and finding her extraordinarily intent on his every word, the usually shy young man took her hand in his, and together they walked toward the low hillsides surrounding her home.

Copper-colored from months of marching under the sun, his skin was clear and smooth. His shiny hair curled in thick waves, dark as charcoal. Bianca was amazed at the muscled breadth of his shoulders – broad for a man who was not much more than five foot six – and that his legs had grown firm and solid as tree trunks.

Massemo described how he'd been moving on patrol through the hills surrounding Mount Etna as part of the army's campaign against bandit strongholds. And he had good news – in the army's attempt to match the power of the Prussian forces with a cadre of young, strong leaders, he'd been chosen for the officer corps. Although he hadn't experienced combat in the hills – his unit always seemed to be behind the last skirmish – he had distinguished himself with his military bearing, his boundless energy, and his gift for understated authority. But a promotion meant that, before the month was out, he would be transferred to the Italian outpost of Assab on the African coast of the Red Sea. And yet, despite his excitement about his new adventure, as well as Italy's chances for securing a prominent place among the emerging European allies, his hopes had been curbed by a private objective: he wanted Bianca to cast aside the masquerade of the ammucciuni and become truly betrothed to him.

Certain that she would think he was acting too rashly, he then launched into an elaborate series of arguments that had been building in his mind in anticipation of this moment. In fact, he was so caught up in trying to convince her that Bianca had to repeat his name several times before he actually heard her speaking.

"Massemo," she said, "would you be willing to marry me now?"

Her surrender was so complete and unexpected that he just stared at her in disbelief, feeling a mixture of confusion and gratitude, and instantly forgetting the entire flood of words that he had raised to break her down.

"Will you, Massemo?" she asked again. "Will you marry me

now, before you leave for Assab?"

As innocent as he was, Massemo was a sensitive man, and he sensed that her urgency meant something more than he was able to understand. But he also felt that if he confronted her, he might risk losing her completely, and he wanted her more than he wanted the truth of anything that may have happened while he was away.

"Bianca, just the thought of you keeps me warm. I will marry you now and become the happiest man in the whole Sicilian army!" Massemo gave her an ecstatic smile and then lifted her off the ground. Tenderly, they kissed in the late afternoon sunlight, Bianca hiding her shame with downcast eyes, and then, arm in arm, they quietly headed back home.

By the next morning, the news had spread throughout the countryside. Massemo went immediately to Father Costello to discuss the banns – the wedding announcement that must be made three times to see if anyone in the community objected. They didn't have much time, so the announcements would have to be made quickly. Though Massemo was a little surprised at the extent of the priest's enthusiasm, he didn't give it much thought – the old man had always harbored strong paternal feelings for the fatherless Bianca.

A huge feast was held at Bianca's house that evening and the engagement celebration began in earnest. Cousins, nieces, nephews, and grandchildren all came to pay their respects. Her mother had been cooking since dawn and as the party progressed and the noise grew louder, Bianca's brothers became so rambunctious that they could only be calmed by the threat of being denied the cannoli made by Palermo's Benedictine nuns.

The company drank toast after toast to their happiness, laughing at Bianca's sudden impatience to become a bride, and teasing her until her capacity for deception began to sicken her. Soon the table talk swirled around her – wedding arrangements, Massemo's commission, Bianca's success with the Contessa, the weather, the crops, all subjects that obsess Sicilian families – and she felt like an intruder in her own home.

Eventually, as the overfed children drifted off to sleep, and the music and laughter subsided, Bianca weakened from exhaustion. She was overwhelmingly tired, as if all that she had felt for Luciano had finally depleted her soul. If any of the women had noticed how little Bianca was contributing to the plans being made, they wouldn't have been far wrong if they supposed that she was hopelessly lost in young love. They were just singling out the wrong man.

WHEN LUCIANO AND the Contessa returned from the continent, Bianca was forced to face the moment she had dreaded: telling the Contessa of her marriage plans which meant that she'd be leaving Santa Matteo, and risking an encounter with Luciano that she wasn't sure she would survive.

Finally, one hot August morning, two weeks before the wedding, she persuaded Massemo to bring her to the manor in his wagon, avoiding the temptation of wandering through the orchard alone. But as they neared the house, Bianca was so reluctant to look in any direction, so afraid of what she might see from a distance that she almost leapt from the cart when, astride his black stallion, Luciano suddenly appeared before them. Moving politely off the cinder track so they could pass by, Luciano smiled and nodded, his eyes boring directly into Bianca's heart. When their cart drew abreast of him, he called to Massemo, "Why is it that soldiers always escort the loveliest ladies? You're a lucky man, Massemo."

"Luckier than you realize," he said, pleased at the compliment from such an important man.

Bianca, her heart pounding unmercifully, locked her eyes straight ahead, wishing that she had the strength to hurl herself from the cart and outrun the horses. They continued on, and soon she heard Luciano's voice shout behind them.

"You'll have to forgive me for staring so hard. I've been spending every morning deep in the orchard, and my eyes are having trouble adjusting to the sunlight."

In another moment, the thunder of Hades' full gallop carried him away.

A few minutes later, Bianca was standing in the doorway to the Contessa's upper chamber. The Contessa, who was vaguely preoccupied sorting through jewelry, bade her to enter. Bianca sat on a small, tufted chair by the foot of the bed and told her about the wedding, saying how sorry she was that her service would have to end. She could no longer live in Santa Matteo; she and Massemo had decided to move in with his family in Corleone, where they would raise their children and work the lands of his aging relatives when he returned from military service in the spring. In truth, it was her decision, not trusting her loyalty to Massemo with Luciano so close at hand.

Expecting one of the Contessa's childish outbursts, Bianca waited patiently for a response. Instead, the Contessa seemed genuinely saddened at the prospect of losing her, and not simply the loss of a dressmaker. In a rare expression of gratitude, she reached into her trunk of Spanish silks and gave Bianca some of the richest samples.

"Here," she said softly. "Perhaps you can find a place for these in your trousseau."

Bianca was so unprepared for this, so moved by her gift and all her conflicting emotions that she dissolved into tears, paralyzing her for several minutes. To Bianca's great shock, the Contessa embraced her, kissed her gently on the forehead, and said, "I know you'll be very happy, my dear. You'll be such a beautiful bride."

Just then, Bianca looked up and saw a fleeting glimpse of Luciano's pained expression in the Contessa's chifforobe mirror. He had been standing behind his mother's doorway, drawn to the room by the sound of Bianca crying. But by the time she could turn, he was gone.

The Contessa had seen him as well, and having also seen the look that passed between them, she stiffened for a moment, then softened again, and touched Bianca's cheek. Stroking her hair, she said over and over, "Such a beautiful bride."

When Bianca rejoined Massemo a short while later, he was waiting with the cart in the inner courtyard.

"This is a wonderful day, Bianca. Even the castle's young master envies me my bride," he said. As they rode away, she held the precious silks close to her body.

IT WASN'T UNTIL Bianca and Massemo had left Brunella's cottage and begun their parade through town that Bianca saw the solitary horseman, riding in the rising sun across a gentle slope in the foothills that surrounded the dusty Sicilian village. Although she knew that Luciano could not see her face, her brilliant white satin bridal gown and prominent position in the white, red, and green wedding wagon would have allowed his eyes to find her. Led by one little girl carrying a bouquet of orange blossoms to lay upon the altar, the long procession moved down the street toward the stone chapel, followed by friends, relatives, and unmarried girls, past all the gathering townspeople. The crowd was modest by wedding standards, less than a hundred in all. But the solemnity and dignity of their approach, along with their spirit of celebration at the feast, made up for any inadequacy of numbers.

To the distant rider, they must have resembled miniature dolls moving through a toy village. Even the wooden cart, pulled by a white burro festooned with carnations, hyacinths, and myrtle, was barely large enough to hold the bride and groom. Still, she could feel the rider's eyes upon her, probing, as always, till he found the center of her being, the secret passion which only he had known, and now, with her final vows about to be locked into place, was closing itself forever.

This was the beginning of life's pattern, Bianca thought, the blends of form and color she had spent so much of her young life sewing into silk.

Massemo put his arms around her shoulders, small and fragile as a child's, in the softly swaying wagon. Noticing her melancholy expression, he drew her closer and whispered, "It is too soon for regrets," as the burro tried to twist his head to nibble at the pink and yellow flowers that encircled his neck. The village children cheered each time he plucked another blossom.

Bianca was careful not to glance westward again, afraid that like Lot's wife in the story the village priest had told her, she'd be transformed into a pillar of salt. Yet, she must have sensed the moment when Luciano turned away from the ridge because she shivered slightly, and in one fading heartbeat, the lace bodice that she had tenderly crocheted, the cluster of tiny narcissus that served as her crown, and even the baby that was growing within her, all seemed to be carved from snow.

That night, Massemo stood at the window watching the starlight, while Bianca prepared herself for bed. He turned just as she was about to snuff the candle.

"No, Bianca," he said, reaching out to touch her shoulder and speaking for the first time since they had come into the room. "Let me look at you. The stars will not show me all I wish to see."

Bianca smiled, blushing slightly, while her heart started to race. Massemo adored her and she didn't deserve him, she thought. But her doubts were stilled as he stroked her hair, then her cheek, and moved his hand along her body. She was a radiant painting become flesh. Raising her gown, he gazed at her loveliness in the golden candlelight and caressed her delicate skin. Then he drew her to him, kissing her lips, her eyes, her throat, and finally their bodies mingled in a warm embrace. In another moment, Bianca felt his hardness against her and he eased down on top of her, whispering promises of love.

Massemo blew out the candle and reached beneath him, spreading her legs, opening her with his fingers. He felt her shiver slightly and gently buried himself inside her. With a few small thrusts, they reached the point of perfect joy. He heard Bianca cry out and kissed her face once more in an echo of continuing passion.

Much later, when Massemo was in a deep sleep, Bianca lay awake, staring at the dark ceiling. The enormity of the secret she had brought into the marriage filled her eyes with tears. Massemo had aroused her, and she was shocked at the depth of her own response. But even as her body gave in to Massemo's once more, she felt the beating of another heart within her.

Thoughts of Luciano burned darkly through the lonely months that followed, and each day brought her closer to spring when the scent of damp grass flooded her body with the memory of their heated moments. But on Easter Sunday she gave birth to a son in a flowering orchard – Giovanni Manzino, the offspring of no one's nobility but his own.

CHAPTER
TWO

It was a special season by human reckoning, the final days of the nineteenth century, but to the natural world, it was another spring, with the cool rains falling once more. Eventually, the early morning chill would send them below to the spoiled-fruit stench of the ship's hold and the two bunks reserved for them there. For the moment, however, Giovanni Manzino and his wife Rosa clung to the railing, staring through the rain's thickening sheets at what had suddenly become their past.

Since Giovanni had never seen the island from this perspective, he was surprised at how high above the waters the island lifted itself. He remembered Rosa's eyes widening when he showed her the faded map he had borrowed, tracing the ship's path across the Tyrrhenian Sea, rounding Sardinia to reach the main expanse of the Mediterranean, and heading toward the Strait of Gibraltar, a line of blue so narrow that she had wondered how a ship could sail through it. Beyond Gibraltar, they could see the vast Atlantic, ever-expanding until it cut off abruptly at the edge of the map. Rosa thought the map had ended because no amount of paper could show the whole of the ocean, anyway.

Now they felt their fears heighten with the stunning sensation of the sea's awesome power. They'd heard tales of other families, tucked into tiny pockets of space among the cargo, who were crushed to death when rough seas had thrown them in between the crates. Still other terrors – of sinkings, of plagues, of crewmembers insulting the women and stealing their passengers' few possessions – were too horrible to consider.

Looking out at the land through the cloudy, gray fog, Sicily seemed like a lost, floating kingdom growing smaller and smaller. Giovanni remembered first seeing the fields from a pack strapped to his mother's back, rising and dipping in the sunlight as she joined Massemo in the harvest. He began to walk with her when he was four, surrounded by women who carried younger children in the same way he'd once been borne. If he had been reluctant, that first year in the fields, to give up the comforts of childhood, he was never troubled by such sentiments again. As a young man, Giovanni had a born dedication to test the limits of his strength and to honor the rituals of tending the land that were the soul of the Sicilian people.

Although every season brought its own demands, the harvests of late summer and early fall were the ones he would remember the most. Those backbreaking efforts of the year were the workers' triumph, even if the landowner did reap the lion's share of the rewards. Still, tenant farmers like Giovanni's parents were able to keep a portion of the harvest for themselves, which saw them through the lean, hard months between harvests. When the weather had been especially kind, the fig trees were bursting with bounty. Golden or purple-black, they were swollen with juice and ready to burst open at the slightest touch. As soon as the dry months came and the ground's black clay became coarse and cracked under a sky that offered little hope for rainfall, sometimes just the memory of their lushness was enough to dispel the taste of dust.

There was wheat as well, but breads and cakes could not be preserved, so most of the grains were pounded and dried into sheets of pasta, then hung from lines of rope like someone's oddly shaped laundry. Months later, boiling water brought back the pasta's suppleness, in a meal that included a whole measure of tomatoes, peppers, and basil.

Giovanni smiled as he recalled the strong late-summer sun

burning down on his shoulders, the laughter of the people as they rode home in the evenings atop donkey-drawn carts. There was joy in these occasions, a feeling of renewed spirit among the men that found its clearest expression in song, buoyed by the presence of so many crystal-voiced women.

> *Mother! I am going to see my fiancé.*
> *I'm going to have my fun*
> *And my pleasures.*
> *I'm going to find my saint . . .*

> *Love, Love, I come by the night*
> *I don't care if it rains.*
> *I don't care if I'm drenched.*
> *I'm going to see to see my fiancé.*
> *I'm going to have my fun*
> *And my pleasures.*

The children sang lullabies, and anyone who couldn't sing hummed softly in the echo of melodies floating in the air. The blend of harmonies seemed to soothe the infants too young to stand on their own. Sometimes the songs were familiar hymns, rising like prayers that the people had locked in their hearts and sun-parched bodies.

If it did not break you, the land would seduce you, and even as he was escaping, Giovanni longed to be back with the dreamers in the fields once more. But his mother had urged him away, afraid that the land would only be satisfied when everyone was buried beneath it.

Giovanni had been a boy of ten when he saw his mother torn by grief at the news that two of her younger brothers – hardly men themselves – had been murdered one after another, on two successive nights. Their battle had been with a new local chief who had tried to extort payment from them above that which their mother was already giving to the landowner's collector. Their deaths, followed only two months later by that of her bereaved mother had changed Bianca irrevocably. Always a dreamer, she had an innate faith in people's goodness – so when goodness failed, she suffered deeply. From the start, she had taught Giovanni that he should hold himself above common sentiments, that he must wash himself of the soil even as his hands were dirtied in it. But her hopes for him seemed to harbor a mysterious expectation. Giovanni saw a secretive side to her nature as she stared out over the hills, or when she woke at night and roamed their small cottage alone. He would hear the tiny creak on the stairs as she descended quietly, followed much later by her soft footsteps as she returned to bed just before dawn. Once he had crept down after her and saw her watching the moonlight, motionless by the parlor's single window.

Increasingly, Bianca spoke of the land as a curse. Giovanni might still have been content to spend his life achieving whatever happiness he could find there, but she had convinced him that Agostino would make that impossible.

Agostino Mulassano was called a *gabelloto* – except on those rare occasions when the people felt safe enough to whisper more venomous words to describe him – someone who leased a large estate on behalf of an absentee landlord, and then sublet it at exorbitant rates to the peasantry. Though there was no formal organization among them, the gabellotos were the first to become associated with the term *mafia*, whose criminal ties were used by the peasants who had come to distrust the established authorities as a source for self-regulation. These were the men who'd been responsible for the deaths of Bianca's brothers in Santa Matteo. They spread their tentacles across the island, and in time came to devour the very people who they were meant to protect.

Agostino had acquired his power as a "strong man" for Vittorio Robbia, a wealthy merchant who was too caught up in the intrigues of Syracuse to be bothered with his holdings in the "insufferable" Sicilian countryside. As domains go, Vittorio's was fairly modest. The lands commanded by Agostino were not that extensive and measured against the vast, verdant fields and forests of other estates, not especially fertile. Although the house he occupied was much larger than the homes of his neighbors, it had none of the grandeur of the manor of Santa Pietro, nor of the nearby Palazzina Reale. But Agostino's authority was substantial enough to make him mayor of the village. He effectively controlled the elections and often the public finances in town. Corleone was relatively poor, however, so there was little glory in its leadership. Yet, for someone who had begun his career as a common laborer, it was a magnificent achievement.

Every day, Agostino mounted his great white horse and rode, ceremoniously, the perimeter of the lands he controlled. In keeping with his position, he wore a uniform of his own devising: gold-striped cavalry trousers and a brass-buttoned blue tunic purchased in Palermo from a military supply shop on the day he accepted Vittorio Robbia's commission. He also wore several gold medals pinned to his chest that signified no battle, no campaign, and no courage. Only his boots seemed less for show than for crushing his enemies.

Giovanni considered him a pompous, arrogant fool, tracking his territory like a *carabinieri*. If Agostino's only offense had been his comical posturing, Giovanni might have dismissed him as one of life's jokes. But Giovanni had fallen in love with his only daughter and Agostino had waged an all-out war against him when he failed to bow low enough in gratitude.

When Giovanni first met Rosa Mulassano, it was a bright summer day. Nicola Bellini, his friend and fellow field worker, had convinced him to come to the wedding feast of Agostino's first-born son, Leonardo, and a local girl from the village, Lia Casale. Leonardo's choice of a wife was inspired by the wish to find a woman from the village who was high enough in rank, yet humble enough in attitude to pay him the proper respect. She shouldn't talk too much, and she should not be too skinny – all the better to deliver him healthy sons. Leonardo, who was rumored to be waiting for Agostino to die so he could take over the estate, emulated his father's domineering style and military bearing but did so only to maintain a position of authority over the peasants. Privately, he thought it was an act. Once he inherited his father's wealth, he'd stop pretending he enjoyed the role of feudal baron and simply indulge in luxury.

A huge wedding party had been thrown so that all those under Agostino's rule could pay their respects. Bianca and Massemo sat at a table in the shade with some neighboring friends, sipping glasses of grappa, a clear wine made from the last pressing of the grapes. Nicola was completely in his element, pursuing every pretty face in the crowd and consuming large amounts of food and wine. Giovanni, meanwhile, was becoming increasingly restless, aware of the fleeting daylight not being devoted to work. A five second pause on the work field was punished with a blow, yet a whole day's labor could be wasted at Agostino's decree. Giovanni stayed long enough to be polite, and was just about to leave when he noticed a lovely young woman in a violet silk dress calmly shaking her head as Nicola tried to lure her into the center of the dancing crowd. With nutmeg-colored hair gathered in a small bun at the nape of her neck, she had a more aristocratic appearance than the other young women, who let their straight jet-black hair fall below their shoulders. But she seemed almost sad or perhaps too shy to join in and Giovanni naturally gravitated toward her.

He had not intended to speak and was only conscious of a mild curiosity. So when she turned her gaze toward him, he nodded out of courtesy, then continued watching the dancers, most of whom were laughing at a drunk young man who kept spinning in place and falling to the ground.

Suddenly Giovanni heard himself saying, "I am not like my friend."

Rosa turned in surprise and gave him an appraising look. "No," she said, "I can see you're not."

Giovanni's first thought was that she was mocking him, comparing his blunt features and social awkwardness with Nicola's physical prowess. But something in the gentle tone of her voice suggested that she might be pleased by the contrast. Soon she turned her attention to the raucous crowd once more, where the man whose pratfalls had been the focus of hilarity was working his way to his feet and now heading tipsily toward her.

"That's my brother, Enzio," she said quickly. "He'll insist that I dance with him, and I'll have to carry him around for the rest of the night." Grabbing hold of Giovanni's arm, she said, "Hurry and dance with me. It's the only way I can escape him."

Giovanni and Rosa held hands for the first time, as they rushed into the circle of festivity, leaving her dim-witted brother blinking his eyes at the place where she had been standing. Giovanni put his brawny arm around Rosa's small shoulders and entered the tarantella, then in full swing, briefly noticing the look flickering across Bianca's face when she saw his choice for a partner. Whatever his mother knew of the girl, Giovanni thought, he was too caught up in the unexpected pleasure of being with her to give it much consideration.

Before the evening was over, he had learned, of course, that she was Agostino's daughter, which explained why the ambitious Nicola had gone against his usual taste for peasant girls and showered her with so much attention. It also explained Bianca's concern, since all the people feared Rosa's unpredictable and frequently dangerous father. But in the space of a few hours, Giovanni seemed to earn Rosa's respect, which is all that mattered to him.

Soon after the dancing wound down and Leonardo and his new bride had left for the privacy of their nuptial chamber in a shower of flowers and rice, Rosa made motions to return home with the other women of the household. As she was about to walk away, Giovanni put his hand on the small of her back and said calmly, "Rosa, if your father would give me his permission, I'd like to call on you."

"Of course," Rosa said, smiling over her shoulder.

Suddenly infused with promise, Giovanni felt as if he'd just leapt from a precipice for some noble cause. The only tiresome aspect was the necessity of approaching one of her arrogant brothers to present his intentions as well. Fortunately, Nicola had often hunted with Cesare, Agostino's second son and older brother to Rosa, so as the wedding feast drew to a close, Giovanni sought him out on the dance floor, where a few couples were still circling. Nicola had his arms around Mara, one of his favored peasant girls, and catching his eye, Giovanni nodded to indicate that he'd like to speak with him. Nicola twirled her around a few more times, then whispered in her ear and took his leave.

"Let me guess," he said as he stopped before Giovanni and laughed. "Rosa Mulassano is the most beautiful woman you have ever seen and you would like to be presented to Cesare."

"Yes," Giovanni said simply.

Nicola, who had realized that Rosa was not interested in him, smiled at his friend. "That can be arranged," he said, glancing sideways at Mara waiting nearby.

CESARE HAD BEEN standing like a watchdog for most of the day and night, so when Nicola and Giovanni approached him, he bristled in true form. "Cesare," Nicola said. "This is my friend Giovanni Manzino. He requests the honor of visiting your lovely sister Rosa."

Cesare smirked, glaring over Giovanni's shoulder at the dwindling crowd, as if he might find someone more interesting there. Then he gave Giovanni a cool gaze.

"So you wish to court my sister, *paisano*?" he said with his usual sneer, though he could have cared less about whom his annoyingly cheerful sister might marry.

"Si," Giovanni said firmly and stood quietly while Cesare issued another expression of apparent distaste, assessing whether Giovanni was showing the proper deference.

"You'll find no fault with Giovanni," Nicola added, anxious to get back to Mara. "We've worked together for a long time."

Cesare said nothing, only smiled a little as if the idea was somehow amusing. "All right," he said finally. "I'll speak to my father."

Later that week Cesare sent word through Nicola that Agostino would be pleased if Giovanni came to his house on Sunday afternoon after the midday meal. Rosa would be there to greet him.

So began their courtship, following a ritual that had existed for centuries. Giovanni would visit Rosa every Sunday, and though the whole family would be present, they'd usually have a chance to sit quietly together in the garden, as long as someone always had them in view. It was there that Giovanni learned of Rosa's mother's early death from cholera and its devastating effect on Rosa's child-hood. In the face of Agostino's icy ambition, her mother's sweet and gentle nature had been the source of Rosa's own goodness. When she died, Agostino became lost in his need for power, the one game whose rules he understood and whose outcome he could control. Giovanni also learned that Rosa's younger brother, Gino, whom she had dearly loved, was killed instantly at age nine during a family excursion to the village of Corleone. He'd run ahead of the family on a dusty street, rushing around the corner in anticipation of the village, and was knocked over by a farmer's horse team com-ing dangerously fast the other way.

After Gino's death, another light went out of her father's eyes. Rosa tried to carry on her mother's role to make up for the sudden darkness. But when it became too much, she withdrew, watching her older brothers and her father become more and more heartless as time went by. Her love for Gino and her mother stayed with her, but she found herself at odds with her family. She wished that she could simply start anew, to create again the kind of life that she had known as a child.

Normally not a talkative man, Giovanni found it remarkably easy to communicate with her, and gradually they came to know one another, expressing most of their affection in silence. Then, one Sunday afternoon, he decided it was time to broach the sub-ject of matrimony and arrived earlier than usual to speak with her father alone.

After waiting for some time in the estate's marble vestibule, Giovanni was finally ushered into Agostino's study by one of the parlor maids. Smelling of burnt firewood, the room was dark and heavily curtained, lit only by a single stained-glass lamp that stood on a carved mahogany desk where Agostino sat imperiously, writ-ing a long list of numbers into a bound ledger. Above his head, the solemn heads of hunting trophies seemed to beg sympathy for their final resting place from anyone who entered. Lining the op-posite wall, a musty expanse of books gave the room an air of cul-tural importance, although none of them seemed to have ever been opened.

Agostino beckoned him forward, motioning toward a large leather chair. "Please sit down, Giovanni," he said, as he put down his pen and closed the ledger with a slam. "Sometimes I wonder what these people would do without me." He gave a great sigh before leveling a hard gaze at Giovanni.

Everything this man ever said or did was a performance, Giovanni thought. He seemed to have a preposterous pose to accommodate every occasion. "Agostino, I have come to request the honor of taking Rosa as my bride," he said, with a tone of formality.

"So you want to marry my little Rosa?" Agostino said, leaning back in his chair and waxing the ends of his wiry mustache until they stood out absurdly from his face. "Tell me, Giovanni, if I consented to such a marriage, how would you protect her?"

Giovanni's expression did not adopt the crafty look of a schemer in sight of his goal. Nor, as Agostino noticed, did he seem to register fear. He simply knitted his brow for a moment, somewhat puzzled by the question, and answered softly. "I would protect her with my life, Agostino, that is all. My family's farm is modest, as you know, but we are hard-working people. She will be safe and happy among us. In time, we will have our own cottage and our own portion of the land, and your grandchildren will be healthy and strong."

Agostino studied the man before him, probing to see if any trace of scorn lay hidden beneath his humble words. Extremely sensitive to any such undercurrents, Agostino had often wondered if there was more to Giovanni than he could intuit. But the man seemed too simple and unimaginative to harbor any secret hostility. He knew Giovanni feared that he might wish to seek a more "suitable" husband for his daughter. But Agostino wanted someone with an honorable reputation in the community since he had an almost paranoid distrust of anyone outside his domain. When Giovanni's background revealed a quiet strength among the villagers, Agostino was especially keen to bring this respected man within his grasp. A local man, raised under Agostino's iron rule, would be easy to manipulate.

"I'm sorry, Giovanni," Agostino said abruptly, "but that will not do."

Giovanni could feel the color begin to rise in his cheeks as his hands clenched the chair's polished arms.

"To give my consent," Agostino continued, "we would have to come to some other arrangement."

"Meaning?" Giovanni asked rather grimly.

For the next several minutes, Agostino scowled and tapped his finger steadily on the smooth surface of the desk. Giovanni remained silent, knowing the wisdom of allowing the other man his conceit. All at once, Agostino bestowed what appeared to be a benevolent smile and said, "Giovanni, I have a proposal for you. As I grow older, I cannot bear the thought of my only daughter deserting the house that has always been hers. Our house is vast, with many wings. Each of my sons lives here, including Leonardo and Lia, in perfect comfort. Surely there is room for my daughter and her husband. I will give you permission to marry Rosa if you agree to become a part of my household and work on the Mulassano lands." Agostino waited for Giovanni's outpouring of appreciation.

Perhaps Giovanni should have realized that Agostino would one day expect more of him than he was prepared to give. As Agostino's passion for military costumes might suggest, oppressing the lives of others was among his most treasured duties. But Giovanni was in love with Rosa, and naively assumed that he could simply marry her and not her family. If to win her without incurring her father's murderous wrath meant living under his roof and working only for him, then he would do so. He knew he'd work harder than anyone else and that he couldn't expect his parents' small farm to support them and the children they hoped to raise. Once he and Rosa were married, they would find some way to distance themselves from this ridiculous harlequin.

Giovanni finally spoke in the same quiet, passive tone, hoping to convince Agostino that his power had extended over still another man. "Thank you, Agostino, I accept."

"It's arranged then," Agostino said with renewed gusto. "You must remember, I know everything that goes on in my village: once you are taken into my family, the people will give you great respect." He reached across the desk to clasp Giovanni's hand in a hearty handshake that seemed as artificial as everything else about him. But Giovanni took note of the implication buried in Agostino's words: without his approval, Giovanni would never earn respect on his own. Agostino's very arrogance will make him easy to defeat, he thought. Such men are always blindest where there is the most need to see.

THE SUN ROSE full and warm, despite the lateness of the season, as the wedding procession headed toward the village church. Despite their feelings about Agostino, the guests were inspired by the sight of Giovanni and Rosa together and embraced the event with open hearts. Everyone gave themselves fully to the music, the dancing, the wine, and the singing, but Giovanni was only conscious of Rosa's beauty, and the dazzling light created by her love. She was a jewel twinkling in the dust, a miraculous presence among so many ordinary villagers. He never imagined he could be this happy, and never so sure of his ability to keep her safe. Because the Mulassano house was so large, with wings branching from the main rooms, Giovanni had assumed that they would still have some semblance of privacy. Although he resented having to live in such close proximity to Rosa's father and brothers, he knew that Rosa would fashion their corner of the villa as she would her own home. As long as they could make it their sanctuary, he'd be able to endure the frictions that were bound to come.

So it was something of a shock when Agostino announced that their rooms would be in the main section of the house, that Rosa's childhood bedroom, bath, and sitting room had been "especially decorated" for them. Now, for the first time with her husband, Rosa entered the bedroom she had thought was behind her forever. Even as a child, the sight of it had always overwhelmed and embarrassed her. Spacious and lavishly draped, it was much too ornate, dominated by gossamer canopies and curtains, and floral patterns that covered every surface. Rosa's developing sense of style tended toward simplicity and this was obviously too childlike for them. At once, she realized the disturbing truth: this was the first of what would probably be an endless number of her father's humiliations. Giovanni would live like a prisoner in a richly endowed porcelain egg, while Agostino chipped away at his manhood.

Giovanni understood Agostino's malice at a glance. A heavy dresser of dark wood had been awkwardly crowded into one corner; a large brass lamp overpowered a delicate white end table; and a painting of a ship battling a storm at sea had been hung over the bed on a wall dotted with tiny African violets. The clumsy attempt to render the room more appropriate had been accomplished with new furnishings that looked pathetically out of place. Giovanni was clearly expected to feel equally incongruous.

Rosa saw the glint of fury in his eyes, but also the strength of his resolve. Instinctively, she pulled him into the room and abruptly slammed the door in the face of a young servant girl who had approached with yet another bouquet of flowers to join the others that were giving their relatively small quarters a musky, suffocating atmosphere. Rosa threw her arms around his neck, kissed him fully on the lips, and then, holding him tightly, whispered, "Giovanni, I know what he is trying to do to us. But we won't let him hurt us. We won't let him win. I'll go to him now, and demand that he . . . ."

"No, Rosa. Won't say nothing about this room — or where we're told to sit for dinner. We'll be like children reluctantly permitted to come to the table. And we won't say nothing at all."

Rosa could feel his body hardening, but his voice sounded remarkably calm. Confused, she pulled back to see if the bitter words had left any expression on his face. As touched as she was by his tolerance, she didn't want him to surrender to her father so swiftly. Giovanni didn't return her gaze; his attention seemed focused beyond her.

"But Giovanni — " she started.

"This is his house," Giovanni continued in the same hushed voice. "I can't oppose him here." He paused, and Rosa felt a sudden stab of despair at the thought that his spirit could be so easily crushed. Then he smiled. "We'll simply have to go away," he whispered. "To America," he said almost as an afterthought.

Rosa felt her pulse quicken. She turned to lead him to her hopelessly frilly bed, and suddenly she saw the focus of his far-off gaze – the painting of the fragile schooner valiantly fighting its way through the rising force of a typhoon.

LIKE ALL COMPLETELY selfish individuals, Agostino Mulassano imagined himself to be very generous. To keep that illusion alive, he periodically showered a few gifts on poor villagers. The village priest woke up to a statue of one of his favorite saints. A widow who had lost her barn to a fire found it being rebuilt the next day. The village children received a pony to share for afternoon rides in the square. As long as the gifts were part of a public event and didn't involve any significant sacrifice, Agostino gave them with a flourish. But no one was fooled. The priest knew that Agostino was completely immune to any moral graces from above. The widow knew that her barn was being rebuilt by the same man who had bullied her neighbors into paying enough patronage for a thousand barns. Even the children would learn that while they pranced on the pony, their parents were desperately struggling to meet the crop quotas enforced by the brutal sons of their benefactor.

Rosa was also aware of her father's conceit and intended to take advantage of it as she and Giovanni began the long-term preparations for their eventual departure. She had no intention of abandoning several cherished belongings to her unmourned past. Fine laces, rare silks, satin garments, precious linens – all the contents of her mother's cedar chest that Agostino had alluded to so grandly as Rosa's dowry when she was growing up – would be hers.

"The women in the village need linens for the church," she said one day to explain the armfuls of immaculate white fabric she was loading into her wagon. "The lace on the altar has yellowed with age and we have more than we will ever need. The congregation will bless you in their prayers, father, when they see your generosity." Agostino simply nodded from atop his horse and then galloped away to roam his lands.

But, of course, the softest silk linens never reached the altar; they were bound for Bianca's cottage, to be stored among her own timeworn linens. Instead, Rosa picked out some ordinary fabric to give to the priest. And yet, for weeks afterward, Agostino nodded proudly as the villagers praised the altar's new splendor – not that he had seen it, since he only attended mass on special occasions.

Or, referring to the forthcoming wedding of a favorite cousin, Rosa said, "We cannot let little Luisa begin her marriage without a proper wardrobe. I've chosen some lovely things that will go so well with her coloring." As before, Agostino merely nodded and returned to his frivolous pursuits, while a few more of Rosa's treasures were secreted from the brightly colored heap and placed among Bianca's drab garments.

Then the tensions that already existed in the house were compounded by a troubling event. Agostino returned from a visit to Messina with a new bride – Adriane, an arrogant, empty—headed woman who imagined that the accident of having been born in a cultured city set her far above the people of Corleone. Rosa suspected that the woman's contempt extended to Agostino as well, but she was willing to suppress those feelings in exchange for his considerable power.

On the other hand, they almost seemed to deserve each other. Adriane's shallow beauty and aristocratic breeding were like Agostino's pretender's uniform – one more expression of vanity, valued only for its ability to impress others. The situation caused Rosa to form an instant antipathy toward her father that poisoned the entire atmosphere, hardening into a cold silence whenever they were in each other's company. Still, there were those who disapproved of Rosa's resentment. Agostino had given her considerable luxury. He'd never struck her with his widely feared hand and he had treated her mother with respect. Rosa, however, looked beyond her own comfort and saw the daily cruelties he inflicted upon others.

When Rosa was a child, the villagers always welcomed her with compliments, but as she grew older, she saw the contempt in their eyes. All at once she knew that she would never be just another pretty child playing in the sunlight. To the people of Corleone, she was the daughter of the man who might, on any given day, destroy them. Once she realized their fear was a judgment of her father and not of her, she began to recognize the realities of life around her. All of her father's wealth was tinged with blood, she discovered, gained from someone else's pain. Families had been driven from their homes and men were frequently beaten for whatever misdemeanor he determined in their deeds. Then, one day when she was twelve years old, Rosa was walking through her father's lands on a dry summer afternoon. She had ventured out further than usual, hoping to find wildflowers under a patch of distant trees. As she reached them, however, she realized that the scraggly olive trees were sheltering a large patch of disturbed and upturned earth, rising in a mound that had been hastily patted down. The ground was a graveyard, she realized, recently and shabbily made. Under the dark and shimmering hills, she felt a cool shiver run through her body. It was the air of death, and it crawled over her skin with chilly slender fingers. Stepping backward, Rosa slipped for a moment in the dust. A stab of fear ran through her, as if she too might be pulled into the bitter bloody earth.

Running home, Rosa lay in her bedroom wishing there were someone she could speak to. But she didn't dare, even though the veiled talk around her was beginning to make more sense. The graves, she knew, were those of men too courageous to surrender to her father's will. The mantle of death fell upon her shoulders as surely as if her own hands had held the rope, the club, the blade. From that day on, whenever a house or barn was burned, or a body was found headless in a field, Rosa saw the Black Hand of Corleone, the secret clan that dealt in fatal vendettas, was enclosed in her father's glove.

And yet, she never imagined that it would be possible to escape her father's rule. His was the only world she had known. Once she became a Manzino, however, the people smiled not only with their faces, but with their eyes as well.

Agostino, meanwhile, would announce to the villagers that Giovanni knew his place and accepted his role as one of the

Mulassano's peasant farmers. His courtship of Rosa had followed every tradition, he said, and his hard work suggested the heart of a man who would never disrupt the pattern of life around him. But no matter how hard Giovanni worked, Agostino demanded more and more menial labor from him that appeared to serve no real purpose. He was fond, for example, of sending Giovanni into the hills on a donkey to gather lemons. Scattered throughout the countryside and thwarted by the scarcity of summer rainfall, they had the maddening tendency to ripen one by one, and never as a full harvest. This meant endless rides over the same narrow trails to catch the actual moment of ripening, and many returns to the village with each meager accumulation. This haphazard harvesting was a job for young boys or old women. To Giovanni, the work was given, it seemed, only to demean him. Yet he was expected to perform it reverently, as if honored to be chosen. Moreover, the donkey was so small and his own body so bulky that Giovanni felt humiliated each time he straddled the poor beast.

He'd also been given other onerous assignments, the most painful one being to act as some sort of family enforcer, which went against everything in Giovanni's nature. He was constantly being asked by Agostino or one of Rosa's three brothers to evaluate the other field workers, identifying those who were shirking their duties and then pressuring them to improve; Agostino was not ingenious enough to impose his authority with anything other than brutality. Giovanni was willing, even anxious, to work himself to exhaustion, but he had no desire to assume responsibility for anyone else. If others chose to fail, that was their affair. To ask him to become their hated overseer was, he surmised, a means for Agostino to reach into his own household and fan the flame of rebellion that could only be doused in a public display of proprietorship. Agostino would have to depend on his sons for policing the fields, Giovanni thought. He refused to make enemies of his friends.

Giovanni particularly despised Enzio, who had never entertained even the possibility of finding some occupation other than punishing workers in his father's fields.

"Only fools work for money," Enzio was fond of saying and

would scold Giovanni for being too industrious. "Even if you accomplish something, you will be old and broken before you have a
chance to enjoy what you've earned. My father has ways to get
what you want while you're still young. I've already told him that
I think you have great potential. Perhaps it's time for you to make
a contribution to the family business."

When Giovanni remained silent, Enzio took it as a sign of
encouragement. "Listen, there's a deal coming through outside
Palermo, an easy heist that will bring you more money in minutes
than you can earn in a whole month of sweat. We take the prize,
then go out for a night on the town with some girls who would
love to bestow their many charms on a man like you, especially
since you're my brother-in-law."

Enzio failed to see Giovanni's fury. Hands forming into fists,
he had to steel himself against his anger and came dangerously
close to exploding. The muscles tightened in his neck and he simply said, "No – Thank you. " Enzio walked away, shrugging his
shoulders, dismissing Giovanni once again from his thoughts.

Then Giovanni and Rosa were subjected to another kind of
anguish. During the first two years of their marriage, Rosa had
become pregnant twice, and each time she had lost the child in
the sixth month. Agostino had announced to the entire family,
and apparently to a great many people in the village, that Giovanni's
seed must be too weak to create children. "Look at my own three
strong sons," he would say, "yet my Rosa has been subjected twice
to failure."

Finally, when Rosa became pregnant for the third time, Agostino
went so far as to declare that if a baby should actually be produced
this time, he would take a decisive role in rearing that grandchild
properly. When word of this reached Giovanni, something changed
deep within him. Agostino was treading upon his circle of intimacy, a line that no man had the right to cross. Suddenly all of
Giovanni's efforts were concentrated on leaving Sicily as soon as
possible. But when the cost seemed hopelessly out of reach, he
turned in desperation to Bianca. Years before, Bianca had told him
that when she and Massemo had returned to their cottage after

their wedding feast, they'd found a miracle lying before them. In a chest of dark cherry wood, someone had left a solid silver tea service for the newlyweds. Everyone was astounded by the enormity of the gift and knew it could only have come from one source: the Contessa Grazella Luisa Santa Pietro. Bianca, however, privately suspected the work of someone else.

"This is my legacy," she had said to Giovanni, trembling slightly as she stroked the gleaming surfaces. "One day you will come for the silver, and it will be waiting for you."

And now, standing in her darkened doorway, looking needy and forlorn, Giovanni knew the day had come.

"Well, you were right, Mamma. I've come to ask for the silver."

He had been infinitely patient, slowly storing fragments of wealth so that someday he and Rosa could set sail for America. Outwardly, they had given no signs of discontent. They had worked each day alongside the villagers, knowing all the while that as soon as they were ready, they would disappear from the village forever. But as Agostino stepped up his campaign to bring him under his heel, Giovanni's patience had run out.

Erupting in shouts of joy, Bianca hugged him as though he had just brought her a room full of silver instead of taking her few pieces away. Giovanni had always known that his mother was different, but as she grasped his hands with surprising force, he felt she had achieved some special victory.

When she was calm enough to speak intelligibly, she said, "You don't know what this means. From the moment you were born, I knew you'd break away from this place, for both of us. It's your destiny."

"I'm not so special," Giovanni said. I'm an ordinary man seeking an ordinary life." He reached out to caress her cheek and Bianca's eyes glimmered with tears. "Massemo!" she called. "Massemo! Giovanni is going to America!" Then she reached up to kiss him. "Go speak to him," she said, "while I get the silver."

Giovanni waited in the kitchen, surrounded by Bianca's blend of aromas. No other room would smell so wonderful, he thought;

it was the scent of his childhood, the aura of a thousand meals mingled with his mother's presence. Here he had found substance for the soul as well as the body, where he and his childhood friends had spoken in hushed tones as Bianca told them stories of the world, warning them of demons lurking in the countryside, of empty graves waiting to welcome fathers and sons whose rivalries would eventually consume them. Only her youngest brother had survived, taken in by a neighboring family in Santa Matteo, one of whose daughters he later married. But no son of hers, Bianca had sworn, would fill a graveyard while she was alive.

When Giovanni emerged from his reverie, he saw Massemo sitting at the kitchen table, staring into the distance with a look of sorrow, his usually calm demeanor marred by a kind of grieved agitation. Giovanni stood in silence, his head bowed.

"When a man becomes too old to work," Massemo began, "his one pleasure in life is to sit in the sun and play with his grandchildren, sipping the wine that was aging when he was a boy. If you go to America, who'll play checkers with me?" His voice dropped away as he finished the words, tears filling his eyes.

Giovanni answered gently, "When that time comes, your grandchildren will be brought to you and I'll beat you at checkers."

Bianca set down a large wooden box on the table. To celebrate the moment, they all drank from a bottle of brandy and dipped into a bowl of plums.

As THE DATE of the ship's departure drew closer, Giovanni became increasingly tense, worried that something might suddenly prevent them from sailing. Rosa, on the other hand, was deathly afraid that they would actually go. Although she didn't want to upset Giovanni by revealing the extent of her ambivalence, the idea of entrusting their lives to some flimsy ship that might be lost forever on a treacherous sea was beginning to seem insane. Rumors that the cargo ships were filled with convicts only increased her anxieties, which became more palpable with each passing day.

The week of their departure arrived and Giovanni traveled to Palermo where he planned to sell the silver and arrange for their passage. He'd been careful to get a recommendation from a friend of a shop known to be honest, and found it hidden in the shadow of the Church of the Santa Maria Della Catena. There, he conducted the business of selling Bianca's treasure, procuring a fair price, and then headed for the waterfront.

Rosa was somewhat right to worry. All the villagers were saying that the cargo ships were run by thieves. Even at the quay, robbers were reputed to be lying in wait to steal the passengers' belongings. Men claiming to be monks sold talismans to guarantee a safe voyage. Posers sold false tickets to the unwary. Giovanni, however, known for his good judgment, found a man whom he trusted instinctively and who made him feel reasonably certain that word of their journey would not reach the ears of Agostino. As it happened, the men at the harbor were well accustomed to the subterfuge of emigrants, usually for reasons far darker than Giovanni's. They also said that the greatest risk for an emigrant to America was not getting lost at sea, but being turned away for health reasons once the ocean had been crossed. Giovanni was instructed to arrive for a seven a.m. departure, bringing only the luggage that he could carry himself. Anything stored in the hold, he was warned, might not be recovered.

Returning home, Giovanni could barely contain his excitement. The trip to Palermo had sent the blood rushing through his veins and he could hardly believe that his dream was about to come true. When he arrived home, he was eager to share his anticipation with Rosa but found her in a kind of daze, her eyes filming over like clouded glass.

"You look like you've seen a ghost," Giovanni said.

"It's nothing," Rosa said. "I've just been to visit Bianca, that's all, and it made me sad."

Giovanni took her hand as they sat at the kitchen table. "She is happy for us?" he said.

"Oh, yes."

She had not told Giovanni that Bianca had asked to see her alone. Bianca always treated Rosa as she would any friend, as if her marriage to Giovanni were just a happy coincidence that had little do with their friendship. Yet when she asked for a private conference, Rosa had a strange sense of foreboding. Perhaps, she had thought, Bianca resented their leaving after all. Perhaps, despite all the times she had insisted otherwise, Bianca expected them to find some way to bring her and Massemo, adding still another burden to their ordeal. Or perhaps, Rosa thought as she was crossing the field to Bianca's cottage, she just wanted to offer some wisdom on the path that lay ahead of them.

Rosa arrived on her doorstep damp from a light rain falling softly through the cold mist, and Bianca greeted her with warmth.

"Come in," she said, and drew her inside. Then she chattered about the weather and set down two cups of strong dark coffee on the table. Only when Rosa had taken a few sips, its bitter aroma filling her nostrils, did Bianca turn the conversation to its true purpose.

"Rosa," she said and smiled, "It's funny. I remember being so frightened when I first saw my son with you, the daughter of Agostino Mulassano. Giovanni had always been so cautious, so unwilling to risk . . . but he was drawn to you immediately, a woman of grace and wealth." Bianca's voice faltered and she pushed her cup away from her. A few moments of silence passed during which Bianca seemed to be concentrating very intently. Rosa sipped her coffee and waited, watching the dimmed focus of the other woman's eyes. Then Bianca cleared her throat and began again, "Rosa, I have never asked you anything about your marriage because your happiness is apparent to everyone. But if you will permit me just this once . . . ." Bianca paused briefly before continuing. "Have you ever felt that there is a part of Giovanni you do not fully understand, some mystery in his makeup?"

Although Rosa had never consciously given the matter any thought, she knew that the answer was yes. Giovanni had some inner fire that flared up when he seemed most at odds with himself. Although most people saw him as they did Massemo – in terms of his simplicity, his quiet strength and endurance, the traditional traits of a laboring peasant – Rosa had recently been aware of another intelligence looming beneath the surface of his placid exterior. The idea triggered so much speculation that she didn't answer Bianca for several minutes. When she finally looked up, somewhat alarmed at how the thought had overtaken her, Bianca was smiling.

"So you have seen something special in him," Bianca said boldly. "Before you leave Sicily, I think you should know why."

Bianca got up to freshen their coffee. "Massemo is not Giovanni's father," she said suddenly. "Giovanni is the son of a lord, the lord of a great manor, whom I have not seen in more than twenty years."

Rosa let out a gasp, almost dropping her cup, then sat facing Bianca feeling utterly bewitched by the effect of so stunning a truth. Her unfinished coffee grew cool as her mind filled with ghosts. Then, throughout the long afternoon, as the shimmering gold of the sunlight made her almost forget the dryness of the dust beneath them, Rosa stared in amazement at the tiny woman across the table as she told the astonishing story of a long ago lover and the child their love had created. It didn't matter that Bianca was telling her things that shocked her, a circumstance that shattered every rule regarding the conduct of Sicilian women. Bianca was describing the most significant event in her life. In a world dominated by the ugly sins of men like Rosa's father, Bianca's sin had a kind of grandeur to it, a beauty that moved Rosa to tears, which now drifted unchecked down her cheek.

Bianca reached across the table and grasped Rosa's hands in hers. "You understand, child, why it is so important that Giovanni never know of this? He loves Massemo. It would devastate him. Who knows what could happen? He might even be driven to seek some kind of vengeance. God knows, he might question his love for me."

Rosa nodded and said, "Yes, of course."

"Then this will be our secret," she said. "I am telling you because you are his wife and you should know everything about the man to whom you are devoting your life and with whom you will one day have children. I would be guilty of the greatest deceit if I did not tell you. My son is special. His sons and daughters will be special as well. It's the reason I have always wanted Giovanni to get away from this place. His family must be given the chance to accomplish great things. In America, his children will find opportunities that God has in mind for them."

Before leaving the cottage, Rosa stood in the doorway for what seemed like a lifetime. The two women held each other closely, crying softly in each other's arms. Rosa's fear of the crossing fled from her mind, and she suddenly longed to be on their way so they could begin to make Bianca's dreams come true.

There was something ceremonial about this meeting Rosa thought, the passing of knowledge between women about the man they both loved. Bianca had wanted her to understand all the mysteries that Giovanni carried within him, ones that he had never been told but would surface as powerful longings and sweep through him like the wind. Giovanni had a special destiny, his mother said, making their trip to America inevitable. It was now Rosa's task to help him fully realize his fate.

And so, on March 19, 1899, as the winds fought in the dark morning sky above them, Rosa and Giovanni slipped out of Agostino's house, carrying only one suitcase a piece – and one bundle of Rosa's precious silks – and hurried down to the front gate where Bianca and Massemo were already waiting to see them off.

Giovanni and Rosa had chosen this day for a reason. It was the feast of Saint Joseph, foster-father of Christ and husband of the Virgin Mary. Also called Father Providence, the Sicilians honored him as they celebrated the change of season. Traditionally, a ring-shaped loaf of bread was made with semola flour to symbolize a measure of providence to the day, and Bianca had baked two of the special loaves for them. She and Massemo could not risk traveling to Palermo with them – Agostino might discover they had abetted their departure – so they had come now to say their final farewells. In a nearby clearing, Giovanni had already secured a horse and cart from Agostino's stables. Paco, a young village boy, was waiting there too – Giovanni had promised him a handsome sum to accompany them on their journey and then return the horse and cart to the stables by nightfall.

After Paco loaded the cart and jumped in, Rosa and Giovanni turned to Giovanni's parents and found themselves speechless at the prospect of being separated perhaps for the rest of their lives. All at once, Bianca stepped forward and pressed her two packages of bread into their hands, then kissed them both. Massemo followed, hugging each of them, and then pulled a hand carved wooden pipe from his pocket, which he gave to Giovanni, his eyes filled with tears. No one dared to speak, as if their whispers might wake the whole village, or unleash an unbearable weeping.

And so, with Rosa by his side in the early morning darkness, Giovanni roused the horse with a gentle snap on the reins and set the cart moving toward the eventual sunrise. The two couples waved until the cart rounded the road leading out of Corleone, and tears began to flow. All was silent save for the sound of Rosa's cries over several miles until Giovanni was able to calm her. They both felt small and alone. The roads were empty at this hour, which at least gave them some feeling of protection.

Several hours later, Palermo came into view just as the light was breaking on the horizon. They arrived at the dock amidst crowds of people bustling about, whole families embracing and periodically weeping. The excitement was intense. Giovanni pulled down their baggage, gave Paco the money he had promised, then nodded the boy to leave. Giovanni took Rosa's hand for a moment and they watched as the horse and cart turned around and headed back home.

"Well," Giovanni smiled to Rosa. "I guess we're off."

They turned to face the great ship docked before them, then picked up their bags. The ship was huge, even ominous, and as they walked up the gangplank, they gripped the rails for dear life. It seemed no time at all before the lines were cast to shore and the ship's engines rumbled beneath them. Suddenly the two found themselves standing on the massive deck, hugging Bianca's loaves of bread, and gazing out over the silver water that rippled toward the hills like tendrils of their own tenuous hold on the future. Neither of them had really believed they would actually leave.

The cargo steamer huffed its way across the calm waters of the Bay of Palermo and as the island diminished in the distance, Giovanni drew Rosa close and they watched together until the shore finally vanished into the fog. Giovanni felt an involuntary shudder tremble through him, as if he were physically shedding his past. Perhaps this was why people watched the coffins of loved ones lowered into the earth, he thought. Only then were they freed from the futile hope that they might return.

"You are taking me to the very edge of the world," Rosa said, as if she were reading his thoughts in the sway of the ship beneath them, "but I have no regrets." Still, she was stricken by the knowledge that Bianca had imparted to her, and by the incipient challenge of turning so great a secret into a private source of healing for Giovanni.

Moving now across the sea, Giovanni searched in vain for a last glimpse of the Sicilian hillside where he'd first seen the silver vision that was propelling them through the water as surely as the ship itself. He remembered how often he had dreamt of this moment as he drifted home under a star-peppered sky after a day of gathering lemons for Agostino. But on one particular night, Giovanni did not have the stars for company. He'd been hot, dusty, and tired, and had stretched out wearily on a blanket against the hill's gentle incline. A cool fog, unusual after such an arid day, had brought a touch of unseasonable chill. Giovanni had eaten his cheese and drunk his cold coffee, tied down his mule and was lying on his back, his body angled toward a small clearing, when he heard some distant suggestion of music. Listening intently, he stared into the clouded, darkening air until he realized that the sounds were coming from behind him, apparently beyond the crest of the hill. He rose from the blanket and turned to face the hillside that was strangely silhouetted by a soft, silvery glow. Puzzled by the source of this mysterious light, he searched the sky for an explanation, but found none, and he knew of no settlements nearby. And yet, the light gained steadily as he climbed the hilltop, unexpectedly silver, as if the moon and stars had been banished by the mist and fallen in a bright, earthbound heap. When he finally reached the crest and gazed out across the valley, he was struck by the vision all at once.

The hills were arranged in a loose circle like a vast bowl scooped out of the earth. There, on the rim across from him, human figures, perhaps thirty in number, danced in a light that seemed to shine from within them. Under their silk and satin skirts hooped in glowing colors of Kelly green, peacock blue, burgundy, and mauve were layers and layers of lace petticoats. The dancing maidens seemed to float as they spun in the mist, their tiny waists bound with bright sashes tied back in bows. They wore headpieces as well, haloes of flowers with long gossamer veils that trailed behind them as they danced in elaborate patterns, laughing and singing with natural grace. At first they seemed to move at a slower pace than the rhythm of the rest of the world – an illusion of the dance, he thought. Or maybe his mind was supplying the melody suggested by their perfect movements. Vibrant colors, almost lost in the glare, were enhanced by the bubbling current of blurred forms that flowed in a star-like stream. Faint music, the high sound of a *friscalettu* or *ciaramedda*, gave the impression of a hundred far-off bells tinkling softly. The rich scent of almond blossoms hung in the air, though he knew they were out of season. Then the image of the dancers faded into the darkness. Giovanni didn't remember falling asleep, but the morning sun awakened him on the still-damp grass.

When he returned to his village a few hours later, he told everyone he encountered about what he had seen, as though he might be describing a storm in the mountains or the sighting of an unusual owl. Some thought he'd been drinking; others just dismissed it as one of many romantic dreams they would hear from young men after a night of imagined rapture. But out of respect for Giovanni, they all listened politely. No one believed him, of course, except Crazy Teresa, who believed everything – whether the hallucinations of the ill, or the signs she imagined in nature's every act. While many in the village dismissed her as a harmless fool, others feared her powers as a witch. She would wander through town, lost in some incomprehensible reverie, and then suddenly point to some individual and announce a prophecy. Even those who were the least superstitious dared not challenge her. Everyone was afraid of provoking her into a *fettatura*, a vengeful power that the people believed could curse them forever unless they carried lucky charms like a red horn, an amulet or even a little red pouch half the size of a thumb filled with grains of salt and hung with a religious medal. It was said that she could cast a spell with one glance from her strangely wandering eyes. When a baby was born, an amulet was immediately concealed on a piece of the child's clothing and worn everyday in case the baby was touched by the evil eye. As further protection, women put their hands in the folds of their skirts, pointing their thumbs downward and tucking their fingers toward the evildoer. Sometimes they spat on the ground and muttered, "God bless," while the men placed their hands in their pockets and grabbed hold of their testicles, then spat also.

And yet, it was Crazy Teresa who finally ventured to interpret Giovanni's vision of the silvery dancers. "One dancer is a king," she said to him. "Another dances in a circle around him, joined by the others, so that he cannot move. The king is a prisoner in his own castle, circumscribed to his own stillness. The other is free from the dusty streets and wants to father many children among the gods. But he is lost in a sea of uncertainty, a storm of raging proportions, until the moment comes when his faith is tested by the strength of his own beliefs." Listening to her speak, Giovanni felt his heart beat irregularly and almost glimpsed the crash of the glimmering surf in her pale blue eyes.

Suddenly the sea had become as beautiful in the sunlight as the fields he had left behind. Then, in a blazing burst of light, thrown back by the water in dazzling flashes, Giovanni and Rosa watched Sicily disappear. The wind rose in the open sea, the air turned bitterly cold, and they stepped down into the ship's hold to rest, Rosa wrapping her arms around the dreamless child within her.

CHAPTER
THREE

GIOVANNI AND ROSA arrived in America deep within a tidal wave of immigrants, millions from Italy alone, answering a call sweeping all of Europe which proclaimed that to truly enter the twentieth century you had to cross the Atlantic and wait for the new age in New York. But as the ship pulled into Ellis Island, all Rosa could feel was disorientation and bewilderment. The journey from Sicily had been so grueling that it seemed like a lifetime instead of a few weeks.

As soon as the ship was well underway, Rosa had felt herself drowning in a sea of nausea that seemed as vast as the sea beneath the hull. Her own swirling sickness from the pregnancy only exacerbated the tension. The pitching ship left her weak from constantly retching. What little air existed in the ship's hold was heavy with the stench of unwashed bodies, fouler each day with accumulated sweat. The smell of urine and excrement mingled with the odors of sausages, salamis, and other preserved meats that could not survive the heat. Since the ship could supply only the barest necessities of water and hard biscuits, the people had brought their own food. Cheeses that no one could bear to throw out spoiled alongside the acidic fruits that ripened one day and became breeding grounds for insects the next.

Rosa had been shy with most of her fellow passengers, but her repeated trips to the railing, where she lost almost every ounce of protein, eventually provided her with a friend. Francesca Secca, a woman far along in her pregnancy, was several years older than Rosa and had a small boy of eight who clung to her compulsively, staring out at the sea in fear and fascination. Rosa and Francesca had just turned away from the railing for the third time in one afternoon when their eyes met as they were wiping their mouths and they began to laugh.

"When are you due?" Francesca asked in a wonderfully familiar dialect that flooded Rosa with joyous relief after many days of near silence.

"In four months," she answered. "And you?"

"Three weeks, I think, though at times today I've thought my baby was trying to climb out of my throat and leap into the ocean."

Rosa glanced down at the woman's belly. "You hardly look as if you're carrying a child at all."

"That's an old story in my family – hunger causes small babies."

"I'm so sorry. I didn't mean to embarrass you."

Francesca reached out and squeezed Rosa's hand with surprising strength. "Hunger is no secret," she smiled. "As you can see, my son, Edwardo, is only covered by the thinnest layer of skin. In America, this will change. I've sworn on every saint in heaven – no more death and poverty for us. I am finished with Sicily forever. My new baby will be born big and healthy in the new world."

They stood together and talked for a long while, each determined to ignore the ship's swaying beneath their feet. Francesca had already lost two children in the six years she'd been married. One had lived only a few hours, the other a month. Both died, she was told, because her own body was too weak and exhausted to provide enough nourishment for new life.

"What made you leave Sicily?" she asked Rosa.

Rosa was reluctant to tell the whole truth of their escape, but she instinctively trusted Francesca and wanted to share her hope.

"My husband has heard so many magical tales about America," Rosa said. "He says that all Americans are the same – rich or poor.

He has a dream to educate our children so they can be equals in the world."

"I am going to meet my husband, Savino, in a town called Buffalo after the baby is born," said Francesca. "He has relatives there who have offered food and shelter in exchange for work on the family farm. But first I will stay with my cousins in a place called Mott Street."

"You're here alone?" Rosa asked incredulously.

"Savino thought it was best for him to go first and secure a place for us."

"You're brave," said Rosa softly. "I couldn't face this journey without Giovanni."

"You'd be surprised at what you can do."

They met every afternoon after that, when the weather was not unbearably cold, to reminisce about the villages they had left behind and imagine their life in America. The time passed more swiftly, but the continual discomfort, relentless as the ocean waves, became more and more difficult to bear. The sea seemed like an angry god determined to sink them, raging against the creaking masts and groaning hull.

Though most people in the steerage slept on a hammock or found a space on the floor, Giovanni had managed to secure bunks for both him and Rosa by plying a crewmember with one silver coin after another. The luxury cabins were only accessible from the crew's quarters — a way for the rich to avoid poverty, Giovanni thought, because they feared it was somehow contagious — but neither he nor Rosa had ever caught a glimpse of the cabins' occupants. Consequently, everyone was truly surprised when one afternoon a visitor climbed down from the first class decks seemingly in search of someone specific.

Professor Marco Marietta, a gregarious little gentleman some sixty years old, was a university teacher from Rome who'd been granted an appointment to teach Italian history at a school called Columbia University. He had come to the steerage because he'd heard from a crewmember that the entire village where he had been born was on board. There, he discovered all thirty-one men,

women, and children who comprised the whole surviving population, with the exception of old man Benedetto, a shepherd who
had fancied himself mayor of the village. Stubborn to the last, he
had refused to join the villagers in the foolish notion of sailing to
the new world, so the people had left him behind – an old goat
among sheep with no one left to bully.

At first, Professor Marietta only wanted to learn about his old
home and see the familiar faces he had remembered from his childhood, but once he was among his own people, he was swept by
sentimentality and had to fight back his tears. He had left the
village at fourteen, but the people were proud of his eventual success which they had heard about from his grandmother who had
remained there until her death. Suddenly gripped with the desire
to help them somehow, the professor wanted to share his knowledge of America, hoping that it would give them some advantage
when they actually arrived. American newspapers had been sent to
him in Rome once a month, so he knew what they would all soon
encounter.

As soon as the professor began to speak, the villagers became so
excited that they immediately brought him outside and a large
crowd gathered around him. Then a huge man came up behind
him and lifted him onto a small crate. The professor, somewhat
flustered by all the attention, straightened his spectacles and pretended he was back in the classroom, now teaching the flipside of
history – that is, the future.

Giovanni listened wide-eyed with the others as Professor
Marietta described the city, how it was organized into neighborhoods, and then talked about the neighborhoods themselves, particularly the ones where the Italians had settled in a part of New
York called East Harlem. The Italians on 104th and 105th Streets
were considered to be of a somewhat higher social class and came
from such places as Placenza. One hundred and seventh street belonged to the Sicilians. The Calabrese from Calabria lived on 108th
Street and the people from Sola Consilena had settled on 109th
Street, between First and Second Avenues. From 111th Street to

115th Street was the market section, with most of the businesses owned by Jewish merchants.

The Red Light District, from 117th Street to 122nd Street on Lexington Avenue, offered hundreds of girls with as many nationalities for as little as fifty cents, or some men amused themselves with dance hall girls in such spots as the Rainbow Garden on 125th Street. However, as their venues were the frequent targets of hold-ups, customers had more than infectious diseases to worry about.

The professor then described a golden age powered by the new god of electricity. He told them that one day New York would have the most modern transportation system in the world with electrified cars moving on tracks erected high above the streets and through tunnels running underground. But the newspapers that spoke of it so rapturously had also reported the many delays caused by engineering disasters and political squabbles. Even the electric cable cars had drawn stubborn resistance from the rich who didn't want cable lines strung through their neighborhoods, and the few colorful little cars in operation had such an alarming accident rate that they had become a joke throughout the city. All of which meant that the twentieth century would be dragged onto America's stage by the same team of horses that had been laboring there for centuries.

Professor Marietta extolled the virtues of Robert Van Wyck, the mayor of New York who lived like a king, causing the villagers to laugh at the memory of old Benedetto. The professor also explained that the city had just combined with several smaller towns – places with strange names like Brooklyn and the Bronx – to form something called Greater New York. But when he spoke about the city's sheer size, many became intimidated by the thought of such enormity. He said that in the past ten years alone, the population of New York had tripled – from a million and a half to three and a half million people. To Giovanni, the figure was inconceivable. How could so many people live together on one island? For the first time, his resolve was truly shaken. Lost in his own enthusiasm, however, the professor continued, saying that precious few immigrants would move beyond the seaport docks because most were cowed by the barriers of language, culture, and experience. They huddled together in tiny ethnic communities and leaned on tradition to reconstruct their lives in resilient bubbles of memory. They were becoming a new class and in most cases they assumed the lowliest tasks, freeing the earlier fugitives of Europe. New ships brought new replacements and the process would go on, often borne in blood.

Professor Marietta then warned them about what to expect at Ellis Island: in addition to the health examination, they would be asked if they had paid for their own journeys and if work was waiting for them in America. Anyone who was brought over under contract with an American company might be deported – since the government was trying to stop the *padrone* system in which foreign laborers were put to work under harsh and abusive conditions. On the other hand, the ability to find work was important because the examiners looked hard at anyone who might become a public charge.

Giovanni grew worried, first that he might not find room for his family in such a crowded place and second, that he would answer one of the examiner's questions incorrectly. Unwilling to hear anything more discouraging, he finally left the professor and returned to Rosa. At least, he thought, they were both young and in good health.

The next morning Rosa woke to a chilly dawn and noticed that the ship was swaying more than usual. Lying on her bunk, she closed her eyes and imagined that she was on a solid piece of land. But the water slammed against the hull, drumming harder and harder in a tribal rhythm, until it was difficult to believe that land existed anywhere, let alone beneath her. The air was stifling. Hundreds of people were crouched in their compartments, and the ship's massive engine was droning nearby.

"Rosa, do you feel all right?" Giovanni asked, knowing when she was trying to conceal her suffering.

"Just a little tired of these waves slapping against us in such an unfriendly way."

"Maybe you should get some fresh air. Why don't you come up on deck with me while I smoke my pipe?"

"No, you go ahead. I'll be fine when the rough water passes."

Giovanni bent over to kiss her on the forehead and then pushed through the passageway and up the staircase that led to the deck outdoors. He could not have been there for more than fifteen minutes when the ship was hit by a ferocious gale, blowing the bow in all directions at once as if the wind was at a fork in the sea and could not make up its mind which path to take. In the pitch of the ship, Giovanni lost his balance and the pipe that Massemo had carved for him flew out of his hands.

The next moment, he was on his knees, reaching with one hand for the pipe that was scuttling across the floorboards and clinging with the other to the bottom bar of the railing to keep from being thrown overboard. A wave of water as high as a castle wall came crashing down on the bucking hull and his fingers slipped from the metal bar. His body slid across the deck, the ship tipping so violently that he was sure it was about to capsize. He grabbed for anything that might slow him down, but the deck disappeared in the swirling rush of black water as his hands locked onto the brass nozzle of a fire hose, unwinding like a threatened snake, just before he was washed under the railing and sent hurtling toward the angry sea. The hose reached the end of its slack and snapped taut, and the brass ripped into Giovanni's fingers. By some miracle, the hose stayed fastened to the ship as his feet dangled within inches of the foaming water, and he was shouting for help, then praying for the first time since he was a boy, grasping the nozzle so hard that it felt as if the brass had been grafted onto his hands, sealed with blood and a horrible burning.

Giovanni hung for what seemed like hours, though it was actually a matter of minutes, until he heard the clamor of voices on the starboard side of the ship. Through the heavy spray of rainfall, he could just make out a huge cluster of hands pulling at the slippery rubber hose. Chants of "Heave Ho!" wafted on the air like the hymns of angels. Slowly his body lifted up a few feet and tossed against the hull until he was able to make one final effort and throw up his legs toward his rescuers before the last of his strength gave out. Someone grabbed hold of his ankle and in one great motion he was hoisted on deck as the ship rolled deeply and Giovanni passed into unconsciousness.

When he opened his eyes the next morning, Giovanni was shaking uncontrollably from a bone-deep chill. The running wounds in his bandaged hands seemed to sear his very being. Rosa was leaning over him with a hot towel steamed in herbs. He tried to talk, but she shook her head, saying, "Stay quiet. Everything will be all right, but you need to rest. You've had a terrible shock. The captain gave you some strong medicine so you won't catch pneumonia. But a guardian angel must have been looking after you." Tears filled her eyes and she tucked him tighter into the tiny bed.

"It was prophesized," he whispered hoarsely.

"Giovanni please stay calm. You are still ill. You mustn't excite yourself."

"It was prophesized," he said again.

The strength of your beliefs, Crazy Teresa had said.

"What are you talking about?" Rosa whispered as her heart leapt inside her chest.

"Crazy Teresa said this would happen," he said and then tried to sit up.

"She never said any such thing. Now, please, you must be still!"

Rosa gently pushed his shoulders back into the blankets and sat by him a long while, measuring his labored breathing, then closed her eyes and thanked God once more for sparing his life. She had been up all night keeping vigil until he regained consciousness. Her fear of losing him had outweighed her own sickness during the seemingly endless storm.

Eventually the ship steadied itself in the water, and the sea became quiet. After making Giovanni as comfortable as possible, Rosa felt confident about going on deck by herself. The cabin was beginning to close in on her and she was desperate to get out. She headed for the metal stairway but had taken only a few steps when she heard a soft moaning coming from below the dark stairwell. There, she saw Francesca writhing in spasms of pain, her young son looking haunted and transfixed at the sight of his ailing mother.

"Go quickly," she said to him. "Get the captain of the ship. He will know what to do." Rosa saw the puddle of water under Francesca and knew immediately that her baby was about to be born, and that unless Rosa did something at once, Francesca and the baby could die.

"Francesca," she said, "lie still. Edwardo is bringing help. Take a deep breath and keep breathing as deeply as you can."

Francesca gripped Rosa's hand and gave her a weak smile of relief.

Nearly twenty minutes went by before Edwardo returned with the captain who said he had summoned a midwife. He brought several blankets and carefully placed one beneath Francesca. Rosa had wanted to move her, but there was no time now for anything except the delivery. Soon the midwife arrived with another crewmember and Professor Marietta.

"Will my Mamma be all right?" Edwardo asked Rosa, his face swollen with tears.

"She's in good hands, Edwardo. Thank God you were here. Please go and sit with my husband at the back of the ship until I call for you. Don't worry, we'll take good care of her."

With Rosa acting as another set of hands, the midwife coached Francesca while the deckhand held a feeble lantern over them.

"Push," she said, "Push harder, then breathe."

Professor Marietta ordered a pail of steaming hot water and a bit of soap to be brought to the midwife and instructed her to wash her hands as well as the pocket knife that she intended to use to cut the umbilical chord.

Suddenly, the baby pushed out amidst the agonizing screams of its mother, and in one sweeping motion, the midwife cut the umbilical chord.

"A girl," Rosa whispered in Francesca's ear. "You've just given birth to your first daughter."

Rosa handed the midwife one of the captain's blankets and she bundled up the slippery child, then placed the infant in the professor's arms while she cleaned Francesca. Ever so gently, the professor washed the tiny creature with some of the warm, soapy water. He had such a tender look on his face that it broke Rosa's heart.

"Never in my life," he kept muttering. "This is beauty beyond anything I have ever seen."

And so it was, in the middle of a hostile ocean, on a ship filled with rotting food, malnourished strangers, and the startling presence of a university professor that Francesca's daughter, Maria Rosa, was born – the first true American among all those pilgrims – named, in part, after Francesca's new friend. As soon as Francesca's condition was stable, she, Edwardo and the baby were moved to new quarters donated by Professor Marietta. Inspired by the professor's remarkable generosity, everyone contributed some prized piece of fruit or dried meat to keep Francesca healthy. They all knew that the baby's best chance for survival depended on the nutrients in her mother's milk.

Meanwhile, the captain instructed a crewmember to move Marco Marietta's belongings to one of his own spacious rooms for the remainder of the voyage. He then announced with a broad grin of partially blackened teeth that he had already arranged for the baby's christening to take place at the end of the week. Apparently, when news of the birth had spread to the rest of the ship, a priest came forward and offered to baptize the child. The sun was shining in the crisp morning air as all the passengers, including some from the upper decks, gathered around Francesca, Edwardo and Maria Rosa. It was the day before they were due to arrive in New York and everyone was in the mood to celebrate. Somehow the women had been able to find enough pieces of lace and white satin to fashion a christening gown and little Maria looked glorious in her mother's arms. Feeling a small kick in her own belly, Rosa had tears in her eyes as she stood by Giovanni, who had finally recovered from his fright.

The people considered the birth a wonderful omen for their future in the new land and they all sang a hymn to the infant Jesus as the priest blessed the child with special prayers. Their song was so loud and joyous that they seemed to be singing so all of America could hear them and know that they were people of God.

The ship approached the harbor at sunrise, and the crowd's expectations rose with the skyline as Rosa and Giovanni stood alongside Professor Marietta, Francesca, and her two children. Rosa felt closer to Francesca than to any other woman she had known, and yet she realized that there was very little chance they would see each other again.

"I'll never forget you, Rosa," Francesca said, as they faced the wrenching moment when the crush of the crowd was forcing them to part. "You, the professor, everyone on board, gave me, my daughter, and even my Edwardo, new life."

Rosa opened her mouth to speak but was so overcome by the moment that she simply threw her arms around Francesca's small shoulders, the child embodying the love between them. They kissed each other's cheeks several times, tears trailing down their faces, then turned to the professor who was shaking hands with Giovanni.

"Thank you, professor, for everything you have taught us," Giovanni said.

Then Rosa and Francesca took turns giving the professor kisses and hugs until he was quietly blushing and a damp mist seemed to cloud up his eyes.

"Nothing in all my years of training could have prepared me for the lessons I have learned on this voyage," he said. "Godspeed, my friends."

Suddenly, in the distance, the immense figure of a woman holding up a torch came into view. But the passengers were so intent on spotting Ellis Island that no one noticed it until the professor shouted, "There she is – the statue of Liberty Enlightening the World!'"

A statue? Rosa thought. A statue of a woman floating on top of the water? Rosa felt her first real rush of excitement.

But the purity of the moment was soon compromised by the sickening smell of fetid harbor water. Hundreds of people converged to leave the ship and waited for the ferry to take them to the docks at the shoreline. Hours went by before Rosa and Giovanni were herded down the gangplank, up a ramp, and into a large, stone building. The mob of people, all dragging their belongings, looked like an exodus of the faithful from a biblical scene.

Rosa knew from the gossip on board that the passengers who held first or second-class tickets had been free to go after a brief inspection on the ship. The vast majority, however, would be processed like so many animals. Here, it is not nobility that separates us, Rosa thought, but wealth. Even so, she pushed the idea from her mind as unworthy. How could she question this new country's justice on the same day that God had brought her safely to its soil?

Once inside the building, they were ushered to the second floor to be examined. At first, some of the very youngest and oldest newcomers were confused, thinking that Ellis Island was to be their new home. But they were quickly corrected by the immigration officials who behaved like prison guards, directing by means of shouts and pushes.

The massive facility had been opened only eight years earlier as part of the nation's attempt to deal with the swelling influx of people. After a fire in 1897 it had only recently been rebuilt, but the building already looked ancient and beaten down by the number of people who were continually passing through its halls. The amphitheater was like a vast spider web, with bare railings forming a network of aisles in which the immigrants stood in alphabetical order and according to nationality. Officials were proud that the system allowed them to examine up to 5,000 people per day.

Nevertheless, immigrants were routinely cheated in the money exchange when buying meals at the processing center. Young women traveling alone were particularly vulnerable and treated as possible prostitutes or public charges. Some inspectors preyed on the ignorant, selling citizenship papers for a very high price that purportedly allowed the newcomers to bypass Ellis Island and go directly to the docks. But there, their papers were often challenged, and once the officials found out they were forged, there was no way to justify their claims.

Waiting in line, Rosa and Giovanni understood the expression that they had heard on board: *L'Isola dell Lagrine* – the Island of Tears, another name for Ellis Island where ripples of fear washed over the crowds when word went around that anyone with a rash, no matter how superficial, would be sent back across the ocean. The ill were placed in quarantine, especially the elderly who were isolated in wretched housing for days or weeks on end until the doctors deemed them healthy enough to be released. Sometimes whole ships were sent back to Europe when an infection was discovered on board.

Hours later, Giovanni and Rosa reached the front of the line where they were examined with a cool eye by a man in a braided blue uniform. Rosa flinched slightly as he reached forward and pulled back her eyelid with a buttonhook to look for signs of trachoma. But both passed their physicals quickly and then Giovanni was subjected to a battery of questions.

Name?

Giovanni Manzino.

Profession?

Farmer.

Do you have work in the U.S.?

No.

Where will you and your wife be living?

New York.

Did you pay for both your passages?

Yes.

THE MOST ARROGANT practice of Ellis Island inspectors was their arbitrary changing of names when they could not understand the immigrants' pronunciation. Many of the foreigners could not comprehend why this was happening, but they were remarkably good-natured about it. Now that they were Americans, they told themselves, why shouldn't they take on American names? Fortunately, Giovanni and Rosa were processed by an American official who could speak a little Italian, so their names remained unchanged. Finally, he handed them their papers and they smiled with relief, then pushed on with the crowds onto the ferry which delivered them to Battery Park.

On the docks, however, everyone's face seemed to express the same desperation that had driven them out of their homelands. For many immigrants, the horrors of the crossing and the humiliations of Ellis Island might have been easier to tolerate had their arrival been able to live up to just a small part of their dreams. As it was, the disillusioned pilgrims found themselves facing a painful sense of homecoming – slammed into poverty only slightly altered from the slums they had left behind. Trapped within the squalor, grime and despair of Lower Manhattan – if anything, this new world was worse. Not only were the streets not paved with gold, Giovanni thought as he and Rosa made their way inland, but many streets were not paved at all and he could see that the new immigrants were expected to pave them. In Sicily, at least, even the poor lived among the richness of nature, assuring them some control over their own survival. But here, it was all flagstone and brick, cobblestone and tar, an unknown landscape in which the innocent were cogs in the mysterious and powerful wheel of progress.

The starkness of America did not disturb Rosa as much as it did Giovanni – at least America offered the possibility of change. But she was stunned by the city's unexpected hostility. Looking around at the other foreigners, she could see in their eyes that America may be the land of opportunity, but not for them. Even the American-born seemed to have given up any claims to fabled wealth. It would take special knowledge, rare skills, and, above all, extraordinary courage to penetrate the core of this new country, she thought.

Giovanni and Rosa walked through the saddened cast-offs on the chaotic streets by the wharf like drifters sifting through human fragments that had broken from the ledges of time. Giovanni would not surrender to some Italian ghetto, however. On ship, he was repeatedly warned against moving to a violent alley called Bandit's Roost in a section of lower Manhattan called Little Italy. And so, ignoring the prodding of the ship's personnel, customs officials, and the pleading of the shrill-voiced street hawkers, all promising to steer them toward shelter for the night, Giovanni led Rosa through the swarm, leaving those who had shared their crossing as determinedly as their family and friends in Sicily. He knew that the single strength he had over the others was nothing more than common sense uncommonly unaffected by crisis. So while hundreds of immigrants blinked in astonishment at a world that had already begun to defeat them, Giovanni stared at the misery around him and did what the others were too submissive to do – he calmly dismissed it.

Toting their few belongings in oilskin-covered bundles, they spent the warm April afternoon wandering through the clamorous area of Canal Street, exchanging a few of their silver coins for American currency in a bank on Broadway, then focusing their attention on a single objective: food. Toward the end of the voyage, the smell of spoiling provisions had made it impossible for them to eat. Now they were standing in the middle of a crowded American street, surrounded by pushcarts blessed with a thousand different scents. Anxious to build up Rosa's strength, Giovanni gestured to the bounty around them, and said, "Rosa, what can I get you?"

"An orange, Giovanni, one fat, juicy orange," Rosa said.

Giovanni walked up to one of the pushcarts overflowing with fruits and vegetables, and returned to Rosa with two oranges and two large red apples. He then ducked into a bakery and bought a warm loaf of Italian bread, two cannolis, two bottles of wine and fresh juice. They had intended to find their way through the throng and celebrate the landing with a picnic, but their hunger overcame them. Attacking the food with both hands, they laughed when they realized how frenzied they'd become and devoured every crumb by the time they reached Houston Street. The sound of their laughter in an alien city made them feel as if their old life was behind them at last.

As they headed north, drinking in the colorful sights, they soon came upon a large manufacturing area, where block upon block of factories seemed to produce nearly everything that the city needed or the means by which they could procure it from the earth or the water. They felt comfortable here, watching the concentrations of émigrés traveling to and from work. Spreading the small blanket that doubled as Rosa's shawl, they settled on a grassy knoll that overlooked the smokestacks busily filling the blue sky with dark clouds, and toasted a bottle of wine to each other and the life that lay ahead of them.

As the afternoon drew to a close, the smoke diminished amid a chorus of whistles and horns, amazingly synchronized yet delightfully out of tune with one another and suddenly the narrow alleys and streets were flooded with people. This was the moment to move, Giovanni thought. If they followed the workers or found someone who spoke Italian, perhaps he and Rosa would find transportation to Harlem.

Giovanni and Rosa followed the flow of workers until they poured into a large intersection where cobblestone streets and muddy avenues scattered in different directions. Dozens of languages and dialects were being spoken all around them, mixed in with accented English. So many vehicles and horses rushed through the streets that Giovanni and Rosa became confused as to which they should pursue. Soon they saw some metal tracks sunk into the road and recognized the trolley routes that Professor Marietta had told the passengers would carry them northward.

Once they had found the tracks, it wasn't long before a swaying trolley came in from the south, drawn by two of the largest horses that Giovanni and Rosa had ever seen. The Clydesdales, Giovanni thought. He'd heard stories about them, even in Sicily. Much too heavy to race, these monstrous animals with their strangely broadened hooves were said to be the strongest working horses in the world. The trolley itself was packed with people, the conductor perched none too securely on the side of the car. They waited at the corner as it came rocking toward them, but when it began to slow down the people cried out – probably in protest at the thought of any more passengers – though their words were lost on Giovanni and Rosa who could not understand a word of English. But the conductor, sweating despite the deepening chill as daylight faded, called to them impatiently in a raspy voice. Giovanni could only guess that he was being asked their destination, so he called back the name of the street that he'd remembered from the professor's lecture: "One hundred twenty five!"

At this the conductor shook his head, waved his arm in seeming disgust, and rattled off a few more phrases in English. He shouted, "Jimmy! Jimmy!" and the man who was driving the horses had them moving once more. Instinctively, Giovanni moved alongside the car, suddenly panicked that they'd be trapped in the lower city with no place to offer them sanctuary. He asked what they should do and how to reach Harlem, but, of course, it all came out in Italian, which meant nothing to the conductor who never looked at him again. Then a woman's voice rose over the crowd. She was speaking Italian with a trace of Bolognese dialect.

"You must go to the el," she said, "This car goes only as far as 86th Street."

"The el?" Giovanni called back, mystified by the strange term.

"The el," the woman responded, "the train that runs above the streets. On Ninth Avenue."

The horses pulled away at full gait and Giovanni watched as the car disappeared. Then he remembered the new transportation that Professor Marietta had described. He ran back to Rosa who'd been waiting on the corner, and told her that they'd have to walk a few more blocks to find the mysterious el. While they could not read any of the English signs, they could understand the numbered ones, and silently thanked the man who had built this enormous city for naming the maze of streets so that even the humblest of people could find their way. Numbers were posted at every intersection leading to Ninth Avenue, and once there, they found the railroad tracks hoisted above the streets – just as the professor had described them – on massive frameworks of wood and iron. They turned onto Ninth Avenue and walked north until they found a staircase winding up to the platform above.

The train that came along the track was a single passenger car, powered by some sort of small steam engine mounted in the front. Giovanni watched the passengers pay their fare – most of them exhausted – looking men in dusty overalls – to make sure that he selected the proper coins for the coin box. Rosa gave out a deep sigh when she was finally able to get off her feet, but when the car moved away swiftly, swaying left and right, she felt her breath catch in her throat. The movement of the car was an uncomfortable reminder of the ship.

Eventually, though, she became mesmerized by the sights. She had taken a seat by the window and was gazing down at the rooftops, at the people and wagons moving on the streets below. The train gradually picked up speed and set off a terrible vibration in the towers supporting it. But the train's engineer apparently knew just how fast to go before the shaking became intolerable because he'd ease off the accelerator until the car rattled more or less smoothly. Looking downward once more, Rosa saw several people shaking their fists as they passed overhead, clearly angered by the smoke, cinders, and noise being showered upon them. No wonder they wanted to bury all the trains beneath the streets, she thought. Soon the city's cluster of buildings began to thin out as they approached a vast meadow rimmed by woods. One of the workmen on board, a black-bearded man with an enormous stomach, heard Giovanni and Rosa wondering out loud if they were passing out of the city and heading into the countryside.

"That's Central Park," he interrupted in Italian. "There's a lovely operetta by Romberg that calls it the big backyard of the city. Isn't it wonderful?" The man crossed the car to join them, introducing himself as Antonio Calandria. "One day," he whispered, with a glance toward the other workers nodding off to sleep in their seats, "we'll do better than all of these people. Just you wait."

Giovanni and Rosa smiled and appeared to agree, though they had no idea what he was talking about, then said a few words of introduction themselves. But there was so much to see outside that they couldn't help staying fixed to the windows. They were traveling by enormous farms, isolated houses of grandeur, undeveloped woods and fields, and many clearings filled with tin and wooden shanties. At one point, while still skirting the edge of Central Park, they saw a huge structure standing alone, looking for all the world like some European castle transported in one piece to this outpost.

"Clark's folly," Antonio said. "A rich man who makes sewing machines spent a fortune building it, thinking he could bring wealthy tenants to this godforsaken part of town. That was nearly twenty years ago, and it's still so far from the center of things that it might as well be across the country in the western mountains. Which is why they call it the Dakota, after a territory so far away that only the Indians would live there. Where are you getting out?"

"125th Street," Giovanni said, "where we hope to find lodgings for the night."

"Morningside Heights. It's quite beautiful there, the new site of Columbia University. You can sleep out on the lawn where they're just starting construction. But take care. The police sometimes attack the people in the camps." On seeing Rosa's alarm, however, he reassured her that the grounds were usually peaceful.

Antonio left them at the next stop, wishing them luck, and they continued for a few more miles through the rapidly diminishing daylight. The open fields provided a clear view of the river, its waters briefly golden. Finally, they arrived at 125th Street, quickly gathered their belongings and descended to the street. They walked past great buildings of stone and marble, as impressive as any they had seen all day, toward the largely undeveloped land where a massive building project was underway just beyond the thoroughfare. Scores of people, most with children, were camping out on the huge expanse of partially wooded property. It delighted them to think of the buoyant Professor Marietta coming here to teach American students about Italy. As darkness let down its velvet curtain, families gathered around tents and cooking fires. Smells of onion and basil hung in the air along with the lilting sound of a single harmonica.

"We'll rest here for the night," Giovanni said, pulling Rosa closer to him.

Rosa counted more than six or seven languages as they walked by small groups talking quietly. With only firelight and starlight to guide them, they found a clearing further in the glade and prepared a place to sleep with several blankets. Just then, Giovanni saw the silhouette of a mounted man in uniform patrolling the perimeter of the grounds, and shuddered to think that Agostino had managed to follow them there in spirit. He remembered Antonio's caution and stayed up for most of the night, watching the policeman like a hunter tracking the scent of his predator.

The night drew steadily colder and Giovanni made sure that Rosa had enough blankets to keep her warm. With Rosa falling into a deep sleep cradled in his arms, he thought: tonight they were a country unto themselves, the stars twinkling overhead like miniature candles and suddenly he saw a blaze of light like silver threads shooting across the heavens and the apparition of the dancers flashed before him, glowing ghosts from a fateful Sicilian sky.

CHAPTER
FOUR

RISING WITH THE first light, Giovanni and Rosa set out to find a place to live on another mild spring day. After stopping for some breakfast rolls at a local bakery, they criss-crossed the crowded streets of Harlem, amazed at the number of Sicilians they overheard walking past them. Giovanni had been told of whole blocks in Morningside Heights whose tenants could trace their heritage to a single village in Sicily. But if he had wanted to be surrounded by Sicilians, he said to Rosa, he never would have left Sicily in the first place. Though he would miss aspects of their old life – familiar songs over wine in the evenings, the crude wooden puppets the children carried through the streets on Good Friday — he needed a future for his family, not a past.

Wandering amidst a rousing array of aromas and dialects, the two turned onto Third Avenue to see great lines of wagons rolling down the street — one hauling bolts of cloth, another with blocks of ice, still another clattering by with bottles of milk. Vendors jostled for space, pushing their carts of fruits, vegetables, silverware, or flavored ices and calling out to prospective customers in a litany of languages. In just a few blocks, Rosa saw more people than in several Sicilian villages put together. Adults strolled through throngs of children playing unusual games with a stick and a ball, while old women patrolled the windows above, occasionally shouting down to the children. The sheer number of shops was over-whelming – a bakery, a café, a shoemaker's shop, and something called a candy store that sold newspapers, cigarettes, coffee and had an amazing display of penny candies. In all the commotion she and Giovanni almost missed the significance of the wagon piled high with furniture and household goods pulling away from a building on East 112th Street.

"Maybe we should try there," Giovanni said, pointing to the five-story building. "It looks as if someone is just moving out."

"But it's so high!"

"The professor said that apartments in America can stretch four, five, or six floors above the ground," Giovanni said. "They're called double-decker or dumbbell tenements and only New York has them."

"But there's no sign in the window asking for boarders."

"Let's try it, anyway," Giovanni said, taking Rosa's hand.

In the middle of the stoop a thin young man had made himself comfortable, smoking a cigarette and reading – with some effort – a newspaper opened on his lap.

"Pardon," said Giovanni, "but could you tell me where I might find the owner of this building?"

The man looked up, squinting in the sunlight and frowning, perhaps trying to place Giovanni's dialect. Shaking out his newspaper, he laughed and said, "The owner? I've only seen him once or twice myself, and then only when he was hurrying to an eviction. He wouldn't be crazy enough to live in his own building. There's a superintendent, though, on the ground floor. Just follow the hallway."

"Why wouldn't the owner live in his own house?" Rosa whispered once they stepped inside the building, where they were instantly swallowed up in darkness. Looking back through the glass-paneled door, the world outside seemed like a bright painting hanging in a darkened room.

"I don't know," Giovanni shrugged, pausing so his eyes could adjust to the murky interior. The single light bulb dangling from a wire in the ceiling was far too feeble to penetrate the gloom. "Maybe because it's too dark."

Rosa tightened her grip on Giovanni's arm as they moved to the end of the hall and Giovanni knocked at the only door. Almost immediately, it was opened by a plump, middle-aged woman who didn't seem at all surprised to see them.

"Yes?" she inquired. A wide smile puffed up her rosy cheeks and her blue eyes sparkled. Beneath her great weight, she seemed remarkably vibrant and strong.

"We're looking for a place to live," said Giovanni. "We've just arrived in America and haven't found a room."

Giovanni twinged slightly as he spoke, afraid that his words sounded as though he was seeking a special favor. He wanted her to know that he was there on a matter of business, not charity. But before he could think of something else to say, she spoke again.

"Well, you're in luck. A family just moved out. They'd only been here three months." She glanced at Rosa's swelling stomach. "They went to sunny California, where all the oranges you can eat are grown outside your front door. The sun is always shining and everyone thinks they can become Rockefellers."

She laughed, and Rosa wondered if she was amusing herself with some private joke. Was there really a place called Sunny California? What did it mean to be changed into rocky fellows? Giovanni was also confused, but he managed to stifle his impatience in order to secure the apartment.

"I'm sure this Sunny California is a wonderful place, but I think I prefer New York City. Maybe we would not feel so welcome in Sunny California."

"Perhaps not. Young people have such foolish ideas. By the way, I'm Gracia Rocca. The rent is four dollars a month, payable on the first day of every month to me. It's a good apartment on the fifth floor, four rooms, nice and clean. The Manfredos were always clean, even with their crazy ideas about California." Gesturing toward Rosa's belly, she asked, "When's the bambino arriving?"

Rosa, despite her natural assertiveness, became surprisingly shy at the mention of her pregnancy. "Three months time," she said in a barely audible voice.

"Good," said Gracia, patting Rosa's shoulder and thinking, this quiet one will need a little mothering herself. "Come," she said and started toward the staircase, "follow me."

Giovanni was nervous about committing himself to a new home in the blink of an eye, but he nodded at Rosa and they both trailed after Gracia Rocca. As they climbed up the narrow staircase, she yelled back at them about a furniture store on Third Avenue where they could buy everything they needed.

"It's not too expensive," she said, "but you'll have to bargain with the man who owns it, Leviwitz. He won't make a deal without haggling, but he's fair and he'll let you pay monthly."

Just as they reached the fourth floor Rosa felt her strength give way. Taking her arm, Giovanni walked her into the apartment and eased her into one of the two wooden chairs that the Manfredos had left behind.

"Rosa, are you all right?"

"I'll be fine," she said, taking deep breaths. "The baby tires me out, that's all."

Beads of perspiration appeared on her forehead and Gracia rushed to bring her a cool glass of water from the kitchen. "She's flushed," she said to Giovanni, placing a hand on her forehead, then looked down at Rosa. "You shouldn't climb up and down those steps too often before the baby is born."

The three waited a few minutes until Rosa was refreshed and handed the empty glass to Gracia.

"Thank you," she said, and turned to examine the new space around her. She had imagined a single, tiny room, or perhaps an apartment that they would share with another family, everyone jammed together as they had been on the ship. But this room was spacious, with a high ceiling and large windows overlooking the street. The floor was not made of dirt, but of solid wood. A marble fireplace was built into one wall and in the kitchen she could see a big, pot-bellied stove.

"Giovanni, it's beautiful!" she said, getting up once more. "Look at that stove. We'll be wonderfully warm."

"You're feeling better?"

"Much better." The other three rooms were equally abundant, with two good sized bedrooms. Coming from a country in which most toilets were outdoors, the toilet in the hallway seemed uncommonly convenient.

"Well," Giovanni said, deciding that this was their first piece of good fortune. "If you're willing to take us, I'll go and find something for us to sleep on."

"Wonderful," Gracia smiled, then said to Rosa. "Would you like a cup of coffee? I'll go downstairs and bring some up."

Rosa hesitated, looking to Giovanni. She knew he didn't like strangers getting too close too quickly, but they would never succeed in America unless they were willing to learn its ways — which meant turning, when necessary, to those who had found their way before them. Besides, Gracia Rocca had a generous spirit that was difficult to resist.

"That would be very kind," Giovanni smiled, nodding to Rosa. "I'll be back as soon as I can."

GIOVANNI WAS INEXPERIENCED at dealing with merchants, but when he entered Leviwitz's furniture store, he learned to bargain in silence, which the impatient Leviwitz interpreted as a shrewd rejection of his prices, and kept lowering them until he felt that he had gone low enough. Then he'd seal each transaction by waving his arms in the air and shouting, "All right, all right. That's the best I can do. It's yours."

Giovanni was able to buy a double bed with a cotton mattress, a sheet, two pillows, and a bed cover for $25.00. He also bought a wooden oblong table and two chairs to go with the two already in the apartment. But even with the help of the boy who worked in Leviwitz's shop, it took several trips for Giovanni to bring it all home.

Arriving with the last load, Giovanni found Rosa covering the windows with sheets that she had borrowed from Gracia.

"Tomorrow," Rosa said, "Gracia is taking me to buy material

for proper curtains at the dry-goods merchant's store. The sheets
will be fine for us tonight."

Giovanni was amazed at his wife's ability to befriend any
woman, as she had Francesca, but glad to know she'd made a friend
in the building. Then he left once more, passing the ice man on
the stairs whom he instructed to deliver a small block to the apartment, and headed for a second-hand store where he picked up
three mismatched place settings, including plates, knives, forks,
spoons, glasses, cups. He also bought two large platters, two mixing bowls and a *scolabasta*, or colander, for straining pasta, as well
as an iron and board so that his shirt could be pressed when he
went to find work in the morning.

He then ordered a modest food supply from the local market
— oatmeal, milk, coffee, sugar, flour, tomatoes, macaroni, and the
apples and oranges Rosa loved. He remembered to bring a box of
matches to light the stove and the fireplace, and in a rare burst of
extravagance, he even gave a peddler a few pennies to bring a small
bouquet of chrysanthemums to Rosa.

Once everything had been arranged in the apartment, Rosa
started to unpack her linens, including several lace doilies and larger
lacework pieces designed to cover a couch or be worn as a shawl.
She brought out the lace coverlet that her own mother had made
for her marriage bed, and which could be folded six times until it
was no bigger than a scarf, as well as her faintly yellowed baptismal
gown — ivory satin edged in creamy lace.

Finally, on a thin piece of velvet, she laid out her heirloom
jewelry: a heart-shaped amethyst stone set in yellow gold, a sap-
phire pendant that hung on a thin silver chain — a wedding present
from her father — a small assortment of earrings including those
she had worn as a child, and a tiny charm bracelet that had been a
baptism gift from her godparents. These, in addition to her engagement ring – a garnet with a small diamond on either side –
and her plain gold wedding band, comprised all her worldly goods.

Soon night came over the city and Giovanni and Rosa fell exhausted into their new bed. It was only their second night in
America and Rosa was so accustomed to sleeping in a swaying ship

that she still felt herself floating as she rocked gently in Giovanni's arms.

WITH DAWN JUST lighting the sky, Giovanni walked briskly through the cold morning air. Professor Marietta had warned the men that employers were reluctant to hire immigrants for anything permanent, so Giovanni was prepared to rely on day jobs for his livelihood. Already he had overheard some men in front of the furniture store saying that a new building project was underway on West 124th Street. Although this would be the first time he had sought work on a large-scale construction site, he had learned the rudiments of a dozen skills in Sicily, where every peasant in the village would work side by side to build whatever the families' needed. Still, he was concerned. Perhaps men were hired according to a special code that he had not yet acquired and would brand him as an outsider.

Giovanni arrived at the site in a matter of minutes and stood nervously among the other laborers, watching the serious authoritative man whom he assumed to be the gang boss for some indication of what he must do to be accepted. Tall and thin, he was writing on a clipboard and would occasionally look up and point to someone, then go back to writing again. "Dolci," he called out.

"Dolci, Dolci, Dolci," a burly, young man murmured next to Giovanni as three others, all heavy-set men with stooped shoulders and their eyes cast down, lumbered forward and through the gate. "The Dolci brothers are related to the backers. They're always chosen first."

Giovanni nodded, perplexed, then asked, "Is he the boss?" gesturing toward the man with the clipboard.

"Just one of their slaves," the young man answered. "His name is Jere Galente, a real prick." Then he poked his head above the crowd and shouted, "Hey Galente, what have they got that I don't?" Everyone laughed, then quieted down as Galente looked up unsmilingly.

"Keep it down, Ruffino," Galente said.

"Thick as planks," the young man muttered, "and they can't

even hammer in a nail."

Suddenly Galente pointed to Giovanni, who glanced around to make sure he wasn't pointing to someone else.

"Yes, he means you," the man called Ruffino said and pushed him forward. "Go on," he said to Giovanni and prodded him again.

Giovanni pushed through the crowd and stood before the boss.

"You're new," Galente said simply.

"Yes."

"Thomas," Galente called out to a laborer behind him. "Take care of this man. Start him on nails." Then he turned back to the crowd and said, "All right, Ruffino, get in here, but keep your mouth shut."

"Yes sir," he said with a smirk.

Thomas, who had the fairest hair and the palest blue eyes Giovanni had ever seen, set down a pail of nails in front of Giovanni.

"Sort them out," he said, as gruffly as Galente might have, and walked away.

No worse a job, Giovanni thought, than hunting for lemons on a donkey. No sooner had he sat down on the building's foundation and started sifting through the nails than Ruffino reappeared before him and stood with one foot on the ground, the other resting on a layer of stones.

"You've never worked on a site before, have you?"

"No," Giovanni said.

"Watch out for Ruffino," Thomas bellowed from across the site. "He likes to give the new guys strange ideas."

"Ignore him," Ruffino said good-naturedly. "Nobody here has a mind of his own." He held out his thickly calloused hand. "I'm Matteo."

Giovanni shook the man's hand and returned to his pail of nails.

"Did you just move here?" Matteo asked.

"We arrived a few days ago," Giovanni said. "My wife and I are living on 112th Street."

"No kidding," Matteo said. "That's where I live."

Giovanni nodded once more.

"You have to jump when they call you," Matteo said. "If you don't, they'll replace you with some idiot like one of the Dolci brothers. It's no different here than in Sicily. Whoever pays the most gets the most."

Giovanni kept his head down. If things were as bad as they were in Sicily, he thought, Matteo would never have been able to speak out the way he did that morning.

As if reading his mind, Matteo said, "Ah, I know what you're thinking–then why would they hire a loudmouth like me? That, my friend, is because of this –." He raised his strong arms and laughed. "I'm an old hand by now. They might not like me, but I get things done."

Giovanni grunted. He didn't want to get involved in someone else's politics. He just wanted to do his job and go home.

Most of the men on the site were Italian and preferred to speak their own language rather than struggle with English that made them all feel inferior. Matteo said it enabled them to insult the boss surreptitiously when he wasn't Italian. He even told one story about an Irishman who had been in the neighborhood for years and had let a whole group of them blabber on about him all morning, then fired everyone without pay at lunchtime – grinning as he delivered his edict in flawless Italian. Giovanni was amused but remained silent, secretly deciding to learn as much English as he could.

At the end of the day, he walked home with Matteo and felt a rush of freedom when he finally reached the steps of his tenement. He would never have to work for Agostino Mulassano again, he thought, then hurried up to Rosa who was calmly cooking dinner in their new home.

From then on, Giovanni was always chosen in the first round. Like Matteo, his physique made him a standout. His broad, solid body, immense hands, his skin darkly tanned from years in the fields made him appear capable of any task. Matteo, on the other hand, was always called last – a little game of humiliation that Galente liked to control.

For Rosa, her transition into the new world was surprisingly easy. In the very first week all the wives in the building, most of whom were Rosa's age or a few years older, came to welcome the couple with cooked risotto, pieces of fruit, crisp loaves of bread, a bowl of steaming pasta pasoli, and even fresh bluefish. While some of them found Giovanni a little aloof, with Rosa they felt quickly at ease. They seemed to appreciate her refined quality and welcomed her every word with delight. Gracia, who'd been especially thoughtful, brought Rosa roasted coffee beans, for which she had developed a craving. Even Lily Dileo, the crippled peasant woman who lived above them, sent down a few narcissus – an expression of spirit that linked her to the land back home.

While Rosa enjoyed being with women her own age, she found herself most drawn to Gracia and Lily. It was a comfort to rely on Gracia's experience. And with Lily she liked to feel that she was helping someone else, if only by providing a little company. The day Lily sent down the narcissus, Rosa went up to thank her personally. Stepping into her small room with a window overlooking the gardens in back of the building, Rosa felt the old woman's sorrow, saw her face pinched with suffering, and knew she led an isolated life. Lily had enough essentials with which to live and eat, but nothing beyond a widow's worn possessions.

"I've come to thank you," Rosa said, stepping toward Lily who was wrapped in a shawl and rocking in a wooden chair. "What beautiful flowers. Did you grow them yourself?"

"Yes, dear, I was a farmer's daughter," Lily smiled. "All the women come to me for advice about their gardens."

Glancing past her, Rosa noticed the window box. All the narcissus in bloom had been plucked from the soil.

"Sit down," Lily said, pointing to the second chair at the table. "Will you start a garden, too?"

"Where?" Rosa asked, sitting opposite her.

"In the backyard. Everyone has a plot."

"I suppose I will, then," she said. "What do you think I should grow?"

"My husband always said our tomatoes were too bitter. But

we found a method to sweeten them. Once they're planted, let me know and I'll tell you the secret."

Lily's husband and only son had been killed in a railroad accident some years before and she had no other surviving relatives. All the women, Rosa discovered, took turns shopping for her. Soon Rosa pitched in as well, and whenever one of Lily's tips proved successful in her recipes, she'd take up a portion of the meal in gratitude.

Gradually their lives seemed to settle into place. Everyone was friendly, but no one intruded the way they did in Sicily – with the possible exception of a few meddlesome old women. A permanent fixture on the steps, they cross-examined Rosa every time she went outside for a breath of fresh air, often asking the same things about her family again and again like a self-appointed jury hoping to catch her in some inconsistency. Rosa managed to be courteous, but she never gave them too much food for thought. As for Giovanni, the neighbors respected him for his dignity, his extraordinary capacity for hard work, and his obvious devotion to his lovely wife, although he never submitted to any conversation with the battalion of women on the stoop. Giovanni's only nagging wish was to find more permanent work, but he rarely had time to investigate other opportunities. Eventually, it was Rosa who stumbled across the first new possibility while she was shopping in Zamboli's grocery store one afternoon in early July. She was filling a basket with vegetables when she overheard Mr. Zamboli arguing with his wife behind a screen at the back.

"No, no, no," Mr. Zamboli screamed, "I am not going to be robbed again! Those construction companies charge too much, they leave the entrance blocked for too long, and they don't care about the mess. If I had the time, I'd get my own crew. But I won't pay those goddamn bastards another penny! They're all thieves!"

In another moment, Mrs. Zamboli emerged, instantly embarrassed that Rosa had been present for her husband's screaming and cursing.

"How may I serve you today, Rosa?" she said quietly.

"Mrs. Zamboli," Rosa said suddenly. "I wonder if I might ask your advice on a business matter?"

"Please, call me Rosella," the older woman said, curious about the business that Rosa might want to discuss. She would not be asking for credit, as so many of her customers did, because everyone knew that Giovanni was adamant about paying for everything in cash.

"It's about your husband's need for a construction worker," Rosa said, a little out of breath from the effort it required for her to speak so boldly about a situation involving her husband. "Giovanni can build or repair anything. Just ask any of the men who have worked with him. He is clean and neat and he is honest. He would never take a penny if he had not done the job properly. He works tirelessly, no matter how strenuous the work. Do you think that your husband might consider him for this task which has him so upset?"

As she reached the end of her speech, Rosa blushed furiously, realizing that Rosella might be angry with her for interfering with a private conversation.

"Wait here," she said, smiling. "It might be just the thing."

Rosa felt her heart beating rapidly while Rosella spoke softly to Mr. Zamboli, her whispering periodically interrupted by some impatient shout from him. But soon the curtain drew back and Mr. Zamboli came out.

"I know your husband, Mrs. Manzino," he said. "At least, I've seen him often enough. I have never spoken to him. But if he is interested in the job, tell him to come to see me this evening after dinner, and we will talk."

Rosa hurried home, filled with excitement. But by the time she reached the apartment, she began to feel guilty as well. Giovanni had so much pride. What if he was offended by her begging for work? What if he hated her for being so forthright? She worked herself into such a state that when he finally came home, she began to cry. Giovanni, frightened by her tears, went quickly to her side and put his arm around her.

"Rosa," he said tenderly, "what is wrong? Is it the baby? Are you feeling ill?"

"No, Giovanni. I'm fine. It's just – " She took a deep breath and said, "I offered your services to Mr. Zamboli, the grocer. He's looking for construction help and wants to meet with you after supper."

Giovanni froze for a moment, a little stunned by the news, which only made Rosa cry harder. Then he softened. "But that's wonderful. I have no steady job, and the work crews are so uncertain. The foreman dismisses us at night with as little pay as possible. There is little continuity from job to job. Most of the workers just take the day's earnings and disappear. This job with Zamboli may be exactly what we need."

The next morning Giovanni was repairing the north wall of the Zamboli grocery, which had never been erected correctly and was starting to crumble. Propping up the roof with lengths of timber, he removed entire sections of stone, filling the spaces with new bricks and mortar to bring the whole wall into line.

Across the street, Nunzio Fazio sat by the window of his pork store, admiring the new wall and the man who was creating it. The wall was so true that it made the rest of the neighborhood look even more ramshackle. Giovanni had completed in a day what a team of others might have stretched into a week. And so, as Giovanni removed the roof supports and began to whitewash the finished wall, Nunzio decided to approach him before the week was out.

Nunzio Fazio was not only the neighborhood's butcher, he was its first entrepreneur, one of those rare immigrants who had arrived in America nearly twenty years earlier with a considerable amount of capital. He was known to be a man with a generous heart – who had never, however, lost his love of profit. He owned shares in many of the local stores, served as a banker to families who had no other sources for loans, and was involved in the construction of several new apartment buildings scattered throughout the locality. With his hand in so many pies, he made it his business to know as much as possible about everyone else's affairs.

But all Giovanni knew was that Nunzio was from Napoli, which meant that he could never be trusted. So when he noticed Nunzio watching him, he set his mind to ignoring him completely. He had no idea why Nunzio was so interested in what he was doing, but he was certain that it must be for some obtrusive reason, and that it would only create problems if he acknowledged his presence.

On the fourth day Nunzio crossed the wide street and stood just a few feet away from where Giovanni was laying another line of brick for the grocery's extension. His pleasant face was quite round and his complexion was fair, with red cheeks and bright blue eyes that augmented his apparent sense of good cheer. About five-foot-seven, he was a bit taller than Giovanni, but considerably broader. Although his body had gone to fat, his arms were heavily muscled from years of butchering heavy meats.

Giovanni paused for a moment, then continued his work.

"Giovanni," he said, in a voice inflated with gregarious goodwill, "I must compliment you on your fine work." Nunzio fully expected Giovanni to respond with gratitude, but not only did he fail to thank him, Giovanni failed to respond at all. It was as if Nunzio had never spoken.

"My name is Nunzio Fazio," he tried again. "I'm from Naples. In my youth, I crossed the bay to Sicily many times. I hear you're from Corleone." He exalted the Sicilian women and hillsides, and described the rich promise of America in solemn, glowing inflections. "Giovanni," he said in the same hearty timbre, "I want you to know that I have had my eye on you."

At this, Giovanni glanced at Nunzio over his shoulder and stared at him blankly, then returned his attention to the brick wall before him. Nunzio was too baffled to feel anger, but since retreat was not an option, he cleared his throat and pressed on boldly.

"I need a dependable man to work for me. He doesn't have to be smart as long as he's strong since I have enough brains for us both. But he must be willing to work long hours. It would be more profitable than simple day jobs. Are you interested?"

For the first time, Giovanni put down his tools. With calm reserve, he asked what Nunzio meant. Nunzio explained that one of his new apartment buildings, only a few blocks away, needed plumbing installed, and he wanted Giovanni to take a wagon up-town, bargain with the coppersmiths, and bring back a load of piping.

Giovanni said simply, "I cannot do that." Without another word, he returned to cleaning his whitewash brushes.

Once again, Nunzio was at a complete loss. Flabbergasted by the refusal, he was embarrassed to realize that his chipper conversation and munificent offer had made no impression at all. "Is it because I am Napoli?" he demanded, his voice growing louder with each word. "Is that why you refuse to work for me when you'll work for anyone else who pays you?"

When this brought no response, Nunzio added, "Is it because I am from the true Sicily?" This final remark, a reference to the long-standing hostility between the Sicilians and the Napoli, was a deliberate challenge: the kind of insult that produced flashing knives in certain Sicilian taverns. But Giovanni only said, "I have no experience with horse wagons, and I do not know the city well enough to find the best coppersmiths. And since I do not know the prices, I could not bargain with any success. If someone else could bring the pipe to the building, I would be happy to put it in place."

Nunzio just stared at him, amazed once more at Giovanni's indifference to anything but the physical task to be performed. Even the ancient rivalries failed to rouse him, and suddenly he was even more intrigued. This man would be able to work free of the bitter squabbling that sometimes destroyed his work gangs, as well as the wall or window they happened to be working on at the time. It never occurred to Nunzio that Giovanni, a simple laborer, was dictating his own terms.

He slapped Giovanni on the shoulder and said, "All right, I'll drive the wagon myself. You can come with me to help with the loading, and next time you'll know what to do. Can you meet me here tomorrow morning at seven?"

"I have only a couple of hours. Then I am working on Mr. Zamboli's store until next week."

"Fine. So you'll come with me to get the copper, then start the work when you're finished with this?"

"Yes," Giovanni said and turned back to the wall once again.

The next morning Nunzio picked up Giovanni in front of Mr. Zamboli's store. As they rode in the wagon uptown, the loquacious Nunzio talked on and on as if he had already had three espressos. He spoke of his ventures in the neighborhood and complained about his workers. Then he told Giovanni that if everything worked out, he could give him a steady job. "And if you work for me," he continued, "you will gain more respect."

Giovanni immediately thought of Agostino, who had said the same thing. Disinclined to respond, Giovanni kept his eyes forward and let Nunzio babble on.

When they arrived at the yard, Giovanni was introduced to Peppino Persicaro, the short, dark-haired dealer who had the same compact body, belligerent stance, and heavy jowled face as the scruffy bulldog beside him. Giovanni looked on while Nunzio and Persicaro launched into a dramatic series of offers and counter-offers, all delivered in a constant stream of words that he could barely follow. Nunzio bargained by combining threats, pleas, and moaning about falling profits with cries of moral outrage. Peppino, who was thoroughly familiar with this style, waited patiently for him to finish before countering his bid. But today his attention kept drifting to Giovanni's unblinking gaze, a new and unknown element. Each time Peppino quoted a price for a particular gauge or quantity, Giovanni repeated the amount softly, his eyes locked on the dealer's face. To Nunzio's surprise, Peppino started dropping the price. Each time he did, Peppino looked to Giovanni for some sign of approval, never realizing that the newcomer's sober manner reflected nothing more than his attempt to understand the bargaining process.

When Giovanni and Nunzio finally left the copper yard, Nunzio slapped him on the shoulder. "Well, my friend," he said. "You did a wonderful job back there. Simply wonderful. Peppino is a very difficult man, but you knew just how to handle him. You saved me a great deal of money, and taught me something about negotiating as well."

Giovanni looked ahead at the road, dumbfounded.

"All my yelling and pleading," said Nunzio, laughing amiably, "and you unnerve him by frowning in silence. Every time he looked at you and saw that Sicilian scowl, the price came down again." Flushed with his greatest triumph as a haggler, Nunzio knew that he had found an important ally whose unusual bearing distinguished him from other Sicilians whom he had come to know and loathe. Giovanni shook his head at the madness of Neapolitans — and started work for Nunzio a week later.

IT WAS THE end of July when Rosa went into labor, and within a matter of hours it was clear that she was not going to have an easy time of it. Sitting beside her, Giovanni felt himself slipping into despair. He was convinced that he had caused the problem: the ordeal of the voyage, all those hours when she had been too sick to move and the ship had been tossed from one mountainous wave to another, not to mention his own brush with death, must have been a terrible shock to her system.

She did not even cry out in pain. She was deathly quiet and seemed so far away, yet too exhausted to sleep. Now and then, her face clouded and he saw that some sharp pain had cut through her body as her small hand tightened its grip in his. But still she did not scream. At times he thought he might go mad, and began to pray to St. Anne, the patroness of motherhood, now that Crazy Teresa had cured his lack of faith.

In what Rosa called "still another miracle," Gracia happened to be a midwife, and so she kept reassuring Giovanni that Rosa was not in any danger. She had taken charge of everything, insisting that Giovanni not worry himself and forcing him to work every morning. When Giovanni hurried home early, he found Gracia hovering like a gigantic angel over the friend she had come to love so deeply.

"She is quiet because she must store up her strength for the actual birth, then she will give you a beautiful child," Gracia said. "You will see, Rosa will not leave you alone."

It was lucky for Rosa that the summer had been milder than

most. After Sicily, the two were accustomed to the heat, but some days in the tenement, Rosa had felt particularly stifled, as if all the buildings stood on beds of embers. But the week had brought a respite, and Rosa was grateful, even in her pain, to feel a soft warm breeze blowing through the apartment. Giovanni and Gracia sat beside her as the half dozen women enlisted as assistants passed in and out of the apartment day and night.

Finally, just after nightfall on the first of August, Rosa emerged from her swoon and, in a few minutes of glorious shouting among all the women, a son — ten pounds and twenty-two inches — was born. Suddenly the long hours of pain were forgotten, leaving joy in its wake, and they named the child Gino, after Rosa's younger brother who had died. Out in the street, Rosa recognized the voices of a dozen children playing and lifted Gino into Giovanni's arms.

Beautiful from the first, Gino soon revealed the permanent color of his eyes: a deep, lustrous green that Rosa knew was inherited from Luciano. Her firstborn son was truly a prince, she thought, with the blood of aristocrats moving through him. Perhaps he would have some natural elegance as well. But in giving her the secret of Giovanni's origin and freeing herself of a lifelong burden, Bianca had passed on the legacy to Rosa — and now as she looked upon her son, she sometimes sighed under the weight of her secret.

For Giovanni, Gino's birth only gave him more motivation to succeed. In a month of working for Nunzio, he had discovered that Nunzio was not only highly successful in his own right; he was also powerful among the neighborhood's community leaders, a core of men who openly or covertly controlled its way of life. But so many Sicilians had emigrated to the new world, it should not have come as a surprise that the powerful gabellotos would have spread their influence there, too. Certainly Matteo had been telling him of their insidious influence since his first day at work. And yet, Giovanni was disturbed at how quickly he had crossed their paths.

"You can't escape them," Matteo said one day, as they stopped to chat on the way home from their different work sites. "I know you'll do your best Giovanni, but they'll get us all in the end."

It was true. Just as in Sicily, no one could truly prosper without the approval of this society of men. Once allied with Nunzio, Giovanni found himself more readily accepted. Although Nunzio was never actually a member of the mob's inner circle, he was a loyal friend to those in power, an "associate" who steered his contacts to the organization's cement and lumber businesses, and offered them gifts from time to time. In exchange, they promised help, if needed.

When Giovanni had won Nunzio's confidence, or what was called his imprimatur – a term the Catholic Church used for the approval of books and prayers – suddenly, the smiles that greeted him were warmer and less guarded. Even the neighbors seemed more anxious to exchange pleasantries. Soon it was obvious that his family would benefit from his liaison with Nunzio. Talking with Rosa, however, Giovanni vowed that he would get no more involved than was necessary to procure steady work. His one mistake with Agostino – albeit an unavoidable one – had been to become unwittingly indebted to him by the terms of his marriage to Rosa. If you took favor, you would find yourself forced to return favor – and not always in the way you might choose.

Several months later, Nunzio brought Giovanni to a meeting with these men, not named but known to everyone in the neighborhood. Speaking in hushed voices, they only nodded now and then at Giovanni. But after several gatherings they began to inquire about Rosa and Gino with the concern of old comrades. Giovanni smiled and thanked them for their courtesy, then stood aside while they discussed business. At no time did he venture his own opinion. In time, the district leaders, including their most visible representatives – the "Mustache Petes" – came to consider him a "neutral," someone who took no interest in local intrigues, nor in their highly profitable but dangerous enterprises. They respected his desire for a simple life that would provide for his growing family. Clearly, Giovanni had become a man of respect, but he never made any move to trade upon this trust. He was content to remain on the perimeter of the dark circle they had formed around the citizenry. Giovanni's only truly uncomfortable moments came when he found himself being introduced to more and more of them individually. Often, the man to whom he was being presented would say, "So, you're the son-in-law of Agostino Mulassano. We heard that you had come to America."

When Giovanni acknowledged that he was, carefully masking the degree to which he resented the connection, the man would smile and say, "Ah, that's good, that's good. We need more men like you in this country. We have to watch out for one another and take care of our own, or the others will take it away from us."

Giovanni smiled and nodded in response, hating himself for having to play along, but realizing that life seldom gave you the choices you wanted or deserved.

As THE AIR grew measurably colder, Giovanni's seven-day work week gave him little opportunity to pay much attention to the seasons. But both he and Rosa looked forward to their first New York winter. In December Giovanni woke to find the pre-dawn city coated with ice. Other times, he and Rosa marveled at the light covering of snow that seemed to turn the streets into marble. Then one morning, just before dawn, Giovanni walked out into a real snowstorm. Two feet had fallen during the night and the entire street was blanketed in white. Nothing had been cleared from the roadway, let alone the sidewalks, and Giovanni found it almost impossible to make any progress through the drifts.

The feel of the snow, as he repeatedly sank to his hips, made him laugh out loud. When he finally made it to Nunzio's worksite, Nunzio told him to go home. No one would be working that day, he said. The whole city was paralyzed. Heading slowly back home, Giovanni then ran into Matteo who told him that this was their lucky day – the city paid more for shoveling snow off the railroad tracks than he'd make in two days. Giovanni grinned at the gleaming snow piling up all around them, and followed Matteo to the tracks to take advantage of their windfall profit.

Before they knew it, Rosa and Giovanni's first white Christmas was upon them. Giovanni was somewhat oblivious to holidays. He never went to church with Rosa, since he worked on

Sundays, and he never particularly liked large celebrations. The neighborhood in which they lived was too poor to present any but the most modest decorations to mark the season, but holly wreaths were hung on front doors all along 112th Street. On Christmas day most people went to work as usual, but then at midday they were let go early. Giovanni walked home among the crowds of festive workers and came through the door to find Rosa's Christmas meal already in progress. Today the pasta had meat sauce, but the real treat was a rich cassada cake.

That night, Rosa gave Gino a bright red fire truck – which made his eyes glow with wonder, though there was little he could do but stare at it. And just as she had lay him down to sleep, Giovanni pulled out a beautifully wrapped gift for Rosa. Her eyes sparkling with excitement, Rosa slipped out of the box a delicate blue glass vase that she had once pointed out in a rickety little store off 112th Street. For herself, she presented Giovanni with two delicately wrought linen handkerchiefs. Of Italian linen, they bore Giovanni's initials, crocheted by Rosa when he was at work.

Only a week later, on an especially cold night, Giovanni and Rosa were jolted awake by an explosion. Gino, who had been sleeping between them, cried out in protest.

"What is happening?" asked Rosa, drawing Gino to her. Leaping up, Giovanni stood still listening. The streets were riotous with noise – horns, bells, and voices shouting. But the most frightening aspect was the booming and crashing of what sounded like bombs and cannons. The air seemed to be deluged by a thousand guns and the screaming of the wounded and dying. Had they come so far only to be slaughtered in someone else's war?

Giovanni pulled the curtains tight against the windows and rushed back to the bed to hold onto his family. Soon he heard a tumult in the hallway, followed by Gracia's voice and the beating of an iron pot. Throwing open the door, Giovanni ran down to the landing.

"Happy new year!" shouted an exultant Gracia. "No, no, not just a new year. Happy new century! The twentieth century is here!"

In another moment, the entire hallway was filled with neighbors, cheering and ringing bells or sounding horns. Many were drunk, and all ridiculously happy at the idea of making so much noise in the middle of the night. Realizing that a bizarre American tradition had overtaken him, Giovanni hurried back inside to tell Rosa that the world was not ending. In fact, in some ways it had just been reborn.

With Gino in her arms, Rosa parted the curtains and exclaimed as the sky lit up with colored flames. "Look Giovanni!" she said, and he came to stand beside her. Each had seen fireworks in some Sicilian fiesta or wedding feast, but nothing equaled this magnificent outpouring from the capital of the new world. "Isn't it beautiful," Rosa said, and held up Gino to the window.

Giovanni smiled to see Rosa so happy and laughed suddenly as Gino seemed to wave his tiny fist at a sudden burst of fireworks. Church bells pealed across the city and as the music from the streets rose up to greet them, Giovanni felt a deep sense of contentment. The century was new, Gino's life was just beginning, and they had made it to America after all.

Meanwhile, in a humble Sicilian kitchen, Bianca read over her latest letter from Rosa, lingering again and again on the sentence describing Gino's luminous green eyes, and found her cheeks streaked with tears as she thought: Sin now transformed into beauty. God has forgiven me after all.

PART
TWO

CHAPTER
FIVE

ON SOME DAYS Giovanni feared that he had torn Rosa away from her real home and brought her to a place that would one day break her heart. It was 1904, four years since their arrival on East 112th Street. Rosa had given birth to three more children – Bennie, age three, Tessie, now two, and Bruno, just three months old. Being one of those small women who managed to remain delicate even in pregnancy, no one could tell with any certainty when Rosa was carrying another child. Her ivory face and coffee-brown eyes never lost their bold innocence, no matter how much energy was being drained from her body, and her shapeless, ankle-length dress and homespun, snow-white apron was always the same.

Bennie arrived when Gino was barely one, but long before Gino was willing to surrender his place at Rosa's breast. The neighborhood women offered weaning advice, some of it fairly bizarre, involving strange-smelling draughts that Gino should be forced to swallow. Most suggested that he use his thumb when in need and showed Rosa how to prepare a sugar-coating mixture that would make it impossible for him to resist. In the end, however, Gino had to suffer through.

While Giovanni had responded to the births of Gino and Bennie with pride, Tessie's birth generated a whole new set of feelings. Gracia had warned him that a daughter stirred a different sense of fatherhood than sons, but he was not prepared for the rush of protectiveness that swept through him at his first sight of her. Perhaps because she was a girl, he believed that she was softer than the others, a more fragile blossom, or maybe his regret at not being able to shield Rosa from sorrow made him fear for Tessie's safety. Whatever the reason, in Tessie he felt that he'd been given the chance to provide a whole new world for her; he'd only have himself to blame if he failed.

In light of this spirit, Giovanni set about fashioning a spectacular crib. Gino and Bennie had each slept in the same small crib – a solid, serviceable structure that had been built with all the charm of a toolbox – but Tessie's crib, he decided, would be enormous, a bed easily suitable for two or three children at once. Using sandpaper and linseed oil, he painstakingly smoothed down the thick, wooden slats so that no splinter could ever blemish her flawless skin, and then painted it a gleaming white, the first item of furniture in the family to be painted. Gracia stenciled the headboard with tiny pink and blue flowers, and Rosa matched her designs by sewing them into the pillow and comforter. The crib became the most beautiful object in their household, reminding Rosa of a lovely velvet jewel box. The feathered mattress was as thick as the one slept on by Giovanni and Rosa, fluffed everyday and sewn in with new feathers every few weeks.

Gino, however, was afraid that such a tiny child might disappear within the crib's vast interior. So one night when the apartment was quiet and Gino heard Tessie making slight crying sounds, he got up from his own small bed, slipped into her crib, and held her hand until she fell asleep. The feeling was so peaceful that he stayed beside her and soon fell asleep himself. This developed into a nightly ritual – and soon Bennie crawled in with them. By the time Bruno came along, however, Gino had grown into a need for his privacy and finally returned to his own bed.

IF ANY OF the women in the neighborhood had realized just how different Rosa's personal history was from their own, they would have found it extremely difficult to imagine her being transported from the luxuries of the Mulassano estate to Harlem's crowded tenements. To them, she was a quiet, lovely woman who devoted herself to the care of her solemn, hard-working husband and four small children. They watched her cultivate the earth behind her building, planting and nurturing anything that the limited soil could bring forth – precious tomatoes, peppers and basil, eggplant and mushrooms. They saw her struggle over her washboard to whiten the bed linen that all the women would hang from heavy ropes on each level between the tenements like steps in a fragile ladder to heaven. They smiled at her flashes of spirit as she corralled her restless children from their street games, brushing off the dust that clung to them, and searching for new scrapes and bruises that needed a touch of iodine or, at the very least, a healing kiss or two. And yet, she refused to be drawn into any of the matters that obsessed them – the frequent jealousies and arguments over every domestic issue from wayward husbands to cooking pasta. She seemed only concerned with one thing: her family's daily survival.

Still, a subtle change of expression would come over Rosa's face whenever the local women touched upon memories of their families in Sicily. Suddenly, she longed to reach out and make contact, however tenuous, with the world she had renounced. Eventually, it was Giovanni's great tenderness toward their daughter, Tessie, that showed her the special capacity of daughters to find softness in their fathers, and a plan took shape within her: she would write to her father and attempt to bring about a reconciliation. Once the decision was made, Rosa began to compose her letter during stolen moments throughout the day. Freed from the constraints of her limited knowledge of English, she was reminded of how much she loved the Italian language and its ability to express the human heart. She wrote draft after draft, her earliest ones laced with flowery phrases that transformed the story of her departure from Sicily and her love for Giovanni and the children into a kind of sad fable about all she had sacrificed. These versions were always destroyed, however, because she didn't regret what she and Giovanni had done and couldn't bring herself to pretend otherwise, no matter how noble the purpose. She could appeal to her father's imagined sense of generosity, but she would never again couch her feelings in a lie. Whatever she wrote would be simple, direct, and honest. The letter, when finished, was remarkably brief.

> Dear Father,
>
> Whenever events conspire to bring about a separation between father and daughter, the only possible solace lies in the cherished hope that the distance might one day be bridged. The greatest gift that God has given us is the family. Our responsibility as God's creatures is to treasure and nurture it. I think of this especially when each morning I look into my children's faces and see traces of the grandfather they have never known. In the five years since you and I have spoken, I have come to realize the complexity of love and its magical ability to endure any heartbreak. So I am reaching to you across the great abyss between us, a separation more of pride than of distance, more of pain than of time, and ask that you try to overcome all our differences and write to me and the children, tell us of your life, and wish us well in the life we have chosen.
>
> I am, as always, your loving daughter,
> Rosa

After the letter was mailed, Rosa counted the days before she could expect an answer. Giovanni and Bianca exchanged letters twice each year, so she knew exactly how long it should take. First was the ship from America to Italy, followed by the boat to Sicily, and then several days' journey on the postman's donkey along the rocky roads to the village.

Soon the appointed time had elapsed and there was no response. Rosa gave her father one more week to assuage his anger, but when that week went by, and the next few as well, her hope gradually slipped away. Disappointment overwhelmed her only once, when she sobbed into the night until Giovanni soothed her to sleep just before dawn. Her father had proven faithful only to himself, and was now nothing more than a phantom from her past.

During this time, Rosa remained inside, using the humid days as an excuse to stay close to her children. Gino's sixth birthday came and went, and her pride in him distracted her from thoughts of her father. Then one night Giovanni came home holding a letter from Bianca in his hand and Rosa felt her heart lift at the sight of it. Her own mother had died so young that Bianca had fully taken her place in Rosa's affections.

Giovanni handed the letter to Rosa with a smile, then gathered the family together to hear her read it out loud. The letter was long and full of poetry. "It is July," Rosa read:

> You remember Sicily in July. Sometimes I sit outside with Massemo and we watch the sky change and the mountains grow dark in the distance. The earth has dried to old brick in the sun, pale around the edges. The dust has settled and the dead grass on the roadside bends in the wind. There are no flowers now, no green grass. But there is green in the olives, the vineyards, the orchards, in the tomato and melon vines.
>
> I have always felt that time is suspended in such light. It floats on the surface of a giant cauldron filled with purple eggplants and shiny green peppers. And the fruit! I wish I could send you a basketful.
>
> Massemo has been struggling a little more this year with the heat. But I tell him it's just as well that a man who has worked so hard be allowed to rest too. He sits outside sometimes in the afternoons and the children come by with the java beans they have collected. They love to tease the old man in his chair. But he helps them shell the beans and they always leave us some, which we cook and wash down with a little wine in the evenings.
>
> But probably I am tiring you with all this talk – telling you of a land that seems so far away. And of course I know you must be happy where you are, free to live as you choose.

Agostino was never an easy man. Even summer does not slow him down. The men grumble that the heat only serves to make him more irritable – though to Massemo and me, he is most cordial. I heard too that there has been some trouble with Enzio, who insists on angering his father at every turn. He has been given a position in the banking office. I saw Agostino in town and he asked after you, Rosa. I told him you are well. You should send him a photograph of you, Giovanni, and the children.

Bianca continued with more news about the town. The next week was the Feast of Saint Rosalia, one of Bianca's favorite holidays, when the whole village came out to watch the parade of the saint's statue in the streets.

GINO UNDERSTOOD ENOUGH to sense the existence of a world that was nothing like his own in East Harlem. There was sunlight and color and open spaces in this far-off land, which made him wonder why his parents had been so willing to leave and come to this crowded and dirty place. But he was most curious about Bianca herself.

"Pappa," he said, "what does my grandmother look like?" He had seen one aged photograph that his mother kept in her bed table drawer, but it was a hopelessly faded sepia print that offered only a fleeting image of a slim woman with dark eyes, who may or may not have been smiling, standing before a tiny house.

Giovanni smiled. "Your grandmother is beautiful," he began, "only your mother is prettier." Then he became wistful as he thought about one of the great sadnesses in his life – that Bianca would probably never see her grandchildren, and that one day she would die without him. "Everyone loves her for her kindness," he continued after sitting silently for a moment, "even more than they admire her for her beauty. You know the stories you love about fairy princesses and the goddesses who live across the sea? Well, your grandmother must have descended from those magical beings, because she exists apart from all other women in Sicily, with their murderous tempers and small-minded gossip."

Gino listened raptly as his father went on, creating an image that fired the young boy's imagination. Although Giovanni described Bianca as a simple woman, Gino embellished his father's words with dreams of his own, visualizing someone in flowing white robes who wore gems in her hair, the consummate saint for whom legions of knights in armor rode out to battle dragons and pirates and wizards. His father's love for his mother was the same pure flame of love that Gino felt for his own. It was the kind of devotion that could never be expressed if you limited yourself to the sometimes mundane reality in which goddesses often became trapped.

As Giovanni finished his impassioned description, Gino felt a deep happiness at the thought that he and his father shared such a magnificent vision of their mothers. A few feet away, Rosa watched both of them intently. She was touched by Giovanni's expression of love for Bianca, and felt painfully moved by the way Gino was now gazing at her. She turned quickly away from the table so they would not see the tears welling up in her eyes.

Later that night, Rosa filled a large copper basin in the middle of the kitchen with hot water. Soon she was humming contentedly as she began to undress in the lamplight. The basin, large enough to accommodate the family's laundry, was a recent gift from Giovanni, something he had found in the copper yard on one of his trips to pick up plumbing supplies for Nunzio. Gino watched his Mamma from behind his bedroom curtain as she stood in the basin, using a ladle to pour water over her body. This glorious sight made everything about his mother seem suddenly mysterious – her hair flowing freely over her shoulders, her skin glowing softly as the water shimmered over her, even the way her stomach completed the roundness and fullness of her body. This vision of Rosa was like that of a heavenly ghost, an angelic presence usually hidden from human eyes. She removed the large copper hairpins that held the bun at the nape of her neck, allowing the liberated hair to expand in the air and cascade down her back, reaching her waist in a swoop that seemed to gather all the light in the room. In a single instant, she was completely transformed, as if her very being had been set free from life's daily restraints. She was now just a girl, a child like himself. After watching for several minutes, this image of perfect loveliness was locked within Gino forever.

It was a hot night and the stale air trapped in the rooms made him toss and turn in bed. So after his mother had dressed in her cotton nightgown, Gino crawled out of bed and begged Rosa to allow him to sleep on the fire escape. It wasn't actually much cooler out there, and the insects could be murderous, but it was a common sight among city children in the summer.

Rosa finally relented and created a makeshift bed with a blanket and pillow on the metal balcony. Gino lay under the stars, his mind still filled with the image of his grandmother as a glittering fairy-princess who loved him from across the sea. It was in this dreaming state that he noticed Yolanda Caruso, a girl his own age, framed in the soft light through her window in the building behind the Manzino apartment. Her skin was golden, her eyes dark and enormous, and her hair, long and auburn. She was brushing her hair and staring into the night, singing, of all things, a Christmas carol in a pure soprano voice. Gino was hypnotized, and then so overcome by the moment that he stood up and leaned against the railing to look more closely. When he tried to move toward her, forgetting that he was four stories above the ground, his bare feet slipped from the narrow perch, the railing flew from his fingers, and Gino began to fall.

Rosa, who was still awake and nursing Bruno, could see none of this, but in a few seconds she heard a crash, followed by a woman's scream and the simultaneous barking of all the dogs who guarded the gardens at night. By the time Giovanni was shaken from his deep sleep, the whole neighborhood seemed to have joined in the chorus. Giovanni climbed onto the fire escape to get a better view of what was happening and heard one of the old women screaming about a baby dropped by God. Although no one in the neighborhood had ever heard him raise his voice, Giovanni started to shout out something regarding working men needing their sleep when he glanced at Gino's empty bed and realized that his son was gone. Giovanni stood completely still for a moment, unable to make the connection between his missing child and the child who had fallen from the heavens. Then Rosa turned on the light, illuminating her naked husband, and they both heard Gino's voice calling, "Pappa! Pappa!" from the darkness below.

Voices erupted in chaos. Giovanni jumped on the rusted ladder of the fire escape, his weight lowering it to the ground with a terrible clanking. Rosa was at the window crying out Gino's name, which started Bennie, Bruno, and Tessie screaming along with her. Lights and shouting silhouettes appeared at every window facing the tiny backyard gardens. But the loudest screams came from the women who had gathered to investigate the ruckus. They started howling and screeching wildly, and Rosa, far above them, slipped into a faint, convinced that Gino had been taken from her in some unthinkably horrible way. Their outburst, however, had nothing to do with Gino. A powerful-looking unclothed man had appeared out of nowhere, running among them, shouting, "My bambino! My bambino!" All the women ran away blindly except Gracia, who'd been the first to alarm the others. She stood her ground and continued her cries, meaning to drive the intruder away, but even she was struck mute by the unexpected sight of Giovanni's muscular body materializing in the moonlight. She lingered long enough as he hurried past her to carry away a memory that would play prominently in her confessions to Father Vespucci for years to come.

As for Gino, he emerged from the tomato plants only a few feet from Giovanni, more or less intact, delighted with the commotion and his father's uncharacteristic display of energy. Other than a few scratches and bruises, he was amazingly unhurt, although the air had been knocked out of him for several seconds. He had fallen straight down, striking the soft tin roof of the building's tool shed some fifteen feet from the ground with a mighty crash, and then rolled down its slant in the loose-limbed way of children. When he ran out of roof, he'd been catapulted into the tomatoes, breaking several stakes and vines as he came to a halt halfway across the patch. He was calmly brushing the dirt from his undershirt when the light had turned on above him and his father had appeared on the fire escape.

Once he'd found his son and realized that he was, by some miracle, all right, Giovanni received an even greater shock when he remembered that his clothes were four stories above him. Tucking the child under his arm, he climbed back up the ladder with a speed that he never would have believed possible, and found Rosa in a swoon on the bedroom floor with Bruno still trying to feed at her breast. Bennie and Tessie were sitting by her side, crying steadily. In a few minutes, Giovanni had everyone calmed down and back in their beds.

Soon the other children were fast asleep but Gino, who had loved every minute of the adventure, was still too keyed-up to drift off so easily. As he lay there with the summer night restored to silence, he became conscious of a low murmuring coming from somewhere in the apartment – the sound of two voices so hushed that they were barely audible. Curious, Gino sat up in bed and began creeping toward the place where his parents slept.

Although no one had ever said to the children in so many words that they should never approach their parents' curtain once it was drawn, somehow they had all understood that this was sacred ground, as inviolable as the space behind the smaller curtain in church where the priest stored the chalice after communion.

A small gap where the curtain did not quite close was still wide enough for Gino's small face to peer through. When the curtain was open during the day, this was just another part of the room, as familiar to Gino as the kitchen; and yet, glimpsed now in the night, the space seemed to contain a hidden dimension. After his eyes had adjusted to the moonlight suffusing the warm, summer air, Gino found himself watching something that even his rich imagination could have never invented. His mother was naked, as she had been earlier when he'd seen her bathing, and his father was naked, too. They were on top of the bed, legs wrapped around each other in a hug that brought their bodies together. His father's face buried in her neck, and hers, in moonlit profile, seemed lost in joy. They were not forming words but seemed to be softly touching in some strange rhythmic harmony, and both of them were moving in unison. The rise and fall of their voices mirrored the motion of their mingled forms, as if they were journeying together to some faraway place that only they could see, with all the time in the world to get there.

Gino watched in fascination as Giovanni's hand circled his mother's breast, feeling his own skin tingle as well. He used to get mad whenever anyone else held Rosa too tightly. This time, however, he felt no impulse to protest. It wasn't fear of his father's wrath, but the sudden realization that he was stealing a glimpse into something larger than himself.

With that thought bringing a blush to his face, he hastily shut his eyes, and pulled the curtain closed. He returned to his bed with the same quiet care that he had left it, and lay down again, trembling and chilled despite the heat. He wondered what it would be like to create such a blissful look on his mother's face and bring out his father's tenderness. He remembered Yolanda Caruso hovering in the lamplight, the melody of her song that seemed to be floating all the way from Sicily, and soon all of these impressions began to swirl together, and Gino faded into sleep at last.

WHENEVER GIOVANNI BECAME involved in one of Nunzio's larger projects, such as gutting the interior of an apartment building, he would leave his house at daybreak. In those first few minutes on clear-lit mornings, when the sun glinted on the crest of nearby tenements, he sometimes imagined the granite structures as the mountains of his youth where he waited for the day to illuminate the fields, dreaming of the sea beyond them. And yet, Giovanni's view of the past was realistic: every man had to suffer no matter how many oceans he crossed. His fellow workers might complain of all they had lost, but he recognized the irony implicit in their disappointments. They had romanticized America as the golden land of deliverance, but now that they were here and found their lives unspared from grief, they had magically transformed Sicily, the tyrannical land they had escaped, into a Garden of Eden.

Always after finishing one of Bianca's letters, Giovanni brooded about leaving her and Massemo behind in a country ruled by petty tyrants. Their absence merely underscored the fact that he had no true companions in this country. The men he knew were all too caught up with their own struggles to be concerned about anyone else's, just as he was too steeped in his own responsibilities to be anything more than a casual friend. The work in Sicily had certainly been hard, but at least he'd felt connected to the faces in the fields. Here, in this city of strangers, he moved from task to task, like a train crisscrossing one landscape after another with no signs of recognition, only the occasional whistle sounding its presence.

For Giovanni, America's main advantage was still summed up in a single detail: the absence of Agostino Mulassano. And now, walking through the early morning stillness, he thought of Agostino as possessing some sort of witchcraft that cast a dark shadow into one's very soul. Even many thousands of miles away, Giovanni could feel his contaminated spirit spread over the breadth of the entire Atlantic.

On his arrival in New York, Giovanni had worried that Agostino might try to vent his rage by striking out at Bianca and Massemo. But in her letters, Bianca had assured him that they were in no danger. Agostino might not forgive Rosa, but publicly he was forced to foster the illusion that he was in control of the situation. Even his daughter's escape had been presented to his neighbors as an outcome he had anticipated. Nevertheless, he continued to approach Bianca in a surprisingly shy manner and ask for news of America. For that reason and to ease Rosa's pain over her father's rejection, Giovanni had decided to take Bianca's advice and arrange for the family to be photographed. He would send one to his mother – and to Agostino as well.

Just the day before, he had rounded up everyone for the ride downtown on the el train to the photographer's studio at the back of an old apartment building, where so many families were waiting to have their picture taken that over an hour passed before the Manzinos were called. Giovanni posed first. His shirt was white and freshly pressed and he was wearing his one good suit. In the fashion of the times, he did not smile at the camera, but seemed to ignore it altogether and stare past the photographer to a distant scene. Watching her husband convey his usual air, Rosa was proud of his strong stance and direct gaze. The honesty she had seen in him at their very first meeting never wavered, and she loved him for his simple purity. Still, his eyes, she thought, had taken on a look of defeat, a darkness hidden from everyone but her. Suddenly, Giovanni stepped away from the camera's eye and organized the three boys around the chair where Rosa sat with Tessie on her lap, keeping her quiet while the photographer popped under his curtain. The boys, in awe of the mysterious event, tried to peek under the curtain to see what the man was doing and had to be yanked back into position by Giovanni.

"Why can't I sit with Mamma?" Gino asked.

"Because," Giovanni said.

"I want a picture with just me and Tessie," Gino said then.

"You'll sit with your brothers like you're supposed to," Giovanni said.

It will be a slightly somber picture, Giovanni thought, at least of Gino, but bring them closer to Bianca and Massemo in spirit.

LIKE GIOVANNI, THE cobbler Carmello Sieppe enjoyed beginning his day before the rest of the city awakened, a habit he'd acquired during his younger years as a farmer in western Sicily. Every day Giovanni would see him bent over a long line of shoes in his lamp-lit store window, the only source of light for blocks around. Usually, Carmello, a crusty old man, would come out to greet him, and the two would exchange idle conversation with all the solemnity of priests conducting mass. Despite the nature of the cobbler's profession, Carmello was always impeccably dressed. The shirt beneath his work apron was white and stiffly starched, his long thin face cleanly shaven, his small, dark eyes alert and glittering brightly, darting about as he spoke. His high-button shoes were polished to such a luster that all his skill and years of experience seemed concentrated in the leather on his feet. Even his hands and fingernails were free from the traces of dyes and polishes that seemed an inevitable insignia of his career. He had a ceramic bowl of water and a large cake of brown soap by his workbench and devoted as much time to washing up as to any of the tools in his shop. He was an odd little man, Giovanni thought, but he was decent and honest, whatever his idiosyncrasies. Whenever Giovanni stopped by to salvage some pair of old boots or bargain for his children's shoes, Carmello would give him a summary of the week's events. Last week, for instance, Carmello had given him a definitive account of why the frequently volatile Rena family had finally fled the neighborhood. Most of the local gossips had already determined that the oldest daughter, Bernadette, had gotten pregnant by some American who she had met through her job at a dry goods store downtown. The word was that she had been tragically seduced, if not actually raped, by the scoundrel. Her brothers had been dispatched to track down the man and force him to marry her or be beaten senseless. But when they discovered that Bernadette had spent quite a few of her lunch hours in intimate trysts with several young men, the family hastily set out for Boston. Bernadette's father had not been able to bear up under the shame. Carmello said that the last time he saw her, she had come to pick up some shoes and one of her eyes had been blackened.

But today, when Giovanni rounded the corner of Carmello's block, he was surprised to see the old cobbler standing outside on some scattering of ice, even though it was August. Only as he drew near did Giovanni feel the crunching of glass beneath his heavy boots. Through the sun's weak light he turned to stare at Carmello's shattered storefront. Shards of glass, like Carmello's polished ebony shoes, reflected the oil-lamp he was holding toward the space that was once his shop window. The entire expanse of glass was gone, most of it lying in heaps on the windowsill and spilling onto the walkway.

"The bastards," Carmello muttered, "the sneaky, cowardly bastards!"

Giovanni's first thought was that Carmello's wrath was directed toward the gangs of young kids, who Americans called "hooligans," that sometimes went on destructive sprees, hurling bricks through windows at random, more for the thrill of the actual crash than from any intention to steal or cause pain.

Sensing what his friend might be thinking, Carmello said, "You know the bastards who did this, don't you, Giovanni?"

Giovanni stared at him but said nothing, realizing now that Carmello must have refused to pay patronage to some group of local thugs. Carmello gestured with the lamp at the crudely painted symbol on the shop's pale wooden door – a hand dipped in black paint.

The Black Hand, as Giovanni well knew, was the sign used throughout Italian neighborhoods to signify the Sicilian vendetta organization. While many who used the sign were just street punks acting on their own, the mere suggestion of it was enough to bring most people to their knees. Giovanni's dismay continued to grow as he realized that the Black Hand was becoming as prevalent in this country as it was in Sicily. In fact, some of the stories seemed too bizarre to be believed. Rumor had it, for example, that the Black Hand would often be found on pieces of paper stabbed into dead, deserted bodies.

"They're parasites, Giovanni, parasites. The minute an honest man reaches a point when he can begin to reap some rewards, these bastards come along and steal them, in tribute to their own depravity." Suddenly beside himself with fury, Carmello kicked a hole through his own front door. "And then they leave this obscene mark behind, as if we are all superstitious old women, afraid of some demon with black hands." The force of the kick almost caused Carmello to fall backward, and he looked with despair at the scuffed toe of his perfect shoe. It was probably the only blemish that the shoe had ever suffered.

Although the Mafia was still a loose-knit group in Sicily, representing the concentration of power shifting from one village and province to another, the Black Hand in America had grown steadily in power and structural unity along with the immigrant population. Still, it was not the fear of bullies and criminals that caused Giovanni to stare with such intensity at the crude outline on the door. Agostino Mulassano, in his obsession with dramatic effect, had signed many of his own warnings and violent acts the same way. So for Giovanni, the symbol represented not only the deeds of brutal men but the plague of Agostino's black heart. As the morning sun emerged from the shadows, he was reminded of the same sunrise he had always known, bringing with it the same injustices. Standing now with his distraught friend on an empty street in East Harlem, Giovanni felt as if all the nightmares from his childhood would, in time, come true, no matter how hard he tried to distance himself, and that somehow Agostino had stretched across the ocean to smear the doorway with his own filthy hand. The plague would always catch up with him, he thought, and with a sad shake of his head, Giovanni picked up a broom inside Carmello's shop and began sweeping debris into the gutter.

Over the next several weeks, Carmello spoke incessantly of the monstrous men who had defaced his property. The only gossip that interested him now was the wealth of stories about the hoodlums who imposed their will on the innocent. Soon, he had fired up the entire neighborhood with a desire to resist them. He was so vocal about his refusal to be intimidated that Giovanni worried his friend's rhetoric would force the enemy to have him silenced. Finally, one morning at work, Giovanni waited until Nunzio was finished explaining a new job to him and broke his customary silence to ask if Nunzio knew anything about the incident at Carmello's shop. Nunzio looked at Giovanni slightly askance, then handed him a tool and shrugged. "Every man must pay his dues," he said and walked away.

Although there were some who dismissed Carmello's impassioned speeches as the false bravado of a little man, Giovanni considered them expressions of courage, even if there was no way to strike back. Gathering in basements or warehouses, Carmello tried to organize groups of merchants to take action against the Black Hand. But they were not warriors, and since the peculiarities of immigrant life bred only fear, suspicion, and hostility toward the city's police, there was no one they could turn to for help. One by one, the merchants spent their anger in speeches and drifted away from the meetings, choosing to appease their oppressors by acquiescing to their demands and paying the weekly amounts that would supposedly spare them further destruction. Only Carmello continued to refuse and went to his shop at the same early hour every morning, half-expecting each day to be his last, waiting for a bomb to be tossed at his feet. If he had ever found out that his friends, ashamed of their own cowardice, contributed a small part of their earnings each week to pay Carmello's share and protect his life, he would have taken his family and fled from the neighborhood in disgrace.

It wasn't long before Giovanni came to understand a great deal more about the forces moving beneath the surface of things. Time and time again Nunzio appeared at the work site with a curious entourage, usually three unsmiling men in large fedoras and expensive overcoats who stayed out of earshot on the perimeter of the project while Nunzio talked – as much with gestures as with words – pointing to the various stages of construction and taking full credit for any nicely rendered detail. Giovanni recognized a face or two from previous meetings with Nunzio, though he was careful not to look directly into anyone's eyes. The workers hated these visits because Nunzio became impossibly short-tempered and would sometimes fire somebody on the spot. He never introduced his companions or offered any explanation of their presence, but everyone assumed they were his backers.

"The number of things he's got going at once," Matteo Ruffino once said, "he must have partners with very deep pockets." But no one ever asked how those pockets were filled; some things, they figured, were better off unknown and Giovanni always remained silent.

One afternoon, while Giovanni was laying floorboards in still another apartment house that was rapidly replacing the vanishing park land, he sensed the pace suddenly quickening around him. Hearing hammers strike nails with far greater impact than necessary, he glanced through an opening cut in the wall and saw the three fedoras huddled around Nunzio at the work site's entrance.

Giovanni set an eight-inch plank into its designated slot and refilled his apron with ten-penny nails to anchor it down. A few moments later, he was surprised to hear the unmistakable sound of Nunzio's fancy shoes carefully finding their footing on the make-shift staircase that linked Giovanni's floor with the workplace below. It was rare for Nunzio to stop and talk with anyone while they were actually working, so Giovanni knew he couldn't trust anything that Nunzio was about to say.

"Ah, Giovanni, here you are," Nunzio called out in his hearty politician's voice. He was puffing and his face was flushed from the climb, but he smiled widely as if denying the strain to his portly frame. Nunzio then directed his attention to the planking on the floor and nodded approvingly. Giovanni paused, a hammer ready in his hand to drive in the first row of nails.

Nunzio cleared his throat and, in a thoroughly unconvincing attempt to sound casual, said, "By the way, Giovanni, have you been attending any of those merchants' meetings in the neighborhood? The ones in the basement of Casca's bakery?"

Giovanni hammered in a nail, then looked up at Nunzio silently.

"Giovanni," said Nunzio, "we are old friends. Surely we can be honest with each other. You will do yourself and your family no good if you become involved with those troublemakers. That loud-mouth Carmello, for instance." His voice trailed off and he began to gnaw at his lower lip, as though distracted by another troubling thought. Then he squatted down next to Giovanni, who continued hammering nails into place, and lowered his voice to a conspiratorial whisper. "Look, old friend," he continued. "Tell the boys to stop making a fuss about things that no one can change." He then patted Giovanni's shoulder a little awkwardly, and without another word, stood up and left, seemingly embarrassed at what he had said.

In the echo of his footfalls, Giovanni considered the few workers' meetings he had attended – those passionate but essentially useless gatherings of powerless men. It had saddened him to think that they were involved in a meaningless ceremony, but now he realized the extent to which they were inviting danger. He started to work a little faster, trying to distract himself, but Nunzio's words came back to haunt him. The Black Hand was free to flourish not because of the strength of those who wielded it, but because of the men whose weaknesses could be preyed upon, facilitated by people like Nunzio. Poverty, he thought, had a deadening effect. At the same time, its low-burning flame could flare up into violence, spontaneous and pointless, like drunken knife fights that ended up destroying what little the people had. Other instances involved a network of shifting alliances, traced roughly along family lines and old world loyalties in which the innocent were always stumbling onto the battleground and getting caught in the crossfire.

Giovanni had seen only a small part of the complex underworld, where leaders and would-be leaders, petty crooks, and gang opportunists all battled for power, territory, and prestige. Too many gangsters, like Albert "the Butcher" Marinucci and Mike "the Torch" Olivetti, vied for control of whole neighborhoods. Some of these men were but extensions of the Sicilian Black Hand. Yet most had not been leaders in Italy or Sicily. Harlem was filled with thugs who had envied the Mafiosos and bandits who had acquired so much power in their home provinces. To escape their domination, they had come to this country, determined to perform whatever horror was necessary to create dominions of their own. Ironically, Mafioso and renegade bandits had made the crossing as well, along with men like Giovanni who were trying to escape them all. The street wars, therefore, had become chaotic, with gunfire and vandalism exploding in ways that made little sense to anyone. There was nowhere to turn for protection, so Giovanni simply walked the line of compromise to keep himself and his family safe.

" . . . . AND SO HERE'S Melissa, all two hundred and sixty pounds of her, eating more lunch than I could carry, much less eat, and asking us in a wailing voice why her husband keeps looking at other women. Can you believe it?" Gracia said, erupting into enormous laughter.

Rosa had been sitting in Gracia's kitchen sharing the one pot of tea they allowed themselves each day, listening to Gracia's endless supply of new stories about the flower factory where she worked three mornings a week. Like many superintendents, Gracia had been given the smallest apartment in the rear of the ground floor in exchange for supervising the building. But it had unusually generous windows that opened out onto a vegetable garden, giving it the illusion of a country cottage. She had painted every item of furniture with the same white enamel and delicate floral pattern that she had painted Tessie's crib. The walls were clean and white and the light had a way of bouncing off every surface. Only the teapot was black, an Oriental souvenir that Gracia had brought back from a visit to Chinatown long before Rosa had known her.

"Gracia," Rosa began when Gracia had quieted down, "how difficult is it? Making flowers, I mean." She didn't mention that the great mystery to her was not the process, but the fact that there were people in this city with enough money to support such a whimsical business. Why would people pay for artificial flowers when the real ones were perfectly capable of creating themselves?

"Difficult? Rosa, how could it be difficult? Carmelina Perrini has been working there for four years, and she's the dumbest woman in Harlem. She may even be the dumbest woman in America. She's late every morning because she keeps forgetting which shoe goes on which foot." Gracia was off again, laughing harder than ever, finding few things as funny as her insults.

"Do you think I could learn?" Rosa asked meekly.

At this, Gracia stopped laughing and stared in surprise at her friend. "Are you serious, Rosa? You mean, you would actually want to work in that place?"

"Well, maybe for a few hours each week, if you think there's a place for me. I can't stand watching Giovanni push himself so hard. Maybe if I earned a few dollars, it would lessen his load. I'd be able to work with you, wouldn't I, Gracia?"

"Of course you'd work with me," Gracia insisted. "They have such a high turnover, they always need new people." Then she paused. "What about Giovanni? Have you told him about this?"

Rosa grinned. "That's my next hurdle. I wanted to be sure it was possible first."

"I don't know, Rosa," Gracia said in a worried voice. "Most

men are very touchy about letting their wives go into the factories. Some would rather see their children starve."

"I'm surprised at you," Rosa said, still smiling. "Haven't you realized that Giovanni is not the same as most men'?"

"I certainly realized it last month in the garden, when he rescued Gino from the tomato plants," Gracia said, giving her friend a wicked look. "He's a fine looking man. Now I know why you begin each morning smiling." She exploded in laughter once more, and this time Rosa laughed just as loudly.

It was several days before Giovanni noticed Rosa's distracted state and overly solicitous attitude – refilling his mug of coffee after every sip, helping him off with his boots in the evening, and stretching her meager supply of flour to make him biscuits for supper. He sighed as he saw how his own anxiety had blurred his awareness of even his family, the only ones who mattered. So one night, as soon as the children were in bed, he approached her. It was the final hour of the evening, and Rosa was rushing to bring a pillow for his back as he sat down.

"Rosa," he said, conscious now of the faint flush of color in her cheeks, always a sign of tension. "What do you have to tell me?"

Rosa stopped abruptly and looked almost frightened. She didn't know her state of mind was so obvious and hadn't prepared an answer.

"Giovanni, I must . . . ." her voice faltered. Dropping the pillow to the floor, she pressed her hands against her face. Then she took a deep breath and sat on the floor beside Giovanni's chair. Giovanni, suddenly convinced that he was about to be told something cataclysmic, waited frozen in place for her to speak.

"Giovanni," she repeated, her voice gradually regaining its composure. "I'm afraid that you're becoming too good a husband and too good a father." She paused as if she fully expected him to understand. Mystified, he could only wait for her to continue. "The hours you work, all the work you do, these burdens could destroy anyone. It is only because you are so strong that you've been able to endure them so well." Then she stopped and her voice grew softer. "I have a way to help," she said, approaching the heart of the matter. "I know that many men are offended when their wives go to work. Something about pride, I suppose." She looked amused for a moment, as if pride was like a card game – another sign of male foolishness. "But Giovanni," she said, looking deeply into his eyes, "I know you are different from other men. You always listen to any idea that might help us and our children. You would have never left Sicily if that wasn't true." She paused, allowing the full weight of her words to settle around him. "I know you will be pleased that Gracia has found work for me at the flower factory."

Rosa smiled up at him, and he felt once again how easily she could melt his resistance. And, in her own quiet way, Rosa knew she had won a kind of victory. She had appealed to the part of him that rejected any absurd posturing so frequently seen among his countrymen who seemed hopelessly obsessed with asserting their manhood by brutalizing their women. Giovanni once said, only weak men needed to enforce their wills, and he never wanted to be considered one of that breed. Rosa is right, he thought. If she could bring in a little money each week, perhaps he could quiet some of his qualms about providing enough for the family. Besides, there was something almost lovely about the idea of Rosa earning money not by scrubbing someone else's floors or being locked behind some enormous loom, but by assembling paper flowers with other women.

Finally, Giovanni smiled and said, "That's wonderful, Rosa. Why shouldn't my own beautiful flower have the chance to make flowers for others?"

Long after Rosa had fallen asleep, Giovanni found himself staring at the cracks and stains in the ceiling, thinking of the numerous flaws creeping into his life. Rosa had spoken so happily about her plan to work at the factory that he could not refuse her. She wanted to contribute in some tangible way. Even so, her offer hurt him deeply. He was humiliated not by some imagined offense to his manhood, but by his failure as a human being: he had brought her to a place where his own efforts were not good enough. He should have accomplished more for his family by now. He had seen the men around him, with the same strength and ambition, who had been here much longer and knew in his heart that no amount of determination could ever scale the blank wall that faced them. Only becoming more involved with Nunzio's men, and the Agostinos of America, could give him material rewards, and the idea repulsed him. Still it was crushing to end each day in defeat.

Closing his eyes, Giovanni took comfort in the knowledge that at least he was respected in the community. He knew the other men would probably interpret Rosa's job as one more example of reconstructing a dream. He let the thought flow through him and decided not to study it too carefully. But he could not dispel the haunting sense that he'd taken one more step toward the bitterness that plagued so many men who lay awake at night staring into the darkness.

ROSA HAD NOT known what to expect at the flower factory. Only two blocks from home, she had imagined a place filled with roaring machines, swarms of oil-stained laborers, and clouds of orange smoke. Instead, she found a warehouse with a glass-paneled ceiling some eighty feet high and so darkened with grime from the surrounding smokestacks that light might have a better chance of penetrating tin. The building occupied an entire city block – so vast, she thought, that it must have been designed for some project far grander than the enterprises that now filled it. Divided into several small assembly areas, most involved with the sewing of clothing, the space was criss-crossed by several rows of tables where, at any given hour, some eighty to a hundred women sat crafting huge rolls of brightly colored tissue into dozens of flower shapes attached to wire stems. The floors were covered with debris, an incredible array of bright colors that made the absence of sunlight somehow irrelevant.

A young girl named Gemma – the daughter of Agostino's brother, Gitano – who'd come over from Sicily by herself a few months earlier, looked after Rosa's children in the morning and brought them to the factory in the afternoon, carrying Bruno so Rosa could nurse him at her workbench. To Gino, the soft piles of bright fragments on the floor were like a marvelous fall of leaves from a coloring book, all composed of impossible colors found only in crayons. Still, the multi-colored paper petals were not enough to distract him from the unmistakable jealousy he felt when he saw his mother nursing Bruno. Rosa understood what he wanted, but her milk was needed for the baby, and, even if there had been enough, she was sure that the other women would be shocked if she allowed Gino to share.

One day, Carmen Machado, a jolly Cuban woman, saw the distress in Gino's eyes and promptly reached across to pick him up, then deposited him on her lap. In one swift motion, she presented him with one of her bountiful breasts and cooed encouragement with phrases in Spanish. Gino understood her offer immediately, and soon he was drawing rich milk from this sweet, smiling woman. The other women all turned in their chairs and smiled at the sight of Gino and Bruno being fed at the same time while Bennie and Tessie sat at their feet, draping themselves in brightly colored tissue and giggling. Perhaps it was then that Gino first realized the world was filled with plenty of women who were willing to offer their caresses in his mother's place.

Once Rosa had become accepted into the group, gossip – which had been a little guarded in deference to the newcomer – regained its customary gusto, veering off into realms that constantly amazed her. Women in Sicily often spoke of sexual yearnings and condemned the sinners in their village, but their talk now seemed innocent compared to the freedom with which women bared their souls in this country.

One of the women, Sara Perri, began talking about a new midwife who knew a special way of avoiding pregnancy. Sara always seemed to be the first to hear stories about such matters, even though she was single, childless, and unlikely to bear children at this stage in her life. At 45, she looked closer to 65, and the proportions of her body were almost comical. She was quite short, and her bosoms were as full as her stomach, giving her an odd, square appearance when seen in profile. Nevertheless, she had a feisty spirit and a cheerful manner. She kept informed on any new developments involving childbirth because she felt that women had to look after themselves since men could not be trusted to show the proper concern.

"This new method," Sara whispered as the others gathered around her, "has to do with a long wire that the midwife inserts carefully into . . . ."

"Oh, that's horrible, horrible!" interrupted Claudia Bennet, drowning out Sara's whisper. "How could anyone do something so disgusting?"

"She must be a witch," said Mary Flynn. "It's against God's law. Only a sorceress could prevent the birth of a child! Only a devil!"

Soon everyone was shouting back and forth, and finally Celia Corvo, the youngest worker at eighteen, her face flushed with feeling, spoke in a voice so filled with passion that she captured their immediate attention.

"I don't care what the priests think, I'm not a machine like my mother, producing a new child every year until my body wears out – ten children in fifteen years, and dead with the birth of the last. I can barely feed my little Pepe as it is. No more babies for me!"

There was a moment of embarrassed silence after this declaration, and then some spoke out in support; others in opposition, as they talked of other methods they had heard – of hot mustard baths and foul-smelling potions to be swallowed by the gallon for days on end. Some had even heard of women who threw themselves down staircases. And yet, they all thought about the wire that Sara had described, and as soon as the shift ended, many of those who had been hesitant to agree with Celia at first quietly sought out the name of the miraculous midwife. It was remarkable, Rosa thought, what women could do after abandoning the restrictions of Sicilian culture along with the olive trees.

Rosa, on the other hand, remained shy among the workers. In her quiet loveliness, she seemed to be just another rural peasant girl who came to this country and was never able to master its language, let alone its accelerated pace of living. So she would sit smiling, as Gracia and the others talked on, listening and learning from what she heard. No one realized that Rosa's reticence embodied a natural reserve and a hesitancy to speak in a language that made her uncomfortable. She was so well-spoken and well-read in Italian, she was unwilling to allow her thoughts and personality to be thwarted by the few phrases she knew in English. The other women, however, were of so many nationalities, English – no matter how flawed – was their only common language. And since most of Rosa's friends spoke Italian only with their families, going home was an adjustment, they said, like succumbing to different pressures under the ocean. Consequently, at the end of the day they often spoke in a bewildering synthesis of both languages before returning that night to their mother tongue.

But no matter how outspoken the other women were, Gracia usually dominated the conversation, peppering long passages in Italian with American obscenities, reversing the way in which the other women mixed Sicilian curses into their English and took secret pleasure in knowing that Americans didn't realize they were being insulted. Even if she weren't so entertaining, Gracia's voice – its sudden swoops and ever-present laughter – would have swept away any competition. It was as earthy as everything else about her. She had no patience with innuendo and was blatantly explicit about sex or any other human function that struck her fancy. In fact, any man who wandered by accident or design into her section of the warehouse would instantly become the subject of Gracia's speculation about the probable size and shape of his penis, complete with appropriately descriptive hand gestures and speaking loudly enough for everyone to hear. However confidently the man may have strode in at first, he tended to leave with a decidedly awkward gait.

One afternoon in late fall, as the women raced home to beat the descending darkness, they were listening once more to Gracia's raucous description of the effect she was having on the young men at work when she used her newest word – tit.

"So when that poor runt, Timmy, came to empty the trash, I called to him: 'Hey, Timmy!' What do you think? Are my tits getting too big for this dress?' And then I held them up like two loaves of bread. The little guy was so scared, I thought he'd go headfirst into the garbage bin."

They were walking down the narrow alley connecting their block with one of the larger commercial streets, passing through piles of uncollected garbage, when a scream erupted from Melinda Moresco, the newest girl who'd just arrived from Sicily. Melinda, whose sense of old-world decorum had not yet caught up with the reality of litter-strewn streets, had approached one of the large metal cans to throw away the orange peels she'd been carrying in a bright blue tissue, and her fingers brushed against something sticking out. She was still screaming and backing away, when the others ran toward her, certain that she'd been bitten by one of the alley's enormous rats. But in an instant they saw the horrifying truth – a human foot, pale and slightly shriveled from the cold, was rising from the debris. Kicking the can with enough force to send it crashing to the ground, Gracia spilled out the body of a small man in a blood-soaked suit, although most of his head remained hidden in the garbage. All the women kept back, afraid of glimpsing a face that would make the horror even greater.

"What do we do?" screeched Melinda, now trembling through a flood of tears.

Gracia, still staring at the figure before them, remained silent. Then, shuddering slightly, she turned to her friends and said in a voice that sounded strange to Rosa, "We do nothing. We must forget that we have ever seen this. It will only bring misery on ourselves." The others nodded, and without a word, they began to slowly walk away. Gracia put an arm around Melinda and tried to soothe her steady sobs.

As each of the women absorbed the shock, none noticed that Rosa, the one who they might have expected to become the most hysterical, had responded to the butchered body with surprising calm. She had seen far too many victims of brutality in her childhood to be overwhelmed by the sight of yet another crumpled human form. But the familiarity of the sight, as well as the nauseating smell that it generated, made her wonder, much like Giovanni, if she would ever escape the pattern of violent death that had engulfed her life in Sicily. Was there some phantom of evil following her from one country to another? By the time she reached home, she was shaking with unaccustomed despair. Falling into Giovanni's arms, she poured out the entire story and pleaded with him to do something. It was sacrilegious, she said, to leave a man to rot like common debris, no matter what he may have done. Death should not be an indignity. Surely, he had a family somewhere, waiting for him at this moment.

"Please, Giovanni," Rosa said, "couldn't we call someone? Someone should know what has happened." Finally, Giovanni left to phone Nunzio from the grocery store.

"Tell your wife not to worry," Nunzio assured him. "I will take care of it." Take care of it, Giovanni thought. Once again, the true nature of Nunzio's subversive role in the city gave him an uneasy feeling. He was still mulling this over when he returned to the apartment and found Enzio Mulassano standing in the doorway, shouting out to Rosa and the children like some triumphant Ulysses home from the plains of Troy.

CHAPTER
SIX

G IOVANNI NEVER LIKED, trusted or respected Enzio. But he tolerated him for Rosa's sake. He knew the day would come when
Enzio would destroy himself with his own blustering ambition
and profound stupidity. His arrogance and weakness of character
typified so many of those who had come to power in Sicily – and
would do so anywhere if given the chance. They dominated by the
only means they understood – deception and cold brutality. To
Giovanni, Enzio had no redeeming values. So it was with stunned
disbelief bordering on despair that he opened the door to find
Enzio, fresh off the boat from Sicily, expecting a place to live.

Gradually balding ever since he was seventeen, his hairline
now receded to a round spot on the back of his head, giving him
the dubious appearance of a monk. About ten years older than
Giovanni, stocky and of medium height, his face was broad and
relatively plain with little talent for expression. More than the
Black Hand on Carmello's door and the dead man in the alley,
Enzio was the first indication that maybe they were doomed after
all. Giovanni stood speechless. Rosa, behind him, went pale. As
the silence grew, a pall fell over the room.

"Enzio," Rosa said, sensing Giovanni bristling with anger. She
instinctively stepped forward and kissed her brother, then brought
him inside as Giovanni held the door open. If Enzio realized his

sister's discomfort, or the danger masked by Giovanni's silence, he simply ignored it. He probably chose to mistake their shocked reception for some kind of nervous respect, Giovanni thought. How else to explain his immediate launch into a babbling monologue, filled with dramatic descriptions of his exploits in Sicily. Unable to believe what he was seeing and hearing, Giovanni refused to move from the doorway, watching incredulously as Enzio eased himself into a chair. Rosa, herself at a loss, returned to preparing dinner, occasionally throwing out questions to keep him talking. If he were to stop, she thought, the pause might be all the incentive Giovanni needed to explode.

Bruno, aged three, had been sleeping in his bedroom when Tessie, Bennie and Gino all trooped in together after playing at the Ruffinos, and for a few moments at least they diffused some of the tension. Fascinated by this strange uncle in their kitchen, they became instant fans, especially when he gave them all little treats and chattered away about his beautiful country across the sea and all the uncles, aunts, and cousins they had never known existed. Bruno and Tessie, both sitting in high chairs, became too distracted to eat their food, which they instead began to push about in circles until Rosa gave them each a soft slap on the hand. Only Gino, the oldest and perhaps already the most perceptive, noticed with some trepidation his father's unrelenting blank expression.

"Mommy," he whispered to Rosa, pulling at her apron as she made room at the table for another plate. "What's wrong with Pappa?"

"Shhhh," Rosa whispered. "He's just had a very long day," then flinched at the popping sound Enzio made while uncorking a bottle of wine.

"Come, come," Enzio said. "We must celebrate being together again!"

Giovanni accepted the filled glass, but he did not drink.

After the shock had worn off, Rosa began to absorb some of what Enzio was saying, and remembered once again how much she had always hated the sound of his voice. Enzio had all the pomposity of her father, but none of the older man's strength.

This, along with Agostino's considerable power, had made his arrogance, if not justifiable, at least somewhat understandable. In a man as weak as Enzio, the voice was as hollow as his soul.

The atmosphere at dinner was so charged with apprehension that Rosa could almost imagine lightning crackling. It made her face tingle, and she tried to keep her attention on serving everyone second helpings.

"And Marisa Tomelli, how is she?" she asked of an old friend, her voice unconvincingly cheerful as she pushed more pasta onto her brother's plate. Her eyes seldom drifted far from Giovanni's, where she could see the storm clouds gathering. The younger children, still oblivious as to the evening's undercurrents, were as flushed with excitement as they were on holidays. The only one who seemed completely immune to the rising pressure was Enzio, who laughed, puffed on an enormous cigar, and drank glass after glass of wine as if he'd found sanctuary in the undisturbed eye of a hurricane.

"So," he continued, "I could see the way money was being poured in and out of the place, and still they expected me to be content with a measly salary." Enzio, as they knew from Bianca's letter, had been working in a banking office in the village – which was actually a clearing house for cash gathered from a dozen different mafia enterprises scattered throughout Sicily. Enzio's name, and his minimal education in the mathematics of bookkeeping, had enabled Agostino to find a place for him there. Agostino had assumed, Rosa surmised, in one of his many miscalculations, that even a man as reckless as Enzio would never be stupid enough to steal from these people.

"They simply underestimated me, Rosa," Enzio said. "A very foolish thing to do, very foolish, and it cost them dearly. I waited for my chance and disappeared with an entire afternoon's receipts before they knew what had happened. How can that be a crime – stealing from the thieves themselves? It kind of makes things right again. They tried to stop me, but I threatened to kill them on the spot. What do you think of that, Giovanni? Didn't I show them the way of the world?"

Giovanni leaned forward in his seat and was about to respond when Rosa rushed in with a torrent of words. "Oh please, Enzio, don't talk of thieves and threats now that you're safe. You'll frighten the children, and I can't bear to think of you in danger." Her face turned crimson as she realized the enormity of the lie, so she hastily changed the subject. "You still haven't told me about Pappa."

"Ah, he becomes more and more crotchety every year. Now and then, when the wine is in him, he tells us over and over how he will never forgive you for deserting him." Then, reaching across the table to pat her hand, Enzio said, "You should be grateful to me, little sister. I gave the old man so much to scream about that he didn't have time to worry about you."

Enzio went on grumbling about their brother Cesare, who was becoming increasingly troublesome. He seemed fed up with Sicily and hostile toward his father and had apparently decided to play no part in taking over as head of the family. Leonardo and Lia seemed content enough, though Lia in particular was restless for her own home and to get her three children out from under Agostino's boots. "Everyone's trying to avoid the old man," Enzio said. "But they're too weak to say anything. I'm the only one with the strength to speak my mind." Enzio sighed like a martyr. "I take the abuse for everyone – for you, for Cesare, for everyone." He shook his head sadly, apparently overwhelmed at the thought that his honor has had to suffer such injustice.

In the brief lull that followed, just as Rosa was forming a silent prayer of gratitude that the meal was ending without catastrophe, Gino suddenly piped up in an excited voice and said, "Uncle, please tell me more about the thieves who were chasing you. Did they have guns?"

The spark had reached the end of its fuse, and Giovanni rose abruptly from his seat. His huge fist pounded the table, scattering dishes and glasses to the floor.

"No more!" he bellowed. "There will be no more of this talk in my house! Not tonight, not ever! I swear to you, Enzio, I will kill you if you ever speak to my children about these things again!" Everyone froze. Bruno, staring for a moment at his uncle, burst into tears. Rosa buried her face in her hands and Gino stared at the floor where the blue vase his mother loved now lay broken in three pieces.

Rosa suddenly moved to take Bruno in her arms and all eyes shot back to Giovanni as he slammed the table once more for emphasis, then sat back in his chair, breathing heavily, and righted the glasses that had fallen.

"I know all about what happened, Enzio. There was a letter from my mother just last month. She told me how Agostino drove you away when you stole from him, and from the only people disreputable enough to give you a place to work. You did it like a creature of the night, stuffing bills into your pockets and sneaking off. How dare you suggest to my children that there was any courage in what you did. You are a coward."

Enzio sat perfectly still, staring at a spot on the distant wall and slowly rearranging the humiliated look on his face until he had restored some of its arrogant sneer. Then he rose quietly from his seat, looked at his sister – now standing with the still whimpering Bruno on her hip – and gave her a brief courtly bow before leaving the apartment.

"Your vase," Gino blurted out, looking down at the floor. Rosa gasped as she saw her precious gift from Giovanni destroyed. Handing Bruno to Tessie, she bent down to pick up the pieces, then laid them out on the table, her hands trembling.

"Rosa," Giovanni said softly, covering her hand with his own. "I am sorry." Picking up each piece, he then turned them over in his hands and said, "I can mend it. You'll hardly be able to tell the difference."

Everyone was silent then, until Bennie, thinking of more important things, asked, "Mamma, we're still having cake, aren't we?"

"Yes, baby," Rosa answered. "We're still having cake."

"And will you save a piece for Uncle Enzio?"

Rosa glanced across to her husband who returned her gaze with a small shrug.

"We'll save him the biggest piece, Bennie," she said. "Because he's our guest. Why don't you help me cut it."

Much later, after everyone had gone to bed, Rosa asked Giovanni why he had never shown her Bianca's letter.

"I was afraid it might hurt you," he said. "No matter how much I hate him, he's still your brother."

"Honestly," she whispered. "I would be happy if I never saw any of my family again. But a part of me still wants them to be happy in their world. It makes it easier not to think of them. Giovanni, I know how you feel, but maybe in this country, away from my father and the rest of his past, maybe Enzio will find a better way. People can change."

"Some people can change, Rosa," Giovanni answered after a moment. "But I'm not sure that Enzio is one of them. For your sake, I will let him stay, but he will have to find a job. I don't want him spending time with the boys, filling their heads with lies."

Beyond the curtain, the children had decided collectively to stay awake until Enzio returned. Bruno and Tessie, however, soon fell fast asleep while Gino and Bennie talked in low voices.

"Gino," Bennie whispered, "why doesn't Pappa like Uncle Enzio?"

"I don't know," Gino whispered back. "Something that happened a long time ago, I guess."

Bennie thought about the candy that Enzio had brought. "Well, I like him," he admitted.

"Me, too," Gino whispered and before they knew it they were both asleep too, images of dramatic robberies and midnight getaways now coming alive in their dreams.

"YOU ARE SUCH a lucky man, Manzino," Paul Gennario said. "You are in good health, you have a wife you love, and you pay for everything in cash."

It was the end of another exhausting day and Paul had come to sit beside Giovanni on a low wooden bench where he was cleaning his carpentry tools. Paul was the most self-absorbed person that Giovanni had ever met, one who spent as much of his work-time as possible talking to anyone within earshot about his endless troubles: the father who hated him, his gambling debts, the three insatiable

women he slept with in regular rotation, (all of whom were demanding marriage), and the growing certainty that he would one
day inherit the heart disorder that had plagued all the men in his
family. He had such a mournful outlook, he seemed willing to
switch lives with almost anyone. Giovanni's usual strategy was to
say nothing to him, afraid that even a grunt might encourage the
man to speak further. Today, however, it seemed to Giovanni that
Paul must have reached a new low. The idea that anyone might
envy him, no matter how inanely, struck him as hilarious. Surprising even himself, Giovanni laughed out loud. He was still laughing a few moments later when he packed up to go, leaving the
bewildered Paul to ponder whether he'd been insulted in some
way.

Ice cream was Giovanni's next thought as he came out onto
the main thoroughfare. He needed something to sweeten up the
dark mood at home now that Enzio was in town. The ice cream
parlor was nestled snugly in the middle of the long avenue, tucked
between the saddle shop and the Columbus Hunt Club. Invisible
behind painted plate glass, the club was a gathering place for block
leaders from all over Harlem. The unofficial kings of a hundred
tiny kingdoms, many of them even dressed like royalty. Their shimmering jewels (often displayed on their hats) and white linen suits
looked absurd in a working-class neighborhood – but no one ever
laughed. In the flash of diamond tie pins and the glow of pomade
in their hair and moustaches, these men killed freely to protect
their territories, and controlled the flow of the only real money
around – profits from gambling, whores, and stolen goods. The
"Mustache Petes" were the most flamboyant of the Mafioso and
the very mention of them could evoke terror in the tenements.
Giovanni considered them an embarrassment to his Italian heritage, but he also knew when to look the other way.

Now passing the Columbus Hunt Club in the late afternoon,
Giovanni saw a whole crew of men sitting outside on kitchen chairs,
drinking coffee and Chianti and reading newspapers. A few were
huddled over checkerboards, and one man, the oldest among them,
was carefully laying out a hand of solitaire on a small wooden

table. How could grown men afford so much free time? When he was old, Giovanni thought, he'd still be struggling from dawn to dusk – as if his labor alone was responsible for dragging the sun from horizon to horizon.

In the ice cream parlor, cool and sparkling with its rich marble countertops and brass fixtures, Lou Sisto, the proprietor, crammed an enormous amount of strawberry ice cream into a single quart container and handed it over the counter.

"You always know what I want," Giovanni smiled, dropping a few coins in the man's hand.

"Isn't strawberry Rosa's favorite?"

"It certainly is, and mine too," Giovanni winked.

Back on the street, he then ran into Matteo. Matteo, who tended to get fired up over even small things, was giving an animated description of the towers being erected downtown.

"They'll carry trains all the way to the waterfront," he said, gesturing in the air.

Suddenly, a commotion outside the Hunt Club made them pivot around to see the immense door of the club slam open. Several men filled the sidewalk, shouting heatedly – including a white puff of a man who was leading his two lieutenants. Nicodemo Grande, Giovanni thought: the man behind the Black Hand, the man who personified the Cosa Nostra from the other side of Morningside Heights.

Grande was storming toward his lavish Packard touring car, flanked by two bodyguards, and hurling curses over his shoulder. Then he stopped, spun around, and roared even louder, gesticulating angrily with his gold-topped cane at an unseen adversary, his great bulk expanding his white silk suit. It was then that Giovanni noticed two men in long overcoats stepping from a large dark car that was pulling slowly away from the curb. Its back window opened and a long pipe leaned out.

Giovanni grabbed Matteo and backed quickly away as a machine gun fired in bright flashes, followed by a pistol's muffled pops. Bullets whistled all around them. One slammed into the throat of a man playing dominoes, hurling him backward through the club's plate glass window. On the sidewalk, the bodies of pass-ersby twisted and fell. Spraying the street with gunfire, the gun-man fanned rapidly back and forth, discharging all forty-eight car-tridges in his gun belt. An old man sitting on an orange crate in front of the bakery was struck dead by three bullets to the skull just as he lifted a bottle of wine to his lips.

Giovanni and Matteo were too stunned to move. For a mo-ment, a lull in the fire seemed to signal the end of the battle. But then the men in long coats opened fire, shooting in a wide arc toward the crowd around Grande. Grande, miraculously unhit, drew his own revolver and fired back as one of his bodyguards was blown against a building. More shots came from the club, shatter-ing the windows in Grande's car.

"Assassins!" Grande screamed, then dove – or hoisted – his heavy body into the Packard. Just then, two bullets ripped into his arm and the splash of blood on his shiny white shirtsleeve was the last Giovanni saw of him: a second later another arm pulled the door closed from within and the car roared, careening, around the corner.

All at once, Giovanni became conscious of a sharp pain in his left leg. As he grasped his thigh and winced, both he and Matteo looked down.

"Giovanni, you've been hit!" shouted Matteo, who dragged him toward the protection of the saddle shop's doorway.

The street was absolutely still. Then, suddenly, everyone was screaming. Crowds of people rushed in all directions. Few, how-ever, seemed to know what to do. In all the confusion, no one heard the soft click of the lock in the Hunt Club's front door.

Wishing only to escape the scene as soon as possible, Giovanni hobbled through the saddle shop under Matteo's arm – disap-pearing out the back door, across the backyard and into the alley leading onto the next block. Giovanni knew the only power to be had with men like these was the sense to stay out of their way. In a neighborhood that had its own rules, they bowed to no higher authorities. Even the police were lame ducks.

Rosa nearly dissolved when she saw Giovanni limp through

the doorway – blood running down his leg and dripping from his boot. Crying out, she rushed forward to help Matteo guide him into a chair. The children spilled out of their room a second later and stopped dead at the sight of their father. Gently ripping away the fabric covering the wound, Rosa had a few more anguished moments before she realized that it was not as bad as it looked; the bullet had passed cleanly through the soft flesh on the left side of his lower thigh, apparently missing the bone.

"It's okay," she said to the children. "Your father is hurt, but he'll be okay." The children stood in their places, too alarmed to move. There was a great flow of blood, so while Matteo applied pressure, Rosa bound up the wound with gauze and tape. Before anyone could be called, the apartment was overrun with concerned neighbors, some of whom Gracia had set to work filling pails with steaming water and scrubbing the bloodstains from the hallway and staircase.

As Rosa smoothed the last of the bandages into place, Giovanni looked at her and said, "Rosa, where is Enzio? I haven't seen him all week."

"He's still with us," she said, momentarily ill at ease. "I thought you realized. He comes here after you've left for work, sleeps a few hours, eats lunch, then leaves again before you come home."

Giovanni stared at her as if trying to puzzle out some mystery. Rosa glanced again at the bandaged leg and guessed his thoughts. He held her gaze, shrugged and said, "I hope he doesn't get mixed up with someone like Nicodemo Grande."

"Oh no, Giovanni," she said at once, "Enzio would never . . . ." Her voice trailed off as she realized that nothing was beyond her brother's capabilities. Giovanni acknowledged her uncertainty with a nod of his head and began to pull on a clean pair of pants.

Matteo, who had been helping Gracia wash the blood off the floor and quelling the neighbors' concern, was finally unable to contain his outrage. The boundless energy he displayed at work was now channeled into anger. Then, one of the neighbors came in to report that Grande had escaped, but both of his bodyguards had died. One of the long-coated gunmen had fallen. There were several bodies inside the club, and on the street. But the most unforgivable loss had been of a seven-month-old baby whose wicker carriage, and life, was shattered right before its mother's eyes.

"This is what we get for looking the other way," Matteo cried. "The only thing these animals understand is death. We must get our own guns and drive them from our streets."

Soon the panic that had swept through the children at the sight of their father's blood turned into a bewildered fear of raised voices from so many strangers. Tessie whimpered as she moved closer to her mother, and the boys looked terrified.

"Please," Rosa said to Matteo. "Let me get the children to bed before we talk more of this. They don't understand these things, and you're upsetting them."

Gradually, the turmoil quieted down, and the crowd began to disperse. Rosa thanked them all, but sighed in relief when the last of them disappeared down the staircase to continue their debate on the street below. The children swarmed around Giovanni to examine his bandaged leg.

"Pappa," Bennie said, in an oddly mature voice. "Are you going to die like Mr. Costello's horse? The horse's leg was hurt too, and the policeman had to shoot him."

Giovanni laughed. "No, my little one, Pappa has no intention of giving up that easily. Do you remember the great wagon they had to put the horse in, to haul him away? It didn't look very comfortable, so I think I'll just stay here in this chair until I'm all better. In fact, I'm beginning to feel better already."

Hours later, when the children were asleep, Giovanni and Rosa talked well into the night.

"We came here to escape the pain and the fear that cruel men impose on everyone else, only to find it all around us again. I wanted something better for you." Giovanni spoke quietly as he sipped the bitter coffee growing cold in his cup.

Knowing Giovanni was about to descend into one of his dark moods, Rosa took his hand and brought it to her lips. She kissed his fingers and his palm, then held his hand to her cheek and said, "Giovanni, people are not meant to escape unhappiness. What matters is what we do with it. As long as we remain strong, it will never defeat us, and you are the strongest man I know."

As his hand moved to caress her cheek, Giovanni realized yet again the true source of his perseverance.

BY THE NEXT afternoon, Matteo had managed to convince several men, including Carmello, to attend a meeting in the battle-scarred Hunt Club. The slaughter had infuriated everyone, so when Matteo made a call to arms, they cheered wildly. And yet, when he spoke out specifically against Nicodemo Grande, denouncing him as barbaric and cowardly, everyone knew he was violating a code by which even the most vicious gang leaders must live. Sitting silently among them, Giovanni noticed how many men began glancing over their shoulders toward the street outside, as if anticipating the cue that would send them all scurrying home. Flushed with his sense of mission, however, Matteo heard only the cheers, and Giovanni realized that his next task would be to protect his friend from his own damning words.

Like Carmello Sieppe, Matteo Ruffino became incensed whenever the Black Hand appeared. But because he was young, or because he lacked discretion, Matteo could never restrain his own recklessness. He now openly protested each new episode of violence or extortion by yelling on street corners or in packed barbershops, defying the warnings from all of his friends that he was saying the wrong things to the wrong people.

"What's the matter with you?" Matteo continued to shout in the club. "We should be using the money you give to these pigs to buy the knives and guns we need to slaughter them! They only push us around because we let them. You are afraid to be men. Were your lives so soft in Sicily that you never developed any guts?"

Giovanni saw several listeners in the crowd quietly take note of the young man's words and disappear out the door. He'd have to ease him away from the others, calm him down, convince him to go home and forget his grievances. Matteo was crossing a line that was far more dangerous for him than for Carmello. Carmello, after all, was a respected craftsman who would be difficult to replace;

even Nicodemo Grande needed to repair his shoes. Matteo, on the other hand, had nothing to offer – he was a day laborer and not a potential source of revenues. A common worker's status in such a situation was simple – Matteo was expendable.

Yet, Giovanni could do nothing to stem Matteo's rising protests. He remembered when the two men were working on the same site, and as soon as their lunch break began, Matteo would run to a cluster of men with his sack and pail, and embark upon his incendiary speeches.

"The worst thing about these bastards," Matteo would intone, "is that they only take from their own. Why don't they steal from the Irish, or the Germans, or the Chinese if they're too fucking lazy to work for a living? What kind of scum steals from their own people, their own village, their families? We should say to hell with them, and buy some ammunition, so the next time they come to our neighborhood, we can give them a run for their money!"

On and on he would talk until some workers moved away, fearful of even being seen listening to such inflammatory words. And now, standing at a distance, Giovanni felt the unmistakable chill of tragedy gathering in the air around him. Soon the meeting came to an end with no solution, and Giovanni walked home with Matteo in a steady rainfall. Still covered with caked mud from the day's work, Matteo was so tired and emotionally spent that he didn't even comment when they passed a partially burned newsstand smeared with ashes in the shape of a hand. Finally, they came to their block. Giovanni gave him a soft clap on the back, and they separated wordlessly for their respective apartments.

Matteo was so weary that as he climbed the stairs to his second-floor flat, he was only vaguely aware of the three men standing together in the dim light by one of the doorways. Then two of them, both taller and broader than Matteo, came up on either side of him and spun him around to face none other than Nicodemo Grande.

"Get your hands off me," Matteo shouted, struggling with his two placid captors, each of whom were wearing dark gloves. "I'm not afraid of you!" But his heart was beating hard. Somewhere in the hallways above him, he could hear doors opening, then closing just as swiftly.

In a voice far softer than Matteo's, Grande said, "We know you won't shut up, you little shit. That's why we're here."

The other two men pushed him roughly down the hall until Matteo was sprawled in his own doorway and all three drew revolvers from inside their coats. Just then the door opened and Nicola, Matteo's pretty young wife, now several months pregnant with their third child, rushed into the hallway. Seeing the guns pointed at her husband, she immediately let out an ear-splitting scream. Her twin sons, Claudio and Dario, rushed up behind her and joined in the deafening chorus. Once again, doors were heard opening and voices called down, which distracted Grande and his men long enough for Matteo to attempt to push his family back inside the apartment.

All three guns fired together just as Nicola threw herself in front of her husband's body. The sound was enormous in the trapped space, silencing all the screams that had preceded it. In one convulsive shudder, Nicola crumpled in Matteo's arms. The twins were stunned by what their eyes could not absorb, then cried wildly as they clung to their father's pant legs. In the dying echo of gunshots, Matteo felt his life sweep away like the final bronze chord that hovers in the air after the Angelus bells have stopped ringing.

In that sacred interior, Grande watched the grief-stricken scene, then folded his arms and spoke in the same quiet voice, "You have done this to her, Ruffino, by speaking against me. I no longer have to kill you because your pain will be far greater. When I was a boy in Salerno, an old priest told me that Hell is not really fire; Hell is the inability to experience and share love. It gives me great satisfaction to know that in dealing with my enemies, I don't give them the cheap commodity of death. I banish them to a very real Hell."

Then he turned and walked slowly down the hall, followed by his two bodyguards, and descended the staircase as Matteo issued a low moan from somewhere within his soul. Giovanni, who'd come running in a stumbling rush at the unmistakable sound of death shattering the evening air, brushed against the men as they were leaving. By the time he reached the top of the staircase, Matteo's cry had become full-blooded.

"Nicola! Nicola!" he cried.

"Mamma! Mamma!" his sons cried in unison. Like two anguished altar boys, they looked at each other through a mirror of madness.

As their cries rose in pitch and intensity, Giovanni stood frozen on the landing. Matteo had dropped to his knees beside his wife's body, and began to sob with his arms hanging loosely by his side. Giovanni wanted to step forward and help him to his feet, to find some way of hushing the children's cries, but all his strength ebbed away at the sight of Matteo's pregnant wife, her body now a limp, bloody blur.

THE MORNING OF the funeral was heartbreakingly beautiful and filled with warm sunlight. The mourners' black garments seemed grotesque against all that brightness, as if together they could darken the day. The wailing of the women ascended to hysteria and a tremendous keening by the time the crowd had gathered around the gaping grave. But those who cried the loudest, it seemed to Giovanni, seemed to know the departed the least. Strangers assumed the burden of the family's grief in one anguished voice, while those closest to Nicola were stunned to near-silence.

Giovanni gazed upon the wreckage of his friend – his final surrender into silence beside the two boys weeping inconsolably – and felt the hand of despair around his throat. For the first time, he found his very foundation shaken. Rosa squeezed his arm as they stood by the grave, trying to control her own tears. It was obvious that Matteo, kneeling by the open grave, was dangerously close to the edge of an emotional precipice far deeper than the pit before him. His entire body was trembling. The moan that issued from his lips in an unbroken monotone was soft, but high-pitched. Every few moments, he leaned his body toward the grave in lurches that caused the other mourners to catch their breaths, convinced that he would pitch himself headlong into it. Then he'd pull back again, oblivious to the hands that reached out to caress his shaking shoulders. As the priest concluded his service and the pallbearers lowered the surprisingly small coffin into the earth on oiled ropes, Giovanni kept vigil over Matteo, who continued to kneel in the same place in a distraught state as the mourners threw handfuls of dirt and flowers into the grave.

No one there was more intimidated by the impact of the tragedy than Gino. He had once gone with his mother to the wake of an elderly neighbor and remembered peeking from the safety of Rosa's skirts at the withered thing in the box. But death had not seemed real to him then. The wake had been in the old woman's parlor, a place he had visited several times, where grownups sat, drank coffee, and talked. The coffin, with its blanket of fresh flowers, had seemed like a strange communication, a bizarre piece of mail that had arrived mysteriously and made everyone edgy, uncomfortable, and sad. But today was different. He had seen Mrs. Ruffino alive and vibrant almost everyday; he couldn't imagine her dead in that small wooden box. Is this what would happen to his own mother and father someday?

Gino watched all the neighbors and occasional strangers gathering closer to the grave. Gracia looked as strong as ever, although her energy was concentrated on maneuvering Lily's wheelchair across the soft, uneven surface of the grass; Lily, clutching a large wooden rosary from the old country, seemed quietly terrified, as if one of the graves would reach out and claim her at last. Mr. and Mrs. Zamboli stood slightly apart from the others, their eyes directed toward the ground rather than at anyone else.

As Gino scanned the faces, trying to measure the sorrow in each pair of eyes, he found himself focused on the twins. They were no longer sobbing, nor calling out "Mamma" in response to the cries around them. They looked exhausted, leaning against one another like matched bookends on a bookless shelf, and staring off toward their father's kneeled and crumpled body. Gino tried to reconcile this image of Matteo with everything that Giovanni had told him about the way men were supposed to behave, but could not. He remembered the time he had stumbled on the sidewalk and bloodied his knee, crying not so much from the pain as from the fright. Giovanni had come to him and pressed a piece of toweling to the wound, then whispered to his son that he was too big for tears.

"Girls are luckier than boys," he had said as he used a second piece of towel to wipe the blood and grit from Gino's leg. "They can cry whenever they want. But men have to learn to carry their pain inside them."

"Why, Pappa?" Gino asked, feeling that this was a grave injustice.

Giovanni hesitated, then said, "Men must go out in the world, and move among other men. If they let their pain show, other men will know they can be hurt, and might find a way to hurt them again. Some men only feel strong when they make others feel weak."

Giovanni had spoken so softly that Gino was certain he was imparting one of life's greatest secrets and was suddenly ashamed of every tear he had shed.

"I'll remember, Pappa," he had said.

Now, watching the shattered man at the graveside, Gino knew that Matteo had surrendered his manhood forever and feared that nothing could protect him from his enemies. Frantically, he tugged at his mother's skirts.

"Mamma," he said, "was Mrs. Ruffino a wicked woman?"

"Good heavens, Gino," Rosa said. "Of course not. She was a wonderful woman. Why do you ask such a thing?"

"If she was good," Gino said, "then why did they put her in the ground? And why do they throw dirt on her? Won't she be cold and lonely, and won't the bugs eat her?"

Rosa placed her arm around her son's shoulders and said, "The bugs will never eat Mrs. Ruffino, Gino. It's only her body that's buried in the ground, and she doesn't need it anymore. Right this minute, she's with God, alive as ever."

Gino looked up at the sky as if expecting to catch a glimpse of Mrs. Ruffino disappearing into a cloud. "But why would she leave her family? Didn't she know how much she would upset them?"

"It wasn't her decision," Rosa said. "God decides these things." Her voice faltered because she knew that she was offering the kind of comfort that may soothe a child, but would sound hollow to Matteo.

"Didn't God know how hurt they'd all be? Isn't he supposed to know about everything and only want to help people?" Gino's voice had risen slightly and Rosa realized that he was really disturbed about this.

"Of course he does, Gino," she said, sounding far more assured than she felt. "But God must have needed her more with Him for reasons we will never know."

With an edge of anxiety still in his voice, Gino said, "But Mamma, look around." He broke away from her and stared at the long rows of headstones. "Doesn't he have enough people already?"

Rosa pulled her son toward her, ran her fingers through his thick hair, and said, "Gino, what has you so frightened?"

The tears he had held back all morning filled his eyes. "What if God should need you one day?" he said. "What would we do?"

Rosa hugged her son tightly, kissed the top of his head, and thanked God once more for her precious Gino, the one gift that somehow made up for all the other ways in which He seemed to betray his human children.

"Don't worry, Gino. No matter what happens, I will always be near you."

Giovanni lingered near the freshly filled grave, then lifted his eyes beyond the departing figures to see Enzio Mulassano, watching from a nearby hillside and smoking a cigarette. Enzio matched his gaze for a moment, then gave a small smile and dropped the cigarette as he turned and walked away. The angel of death, thought Giovanni, like his father before him, always drawn to someone else's suffering.

In the next weeks, Matteo gradually vanished before everyone's eyes. Always a thick-bodied man, his flesh withered a little more each day as if he were steadily being devoured. Eventually, he became a stick-figure who wandered the streets with no apparent purpose, lost in his own private hell. The relatives who had temporarily taken in the children soon absorbed them permanently into their already sizeable family, shaking their heads each time they encountered Matteo drifting along the avenues like a gray ghost, his spectral form enclosed in the same dark overcoat that he had worn to his wife's burial. No one ever knew where he slept or ate, and finally he disappeared altogether.

CHAPTER
SEVEN

Enzio lost no time in exploring the darker side of street life. Within a few short months, he had managed to become involved in dozens of schemes and penny-ante hustles. Although he was perfectly willing to serve as a distributor of stolen goods — primarily truckloads of merchandise taken from break-ins of warehouses and storerooms — he wouldn't do anything that required brute strength. Fancying himself to be some sort of aristocrat, he never submitted to dirtying his own hands. His arrogance was so complete that he was even known to wait for storekeepers to open for the day so he could sell them back the goods that someone else had stolen from them the night before.

One evening, while Enzio was in one of the dingy saloons on Metropolitan Avenue, playing a hand of solitaire and nursing a glass of brandy, one of the tavern regulars, a crafty alcoholic named Nick Mastragiacomo, spotted him from the doorway and hurried toward him. He knew that Enzio always had the price of a drink and would save him from another night of withdrawal if he could only steer him toward another shady opportunity.

"Good evening, Mr. Mulassano," he said, with the exaggerated courtesy Enzio always welcomed. "How fortunate I am to find you here when I have such interesting news." Nick had to pause for a moment because the smell of whiskey was making him dizzy. Enzio laid out his next card, ignoring him completely. Nick would get to the point eventually.

"Don't mind if I do," Nick said, taking the seat next to Enzio as if it had actually been offered. "I happen to know a shipment of olive oil that's been separated from its owner," he whispered, "and there is someone who will pay well for it." Besides his love for drink, Nick also treasured the illusion that he was part of a grand fraternity that dealt exclusively in secrets. But the fantasy was so weak that Nick feared even Enzio wouldn't listen.

Without looking up from his columns of cards, Enzio said, "And for enough whiskey, you will allow me to be the courier."

"Yes, yes," said Nick, deeply relieved.

Only a few more words passed between them before Enzio left money for him on the bar and headed for the truck that Nick had told him was carrying the load of olive oil. It was just a few blocks away and Enzio whistled as he walked, tossing the keys into the air, and catching them smoothly. The truck was exactly where Nick had said it would be, so Enzio climbed in and began the drive downtown with the buyer's address in his shirt pocket. The warehouse was in a disheveled section of the city near the waterfront, where all the railroad tracks converged to access the goods arriving on ships from all over the world. But the streets were a hopeless maze. Soon the whistling gave way to curses as Enzio got lost down narrow alleys and had to turn the clumsy truck around again and again. By the time he finally found the right street, both the whistling and curses had been abandoned for a steady stream of Sicilian invectives directed at Nick Mastragiacomo and the mysterious buyer who had been stupid enough to set up offices in a place that no one could find.

He was so exasperated, in fact, that when he screeched into the empty lot, he almost ran into a man standing at the warehouse's back entrance. Leaning through the window, he was about to shout at him to get out of the way when Enzio noticed a shotgun cradled in his arms. Suddenly losing his bluster, Enzio called out simply, "Where's the man in charge?"

"Through there," the sentry said, knowing very well that Enzio had just restrained himself from cursing at him wildly.

"Through where?" Enzio repeated, confused. The guard paused, thinking to toy with the man for a moment, then decided he wasn't interesting enough.

"There,' he said, and pointed to a break in the chain-link fence that surrounded the property.

"Right," Enzio said, and reversed the car, swerving around to park next to a loading platform. Climbing down from the truck, he headed toward the building, indistinguishable from those around it – five stories of badly discolored brick with small windows encased in wire mesh. Smoothing down his clothes he walked through the back door, stepped briskly down the brightly lit corridor toward the office at the other end, and passed another armed man who seemed to be staring at him in amazement. Enzio's curiosity was piqued at all the heavy artillery and he momentarily wondered who the "buyer" might be.

Knocking first, then entering the office with a flourish, Enzio was ready to strike his deal by impressing the man with a hard bargain. But the man who sat before him was an ominous sight. Raising his massive, scowling head, he revealed a set of stony features in which the only sign of life was a tiny pulse beating at his temple. Enzio, who had never been one for subtleties, exhaled impatiently as he approached the man's desk.

"I must interrupt," he said in a hurried voice. "We are all busy men, but I have a business matter that must be disposed of as quickly as possible. I believe I can do you a great favor. I have just come into the ownership of a hundred gallons of the finest olive oil." Enzio paused to let his words sink in, then continued with an undiminished swagger. "It can be yours, this morning, if you offer me a fair price."

Slowly, the man stood and introduced himself, as his two beefy associates in gray suits looked on in disbelief.

"How nice. My name is Nicodemo Grande. And what, may I ask, is yours?" Grande had decided to put the man at ease to see what, if anything, lay behind this incredible blunder. But the silence that followed was palpable. Enzio felt as if the floor had given way beneath him; his skin crawled and lifted the small hairs on the back of his neck.

"It is very fortunate that you have come to me this morning of all mornings. Carlo here was just explaining to me about the delay of a shipment of that same amount of oil. God truly works in mysterious ways, no?"

Enzio shuddered. "Mr. Grande," he said in a broken voice, "I have been betrayed. I have been deceived into offending a great man."

Grande gave him an icy smile. Enzio's sudden dive into submission had not been lost on him, but he also knew that nothing the man said could be believed. Still, he was curious as to what shape the fool's story would take.

"I ask for the chance to make it up to you," Enzio said. "Let me give you the man who has done this terrible thing to both of us."

Although Grande's fury was known to erupt spontaneously, his real power lay in his ability to wait. He had nothing to fear from someone as pathetic and inept as Enzio, so he could give him a long leash with which to hang himself.

Staring intently, with an expression that was almost bemused, Grande said, "You have exactly one hour to bring me the man responsible. When that hour has elapsed, I will kill you in his place."

Enzio nodded, bowed slightly, and nearly ran away. Feeling the panic rise in his throat, he found his way out of the building, but once outside he stopped in his tracks. Where could he hide in so short a time? In Grande's presence, the prospect of one more hour of life seemed an impossible blessing. Now it seemed a cruel joke. *An hour.* Blindly, Enzio made for the truck. Even without his urgency, however, he probably would not have noticed the darkly clothed, stocky man who had already begun to follow him.

Enzio made his way out of downtown much more quickly than he had arrived, and soon found himself at Rosa's door again. Used to seeing him only in the mornings – and certainly not when Giovanni was home – she greeted him with some ambivalence.

Behind her, Giovanni looked up from the kitchen table, his expression dissolving into a contemptuous stare.

Today, however, Enzio was in no mood to ignore his hosts.

"Giovanni," he said as soon as he was safely inside the apartment. "You must find some way to hide me. Nicodemo Grande has threatened to kill me!"

Rosa saw Giovanni's face move from shock to rage, then watched the way he masterfully veiled it with an impassive stare. Before her husband, Rosa sometimes forgot her own feelings completely. Her emotions were nothing beside his powerful and righteous temper. Both she and Enzio – himself now sweating profusely – held their breath as they waited for him to speak.

"You are an idiot, Enzio!" Giovanni exploded. "You have brought the wolves to my door and put my family's lives at stake. I cannot forgive you this. Get out on the fire-escape like the jackal you are and stay away from us. Otherwise, I will bring you to Grande myself."

The sound of footsteps echoed on the stairway as Enzio clambered out the window and pressed his back up against the tenement wall. Giovanni rose to the door, opening it just in time to see Grande's man, Savarese, reach the landing. Cautiously, Giovanni walked out into the hall, wearing rough trousers and an undershirt that revealed his muscular chest and arms. As he closed the door behind him, Savarese – who liked to equalize his position with stronger men – drew out a large pistol.

"My friend," said Giovanni, "I must ask you not to bring out that gun. My wife and children are close by, and the neighbors are peaceful people. The man you are looking for is gone, and he will never come to this place again."

Giovanni's manner was calm, reasonable, even kindly. But Savarese was not the sort who needed provocation to use force. Attempts at appeasement only assured him of his own invincibility; and he could never resist the delight of pressing his advantage. Stepping toward Giovanni, he promptly poked his pistol into Giovanni's midsection.

"You don't understand," he said, "I have come from Nicodemo

Grande and I want that blubbering idiot delivered to me now. Otherwise, I'll kick open that door and you will see what large holes this gun can make in small children."

Giovanni sighed, his body sagging for a moment in apparent surrender. But the gesture was only one of resignation: he would have to become far more involved with this than he intended.

Giovanni's right hand slapped the gun away, sending the pistol over the railing and down the stairwell. A second later his massive left fist rushed forward, jabbing into Savarese's groin. As the sudden blow brought Savarese forward in agony, Giovanni grabbed a handful of his hair, lifted the man above his head, and flipped him over the railing. Savarese screamed the whole five floors until the sound was cut off by the snapping of his neck on concrete.

Giovanni stood by the railing, staring across the empty space at some canyon far deeper than the one into which he had pitched Savarese. His muscles tensed and his hands gripped the balustrade. Any man who kills strangers at another's bidding is no longer a man, Giovanni thought, and so he felt no remorse for the life he had destroyed. How many nights had he been convinced that some dark force was intruding on his dreams – and now his own brother-in-law, a hapless villain, had single-handedly put his family in jeopardy. It was time to deal with him, once and for all.

Giovanni re-entered the apartment, coiled to strike.

"Where is . . ." Enzio began. "I mean, what happened to . . . ."

Giovanni cut him off with a stream of words so brutal that Enzio staggered back as if struck. Giovanni spoke in the Italian of field workers and peasants who knew a thousand phrases to damn the maggots they crushed beneath their boots. Giovanni spit out the words with a venom that shocked Rosa, and the children, too. Only Rosa understood the words, but the children felt his fury as if it slapped them across their cheeks. Their father had become a monster, she thought, recalling the God-crazed prophets who spoke in tongues.

Enzio backed up against the wall, but Giovanni never moved toward him. On the other side of the kitchen, Gino threw one protective arm around Tessie's shoulders. The color rose in his father's face, and the muscles in his arms and chest had gone steely with rage. If the fight didn't end, he thought, Enzio was sure to jump through the window to the street below.

Then, suddenly, Giovanni stopped speaking – leaving a deadening silence in its wake, as threatening as his furor. Slowly, his breathing returned to normal. Enzio was motionless, too weak to make the enormous effort it would require to reassert his dignity. Then, speaking once more, Giovanni delivered his last words with careful deliberation.

"Enzio," he said, "you are exactly what your father was before you – too selfish to think of anything but your own desires, and too stupid to realize the damage you do to others. This time, what you have done is unforgivable. You have brought the devils to the door of your sister and her children. From now on, nothing you do, *disgraisada*, will ever touch them. You will leave our house tonight and never return. If I ever see you here again, I will kill you with my own hands, and leave your rotting carcass in the street for Grande and the other maggots to feed upon."

These words, spoken in a near-whisper, seemed even more powerful to Gino than the barrage that had preceded them. He'd seen his father's great reservoir of strength, and it far was deeper than he had ever imagined. Watching him now, Gino felt a dizzying mixture of fear and pride. His father seemed capable of destroying any threat they might face, and Gino loved him so fiercely that it took his young heart by surprise.

It was Gracia who broke the silence, rushing breathlessly into the apartment. "There's a dead man in the hallway," she finally managed to say, "all bloody and broken. And there's a gun lying next to him. Where in God's name did he come from?"

Giovanni gave Enzio a hard look, then turned to search the eyes of his son. Gino felt a flash of fire pass between them and a moment later was following close behind him, in a spiraling descent to the shouting mob below. As Enzio sighed in relief, Gracia looked at him suspiciously, then moved to Rosa, now holding a cloth to her forehead and shivering uncontrollably by the stove.

When Nicodemo Grande came to America, it was not because he had been unable to rise to power in his home province of Salerno. In fact, his power there had been absolute. While rumor had it that the Italian army had driven him from Italy in response to several of his more outrageous crimes, his real reason for crossing the ocean was boredom. Once he had destroyed all his enemies, there was nothing left to do. For Grande, the contentment of living like a king could never compare to the exhilaration of winning his kingdom in a battle.

To maintain his thrill of conflict, he came to Harlem in 1898, just a year before Giovanni and Rosa made their crossing. With a refined talent for stealing, he soon amassed a great fortune and a small army of loyal soldiers. The fact that most of his victims were his own countrymen did not deter him from betraying them. Instead, he was grateful that these new Italian-Americans could be so easily manipulated and fall so routinely into patterns that had sealed the miserable fates of their Sicilian ancestors.

So accustomed was Grande to mastering the lives of others that the next morning's news almost amused him. His reaction to hearing that Savarese's crumpled body had been found in a tenement stairwell was hardly the unbridled fury that his henchmen had expected. Always inspired by a challenge, Grande's curiosity was aroused. Who was this man, he wanted to know, who had been crazy or courageous enough to have stopped Savarese so effectively.

Sipping his mid-morning brandy at his desk, Grande turned the question over and over in his mind, until a small boy, cap in hand, knocked politely on his half-opened door. Grande gestured for him to enter and the boy, who must have been nine or ten, announced, "I have a message for you from Giovanni Manzino. It's about the man who fell."

"What is it?" Grande asked.

The boy fidgeted with his cap.

"Well," Grande said, "I'm listening."

"He wants you to . . ." The boy paused, his face twisted in concentration, then began again. "He said to ask you very respectfully if you would meet him at three o'clock at Fazio's coffee shop on Amsterdam Avenue." The boy seemed pleased with himself for having such useful information to impart and smiled brightly. "So, will you meet him?" he continued. I'm supposed to find out."

Grande flipped him a shiny fifty-cent piece. "I'll be there."

The boy looked down, staring uncertainly at the coin. "Mr. Manzino already gave me a nickel," he said.

"Just remember who gave you more." As the boy left, smiling even more broadly, Grande summoned one of his guards and told him to find out whatever he could about a man named Giovanni Manzino.

That afternoon, precisely at three, Grande looked up from *El Progresso*, his Italian-language newspaper to see a large man in laborer's clothes stopped in front of him. Grande's eyes flickered briefly to his left where two men sat together in a corner booth, then to his right at a third man alone at one of the small circular tables. Each one slid a hand around the revolver tucked into their belts.

The laborer blinked and narrowed his eyes for a moment, adjusting them to the dimness of the shop.

"Good afternoon, Signor Grande," the man said in a clear, accented voice. "I am Giovanni Manzino. We have a very serious matter to discuss."

Grande raised his fingers in a brief gesture toward his bodyguards, indicating that they could relax. Six hands rose from their heavy revolvers and returned to their pastries, although all eyes stayed on Giovanni. Meanwhile, Grande studied the man carefully. He had spoken politely, yet had no subservience to his manner, none of the groveling that Grande usually observed in men who approached him as informers. He seemed to speak with the kind of courtesy that existed among equals when they had significant business to conduct. Grande normally felt contemptuous of the spineless peasants who fearfully humbled themselves. Still, he resented the unmistakable implication that this man would never bow before him. Gesturing at the chair opposite his, he invited Giovanni to sit down, even going so far as to force a smile of welcome. Giovanni nodded and balanced his imposing body on the incongruously delicate wrought-iron chair.

Abruptly, he began, "Last night a man who worked for you threatened my family. He left me no choice but to kill him." There was no trace of apology in his words. His tone was that of a man simply acknowledging one of life's more unfortunate circumstances, which any reasonable man would understand.

Grande was impressed by Giovanni's frankness and reserve. After a few hurried inquiries, he knew of Giovanni's unshakable reputation for independence and personal honor. It was also known that he was particularly disinterested in his brother-in-law and would have never assisted him in anything. In fact, Giovanni had always steadfastly refused involvement in any "local business."

"Tell me how it happened, Signor Manzino," he said, slipping into Italian, the language of their shared homeland.

"I don't know what he has done, but Enzio Mulassano, my wife's brother, has apparently aroused your anger. He has just recently arrived from Sicily and has been staying with us, in our home. It is only in regard for my wife's feelings that I've tolerated his presence at all. Nevertheless, he was with us, unarmed, when Savarese came to our doorway – and so were my wife and children. This man Savarese drew his weapon and intended to storm my apartment." Here Giovanni paused, as if giving Grande time to absorb the enormity of Savarese's offense. Then, in an elaborate shrug, Giovanni added, "I threw the gun down the stairs, but that was, at best, a temporary measure. I had to throw the man over the railing as well." His story completed, Giovanni gave a mildly apologetic look, as if he'd accidentally bumped into Grande on a crowded sidewalk.

Grande stared back quietly at this extraordinary peasant, but his mind was racing. There would be little glory in killing such a man, Grande thought. He might even lose face in the neighborhood, ultimately diminishing his power in the community rather than enhancing it. Giovanni was well-respected by his neighbors, and by now every Sicilian in the city would know that he had acted heroically in defending his family against an armed intruder.

If Grande were to kill him, he would only compound Savarese's stupidity and risk alienating these hopelessly sentimental people. They were already crucifying him for shooting that damned Ruffino woman who had stepped in the way of the bullets meant for her husband. True, he wanted these people to fear him, but the fear had to embody some respect or it was ultimately useless. Clearly, any action taken against Manzino might backfire. And so, Grande was prepared to make concessions of which few would have imagined him capable.

"Signor Manzino," Grande began, "between you and me, as gentlemen of the world, Savarese was an embarrassment, nothing but a street hooligan. His job was to hunt Mulassano, not your family. He was far too pushy, anyway," he continued lightly. "He killed when it was far more efficient to terrorize and, frankly, I'm well rid of the bastard. I hope that your wife will accept my apology for the disruption of her home."

Giovanni remained silent, reluctant to say anything that might upset the balance that he had somehow achieved. "May I offer you some espresso?" Grande said, gesturing now across the room to Fazio standing speechless on the other side of the marble counter.

"Yes, thank you," Giovanni answered, subdued but still suspicious.

Fazio immediately brought over two fresh cups.

"There is, of course, still the problem of your brother-in-law," Grande said, anxious to reassert his authority, if only for the sake of the bodyguards who had begun to eavesdrop on their conversation.

"Yes," said Giovanni, sipping the steaming coffee. "There is always the problem of Enzio."

"Does his life matter to you?"

"Not to me, but it matters to my wife."

Grande nodded gravely. "All right, then," he said at last. "He is my gift to you. Tell your wife that her brother lives, with my compliments, as a way of offering restitution." His smile faded slightly, then Grande leaned forward. "However, if this man offends me again, in any way at all, this dispensation is ended. I shall kill him where he stands."

With an elaborate shrug that reminded Grande of all the peasants he had ever known in Sicily, Giovanni answered, "If it should come to that, I am sure he will have deserved his end."

PART
THREE

CHAPTER EIGHT

IT WAS ALMOST impossible for the children to appreciate the enormous change that their parents had undergone in moving to America. If they had, it might have been easier for them to understand their increasingly remote father. Giovanni's days at the construction sites were long and exhausting, and when he wasn't working for Nunzio, he was acting as superintendent for the apartment building next door. Since Nunzio paid him only nine dollars a week, he was forced to take on more work whenever possible and, consequently, was spending less time at home.

Yet no matter how much he toiled, he could never get ahead, though he seldom communicated the depth of his frustration. To Rosa, he was always open, tender and caring, but his growing distance began to frighten the children. As soon as he came home, everyone would turn solemn while the weary man sat sternly at the head of the table. By now they'd all witnessed his full temper, and the fear of it caused them never to counter his word. For Rosa, Giovanni's darker moods only aroused her tenderness. It grieved her to see him so tired that he could barely show his love for the children whose lives he protected from hardship.

Each day started early with a little milk over oatmeal that Rosa said "grew while you ate" and which they used for dunking her homemade bread – the best bread in the neighborhood, filling the whole building with its aroma at baking hour each day. Butter was too luxurious. Afterward was the daily teaspoon of cod liver oil, which, if you were lucky, you could pour down the sink without Rosa noticing. Giovanni then left for work and soon afterwards, Gino and Bennie went down to the street. Though Giovanni grumbled, the boys really did contribute to the family. Each Saturday, Gino took the train with Giovanni to the Bronx where they filled burlap sacks with wild greens in the fields. During the week, the boys were expected not only to do chores and errands but to bring in any extra pennies or milk or supplies. For them, the hunt for tips and money became as much of a game as anything else.

In the summers, they delivered ice for the iceman Mr. Monefusco. Rosa worried they would break their backs carrying huge blocks up tenement stairs, but Gino assured her that on hot days much of it melted before they got it half-way up. In winter, wood was always needed for the stoves, so the children loitered around the furniture stores on Third Avenue and pilfered empty crates.

When they weren't scrounging for pennies, the boys used the streets as playgrounds. At first Rosa was horrified at their playing fields. The concrete underfoot was hard and unyielding. The drivers of trucks, cars and wagons were notoriously impatient. But the boys loved the excitement. Striking trolley tracks and cracks in the cement, balls hurtled in wild directions. Hitting the el train meant an automatic home run. Bennie, whose body was stockier than Gino's, soon became a minor star, outperforming everyone in the power of his swing.

By the time the boys arrived home, they were invariably covered with dirt and several new scratches. To them, it seemed that Rosa and Tessie must have been sitting on bed all day reading stories. What else was there to do in the house? Gino couldn't understand how it could take all day to clean a few things and make their evening pasta. Certainly, he thought, it must be horribly boring to stay at home all the time. Rosa laughed and tousled his hair when he said that. "There's more going on out this one window," she said, "than there ever was in the village where I grew up."

In fact, Rosa sometimes thought, the hardest thing in the new world was actually to find any solitude. All along the Manzinos block were six-story buildings filled with families in which Rosa and Giovanni's was considered a tiny one. Below the apartments were cobblers, bakers, barbers, blacksmiths and grocers. Despite the crowds, all the neighborhood people knew each other. Going grocery shopping was like stepping out for a Sunday promenade in an ancient village: full of greetings and waves and the tipping of hats. "Mrs. Manzino," the shopkeepers would say, smiling and pointing out the day's specialties. There was always a candy stick for Tessie too, or perhaps one of the tiny apples she liked to roll in her fist.

Back in the apartments, it was always wise to be prepared for a visitor. It was a tradition that whenever someone came to the door, even a neighbor seen every day, plates of food would come out to the cry of "Mangia, Mangia." The front door wasn't the only entry point for visitors either; there was still the fire escape. One spring day, when Rosa was kneading dough in the kitchen, she heard a strange noise outside. Turning just an inch, she saw a man on the fire escape and heard shouts from below. Assuming it was none of her business, Rosa ignored him and went on with her work, figuring he would leave in his own time. He did, but not without crawling over Rosa's windowsill, landing on the floor with a thud, and bolting through her front door. Tessie, who had come out of the bedroom just as he ran by, stared at him and then at her mother. "Who was that?" she asked. But Rosa simply shrugged.

For Tessie, life at home was far from boring. From the first, Bruno was a demanding baby who had to be watched over constantly; if he himself couldn't take part in an activity, Tessie had to set him up where he could see it. Even then, if left alone for a few minutes too long he'd be tearing up paper underneath the sink or banging on the stove with sticks. Besides Bruno and the daily cooking and shopping, each day brought something new. Twice a year, the cotton mattresses had to be washed. Rosa emptied all the cotton batting onto a sheet, then washed the ticking, dried it, stuffed the cotton back into the mattress, and sewed it up. The killing of bedbugs was a regular job that Tessie hated more than anything. Each time Rosa went for the hammer and basin of water, Tessie screamed. When Rosa banged on the springs and the first bug began to fall, she ran away to hide – often under Bruno in his crib.

As there were few extra sets of clothes, not even of Giovanni's work clothes, washing had to be done every day. After boiling all the clothes in a tub on the stove, Rosa used washboards for stains, then wrung and rinsed out each garment by hand. Tessie's job was to hang all the fresh clothes on the laundry line that criss-crossed the back of the apartment building along with all the neighbors'.

There were so many large families in the buildings that births were quite common. No one ever went to a hospital; as soon as someone went into labor, a midwife arrived with a satchel. For a long time, Tessie thought the baby arrived in the satchel too. But no one ever spoke of such things and she never dared to ask. Doctors were almost unknown in the neighborhood and if a home-made remedy didn't work, a visit was paid to the local healer on 109th Street. Mrs. Anna Randazzese lived at the top of a five-story tenement. Her workroom was her kitchen at the back of the building; sunlight streamed over the potted flowers in the windowsill and fed all her magic herbs and weeds. The cupboards overflowed with bottles and jars of ointments and lotions and dried herbs. Dressed in black ever since her husband had died (more than ten years ago now), Mrs. Randazzese looked to Tessie like some fantastic witch out of one of Gino's books. Even her name sounded mysterious, while her cures were as strange as witchcraft. For a fever, she rubbed the hand muscles and pulled a finger. For sore throats, she massaged the glands and yanked out a piece of hair. When Bennie sprained his arm in yet another street scuffle, Mrs. Randazzese took a length of twine, dipped it in the white of an egg, and wrapped it around Bennie's wrist with a piece of cloth. In two days, it had miraculously hardened into a cast.

Another time, when Tessie had headaches for a week, the healer recited prayers over her. "Let me pass your head," she said, then made a sign over Tessie's forehead. "My child, you are overlooked." That night, Tessie had been amazed that she felt completely well again – though at dinner Gino told her that she too was turning into a witch: hadn't she noticed how her eyes were starting to flash like knives?

"It's true," Tessie said, cheered by the return of her health. "And if you don't watch out I'll pour love potion in your ears when you sleep and you'll fall in love with a bedbug."

It wasn't long before Rosa came to see what many mothers had before her: that the basic characters and alliances of children form early on. From the first, Gino and Bennie were particularly close. Gino was much quicker than his younger brother, and Bennie more of a street brawler. Yet despite their differences, they had a natural affection for each other. The loyalty between them was a kind of ease; no matter what happened, Rosa realized, these two would always protect each other.

As the only girl, Tessie doted first on her father, and then on her eldest brother. As a baby, Bruno was everybody's favorite – as Tessie was rarely without him, Rosa began to joke that Bruno had two mothers. His relentless need for attention, however, ultimately exasperated both of them. It was as if God had forgotten that all humans are supposed to sleep, Rosa said; Bruno had more energy, and required more work, than the other three put together. Four and five years older than he, Gino and Bennie would always be far enough ahead to move in a slightly different crowd. But Bruno was always around the next corner.

One thing you couldn't say about the Manzino children, Giovanni thought, was that they were boring. Each of them had his own unique will. Not to be outdone because she was a girl, Tessie could be as assertive as any of them. As quick-witted as Gino, she was always engaged in little taunts and teases. As willful, Giovanni thought, as her grandmother Bianca, she went unswervingly for what she desired. When she was five, Giovanni caught her using the crucifix from her bedroom wall to stir some watered-down tomato sauce she planned to serve her doll for dinner. While the doll ended up in a cabinet above the sink – banished without Tessie's nourishing meal – Tessie was not to be defeated. Waiting until everyone was asleep, she crept out of bed and climbed onto the kitchen shelf by moonlight – certain that her baby could not sleep amid so many dishes. Just as her fingers closed around the doll's foot, however, her grip on the cabinet gave way and she crashed to the floor. Rosa, who reached Tessie first, found her sprawled on the tiles, holding the doll aloft so it wouldn't suffer the same pain.

"This is what God has done to remind you never to disobey your father," Rosa said.

For her part, Tess only wondered what kind of God would strike with such malice at so small a sin. Something was very wrong with the world, she decided.

Her sixth birthday had been no exception. In a household where the children kept their worldly goods in one box each, big presents could hardly be expected. Still Tessie knew that her father would have a treat for her, and drove Rosa to distraction all day. Nothing could hold Tessie's attention – not even baking her own loaf of bread in the oven. Finally Rosa sent her downstairs to play with her friend Madeline Benina. In ten minutes, however, Tessie reappeared. "Okay," Rosa said, exasperated. "Go down and play with your brothers." Tessie grinned, as both knew this is what she had really wanted all along.

"And take Bruno with you," Rosa called, as Tessie scampered for the door.

When Giovanni arrived home at six o'clock he found his four children sitting in a row on the front steps. Everyone, even four-year-old Bruno, was panting and flushed from playing handball in the heat.

"And what trouble are you up to today?" Giovanni asked.

"No trouble," Gino and Bennie said in unison.

Now that her father was home, Tessie had little need for her brothers, but took Bruno by one hand and her father by the other, rushing upstairs for her present. Once there, Rosa had to smile at

Tessie's beaming face as Giovanni placed a soft package wrapped in white paper in her hands.

"This," Giovanni said solemnly, "comes from your grandmother in Sicily, thousands of miles across the ocean."

Quickly tearing off the paper, Tessie stared in amazement at the doll in her hand. It was a tiny creature, fashioned from scraps of discarded cloth like a quilt. Its crude face and odd blend of fabrics might have seemed comical to some, but to Tessie it was the most beautiful doll she had ever seen. Her grandmother, Giovanni told her, had been a seamstress who once worked for a great Contessa. Amazed at the tiny stitches and wonderful work, Tessie carried the doll constantly from then on, swearing that it could only sleep if she sang to it and forbidding her brothers from ever touching it.

While they teased her constantly, Tessie could hold her own. She was never a tomboy exactly, but she definitely had a stronger calling than most girls for boys' games. After a few years, Tessie was as likely to be playing handball with her brothers as dolls with Madeline. Rosa was proud of Tessie's smartness: no matter how she and Giovanni tried to protect her, she thought, it was a big dirty city that they lived in, with plenty of strangers.

To her brothers' annoyance though, it seemed that Tessie could use her girlhood either to get out of things she didn't want to do, or to do those she did. When she joined in at stickball, she played so fiercely that the neighborhood boys nicknamed her Tess, which she called herself from then on. When the boys had to carry some wood upstairs, however, she quickly ran ahead "to help Mamma with dinner." At the movies, which were so popular many sat through all shows twice, and ate their dinner in the theater, Tess enjoyed her moments of power as she ceremoniously doled out Rosa's packed meals to her brothers — but only when she decided they were hungry enough. This infuriated Bruno and Bennie; only Gino was more amused by his sister's antics than bothered by the hunger in his stomach. "Tessie," he would say. "The little witch of 112th Street."

"The good witch."

"Huh," Bruno would say, banging on her dress with a drumstick.

One October afternoon, Rosa stood watching Gino, Bennie, Tessie, and Bruno in the backyard below their window. Most of the earth was filled with vegetables, but they had found a rare empty patch and carved out a circle to play marbles. Looking down over them, Rosa had a sudden sense that something was odd about the neighborhood. She tried to puzzle it out, following the drift of a few fugitive leaves from the block's half-dozen trees across the patchwork of fence lines and garden rows. The air was warm despite the rising breeze, but the copper-colored leaves reminded her that she would have to find heavier clothes for the children before winter. Then suddenly she realized why the neighborhood seemed so strange – all the children but her own were gone! Every day, the number of children grouped around the same game of marbles had grown smaller and smaller, as though the circle had swallowed them up while her back had been turned.

Later, as she, Tess, and the three boys made their Tuesday afternoon trek to the shops on Metropolitan Avenue, she asked them where their friends had gone. "School," they answered in unison, all except Tess, whose mouth was too full of marbles to mutter anything. Rosa bent down to tap the back of Tess's head so she would spit them out into her mother's outstretched hand, a daily ritual since the marble season had started in August.

"I just like the feel of them in my mouth," Tess would say. Or, "I'm cleaning them for my brothers." Better yet, "I'm trying to top my record for how many I can hold at once."

School? Rosa felt a rush of anxiety. How could she have forgotten to enroll her children in school? Like so many immigrants, she and Giovanni had carved out their own sanctuary and stayed religiously within its boundaries. But outsiders always encroached on their little world: fire inspectors looking for bribes, politicians looking for votes, and dozens of other intruders. Rosa remembered the severe woman in a badly cut matron's uniform who had appeared toward the end of the summer, stopping children to ask their names and then scribbling them down in a small notebook. Whenever she came across a mother, she had warned her that all children over seven would have to be registered and in school in September. As with most strangers, Rosa had instinctively avoided the woman who had obviously been overwhelmed at the number of children swarming in the streets and shouting in dialect from stoops and rooftops. But she must have made some impact, Rosa thought, because the children were nowhere to be seen.

Thinking now of how she had avoided the schoolmistress – if that was what she was – Rosa then felt suddenly guilty. She had always meant to send her children to school. But she supposed that somehow she had not wanted to part from them quite so soon. They were growing so fast. Stopping in to see Gracia, she found her scrubbing her kitchen floor – something Gracia did so often Rosa always felt ashamed of her own. Rosa immediately asked what would happen if she didn't send Gino and Bennie to school this year.

"Why, nothing, I suppose," said Gracia. "But why wouldn't you?"

Rosa was too embarrassed to admit that she had forgotten.

Gracia hardly noticed though, but launched into an entire litany of reasons to send them: older children grew too restless at home and only got into trouble; it was good to get them out from under your feet now and then; at school they can play games with other children and get free milk every afternoon, thanks to a young congressman named La Guardia. Rosa couldn't help noticing the one thing that Gracia hadn't mentioned.

"And I suppose they might even learn something worthwhile?"

Gracia wrinkled her brow for a moment and gave a broad wave of her hand. "What's to learn?" she said, and refilled her soapy bucket. Like most women from Italy, Gracia had no experience with schooling beyond the priest's preparation for communion. In her childhood, much like Giovanni's, children had to work along-side their parents in the farmyards and fields; school was some-thing for her cousins in Rome or Florence or Palermo. It wasn't surprising then that she couldn't see any value in it. But Rosa knew that the one good thing her father had done for her was to hire a tutor while she was growing up. At a very young age, she could read and write, and had entered the worlds of history, art, and literature.

That night she spoke to Giovanni. At first, he had more misgivings than Rosa had, but she soon convinced him they would fall behind the other children and maybe never do well in this new world. Giovanni was grudging. But knowing how difficult his own life was, he soon gave in. The very next morning, Rosa led Gino and Bennie, dressed in their only clean shirts and trousers and smelling of brown laundry soap, to P.S. 168, the new school building three blocks away. Made of red brick, it stood on a stretch of open land only recently cleared of trees and shrubbery. Speaking to several other mothers walking with their children, Rosa learned that they were lucky to have a new school so close to home. In other neighborhoods, schools had been hastily set up in factories, storage warehouses, pool halls, and even prisons. Often they were airless, sooty, hopelessly gloomy, and even dangerous. Children had disappeared down forgotten freight-elevator shafts and been attacked by enormous rats when they tried to use the building's crude toilets.

When the three entered the school's main corridor, classes had already begun for the day. Walking down the long halls to the registrar's office, they were awed at the scores of silent children in the classrooms alongside them. The silence actually seemed louder than the caterwauling of the streets that they were used to. Bennie was intimidated by this strange force that kept his friends struggling with pencils in their seats. It felt like church, where there was always some old woman to slap his hand if he poked the boy sitting next to him. Drawing up his lower lip in a pout, he put on his best they-won't-tell-me-what-to-do expression. Catching sight of him, Rosa reached quickly pinched his cheek, whispering, "Stop that, Bennie!" Robbed of his belligerent mask, Bennie feigned the next best thing – boredom.

Gino, meanwhile, had none of his brother's fears. He had felt self-conscious when his friends had asked why he wasn't going to school. Now he was thrilled by this huge leap toward growing up.

His heart pounded and from the tingling in his cheeks he knew that he was blushing too. In the registrar's office, they found a young woman poring over a ledger book. Looking up from her desk, she smiled at Gino while Rosa turned to an older woman who seemed to be in charge. Leaning across a large countertop, the woman gave Rosa a series of papers to sign, speaking with the exaggerated care that one gives small children. After several minutes of this, Rosa suddenly spoke out sharply. "I am perfectly capable of filling out the forms myself."

Startled, the woman moved back slightly. "I'm sorry," she said. "It's just that so many of the mothers . . . ." Too embarrassed to continue, she nodded and returned to her office. A few minutes later, a young boy came to bring Gino and Bennie to their classrooms.

From the first day, Gino loved school. Though independent, and even a little aloof, he liked being with so many children his age. He never tired of studying their voices and their mannerisms, of imagining what they were thinking and feeling. Then too, he fell immediately into the routine of his lessons. Already, he knew he had to make money someday if he ever hoped to achieve anything; all these words and numbers would only make it easier, he thought. Reading came easily, and he loved each clean piece of paper issued by his teacher, Miss Reilly. He also loved practicing the elaborate signature he would need if ever he became important.

On most days, however, Gino gave little thought to the usefulness of his lessons. The building itself was marvelous to him — so large, with so many hallways and stairways to explore. Whole corridors of classrooms were still empty, waiting for more children and kept closed to save the cost of heating. Every surface was clean. The aroma of thick wax on wooden floors reminded him of the caramel apples sold by vendors on the street. He loved the smell of large wooden pencils and the deep purple ink in his inkwell, though the knife-edged pens were difficult to use without tearing the paper. It was a good thing that Bennie wasn't allowed to use them yet, Gino thought. He was so clumsy he might drown his class-mates in ink.

Above all, he loved Miss Reilly. Some of the other children referred to her as Old Battle-Axe or Miss Prissface, but then children were expected to insult their teachers. To Gino, her every gesture was special. She was tall and slender, with long, dark skirts that swept to the floor and hid all but the tips of her buttoned shoes. Her white starched blouses rose to a high stiff collar and her thick hair was drawn into a bun that added still more inches to the top of her head. Despite her severity, which she needed to survive a class of so many budding hoodlums, Gino knew that Miss Reilly had great softness. When she moved across the room, he could sense the shifting of full breasts and the roundness of her hips under the folds of black wool. When she came to check his work, especially toward the end of a long and exhausting day, he could catch the scent of roses mingling with perspiration as she bent down to his desk. He wanted to unpin her rich auburn hair and watch it tumble across her shoulders. Sometimes, when she stood by one of the windows on a clear morning, the sunlight sparkled in the wisps of hair that had loosened from her bun, as if they had reached out and taken hold of tiny jewels. She brushed the strands away as if annoyed by her rebellious hair but too busy to stop and pin it back. What may have endeared her the most to him, how-ever, was the unmistakable flush that penetrated the talcum she dusted on her cheeks, a flush he noticed at odd moments, particu-larly when she read stories that stirred her, such as the knights of the round table. On one such occasion, as she read a passage about the Holy Grail and a blush rose to her cheeks, she glanced quickly at the class, perhaps to be sure that no one noticed. Suddenly she and Gino were staring directly at each other. His face immediately became inflamed, as if he were answering her color with his own echo. She smiled so gently at him before returning to the book; the memory was like a gift of roses. Gino loved her, but never had the courage to say so.

Caught between pride in Gino's success and exasperation at Bennie's refusal to study, Rosa knew that one day both would have to drop out and help their father in the struggle to survive. Despite Giovanni's long hours and Rosa's job at the factory, the family always seemed a step beyond their means. Even the school lunch, only five cents a day each, was more than Rosa's budget could bear. With both Gino and Bennie in school, this meant fifty cents a week. Instead, Rosa made them each bologna sandwiches from vegetables and five cents worth of meat that she sliced very thin. But she was determined to keep them in school for as long as she could.

Her only real concern was over the fighting in the school playground. Not unlike their parents, the dozens of children divided themselves into small clusters, most of them representing individual families. While many were Italian, there were also Polish, German, Jewish, and even a few Chinese children. All seemed to coexist with little trouble, until the Haggerty brothers arrived – all five of them. Even Giovanni knew their father: Jimmy Haggerty, a laborer with a drinking man's bravado and a boxer's body. Not just one man had crossed paths with him after a night of carousing – and regretted it. His sons, collectively, were obviously trying to copy their Dad's image. It would have been impossible for just one of them but as Giovanni said: cowards find courage in crowds. Knowing already how tough kids liked to pick on him for being too pretty, Gino gave them a wide berth, and advised Bennie to do the same.

Unfortunately, Bennie had not yet learned how to rise above the baiting of others, and one day during mid-morning recess, Gino came out of the classroom to see a small crowd gathering by the wooden fence at the sidewalk. Usually, boys and girls played on opposite sides with several games going on at once – jump-rope contests, ball tosses, jacks, marbles, even a footrace around the schoolyard's perimeter. Both girls and boys were gathered together now though, and Gino knew immediately that the Haggertys were at it again. Crossing the playground and peeking through the crowd, he was shocked to see them in a circle – and Bennie in the middle being tossed around like a medicine ball. Smaller than all the others, Bennie could swing his fists all he liked but they could still keep him off balance.

"Hey, you skinny dago," one said, shoving him to another brother, "why don't you hit me?"

"Wop! Watch out for the grease!" the next said, bouncing him along to someone else.

The kids were cheering them on, more out of fear of becoming the next victim than out of any respect. They didn't notice Gino pushing through the crowd until he suddenly stepped forward and caught Bennie in his arms.

"Another dago! What's the matter, grease ball? Afraid he can't fight his own battles?" shouted James, one of the Haggerty nine-year-old twins.

Bennie tried to break free and throw himself at James, but Gino held on and said, "That's exactly what he's going to do, but not now. The monitor will be here in another minute and he won't be able to finish you off in time." Gino's voice was so calm and confident that a hush fell over the other children, and a few looked over their shoulders for the recess teacher. "You're bigger than he is, and he can beat you all. But it'll have to be one at a time. Unless, of course, you're afraid to face him by yourselves."

The challenge hung in the air for a long minute, and then Jackie Haggerty, the eight-year-old who had started the day's fight, said, "Just name the time and place. Only it better be today, and you better show up."

Gino smiled, with a calm that made the Haggertys look warily at each other. "The lot across from the Armory at 3:30. We'll wait for you." He then walked through the crowd with his arm on Bennie's shoulder just as a teacher hurried toward them. With the calm of seasoned veterans, all of the children instantly dispersed, looks of wondrous innocence on their faces.

Bennie, looking back over his shoulder, whispered "I wasn't afraid, Gino, honest. But they had me cornered before I knew what was happening. We'll get them later, right?"

"Right, little brother," Gino said, tousling his brother's unruly hair. "Just stay calm till then."

The crowd at 3:30 wasn't quite as large as the one at the schoolyard, but everyone was much quieter – no one wanted to miss any part of the drama.

"Remember," Gino said, as the Haggertys gathered around him, "one at a time."

No one questioned that Gino had somehow become the one in charge, and soon Bennie and Jackie moved toward one another in the circle. Over at the Armory, a few uniformed men sat on the steps, watching the show and laughing at the boys' gravity.

Whatever Bennie lacked in size, he made up for in fury. In just a few swift blows, he had sent Jackie sprawling to the ground with a split lip and a great deal of blood. Steven, the second twin, jumped in with a headlong rush at Bennie's midsection, but Bennie twisted to the side, leaving Steven crashing to the dirt. In a moment Bennie was on his back, pounding away at his head with tiny fists. Forgetting the one-at-a-time rule, and unable to stand his twin brother being pummeled, James darted forward and kicked Bennie in the chest, sending him flying with the air whooshed out of him.

Victory was short, however, because Gino grabbed James by the shoulder, spun him around and sent several sharp blows to his face. He fell back onto the ground next to Bennie, a small chip of one front tooth disappearing in the dirt. Brendan and Dennis, the two oldest Haggertys, then started toward Gino, but he held out his hands and said, "One at a time, remember?"

Someone in the crowd took up the cry, "One at a time!" and the remaining brothers, sensing the crowd would move against them if they all jumped on Gino, backed away. Gino helped Bennie to his feet and said, "Three down, two to go, little brother. I'm proud of you."

During the next few minutes, Bennie went up against Brendan and Dennis in turn. They were big boys of ten and eleven, and probably could have hurt Bennie very badly if they had put their hearts into it, but Bennie was so vicious and swung his fists so wildly that everyone was a little afraid of him. They each swapped punches with him for only a few minutes before tearing free, and shoving him clear. Still Bennie was covered with bruises by the time Dennis called a halt, blood pouring from his nose. Grinning like a madman, he didn't seem to feel a thing though, but ran over to hug Gino.

"I did it! I did it, Gino!" Bennie shouted. "We showed them all!"

Looking almost pleased that they had finally come up against someone who had challenged them, the Haggertys offered their hands in a way that was almost comically formal. Gino and Bennie shook hands with each of them, and the crowd applauded, as if it had all been a show for their benefit. The Manzinos and the Haggertys would now be allies for a while, until someone had a mean-spirited moment, and the war erupted again. Most schoolyard truces had little chance of lasting too long.

From then on, Gino's social position in the school was defined by his quiet strength, his independent attitude toward any other skirmishes that broke out, and the way girls were aware of him wherever he went. Comfortable now with his status, he set about acquiring the skills that would give him an edge over others lacking his self-discipline. A diligent worker, he took extra satisfaction in Miss Reilly's apparent pleasure in him. For her part, whenever she realized he was staring at her, she felt a telltale blush and hastily distracted herself with some piece of class business.

Bennie, meanwhile, though now commanding quite some respect in the playground, seemed doomed to fail in the classroom. On their walks home from school he complained bitterly to Gino that he had been forced to wear the conical cap of the dunce once again. But Gino was not especially sympathetic. Bennie wasn't the smartest, but he wasn't the dumbest either, and the teachers never made anyone wear the dunce cap if their only sin was to be truly slow in learning. The cap was for those who refused to learn and Bennie was apparently particularly gifted in that. Not only did he waste time in class and try to encourage anyone within earshot to waste time as well, he was constantly pulling pranks, like rolling up wads of paper and ink and launching them at the girls. Sometimes he disappeared from the classroom altogether – even when Rosa had Gino deliver Bennie to his teacher in person.

Rosa knew that Bennie had been excited about his lessons at first. But when they had proved difficult, he suddenly wasn't interested anymore. If he couldn't be as smart as Gino, he pretended he couldn't be bothered. "Why should I stay in that crummy place?" Bennie argued with Rosa. "I can make twenty cents a day when I work with the ice man. The ladies tip me!"

Rosa tried to talk him into trying again, and stubbornly insisted he return to school. But when his attitude remained unmoved she realized the situation was probably hopeless. When he succeeded in being held back a grade and found himself among even younger children, she knew it was only a matter of time before the streets became his only form of education.

CHAPTER
NINE

ONE AUTUMN DAY after school, when Gino was exploring the forbidden territory of the cellar beneath his building, he came upon the unexpected sight of a large man bleeding on the coal pile. Dominick Bazzano, in a gray suit and bloody white silk shirt pulled open to his chest, was obviously in pain and concentrating on changing a wad of packing around a stomach wound. Gino watched him for several minutes from just beyond a pile of old cartons, then stepped out into the dusky basement light.

Looking up, Dominick jumped slightly at his presence, then returned Gino's stare. Since he had shot a man in a robbery and the police were hunting for him, he shouldn't let anyone see him. But Dominick was fond of children, and had no desire to hurt the boy. Two days earlier, he and Ralphie Necci had robbed the receipts from an Italian restaurant several blocks away. They had eaten there many times and were constantly amazed at the number of customers that frequented the place. So they had burst through the door and emptied the register right before closing, disguising themselves with bandannas over their faces. Even so, Dominick's bandanna could not have fully hidden him; the owner could still recognize his immense bulk, his halting speech, and lumbering walk. Ralphie, much smaller and rather nondescript, might have never been identified. Dominick made his mistake, however, when he wandered back into the restaurant with today's lunch crowd, much too enamored with the cook's scungilli hot sauce to stay away any longer. The owner spotted him at once. "Thief," he screamed. "Thief," and came rushing at Dominick with a carving knife. Dominick, who had just been about to sit down, instead had to shoot his way out – but not before the knife plunged into his stomach. His greatest regret, as he stumbled towards Ralphie's room in a nearby tenement, was that he had killed the cook who made such wonderful food.

Hearing Dominick's pounding at the door, Ralphie pushed aside the woman on top of him to find his friend grinning with embarrassment, pressing his hand into his bloody stomach. "You idiot!" Ralphie cursed, and not even bothering to ask what Dominick had done, rushed him out of the apartment and down the street into the basement of Gino's building. It was there that Dominick was now waiting for Ralphie's return.

"What happened to you?" Gino asked.

"Someone cut me," Dominick said, "but you have to promise not to tell anyone. I'm already in a terrible mess, and if anyone finds out, I'll be in even more trouble."

"I won't tell," said Gino, backing toward the stairs. As he did, he suddenly bumped into a body behind him. Whirling around, he saw a man with a paper bag in one hand and a pistol in the other. His body was small and wiry, his eyes agleam even in the darkness. "Sorry kid," Ralphie said. "But you're not going anywhere." Ralphie did not share his partner's sentimentality about children.

"C'mon, Ralphie," Dominick said from the coal pile. "He won't say anything."

"Shut up, you big idiot. You got us into this and I'm the one who has to get us out." Dropping his brown paper bag to the floor, Ralphie leveled his pistol at Gino. Gino stood transfixed as Ralphie pulled the hammer back with his thumb, then suddenly lurched forward at the muffled sound of a gunshot exploding in Ralphie's right temple. While its force flung the man against the cinderblock wall – where he collapsed into a bloody slump on the floor – Gino was still standing as if paralyzed. The sight of Ralphie's head drooping into his chest with blood streaming thickly down his face and neck, made him suddenly ill. For a moment, he wondered if he might be sick, then if he would pass out. Then a chill spread throughout his whole body, lifting, it seemed, each hair on his head. After the first shock passed, the second was in realizing that if Dominick had not shot first, it would be Gino looking as Ralphie did.

"Ah I'm sorry kid," Dominick said quietly. "No kid should have to see a sight like that." It was then that Gino understood that not all murderers are alike. Dominick was one, but hadn't it been to save him? Gino only realized how tense he was when his body suddenly relaxed with relief and gratitude. He would have to help this man, he thought. The first thing would be to get him some proper packing for his stomach, then to get rid of Ralphie's body somehow.

Dominick, however, had managed to stop his bleeding for the moment. He had propped himself up against a wall, and his primary concern was something else. "Bring me that bag he dropped will you?" Dominick asked. "It's my lunch."

Gino felt the life rush quickly back into his body, as he almost ran for the bag and delivered it to Dominick.

"Don't feel bad about Ralphie," Dominick said, unwrapping a huge roast beef sandwich. "He was always yelling at me anyway."

IN THE NEXT few weeks Gino helped hide Dominick until he was safe. First they had to get rid of Ralphie. Because Dominick was weak – with Gino half-expecting his lunch to drop out of the hole in his stomach at any moment – Gino thought of finding a few friends to help. This, he soon realized, was in their situation impossible. Besides, Dominick insisted that he was fine and would rest fully once the task was over.

Then Gino remembered seeing an old piece of carpet out at the dump and, telling Dominick he would be back soon, ran out to see if it was still there. It was, though by the time Gino was half way through lugging it back to his building, he wished he had thought of another idea. Whenever he felt like giving up though, he just thought of the body, which gave him a little more energy. Finally he hid the rug in an alley by the Manzinos building, approaching from the back way so no one could see him. He then went home for dinner and to bed, seemingly as usual. It was 3.a.m. when he tiptoed out of the apartment, not having slept at all, to join Dominick. He had wanted to bring Bennie in on the secret to help, but Dominick told him absolutely not. One kid knowing his whereabouts was enough. No matter what Gino said, Dominick was adamant. So it was just Gino and Dominick who had to drag Ralphie's body out into the alley, then wrap it up in a rug and leave it there. Of course the rug and its contents were found three days later, but the police had heard of this trick before. They assumed someone had dropped it off in a car. No murderer would be stupid enough to toss his victim out right in his backyard.

Once the ordeal was over, Gino set out to make Dominick comfortable in his hideout. He found some foam from a car seat in the dump, which served as a mattress. From the bathroom cupboard he took an old sheet that Rosa had decided was too worn for regular use, but not quite ready for rags. They fashioned a card table from a crate and – with a candle, a stack of magazines and an assortment of bread, milk and cheese from Gino – Dominick was content to lay low for a while.

Many evenings, when Rosa thought Gino was out playing in the streets with his friends, he was actually down talking to Dominick. He would never be like Dominick, this much Gino already knew. He could not imagine himself ever getting into a situation where he would have to shoot his favorite cook and a friend. Still he found Dominick's stories fascinating. He, like Uncle Enzio, lived in a whole separate world from Gino's father, a world where one could make a lot of money – according to Dominick – if one just got in with the right people and learned the rules to their games. Days were early and opportunities many for the right men.

One night, for no real reason, Gino suddenly found himself asking what Dominick's father had been like. Gino could still not understand how his own father thought, what he was like and what he even felt sometimes. Rosa was easy to understand; she was always smiling and asking him questions. But Giovanni was so distant. He hardly ever spoke to Gino, and Gino, when he wanted to speak to his father, never knew what to say.

"Gino," Dominick said, leaning forward over the table where the two were playing cards. "You are Sicilian, and I am from Milan. Which means we are both different and similar."

"Yes," Gino smiled.

"I do not know what all people are like. But I do know my people. We are not easy! No one explains anything to the young. Especially not the parents. We are just to learn!"

"Yes," Gino smiled again.

"In the old country, you would see men who would rather beat their sons than explain anything to them. Does your father do that?"

"No," Gino said.

"But he is hard in other ways?"

Gino looked down and did not answer.

"When I was a boy I thought my father did not like me. I thought no man who likes his son beats him. But that was just the way he was taught. Then when he tried to give me advice, I would not speak to him. I grew big too soon, and too sure of myself. I said I don't need to listen to anyone — least of all an old man. I left home at thirteen. But you know — well, I have made mistakes.

"Fathers only want the best for their families. They do everything for their families. It doesn't always seem that way, but it is true. One day you will wake up and realize it is true."

Dominick leaned in. "The trick Gino is to listen, always to listen. To listen even when no word is being said. That is how you learn."

BY THE TIME Dominick was well, and the police chasing someone else, Gino was sad to see Dominick go. It was night, and when Gino came down to the cellar, Dominick had packed up his bed, turned his card table back into a crate, and stacked up his magazines against a wall. He had been wearing some old work clothes Gino had brought him, but now was back in his suit — with the work shirt replacing the silk one he had earlier bled through.

"My boy," he said, giving Gino a firm hug, "I hate to say goodbye. Here, you can visit me sometime. This is Belvedere's, a bar a friend of mine owns," he said, giving Gino a piece of paper with an address on it. You can always find me there, if you ever need anything."

Gino smiled and shook Dominick's hand. "I'll watch out for you," he said. "You watch for me too!"

So Dominick disappeared into the night, leaving almost as suddenly as he had arrived. Still, Gino would have reason to think of him again much sooner than he guessed — it wasn't long after he left that Gino decided to quit school. While Rosa would have preferred him to keep going, Gino knew his family needed his help. Besides, he thought, now that he knew math and English, he could learn everything else himself. Gino's teachers had given him his love of reading. But from visits to his friends he discovered that the homes of wealthier families invariably had stacks of books lying about and in shelves. Convinced that reading had something to do with success, Gino had begun borrowing constantly from the library, sitting at home with his feet propped up on the oven and reading for hours.

His determination to succeed became more and more fierce — the more so as he discovered that life held more than the struggles of the Harlem tenements. Determined to do whatever it might take to achieve his own fortune, Gino then decided starting work would set him on his right road. He could always read at night. Now it was time to earn more than the iceman's tips.

IN THE FALL, when school started again, Gino was combing the streets asking for work. Finding nothing in the neighborhood, he suddenly struck upon the idea of calling on Dominick. Who knows, perhaps there was a job for him amongst Dominick's many and varied friends. The bar address Dominick had given him was on 116th street, just below the Red Light District. Gino walked in one warm afternoon in early September to find a tall good-looking Italian man cleaning glasses behind the bar. "Excuse me," Gino said, "Have you heard of a Mr. Bazzano?"

"Who's asking?"

"My name is Gino Manzino. I am a friend." The man, who had unusual bright blue eyes, slowly wiped his glass.

"A friend, eh?," he said, "From where do you know Mr. Bazzano?"

Gino flushed, unsure of how to answer. "From 112th Street," he said finally.

Suddenly the man laughed and set down both his glass and dish towel. "Ah-ha," he said. "You are the boy Dominick told me about. The one Ralphie wasn't so fond of, yes?"

Gino smiled. "Why didn't you say so?" the man said. Then he called over his shoulder to the kitchen out back. "Hey Louis," he said, "We have a friend of Dominick's here."

Louis came out of the kitchen wiping his plump white hands on an apron around his stomach.

"This is Gino," the bartender said, "the one who kept Dominick company on 112th Street."

"Ah," Louis smiled. "A pleasure to meet you." He stepped forward and gave Gino a long handshake and broad smile. "Dominick has moved away for a while. To the country, for a change. But he told me all about you. How can I help you?"

Gino tried to hide his disappointment. "Do you know when Dominick will be back?"

"Not for a while," Louis smiled, lifting his heavy eyebrows at the bartender. "Did you have something to tell him?"

"No," Gino said, shaking his head. "I just – is Dominick all right?"

"He's fine. He'll be back soon enough."

"Dominick said for me to reach him here. I have just left school and am looking for a job."

"Well," Louis smiled. "You are in luck my boy. Paolo here has been complaining about the boy who helps him with his dishes. Apparently he is not so gentle with his hands," Louis laughed.

"You'd have to be good at washing, and help get our supplies from the warehouses. But from what I've heard you are an honest boy, with a good mind. And you are also quite resourceful," Louis laughed, and Gino looked down, smiling a little but not sure whether or not he should.

"When can you start?"

"Today," Gino said.

"Tomorrow," Louis said. "You come at eight. Paolo will tell you what to do."

So Gino began work for Belvedere's, cleaning the floors, washing the glasses, riding with Paolo to pick up liquor at the warehouses. He liked the atmosphere in the bar in the afternoons, when customers were few and he and Paolo could talk together while washing up. He liked riding through the busy streets in the wagon, picking up the boxes of liquor, then stacking the bottles in the gleaming bar with its long strip of mirror behind it. Although he never worked at night, he enjoyed feeling as if he were inside a slightly dangerous world, one where laborers sat and smoked, or men in fancy suits ordered rare liqueurs in the late afternoon, talking in quiet voices around the bar's few small tables.

When Gino had first told Giovanni of his job, Giovanni had been pleased about the work, but not about the bar. His contempt for the likes of Enzio extended to the whole underground world, in which bars played an important role. Gino, however, convinced him that really he was not working in the bar when it was open, but helping with cleaning and preparation and supplies.

Still one day Gino had another rude awakening. It was early in the afternoon and he and Paolo were both working behind the bar. Louis was out in the kitchen preparing for the evening meals. That day, however, two slick-looking men in suits and hats came in at three in the afternoon and demanded a meal. Paolo nodded – as if he knew the men, Gino thought – then walked out back to Louis. Gino noticed a certain gravity in him, and stared at the men and their bright gold watches as they sat a table in one corner. Soon Louis came out with two elaborate meals such as Gino had never seen him serve. There were pasta dishes, and meat, and salads and an extra bottle of wine – a special wine, Gino knew, as he recognized it from the cellar.

The two men hardly seemed to notice Louis, but only grunted a little when their food was set down. For the next fifteen minutes, while they ate, everything in the bar was silent but for their occasional murmurs, the click of forks on plates, and the squeak of cloth on brass as Gino polished the rail behind the bar. Then, as Louis was making coffee for them, a quick sharp shot rang out and seemed to echo around the room. Stiffening, Gino looked up to see a man walking, hat on, out the door. Behind him, arched backwards in his chair, was an all too familiar sight: a dead man with a hole in the head and blood flowing fast.

Paolo leapt over the bar before Gino could say a word. "They got Stefano," he called out. Louis had arrived from the kitchen and stood shaking his head as if at another spilt dinner. "Why must they come here for their wars?" he finally said. Then spying Gino, he told him, "You've seen enough, boy. We'll see you tomorrow."

Gino tried to protest, shaking his head while unable to take his eyes from the bloody man before him. But Louis insisted, and soon Gino was walking home – feeling a little less sick, he noticed, than the time Ralphie was shot, but still suffering from a knot in his stomach. This was the second murder he had witnessed and he was not about to tell Rosa and Giovanni about it.

Fortunately, he didn't have to be reminded of it too much, as the next morning all was quiet again and back to normal. When Gino asked Paolo about the man, Paolo said, "Don't think of it again. It's over." This was the way, Gino thought, that Dominick had been about Ralphie. For a while he feared such violence would be a regular occurrence. Fortunately, however, the whole next year went by with nothing more bloody than fistfights.

CHAPTER
TEN

IT SEEMED NO time before a year had passed, and Bennie had scraped through yet another dismal class at school, with only Bruno now matching him for poor performance. It was only natural that Bennie would soon follow Gino into working life. As Bennie searched for a job, however, it looked like Gino had found one of the better ones. Never known for his diplomacy, Bennie had no luck with the local merchants while the factories and warehouses weren't hiring. Finally, Bennie was taken on by a fish market. It was such a messy smelly place that jobs came open more frequently than elsewhere. So Bennie, alongside several other neighborhood boys, started working life washing and scaling fish. Surprisingly to everyone, however, he actually liked his work, and was less lazy when not required to think all the time. Bennie's fury as a child had always concerned Rosa. But he had never developed into a bully. His was the sort of rebellion fueled by frustration – notably at not being able to perform. Once he was working, some anger at his own inadequacy seemed to be eased in him.

It was an odd twist that as Bennie seemed to right himself, Bruno became more and more obviously the black sheep of the family. Simple like Bennie, he was far more dangerous, as his anger was laced with cruelty. It was Tessie, at first his greatest champion, who felt this effect the most. As Bruno's older sister, she had at first treated Bruno much like her own doll or baby, taking him everywhere, watching over him in the house, even bathing him for Rosa. Before he could even speak, however, Bruno revealed a personality kink not seen in his other siblings. Beyond needing constant attention, Bruno went to curious lengths to get it. Besides his penchant for making loud noises, he seemed to enjoy terrifying others – most notably by leaning out the window until Tessie or Rosa saw him and screamed, or swinging on the banister in the hallway. Tessie and Rosa both found their affections drained, and by the time Tessie went off to school she was relieved to get away from him. Whether what Bruno did then was meant as a joke, or as punishment for her going away, Tessie would never know. But she never seemed to recover from what six—year—old Bruno did to her doll.

Coming home late one afternoon, Tess walked into her room to find Bianca's doll pulled apart into five pieces. The legs were in the pair of shoes at the end of her bed. The arms were sticking out from under the windowsill. The body was half hidden under the blanket, and the head was placed squarely on Tess' pillow. Tessie's sobs could be heard all night, despite Rosa's promise that they would find someone to sew the doll back together. Though Giovanni, in the tradition of his ancestors, gave Bruno the first beating of his life, what disturbed Rosa most was the way Bruno still smirked at his sister with his face swollen from tears. Even Gino and Bennie, who at first thought the incident slightly amusing, were shocked that Bruno was really happy at Tessie's distress. Rosa had an expert seamstress repair the doll and peace was reestablished in the house, but never again would Tessie trust her brother as she had.

Initially, Tessie had insisted on going to the local school with her brothers. Though a good student, she was easily distracted, which Giovanni blamed on the presence of too many boys. Once Gino and Bennie had left, she was more easily convinced to transfer to a girls' Catholic school, St. Cecilia's. Herself a feisty child, Tessie's willfulness never caused real harm to others though. Her spirit gave rise more to exuberance than to trouble. At first Giovanni worried that she might go astray, but it was stimulation that Tess sought. At St. Cecilia's she was fascinated by her new world. She loved the beauty of the masses, the flowing robes of the priests, the candles and hymns and banners hanging from the rafters. She started reading the lives of the saints, and even dreamed of becoming one herself – something which Gino soon teased her about unmercifully.

Church attendance in Harlem was unusually high and children were raised with strict moral codes. They were especially taught the importance of *rispetto* – the code of respect, especially for one's parents and the family. If family rules or moral codes were broken, the offender might be cast out of the family, the worst exile possible. Tess liked to remind everyone she knew of such rules, especially Gino.

She also loved the neighborhood church: Our Lady of Mt. Carmel on 115th Street. The largest in Harlem, the church was built in 1884, largely with funds from the German and Irish communities. Until 1919, Italians, relative latecomers to the neighborhood, were relegated to worshiping in the basement.

Children, however, had a little more freedom and Tess loved to venture up into the atrium to see the church's jewel-laden Madonna statue. In July, she rounded up a group of her school friends to attend the festival for it. Thousands of pilgrims, many of them barefoot, came to the neighborhood for a parade of the statue through the streets. All followed in the Madonna's wake, carrying money or candles to honor her. The candles weighed as much as twenty pounds each and were shaped like hearts, arms or legs, depending upon the particular grace sought from the Madonna.

When the boys dared to make fun of Tess' new devotion, Tess promised to say a prayer for them. While Rosa thought her devotion a little too strong, Giovanni was happily impressed by the new Tessie. Reading of the saints, he said, could certainly harm no one. And in most people's cases it could help a lot.

EVEN THOUGH GINO was working, he still found time to play stickball with the neighborhood boys – or simply to hang out and get into mischief. Most of their games were innocent but occasionally they turned violent. Trapped on crowded and impoverished streets with an excess of energy and little imagination, the boys grew restless, then disruptive. They harassed storekeepers, fought among themselves, and generally made a great deal of noise. Gino seldom sought to play any part in their schemes. He preferred going his own way, and was unusually happy for a loner. Occasionally though, he got caught in the middle – and when he did, he proved capable of handling any dispute. Quick, strong and fearless, he also had another distinct advantage over his opponents – he was usually smarter.

One afternoon, however, not long after his tenth birthday, Gino came home in tatters. His shirt and pants were torn and filthy; his face was swollen, with a gash under one eye. Though he tried to sneak into his bedroom without being seen, Rosa was too quick for him. "Gino," she said, pulling him back by the shoulder, "what happened to you?"

Whenever Gino fought, Rosa became distraught. When Giovanni found out, he unleashed a fury that created more pain than the bruises. So Gino looked at her, his eyes wide. "I was running in the street," he said, quickly saying what he had rehearsed on the stairs. "I was going so fast my foot slipped on the curb and I fell in the gutter." Rosa shook her head, feeling slightly ill at the sight of his bruised face. "It must have hurt terribly."

Gino shrugged, though Rosa noticed a tremor in his lower lip. "It's okay," he said.

"Come here," Rosa told him, and led him to the kitchen table. "Sit down so we can clean you up."

As Rosa filled a bowl with warm water, Gino silently thanked God that his mother believed him. He thanked Him again when he was able to fill in his story with more details before Giovanni came home – as he had little faith in his ability to lie before his father. Rosa took his torn clothes and washed his wounds. So relieved that nothing was permanently damaged, she never even noticed that his injuries weren't quite consistent with a fall into the street. But by the time Giovanni walked through the door, Gino had been restored to such respectability that even to him his story sounded reasonable.

It was just a few hours later when Mrs. Salvio, a neighbor from the other end of 112th Street, stopped by after supper. All the children had gone to bed, including Gino, and a late night visit usually meant Mrs. Salvio was harboring some item of gossip. Tonight proved no exception. As soon as Rosa had set down coffee on the kitchen table, Mrs. Salvio began to speak. "What do you think of that Carmine DeVito?" she asked, then promptly answered her own question. "He is a scourge on our streets – that's what everyone says, and I think they are right. Any time you see him he has a horrible scowl on his face. He's always fighting with the storekeepers, trying to get a special price or just losing his temper for no reason. And his children are no better. I don't know what Mrs. DeVito does all day, but her children are running wild. I keep my little boy right away from all of them."

Neither Rosa nor Giovanni knew why she was so worked up. Only Gino, listening in the next room, knew exactly where her story was leading. He was so frightened he instinctively pulled the blankets over his head.

"Rosa," Mrs. Salvio said, after taking a breath, "you haven't told me – how is Gino's beautiful little face? I just can't imagine how a grown man could interfere in a fight between two small boys. If I hadn't seen it for myself, I never would have believed even a bully like Carmine DeVito would punch and kick a little boy like that. Why, even his own wife said . . ."

At this point she bit off the end of her story because Rosa cried out and dropped her coffee cup to the tabletop with a crash. Giovanni rose from his chair, laid his huge hands on the table and leaned in.

"Are you saying," he said in a deep, slow voice, "that Carmine DeVito hit my son?"

Mrs. Salvio looked from Giovanni to Rosa in confusion. Not only had Giovanni never spoken to her directly before – keeping himself to occasional greetings or mutters – but it had never occurred to her that the Manzinos didn't know what had happened.

"Yes, of course," she answered uncertainly, "we all saw it happen. He hit him several times."

Although Giovanni remained calm, Rosa knew at once that her husband was seething. As he moved past Mrs. Salvio toward the door, Rosa threw herself at him, grabbing his arms, his suspenders – anything to keep him in the apartment. Suddenly all the children were awake, crying at the sound of their mother's pleading. Mrs. Salvio sat in shock at the pandemonium she had unleashed. Only Gino, coming quickly to the kitchen doorway, understood the implications. When it came to neighborhood disturbances, he had learned one rule: if there was any dispute, the boys were wrong. Yet there was something in his father's tone of voice that made this time seem different. Carmine DeVito had stepped irrevocably into family territory – he'd been arrogant enough to hit another man's child and stupid enough to choose Giovanni's.

Shaking off Rosa, Giovanni left the room, strode down the stairs, and moved swiftly across the street to the DeVitos, a fifth floor apartment in the rear of the building. As he took the stairs two or three steps at a time, Rosa sank to the floor where Bruno and Tessie were crying. Both Bennie and Mrs. Salvio looked on helplessly while Gino hesitated for a moment, then ran out, naked but for the trousers he quickly pulled on.

By the time Gino reached the fifth floor, a terrible pounding was filling the hallway and doors were opening on every floor. Having found the DeVitos door locked, Giovanni was slamming at it with his fists. He then kicked it open, as the family within shouted at what they believed to be a madman. Just as Gino came to the top of the stairs, moving as quietly as possible so his father's fury would not turn back on him, Giovanni came face to face with Carmine DeVito. A large man with hanging jowls and an almost completely bald head, he had no idea how to respond. With his wife and children gathered behind him, he stared in bafflement at the stranger who had broken down his door.

Coming up behind his father, Gino ducked back against the stair railing as his father hurled his fist into Carmine's face. Carmine was lifted inches from the floor, flowing backwards in what seemed like slow motion, landing face up on the polished wood floor. Luckily for him he was immediately unconscious, shielded from the coming pain of several broken bones in his lower jaw.

As Mrs. DeVito came rushing to her husband's side, Giovanni nodded to her, then turned swiftly on his heel. It was then that he saw Gino, pressed against the railing with his hands gripped fast to it. "Come over here," Giovanni said, pulling him by one wrist and then placing his hands on Gino's shoulders and leading him down the stairs. Doors were still open on each floor, and seeing curious eyes behind them, Gino wished a wind would come to slam the doors on each one of them. Neither he nor Giovanni said a word until they reached the street. Then Giovanni stopped and held Gino at arms length.

"Don't you ever keep a secret like this from me," he said, still shaking with suppressed anger. "No man hits a son of mine."

"Yes, Pappa," Gino said.

Giovanni gripped his shoulders tighter. "And no son of mine creeps around hiding his wounds either. I won't have it."

"I'm sorry."

"Don't be sorry. You can always come to me when there is trouble. Do you know that?"

"Yes," Gino said.

"Let's go home."

When they reached their apartment, Giovanni went to comfort Rosa and the children – while Gino went immediately to bed and Bennie quickly followed him. Gino was too upset to answer many of Bennie's questions, but told Bennie to go to sleep, that he'd tell him everything in the morning. As Tessie and Bruno were put to bed, too, Gino felt his mother's hand on his forehead and a gentle kiss there. Still, Gino lay in the dark, not sure why he felt so wretched. He should be grateful: his father had acted so heroically; by morning, all the neighborhood would know he had broken DeVito's jaw in Gino's honor. The Manzinos would be looked upon with new respect. Still, Gino felt ill at ease.

He replayed the moment over and over – crouched by the

railing as his father gave vent to his rage. Gino had always sensed his father's power, but he had never seen it expressed in full force. Carmine DeVito's actions had been unforgivable because he had hurt a member of the Giovanni's family. The offense was to Giovanni, not to Gino, an issue of honor between two heads of families in which Gino's role had been secondary.

Giovanni believed his father meant Gino could come to him at any time. But the truth was Gino wouldn't want to – especially if he were in real trouble. Giovanni's rage could be re-directed at him too, no matter who said otherwise. Then too, Giovanni hadn't even asked Gino what had happened with Mr. DeVito – or looked to see how much Gino had been hurt. Gino remembered what Dominick had told him about listening to his father. But still Gino couldn't escape the fact that it was easier to keep his distance from his own. He could never be sure what to expect. And then Giovanni was so worried and troubled all the time; no one wanted to upset him. At the end of it all, Gino realized that more than ever his goal was to fight his battles alone.

CHAPTER
ELEVEN

IN JUST A few weeks, the DeVito family picked up and moved –
never to return to the old neighborhood again. At the same
time, Gino's independence was causing some resentment in the
other boys. Insulted that Gino didn't seem to need their company,
they also envied his good looks. He was much too "pretty" for the
street, and too neatly dressed. With Rosa's dark hair and eyes, his
ancestry linked him to Sicily's Greek heritage and made him seem
better than everybody else. They interpreted his delicate appearance and gentle charm as displays of arrogance. The neighborhood
women, however, weren't so critical. Watching from the windows
and stoops, they remarked upon his ease and grace. Besides beauty,
Gino had some quality in his eyes and manner that suggested a
deep sensuality, and the women smiled at each other as daughters
and nieces and shop girls all fell in love with him.

Like many girls in the inner city, Anita Columbo had the kind
of experience with sex that would have been all but impossible in
an Italian village. At seventeen, she had already won the interest of
many young men, but lately she had found herself increasingly
attracted to twelve-year-old Gino. Working in her father's bakery
on 113th Street, she sometimes saw Gino passing by, and occasionally he came in to pick up some bread or a pastry. His body
was already strong and slim, and when she handed him his change,

Anita thought she detected a special warmth to his skin. She knew Gino liked her, always returning her smiles with a shy one of his own. It thrilled her to think of being his first lover and she soon began devising a way to bring it about. The enormity of what she intended to do caused her to hesitate, so she waited as long as she could. Then, one warm evening in April when she could no longer bear the supple feeling in her body, she decided it was time.

Watching as Gino left the bakery, Anita set down her apron and told her younger sister Angela that she'd be right back. She then ducked out after Gino and, rounding the corner, saw him enter his building. "Gino," she called in a strong whisper, stopping in the vestibule as he froze for a moment three steps up the unlit stairway. "Come to me, Gino." Something in the intensity of her voice made Gino turn and move instinctively to her and as he reached the bottom of the stairs she led him quickly into the dark hideaway there. The space was larger than he expected, and darker; Gino felt a rush of blood and knew he was blushing deeply. The busy street he'd just left seemed a thousand miles away. He couldn't see her, but she found him with her hands, and he heard her breath deepen when she touched him.

She was incredibly gentle, her fingers brushing lightly over his face, neck, arms. Though she never spoke a word, Gino was guided by her touch and the excitement rising within him. Taking his hands, Anita drew them to her, and filled them with her breasts. All at once, she was naked and he was overwhelmed. She kissed his eyes, his throat, his lips, then undid the rope that served as his belt and moved her hands to the front of his body before the loose trousers could touch the floor. Her breathing changed once more when she found the hardness there and, while he held her tight to fight his dizziness, she lowered herself to the blanket she had earlier laid out in the darkened alcove. In one motion, she drew Gino down, and soon he was gently inside her.

From start to finish, it couldn't have lasted more than eight minutes. Then, Anita dressed both Gino and herself, and sent him upstairs to supper while she hurried out of the building, smiling back at him as she went. Gino was amazed that so little time had passed. His life would never be the same, he thought, now moving in a time of its own, marked by his and Anita's altered breathing. As supper slowed to a crawl, Anita's world rushed on inside him. And yet, however radical the experience, no matter how jangled his body felt, he was still a young boy a few minutes late for supper, facing his ziti and broccoli.

As always, the supper table was a little chaotic. Bennie was teasing little Bruno with a piece of pasta, Tessie was chattering to no one in particular, and above the hum of them all Giovanni and Rosa were trying to have a conversation about the day's events. At first, Rosa had tried to impose a rule of silence at supper, an approximation of the kind of decorum that had surrounded her own childhood dinners in Sicily and a form of respect for Giovanni after his long day at work. Like so many traditions, however, it had soon broken down when confronted with the realities of family life. The children's spontaneous energy was irresistible, and Giovanni hadn't the heart to squash their innocent outbursts. Though at times he was too weary to do more than eat in silence, at other times he smiled at both their laughter and their squabbling. Soon Rosa understood that this, not some pointless exercise in formality, was what he needed at the end of a wearying day.

Tessie in particular seemed to view all silences as personal invitations to fill the air with conversation, no matter how senseless. As Gino slipped into his chair, Tessie piped up, "Gino, where were you? I kept calling and calling down the stairwell. I was about to come down and find you." Fighting back the flush that was once again crawling up his neck, Gino started stuffing his mouth with ziti. But Tess was not so easily discouraged. "Didn't you miss me?" she asked, giving him what she considered to be her most dazzling smile.

Knowing his part in her ritual, Gino managed to smile back and say, "Every moment, Tess." Always fair-minded in her flirtatiousness, Tessie tended to dispense her affections equally among her three brothers — though Bruno had yet to regain the stature he knew before shredding Bianca's doll. Tonight, however, Tessie was focused on Gino. Everyone knew that her father was her greatest love and always the intended audience – though Rosa said Tessie's backtalk was practice for future boyfriends. Whatever it was, Gino was greatly relieved when his response seemed to satisfy her and she went back to her own dinner. No one else seemed to be taking any special notice of him, although Gino kept stealing glances at his mother just to be sure. His head was buzzing, and the lower part of his body was still tingling. It was as if the nerve endings were remembering the sensations Anita had aroused, while his mind was trying to banish the memory – at least for now. Gino was sure that if he let Anita's image of her take hold of his imagination, everyone at the table would know exactly what had happened. But his body mocked the attempt, and the effort of keeping his visions at bay made it impossible to follow any of the conversation. Then, just as he was beginning to relax, Bennie turned to him and said, "Gino, you smell funny." Gino instantly punched Bennie in the upper arm, perhaps a little harder than usual, which started Bennie punching back.

"Stop that," Giovanni voice commanded. It took Gino a few anxious seconds to realize he was safe, and that nothing in the exchange seemed out of the ordinary. Even Rosa, who was usually more sensitive to Gino's moods than he was himself, paid no particular attention to him that night.

Later, as Gino lay in bed, the tension in the air when his parents looked at one another began to make sense. And the time he had seen his father caressing his mother in the dark – no wonder he been overwhelmed. There was a pattern to it all, to the longing he saw in the eyes of the women who watched him on the street, to the secret meetings of the older boys and girls as they rushed to alleyways and rooftops and cellars, to the flash of anger in his Mamma's eyes whenever her friend, Maria Mancuso, grabbed Gino in the hallway and pressed his face a little too insistently into her ample breasts. As Gino drifted off to sleep, he felt immensely grateful for discovering all he had missed.

Something must have haunted Anita, too, for it wasn't long before she sought out Gino again. He had been in a constant fever, reliving the moments over and over, wondering if the bliss he had felt would be a miracle that occurred only once in his life. He was too nervous to go into Anita's store, afraid her father would come at him with a stick or that Anita might slight him. But soon Anita ducked out of the bakery once more, stopping him on the corner of the street and whispering quickly "meet me after supper – in the lot." She said nothing else and, for his part, all Gino could do was nod.

For the rest of that afternoon, his nerves were in a jangle. The world was full of hidden pleasures and, apparently, this was the way to reach them. Supper was once again an ordeal; he hardly ate, almost convincing Rosa that he was sick and shouldn't be allowed to go back outside. But finally he was free and found his way into the wooded lot at the end of the block. Entering the grove of trees just as the sky was beginning to darken, he found Anita in a clearing, lying on one hip in a black cotton dress, a worn blanket spread out beneath her. Completely silent this time, she undressed him immediately, her breath returning to the rhythm that he had remembered so well. Then she slipped off her dress, shook out her hair and smiled. The dress was all she had been wearing, and Gino was awed at her nakedness in the falling twilight.

It was then that he discovered, as he was guided again inside her, that the thrill he had known could be rekindled again and again. A new contentment flowed through him, and he moved with Anita in response to her body so she moaned wonderfully, pressing down with her hands on his lower body to bring him in even deeper. Never had he felt so strong. Afterward, she hustled into her dress and was out of the clearing before he even had time to put on his clothes. He wondered briefly why they never spoke, except for the indistinct words she would murmur at the end. But he was much too happy and sleepy to worry about it and made his way home at a slower pace than usual, smiling all the way.

Though Gino usually shared everything important with Bennie, Anita had left him suddenly speechless. Lying in the bed beside his brother, just across from the sleeping Tess and Bruno, Gino wanted to talk to Bennie, but knew he should say silent – at least for now. It wasn't that he couldn't trust Bennie, but that his experience would somehow be lessened by talking about it so soon – or might, even to Bennie, seem like bragging. Most importantly, however, Gino realized how important secrecy would be to Anita.

For the neighborhood girls, reputation was everything. As with Tess, the girls were raised to follow strict moral codes, both by their parents and by church. Although their parents might have come from countries in which all the young people traveled on bikes, here both bicycle riding and roller-skating were prohibited as not ladylike. When girls worked outside the home, they were also expected to learn how to sew, clean house and cook.

If a girl was seen even talking to a boy, it was assumed that something was going on. Between him and Anita, Gino realized, something certainly was. But if they were caught it would be Anita who suffered most. Gino had heard of girls who had ruined their reputations even by dating more than one man – and had then been forced to move to New Jersey, or anywhere else that her family had relatives to take her in. Gino was amazed that Anita was obviously not too worried about any of this. He also wondered if he should stop it from happening again. But how could he, he thought, as he drifted off to sleep. It felt so wonderful . . . . and then, hadn't she come to him?

As it turned out Gino did not have to worry about Anita. They had been together twice and the next time would be the last. It was then a hot July day and Tessie's favorite parade, Our Lady of Mt. Carmel, was underway. Every family in the neighborhood was in attendance, so it was easy for Anita and Gino to steal away once the music and wine and heat had blurred everyone's senses. As the immense giglio made its way through the streets on the shoulders of men, including Giovanni and Anita's father, Anita and Gino slipped into bed on sheets that smelled of her. She helped him undress and told him to lie on his back. With her clothes still on, she moved up and down his body with her kisses, eventually taking his rising penis into her mouth. At the touch of her tongue, Gino could only think how beautiful the world seemed. Then Anita slipped out of her dress, but Gino gently resisted when she started drawing down on him again. Instead, he began to explore her as she had explored him. Confused at first, Anita gave a soft laugh of surprise when she realized what he was doing, and then surrendered to his slow and gentle caresses. When he finally entered her with his tongue, she responded with a frenzy so extreme that he was momentarily frightened.

"Oh, Gino," she cried, in a voice touched with panic, "don't stop, please God, don't stop." Her fingers dug into the back of his head, and she shuddered beneath him as she squeezed him between the soft flesh of her inner thighs. Afterward, Anita was unexpectedly reluctant to let him go. She stayed still, holding him close and actually talking in a low, sad voice. She told him of her family, her friends, and her plans to one day find a job in another section of the city where all the women wore pretty clothes to work every morning. Then she told him she would never be with him again.

Gino was sure her decision was because of her reputation. He therefore offered no resistance. However desirable Gino was becoming to women, he was too young to launch a full-scale pursuit of lovemaking. And so, soon after he lost Anita, his normal sunniness gave way to a mood that had Rosa terribly worried. Even the herbal tonics she brewed for him had no effect, and he refused to speak to the priest. Gino respected Anita enough to make their parting as easy as possible. But though he stayed away from her store, their occasional crossings on the street filled him with longing. The rush of her skirts brought her sweetness back to him and he had to look away.

Then one afternoon, Tia Gallina, a scruffy little six-year-old girl who lived in the next building, approached Gino as he was playing alone in a vacant lot beyond the row of tenements. He was throwing a hard rubber ball against the side of the building, keeping track of the points he scored according to his own elaborate system: ten points each time the ball struck one of the darker bricks above the second floor, five points when it bounced off one of the metal pipes that emerged here and there, and two points lost if he allowed the ball to touch the ground before catching it.

He was having an exceptional run, scoring 38 points in an hour, when Tia called, "Gino! My sister Ursula wants to see you. She says you should come upstairs right away." She then gave a strange giggle, turned, and ran away. Gino was mystified. Ursula Gallina was one of the older girls, one of Anita's crowd, who had never spoken to him that he could remember. After a few minutes of wondering if Tia was trying to involve him in some prank devised by the younger children, he started for the Gallina apartment.

He knocked on the door a few moments later and Ursula ushered him in. Mrs. Gallina worked every day at the glassworks factory downtown, so there was no one else there. Mr. Gallina had left so long ago, even before Tia was born, that even the neighborhood gossips could no longer agree on what he had looked like, much less why he left.

Gino was standing in one of the apartment's two rooms. The stove and icebox on one side identified it as a kitchen; the soiled sofa and floor lamp comprised a "parlor" on the opposite wall. Ursula, wearing a navy blue robe, was standing in the doorway to her bedroom.

"Gino, come here to me."

He obeyed out of reflex, having no idea what she wanted. In another moment, she had taken his arm, led him into the musty room, and closed the door. She then removed the robe. Standing naked before him, she said, "Well, Gino? Aren't I as pretty as Anita?"

Gino was formulating an answer before he could even let himself acknowledge the question. No doubt she was considered far prettier than Anita – her hair was thicker, darker, her body fuller, and she had a way of using her eyes when she spoke to men that always seemed to excite them. In fact, the old women whispered "Butone" whenever she walked by. In comparison, Anita was somewhat thin and a little pale. But that had never mattered to Gino. He had already learned that there was a great deal more to people than their appearance.

"Let me help you with your clothes, Gino," Ursula said, beginning to unbutton his shirt. In response to some impulse still unclear to him, he pushed her hands away. He was sure that Anita had never told Ursula anything about him. But in a block as crowded as this, gossip could flash like heat lightning, however small the spark that started it, and they must have risked being together too often, he thought. Gino instantly resented Ursula's attempt to intrude on their secret, as well as the self-possessed way she seemed to dismiss Anita's importance. He wasn't going to be used by her.

Puzzled, then annoyed when he backed off, Ursula grabbed him by the shoulders and said in a hard-edged voice, "You're not leaving here, Gino. No man on this street would say no to me, and I will not let a little boy . . . ."

Her voice, rising in anger, broke off sharply when Gino punched her in the soft center of her stomach. Her breath fled from her body and she sank to the faded rug on the floor as Gino turned and ran from the room. By the time he reached the street, he was proud of his determination not to bend to someone else's will. Quietly, he re-engaged his war against the wall, occasionally glancing back toward Ursula's apartment, as if the blow he'd struck against a girl would bring some sort of retribution, but nothing came.

Soon Gino was going through the same sexual initiations as his friends, giving no outward sign of having ventured somewhat further on his own. Occasionally, he and some adventurous girl would undress and stare longingly at each other's bodies, but they never surrendered to their feelings. Usually, the only girls he spent any time with were close to him in age, allowing him to touch them beneath their clothes for long stolen minutes during neighborhood parties. On one such night, he and two pretty girls left a party and sprinted two blocks to sneak into a machine shop through a broken door on the roof. In the manager's office they then spent a wonderful hour sitting naked on a small rug. The girls loved watching Gino's body respond to their caresses; in turn, they allowed him to feel any part of them, using only his hands.

CHAPTER
TWELVE

B ESIDES DISCOVERING THE opposite sex, Gino began to enjoy his work more as he grew older. Paolo and Louis gave him more responsibility, and Paolo had begun teaching him how to mix drinks. Gino was not really allowed to serve as he was underage but sometimes Gino helped out Paolo behind the bar, which Giovanni wouldn't have liked at all but which no one else seemed to object to.

Gino began to learn about the underworld that he had so far only glimpsed. He knew full well of his father's contempt for the Cosa Nostra: of how he and Rosa had fled Sicily to escape it, and of their mutual dislike for Enzio. Then too, no one grew up in East Harlem without discovering its dark threads running like tendrils through the crowded streets. For the most part though, stories in the neighborhood were told in hushed voices, with rumors and accusations passing from person to person. In Belvedere's, talk was less guarded. Gino became aware of a vast network of operations and businesses beyond the small one in which he himself had always lived.

Like Giovanni before him, Gino came to see the signs of the Black Hand in his daily life. When certain men came into the bar, Gino noticed that others were particularly respectful in their presence. From their talk, he discovered that the killing Gino had seen was only one of many on these streets. Only now did Gino fully grasp the story behind Matteo Ruffino and the terrible death of his wife. Gino also realized that merchants and shopkeepers were expected to pay protection – and Louis was not exempt. Every so often Gino noticed a heavy set man in a dark suit walk into the bar, take off his hat and nod simply at Paolo. Paolo would nod in return, then disappear out back to fetch Louis. Over time, Gino realized that Louis was paying the man, and that if he didn't, retaliation would ensue.

Gino also came to understand that no one ever admitted knowing anything – and that everyone, including his bosses, knew enough to keep quiet. Just as when you were a child and had to fight someone to establish your right to respect, so the adult world was ruled by the same mixture of respect and fear. These were the same rules Gino knew from his family, brought home to him most strongly from seeing his father fight Mr. DeVito.

By instinct, Gino kept his discoveries to himself. Fearing how Rosa and Giovanni would react to such stories, he downplayed his contact with men his father would despise. Though he told himself that this was to preserve the peace, somewhere inside Gino secretly knew that the underworld excited him. It was the challenge he had always looked for – and even if it was dangerous, it was worth it if he could escape such a crushing life as his father's. Gino had watched as Giovanni became more exhausted and joyless as the years went on. Though he and Rosa might consider their lives enough, Gino began to look upon each day at Belvedere's as training for his future. The secrets he kept from his parents only revealed his development.

Sometimes after work, Gino headed back to the neighborhood for a game of street soccer or stickball with Bennie and his friends. On one such day, Gino was in the midst of a particularly heated and hazardous soccer game. As usual, the playing field was cement and the runners had to weave their ball through hurtling trucks, cars, and wagons. Gino played well: what he lacked in bulk, he made up for in speed and daring. But on this day, as he dashed with the ball up the sidewalk, outflanking the players in the street, one of the smaller boys delivered a low body block from behind a parked car. Gino's forward motion deflected sharply to the left, sending Gino into a collision with a bunch of trash cans by the staircase to a cellar apartment. He was moving so fast and hit the cans with such force that he toppled over them and down the stairwell. Halfway down, as his body tumbled, his left leg slammed down on one of the iron spikes that formed the railing for the stairs. The spike penetrated three full inches into the soft flesh under the knee, stopping Gino's fall with a jolt as the spike locked into him. Aware of the blinding pain for only an instant, he then fell unconscious. He didn't even have time to scream.

Fast after Gino were the rest of the players, crowding down the staircase to see if he was all right. "Let me through!" Bennie yelled, frightened by the dizzying speed at which Gino had fallen. The boys moved aside and Bennie leaned down over his unconscious brother. Seeing his pinned leg, Bennie felt a shudder go through him. "Get some help!" he called up immediately.

A group of men passing on the street were hurried down the stairs. So was Pauletta Benina's mother, who lived below the Manzinos and had been passing by with her shopping. Two men held Gino's body while a third worked the leg upward from the wrought iron. Bennie had moved everyone else back to the top of the stairs, and looked on with horror. The only consolation was that Gino was not able to feel the pain. The spike was considerably wider an inch below the point, so the hole in Gino's leg was enormous. To stop the terrible flow of blood, Mrs. Benina tied the wound with a shirt one of the men had given her, but it was soaked through almost at once.

"Quick," she said. "Take him to the hospital. Bennie, you go with them. I'll fetch Mrs. Manzino." The men nodded, quickly carrying off Gino's limp body. Not wanting to alarm Rosa, Mrs. Benina tried first to settle her own nerves, then, greeting Rosa calmly at her door, told her only that Gino had fallen playing ball, and had been taken to the clinic. By that time, however, the doctors in the emergency ward were desperately trying to stitch up the wound and replace all the blood Gino had lost. Gino was still unconscious.

Rosa arrived at the hospital with Tessie and eight-year old Bruno. Finding no one at the admitting desk and a crowd of weary and wounded people in the waiting room, Rosa walked promptly through the door to the office. "My son," she said to the first nurse she saw. "Gino Manzino, he has been wounded. Can you tell me where he is?"

Though at first annoyed at the intrusion of three people into her inner sanctum, the young red-haired nurse recognized the dark good looks of the boy who had been brought in unconscious.

"Your son has the hurt leg?" she asked.

"Yes," Tessie jumped in.

"He is with the doctor. You must wait."

Usually Rosa submitted to the customs of her new world – or lived her life so they did not affect her – but in this case she could not entertain the idea of waiting apart from her son.

"Please," she said. "I must see him."

From past experience, the nurse knew how obstinate her clients could be, so looked at them for a minute and then held up her hand. "One minute," she said.

Disappearing through a large metal swinging door for a moment, she then came back and said, "Your son has been moved. He is still critical, and under observation. The doctor will be out to speak to you."

After what seemed an interminable time, an overworked looking man of about fifty came out in a white coat. "You are the doctor?" Rosa said, moving quickly towards him.

"Yes. Dr Matthew Murphy."

"You have seen my son, Gino Manzino?"

"You are his mother?"

"I am. How is he please?"

The doctor motioned to a door off the admitting room, a small office where they could speak in private. Rosa held Bruno's hand while Tess stayed close on her other side. Though there were chairs, everyone remained standing.

"Your son has had a nasty accident. He fell onto a spike that unfortunately was very thick and went very deep. We have sewn up the hole, but if it becomes infected, it could be serious. Don't worry," the doctor said, not wanting to upset them too much. "It could be fine. We just need to watch him closely for the next few days. With good luck, and the strength of youth, he should recover completely."

Rosa was sickened by the thought of such a hideous accident. No nastier weapon could be found in innocent play, she thought. Even picturing the spike in his leg made her tremble. Still she suppressed her emotions, wanting to see Gino immediately. Gino was on the first floor, the doctor said. "He was conscious just before the surgery, but I put him to sleep again, for the pain. He should wake up shortly. It is Room 105; I believe another of your sons is with him now."

When Rosa and the children found Room 105 the first thing they saw was Bennie sitting on metal chair at the foot of Gino's bed, leaning over with his elbows on his knees and staring intently before him. Looking up at their approach, he was obviously relieved to see some familiar faces. At this point, Bennie had probably been more affected by the accident than even Gino had: Gino hardly knew what had happened while Bennie had watched it all. Rising quickly from his chair, Bennie went to his mother and said, "It's okay. The doctor said they sewed up his leg and he'll be okay."

"Yes, Bennie. I spoke to him on the way up. I am glad you were here." In the small antiseptic room, Gino's face was drained and white in the dim light. An IV was hooked up to one arm with bottles feeding both blood and a clear liquid into Gino's veins. Though Gino was covered by a white sheet, the thick bandaging on his leg, from ankle to thigh, was easy to see. As none of the Manzinos had been in a hospital before, they were shocked by how fragile Gino looked under the swaying bottles in the sterile metal bed.

Rosa had an immediate impulse to sit beside him on the bed, but knew this might hurt his leg. Bruno, however, rushed up im-

mediately, looking as if he were about to land forcefully beside
him.

"No, Bruno," Rosa said, reaching out to grab his arm as he
passed her. "Don't sit down. Gino's hurt, and he is sleeping."
Stopped just short of the bed, Bruno opened his round eyes wide.

"Why is he sleeping?" he asked loudly.

"Because he is resting." Rosa said.

"Can't we wake him up?" Bruno asked just as loudly.

"Bruno," said Bennie in a sharp tone.

"Gino has had a very bad accident," Tessie told Bruno more
gently. "We mustn't disturb him."

"Is he going to die?" Bruno asked.

"Of course not," Rosa said, a little sharply this time herself.
"He hurt his leg, that's all."

"Jerry Espanso died and he only hurt his leg too."

"Bruno!" Rosa said. "Jerry Espanso was run over by a train.
This is just an accident."

"Oh," Bruno said, looking deflated.

The Manzinos fell silent then. Bruno promptly placed himself on Bennie's former chair, but the others stood around Gino's
bed immersed in their own thoughts.

When Giovanni walked in, he thus found his whole family in
an unusual silence. Rosa quickly led him into the hall, told him
what had happened and how the doctor had said the only danger
was an infection. Giovanni, who had only received a message from
Rosa though a neighborhood boy, was relieved that the worst seemed
to be over. Terrible accidents happened to children, but Gino
seemed the kind to pull through anything. Giovanni reminded
Rosa of the time Gino fell from their fire-escape, and emerged
without a scratch from the tomato patch.

Oddly, Gino regained consciousness only a few minutes after
Giovanni joined his family in his room. Opening his eyes heavily
and blinking for a few moments in surprise, Gino asked, "Why are
you all watching me?"

Rosa, smiling in relief, took his hand while Giovanni spoke.

"Gino," Giovanni said. "You have had quite the accident."

"I have?" Gino asked. He was so hazy from the drugs and the shock he could only remember playing soccer, running, and now being here.

"You managed to put a big hole in your leg from what your mother tells me. But apparently they have sewn you up just fine."

"That's why it hurts," Gino said, suddenly realizing his pain.

"As much as falling four flights from a fire-escape?" Giovanni asked, and the solemn atmosphere of the room lifted a little as everyone laughed.

For the next three days, the Manzinos kept a constant vigil over Gino: Tessie and Rosa and Bruno watching him during the day, and Bennie and Giovanni in the evening. While they had managed to play down the accident in front of Gino, secretly all were terribly worried about the possibility of infection. Only Bruno, who had a curious detachment from all personal ups and downs around him, seemed relatively unaffected.

"It's just a hole," he said to Bennie after dinner one night. "Why does everyone go on and on all the time?"

Bennie, who had, at Bruno's prompting, shown Bruno the offending spike in the stairway just that afternoon, knew Bruno could not be stupid enough to think this was only a little accident. Now he looked at his younger brother and felt for a moment like a complete stranger. He and Gino, only one year apart, had naturally been better friends. Yet Bennie knew it wasn't just Bruno's age that separated them, or separated Bruno from others, but the strange way Bruno had of deliberately antagonizing people.

Tess had still not forgiven him for what he had done to her doll. Doubtless she would have – except that she didn't trust Bruno not to do it again. Instead she lavished her affection on her older brothers, especially on Gino. She was at the hospital immediately after school, talking and reading to him from several books he had asked for from home. Then Rosa arrived with Gino's home-cooked dinner.

On the fourth day, when Gino suddenly slipped into a fever, everyone's greatest fears were realized. Rosa arrived at eight in the morning to be stopped by a nurse in the hallway.

"Doctor Murphy has asked to see you," she said. "And your husband."

"Is my son all right?" she said quickly.

"Yes," the nurse said, not looking at her. "Only there has been a complication."

Rosa sent Bruno to fetch Giovanni immediately. When the two were finally in a closed room with Dr. Murphy, he asked them to sit down.

"Is Gino all right?" Rosa asked again, unable to contain herself.

Doctor Murphy looked quietly at them. He had had to break bad news to many a person.

"I am sorry," he said. "It is as we feared. The spike was simply too big, and went too deep. Gino's leg is infected. We have tried to prevent it, but gangrene has set in and your son has developed a dangerous fever. Severe action is necessary immediately . . . We have no choice but to amputate."

"Amputate?" Rosa repeated.

"Yes," the doctor said firmly.

"Amputate what?" Rosa asked, groping blindly in her distress.

"His whole leg," the doctor answered. "To the hip. Otherwise the infection is likely to spread. Your son would die."

Giovanni had been completely silent in his chair, too incredulous to react. Now he felt a rush of anger through his body.

"Likely to spread!" he said. "The infection is likely to spread – which means it may not spread – and you want to cut off my son's leg!"

"We see no other way."

"No," Giovanni said. "This can never happen. Never!" A picture of Gino crippled flashed through Giovanni's mind. Gino would rather die. Giovanni could have slammed his fist into a wall, or knocked everything from the table before him. But he managed to suppress his rage to ask his question one more time.

"You can see no way to save the leg?"

"I am sorry," Doctor Murphy said.

"Then we will leave your hospital," Giovanni said stiffly.

TURNING TO ROSA, he realized she had begun crying steadily, that her whole body was shaking. As he led her swiftly through the hospital corridors, she let out several terrible sobs. "You must not give up hope," Giovanni told her when they stepped outside. "This is only one doctor. One hospital. Someone else will be able to help us."

With this, and Giovanni's comforting assurance on the walk home, Rosa managed to quiet herself, if only to lessen the impact of the news on her other three children.

ONCE GIOVANNI HAD Rosa safely inside the apartment, he took the blanket from their bed and hurried out of the building. He went directly to Enzio, the only man he knew who had a car he could borrow.

By this time, Enzio was managing a moving and storage company financed by the Sicilian Mafia, hiring only black men to do the work and paying them as little as possible. He knew they were powerless to object and that there were plenty of others to replace them. He gambled extravagantly, wore flashy clothes, and cheated on his wife Maria with several whores, often showering them with stolen jewelry while Maria had to account for every penny. Giovanni knew all this both from Rosa, who visited occasionally, and from talk in the neighborhood. He himself had never visited Enzio's home and did so now for Gino's sake.

Luckily for Giovanni, Enzio had had a particularly hard night of drinking and had not yet left the house to go to work. When Maria opened the door she looked frazzled and uneasy, yet immediately greeted Giovanni warmly. For a man so extravagant, Enzio's home was sparse, with few luxuries. The sight of Enzio's stylish hats on a rack immediately aroused contempt in Giovanni. Rather than exchange pleasantries, he told Maria simply that Gino had had an accident and he needed to borrow a car from Enzio. Did Maria know where he could find him?

"Oh" Maria said, averting her eyes for a moment, "he is here. He was not feeling well. Is Gino all right?"

"He is quite ill," Giovanni said.

Just then Enzio, having heard the voice of a man in the living room, opened his bedroom door and looked out – wearing only his underpants.

"Giovanni," he exclaimed, obviously surprised and embarrassed to be caught looking so disheveled at this hour.

"Why didn't you tell me he was here," he then snapped to Maria.

Maria started to speak but Enzio cut her off with a wave of his hand. Pulling on a robe, he came out of the darkened bedroom blinking at the light, stubble shadowing his swarthy face.

"Excuse me," he said, "I have a stomach problem. Maria is still learning how to cook, aren't you?"

Maria, obviously frightened, said nothing.

"But she can make coffee, yes Maria?"

"Yes," she said, and quickly moved out of the mens' way and into the kitchen.

Letting Enzio's obvious hangover go unremarked, Giovanni explained what he needed. It was the only favor Giovanni had ever asked of Enzio and both knew how much time Enzio had spent leaning on Rosa and eating the Manzinos food. Pleased both that Giovanni had come to him – and that it made it obvious who was the more successful man – Enzio gave him the keys at once. Though the two would never get along, Enzio at least had a grudging respect for his righteous brother-in-law.

A short while later, the staff at the public ward were trying everything possible to stop the silent and stern man from forcing his way into Gino's room. Once there, Giovanni stared solemnly at his son's broken form, then wrapped him in the blanket, and forced his way out with Gino cradled in his arms.

"You'll kill him," Doctor Murphy shouted. "If we don't amputate now, he won't last a week!"

Several miles away, Giovanni delivered his son into the arms of the nuns at St. Vincent's Hospital. Perhaps this was one time when God could make a difference, he thought. The sisters, however, had far less confidence in the power of prayer to intercede in such cases. Too many people had died within their walls, and the plight of a boy who'd been "rescued" from surgery became a crisis for the entire staff.

By chance, a young doctor named Adam Perrault was working that evening in the hospital's emergency room. A recent graduate of Harvard Medical School, he supplemented his private practice on Park Avenue with volunteer work in the evenings at St. Vincent's. The moment he heard the nuns fretting about Gino, he quickly finished his task of setting a workman's shattered ankle in a cast, and asked to see the new patient at once. Dr. Perrault, who was deeply interested in a number of new medical techniques, thought that Gino might be a candidate for one of the new antitoxins which were known to attack buried infections.

When Giovanni came home that night with the news everyone was overwhelmed with both fear and hope. Even Bruno understood the gravity of the situation and whispered to Bennie at night that he never thought Gino would die. Both Rosa and Tess went to sleep with prayers for Gino on their lips.

When the whole family arrived at St. Vincent's in the morning they were told that Gino had responded to Dr. Perrault's treatment almost overnight and the need for amputation vanished. Despite all the doctor's efforts, Rosa insisted that the cure was a case of divine intervention. Gino was a miraculous child whose nature it was to attract further miracles. Even the nuns shook their heads in wonder at the extent of her faith. "God gave you four children, but you only have eyes for one," they told her. Rosa smiled and blushed and thought how lucky she was to have such a special son. She loved all her children, just as she loved her husband and her home, but these were the things a woman expected of life. Yet, from the very beginning, Gino had exceeded all her expectations. Each time he smiled at her, she felt that God had blessed her with a happiness her friends had never known. It was more than the fate of his being first born. They had a communion of the spirit and she was terrified of losing him.

The new treatment meant several more weeks in the hospital. By the third week, Gino's eyes had regained their shine, the color had returned to his complexion, and most of his spirit was back. While there were many who came to care very much about Gino's dramatic reversal, among those watching him was a lay nurse named Kathleen Donovan. Small in height, with a voluptuous figure, shining almost white-blonde hair and large round blue eyes, Kathleen had an alluring mix of maturity and childlike beauty. Other boys in the ward, especially the older ones, would whisper about her endlessly, concocting excuses to call for her help. They were especially enraptured with the way her white skirt caressed her thighs a trifle too tightly, a predictable response given their age and the number of women on the wards who were nuns.

Kathleen studied Gino with eyes that were decidedly less sentimental than the others. Through their astonishing blue, Gino noticed a sadness, even when the rest of her face was smiling. Since Gino had grown up in a neighborhood filled with sad, dark eyes, he'd assumed that anyone with such big blue eyes must be happy. But Kathleen was not happy, though she was pretty, good at caring for people, and married.

Her husband, Michael Donovan, was a shipyard worker who had wanted to become a priest. He was almost neurotically pious and looked upon his worldly responsibilities as interruptions to the richer life promised by religion. Unfortunately for Kathleen, this attitude included his sexual life. He made love dispassionately, out of some vague sense of duty, hoping that his indifference would make it less offensive to God. Preceded by years of terrible poverty, her life was strangled by despair.

The first time she looked into Gino's eyes, Kathleen saw many of her own feelings reflected. Soon she looked forward to seeing him on the ward each day, despite the stares she received there. As Gino continued to gain strength, she felt herself being drawn along the path of his recovery. At fourteen, Gino's intensity made him markedly different from the horde of boys who usually came and went. As his energy grew, so did her infatuation, and each time they spoke, however briefly, the sense of intimacy between them increased. When one afternoon Katy said that she'd be back later that night, it seemed entirely natural.

238 •   LANA SANTORELLI

Most of the boys were asleep when she returned to the dark-ened ward. Gino's bed was the last in a line of twenty, with a wall on one side and a recently emptied bed on the other. He was lying on his back, one leg immobilized by bandages and tubes, still wide awake when she silently stretched out the portable screen to con-ceal her presence. Then she kissed him softly and reached beneath his hospital gown to arouse him with her fingers. Lifting her skirt above her hips, she climbed up on his bed and slowly lowered herself onto him. Moving ever so softly, she allowed her body to bring them both to a silent climax, his fingers tightening suddenly on her breasts in the final moment.

From that night onward, Katy's eyes brightened, at least enough for Gino to see. Although she never came to him again in the re-maining weeks, the smiles they exchanged filled him with con-tentment. Lovemaking had healing powers, Gino thought, that had nothing whatsoever to do with guilt.

CHAPTER
THIRTEEN

Growing up, Tess watched the development of her own beauty with deep uncertainty. A lovely young woman was emerging from the child, and looking in the mirror was almost like watching a stranger. Already, others were responding to her differently. Mens' eyes moved from her face to her body, to her face again, with a smile that seemed somehow unclean. Women watched her with envy and suspicion. She was not yet thirteen when she began to fill out; now, at fourteen, her child's clothes did little to hide her maturing body. Realizing that she caused a stir every time she walked home from school, Tess went through a period of deep embarrassment in which she tried to hide her body from the world. She wore oversized blouses and hunched her shoulders as she walked, but it never seemed to help. The boys, many of whom gathered outside St. Cecilia's in the late afternoons, still responded to the swelling of her breasts and the soft curve of her hips. The more she tried to blunt the effect of her beauty by adopting a severe expression, the more alluring she became, a touch of dark mystery among all the giggling schoolgirls.

Eventually, Tess tired of resisting nature. Her childhood wish to be like the boys was finally given up so that by the time she turned sixteen, Tess was able to exchange graceful smiles with the people she met, wear modest clothes that still enhanced her body, and walk with her shoulders straight and proud. An inner voice kept whispering that it wasn't fair; she shouldn't be defined by the way she looked. This, of course, was something that her religious training had made clear to her. Though Tess had long since given up her desire to be a saint, and went to church no more frequently than any other girl her age, she was disturbed at the way the world was changing for her. She did not like being used in the fantasies of men and at times this sense of injustice distracted her from her normally carefree sense of the world: the outgoing Tess was at times so withdrawn that sometimes she scarcely seemed aware of her surroundings.

ONE CHILLY AFTERNOON in late February, while Rosa was haggling with an elderly Russian storekeeper over the price of several yards of rose flannel, Tess wandered across the street and into a group of schoolmates trying to peer through a blackened pane of glass into an old, abandoned warehouse. Tess had been lost in thought, and the girls were younger than she, but Tess was curious when she noticed their hushed excitement.

"What are you doing?" she asked no one in particular.

"Looking at the gypsies," said a small blonde haired girl, turning to glance briefly at Tess. All of the girls were about twelve and still, Tess noticed, in their school uniforms.

"They live wherever they can until the cops chase them away. My father says they all have long knives and hunt cats for dinner – and they can even see into the future."

Tess tried looking over everyone's shoulders, but all she could see was someone moving about in a vast room in the shadow of a single lit lantern. Suddenly, the door to the gypsy lair opened and an enormous woman, dressed in what seemed to be a large circus tent, shouted at the girls in a bizarre language. They all scattered away, except Tess, who stood there thinking that the woman seemed more worried than angry about being spied upon.

The woman stared at her for a moment, then made a "humph" sound, and disappeared as abruptly as she had come. It was then that Tessie realized someone else was watching her. Leaning against the doorframe of yet another doorway to the huge warehouse, was a mysterious boy smiling at her.

He had very thick, dark hair, brown skin, and the blackest eyes she had ever seen, like large olives. He was probably her age but slightly taller, and she loved the way he looked – like the boy in *The Jungle Book* she had read in the library dozens of times. They smiled at each other for several minutes until Rosa came out of the shop across the street, calling her name. Tess lifted her hand in the air, as if to say goodbye, blushing suddenly as she realized how long they had looked at each other. Then she turned and quickly crossed the street.

Over the next few weeks, Tess accompanied her mother to the dry-goods store quite a bit more readily than usual. But she never saw the gypsy boy, even though the warehouse was still filled with his people. Then, one spring afternoon, Tess ventured to the block on her way home from school and found him feeding a large litter of puppies in the vacant behind the warehouse. Stopping still when he saw Tess, he gave her the same provocative smile.

"The girl who doesn't run," he said, and Tess flushed. She was half-surprised that he spoke English, and his accent was foreign to her. "Do you like puppies?" he asked then. Tess looked at the beautiful little dogs, chocolate brown and shining and falling over each other as they scrambled for food. "Here,' he said, gesturing to several bags of dog food below them, "I need to fill some more of these bowls. You can help if you want." Tess immediately fell into step with this boy, spending the next half hour helping him feed and then begin to groom the dogs one by one.

"The dogs like you," he said. "You are very gentle with them. Perhaps you would like one to take one home?"

"Oh no," Tess said. "We couldn't have a puppy in our house."

"No?" the boy said. "Why not?"

"Well," Tess said, watching him as he set down one of the brushed puppies and lunged quickly to pick up another. "We live in an apartment, my three brothers and my parents and I, so there is no room for a dog."

"Well you must visit mine then," the boy said, and smiled

again. His voice was so warm, his movement fluid like dancing, that Tess immediately thought he must have lived much of his life in the country.

"You have never lived in an apartment building have you?" she asked.

"Of course," he said. "Sometimes I think I have lived everywhere."

"Is that because you are a gypsy?" Tess said, then blushed, embarrassed that she had been so rude.

The boy, however, did not seem to mind. "That's what people call us," he said. "Because we move from place to place. But not all gypsies are alike, and many other things they say of us are also not true."

"What sort of work do you do?"

"Many kinds. We breed animals, like these. Some of our men do ironwork and carpentry and some women even tell the future."

"The future!" Tess exclaimed.

"That's what they say."

Tess was embarrassed suddenly that she had asked so many questions of a complete stranger. The boy seemed to read her thoughts, leaning slightly closer to her and saying, "You know you have not told me your name."

"Tess Manzino. It's really Tessie but I have been called Tess since I was a girl."

"Tess," he repeated. "That is a heroine in a famous book. She travels like the gypsies and is very brave."

"Really?" Tess said. "I'll have to read that."

"And you are Italian?"

"My parents came from Sicily."

"My family is from Bulgaria. My name is Carlo," the boy said, holding out his hand to her. Tess noticed immediately how different it was from her own: so much darker from the sun, the fingers slightly swollen the way her fathers were when he had been laboring. Feeling his fingers against hers, Tessie felt strange and unexpected longing.

Again, as if knowing her well, Carlo held her hand and spoke quietly to her as the puppies worked away at their dinners. "You really are the girl who does not run, aren't you?"

Tessie gazed back at him.

"I knew you were when I saw you that day. I hoped we might be friends." Carlo grinned happily, breaking the seriousness of the moment. "Would you like to come to have lunch with me tomorrow? I often eat here out here in the sun."

"I could," Tess said, hesitating. "But I have school. I could only come for a little while."

"A little while then," Carlo smiled. "What time?"

"Just after noon," Tess said. "But I won't have very long."

That night Tess could not stop thinking of the mysterious Carlo. When she rushed out of school the next day the secrecy of it all made it even more exciting.

Carlo was waiting for her in the doorway again, just like the first time. In the lot he had placed a little table and two crates for chairs. Tess sat with her hands in her lap, while Carlo brought out plates filled with figs and sweet cakes: a most exotic lunch to Tess. They also had black tea, a little bitter to one who had never tried it, but still wonderful to Tessie.

"This is so different from our food," she told him.

"What do you eat?" Carlo asked.

"Oh pasta – and pasta – and more pasta," Tess laughed.

Carlo asked her then what she was studying in school, and what she would do when she left. Tess shrugged. "I am not sure," she said. "Though once you know I wanted to be a saint."

"You did?" Carlo asked.

"When I was about nine," Tess laughed. "But now, well I will wait and see. What about you?" she asked. "Will you travel always as you do now?"

"Not forever, I think. I will stay with my family as long as I am happy but perhaps one day I will settle down into a city like yours."

Before the two knew it, Tess' time was up. Carlo and Tess rose together and stood looking at each other under the blue sky. Tess thought his eyes were the most beautiful she had ever seen: black as night, warm like the sun on her skin. Just before she hurried away, Carlo leaned toward her and kissed her on the mouth, gently touching the back of her neck with his hand as he did so. The kiss was brief and chaste, but Tess had never been kissed, and was overwhelmed. The memory of his touch and the taste of his lips stayed with her all afternoon and night.

Over the two weeks Tess met Carlo after school almost every day. He was so different from the other boys she knew: the friends of her brothers who laughed nervously when they saw her, the boys outside St. Cecilia's who only found courage in groups, the men on the street who sickened her with their probing looks.

IT SEEMED TO Tess that Carlo was not interested in her solely for her new beauty. There was a deeper understanding between them. Both wanted to know everything possible about the other's life. Carlo asked her to describe all her brothers, and her parents, and what it was like to go to a Catholic school and live all one's life in one place. As this was the only world Tess had known, she loved seeing it through the eyes of a stranger.

Carlo told her how hard it was to pick up and move all the time. At first he had thought he would stay in touch with the friends he made throughout the country, but even the best friends forgot you if you were gone for too long. Now he preferred to stay with his own people, rather than leave new friends behind all the time.

"But sometimes," he grinned as the two sat next to each other on crates watching the puppies again, "There is one too special to ignore."

Tess knew that Carlo would leave New York one day. She also knew that Giovanni would never let her go out with a gypsy boy. She had had to keep their friendship a secret, saying she was staying late at school or that she was with her closest girlfriend, Madeleine Morgano. But she loved the idea of being liked by someone so different from anyone else.

CARLO TOO HAD kept his feelings for Tess a secret from his family. Although it happened all the time, no one liked to see a local girl picked up by a man for a few weeks and then forgotten when they moved on. The gypsies had learned to keep their private dealings with those outside the group largely to themselves.

Sometimes, however, when a particularly close or interesting friend was made, guests were invited into the gypsies' world. One afternoon Carlo offered such an invitation to Tess. Could she get away for dinner the next evening? Tess managed not to lie too badly – telling her mother she was having dinner with Madeleine. The two did occasionally spend an evening together, so no one suspected anything.

The next day Tessie and Carlo sat in the lot that had become their private world, holding hands until dark. Carlo, though as experienced as Gino with girls and women, knew Tess was not ready for such things. As they kissed, both felt an almost painful longing. Pressing his lips against Tessie's closed eyes, Carlo sighed, then rose and led Tess by the hand into his warehouse home.

Tess found herself in a strange, self-contained world made up of multi-colored carpets that cut the huge space into dozens of rooms. Hanging from ropes that crisscrossed the ceiling, they had transformed the area into a tented city. Only the yellow light of old lanterns, the scent of candied fruits and incense filled the air. In the middle of the room a group of about twenty men, women and children were sitting on stools and on the floor preparing vegetables and some kind of meat on a propane stove.

The introductions were over quickly. "Mother, father, this is Tessie Manzino," Carlo said, then turned to everyone else. "Tessie is a good friend of mine." Carlo's parents, both small slim people with a slightly nervous look about them, stepped forward to shake her hand. Still they both smiled strongly at Tess while others of the group called out greetings.

In her nervousness, Tess found herself staring at the meal on the stove. "Is that cat you are cooking for supper?" she blurted out. Luckily everyone laughed and Carlo's father placed his stool by Tess and gestured for her to sit down.

Like the Manzinos, the gypsies were poor, but they had enough to be eating chicken and vegetables that night. As everyone had been silent when the two walked in, Tess wondered if they would stay that way all through dinner. They did not, she soon found out.

They did seem to talk in a much quieter way, but everyone asked her questions. Tess told them again about her family, and where they were from and how she liked living in New York. Her questions to them, she noticed, were treated a little more guardedly. "It would take many years to understand our ways," Carlo's mother said so that everyone laughed.

After dinner, Tess suddenly noticed Carlo's father lifting a long knife from under his chair. Hadn't that little girl said something about gypsies with long knives? She gasped noticeably, drawing everyone's attention to her. Then, as Carlo's father used to knife to peel his orange, it was Tess' turn to laugh. By this time Carlo was sitting beside her and the conversations broke down from one into many between different people. Lifting her eyes to Carlo, Tess said, "Oh, I am so embarrassed. I didn't think he was going to do anything — it's just that everyone talks of the gypsies' long knives."

Carlo laughed. "And of the way we eat our cats for dinner? I suppose that someone very poor might eat a cat but I'm sure our puppies would taste much better."

Tess squeezed Carlo's hand. "What about the future," she said, excited by the exotic world around her. "Can you really tell the future?"

"Perhaps you will decide for yourself," Carlo asked, taking her hand suddenly and smiling. "Would you like to have your fortune read?"

Tess had a little trepidation. What if she heard something bad? Her curiosity, however, overcame her. Carlo led her over to a heavy woman in a long skirt and billowing black blouse. The woman did a host of strange things, turning over Tessie's hands, gazing into her eyes, laying out strange and colorful cards before her. Finally, she spoke. "You are a strong girl," she said, "a girl of passion." Tess glanced briefly at Carlo, embarrassed yet not ashamed. "Your life will be a full one, with happiness, dancing, but also sorrow." Suddenly the woman, who had closed her eyes and was looking inwards, was troubled, "I see dancers. They are way up on a hillside. They are silver in the light and beckoning for someone to return." The woman opened her eyes and smiled. "It is up to you to interpret this dream for me."

When Carlo walked Tess home the few blocks to her house, Tess was deeply stirred and lost in thought. Rosa had told her of Giovanni's vision of the silver dancers. Did the fortune mean that Tess was being called back from Carlo and the gypsies to her people? Or were the Manzinos meant to return to Sicily? So much had happened this night she could no longer think of what to say. Leaving Tess in the shadows just a few doors from her house, Carlo brought her back to earth, whispering how beautiful she had looked all night, and how she was not to worry about anything. As it turned out, however, Tessie did have to worry. When Enzio came to dinner one night, everyone was far too preoccupied to notice Tessie's reactions to his news. Massemo was dying, he had heard, and Giovanni should visit him now. Sitting at the table as her father heard this news, Tess gasped. She wished she could tell him of the gypsy woman's reading, but it would only reveal her friendship with Carlo and create more trouble. Tessie was sad for her parents, and for Massemo, but as she had never met her grandfather she could not truly grieve or him.

Her greater worry became the increasing love she and Carlo were feeling for each other. Despite her maturity, Tess was still only a girl. Even if Carlo had been Sicilian and Giovanni approved of him, they were too young to marry. Carlo too was already used to women who gave themselves immediately to him, so as their affection deepened, so did their frustration. Tessie even wondered how long they could continue on this way – in secret and with no prospects for the future.

One day when she and Carlo had escaped to the movies, sitting in the back so they would not be seen, Carlo noticed that she was quite forlorn. Sadly, he turned her face to his and kissed her, then gently ran his finger down her cheek. Tess, even with Carlo beside her, was realizing the difficulty of her feelings for someone she might never be able to love fully, and the pain seemed sud-

denly too much for her. Then, just two days later, Carlo pulled
Tess into the warehouse as soon as she arrived, bringing her for the
first time to his bed, a small space tucked away in darkness and
with a light blanket for a mattress.

"Tessie," Carlo said, when both were sitting cross-legged and
facing each other. "We are leaving tomorrow, for Philadelphia."

"No," Tessie cried out, stunned. "You can't!"

"We both knew this day would come. But we don't have to
part. You could come with me, Tess. We could be together always."

Hearing this only made Tess more miserable, and she began to
sob, struck with the terrible thought that she would never see him
again.

"Oh I can't," she said. "We are too young. Our families are so
different. You know it is impossible."

Carlo did know it was impossible. And perhaps better than
her he also knew that she would forget him in time. This was a
truth all of the gypsies had learned and it made them both loving
and hard at the same time. Still Carlo did not plan to make her
forgetting easy.

"Then you will hear of me again one day," he said. "You must
never forget me." Then he moved to hug Tessie to him, and they
both lay back together on his blanket, holding each other while
Tessie continued to sob, not caring if anyone heard or found them.

CHAPTER
FOURTEEN

E AST HARLEM, AS Gino had discovered, had more than one king-
pin. Yet it was Nicodemo Grande who continued to exert the
most influence on the Manzinos. Since his disastrous encounter
with Grande years before, Enzio had attempted to keep a low profile around the neighborhood, hiding his second life of gambling
and drinking with pretenses at being a family man. Yet Giovanni
and Rosa both knew – if only from the increasingly weary look in
his wife Maria's eyes – that Enzio was far from reformed. Rosa
simply ignored these implications, keeping up her friendship with
her brother over casual lunches and chats with Maria. But Giovanni
had exchanged no more than a civil sentence or two with his brother-
in-law since borrowing Enzio's car during Gino's accident.

It was no real surprise to Giovanni then, when Maria arrived
at the Manzinos one evening in a state of distress. It was winter,
and the snow on the streets was packed into solid ice. The Manzinos
had just finished dinner and their apartment was still warm from
the oven. Hearing a knocking at the door, Rosa turned from her
place at the table.

"Are you expecting anyone?" she asked Giovanni.

"No," he said, glancing around the table as he stood up. None
of the children, however, indicated that they were either.

Opening the door, Giovanni found Maria, her hair loose around her shoulders and a shawl draped haphazardly around her heavy black coat. Her skin was white with the cold, and her hands, with no gloves, almost blue.

"What is it Maria?" Giovanni asked. "Come in. Come in."

"It is Enzio," Maria said, sobbing as she spoke. "He has gone."

"Gone?" Giovanni asked. "What do you mean he is gone?"

"He has disappeared." Rosa came quickly from the table and led Maria to a chair, forgetting in her surprise to remove her coat and shawl.

The Manzinos listened as Maria said Enzio had gone out one evening, five nights ago now, and not returned. She had decided to wait awhile, as Enzio had disappeared for up to three days at a time before. But now it was the fifth day, and she had not heard a word. He would never, she knew, go that long without telling her where he was.

"We must ask everyone we know to look for him," Giovanni said quickly.

"I'm afraid he might have gotten into trouble again – real trouble this time," Maria cried.

Over the next few days Rosa kept Maria company as often as possible, while Giovanni walked around the neighborhood trying to get news. The last report he heard on Enzio was not encouraging. In a drunken spree one night Enzio had boasted of how he had escaped Grande's hand once, and would do so again. He dared Nicodemo to pick a fight with him. "He knows a match when he sees one,' Enzio had bragged, "that's why he stays away from me, the fat old man is scared." Sitting at a table just next to him was one of Nicodemo closest cohorts. He stood up from his chair and stared at Enzio, then quickly left the bar. Enzio, who should have known better, had a tremor of worry, but brushed it off. Grande's warning to him should have kept him silent for the rest of his life. But that was his problem. He had never, Giovanni knew, discovered humility. His arrogance, inherited from his father, could not be frustrated – no matter how often the world showed Enzio his true place.

Grande had promised to kill without hesitation if offended

again. And as everyone knew, Grande kept his promises. No body was ever found, but when the weeks turned into months there was little doubt about Enzio's fate.

In time, Maria would find that living without Enzio was actually a relief. The most difficult thing was not knowing for certain whether or not Enzio was alive. If only for her daughter Despina's sake, however, Maria kept her spirits up. When she eventually found work at a clothing store, she found new interests and friends that actually made her life happier than it had ever been with Enzio. Even Rosa, who had loved her brother, recognized that his absence meant a certain measure of peace.

The next surprise for the Manzinos would prove more fortuitous. Cesare Mulassano was Rosa's second eldest brother and ten years older than she. They had never been close, as when Rosa was growing up Cesare was already at work. From the first, he seemed destined to follow in his father's rule. By his twenties he had developed the same superior air. A stocky man of about five foot seven, he had deep brown eyes, dark hair and dark skin bleached by the Sicilian sun. He differed from his father only by his nose, which was long and thin and gave a slender Greek appearance. While he didn't exhibit the same overt pleasure at exercising the family power, he seemed happy enough to assume it.

By the time Giovanni courted Rosa, the couple both treated Cesare much as they did Agostino – with caution. Cesare would brook no criticism of his father and condescended to Giovanni as his father did.

It had now been many years since Rosa and Giovanni had seen him, and all their news from Sicily told nothing unexpected – except, perhaps, that he had grown quieter. What they did not yet know, however, was that Cesare, over the years, had grown into a more thoughtful man. He had married a sweet-natured girl from the village. Like many men, he had also come to see how he had taken on his father's role almost blindly while young. He had chosen to ignore his father's crueler side. Having fewer family members to control, Agostino exerted more and more pressure on the villagers, exacting all their energy and destroying any goodwill.

Cesare saw all the people leaving the village, and the fields dying from lack of care. He had done his father's bidding all his life, and suddenly he wanted to be his own boss, not wait for his father to die. Agostino had never been that warm to him anyway. Eventually, Cesare decided that he too could make a better life for himself in America. Not even Bianca and Massemo could have told Rosa of these changes in Cesare. Unlike Enzio, Cesare kept his feelings, and his change of heart, to himself.

IT WAS LATE spring when Cesare and his wife Teresa boarded their ship. As Cesare was older than Giovanni and Rosa had been, and a wealthy man, his fears were not the same. His only worry was that life in America might not bring him better fortune than wealth at home. Standing on the ship's stern, seeing Sicily slowly disappear, Cesare felt far more excitement than fear however. The greatest chains, he thought, looking back at the yellow fields, are those we fashion ourselves.

Cesare and Teresa first found a furnished apartment downtown, near City Hall. One day, pausing for lunch while out looking for work, Cesare heard a man giving a speech in Italian. Orange in hand, Cesare moved closer to listen.

Congressman La Guardia, a first generation American of Italian and Austrian parents, was a champion of Italian immigrants and elected to congress five times before becoming Mayor. He was the immigrants' first powerful advocate in the new world, a man who not only helped the immigrants, but drew his strength from them. He tried to intercede when they bumped guilelessly against the hard edges of the legal system and he worked ceaselessly to ease their transition to America. La Guardia could hear by Cesare's voice that Cesare had only just arrived. As they spoke he knew that Cesare was just the kind of man he looked for: one who had experience, intelligence and a desire to succeed. Such a man could be an asset to the Italian-American community.

Listening to La Guardia, Cesare himself was moved by this obviously successful Italian. La Guardia had a warmth to him, a good-natured aura that made Cesare comfortable. The two ended up taking a walk together, standing by the river and talking for an hour. La Guardia asked Cesare to meet him in a few days for lunch. "Wear a suit," he said, "perhaps we'll meet someone looking to hire a man like you."

When Cesare came back, he instead told La Guardia that he was interested in buying a business in New York. Over a dish of spaghetti in a local Italian restaurant, La Guardia advised him on the various industries he might consider. "You are used to being in command," he said. "That need not change here."

After then Cesare and La Guardia became fast allies, meeting for lunch in their favorite restaurant. There was nothing La Guardia liked more than to see an Italian immigrant succeed.

After some thought, Cesare decided to enter the moving and storage business and began seeking his location. At the same time, La Guardia asked Cesare about his sister in America. Hadn't Cesare said that she was in New York? She was, Cesare said, but he had no idea where.

"What is her name?" La Guardia asked.

"Rosa Manzino."

"And her husband?"

"Giovanni Manzino."

"Well," Cesare smiled, patting Cesare on the back, "Leave it to me. I will find the Manzinos for you."

True to his word, La Guardia had the assistants at his office conduct a search. As the Italian community was quite small, and the Manzinos already entrenched in it, it was only a week before La Guardia gave Cesare the news that the Manzinos were on 112th Street.

He then told him that he had personally visited Giovanni at work one day, informing him that Cesare was now in America and would like to meet them.

"I bet that gave him a bit of a shock," Cesare said.

"He invited you to dinner this Saturday night at seven."

It was true, Giovanni had been shocked, and not so pleasantly. Approached by the Congressman while on lunch break, he had felt his heart sink upon hearing Cesare's name. Was he in trouble again because of a Mulassano? Finding he was not, he still bristled at the thought of another of Rosa's brothers in America. And Cesare just as much a criminal as Enzio.

Still he did not betray any of this to La Guardia, only asked if he might relay a message to Cesare for him.

"Certainly," La Guardia said.

"Please be so kind as to tell Cesare that he will be welcome at our house this Saturday at seven."

"I will Mr. Manzino. May the reunion be a happy one."

Cesare and Teresa arrived on 112th Street with some trepidation. No one knew whether the dinner would be a disaster or a beginning. When Cesare and Giovanni shook hands, Giovanni remembered how Cesare had first greeted him. "Paisano," he had called him. Ready for some slight, Giovanni was pleased to discover a level gaze and firm handshake.

"Giovanni," Cesare said. "It is with great happiness that I visit you now in your new home."

Giovanni smiled, as did Rosa behind him.

"Of course," Giovanni said, somewhat warily. "You must make yourself at home."

Rosa, in her excitement at seeing one of her brothers, immediately forgot all of her misgivings about Cesare. Perhaps, she thought, they might return, but it was also possible that Cesare had changed. After all, he had moved to America.

Embracing her brother, she promptly had Giovanni pour everyone a glass of wine. Only five minutes later, she had dinner on the table, replete with her famous bread. As they ate, Cesare told the Manzinos about Sicily. The first, and most important news, he said, was of Giovanni's parents. "Your father, Massemo, has been very ill."

"We thought so," Rosa said quickly. "From Bianca's letters. She never says too much, but each time she writes it seems that Massemo is worse. Also, Enzio told us – before he disappeared."

"He has not worked at all the past year," Cesare said. The month we left he had become very thin and was kept in bed, quite weak, almost all day long. Perhaps," Cesare said, looking at Giovanni, "you would like to visit."

Giovanni looked pained. He still had little money, and Sicily was so far away. Yet if Massemo were truly ill, as it seemed, he would have to find a way.

"Yes," he said slowly. "Thank you for bringing the news."

"Perhaps we will go together," Rosa said, placing her hand on Giovanni's on the table.

"Perhaps," Giovanni smiled.

"And how is our father?" Rosa asked then.

Cesare set his wineglass on the table.

"He was always a difficult old goat. Now he's worse. The villagers hate him. And as for his family – he feels all the people he loved turned on him for no reason. We were full of malice and jealousy, he says, since we were children," Cesare laughed.

"His wife has left him, though he pretends she just likes the city life in Palermo. It's a sorry state for him I suppose."

Rosa thought suddenly of Enzio. "You did know that Enzio disappeared?" Rosa asked Cesare.

"Bianca told Agostino."

"He was reckless," Rosa said.

"Yes," Cesare answered.

"They think he was murdered, finally . . . You must meet his wife, Maria, and their daughter Despina."

"I will," Cesare said.

"And what about Leonardo? He is still in Sicily?"

"He went to Naples to handle some business. He started spending more and more time there and eventually he moved, with his wife and six children. He still handles work for father, but only returns for vacations."

"So father is alone?" Rosa asked. "I wonder if he would have been different, if Mamma were still alive."

"I'm sure." There was a moment of quiet then as both Rosa and Cesare and even Giovanni thought how the family had disintegrated, how things had changed so drastically. But then, Rosa thought, Agostino had driven off his second wife too – a woman only ever interested in wealth and rank. She wondered how they had parted. Rosa stood up then, breaking the moment's somber mood and looking at the children.

"Who is ready for dessert?"

Rosa brought out a rum cake baked that afternoon, while Cesare's wife Teresa presented two dozen cannoli, her specialty, With more wine and food than they had had since Christmas, the dinner turned into a celebration, with even Giovanni relaxing into ever more light-hearted conversations.

THOUGH GIOVANNI HAD always shied away from accepting the help of strangers, he knew certain people came as gifts into our lives. Such a man was La Guardia, who with his easy smile and generous spirit put everyone at ease. Because he had reunited Cesare with Rosa and Giovanni, Cesare had them all over to dinner one night in his new apartment. La Guardia liked Giovanni immediately – seeing through the reserve to find a man who was honorable in all ways.

La Guardia also then arranged for a passage to Sicily for Giovanni at no cost. Giovanni need only transport some papers to Palermo at sometime during the journey, in exchange for a first class passage. Before he left, the family once again went for photographs to show to Bianca. As he watched his now well-grown children before the camera, Giovanni felt both a pride at their good looks and high-spirits, and a sadness that he could not bring them to Sicily with him. It looked as if Massemo had been right: he would never see his grandchildren after all.

All the Manzinos rose early to accompany Giovanni to the ship. On the train downtown the children were especially quiet, dreaming of the homeland their father was returning to. Walking west to the docks on the Hudson River, Tess asked her father to tell Bianca that she still kept her beautiful doll tucked high on a shelf, safe from danger.

Standing at the railing on the highest deck of the ship, Giovanni waved to his family below. Behind them New York stretched out in the warm summer air. Though not Sicily, it was still beautiful,

Giovanni thought, with its crowd of red brick and white stone buildings, its cobbled streets and its vast expanses of trees. There was a certain mystery to it, he thought, something that gave one hope. It really was a new world, a great experiment whose history he and his family were a part of.

During a long, quiet passage, Giovanni kept mostly to himself. Never one for talking, he enjoyed the days of privacy. When the ship finally came in sight of Sicily he was standing on deck alone, the salt wind cooling what was otherwise a hot July day. It was early in the afternoon and Giovanni could just make out the shapes of men reaping wheat in the hills. Their sickles were black against the stark blue sky. Most of the streets were deserted, save for an occasional woman carrying a loaf of bread or a few groceries. Giovanni felt the slow quiet of the country come back into his veins. The hills looked ancient under the bright sun, the trees impervious to any of man's adventures.

Giovanni remembered a work song the farmers used to sing:

I passed down a road early in the morning
And saw a plot of carnations in the field
I called to the owner and asked her for some
But the owner told me no.

Late at night I went back there
And ravaged the ground with my bare hands
I stripped the plots of every carnation
And when I was finished I left.

Beautiful and harsh, Giovanni smiled: that was Sicily. As the lines were cast down to the dock, he felt a rush of excitement. He was home. He might never live here again, but still it was home. No letter had been forwarded announcing his arrival; there had not been time. So Giovanni came off the ship alone and made his way, through the town and the valley, up to the home where he had been born. The roads were dry and dusty and the sun bright on his back. The mulberry trees shone with black fruit and figs hung low in the trees beside the road.

As he rounded the curve leading to his house, Giovanni had an impulse to sprint the rest of the way like a boy. Instead he came quietly upon the old stone house in the shade of an almond tree. Finding it quiet, with no one outside, he stopped at the front entrance and called out "Mamma." There was a silence.

It may have been 16 years, but Bianca knew her son's voice. "Giovanni?" she called, and stepped into the doorway. Giovanni knew immediately that Massemo had already died. Bianca was in black, and she looked so much older and more delicate than Giovanni had imagined. Her hair was white now, and her eyes darker, as if they had absorbed all the sun of her life.

"Mamma," Giovanni said, in a rare cry of emotion. "I am too late."

"You are never too late," Bianca said. "You have come to comfort me."

Giovanni stepped into the kitchen, which was quiet and still. He sat at the table as Bianca made them a cool drink of lemonade. Then Bianca told Giovanni that Massemo had died two weeks before. "You could not have known when it would happen," she said. "He simply grew weaker the past few years."

Looking at his mother, Giovanni knew too that she had grown weaker: that while our children come to strength our parents return to fragility. Taken aback by Giovanni's unexpected arrival, it was several hours before Bianca believed he was not just an apparition.

As Giovanni lifted his photographs from his jacket, however, Bianca's face broke into a great smile. She pored over each picture with a child-like happiness. "They are beautiful," she said, "all of them." Though she did not say so, she was especially struck by Gino – who with his fair eyes, dark hair and lean body, resembled so very much Luciano.

Just before dusk, Giovanni slowly walked with Bianca up the hill to Massemo's grave. Still fresh, it was laden with flowers, which in the hot sun had begun to turn crimson and orange and burnt yellow. As the sun slowly settled behind the hill, Giovanni thought again of his pictures. He had taken Massemo's grandchildren away. He had come too late to say goodbye. Still, in the serene quiet of the hills, in the faint light and the stirring of the evening's soft breeze, he knew Massemo had never felt anger for him, nor did Bianca, who now held his arm.

The next day Giovanni visited Agostino. Despite his misgivings about the man, he was Rosa's father and Giovanni knew Rosa would be hankering for news of him. He arrived at noon, when Agostino would probably be in for lunch. Bianca said Agostino's wife had left years ago. Being a social woman, country life ultimately bored her, and Agostino had bought her a villa in Palermo. This, Giovanni thought, stepping into a cool and empty hall, explained the silence of the house. He stood awkwardly inside the front door and at last called out "Signor Mulassano." His voice seemed to bounce off the clean white walls and cool tiles.

Suddenly a young woman appeared, scarcely more than a girl. She looked a little like Rosa had, Giovanni thought, when he had first met her. An apron was tied around her waist. "Sir?" she asked.

"My name is Giovanni Manzino. I am looking for Mr. Agostino Mulassano."

The girl nodded, help up her hand to signal that he should wait, and turned back down the hall whence she had come. A few minutes later Giovanni heard Agostino's voice booming towards him. "Mr. Manzino. What a pleasure." Agostino was wearing all white, including a large straw hat. He held out a soft white hand, coming to a stop before Giovanni.

"Mr. Mulassano," Giovanni said.

"Are you here alone?"

"I was visiting my mother. My father, Massemo, recently died."

"I heard," Agostino said. "My sympathies."

There was a pause as the two men gazed at each other. "Please," Agostino said then, waving his arm towards the hallway. "I was just sitting down to lunch. Come join me."

Agostino could, Giovanni thought, be charming when he wanted to be. What was annoying was that his niceness was usually aimed at achieving a certain end. Still, Giovanni thought of Rosa again, and knew he was the bridge between father and daughter.

The two passed down the long white hallway Giovanni remembered from years before, then into the massive dining room that had once been crowded with young people and servants. Now, however, there was only the sun through the small windows and one place set at the head of the table. The girl quickly brought another and Giovanni sat down. When Agostino made no mention of his wife Giovanni felt sorry for him – even as he wondered that he could.

The lunch was the best the village could offer. Agostino had always liked good food as a pleasure he could rely on. After salad with pecorino cheese, soup of cucuzza summer squash and fresh pasta, came the season's fruits: tiny pears or peruzzoli, in homemade red table wine.

For a time, Agostino seemed most concerned with business in America. How was it for Sicilians, he wanted to know. What were the opportunities and how did they live? Giovanni described the neighborhoods, the Mafioso, the politics of America that usually did not affect the Italians.

"How is Cesare?"

"Very well," Giovanni said, feeling slightly uncomfortable.

"He's found work?"

"In the moving business."

"Maybe I could do that."

For a moment Giovanni feared Agostino planned to follow his children to New York. He relaxed, though, as Agostino said Sicily was the only place for him. "I think a man like me would do well in your country," he said. "But I am happy here. At a certain age one is happy to enjoy the sun on the fields, yes?"

From what Giovanni knew, the sun flogging the backs of the laborers was more like it.

"And Enzio – have you seen him?"

"No."

Giovanni had no idea what Agostino did or did not know about

Enzio's disappearance, but he wasn't about to introduce the subject. Agostino must have known it, because he let it go.

After the main course, while waiting for their fruit, he finally asked after Rosa.

"She's well," Giovanni said. "Busy with the children, of course."

"She wrote to me a few years ago now. I wrote her a reply, but I guess I forgot to mail it."

Forgot, Giovanni thought. He didn't forget.

"Wait a moment," Agostino said and got up from the table, pushing his chair back and moving quickly out a door to where Giovanni remembered his study was. A few minutes later he reappeared, waving a faded envelope in his hand. "Perhaps if it is not too late you will give it to her."

Giovanni slipped the envelope into his pocket.

"We fathers have a lot of pride. Perhaps you will understand one day. What it is to lose your child in the middle of the night."

Giovanni stiffened. As Rosa's husband, the implication was that Giovanni had stolen her away. But Agostino, Giovanni knew, could not help himself. And on some level – as the letter proved – he was trying. Giovanni's fingers brushed against the photographs in his pockets. He drew them out. "Would you like to see pictures of the family?"

"Why not?"

He hid his emotion relatively well, Giovanni thought. Though the curiosity in his gaze made even Giovanni smile.

"The girl's a beauty."

"She is," Giovanni said.

"How old?"

"Sixteen."

"She'll be a mother herself soon."

"Not too soon, I hope."

"How long will you be in Sicily?"

"I'm traveling to Palermo to deliver some documents, so about two weeks, I think."

"Feel free to borrow my horse and cart."

Giovanni hesitated. He knew Agostino's charm could turn to

deceit. But who was left for him to hurt? Giovanni would take the cart, and be glad he was no longer Agostino's laborer, as he had been all those years ago, picking up lemons from the dry and dusty hills.

Giovanni completed his journey swiftly. Having no love for crowds, he delivered his documents and returned the same day. Leaving the cart in the stables he suddenly saw Agostino watching him from a window. Agostino leaned out and smiled at him. "Just like the old days, eh, Giovanni?"

Giovanni bristled, then shrugged his shoulders. What use was it to argue with a man whose house was empty?

DURING THE NEXT week, Giovanni spent most of his time out in the open air. He hiked the small hills behind the village, then down and up again into the mountains. He gazed at the blue sea, and picked figs, dark and fully ripened, from the branches along the way. He watched the farmers in the fields and even took the sickle from one tired workman, just to feel the old stretch and pull of his muscles under the iron weight.

The village was not as full as it had been. Many young people had been drawn to the cities: to Palermo and to the mainland. Those left behind were a quiet, more subdued group he thought. One generation became another and with age Giovanni could see the old woman in the young, the man in the child. He thought of his children, of Tess at St. Cecilia and Gino at the bar and both Bennie and Bruno still running around creating trouble – though not Bennie so much these days. How would they have been, raised here? Giovanni did not know. Yet he envied his children's curiosity, Gino's love of books and even Bennie's eagerness to get out and work. Theirs was the chance to follow any calling, not to be thrust into one by force or necessity. In the best of worlds, he thought, we should have all these things: the beauty and serenity of the land, the learning and opportunity of the city. He wished only that he could have all his children here, high on this hill where he saw the silver dancers as in a dream. It is visions like those, he thought, gazing at the valley below, that sustain us.

Coming back early one evening, Giovanni saw an aging, elegant man stepping out of Bianca's cottage. He was tall and slim and wearing clothes that were far too expensive for a farmer. His shirt was crisp and white, with pressed cuffs and a stiff collar, and his shoes were polished and shining. His eyes, unusually, were green like Gino's.

"Sir," the tall man said, dropping his head in acknowledgement.

"Giovanni Manzino," Giovanni said.

"I have just been visiting your mother. We are old friends. Do excuse me."

"Of course," Giovanni said, stepping aside to let the man pass. As he did, he noticed that the man never took his eyes from Giovanni, but stared intensely at him. Of course, Giovanni realized, he was staring, too. There was something about this man, he had a quality which reminded him of something—.

Inside Giovanni found his mother's bedroom door closed. She was resting, Giovanni thought, pouring himself a glass of water and sitting down at the kitchen table. It was then that he discovered several new bills and a box of groceries with certain luxuries Bianca would never buy. Orange chocolates, for example. And special cheeses from overseas.

"Who was that gentleman?" Giovanni asked Bianca when she appeared at the kitchen door a half hour later.

"That was the man from the estate I worked at when I was a girl. His mother, the Contessa, was very fond of me. She left word that her son, this man that you met, should keep an eye on me." Bianca laughed, tossing her head almost as if she were a girl again.

"Life is full of strange things isn't it Giovanni? Who would expect that an angel would care for me on earth. He has blessed us all in his way."

Giovanni watched his mother slip into a sort of reverie, talking as if he were not even there.

"How much does he give you?" he asked.

"As much as I give you, my son."

Giovanni shook his head. He would have liked to ask more, to follow the man down the road and talk to him. Yet it was almost dark now, and probably the man would be gone.

On his last night Giovanni wandered up into the hills again. In the back of his mind he thought he might see the silver dancers. Instead he had images only of his mother, of Massemo, and this strange man with the orange chocolates. Who knows, he thought, if our true guardians are in the skies or on earth? As the sun set on the glowing fields he felt a sadness that he might never see this land again. Yet someone, perhaps his son, perhaps a grandson, would return to gaze upon this scene again.

> *Butterfly or dove*, said the song of the fields:
> *You fly with the wind. Don't run out of breath.*
> *In the morning when I rise up anxious*
> *I go to find my saint; the way is very long*
> *Then I hear a joyous sound, from the distance.*
> *I hear a precious song."*

CHAPTER
FIFTEEN

IN SOME WAYS Giovanni's return to Sicily closed a door on the past. Knowing that his father was dead, and his mother being cared for by a gentleman, placed him more squarely in the new world. The night he returned, Giovanni gave Agostino's letter to Rosa, telling her that it had been written many years before. He had not yet read it, but waited as Rosa opened it with a trembling hand. Despite her long suffering over father's silence, Rosa still loved the man she had known as a child. Somewhere in Agostino that man still lived and though she herself had no desire to return to the past, still Rosa took solace in Agostino's words. The letter could have been written yesterday:

My Rosa

You cannot imagine what it is to wake up in the morning and discover that your daughter has fled like a thief in the night. I felt as if a wild boar had ripped my heart from my chest. I cannot understand why you did not come to me with your grievances. Perhaps your husband was not happy here, but if you had talked to me we might have found another solution. So often I looked at you and saw my own wife's image, your mother's image. I wished only to protect you. Now though, your need for me is gone. Your lack of trust in me, your choice to run away in secrecy will haunt me always. Still, I send you blessings for your new life, because I only want your happiness.

To Giovanni, the letter revealed Agostino's selfishness and inability to perceive anyone else's condition. Rosa's actions were related only as they affected Agostino. To Rosa, the letter was a proof of her father's ultimate, if awkward, love. Despite his stumbling, Agostino had given her his blessings.

Another result of Giovanni's journey was that it heightened the Manzinos friendship with Cesare and his family. On holidays, Cesare and his wife Teresa at times came for dinner, after which Rosa and Teresa talked in the kitchen while Cesare and Giovanni shared an extra drink in the living room. Though Teresa turned out to have a loose tongue, Rosa kept herself to listening. Words stung worse than a bee was her philosophy. Eventually Cesare and Teresa moved to a luxurious apartment on 104th Street.

Cesare enjoyed his new life: the freedom of doing what he liked, the pleasure of not having to account to his father. Sometimes as the nights and years passed, he and Giovanni would reminisce about the good things they remembered. Rosa might bake a rum cake and Teresa bring out biscotti for dunking in black coffee or wine.

La Guardia also came to dinner several times, bringing along a bottle of fine wine each time. Always on the lookout for the prospects of Italian immigrants, he also began to take quite an interest in Gino. "You have a live one here," he told Giovanni one night, noting the gleam in Gino's mischievous eyes. Hearing about Gino's job at Belvedere's, La Guardia was skeptical. "We must all learn the facts of the world," he said, "but I think Gino might take a different path."

Gino laughed at the conservative La Guardia, who wore hats and dressed in dark suits and was always so courteous. "Should I become a politician like you?"

"Only the girls would want to vote for you," Tess called, overhearing them from the kitchen.

Gino blushed and Cesare rumpled his glossy brown hair with his hand. "A live one," he winked at Giovanni.

Cesare too was impressed at Gino, at his ability to work and at his good effect on both men and women. Something in Gino warmed him —not enough to loosen his pockets, but enough so that Cesare began to feel Gino should have been his own son. Cesare had been saddened at his wife's inexplicable inability to have children, but over time the two had come to accept their lot. Though he liked Giovanni well enough, Cesare began to wonder how it was he could have produced such a splendid son. Then it dawned on him that Gino had his own Mulassano blood in him.

As Cesare was wealthy, and Giovanni poor, Cesare began thinking that it might be fitting for him to adopt Gino, relieving Giovanni of just this one child. After all, he did have four. Gino could come and work for him, and live well with him and Teresa. One evening, Cesare took Giovanni aside to present his idea. "Now Giovanni," he said, attempting to approach a graceless subject gracefully, "I have a proposition for you." When Giovanni heard the proposition, however, he was not impressed. He was deeply insulted – a possibility Cesare hadn't even imagined. Sometimes, it seemed to Rosa, who heard all this later, people forgot what a man of family honor Giovanni was – until they put a step wrong. "I would rather throw my son in the sewer," Giovanni told Cesare, "than have it said that I cannot care for him."

"But I'm his Uncle," Cesare said. But Giovanni wouldn't hear of it. Cesare had to settle for remaining only Gino's uncle, though already he sat musing at how nice it would be to have Gino working for him one day.

IT WASN'T JOB prospects, however, that now concerned Gino. Completely caught up in the concept of America, he, along with most of his friends, developed a covetous relationship with that center of American culture: the automobile. Although they lived in the depths of a city where a car was a terrible burden, all the immigrant sons stared long and hard at the sleek machines that moved through the teeming streets en route to wider boulevards. Most of the boys, however, had no official status – no passports, work permits or citizenship papers – so they couldn't get licenses to drive, let alone registrations and legal bills of sale. For Gino and the young Turks prowling the streets, however, such limitations were easily overcome. Hot wiring was the answer. "Angel Hair" Sedutto stole fourteen cars, including a police cruiser, the summer he turned seventeen. With soft blond curls that had given him his name and a childlike smile, he seemed an unlikely felon. Nevertheless, he left the neighborhood at least once a week to scout the city for his next acquisition, carrying the lunch his sister had packed in exchange for the promise of a weekend ride. By nightfall, he'd return to the block, to the cheers of his friends, with another car more fabulous than the one before. Soon he'd be racing through the streets, eventually drawing the attention of an officer. Gaining a lead of two or three blocks, he would abandon the car at an intersection with the motor still running. Once, he stole a beautiful new hearse, but as none of the girls would drive with him – let alone take advantage of the spacious cushioned rear area – he left it on a road in Central Park the next morning. Angel's joy rides came to an end when he managed to steal a bulldozer from a construction site and disappeared from Manhattan to the farmland, never to be heard from again. Decades later, Gino thought how proud Angel would be that they had invented a new pasta called Angel Hair, light as a feather.

Gino's scrapes were never quite as dramatic as Angel's, but they were certainly colorful. He drove his first car, an old Cadillac, with no legal sanctions at all. Whenever he was stopped, he was usually brought into the station house. Gino never resisted, but hid his resentment beneath the mask of bewilderment that so many immigrants had mastered in the face of authority. After the first incident and the precinct sergeant's exasperated warnings, Gino's car was impounded and Gino thrown into jail where he waited patiently for La Guardia to get him out.

La Guardia would never assist a criminal, no matter how well connected. But he did try to help immigrants whose foibles sometimes got them into trouble. Since Gino was usually picked up in the small hours of the morning, this meant waking La Guardia from his sleep. Though he was out of the district, he was powerful enough to have his bidding done over the telephone. Gino always felt chagrined, knowing that losing out on his already brief hours of sleep, didn't warm La Guardia's heart any.

After being tracked down on one particularly bitter winter night, La Guardia had his car take him to the station where he took Gino aside and said, "Listen, Gino, I'm glad to be able to help, but could you manage to get arrested in the early afternoon? And, whatever you do, don't antagonize these Irishmen by letting them see how much luckier you are with women."

This last remark referred to Gino's most recent arrest – and explained why the arresting officer had been so determined to have Gino locked up. Gino had actually been driving too slowly. His date for the evening, Louisa Belladonna, had unzipped his pants and buried her head between his legs, so distracting him that he had passed through a red light at an empty intersection. As soon as he saw the flashing light of the police cruiser in his rearview mirror, Gino had muttered, "Oh shit" and pulled over to the curb. Louisa misunderstood and became even more frenzied, despite Gino's urgent pleading. She was still feverishly at work when the cop shined his flashlight into the car's side window.

No such event had transpired this night though. Gino had simply, he told La Guardia, been pulled over with no papers again. Leaving the station, Gino walked with La Guardia through the midnight streets. La Guardia would be up again in four hours, but pushed open the door to a diner. There he had breakfast of eggs with cheese and parsley and toasted bread delivered to the table. Sometimes he did the talking, cautioning Gino that errant ways can lead to errant lives. This morning, however, he listened as Gino told him he was growing tired of his present life. "I've been at Belvedere's for six years," he said. "I don't want to end up tending bar forever like Paolo."

Sipping from his large mug of coffee, La Guardia laughed. "I don't think you will Gino – but perhaps it's time you did something about it."

CHAPTER
SIXTEEN

GINO WAS DETERMINED to go beyond the harsh realities of the tenements – not only in terms of material goods, but in experience. He knew the extent to which his home life had been more fortunate than that of others. Yet his ambition came from a conviction that a better life belonged to him somehow by birthright. By the time he was eighteen, Gino's drive made him seem all but incapable of failure.

It was then that La Guardia sent a message through Cesare that Gino should apply for an open position as a bellhop at the Commodore Hotel. This was the finest hotel in New York City, located on 42nd Street between Lexington and Park Avenues. Gino promptly put on his best clothes and walked downtown. Doubtless La Guardia had put in a good word for him, but it was Gino's simple confidence that landed him the job. Just eighteen, with eight years of service behind him, he was an unusually strong candidate.

All prospective employees were interviewed at length and asked for references. Gino waited all afternoon until the hotel manager made his decision. When his name was called, he stepped into the manager's office to receive a handshake and a new uniform: a vest and shirt, trousers with piping and a short jacket with epaulets. Dressing for his first day of work gave Gino a thrill that he had never felt before. It wasn't just the prestige of joining the Commodore staff that delighted him. It was the realization that for the first time, he was meeting men who epitomized success.

American and European businessmen, politicians and lawyers, all stayed at the Commodore. So did the greatest actors and musicians of his time. Being a bellhop, Gino saw how these men moved in the world: how they dressed, spoke, ate and drank; where they went in the evenings, and with whom.

So far Gino had seen only a certain level of neighborhood hustler. The men he watched now had a quieter style. The actors and musicians were flamboyant, and Gino frequently helped them stagger both into and out of cabs. Known for their parties, these men could certainly get carried away. One early morning when the sky was still dark, a very drunk and famous musician asked Gino to escort him to the top floor. Gino knew better than to question a client – especially a drunk one. So he escorted him up. Once there, however, the man dashed off in search of the roof. Alarmed, Gino followed him up and caught on to his sleeve as the man veered towards the roof's edge. "Sir," Gino said, "I cannot allow you to do that." The man looked at him, surprised, then let Gino lead him down to his room.

The men with real power, Gino learned, did not attract attention by noise but, more often, by silence. Gino was astonished at how much luggage they brought: cabs arrived from the train stations with huge sets of expensive suitcases and hatboxes. Though they wore the finest suits, however, though their shoes were polished and their hats brand new and their fingernails carefully kept, their real power was in their presence: in their indomitable authority and ease. Whereas the men at Belvedere's could be demanding – calling for a drink or an ashtray or a match as if Gino were their own personal kept boy – these men were always polite, thanking Gino as he helped them from their cars, quietly pressing bills into his hand when he carried their bags. Whenever a rich Italian stayed at the hotel, he picked out Gino immediately. One man, in particular, was Gino's favorite. A tycoon in the paper industry, he traveled the country constantly. Saying Gino reminded him of his own son – whom he seldom saw – he gave Gino tips almost as large as his paychecks.

Gino also studied the women: the ones men married, the ones they didn't. In East Harlem, people looked the other way when witnessing arguments. Belvedere's had been good training, but the Commodore perfected Gino's understanding of the rules of silence. Here he had to look the other way with eighty percent of the women. This was hard to do: the girls who appeared out of the night on these men's arms were often bright and shiny things, their hair glossy and their clothes silken. As with the men, however, Gino found it was more subtle women that commanded ultimate attention: those who, like their husbands, walked gently in and out of the night.

Gino himself walked gently with them sometimes. His allure was not confined to his own neighborhood. Indeed his good Italian looks were even more attractive at the Commodore for being exotic. Both wives and girlfriends adored him. One woman beckoned to Gino from her doorway while he carried another's bag. One slipped him a note in the hotel lobby as she passed by en route to the elevator. Once, he was summoned upstairs by someone who claimed he had lost one of her bags. The woman hustled him inside her room, then promptly ushered him to a sofa where she asked if he would like a drink.

As long as the woman was pretty, with no husband in sight, Gino considered himself most fortunate. His discretion was part of his success. Despite all of his liaisons Gino never had an angry husband after him.

After several months at the Commodore Gino had earned enough money to rent an apartment of his own. Giovanni didn't like Gino's odd hours, and Gino didn't like being told what to do – especially when he gave most of his money to the family. Giovanni expected no less from his son – reminding him more than once, "I gave you life." Gino didn't mind this so much; he was making such good money, most of it from tips, that he always had more than he needed, and it made him smile to see Rosa still leaving fifty cents on the mantelpiece for him each week. But Gino, who would go on giving his mother his bankbooks for several years, was yet restless for bigger things.

Then, one night in springtime, he ventured out with Jimmy Sullivan, another bellhop at the Commodore. The two headed to 45th Street on the West Side to a nightclub known for its dancers. Sitting at a table on the right side and in the front row, Gino had a close view of each girl who came down the stage towards him. Their dance was hardly burlesque, but it was certainly provocative. Gino had never seen such elaborate and colorful gowns: the girls appeared for each dance in newer and more fanciful dress. About half way through the show Gino spotted a lithe woman, in her late twenties, with glossy dark hair and a certain sensitive and intriguing look. Staring at her for the rest of the night, Gino's eyes seemed to draw her glance to him. Their attraction was immediate. Later, Gino thought nothing of approaching the maitre d' to learn the young woman's name. When he did, he promptly went backstage where she received him in her dressing room with a calm smile.

That very night Gino accompanied her home to her room in an apartment block nearby. Her name was Rita Stewart, and at age 28, she had already been married, borne a child, and been divorced. Her son, aged six, lived with his father and his new wife out of the city and Rita claimed she had been too young for marriage: her dancing had always been her greatest passion.

Rita's intense lovemaking enticed Gino for that first night. But it was the undercurrent of their affection that held him. Neither she nor Gino were sentimental enough to confuse their attraction with romantic love. Rita wasn't truly interested in a young man and his demands. She also had enough experience of life to protect her from having any illusions about Gino. When his time for marriage came, Rita knew she would not be the girl.

Even when they agreed to live together, both knew it was somewhat a matter of convenience. Rita's room near the club was small with little sunlight and she had already been searching for a better place. The two could help each other in a time when neither wished to live alone.

Gino considered moving near the Commodore, but East Harlem was still his home, and Rita didn't mind moving out of the theater district. So, without mentioning Rita to his family, Gino found an apartment with a bedroom and living room on Cesare's street: 104th Street. Already it pleased Gino to be amongst the slightly better-off immigrants. It occurred to him that until the Commodore he had never known just what he was yearning for in life. While Bennie had now been at the fish market for years, and was happy to have been moved up to assistant manager, Gino needed more. His vague hankerings had been only that until the Commodore showed him a new world. Now that he knew what he sought, it could only be easier to attain it.

CHAPTER
SEVENTEEN

WHILE GINO AND Bennie were making their ways in the world, and Tess was still at school, their youngest brother Bruno seemed to be following Uncle Enzio's footsteps. Even less fond of school than Bennie had been, Bruno had a more pressing reason to leave: he was expelled. A bully from early on, he only grew worse with time. The schoolyard seemed to represent a fighting ring to him, and when yet another boy had been pummeled by his fists, the schoolteachers decided they had had enough. Calling in Giovanni and Rosa, they recommended a special school downtown for boys who needed more discipline. Although they knew Bruno was difficult, however, Rosa and Giovanni thought this was too much for a still young boy. Besides, the belligerent Bruno wouldn't hear of it. "I'm not going to any prison school," he said. "I never wanted to go to any school. I want to make money like the others." Even Rosa knew that if they forced Bruno to go he would only play truant.

Age ten when he left school, Bruno began selling newspapers at the railroad station. His loud voice and presence drew him more attention than the other boys. Eventually, however, Bruno was fired when the owner suspected he was not handing in enough money. Indignant, Bruno said the work was too boring anyway and soon, whether by choice or by necessity, was bouncing from one job to another throughout the neighborhood. For a few months, he joined Bennie at the fish market. Bennie, however, was horrified at Bruno's rudeness. It was all he could do not to tell his own brother to quiet down and start working sometimes. When their boss fired Bruno, Bennie was secretly relieved. Not even Cesare would hire his nephew.

Instead, Bruno moved on to stacking goods at a grocery store, then became a busboy at a restaurant. For a time, Rosa hoped he might become a chef. Fired from that job, however, Bruno was next packing furniture at a warehouse on Third Avenue.

By age fourteen, Bruno's already stocky body had grown muscular with physical labor. Small in height, he wasn't graced by Gino's slimness, but instead developed a tough boy swagger that made it surprising to find these two were brothers. Bruno's face had the heaviness of a seasoned fighter, with none of Gino's refined features. When Gino went out to live on his own, he became more removed than the rest of the family from Bruno's dramas. With his own apartment, however, he also became subject to Bruno's surprise visits. Gino was uneasy about Bruno seeing Rita. He did not want his private life with her discussed. In this matter, at least, Bruno seemed capable of remaining quiet. To him it meant that he and Gino had a special bond, a secret that attested to their superiority. At the same time Bruno liked to show off to his eldest brother, making fun of Gino's swanky uniform and saying no one would ever tell him what to wear. Gino only let Bruno in when Rita was working, so Bruno was also free to brag to Gino about all the neighborhood girls – implying personal relationships with them all. Gino listened without saying anything, until Bruno eventually tired of the sound of himself and left. Before he did, though, Gino always slipped him a few bucks, feeling a pang of pity for his hopeless brother.

Bruno was satisfied by his warehouse job for several years. But he was also one of the crowd that spent breaks smoking cigarettes and inventing schemes to make extra money. Gino heard quite a few of these plans over the years, but as he never heard of any good results, assumed they had not gone well.

One night, however, when Bruno was sixteen, he stopped in at Gino's after work. Rita had already left for the club. Gino was working the night shift and getting dressed for work. "Are you leaving?" Bruno asked with some urgency. "I have to tell you something."

"I have a minute," Gino said. "I'm just getting ready."

Bruno sat a chair at the entrance to Gino's bedroom, where Gino was pressing his shirt.

"You'll never believe this," he said. "I've got an unbelievable chance to make money on some guys."

Gino raised his eyebrows.

"These Russian guys came up from downtown. I met them in this bar over on Second Avenue last night and the bartender – I know him – he came and told me they were looking to buy some guns."

"Guns?" Gino asked. "What do you know about guns?"

"Not much," Bruno smiled, taking out a coin and playing with it in one hand. "But neither do they, see?"

"Then why are they looking for them?"

"That's the point. They need some but they don't know anything about them." Bruno paused. "Anyway, I asked around with some guys I know from the warehouse. They told me I can get some real cheap, then hike up the price. They'll never know the difference."

"Where are you going to find cheap guns, lying in the gutter?"

"There's this place, on 118th and Pleasant Avenue. Some old guy at this pawn shop buys guns from people who, you know, have to sell them quick."

"You had better not pass on someone's piece," Gino said.

"Oh come on. By the time this guy sells them to me they'll have been sitting around forever."

Gino sighed. "If they were safe they wouldn't be getting rid of them."

"Oh come on. You've got to take risks sometimes. You can't go around opening doors for people all your life."

Gino laughed. "Maybe," he said. "But no one wants to end up

under a moving train either."

"Ha," Bruno laughed. No one talked much about Bruno's escapade of the year before, doubtless because no one wanted to bring up the fact that Bruno was a thief. He had stolen a wallet from a man in the first car of the Third Avenue el, fled through the train, and slipped between the fifth and sixth cars. Grabbing onto a length of chain as he went down, he was dragged beneath the cars, bouncing off crossbeams for three city blocks before the train reached the next station. He spent the next four months in a hospital and laughed the whole time. "They never got the money," he boasted to Gino, "I hid it in a grating at the station, and when I went back it was still there."

Gino looked hard at his brother, no more than an oafish child. "Stay away from those guys, Bruno. I used to see guys like that coming into the bar. They're trouble."

"You play too safe Gino. It's a no-risk deal."

Gino shrugged. It was tiresome trying to help someone who couldn't listen. Bruno walked him down the stairs and to the subway though, going on about the great chance this was.

"Don't do it," Gino cautioned one last time. Then he stepped onto the train and raised his arms. "If you do," he said, as the doors closed, "I don't want to hear about it."

Gino did hear about it though. And sooner than he thought. Only two nights later he was called to the phone at the Commodore.

"Is this Gino Manzino?" a voice asked in a thick accent.

"Yes. Who is this?" Gino asked.

"We are looking for your brother, Bruno. Do you know where Bruno is?"

"Why do you want him?"

"We have some things of his. He's made a big mistake."

"I don't know what you're talking about," Gino said, "I don't know where Bruno is."

"Tell him we will find him," the man said, then hung up.

Gino was incensed. Not only had Bruno once again done something stupid and dangerous, but he had put Gino at risk too. Pulling on his coat, Gino was at least glad it was a quiet night at the hotel. "I'll be back," he told Jimmy Sullivan and rushed out the door.

Gino was gone for almost two hours, checking first at the Manzino home, then at the bar Bruno had mentioned, and finally with some friends of Bruno's at Augie's pool hall on 110th Street. No one had heard from him though, or seen him, and Gino became increasingly angered.

Only an hour after he returned to the Commodore, another phone call came in at midnight. "Bruno Manzino had his throat slit," said a hurried voice. "He's still breathing, behind Augie's."

Gino pulled on his coat again. Luckily, his shift was over, so he made straight for the door and uptown. He found Bruno lying on his back in an alley, holding a blood-soaked handkerchief to his throat. When Bruno tried to speak, all that came out was a blood-filled gurgle.

Gino knew he should have felt some compassion, but Bruno had brought this on himself. It was hard to feel sorry for someone who was so intent on destruction. "Stay here Bruno," Gino said, then slipped into the bar to get help. At first he recognized no one, but then a familiar-looking heavy-set Irish boy made his way over to him. With a shock, Gino realized that this was one of the Haggerty brothers whom he and Bennie had fought and despised years ago in the playground. "Are you looking for Bruno?" Jackie Haggerty said.

"Are you a friend of his?" Gino answered.

"Yeah. I was supposed to meet him here an hour ago. We work together." Disgusted that Bruno could have picked a Haggerty for an ally, Gino nevertheless didn't have time to do anything but shrug it off.

"Bruno's out back," he said. "He's been hurt."

"Shit," Haggerty said.

Together the two went out back and managed to carry Bruno the few blocks to the local hospital. Leaving Bruno in the emergency room, Gino then went to his parents.

Waking Giovanni, he told him in the living room what had

happened. Soon Rosa was up too, then Bennie and finally Tess. If Gino was angry, his father was livid. "He is a stupid, bull-headed son-of-a-bitch," Giovanni said.

"It serves him right," Bennie interrupted.

"Don't say that," Rosa said, pulling her coat over her night-gown.

"Oh Mamma, you know he'll just do these things until they kill him."

"Well they've really hurt him this time," Rosa said.

Bennie, who had never forgotten Bruno's curious indifference to Gino's accident with the spike years before, rolled his eyes and headed back to bed. Even Tess, who had once coddled her younger brother, had long ago come to dislike him for his arrogance with her and her girlfriends. Though Bruno confided in Tess sometimes, Tess only trusted Gino. "Can I go back to sleep too?" she asked. "I have a test in the morning."

"Yes you can," Rosa said. "We'll be back soon."

It was just Gino and Giovanni and Rosa who walked out into the midnight air to the hospital. Gino couldn't remember the last time his father had been so angry, and was surprised that he was even going to the hospital. "You don't need to come," he said. "I can take care of this."

"I'm going for a reason," Giovanni said abruptly.

They found Bruno lying back on a white hospital bed. His throat, now covered in white gauze, had been sewn together by emergency room surgeons in much the way Rosa might have sewn a chicken. Smiling like a beaten fighter who believes he has won a fight, Bruno managed to whisper, "I told you those Russians were stupid, Gino. Not only did they believe I could get them top guns, they even believe I am dead!" He then laughed wildly, his usually high-pitched chuckle reduced to a rumble by the hole in his pipes. Gino, like his father, stared at him. I'm dealing with an idiot with a death wish, he thought, a madman. Yet Gino knew that every bad thing Bruno did hurt his mother more, so he tried to have some sympathy and help his brother stay out of trouble. Tonight though, Bruno had worn everyone's patience thin.

It was Giovanni who broke the silence. His voice was so tense, it seemed difficult for him to get out his words. "Bruno," he said, "You treat yourself and your family with no respect. I will not allow your stupidity and arrogance to infect my house anymore. I want you out of my house."

Bruno's eyes seemed to bulge in his white face. All he could whisper was "But – ." Rosa went and stood beside him, taking his hand. "Giovanni," she said, "You are being too harsh. It was an accident. You must give Bruno another chance."

"Accident! This was no accident. He deliberately carried out a stupid scheme to cheat men and put others in danger. Bruno is sixteen years old. He works. He has money. He does what he likes and he contributes nothing to this family. He can live with the dogs in the cellar – not with me. Come Rosa –. "

Seeing Giovanni's conviction, Rosa knew there was no arguing with him now. "Things will be all right," she said to Bruno, and squeezed his hand. "I'll see you when you come home." Giovanni snorted by the door, waiting for Rosa and then leading her away. Giving a slight wave, Gino followed them out, saying to Bruno as he left, "You're lucky you're alive." From down the hallway, Gino heard Bruno laugh, or try to – a sick curdling laugh that trailed down the hallway like a terrible curse.

CHAPTER
EIGHTEEN

Rosa's attempts to soften Giovanni had no impact. "He has gone his own way," Giovanni said wearily, and Rosa realized he was right. Allowing Bruno to live on at home was only condoning his reckless behavior. He had to learn to live with the consequences of his actions.

Bruno, however, was not worried at his parents' decision. He laughed at it, as he laughed at everything else, and with his even more pronounced swagger moved into an apartment with Jackie Haggerty and another warehouse packer. No one in the family liked to visit there. It was dark, dirty, and smelled of the opium the boys liked to smoke. Gino didn't know how Bruno could tell the new food from the old, the clean clothes from the dirty. The three boys paid little attention to their surroundings. With enough money to drink at the bar, play pool and make up stories, they were content to wait around until the next get-rich scheme came along.

Although Bruno's encounter with the Russians had obviously gone awry, the memory of all those guns at the pawnshop kept returning to him. Surely, he thought, the shop's owner could do more than sell them for a few dollars. And if the guns were hot, wouldn't he know where they came from? Wouldn't the police be interested in knowing too?

Bruno mulled this over while lying around and drinking during his convalescence. He then paid another visit to the pawnshop. "I'm interested in starting my own shop in East Harlem one day," he told the old scraggly haired owner. "But I need some experience. I could work at night, maybe, or a few hours a day, if that's all you need."

The old man looked at Bruno, noticing immediately the raw red scar on his throat. There was something shifty in his eyes too, which he did not like. Then he noticed Bruno's brawny arms and strong shoulders. "Maybe," he said slowly. "I need to do some inventory work. It's a lot of moving and cleaning; things haven't been organized around here in years. Can you do heavy lifting?"

"Sure," Bruno said. "Anything you need. I just want to learn."

"I can only pay you by the hour."

"Fine," Bruno said.

"We'll just see how it goes."

"Sure. And the more you could explain to me, about the business, the better."

"My name is Harry Fienstein."

"Jerry Manzino."

"Manzino," the owner paused. "Aren't you the guy who bought guns from me last month?"

Bruno laughed. "Oh, that was my brother. We look alike. He's the one who got me thinking about this pawn shop business."

Harry looked at Bruno skeptically, then shrugged his shoulders.

Bruno smiled. He had worried about being recognized by the owner, not knowing if the Russians had tracked the guns down to him. It was just as well that he lied about his name, he thought. You could never be too careful.

So Bruno began working for Harry Fienstein in the evenings. With his mission in mind, he was cheerful even when sorting through all the dusty odds and ends from Fienstein's store and backyard. He had never seen so much junk in his life, and enjoyed giving Fienstein advice on what they could sell, throw out, or destroy. He derived a certain pleasure in watching the old women and men of the neighborhood come in to pawn their prized belongings. It was pathetic, he thought, how when they came to sell their dearest possessions, they pretended they didn't care about them. Not one for sentimentality, Bruno could, he realized, be good at this business. Of course, he wasn't really interested. He just kept waiting for the right customers.

One bitter night when the cold had Bruno wearing a scarf and hat indoors, a burly man in a heavy wool coat and hat burst through the front door, bringing the cold wind with him. Fienstein was out back, so Bruno called to him, then studied both men carefully. Fienstein shuffled to the front counter, neither friendly nor rude, just doing his job. The man in the coat quickly pulled out a large black gun and placed it on the glass counter. "What will you give me for this?"

Fienstein turned the gun over in his hand. "Is it new?"

"Yeah."

"It looks like the last one."

"Yeah."

"Twenty bucks."

"All right," the man said, looking around. Catching sight of Bruno, who was standing on a stool pretending to check over some radios on a top shelf, he stared hard at him for a second. "Who's this?" he said to Fienstein.

"My new boy."

"Tell him to keep his eyes to himself." Bruno looked away, but secretly he was smiling. All he needed was now was this man's name — and he'd be dead.

Bruno let a few days pass before bringing up the man with the gun. Then, while cleaning some furniture out back, he said to Fienstein, "That was a strange looking man the other night."

"Who?"

"The one with the piece."

"He's a customer."

"A regular?"

"You could say that." Bruno, for once, had the sense to say no more. Two weeks later, however, another man came in, also at night, and quickly laid a gun on the counter. He was more nervous than the first, Bruno thought; this didn't look like a usual occurrence for him. He seemed relatively uninterested in how much he would get for his weapon, but only wanted to get out of the store. Bruno said nothing about him afterwards, only went to look at the gun when Harry had gone for coffee. It was smaller, and blackened in the barrel, meaning, Bruno figured, it had been fired. He picked it up. He liked the solid weight of it, the way it slipped right into the groove of his hand. Squeezing his fingers around the trigger gave him a rush of strength. "I could get used to this," he thought, then quickly put the gun back before Harry returned.

It was another month before Bruno saw the first man again. He came in with some men's jewelry: a watch and chain. "Johnny," Fienstein called him, and Bruno kept his eyes down. Later he looked closely at the watch and found two initials on the back. CS Who, he wondered, was CS? The next night, Bruno was at his old bar with his friends when he glanced at a newspaper on the bar. Sly Charlie Gunned Down, it said. Sly Charlie. Bruno, not one for reading, immediately opened up to the story. "Business mogul Charlie Sirano was gunned down outside his apartment last night. Nicknamed Sly Charlie for his elusive lifestyle, the gangster controlled a network of underground crime in downtown Manhattan. Police are looking for his assassin, but with suspects so many, fear his death may be just another in a chain of ruthless murders."

Bruno felt his face flush hot. Charlie Sirano. CS. He was sure this Johnny was involved, probably the assassin himself. In a reverie, Bruno dreamed of walking into the police and receiving a hero's reward for turning in a major criminal. His name would be in all the papers. Everyone would talk about him. Probably he'd be given a reward. Then he realized he didn't know Johnny's full name. And the best way to cash in on his discovery would be to go to Johnny himself. All he had to do was tell him what he knew, and how much it would take to keep him quiet. The man would be so scared, Bruno laughed, he'd do anything he asked.

As Bruno waited for Johnny to come back to the pawnshop, however, he couldn't stop himself from talking. At first he told only a few friends of his plan. In a few days he had told a whole barroom, and they had told their friends. Even Jack Haggerty told him "Bruno, don't you think you should keep this quiet?"

But Bruno just slapped him on the back. "It'll just make him more scared," he said. "He'll be shaking by the time he sees me."

Johnny wasn't shaking though. Johnny was very calm. He walked into the store one afternoon, looked at Fienstein and said, "Where's the boy?"

"In the yard," Harry said.

"Good."

Johnny walked straight out back, found Bruno sitting in a chair smoking and kicked the chair straight over. Bruno, landing on his back with his legs in the air, called out "What – "

"What, what what," Johnny repeated, standing above him and taking out a gun, pointing it at him.

Bruno scrambled out of the chair, but Johnny stepped forward and kicked him in the behind, then the chest.

"You little bastard. What have you been saying about me?" he asked.

Bruno stammered, flat on his back. "You've got it all wrong," he said.

"Is that right?" Johnny said, then kicked him in the head. "Is that right?" then kicked him again. Bruno's face was bleeding and he had tears in his eyes.

"What a child you are," Johnny said, and again raised his gun. "Too stupid and pathetic to kill really. The kind who needs a long life to suffer in." He laughed again, walked over to Bruno, took his head in his hand and pressed it back into the ground. He lifted it, and slammed it back, once, twice, three times, each harder than the last. "It hurts me to kill such a stupid boy," Johnny said. "It really does. It's too much trouble for me, the body and all. I want you out of this town, out of this city. If you're here tomorrow though I'll have to kill you. Understand?"

Bruno nodded, unable to see for blood and tears and his throbbing head. Johnny gave Bruno another violent kick to the stomach. "Stupid stupid stupid," he said and walked out.

Bruno was lucky that Fienstein was there. His family would not tolerate any more violence. Fienstein, however, had seen the only good side Bruno had ever presented to anyone and so bandaged him up and fixed his wounds and told him he'd heard what Johnny said. Bruno had to leave immediately. "Do you have family, friends, anywhere else?"

"No," Bruno mumbled.

"None?"

"No."

"Then you can join the army. The recruiting station is downtown. You look bad, but they've seen worse."

Bruno shuddered, his whole body crying out. "I'm not running away," he almost screamed. "I'm going to kill that bastard first."

"You'll be dead first."

"Just give me a gun. You'll see."

Fienstein, watching him, felt the same disbelief Bruno's family had known. Such obstinacy could only lead to a violent end. Still, suffering so much from his wounds, Bruno at least wanted to stop the pain. So he let Fienstein take him down to the recruiting station. The officer was not impressed at his condition, but Fienstein explained that Bruno was the victim of a neighborhood gang that tormented good working boys like Bruno. As Bruno was too dizzy and sick to speak, he was silent long enough for Fienstein to have him conscripted. Officially known from then on as Jerry Manzino, Bruno let an officer lead him away and onto a bus that left that very evening for training camp.

Three weeks later Rosa and Giovanni received a postcard from a private Manzino and Bruno missed the wedding of his older brother Bennie – the first Manzino wedding in the new world, to the healthy young Sara Callo, already three months with child.

CHAPTER
NINETEEN

Between the Commodore and Rita, Gino didn't have much time for the old neighborhood. But he was also anxious to move up in the world and when Uncle Cesare offered him odd jobs, Gino was glad for the chance to see his uncle's operations.

With his moving and storage business thriving, Cesare had bought the apartment building he and his wife lived in on 104th Street. Everyone knew that Cesare's business dealings were not always straightforward. Like Enzio years before, he hired blacks whom he paid little and gave backbreaking work. He had increased his wealth by discriminately stealing from the loads of goods he was hired to move and store. If not well-liked in the neighborhood, Cesare was still a man of respect, one with an eye for life's finer things, including the ladies.

In his free time Gino began working directly with Cesare. Since the time he had asked Giovanni if he could adopt Gino, Cesare had still felt paternal towards his nephew. This did not, however, mean that he was going to give away his money. Even Gino had to press him for his pay, which Cesare sometimes withheld completely.

One Saturday morning, Cesare told Gino that he needed him to drive to New Jersey for the day. Two of his cousins owned a convenience store there and had cheated Cesare out of money. On the drive out, Cesare was detached and quiet. When Gino swung in front of the store, Cesare nodded, indicating that Gino should wait in the car. Gino watched him walk swiftly into the store, then, just a minute later, heard four shots ring out in quick succession. When Cesare emerged from the store just a few minutes later, he was closing his jacket with hand and pulling his hat down with another. "Let's move," he said to Gino as he got in.

On the long drive home, neither mentioned the gunshots. Then Gino asked if Cesare would pay him money he owed him. Cesare was notorious for his tight fist with cash. "You are too impatient," Cesare said, looking out the window. "You must not be so greedy in asking for things." Outside, Manhattan glowed in the late afternoon light and Gino took a deep breath, increasingly annoyed at the way his uncle expected him to work for nothing. "One day," Cesare said, "everything I have will be yours."

Gino knew that Cesare wouldn't say this lightly. Yet Cesare didn't seem bothered by the fact that people lived on money. So he wasn't about to leave his job at the Commodore. Besides, he had only recently left home, and liked the freedom of his own work and his own life. He still gave a good portion of his earnings to Rosa.

It made Gino uneasy that Giovanni didn't like him doing even small jobs for Cesare. He had also noticed that the friendship between La Guardia and Cesare had suddenly ended. Though Gino did not know the cause, he did notice that neither man spoke of the other to him. In 1921, when La Guardia began his campaign for mayor, Gino served as an organizer of the neighborhood vote. Not being registered to vote, he felt the need to compensate by enlisting dozens of others. One night, however, when Gino was working at the local polling house La Guardia came in to see him. "Gino," he said, "let's go outside for a moment."

By his even occasional association with his uncle, Gino had effectively crossed the line into actual crime. La Guardia believed strongly in his role as a reformer, in cutting away all the webs of corruption smothering his people. Once it was clear that Cesare and hence Gino had chosen to live outside the law, however, La Guardia had to severe their relationship, however regretfully.

"Gino," he said. "I have always told you that you will do well. But I had hoped you would do so within my domain. I will no longer lecture you on how to live, and who to work for. It is for you to choose. But I am dedicated to the unity of this city, and to the laws that govern it. I had hoped that perhaps you would be a part of it. Now that you have chosen otherwise, however, I must tell you that I cannot continue to see you, just as I see no one else who lives outside the laws I respect."

La Guardia spoke so sadly that Gino experienced his conscience stirring again. He had never believed that the law contained anything he could not live without, yet now was suffering his first real consequence. It was his final parting from his prominent man, and though he did not protest – only shook La Guardia's hand and said he understood – Gino felt that he had alienated himself, perhaps forever, from a certain form of human decency.

That night Gino left the polling station early. Rita was at work, and he did not feel like being alone. Instead, he decided to visit his sister Tess, now nineteen and still living at home. Tess had stayed in school until she was sixteen. Whereas in Sicily she might have received only the barest of elementary schooling – which for girls was often reduced to instruction in sewing, in America she had been received as much education as Rosa with her governess; as a result she had a real sense of belonging in the new world. At seventeen, once her long bout of lovesickness over Carlo had passed, Tess became a remarkably self-possessed young woman; at 19 she had a confidence that gave her a unique sense of style. As Gino turned down 112th Street, he smiled thinking about the flamboyant large hats Tess had recently added to her wardrobe.

When she first left school, Tess had sought work for several months, causing some of the neighborhood women, including Gracia, to grumble that schooling obviously served no purpose at all. Then, Tess surprised everyone by getting a position as a sales clerk at the city's largest department store, Macy's on West 34th Street. As the Commodore and Macy's were not too far apart, Tess and Gino occasionally met after work: especially when Gino needed help buying a small present or a pair of shoes.

As it was not late in the evening, Tess and Gino had a last cup of coffee together in the kitchen. Tess, who had always adored her eldest brother, put Gino at ease. She never asked more of him than his company and the two were happy just to sit or walk together without speaking at all. Seeing that Gino was worried, Tess did, however, ask him what was wrong this evening. When he shrugged it off, however, she did not press, but simply kept him company as he struggled with the feelings La Guardia had aroused in him. Ultimately, sitting there in the kitchen with Tess, Gino decided to continue his life in the same vein, refusing to work with Cesare until he was paid like a real man.

CHAPTER
TWENTY

WHEN FILOMINA LAROCCA first ran into Gino Manzino, it was early afternoon and she was walking home from work with her friend, Carmela Colleti, listening to her talk on and on about her latest crush. As they turned a corner, she halted abruptly. A young man was blocking her path, staring at her with such intensity he completely unnerved her.

"Excuse me," she said, as she recovered her composure and walked around him, hoping that he hadn't seen her blush.

Gino simply stared after her; she was walking so fast, Carmela had to race to catch up with her. Finally, his friend Paulie Vitelli had to push him from behind to get him jumpstarted again.

"Hey Gino!" Paulie said. "What the hell's the matter with you?"

Gino didn't answer. He was ruminating over the color of her eyes – an astonishing shade of blue, a rare find among Italian women. It was a color from another world, he thought, one that he associated with Katy's eyes from the hospital, and a face that still haunted him.

"Who is she?" he asked.

Paulie just shook his head and laughed. "Man, you're incapable of seeing a girl and not wanting her. Why don't you give it a rest? I don't care how big her chest is, she's just a kid. Besides, she's no bimbo. Her two brothers are in my school and her family just moved here from Mott Street a few months ago."

"Paulie, I'm going to marry that girl someday," Gino said, matter-of-factly.

"Just like that, huh?" said Paulie.

"I mean it Paulie. What's her name?"

"Sure, don't rush it. First find out her name, then marry her. Jesus Christ, Gino."

"Come on," he insisted. "What's her name?"

"Filomina LaRocca. But I'm really beginning to think you're crazy. Beyond the fact that you never saw her before, have you forgotten about Rita?"

As a matter of fact, Gino had forgotten. In a single glance, Filomina had shattered his complacency, her one glance suggesting that love could offer more than he had imagined. It was days before he could bring his inner turmoil under control. Rita realized there had been a change in Gino, however much he tried to hide it. As chance and fate would have it though, it would not be long before another force changed both of their lives forever.

In the next months the memory of Filomina drifted before Gino like a leaf floating gently toward some distant forest floor. At times, Gino would wonder how much of the image he held of her was memory and how much was fantasy. But however real or imaginary her beauty had been, he was never able to completely let go of the feelings she had aroused in him. Some mornings he woke thinking of her so hard he would literally think himself hard. Awakening beside him, Rita would assume that his obvious longing was for her, and was only too happy to accept his morning gift fully. As his dream of Filomina blended into the body of the women beneath him, he felt a vague whisper of guilt, as if he were being unfaithful to one of them somehow. Or perhaps to both. It wasn't that Gino was using Rita, at least not in any conscious sense. It was just that, if there were one area that revealed how much more mature she was in her understanding of life, it was in their sense of time. Gino was very happy with Rita in the present they shared so easily. Like anyone who was still basically a child, he never really developed any sense of the future. He had no interest in the past — though he had not yet learned that time could not be so easily wished away. If he and Rita were happy now, why need anyone worry about what might come? Only she knew the one certain thing that lay ahead. Only she felt the distant chill.

It was not long before this future arrived, in a way Gino never expected. It was a humid summer evening. The sky was filled with the distant rumblings of a storm that would wash the city clean, and Gino was approached by Gussie Allesano, a major force in the streets for as long as Gino could remember. What marked Allesano was that he managed to maintain his position of strength with remarkably quiet dignity.

Gino was sitting with several young men on the weather-worn bleachers in one of Central Park's many meadows, watching a fairly violent baseball game between two teams of younger neighborhood boys. They were all drinking beer although Jimmy from the Commodore, the one Irishman among them, insisted that since it was Rheingold it wasn't really beer.

"Only Jews and Italians could think this was beer," Jimmy grumbled, mixing Guinness stout and Schaeffer in a large cardboard cup to make his own black-and-tans.

Gino and the others weren't particularly concerned with the finer points of beer. The Rheingold was doing exactly what they intended it to — easing the thirst the balmy evening had given and keeping them more or less drunk. They didn't have enough energy for much else, although they did manage to cheer and boo both teams on the field now and then. Gino had just about decided to head downtown to see Rita, when he saw two large men in dark suits approaching the bleachers with stony expressions. Gino's eyesight was a little blurry from the beer and the heat, but he recognized the two immediately. They were Gussie Allesano's bodyguards.

Some twenty years older than Gino, Allesano was a small and delicate man, the richest of the local bosses and rumored to be a descendant of Italian nobility. His clothing was impeccable but understated, almost British in style, and the perfect complement to his fair skin, green eyes, and thick head of prematurely whitened hair. Though he had none of the flamboyance common among men of his position, onlookers invariably described him as a "dapper little man," who could be mistaken for a banker, which was not far from the truth. While many men rose to power through muscle and guns, Allesano's strength lay in the manipulation of money. In his own quiet way, he was a genius at investing capital, whatever its source, and making it blossom. He handled property acquisitions, loans, stock investments, and a dozen other spheres of activity with such brilliance that he had earned the respect of most people in the neighborhood. Flanked by his enormous bodyguards, he smiled shyly at those he passed, as though embarrassed by the monsters at his side. Still, no one ever doubted the iron will within. A measure of the amount of respect he commanded was the extent to which he was feared.

Gino watched the two men with curiosity, even enthusiasm, until he realized they were not just approaching the bleachers; they were approaching him. The awareness stripped him instantly of his inebriation. Glancing nervously toward the field once more, he wondered if he'd been inadvertently booing one of Allesano's relatives. But before he could decide on a likely candidate, one of the men called out to him.

"Gino Manzino," he said, in a strangely high-pitched voice. "Mr. Allesano would like to talk to you."

All eyes in the bleachers turned toward Gino with the kind of look you'd give a man who was falling off a cliff. They remained locked in that position during the long moments it took for Gino to climb down from the bleachers and walk with the two men across the meadow to the gravel parking lot where a black limousine was waiting, its door open. Even the players on the field stopped their game to watch him move away through the dusk.

Gino was directed into the back seat, still too numbed by the suddenness of it to even imagine how he might defend himself. Then the door closed behind him and he found himself sitting alone with Gussie Allesano. The scent of Allesano's subtle cologne mingled with the rich smell of the leather interior, which made

Gino feel particularly loathsome; he knew he smelled of sweat and beer. Nonetheless, Allesano extended his hand and gave him a characteristically shy smile.

"Mr. Manzino," he said, "I've been looking forward to this conversation for some time. It concerns Rita Stewart."

If this unexpected summoning had shocked Gino, the mention of Rita's name completely undid him. It was several minutes before he understood Allesano's explanation. The little man spoke in soft, measured tones with the same courteous manner he might use when offering someone investment advice. Only the inner light dancing in his eyes hinted that he was actually revealing his innermost heart to a perfect stranger.

Allesano had known Rita for many years. He had been present for almost every performance she had given, beginning with her first anonymous work in the chorus of a relatively modest nightclub up to her current success as a featured dancer in one of the more extravagant revues now making its rounds through some of the larger clubs in Manhattan. He praised her grace and her beauty, describing his devotion like some courtier from another century giving homage to a princess. Gino was fascinated and remembered how often Rita had spoken of what the dancers referred to as "stage-door johnnies." In addition to all the crude characters who called out obscenities as they waved hundred-dollar bills at the chorus line, there were always a few gentlemen who sent bouquets of roses and bottles of champagne to their rooms, accompanied by polite requests for the privilege of buying them dinner. Most of these men were older, more reserved, and far wealthier than the usual run of admirers. A dancer's company for dinner was all they expected in exchange for their generous gifts. Gino could easily imagine Gussie Allesano smiling quietly in the darkened nightclub as Rita enchanted him with her every gesture and movement.

Allesano paused to look with sudden intensity into Gino's eyes, studying him as if he was trying to measure Gino's character before taking some irrevocable step.

"Mr. Manzino," Allesano said softly. "Perhaps I should simply tell you my problem. I love and respect Miss Stewart more than any woman I know and wish to offer her everything I possess if she would consent to marry me. She is aware of my intentions, but her heart, it would seem, is not free. I would like you to stop seeing her. After all, you have not married her."

Gino didn't know how to respond. He felt as if he was being challenged about the sincerity and purity of his intentions by some powerful protector of womanhood. For a moment, he felt the hair rise on the back of his neck as he imagined this courteous, old-world man calmly removing a rival by the most expedient means. A small bullet, perhaps. Seeing the thought flicker across Gino's face, Allesano smiled and rested a reassuring hand on Gino's shoulder.

"Don't misunderstand, Mr. Manzino. I have no wish to hurt you. Only to fulfill certain desires of my own."

Everything the man said overwhelmed Gino still further, but now he was also feeling guilty. Here was a man willing to give Rita a full and happy life while Gino went along from day to day offering her nothing for the future. In his heart, Gino knew he did not wish to marry Rita. Compared to the man beside him, he felt incredibly selfish and inadequate. The scope of Allesano's passion was astonishing; Gino's moments of affection and desire seemed feeble in contrast.

"Of course, you don't have to answer me now," Allesano said, sensing Gino's turmoil.

With that, he nodded his head, seeming to signal that their conversation was over. Gino got out of the car, passed by the bleachers to assure his friends he was safe, and then walked home slowly in the fading light.

For a day Gino said nothing to Rita, only contemplated the task before him. Should he tell her the truth about Allesano, or should he simply tell her he wanted to move out. His trust and affection for Rita won out and in the end he told her everything Allesano had said. He admitted that he did not feel ready for marriage, and was not sure he would ever be. Rita did not press him, but told him that Allesano had told her of his hopes also and that she had been considering his proposal.

"So you would marry him," Gino said. Rita, who would love Gino more than Allesano in many ways, yet knew how to choose wisely for herself.

"Not without missing you," she said.

A week later the two had a sad parting but consoled each other with their still great affection. Gino moved into a new apartment, also on 104th Street, and it was only a month before Rita moved out, officially betrothed to Allesano.

For a while after Rita, Gino became irresponsibly involved with a number of women again. So irresponsibly in fact that Filomina herself became witness to one spectacle his excesses had created. Filomina never knew the connection to the beautiful young man she had seen on the street a year ago, but as she was walking one evening from the job she had just begun at a factory, she saw a huge crowd gathered at the end of her street. Since many of the onlookers were laughing and cheering she assumed it wasn't a truly violent scene, so approached the crowd curiously. As soon as she was close enough to see, she understood the festivity. A terrible fight was underway. But since it was between two young neighborhood girls, there was a circus atmosphere in spite of the real blood flowing.

As the two young women rolled on the sidewalk, fingers locked in one another's hair, the men who watched were the most enthusiastic, probably because both of the girls were pretty and their struggle had brought their dresses high above their hips. But Filomina could see their badly scratched faces, and their looks of desperation. When an older woman succeeded in wrenching the two apart and the crowd began to disperse, Filomina slipped into her old preoccupation with life's inequities. Men fought in the streets, however senselessly, and were admired for their courage. Women fought and were disgraced and ridiculed. Just then, she heard one of the young men whisper to another, "It's Gino Manzino again, they were fighting over him."

The name meant nothing to Filomina, but she was immediately fascinated at the idea that a boy could be so desirable that two lovely girls would end up trying to kill each other in sight of the world. What could he be like? She was much too curious about the phantom lover who had caused all this than to worry much about its philosophical aspects.

The name stayed with her though, as had the face of the man she had seen on the street, and within a few months the two were brought together in a moment that was to shake her more deeply than anything had before. Filomina and Carmela were sitting at a soda fountain not far from the textiles factory where they both worked. As usual, Carmela was talking about men, and Filomina was only half-listening. Although fairly pretty, Carmela had none of Filomina's special beauty and had learned early on that Filomina's loveliness could help her; Filomina drew attention wherever they went and since Filomina was never interested in any of the men who were bold enough to approach them, Carmela could offer herself as compensation. She had created an extremely active social life this way.

While Carmela whispered – she always whispered, as if the world was trying to overhear her most intimate secrets – Filomina's mind wandered away; the only chances she had for marriage seemed like deadly traps, and she wasn't willing to surrender herself so easily. Every one deserved a better life, she thought, than the one they sometimes settled for. But there were days when she deeply regretted this knowledge.

She looked up just as Carmela was saying, "Filomina, this is Gino Manzino." Carmela made it a point to know all the neighborhood business, so Gino had long been a part of her special landscape. It was surprising that Carmela hadn't mentioned Gino to Filomina before, but Filomina didn't concern herself with people out of her immediate realm, so Carmela had never had real reason to bring him up.

Filomina was immediately struck by his good looks and sweet deep smile. He was almost too perfect, she thought. What would it be like to be so perfect?

Gino himself was similarly overwhelmed. Filomina's hair, long and shimmering, contrasted sharply with the fairness of her skin. She seemed to be made of porcelain, a precious china doll that had

somehow come to life. She was barely five feet tall with feet as
beautifully shaped as a child's. Her waist, despite the fullness of
her breasts and hips, was so small, Gino imagined placing his hands
around it and his fingers touching. But the eyes superseded everything – a blue shadow cast by long, black lashes. After introducing
Gino, Carmela went on to introduce his friend, Paulie Vitelli. Paulie
was a dare devilish sort of boy Gino had met in the neighborhood.
Though not as agile as Gino, he too was popular with both women
and men, and so a natural friend for Gino. He was also, of course,
on Carmela's list, as she knew several girls he had courted.

Suddenly realizing they had to leave or they'd be late punching in, Filomina asked for the check. But Gino interrupted, saying, "We already paid for your sodas."

"You shouldn't pay for me, Gino," Filomina said, blushing a
little at how easily his name rolled off her tongue. "I don't know
you."

"You will," Gino answered, solemnly.

After a garbled "thank you," Filomina grabbed Carmela's arm,
and they hurried away.

One month later, Filomina rounded a corner on her way home
from work, and Gino fell into step beside her. Since then, Filomina
had found out a thing or two about him – mostly from Carmela –
and had decided to be careful. She wasn't about to fall into her first
suitor's arms, no matter how charming and good looking he was.
Still she hadn't been able to shake him from her thoughts. And
even now he was disarming, a little nervous for some reason, but
still wonderful, she thought – tall, slim, and incredibly clean, with
thick dark curls and green eyes.

"Remember me?" he asked, "from the soda parlor?"

Each night for the past twenty-nine days, she had seen his face
every time she closed her eyes. Even passing through the streets,
she had looked for him, always expecting him to appear at her
side, the way he just did. Even so, with all of her tension locked
behind cold blue eyes, she only answered,

"You're Carmela and Paulie's friend."

Her attempt at a calm response was so successful that Gino

momentarily lost his step. He was used to a much heartier response from the women he knew, but he knew instinctively there was more at stake this time – some special link existed between them, and he felt terribly confused when she spoke so stiffly. And yet, responding in such a strange way was oddly pleasing; it verified that she was different from the other girls he knew.

"May I walk with you a ways?" he asked.

She shrugged, without smiling, as if to imply that the streets were public thoroughfares, and she had no way of stopping him. Neither of them said another word until they reached her apartment building where she paused briefly before continuing up the stairs.

"Wait!" Gino called, a little more loudly than he intended. A few people passing by turned to stare at him, so he waited until they moved on.

"Look," he finally said, "I'd like to be able to take you out some night. For dinner, perhaps, or to dance, or . . . ."

"I'm sorry," she said, "but I have a beau, and he wouldn't like me seeing someone else." She had conjured up this imaginary suitor before, to discourage many boys who seemed reluctant to accept her simple "no" when they asked her for a date. But why, she thought, am I doing this now? How can I think of sending him away? She was as frightened as she was drawn to him, and some self-protective impulse told her to hold on to some distance, knowing full well that any obstacle between them, real or imagined, would one day fall. Today, however, she practically ran upstairs. But the next afternoon, he waited for her again, as he did every evening for the next two weeks.

On hearing that Filomina had a beau, Gino was for a brief while crushed. It didn't surprise him, of course; she was so beautiful. But who was he? Whenever possible, Gino tried to find out about him. But as the days passed and he heard no specifics he decided that if he did exist he couldn't have been that special; if he were she would have been proud to name him. So he gradually put the "suitor" out of his mind, and decided instead to show how earnest his intentions were.

Filomina meanwhile hid behind a calm reserve, politely declining his many invitations. She tried to account for Gino's effect on her, why she was so afraid of showing him any vulnerability, and on the face of things, there were a number of "explanations." He was Sicilian, for one thing, and her father had warned her about Sicilian boys – how they abused and abandoned women. On those occasions when they did marry, he'd say, they treated their wives with even greater cruelty than they had their girlfriends. There were exceptions, of course, but Gino's reputation hardly suggested that he would be one of them. None of the other boys in the neighborhood had earned such notoriety as a lover. Gino always had a dapper appearance and spent money so freely on women, few doubted he'd found shortcuts to making it, especially since the organized network of criminal activity was increasing its power in the neighborhood every day. In addition, though her father never mentioned it, the fact was understood – Gino's skin was conspicuously dark.

But even as she noted these objections, Filomina realized what truly frightened her was the inescapable feeling that Gino would take absolute control of her life. She wanted him, but she couldn't give up her future just yet. Still, she couldn't help herself – every time they walked through the streets in near-silence, she became more and more lost in anticipation of his kiss, his touch, no matter how much her mind was reprimanding her desire.

For his part, Gino was becoming increasingly more confused. Attired in his Commodore uniform, managing to sneak in his visit with Filomina before rushing to work himself, he felt like Filomina's escort. Frustrated and humiliated by his inability to break through her reserve, Gino vowed over and over that he would not return for yet another awkward meeting. But when the final whistle blew, he found himself on the same street corner, nervously smoking a cigarette, waiting for his first glimpse of her amidst the crowd of lesser faces. His sense of foolishness robbed him of his gift for persuasive talk. He walked swiftly, to get the ordeal over with, and then experienced a small panic when his few moments with her had ended once more. At night, unable to sleep, he examined the time they had spent together, imagining what it would be like to kiss her perfect mouth, to touch and enter her perfect body, to taste her porcelain skin. Filomina, on the other hand, never suspected his turmoil. All she saw was a tall young man consumed with a brooding intensity. When he crossed the street, his body held at a kind of attention, she was thrilled by the thought of his old world courtliness.

The fact was, Gino had lived for so long with the common conviction that there were two separate races of women – the ones who formed the foundations of families, and the ones who aroused men's desires – that his feelings for Filomina took away his sense of balance in the universe. When he walked with her through the dirty streets, her innocence and childlike grace told him that this was a life he should protect. He worried constantly about something happening to her, becoming inwardly enraged each time a man glanced her way, living in fear that some womanizer might one day win her trust. It never occurred to him that the most dangerous womanizer on the streets had already come to her side.

By the second week of their evening walks, he was wracked with guilt for wanting someone so pure, yet terrified of losing her. Stung by her persistent refusal to go out with him, he would just say goodbye, bow slightly, and leave. Finally, one night, in a moment of desperation, Gino turned back as she was climbing up the steps.

"Filomina," he called, "Have you ever been to the Cloisters?"

"No," Filomina said.

"It's a very special place. I'd like to take you there. Would you come with me on Sunday?"

She paused for a moment. "I'll have to bring my sister, Sonia. Is that all right?"

Smiling for what seemed like the first time in weeks, Gino said, "Sure, that's fine." Filomina smiled back, waved, and then went into the building. Gino stood on the street, whistling softly, almost dancing. Happiness, he thought, was largely a matter of timing. Wait until she saw his car. He laughed as he remembered the look in Ciro Salvemini's eyes the first time he had seen the magnificent machine.

GINO'S NEIGHBORHOOD, LIKE all urban neighborhoods, had its share of elderly people who seemed to pass their entire lives in upstairs windows, staring out at the streets below with quiet concentration, as though they were afraid it would all disappear if they glanced away for a moment. For many of them, this window vista was all they had seen of America.

Ciro Salvemini was one of these ancient watchers. His face and hands were so wrinkled, his body so stooped and shrunken that no one, perhaps not even his own family, could accurately assess his true age – though most people thought he was at least a hundred. He'd come over from Sicily with his two sons and their wives, a silent addendum to a bustling family, and seemed content to sit at his window, ignoring the greetings of most courteous passersby. Although he watched the activity below indiscriminately – children running at their games, men and women coming and going in all seasons – it was the sight of automobiles he waited for, secretly delighting in how they had replaced the old horse-drawn wagons. Only his daughter-in-law who brought him coffee now and then knew of his obsession. "I saw two Chryslers today – two new ones," he'd say. Or, "A real Daimler passed by. Imagine that!" The harried young woman, who knew nothing of automobiles, only muttered before returning to her household duties.

Ciro wasn't the only man obsessed with automobiles. For years, cars had been the toys of the rich, but Ford's model T and its imitators had brought the automobile within reach of the middle classes, and then within the range of even lower echelons as the battered early models were traded in for new editions or simply abandoned on roadsides. Despite Ford's success, however, Americans were still surprisingly behind European manufacturers in designing cars that truly blended beauty and function. Hundreds of automobile companies sprang into existence and then just as quickly dissolved, often before the first car ever reached the highway; others produced cars that fell apart on the first rough road.

Manufacturers like Buick, Chrysler, and Packard were beginning to learn from their mistakes and slowly duplicating Ford's triumph, but the vast stretches of unpaved roadways spanning the continent seemed to discourage a national commitment to this new industry. For the moment, all the flash and excitement of the automotive age could be found only in the cars of Great Britain, France and, especially, Italy. The Americans of the prairies had to be content with utilitarian designs – boxes on wheels that had all the imagination of farm machinery – while New York's city streets were filled with Marchands, Renaults, Rolls-Royces, and Isotta Fraschinis. But no automobile was more impressive in appearance and performance than the 1908 Lancia "51", and no one was more aware of this than Ciro Salvemini.

In the small village in Sicily where Ciro had worked as a machinist repairing bicycles and farming implements, an automobile was a great rarity, but one summer afternoon, a local landowner had driven the only automobile within a fifty mile radius into the village square, only to have it sputter noisily to a stop, blocking all the horses and oxcarts. Ciro was summoned to push the contraption out of way and "do something with it," although he didn't have the slightest idea as to what that something might be. Still, he was mesmerized by the device and spent hours tinkering with it, studying the intricacies of the temperamental motor, until he actually fixed it. For months his dreams were filled with images of carburetor systems, gear mechanisms, and a wide variety of pistons and cylinders. He sought out every known automobile in that part of Sicily and talked endlessly to anyone who ever had contact with one. It was not surprising, then, that he went into near-ecstasy when he looked down from his window and saw the Manzino boy and one of his friends pushing a genuine Lancia into the alleyway separating two of the apartment houses across the street. He was so excited that he nearly toppled out of the second story window; instead, he ran out of the apartment. His confused daughter-in-law came running after him, screaming in panic, convinced that only a natural disaster could have inspired the arthritic old man to leap up from his perch and fly from the room.

Ciro dashed across the street, leaving his flustered daughter-in-law in the dust, and shouted at Gino to wait. Shocked to see the familiar window-inhabitant actually moving, let alone calling his name, Gino and Paulie watched Ciro, the usually silent stick figure, become a wildly animated old man showering the car with praise and asking a torrent of questions about where they had found it.

Gino was sure that finding the Lancia had been fate. He'd been racked with indecision ever since he'd decided to buy a new car. He wanted something impressive and had narrowed his choices to one of the American cars that had enough style and polish to satisfy his adventurous spirit without exhausting his available funds. But when he went back to the garage on upper Broadway for a second look at a year-old Chrysler, he spotted the Lancia huddled beneath a burlap blanket.

Gino loved everything about the car – its lacquered surface, the richness of the wood and leather interior, the brass lanterns and trim. "This car," the owner had intoned, "is not simply a great car. It is the pride of Italy, the one machine that has won respect for Italians throughout Europe." Gino had never thought consciously of nationalistic pride, but it suddenly seemed essential to drive an automobile created only by the mind and hands of fellow Italians. A short while later, however, when Paulie was cursing him for buying an undriveable vehicle, he began to wonder if his romantic imagination hadn't gotten the better of him this time.

Ciro practically begged Gino for the chance to help, confident that he could find a way to make it perfect. The needed parts could be found, if you knew who to ask, and what couldn't be found could be invented, fashioned from parts of other cars. For the next few weeks, with Gino acting as his bewildered assistant, Ciro poured his soul and every waking moment into the car, often thanking Gino for making him feel alive again.

The day it was completed, Gino started the engine for its first official journey, and a cheer went up from the neighbors who had assembled for the ceremony. Every surface gleamed – even Gino in the new suit he had bought for the occasion. Sitting happily at the wheel, listening to the deep, resonant hum of the powerful engine, he looked around for Ciro, and saw the old man standing a few feet away with tears in his eyes. It took a few minutes for Gino, touched by the old man's emotion, to persuade him to get in the car, the only passenger in the Lancia's maiden voyage.

FILOMINA COULD NEVER tell her Mamma and Pappa that she was riding with Gino on Sunday, but Sonia was more than happy to invent a plausible story about an outing with some of her friends. She never had any conspiracies of her own and enjoyed creating one with her younger sister.

Filomina loved it all – the car, the drive to the Cloisters, everything about their afternoon together. Even the presence of Sonia in the rumble seat became a part of the magic. She was their chaperone, and the day turned into one of those courting scenes from the old country that Mamma would describe. The medieval church and the riders on horseback through the Cloisters' unspoiled parkland only reinforced the notion of having slipped backward in time, as did Gino's white suit and his special charm.

Gino was also struck by their escape into another realm. Filomina stirred feelings in him that melted away the concerns of the contemporary world. She didn't seem to belong in the dirt and noise of the city. Gazing across the meadows as he sat on a stone wall, Gino found himself thinking about an his father's story about a group of silver dancers on a hillside.

Neither Gino nor Filomina felt any of their usual awkwardness with each other. They were entirely natural, talking as quietly and openly as children. By the time they returned to the city and Gino had dropped Filomina and Sonia at the corner, Gino and Filomina were breathlessly aware of their love. Sonia, of course, could see it as well, and whispered to her sister that she would do whatever she could to help them be together.

Over the next few months, the two met whenever they could. Filomina's certainty that her family would prohibit and perhaps prevent their relationship was not imagined. Her Pappa had little else in his life but his prejudices and held onto them tighter each day. He spent his nights with jugs of homemade wine, polishing his hatreds the way someone would scrub the old blade of a knife.

Gino and Filomina worked hard at submitting to this need for secrecy, Sonia leaving with Filomina in the evenings and meeting up with her an hour or two later so that their parents would think they'd been together all night. Sonia thought it was all very romantic, a Romeo and Juliet story right in her own family. Gino and Filomina, however, had little interest in living out someone else's drama. Their need to be together was real, a desire that should not be subjected to such absurd restrictions, and as their passion deepened, their patience eroded. And yet, Gino had not made love to Filomina. He had kissed her, held her, and felt her tremble in his arms, but he refused to let them surrender. He loved her and wanted to protect her from all the dangers in the world, but he was afraid that if they made love, he would become one of them. There was only one way to solve the problem – marriage.

And so, one April morning, with as little fanfare as if it were just another country outing, they drove out of the neighborhood and were married in a judge's chambers in Tarrytown. By mid-afternoon, they were in Gino's apartment, grateful for the chilly rainfall that made them feel all the more sealed in shared warmth. Gino was more gentle than he had ever been in love, but Filomina responded to him so intensely that, by the end of their first hour together, they were locked in a frenzy that pushed them far beyond anything they had anticipated. But, even though they were married, Filomina was forced to return home that night and hide her copper wedding ring at the bottom of her dresser drawer.

The next two months passed with a terrible slowness. Gino and Filomina hid away in his apartment during all the moments they could steal, but the time in between was endless. When Filomina disentangled herself from Gino in the late afternoons and hurried from their warm nest, she was not just a lover returning to the life that always waited beyond the limits of passion. She was Gino's wife, and she was leaving what had become her new reality to participate in an empty charade. It was madness, and soon Gino's capacity to deal with it came to an end. He told her that he could almost accept the secrecy, perhaps even romanticize it for the time being, laughing at the way they had managed to create their own world right under everyone's noses. But what he couldn't accept was the way Filomina became overwhelmed with shame every time she thought about being discovered. She was still her parents' child and had yet to become the woman who had chosen to share her life with him. Their marriage was meaningless, he said, which cheapened everything that happened between them.

Listening to him, Filomina felt as if everything she loved were at risk. She knew Gino was right, but she didn't have the courage to tell her Mamma and Pappa what she had done. She couldn't bear to see the disappointment and hurt in their eyes. Gino didn't seem to understand what a lifetime of submission to the will of others could do. His experience had been so different. Rosa would forgive him anything. Her love was unconditional; it had no limits. And although Giovanni was aloof, even disapproving, at least he had let his son choose his own path.

Finally one morning, after still another sleepless night, Filomina was heading toward the door when, to her own disbelief, she turned to her mother and said, "Mamma, I'm leaving now. And I won't be coming home tonight. Or any night."

Her words were so unexpected, so beyond sense, that Concetta, her mother, might have simply dismissed it as a joke if not for the tremor in her daughter's voice. She turned from the morning dishes and stared at Filomina.

"What do you mean you're not coming home?" she asked and then became eerily quiet. She had slipped into Italian, a sure sign of the gravity involved, her voice tightened more by panic than anger. Filomina was just about to step into the hall, tears already forming in her eyes, when she said flatly, "Mamma, I'm married."

Her mother staggered back, like someone who'd been struck, and screamed, "Have you gone crazy? Have you lost what little sense you had in the first place?"

Filomina ran down the stairs, stopping up her ears so that she wouldn't hear any more. When she got to the bottom floor, she banged on her sister Bella's door and shouted, "Hurry upstairs to

Mamma! I think she's sick!" Then she was gone, fleeing from the apartment and from the block, sobbing so deeply, she was close to hysteria. By the time she reached Gino, jolting him out of a sound sleep, the shock waves had begun to radiate throughout her body.

That night, Vincenzo, Filomina's father, came home from the subway tunnel construction site to take immediate command. His first step was to initiate a thorough interrogation. Each of the children was subjected to intensive private questioning as he hunted for a name or any clue that might determine the bridegroom's identity. Jennie, the youngest, told him that the day before she'd been looking for something to write with and found a ring in Filomina's dresser drawer. She had taken it to school and traded it for a brand new pencil.

The other LaRoccas responded with unmitigated fear to their father's furious cross-examination. In desperation, they gave him every name they could think of, implicating everyone from a senile parish priest to a seven-year-old boy on the next block who used to whistle at Filomina every morning as she hurried to work. ("It was a real dirty whistle," little Eugene insisted.) Vincenzo was beginning to despair of ever isolating a believable candidate when he looked at Sonia and saw her squirm.

As long as her sister's romance was a game, a schoolgirl's rebellion against restrictive parents, Sonia was the most loyal of allies. But once brought face-to-face with her father, in what he kept referring to as the family's hour of shame, she fell apart. He had barely finished phrasing the question when she blurted out "It must be that awful Gino Manzino" and then collapsed into tears and a high-pitched wail. Vincenzo sat back in his chair, wishing that he had Concetta's tendency to pass out when she became upset.

Filomina was the seventh of thirteen children, the middle of an extended family that included not only her six brothers and six sisters, but dozens of uncles, aunts, cousins, and in-laws who were scattered throughout the city. As word of Filomina's act of betrayal reached them, the entire clan converged on the LaRocca household like an army hastily recruited to defend the family against an unexpected enemy. In fact, people from all over the neighborhood debated the LaRocca crisis in social clubs, kitchens, saloons, and living rooms. Bets were even wagered as to whether Filomina was pregnant and whether Gino Manzino would leave town.

When the name, Gino Manzino, was put before the men of the family, some talked about his disreputable street dealings, his high-life at the swanky Commodore, and the dangerous crowd that hung around him and his Uncle Cesare Mulassano. Others told stories about his legendary sexual adventures. Everything Vincenzo heard only deepened his sense of outrage. "Sicilian scum," he muttered as more and more details were added to the portrait of this monster who had violated his daughter, "always the Sicilian scum."

Gino was relieved that at last the secret was revealed and assured Filomina that she was exaggerating the damage it had caused. Of course her Mamma would be upset, he said, and her Pappa would feel a certain amount of resentment, but soon everyone would accept the situation and they could begin a normal married life. Two days later, however, after Gino had left for work, Filomina opened the front door to find a tearful Sonia waiting outside. Numbed by all that had taken place, Filomina had almost persuaded herself that perhaps Gino was right, the worst was over. But one look at Sonia and she knew that it had only just begun.

Robbed of the will to resist any further, Filomina followed Sonia home, only half-hearing her sister's garbled account of all that had happened. Dazed and frightened, Filomina reached the apartment and entered a world that had been totally transformed since her departure. There were people everywhere, including many she didn't know, all of them staring at her as if she had walked in on her own funeral. And yet, despite the dozens of people crowded into the parlor, the air was suffused with absolute silence.

Filomina sat quietly in a corner, trying to make herself disappear, as her sisters told her why so many of the people were strangers. All of her family had been summoned, some from as far away as Brooklyn and the Bronx, and the Manzinos, too. The only person missing was Gino. Various people had been sent to find him, but Gino wasn't in any of his usual haunts. As it turned out, he had spent the afternoon in Brooklyn doing a favor for a friend and on his way home, he had decided it was time to speak to his parents, so he'd gone directly to his old neighborhood. But the streets were oddly deserted for so early in the evening, and no one was home at the Manzino apartment. Finally, Gino ran into a friend of his mother's on the street who told him where Rosa, Giovanni, and everyone in his family had gone.

Gino was overwhelmed by the sheer numbers of men, women and children filling every inch of space in the LaRocca household. The gathering had evolved into a ritual so formal that even Rosa was held back from her natural impulse to run forward and hug her son when he arrived. As all eyes turned toward Gino, people stepped back to open a narrow aisle through the crowd that led directly to Vincenzo LaRocca. Filomina was standing behind him, her lovely blue eyes looking like oceans about to overflow.

Everything depends on how I act at this moment, Gino thought. Like a bullfighter, form is all that matters. As he stepped forward he caught sight of his mother and father, standing together near Vincenzo. It seemed to Gino that they too were waiting for their son to prove his honor. He would not put them to shame, Gino told himself. Holding Vincenzo's gaze, he approached with a slow and easy grace. He dropped to one knee and humbly kissed the patriarch's hand. In a clear voice, he expressed his deep remorse for the terrible offense he had committed and begged for Vincenzo's forgiveness. Filomina watched her husband with fascination, awed by his courage and strength. Gino was being preposterous, of course, and everyone knew it, but they also respected his purpose. Tradition was the only means to conquer life's tragedies.

Gino's display of humility appeased Vincenzo's pride and diffused all the tension in the room. He was not overjoyed to have a Sicilian son-in-law. He would rather Filomina had stayed within her kind. But seeing as the two were actually already married, he might make some exceptions. Besides, Gino was obviously enamored of Filomina, would take care of her and protect her with the resolve he showed this very day. What was important now was to have the posting of the marriage banns as soon as possible so that Gino and Filomina could be married in the eyes of the Church. After all, what is the good of having nephews as priests if not at a time like this?

Through the intercession of Paolo, son of Vincenzo's brother Antonio, Filomina and Gino were married before God on May 29, 1930. As Gino left St. Cecilia's that morning, he couldn't help musing on the miracle of religion. In one hour of incense and murmuring Latin phrases, a family's moment of dark disgrace had magically become a joyous triumph.

Only Giovanni remained openly stern. Gino was right; Giovanni had only been truly concerned before Filomina's father; as with Carmine de Silvio who had hit Gino when Gino was a boy, it was Giovanni's honor that was, for him, at stake. Giovanni had been proud that Gino had managed to right what the entire neighborhood would rightfully construe as a wrong – even a wrong for love. But he secretly resented Gino's freedom, that he had once again gone his own way – never thinking to ask his father's opinion. Though Giovanni congratulated Gino on his beautiful wife, once again he felt a stranger to his oldest son's life, the very son he had crossed the ocean to give a new life.

Gino was too overjoyed at his happy bride to notice his father's secret thoughts. If he could have told his parents of Filomina he would have – but he was protecting her, and as he watched her beaming face, Gino knew that was the most important thing to him now.

The priest was given a bottle of wine for payment, and the same crowd who'd stood in angry vigil just days before, now returned to the LaRocca home for a happy reception. A procession of relatives and friends filed past the couple, presenting envelopes called *aboosta*. Gracia was there, now almost sixty and slowed to a dawdle under her great weight. The grocers, the Zambolis, were there, and Jimmy Sullivan and Paulie Vitelli and Carmela. Bennie and Sara were there with their four children, and Tess who stood guard over Filomina's delicate train. Everyone wanted to contribute to their new start in life and back in their own apartment,

Gino and Filomina counted the legacy – fifty dollars. As Gino drew Filomina to him in their now-sanctified bed, he promised her that this was only the beginning of having everything she would ever want. A few months after their wedding, however, their dreams were already slipping away as the dreary pattern of survival hardened against their brightly imagined future.

CHAPTER
TWENTY-ONE

EVENTUALLY, A GENUINE, if hesitant, friendship evolved between the Manzinos and the LaRoccas. Rosa welcomed the new influx of in-laws, feeling they gave her the extended family she had left behind. The women from each clan shared recipes, gossip, and afternoon coffee. Though Giovanni tended to keep his distance, Vincenzo was anxious to justify his acceptance of his daughter's marriage in the eyes of the community and make it appear that he had chosen the situation, instead of being forced into it, so he would praise the Manzinos, particularly Gino, at every opportunity.

In their first months together, Gino was at the Commodore and Filomina had her factory job. The long-sought blossoming of their passion was so powerful that their doubts about the future seemed insignificant, as harmless as an old superstition that had no place in this country. But within a few months, Filomina was pregnant, and the timing couldn't have been worse. Gino's job had weathered the worst of the depression, but ironically, it was a jealous manager, coveting Gino's superior tips, who fired him. Since pregnant women were prohibited from the work bench, Filomina's meager contribution to their income also ended. Soon their tiny cash reserve was exhausted, and they were forced to abandon Gino's furnished apartment.

With little more than the clothes on their backs, they appeared at Bennie's doorway, where he and Sara now lived with their five children. Gino's brother had agreed to allow the suddenly destitute couple to sleep there, but Bennie and Sara's own plight made it impossible for them to share their food. Gino was grateful to his brother, yet a part of him inwardly trembled. He could no longer act independently, and this awareness gave him his first taste of an unwelcome and unfamiliar bitterness. In the moonlight that streamed through their window, Filomina lay awake at night, watching tiny insects race across Gino's sleeping body, cracking them with her fingernails, one by one. Rising early in the morning, she went to her Mamma's house to eat breakfast; on most days, she skipped lunch. Meanwhile, Gino searched for any work he could find, eating an occasional piece of fruit stolen from a street vendor.

In the evenings, Gino and Filomina thanked God for their families. They survived by rotating dinner among family members; with meals built around pasta dishes, the supply could always be stretched to include one or two additional mouths. Everyone, especially the children, looked forward to these sharings; they made normal suppers into festive "company" occasions. But Gino could never shake the feeling of dread as they sank deeper and deeper into debt. He accepted the hospitality by bringing some small gift — tobacco, fruit, sugar — and vowed to repay every favor.

By the time Filomina was six months along, Gino was making six dollars a week unloading produce trucks before the stores opened in the mornings. When it was clear they could depend on at least this small amount, Gino paid three of the six dollars to his brother in exchange for the room and fifty cents for each meal.

Then Sara found that she was also pregnant and she'd be needing their room for the baby. Bennie hated to ask his brother to move, but with so many in the house could not see any other way to manage. He knew the street where Gino worked, and rather than talk to Gino at home, sought him out on the way to the fish market. He found Gino in the midst of a truckful of crates, and stood watching him uneasily, not knowing how to interrupt. Gino, suddenly spotting him, had a moment of alarm. "Was something wrong at home?" he asked, signaling to the other workers that he was taking a break. Bennie shook his head, embarrassed.

"Is everyone all right? Is someone sick?"

"No," Bennie said again. "Everything's fine. I just wanted to speak to you."

The two had stopped in front of a restaurant where Gino put his hand on Bennie's shoulder.

"What is it?" he asked.

"It's just that Sara's pregnant again, and with the five other children we have nowhere to put the baby . . ."

"You need our room," Gino said. "Filomina and I can find another place. Don't worry about it, Bennie."

Bennie was relieved that his task was over, and sorry to put his brother to more hardship. Gino too, of course, was secretly worried, but as it turned out Filomina's own sister, Bella, had a room spare, which she was more than happy to give to Filomina and Gino.

Bella, three years older than Filomina, was a warm, goodhearted woman trapped in a loveless marriage with a man named Nicky Covio. However great her own disillusionment, she was always able to provide a happy life for her two children. Her boundless capacity for hope made Gino and Filomina's lives a little brighter, and once Gino saw that she really did enjoy having them with her, much of the strain on him eased.

Gino slept on a fold-up bed called a *bronda*, and Filomina, now eight months pregnant, slept on the parlor's tiny couch, with straight-backed chairs drawn close to prevent her from falling in the night. But the conditions were immaterial. Filomina, still eighteen years old, was so glad to be back with her own family again – her Mamma was only two flights away – she found herself sleeping for the first time in weeks. As much as she loved Gino, she felt a reserve in his family that always kept her apart from them, a strange formality that puzzled her. Tess was kind to her, her sympathy having been aroused at Filomina's fraught beginnings. Rosa, too, was wonderfully sweet, but the intensity of Gino's devotion to her made Filomina slightly uneasy. Back home, she realized how much she missed her own mother; she'd forgotten how much she loved the smell of her Mamma's house.

Her Mamma and Bella fussed over her constantly, bringing her tiny portions of strange foods and broths. "Here," they would say, "eat this for the baby. You don't want the baby to be born with the mark." There were so many superstitions; women could never fully dispel them and even the priests were reluctant to forbid their accompanying rituals.

By the time she reached her ninth month, Filomina had ballooned to 142 pounds, almost forty pounds more than her usual weight. How, she wondered, had Mamma found a way to have baby after baby and still continue the endless cycle of cleaning, cooking, and mending? Filomina gave birth on Bella's parlor couch with an audience of three women, as well as a doctor, whose presence Mamma found entirely unnecessary. Mamma coached Filomina in Italian, warning her not to listen to a word Dr. Pellegrino was saying because Mamma knew best. Bella and her six-year-old daughter, Sandra, hovered around the makeshift bed, blocking the doctor each time he tried to touch his patient.

Beautiful and pink, Angela came into the world on a cold December morning, just two days before Christmas, and Gino's desire to create a new life took on a sharper edge. New fathers were like boys on their first day of school, with spotless, pressed clothes and scrubbed faces, their pencils – shiny and pointed, their notebooks – endless pages of unblemished white. Every entry was correct and completed ahead of time. To Gino, Angela was the greatest gift he'd ever imagined, which gave a different quality to his determination; it was a kind of holy cause, oblivious to the possibility of failure.

One afternoon, Gino was in an uptown social club with the other young men who couldn't find work. The bitter cold had shut down all the construction projects, public and private, and the club was crowded with men who needed a warm stove, some hot coffee, and a few hours of escape from their women and children. As he sat at a table, half-heartedly playing cards with a few

friends, Gino spotted Aldo Testa across the smoke-filled room. It
had been almost ten years since he had seen Aldo. About five years
older than Gino, Aldo had been just 19 when he made his living
delivering his uncle Giuseppe "Pepe" Testa's gin to bars and restaurants such as Belvedere's. Gino had helped him unload his good
over the years but had never thought too much of the eager yet
somehow goofy young man. Now, however, Aldo was wearing a
dark cashmere coat over an expensive-looking blue-pinstriped suit
and a red silk tie. Gino wasn't by nature an envious man, but he
was amazed that Aldo could be so prosperous in the face of so
much poverty.

Aldo knew how little most people thought of him, but he
couldn't resist parading his success while former companions muttered curses behind his well-tailored back. As it happened, his
wealth was an accident. Aldo's uncle had no sons of his own, so as
his only brother's son, Aldo was working as the eventual heir to an
immensely powerful organization built on bootlegging. Watching
Aldo strut across the room, Gino wondered for the thousandth
time why so much in life depended upon blind luck.

When Aldo caught sight of Gino, he hurried toward him with
a wide smile and babbled on about his racehorse running at Aque-
duct this spring. Gino listened patiently. Then, completely out of
the blue, Aldo presented him with a proposition. His Uncle
Giuseppe's entire network of trucks, running between lower Manhattan and Newark, had to operate three or four times a week
despite the ever-increasing dangers of police blockades and
hijackings by rival gangs. The former driver, "Chickie" Maggio,
had recently begun an extended vacation of five to ten years in
Elmira penitentiary and the backlog of undelivered booze was
making everyone nervous.

"How about it, Gino?" Aldo asked, offering him the chance to
fill the vacancy, "for old times' sake."

Gino smiled, knowing that the offer wasn't remotely as generous as Aldo was making it sound. A new driver wouldn't survive
more than three or four trips without being killed or caught. The
Testas were just trying to move their merchandise until they could

set up a new system. Still, Gino knew that he could make a great deal of money for each run, money for his family which now seemed worth the risk.

The night of the first ride, Gino discovered that the most frightening aspect of the job wasn't any obstacle in the road or a foreseeable block. It was the fact that disaster could fall at any second during the long ride at night. The driver was always expendable, disruption of delivery and even destruction of his goods the goal. Sitting behind the wheel, Gino remembered his old car thieving buddy Angel Hair, how oblivious and content he had looked while charging out of Manhattan to his doom. The worst was knowing that he was powerless, Gino thought, that his last act could be turning the key in the ignition, or turning off an exit where a car might be waiting, or arriving at a destination that might itself be a trap.

After the first uneventful night, driving from a Harlem warehouse along a prescribed route to Newark, Gino realized that no good would come of unsettled nerves, and soon convinced himself that this opportunity was divinely inspired to help him and his family at a low ebb.

Filomina knew only that Gino's new job involved driving, and when he started coming home with larger and larger handfuls of cash, she praised God for allowing her husband to find honest work that paid so well in such perilous times. By the time Angela was three months old, Gino was able to rent an apartment for the huge sum of $18.00 a month, just three blocks from the LaRoccas. Everyone was excited about Gino's good news; Rosa orchestrated a family celebration. Gino even brought a large bottle of illegal wine to toast the future.

While the rest of his family was buzzing about his new success, however, Giovanni was strangely silent. So much money, he thought, could only come from a life of crime. Denied his father's approval, Gino's only response was to look directly in his eyes and give him a self-possessed smile, that of a man who had moved beyond old frustrations. Giovanni ignored his son's challenge and the evening proceeded without incident, although Giovanni refused to drink the wine. Seeing it was imported and not home-made, he called it gangster wine and drank only black coffee.

The next few months brought Gino well beyond any concern he might have had with what his father thought of him. Filomina filled the apartment with furniture and a real carpet was on the floor. Most of their things were second-hand, bought from families who needed money for food, but they were wonderful anyway, and Filomina, her energy returning as the baby grew, kept every inch of her first real home spotless. Gino came home each night, feeling as though he were entering a mysteriously enlarged dollhouse, or one of those perfect little rooms inside the porcelain Easter eggs that his Mamma's friend, Mrs. Verdicchio, had brought over from Sicily.

Over the next few years, Gino's star continued to rise. Angela was a constant joy; every time she smiled at him, or grabbed his finger in her chubby little hands, any guilt he might have felt about the dangerous world to which he now belonged was eased away.

But it didn't take Pepe Testa long to realize that Gino was too valuable to risk losing on the road. The lines to Canada were being closed off by Federal agents, and fewer and fewer shipments were getting through the customs officials at the docks. As a result, violence on the streets was escalating wildly as more and more people tried to get their hands on the few available shipments of quality liquor. Too many poisonings in speakeasies had discouraged the high-rollers from depending on basement-brewed gin. And soon Gino was moved to a position of greater responsibility within Pepe's growing empire. By the time Prohibition ended, collapsing the bootlegging arm of the Testa organization, Gino had become safely ensconced in loan sharking and the disposal of stolen goods.

Whatever doubts Filomina once had about being fairly treated by the Fates melted away during these blessedly untroubled years. There was plenty of money, so she could care for her family free of the terrible anxieties that had burdened them during the first few months of their marriage. Perhaps if she had suspected the real nature of Gino's business, she would have found fresh ground for her old fears. But it never occurred to her to question Gino; she had complete faith in him and simply assumed he was receiving the success he deserved.

Meanwhile, Gino, missing the sexual adventures of his earlier years, had begun to visit other women. It hadn't happened very often, and he was always discreet, but the incidents were gradually forming a pattern. He truly believed that his infidelity in no way diminished his love for Filomina. He was not seeking romance or manhood with the other women he knew. It was just that, in the years before he fell in love with Filomina, his sexual life had been an array of richly varied experiences and exotic approaches to lovemaking that he believed must never take place with Filomina, the wife he honored and the mother of his children. He enjoyed possessing her, but only in what he considered to be "decent" expressions of sexual passion. When other desires swept over him, he resolved the conflict by turning to others.

Gino's first affair happened unexpectedly. One of Testa's lieutenants had given Gino an address in Little Italy, where he was told to collect an old debt of four hundred dollars. He was given no further information, but instructed to have the money within the week. I'm being tested, he thought. Gino never felt he was completely trusted, perhaps because his only well-known criminal relatives were Enzio, his bungling long-lost uncle, and Bruno, an early discharge from the army who had recently been spotted in Boston.

The lovely woman who opened the door had the look of someone whom life had beaten down. Her skin was pale, lined with fatigue, and her dark, shapeless dress seemed consistent with the musty smell that escaped from the cheerless apartment. And yet, her simple beauty – its dark features, the fullness of her breasts, and the look of ageless wisdom within her brooding eyes – had enormous power.

"What is it that you want?" she asked in a husky voice that seemed to capture the darkness of the woman and the room.

Gino cleared his throat in a unconscious attempt to rid himself of his stirrings of desire, and said, "My name is Gino Manzino. I am here for Mr. Testa."

The woman's name was Anna Zarra, and she knew why Gino had come before she had asked. But his well-groomed appearance and expensive suit seemed at odds with her image of a loan shark's bill collector. She stepped back to allow him into the apartment, keenly aware that the fear she first felt was beginning to soften.

"The debt was my husband's, and he's dead. The money's gone. I don't know what I'm supposed to do next," she said, as Gino surveyed her one small room.

Wonderful, Gino thought. No wonder old man Ferucci had passed this job on to him. When a man owed money to Testa and died before he could repay, his surviving family inherited the debt and Testa would take any measures he saw fit to conclude the matter. This clause was essential to all loan agreements; otherwise, too many of Testa's clients would choose death as an alternative to life-long bondage; few men, no matter how desperate, would leave their wives or children to become Testa's permanent instrument of repayment. It was now Gino's task to find some way of exacting money from the woman, or inflict the kind of punishment Testa's reputation demanded. And though the prospect of violence had never deterred him, however much Gino might prefer to negotiate a solution, it had always been in response to someone's intent of hurting him. How could he take action against someone like Anna Zarra?

"How did your husband die?" he asked quietly. The unexpected courtliness of his voice and manner distracted her for a moment, but then she realized what he had said and felt a flash of anger.

"The same animals who made him borrow money so he could keep playing cards shot him over a hand they had lost. At his funeral, at his *funeral*, someone walked up to me and told me what I owed. He said that after a respectable mourning period, someone would be around to collect it. Three weeks later, they sent that guy Ferucci, and now you're here." She gave a half-smile. "I guess three weeks is what they call respectable. And, of course, I was charged interest for the time. That's why it's up to four hundred dollars. He only borrowed two hundred."

Gino hated this. The people who borrowed from Testa knew the cost, and knew the risks if they failed to pay. Their families, however, were always the last to know anything.

"What happened with Ferucci?" he asked. His voice was still soft, a quality which calmed her.

"He was old and nervous," she said, "and once he saw my daughter, he knew he could never hurt me. But you're young and strong and my daughter is in school. So what happens now?"

For a long moment, they stared into one another's eyes until the air seemed to thicken around them. Then Gino finally said, "Your debt is cancelled, Signora."

Apparently both of them were shocked by this pronouncement because a stunned silence followed. With an embarrassed smile, Gino bowed slightly and turned back toward the door.

"No, wait!" she said, rushing forward and placing her hands on his chest. "I don't understand. How could it be cancelled?"

"I have cancelled it," he said. "You won't be bothered anymore. But please don't mention this to anyone." No debt to Testa could, of course, be cancelled; Gino knew he would have to pay the money himself. In fact, he'd have to hurry if he hoped to get the full four hundred by the day's end.

"No, please wait," she said again. "Please." In the next moment, her hands passed down his body, swiftly and gently, unfastening his trousers as she dropped to her knees in front of him. He was caught too off guard to protest, to say that she didn't have to do this. Still, he was hard by the time her fingers found him, stiffening so rapidly that she pulled back momentarily in surprise. She gave a small smile, then closed her lips around him and began to stroke him with her tongue. As he quickly surrendered, Gino realized why the mustiness in the room seemed so familiar. It was the same scent that had filled the back cellar of his parents' apartment, the tiny crawlspace with the damp mattress where he'd once taken so many young girls.

The long weeks of remorse gave him many sleepless nights of

secret shame. Each time his beloved bride kissed him or touched him, he felt unworthy. He rose from their bed in the middle of the night to sit in the darkness, sipping at a large tumbler of wine. Yet, beneath his troubled conscience, he'd become aware of something else – that brief moment of lust had awakened a part of him that had nothing to do with his home, his family, or Filomina.

From then on, Gino had trysts with a long succession of women. Perhaps his boldest adventure was with a black girl he had met at the Park Lane nightclub. Like Rita, Dolores was a showgirl. But unlike Rita, she only saw Gino as a handsome young fan with a fat wallet. It came as a surprise to her to discover that Gino enjoyed making love to women as much as he did receiving love. Breaking his own rules, Gino soon had Dolores set up in a private dressing chamber, replete with a long sofa and an extra suit of Gino's in the closet.

Six months later it was English Nellie who seduced Gino in her own restaurant Nellie's Bar and Grill on Mott Street. A tall slim glamorous blonde with private rooms above the bar, she most attracted Gino with her legs, so often ascending her iron staircase in silver high heels. It took a while for Gino to climb the stairs after her, but by the time he did, his guilt over Filomina had been all but suppressed. In his mind, Gino had created a new inner space for a new set of secrets. Even so, when Filomina reached for him, he occasionally felt a wave of self-loathing sweep over him. He had vowed to protect her from the darkness in the world, but saw that some of that darkness was in him.

As for Filomina, she eventually came to realize that some part of Gino had been lost to her, and one morning she woke up with absolute certainty that other women had existed for a long time, though nothing in Gino's manner justified her suspicion. True love makes many women blind; in Filomina's case, it made her see. And yet, no matter how much pain this knowledge caused her, she never spoke to him of what she knew. Though it was understood among all the wives never to question their men about anything they did away from home, that was not what kept her silent. Nor was it the fear of what she might find out, since she had already accepted the worst. The fact was, Gino loved her, and she knew he would never leave her. He must do this for a reason, she thought. Perhaps, there was something missing in the way she made love that drove him to other beds. The answers lay in a realm that eluded her, a world, like all worlds that must have its share of pleasures, but ones she had never experienced.

Only once did Filomina stumble across any hint of the darker side of sexuality. Lena Piccolo, one of Filomina's childhood friends, had come to the Manzino's latest and most luxurious apartment for tea, and the talk turned to love. It was one of those days when Filomina was feeling a vague sense of sadness and loss. The family was prospering, the children were healthy, and Gino was cheerful and affectionate, but looking into his eyes, she sensed more distance than usual. Lena always said that she and her husband, Marco, had a wonderful love life, often adding a suggestive laugh that puzzled Filomina into thinking perhaps Lena knew something she didn't about love's mysteries.

"Lena," she asked, after a pause in their conversation. "Can I ask you something personal?"

"Of course you can," she answered, smiling as she watched the color climb into Filomina's cheeks.

"You say that Marco loves you. But how do you know?"

Confused about exactly what her friend was asking, Lena began, "Well, he tells me all the time. He's always good to me, and generous, and . . . ."

"But Lena," Filomina broke in, "how do you really know?"

Lena stared at her for a moment, taken off guard by such an unusual question, coming from Filomina. Finally, she said, "And, I suppose, there's what happens between us in bed."

"Do you mean making love?" Filomina asked.

"I mean the way we make love," Lena said, still hesitant to speak of sex with someone as old-fashioned as Filomina. "You know," she added, "the different positions."

Trying hard not to let her bewilderment show, Filomina thought, The positions? What positions? But to Lena, all she said was, "The positions. Yes, of course." Then she smiled conspiratorially and asked, "Tell me, Lena, which positions do you and Marco like the most?"

"Filomina!" Lena cried out in shock. "You mean, all these years I thought you were so innocent, and you were secretly . . . ." She covered her mouth and giggled like a schoolgirl. "You really had me fooled. I can't believe it." Filomina blushed and laughed with her.

"Well," Lena continued, getting down to business, "he's been trying a lot of new ones lately. I got so excited when we did it doggie style, in the last few weeks, we've tried some of the others. You know, the swan, the duck, and . . . ."

She went on enthusiastically for some time, while Filomina hid her astonishment behind a silly grin that felt nailed to her face. Lena spoke of positions, tonguing techniques, special implements, and creams. Filomina found it so incomprehensible, she became fearful. Fortunately, the children came in and Filomina was spared the impossible task of finding some way to contribute to this bizarre conversation.

That night, as soon as Gino came home, he could see that Filomina had been crying. She was highly agitated; her immense blue eyes were brimming with tears, and she spoke in a voice so rushed between sobs, so touched with hysteria, he could barely understand her words. The only phrase he could clearly distinguish was, "Why don't you love me the way Marco loves Lena?"

Gino held her close until her crying lost its edge of panic, and then she gradually told him what Lena had said, or what she could remember of it.

"It is nothing," Gino whispered. "Lena is a very foolish woman. Don't let her upset you." He eased her onto their bed, gently stroking and caressing her until her tears subsided. Kissing her forehead, he whispered, "Go to sleep, my love."

The next afternoon, Gino went directly to Marco Piccolo's home. Marco was surprised to see him and a little nervous; Gino rarely came by unannounced.

Without a greeting, Gino asked him if they could step into the den to discuss a private matter. The parlor was filled with

Marco's family. Still puzzled, Marco led him into the other room. Once there, Gino said coldly, "Don't you have any control over your wife's big mouth?"

"I . . . I don't know what you mean," Marco stammered.

"You can fuck your wife any way you wish, but don't you have enough sense to keep such things in the bedroom? How can you let your wife talk to Filomina about dog and swan positions?"

Stunned, Marco leaned on his desk to ease his weakened knees. With deep embarrassment, he listened to Gino's summation of Lena's indiscreet boasting.

"No decent woman," Gino said with contempt, "should have to hear such filth. Keep her away from my wife."

As Gino left the apartment, he could hear Marco shouting amidst Lena's shrieks.

PART
FIVE

CHAPTER
TWENTY-TWO

B Y 1936, GINO and Filomina's life had settled into a pattern that they assumed would more or less define the balance of their lives. Three more children were born to Filomina in the next five years. When Angela was born, Gino had showered her with all the adoration fathers felt for lovely daughters. Then Carla came along one year later, with beautiful dark Sicilian skin and eyes that echoed her mother's, blue as the sky. Vinnie was just as beautiful, but Filomina noticed a darkness in his stare that scared her every time she looked at him too closely. Everyone said that Philip, or Philly, who came six weeks ahead of schedule, should have been a girl, with his magnificent, small features and gentle, angelic personality.

Angela was born into a modern world, an increasingly prosperous family, and sought nothing more than to become the living embodiment of old values. In school, she was brilliant, and the nuns praised her intelligence as she won one academic award after another. But she never seemed to carry her intelligence into any other part of her life. Away from her books and the classroom, she became nervous, almost frightened, and longed for the security she believed could only be found by following her mother's example and accepting the domestic role traditionally filled by generations of women in the family.

In Carla, Gino saw all of the qualities he had hoped to find in a son: independence, intelligence and, above all, the courage of her convictions. Although he was astute enough to recognize these qualities in his daughter, he couldn't tolerate the concept of a world beyond the home belonging to women rather than men. He'd been anxious for a son and was already looking forward to Filomina's next pregnancy; vague plans for a dynasty had been forming in his mind. But Vinnie, his first son, was all rough edges, a natural brawler who would eventually become the victim of his own violent impulses.

With the birth of Filomina's fourth child, Philly, his sisters, Angela and Carla, were happy to have a baby brother to fondle and tease, particularly one who didn't have Vinnie's explosive temper and the physical strength to inflict bodily damage. Philly was so gentle that he might have become an easy target of his brother's terrorizing if it weren't for the principle their Pappa had instilled in them early on that brothers must stick together and be ready to defend one another from outside threats. It was their first exposure to the concept of family honor. Even so, Philly never inspired any of the rivalry that often stirred bitter conflict between brothers. They were never interested in the same things at home, in school, or in the neighborhood, so there was no arena for competitiveness. Vinnie tolerated his passive brother, though he did spend a lot of time making fun of him. In fact, since the dangers of street life often spilled into the classrooms, Vinnie was frequently called upon to defend him in one confrontation or another. But he didn't really mind. It made him proud of his strength.

When Philly was old enough to consciously evaluate the world into which he'd been born, he detected a certain tension between his parents that was difficult to characterize, no matter how much they appeared to love each other. Unlike his Mamma, Philly fully recognized what his Pappa did to earn the living that had given them such an impressive home and so much prestige in the neighborhood. Yet whereas Gino showed no shame, to Philly his lifestyle was simply one of crime, a sin he had no desire to share.

Gino's heightened ambition had pulled him further and further from the family circle for longer periods of time. Uncle Cesare may have been cheap, but when he realized that Gino was fast becoming a valued member of the Testa organization, he had suddenly found a suit with deeper pockets. As he had never fully trusted the Testas, Gino was glad to go to work again for Cesare, and this time with respect. His long years of training at Belvedere's and the Commodore, as well as his bootlegging experience, gave him a distinct advantage over other men of his age. Gino also had refinement, a charm and authority that opened doors. As the years slid by as on a finely oiled machine, so did Gino's wealth and status steadily increase. Filomina was also right in suspecting an increase in his episodes of infidelity, but rather than confront him, she turned her attention to her children, allowing her husband to slip further away. In the end, it was probably unspoken guilt over his numerous affairs that explained Gino's reluctance to interfere with Filomina's growing attachment to Philly. His difficult breech birth meant that Filomina's childbearing days were probably over and Gino saw her special love for Philly as an echo of Rosa's love for him. Even now, the few moments he spent with his mother every week were some of his most precious. Unlike with Filomina, Gino never had the fear that he might one day disappoint her.

Meanwhile, Vinnie banged his way through school on one athletic team or another, steadily losing academic ground until dropping out of school several months before graduation. Philly, however, excelled in his classes, and not simply because of aptitude. In books, Philly found a vast new world in which he felt completely at home. So when the time came for him to choose the way he would spend his life, he found school untainted by the corruption that dominated Gino's world. Eventually he approached his Pappa with a request to become the first Manzino to attend college.

Gino never quite knew how to respond to a son so lacking in masculinity. He feared that he had somehow contributed to the boy's strangeness. For his part, Philly simply believed that his father's warmth was oddly blocked in his case. There was no anger, but there seemed to be a failure of affection. And so, regardless of his Mamma's encouragement, Philly was extremely nervous about asking his father for a favor that would be so expensive and so at odds with the normal expectations of the family.

To his great surprise and relief, Philly found his father willing to finance his son's plans. At first, Philly thought his mother had interceded for him and made some kind of private bargain. But she had said nothing to Gino, suspecting that he might resent her intrusion into an issue that concerned only father and son. Despite the differences between them, Gino genuinely loved Philly. He wanted happiness for his son, as he did for all his children, and he somehow understood that Philly needed a life apart from his father's world. Perhaps, Philly thought, it also had to do with pride – as certainly Gino knew that Philly was likely to be successful there.

When Philly entered Boston University as a liberal arts major, there was a new American emphasis on attending college, where all the brightest and most creative of the emerging generation found common ground. Boston University offered all the academic challenges any young intellectual might require, as well as a festive social life that made even the hard work seem painless. Philly loved it all – the classes, the parties, the all night study and bull sessions. He learned to love coffee and beer, and wine that hadn't been crushed in a neighbor's basement. He loved the books, the library, and the writing. He especially loved the writing. It was through writing that he first came to know James Kilkenny.

Professor James Kilkenny was Philly's instructor in freshman composition. Because Philly had come from an inner city high school, he'd been mixed in with a group of underachieving athletes and over-celebrating society kids. But soon he stood out in sharp contrast to the other students who were either too limited or too lazy to produce anything meaningful. Philly wrote extensively and beautifully; it wasn't long before Professor Kilkenny recognized his talent and realized that he'd been ridiculously misplaced in his class. But Kilkenny was reluctant to let him go and have him placed with another professor. He finally came up with a plan, approved by the English Department, which allowed him to take

Philly out of the group and assign him to an independent writing project for course credit. This involved a series of private meetings so Kilkenny could monitor his progress and evaluate his work individually. Philly wrote poetry, formal essays, short stories, journal entries – anything to keep his creative energies churning – and he looked forward to their conferences more than to any other part of his curriculum. Kilkenny had become his advisor, guiding him toward courses and readings that would enable him to truly achieve his potential as a student and as a writer. By the semester's end, they had developed a close friendship and Philly began to show him some of his personal writings that he had always considered too private to be shared with anyone.

Then, in the spring of his first year in Boston, Philly accepted Jim Kilkenny's offer to come to his apartment one evening for dinner.

"On one condition," Philly said, then smiled, "I do the cooking."

He kept Filomina on the phone for a full half hour so she could dictate the details of one of her special recipes. Of course, Philly's inexperience in the kitchen seriously handicapped his attempt, but the end result was delicious anyway. Even a reasonable facsimile of one of Filomina's meals was a dramatic improvement over most of the Italian cooking available in Boston. They consumed a considerable amount of wine during Philly's clumsy struggles with the stove, which helped to transform the entire evening into a pleasant blur.

When, on the second meeting, Philly and Jim became lovers, it seemed like the natural next step, both in terms of their developing affection for one another and Philly's new understanding of what made him so different from other young men. If he had any guilt at all, it was in the knowledge that he had committed himself to something he could never imagine anyone in his family understanding, particularly his father. Still, only his mother's approval really mattered.

Actually, all of the Manzinos were far too lost in concerns of their own to worry much about Philly's isolation from the family.

In years of scrambling for his own power, Gino had created a solid base of wealth and influence. But the dangerous world through which he moved was beginning to drain him of his energy and capacity for joy, and this slow deterioration was exacting its toll at home.

If Gino had been less talented, he might have settled into a life with Filomina and their children and discovered the kind of contentment that would have been consistent with his buoyant, optimistic nature. But when he realized how well-suited he was to conquering the violent world of the streets, he found himself taking larger and larger risks. The demands of his profession were distasteful, but it excited him to be able to prove his worth time and again. After a while, he became as conscientious about loan-sharking and enforcement as any businessman might be about a legitimate career.

Filomina could hardly remain unaware of the dangers Gino faced every day. Gradually, he began to entrust her with some of his problems from beyond the home, knowing her talent for judging people's character. She was never deceived by appearances, nor did she have any personal entanglements to cloud her judgment. In fact, Filomina stayed home only because she knew enough about the world to choose to live apart from it. Still, Filomina never asked him about his work directly, which appeased Gino's Old World sense of things. If there were some matter he wished to discuss, he would bring it up in normal conversation as if he was idly speculating about the day's events. Filomina would then offer her opinion in the same curious way. The charade was carried out with increasing frequency over the years so that eventually she became his only consultant and confessor. But they were together for a very long time before he began to speak to her freely.

There was a time when Filomina's instinctive understanding of human nature had made Gino uncomfortable. If Filomina could see through him, he thought, how could he be sure of keeping her? Soon he came to realize that it was precisely because she could see into the heart of things that he could feel secure in her devotion. Strangely, this realization did not ease his concerns. The strength of her love created a frightening sense of responsibility. And yet, without her special understanding, he knew that his own passion would have never become all that it was.

Finally, one afternoon he told her that Mr. Impallazio, an elderly merchant, had borrowed a few hundred dollars from him and then disappeared from the neighborhood, missing his first interest payment. Gino had approved the loan himself, but the man's tailoring business had been closed for over a week and no one answered the door in the tiny apartment he maintained on the shop's second floor. Gino described the situation to Filomina in a casual conversation over coffee. She smiled, reached across the table to hold his hand, and said, "Perhaps I can find out where he's gone." Gino only shrugged, as if acknowledging he had asked her for help would have made him appear indiscreet.

Early the next morning, Filomina asked the neighborhood women about Mr. Impallazio's closed tailor shop, tapping into a vast network of information routinely closed to men. By mid-afternoon, the answer had found its way back to her, and she presented it to Gino with the evening meal, as casually as she might report any neighborhood gossip. Mr. Impallazio's daughter had been arrested in Albany for prostitution. It was taking him longer than he expected to arrange her release and find her a real job. The poor man had needed the money to get his daughter out of jail. He'd be back by the weekend and planned to find some way to pay back Gino out of his shop's meager profits.

Gino smiled as he listened to Filomina's tale, particularly noting the way she kept referring to Mr. Impallazio as "that poor, poor man". He was greatly relieved, however, not only because he had done the right thing in trusting the old man but, more important, he had done the right thing in trusting Filomina.

Although the dark nature of Gino's dealings contrasted sharply with Filomina's sense of decency, she never saw any conflict in helping Gino. She understood that he moved in a world opposed to the law, but the law was an empty concept to most immigrants. The law was for Americans, and she was part of a community that didn't think of itself as belonging to America. Most of the people she knew and loved had never been granted entrance into American life and so they had built their own world on America's perimeter. They did whatever was necessary to survive. Life on any hostile frontier demanded desperate acts that would never be condoned in a country run fairly.

While she would never understand how the word "political" could possibly apply to her, Filomina's acceptance of Gino's life was really a political act. From her perspective, there was nothing criminal in striking back at a corrupt system. This belief existed in Gino's attitude as well, but his was blended with elements far less innocent. He had long since gone beyond what was merely required in the struggle against America's injustices. Still, the superiority of the outlaw's cause allowed him to pursue his objectives guiltlessly. And yet, the notion that any of these feelings might be described as political ideas was incomprehensible to the Manzinos. Their only sense of history was their own. Politics was a word used in the old country by local chieftains to manipulate power and maintain the elaborate systems of intimidation and patronage. In this country, it referred to the well-dressed men who appeared in the neighborhood from time to time to smile, shake hands, and make entertaining speeches, often in Italian. As these men spoke earnestly of all the people would gain by voting for them, the crowd would listen politely, sometimes enthusiastically, and break into cheers at various points in the speech, even though no one in the audience was registered to vote; in fact, many of them weren't even supposed to be in the country. But no one wanted to spoil the celebration that had taken them away from their afternoon's work. Besides, on summer afternoons, the candidates usually brought trucks with free ice cream for the children. To them, politics in America was a harmless hour of amusement, intended for other listeners.

Of course, Fiorello La Guardia had punctured a sizable hole in the protective armor that immigrants such as Gino liked to wear. Once Gino had joined forces with Cesare, his friendship with La Guardia had been severed – and because Gino knew La Guardia's decency first hand he could hardly dismiss him when he saw him on billboards or giving speeches to cheering crowds. It was living with such contradictions, or in spite of them, that hardened Gino and even Rosa in ways that were subtle and yet long-lasting, wounds that never quite healed – much like the pains of Gino's infidelities or of Giovanni's secret anger when Gino went to work for the very Mulassano family whom he had left Sicily to escape.

In the end, Giovanni's arch-enemy, pompous Agostino Mulassano had died much as expected: alone in a house of hired servants, his burial attended to only by the churchmen he had already hired for the occasion. A few weeks later, Rosa's brother Leonardo returned from Milan and set about carrying on the Mulassano rule. By that time, however, Giovanni and Rosa looked back to Sicily only in daydreams. After Agostino's death came Bianca's, a peaceful one, according to the letter from Leonardo – yet one that for Giovanni would never seem quite real. He would never return to Sicily, and never see Bianca's grave – but neither, he realized, did he want to.

Giovanni still deeply regretted not having being able to have Massemo and Bianca meet their grandchildren. Years of pitiless labor had given him a bitterness that not even Rosa could soften. For her part, if she ever missed the luxuries of her youth, she only had to remember the countless nights she and Giovanni had lain beside each other, laughing as they recounted in every hideous detail the marital bedroom Agostino had so long ago prepared for them.

For Gino and Filomina, however, their one insurmountable problem was not their home country or their parents but Vinnie – the son who wanted desperately to become his father's champion and heir, yet saw his dreams slipping further away each day. Almost from the beginning of his adolescence, Vincent Manzino was a disappointment to those who loved him, and Gino took most of the blame. In naming Vinnie after his own maternal grandfather rather than after himself, he had hoped to encourage his son to form his own individuality, and not just become his father's shadow. He'd given Vinnie responsibilities well beyond his experience, encouraged him to assert himself despite any errors he might make, praised him even when he'd done little to deserve it, and always spoke to him with a seriousness reserved for adults.

Given this unconditional endorsement, another boy might have grown into the kind of man who deserved this confidence. But Vinnie lacked some basic necessary quality. Much like Gino's lost brother Bruno, he was always being caught in some lie or mean-spirited scheme, usually directed against one of his sisters. As these incidents seldom involved anything serious, Gino managed somehow to dismiss them, even to the point of claiming amusement at his son's cleverness. Filomina, however, was not so easily assured. What disturbed her was that Vinnie seemed to enjoy the lie for its own sake. When he did something to hurt one of his sisters, it was always something unnecessarily cruel, serving no purpose other than to satisfy some sadistic impulse.

When Vinnie finally reached manhood, in years if not in character, Gino found a place for him in his growing empire – a move that some, even then, found almost delusional. By then Cesare had suffered a stroke, and returned to Sicily with Teresa, leaving Gino in entire and personal control over the American arm of the Mulassano business. But if Gino was hoping to turn his business into a Manzino dynasty, he was pinning his hopes on the wrong person.

For as long as he could, though, Gino refused to attach any significance to Vinnie's transgressions, choosing to believe that the boy's sneakiness and mean streak would mature into resourcefulness. Friends who had for years helped Gino to build up his business watched with sad eyes as Vinnie made one mistake after another, many of which cost money and a few of which cost lives. No one thought that Vinnie could be transformed into a leader. Even Gino couldn't attempt to justify his son's actions. Instead he sighed with disappointment when Vinnie failed, and his friends felt as if they were watching a man who'd spent a lifetime accumulating a collection of glass allow a clumsy child into the room. They held their breath each time the boy shattered another piece and helped Gino sweep up the broken shards.

Vinnie's other great problem was his utter inability to see beyond the here and now. However clearly Vinnie might assess the situation before him, even penetrating the moment with the fierce light of his ambition, he had no understanding of the larger truths. He never perceived the patterns that moved within events, nor the ways in which the future could be shaped by the present. To Vinnie, life was a series of disconnected episodes, complicated in themselves but nothing more. Gino could not make him realize that survival depended on strategy. For a brief while, Gino even tried to use the game of chess to break through Vinnie's handicap. As Gino, Bennie, Tessie and Bruno had become adults, with Bruno disappearing and Tessie removing herself to midtown New York, they also seemed to lose common ground. This wasn't a village like Corleone, and different lifestyles soon pulled them far apart. One of Gino's true pleasures in life, however, was helping those who had earned his trust. So when Bennie came to him one year with a plan to quit the fish market and open his own grocery store, Gino was quick to offer help. It was Gino – with his fond memories of Belvedere's – who proposed opening a cafe and restaurant above the grocery store. MANZINOS it would be called, and Gino, over-riding Bennie's protestations, spared no expense. At completion, MANZINOS consisted not only of the cafe and restaurant up front, but a room for Bocce, and a backroom for the local men to while away quiet hours playing chess, sharing Italian language newspapers and smoking their countless cigarettes.

Giovanni at first took to stopping by for a coffee after work. Bennie and Sara employed each of their five growing children throughout the establishment, and Tessie and Gino even shared an occasional game of checkers together. Gino had learned to play checkers from the old men in the social clubs who were always looking for new partners, and many years ago had taught Tessie to play against him. Eventually, however, his intelligence and ambition led him to the more complex challenges of chess. Hoping to demonstrate the importance of planning all moves several steps in advance, Gino spent many nights with Vinnie at a chessboard in MANZINOS, accepting espressos from his sister-in-law, and the biscotti that would mysteriously appear from time to time on his saucer from the tiny hand of Gino's niece Tina. But no matter how patiently he tried to explain the principles that produced victory, and no matter how gently he responded to Vinnie's reckless moves, Gino soon learned that his son was incapable of winning any game that required foresight and self-control. In the end, Gino was the only person who would ever play chess or checkers with Vinnie, and in later years, each time Gino found himself pulling Vinnie back from the edge of some disaster, he would remember his final chess lesson. Overwhelmed by frustration as his game collapsed once more, Vinnie had swept the pieces from the board in a single gesture, scattering them across the room. His father looked on wearily which only angered and frightened Vinnie further. From then on, Gino surrendered his dream of a natural heir and like a chess master began to construct situations in which Vinnie could move through life without bringing the whole world down on top of him.

One of Gino's first plans was to suggest that Vinnie become a lawyer – channeling his volatile energy into something structured. Gino was farsighted enough to anticipate the battles that he'd eventually have to win in the courts, not the streets, so having a lawyer in the family would be to his advantage. If Vinnie could learn to handle the demands of such a field, Gino thought, he could acquire some sorely needed self-discipline.

The fact that Vinnie had been unable to complete even high school was something Gino overlooked. Vinnie simply began law school with a high school diploma obtained through political influence. The last person to be bothered by this was Vinnie, who figured that law school would at least free him from his father's domination for a while. It wasn't long, however, before Vinnie was expelled for a number of offenses involving sexual transgressions and assaults against the underage or unwilling. Even when women had made themselves available, Vinnie would push them beyond the limits of their willingness. All this was an extension of his neighborhood escapades, where at first the people had made the mistake of seeing Vinnie as having inherited his father's reputation as a gifted lover. But there was nothing of the romantic in Vinnie, nothing of the joy of physical love. In sex, as in other matters, he was an abuser, a crude taker of what hadn't been offered to him.

By the end of three years, no matter how much money and pressure Gino had brought to bear on the situation, Vinnie had managed to have himself thrown out of four progressively less impressive colleges. His first expulsion at least mentioned academic grounds and a series of miserable course failures, despite the most expensive tutors. In the other three schools, he seemed to pursue banishment, accumulating so many charges of violence and excess that his ousting from the institutions was the only alternative to criminal prosecution. Finally, having failed to mold Vinnie's instincts into what he wanted, Gino watched with growing resignation as his son deteriorated into true wickedness, thinking more and more of his brother, Bruno.

Bruno had been the only person to drive Gino to the same level of despair, who actually made him feel contaminated by another's craziness. He had moved from disaster to disaster, laughing his way through injuries that would have killed anyone with a normal constitution. Even when Bruno was young, one of the old men in the neighborhood used to say, "Bruno was probably killed years ago, he was just too dumb to lie down." If Bruno had only hurt himself, Gino might have been able to help him, but as it was Bruno lashed out with sometimes devastating results. The last time Gino had seen him was just after Bruno got out of the army. Bruno had come to live with Gino's family, and soon began drinking heavily. Then one afternoon, Filomina and the children, all toddlers at the time, had sought out Gino in his warehouse office to tell him that Bruno was drunk again and had ordered them out of the house, telling them to sleep in the street and screaming that he needed quiet. Gino ran back to the apartment and stormed through the door, remembering the dozens of brawls he and his brother had gotten into over the years. Bruno had been waiting behind the door with a chair and brought it down on Gino's head, laughing insanely. The fight that followed put them both in the same hospital ward, but they had to be separated immediately because Bruno kept staggering out of bed to pull the tubes out of

Gino's arms. Eventually, Bruno had worn down any belief Gino had had that brothers stick together under any circumstances. Bruno had finally run off to Boston. After more than a year had passed, Tessie received a scribbled postcard from him. Three years later, a photograph arrived of Bruno and his wife, a buxom black woman raised in Harlem who worked as a nurse's aide. Bruno had finally opened up his own business, he wrote, a second hand furniture store.

As GINO WATCHED Vinnie act with Bruno's same recklessness, he felt a terrible sadness and fear for the future. Setting a crooked man straight seemed an impossible task – whereas others, like Bennie, could scarce be corrupted.

When he looked back, Gino had to admit that he and his brothers seemed to have followed almost predestined lives. Their characters had changed little from their earliest years, leaving Gino to wonder how much of a man's actions are of his own choosing. Only Tessie had diverged from an expected path, and without the best results. Gino saw how his daughters Angela and Carla romanticized their flamboyant Aunt Tessie. To them, Tessie was a glamorous woman with her own career and apartment and private life. They knew vaguely of Tessie's marriage, at 23, to an American Indian who had moved to New York from a reservation. He had been a remarkably bright man who had become a Macy's store manager in just three years. But he died just two years into the marriage, stepping out of the store at lunch-hour to be struck dead by a speeding car. What only Gino knew, however, was that since her husband had died, Tessie had gone through a terrible year of grieving from which she never truly recovered. In a strange twist, she had become much like Gino himself, moving from one lover's arms to the next in search of some elusive cure. Informed of Tessie's liaisons by various friends around the city, Gino grew increasingly alarmed, sure that Tessie was not acting out of any free spiritedness but a real and twisted grief. Occasionally, he had his car pick up Tessie from work and drive her uptown to MANZINOS, where the two sat over a cappuccino or a glass of wine in the early evening.

It was an irony not lost on Gino that he had always tried to set up Tessie with one of his Italian friends – but when Tessie finally did choose an Italian boyfriend it was a rakish hustler named Eddie Cordasco, a slick lanky man five years Tessie's junior and all but raised in a pool-room.

"Why can't you find a nice man," Gino reprimanded Tessie, "Someone who'll look after you?"

"Like you look after Filomina?" Tessie shot back with a bitterness that was becoming more frequent in her. Gino took a sip of his wine.

"Like me," he said, calmly. "Like Bennie. But you always like the wild ones, the long shots like that gypsy boy."

"You mean Carlo?" Tessie shook her head. "That was fifteen years ago. How did you know about him?"

Gino smiled. "I knew," he said. A few years ago, Tessie would have followed up on such a statement, but that was the problem with her lately: she didn't seem to care.

"Did he ever come back to the city?" Gino asked.

Tessie looked down, then smiled the most wistful smile Gino thought he had ever seen. "He did come back. It was about five years ago, just before my wedding. He found me at Macy's." She shrugged. "He's a dog breeder now, in Long Island. He had a litter of his own, too: twin girls, and two little boys, and an Italian wife. He gave me his address in case anyone wanted to buy a dog." Tessie laughed, but Gino couldn't help but sense some terrible sense of loss in her that frightened him. Only time could help her, Gino thought, and only then if she did not compound her sorrows. However much Gino tried to warn Tessie off Eddie Cordasco, though, she could not be influenced. As she stood to leave, donning her large black hat and lifting her stylish handbag, Gino saw a flash of the stubborn Manzino will that could either make a life or destroy it.

Whereas Tessie brought Gino a strange unease, Vinnie brought him – for perhaps the first time in Gino's life – true defeat. By the time he was thirty, Vinnie had been married and divorced twice. At 24, he had married Leslie Wolfe, a hatcheck girl of 31 who moonlighted as a call girl. The two had known each other for two weeks when they drove to Maryland and were married by a justice of the peace who required his cash payment up front. Even Vinnie didn't pretend that his marriage represented an infusion of love. They'd been screwing for fourteen days, and the impulse to marry was more an attempt to keep the frenzy going as long as possible than anything else. Gino was predictably outraged.

"You'd already paid for her," Gino told his son. "In fact, you overpaid. Why in God's name would you marry her? Do you want a whore to be the mother of my grandchildren?" But Gino's reaction just pushed Vinnie deeper into rebellion. The marriage lasted six months, but he would have kept it alive longer if Leslie hadn't made it impossible. She had given up being a call girl, but she hadn't stopped jumping into bed with strangers free of charge. She allowed every delivery boy and maintenance man in the building to slip inside her, and eventually Vinnie realized that the arrangement was doing little to enhance his status in the neighborhood. Besides, he'd decided to re-establish communications with his father; without him, he had no future. So, when he came home one afternoon to find Leslie in bed with a sixteen-year-old boy from God knows where, Vinnie took advantage of the moment to end it all in a rampage. He threw the naked kid down the stairs, and then beat the hell out of Leslie. In retribution, she turned back to him as she was leaving and said, "You know, I really thought that Gino Manzino's son would be a hell of a lot better in bed. I only wish I could have had Gino instead. I would have cleaned out his pipes. He would have made my back ache for a week," then slammed the door behind her. But instead of becoming even angrier, Vinnie collapsed to his knees and sobbed, too exhausted and ashamed to chase after her and hit her again.

Within a few months, he had reconciled with Gino and was working again, coming into MANZINOS to chat with Bennie and pat his nieces' hair. He had also returned to the wild life of drinking, knife fighting and seamy sexual exploits. Yet, somewhere in the midst of his debauchery, he remembered Gino's words about marriage and grandchildren and realized that he'd have to arrange a real marriage if he ever hoped to gain his father's respect.

Vinnie Manzino met Rosanna Bogardi at the wedding of a neighborhood friend. She was eighteen and had only been in the country for a few months. Her old world innocence and shyness, coupled with a fresh, natural prettiness, attracted quite a few of the younger men at the wedding. But to Vinnie, the fact that she was such a recent arrival from Italy meant that she wouldn't know much about his reputation and would be too naive to see through him. He also knew that his father would respect her young purity.

Rosanna was overwhelmed to find herself being rushed into a courtship by a man who was not only older but seemed so successful. Vinnie dressed impeccably and observed every formality dictated by tradition as part of the courting process. Rosanna's American relatives were extremely supportive, anxious only for her to have a prosperous marriage, and since she didn't have the insight or the experience to see the cruelty that lay behind his eyes, she thought that Vinnie was the handsomest man she had ever seen.

And so, Vinnie and Rosanna were married with full pomp and circumstance in a high mass at St. Teresa's. Rosanna looked lovely with her green eyes, long auburn hair, and flawless complexion. Watching her move within the silk brocade, Vinnie saw her as a gift yet unwrapped. The reward for having been forced to keep his hands off her would come tonight, he thought, as he stood at the altar, smiling at her in anticipation. Smiling back, Rosanna imagined herself to be the most fortunate of brides.

Her love for Vinnie was so perfect in its childlike way that, with any gentleness at all, he might have ensured her lifelong devotion to him, whatever his faults. But on their first night together, when he was presented with a virgin who would need patience and tenderness, Vinnie shattered any chance they might have had with his brutality.

Finally alone in their hotel suite, Rosanna was still humming a tune from the wedding reception and spinning slowly in place when Vinnie hurried out of his clothes and then suddenly stood naked before her, demanding that she get undressed.

"What the hell are you waiting for?" he asked roughly. "Haven't I waited long enough?"

Rosanna stared at him, at his grotesquely swollen member, and was shocked to the point of actually fearing her own husband. As she stood frozen to the spot, he said, "Shit, I'll do it," and with one motion tore the gown from her body.

Within seconds, she was thrown on the bed, her legs forced apart as he climbed on top of her, searching roughly with his fingers for the space inside her. In the brief moment she had before the pain of his entry, she tried to understand what she should do with her body to accommodate his onslaught of passion and thought sadly of the nightgown of pale pink silk still folded in her suitcase. Her Aunt Louisa had told her how lovely she would look in its shimmering silk. And then the pain came at once, the terrible tearing blotting out everything. Rosanna clung desperately to Vinnie's heaving shoulders, fighting back screams and remembering what her aunt and other older women had told her about the initial "discomfort" of lovemaking that would give way to acceptance and, in some women, to bliss. But the agony grew and she sobbed her way through the rest of the assault.

Toward the end, when Vinnie felt a sudden rush of warm liquid, he muttered, "There you are at last. I knew that you wanted me," and then he swiftly climaxed. A few minutes later, when he saw it was blood she had surrendered, he cursed and struck her across the face. She fled to the bathroom and locked the door, eventually crying herself to sleep, a towel soaked in cool water pressed between her thighs, curled up on the floor under the other towels. By then, Vinnie was downstairs in the hotel bar, drinking through what remained of his wedding night.

Vinnie was sprawled asleep, fully dressed across the bed, when she quietly came out of the bathroom early the next morning, hurried into her clothes, and slipped from the room. From the cafeteria across the street, she sipped coffee, her face turned to the side, hoping that by keeping her face toward the window, she could hide the bruises and red-rimmed eyes from the few people there eating breakfast. Crying softly most of the time, she reminded herself that she was an American bride, and if that privilege involved a price she had never imagined, she must not disgrace her family by failing to pay. Other women had survived; so must she. Instantly flooded with guilt, she ran from the cafeteria and back upstairs to their room, managing to slide into her pink nightgown before Vinnie had stirred. When he reached for her, she remembered once more her romantic expectations for the night and felt her stomach cramp and tighten.

"Vinnie," she pleaded, "I'm all torn inside. You can't come inside so soon."

He just smiled at her as he undressed, and suddenly she saw a gleam of ice in his eyes. "That's fine with me," he said. "I wanted your mouth this time anyway."

She didn't understand what he meant by this, until he pushed her head toward his penis.

"Suck on it! Suck on it!" he commanded as she drew it into her mouth, certain that she was committing some awful sin and would never be allowed in heaven.

"That's it," Vinnie moaned. "Your cunt was too tight anyway." Seconds later he exploded into her mouth, and she held his bitter seed there for several minutes, terrified that he would hit her again if he saw her spit it out. Then she slowly got out of bed, went into the bathroom, closed the door, and quietly vomited into the sink. The nausea she felt was somehow worse than the pain she had felt the night before, but her fear and shame were even greater which made her feel somehow to blame.

Over the days and nights that followed, Vinnie "instructed" his bride in ways to please him involving new and more humiliating sexual forms. Although he kept adding refinements, her mouth was the opening he most wanted to fill. The positions kept changing and he taught her how to insert her fingers deep inside him and move them around as her mouth and tongue worked endlessly over him. She slipped into a kind of numbness, and when he began plunging inside her again before she had healed, she endured the pain with no outcry. Her mind had disconnected from the body being brutalized, and pitied it from a distance. On those rare occasions when Rosanna resisted some new humiliation Vinnie had devised, he beat her into submission. However hardened her emotions had become to the daily torture that now comprised her life, her pale skin remained delicate and vulnerable, and she was forced to remain in the apartment so no one would see her darkened scars and bruises. She was happiest during those blessed periods when Vinnie left her alone to pursue business, drinking, and other women – women, he was fond of saying, who knew how to fuck a real man.

For his part, Vinnie felt satisfaction in knowing that his behavior was perfectly consistent with the drunken advice of the aging womanizers in the neighborhood social club: "Spend the first years teaching your wife how to excite you every night of your life." Had he felt any sensitivity toward Rosanna, he would not have been thrilled every time she cried. Her childlike anguish aroused him more than anything ever had. With her, he found a way to strike back at all his failures and ultimately his father as well.

With time, Vinnie also learned how to strike her without leaving any visible marks, so he could continue the charade that suggested his marriage had changed him for the better. He displayed Rosanna with apparent pride at family gatherings and neighborhood parties, always praising her cooking and the children she would one day give him. Rosanna played her part meekly; few had known her well enough to see that the special light in her eyes had disappeared. Only Filomina watched her carefully, sensing sadness beneath her quiet exterior, but not knowing what to make of it. Vinnie even kept the promise he had made to Rosanna when she agreed to marry him: he sent money to Amalfi in Salerno so her parents and two younger sisters could arrange for their migration to America.

Once Rosanna knew that her family was coming, she found the strength to hold on a while longer. Suddenly she had the patience, if not to embrace her husband's unnatural desires, then at least to submit to them without tears. All that mattered now was not to provoke him and make her situation worse. She had to survive until her parents crossed the ocean and could save her. Vinnie simply assumed that the subtle softening of Rosanna's resistance meant she had "come around" at last.

The moment Rosanna saw her mother's face again in her Aunt Louisa's parlor, she fell apart. All the horror she had somehow contained poured out uncontrollably, and she threw herself across her Mamma's lap, sobbing and pleading for rescue from the marriage that was destroying her.

The men and children were ushered from the room and, in broken phrases and soft moans, she told the women gathered there of the months she had spent in a private hell. As soon as her mother shook off the initial shock, she went to Rosanna's father, who was waiting in a silent rage in the apartment's tiny kitchen, trying to absorb this vision of the new world as a land of primitive predators. His wife told him of the atrocities his daughter had survived and his anger had only one focus – Vinnie Manzino.

Aunt Louisa tried to explain the power that Gino Manzino wielded over the neighborhood, but it made little difference. Amalfi had been filled with such men, and yet, however impoverished his position, Benito Bogardi had never allowed any of them to dictate how he should live, which made his departure for America far more than a gesture of mere restlessness – it was essential for his family's safety. But he would be damned if in his first hour on these shores, he allowed some Sicilian immigrant to intimidate him and violate his daughter.

His wife could only calm him down by reminding him that Vinnie was responsible for them being here, and they were in this country illegally. If he offended someone as important as Vinnie Manzino, he could end up dead or back on the beaches of Salerno.

"But Gino Manzino," interrupted Louisa, "is supposed to be an honorable man, no matter how monstrous his son might be. We will call for a formal meeting of both families, and Rosanna can present her testimony against Vinnie to his own father."

To arrange for the meeting, four of the Bogardi women, including Rosanna and her mother, went to see Gino and Filomina at their home the next afternoon. Gino had already suspected that something was terribly wrong. Vinnie had been acting oddly and was even more evasive than usual.

Vinnie made one attempt to call the Bogardi household, but the phone was hung up the moment he identified himself. He didn't try again and he couldn't face his father with the news that his wife had returned to her aunt's home, leaving only a scribbled note that said, "I am at Louisa's. Stay away."

When Rosanna's Aunt Louisa explained in calm, measured tones what had been going on for these last months between Rosanna and Vinnie, without disguising her bitterness, Gino felt a shame so deep that it briefly held his anger at his son in check. He even shared Benito Bogardi's longing to tear Vinnie apart with his own hands.

As the terrible story unfolded, Gino exchanged troubled glances with Filomina, who had begun to cry softly, and then turned his gaze at the Bogardi women. Rosanna's mother sat stunned, as if the retelling were making it happen right in front of her eyes. Louisa simply held and patted Rosanna's hand mechanically, murmuring softly, but Rosanna seemed untouched by the comforting. Perhaps hearing the horrors described in this lovely, civilized room, and spoken of in the past tense had diminished her anguish even as her mother's had increased, because she looked surprisingly composed and her face seemed almost serene. She looked like a lost child on her first day home, Gino thought, and far prettier than he remembered from their few meetings.

In another moment, Filomina crossed the room to embrace Rosanna and the other women gathered closer around her and began to cry openly. In a sad, gentle tone, Rosanna joined the crying at last, slipping back into the couch as the others crowded forward. Her skirt parted and moved upward, and Gino suddenly saw the soft skin of her inner thigh and a long finger-shaped bruise that started well above the bend of her knee and disappeared into the darkness beneath her skirt. The image transfixed him, and he felt as stirred by the blue-black mark as he did by the silken skin surrounding it.

Then he rose with a sudden shock of revulsion. His face flushed and he rushed outside. By the time he found Vinnie in his usual watering hole, Salvatore's in upper Harlem, the wave of conflicting passions had become a blinding fury. Vinnie stood to meet his father, and Gino struck him with a blow that carried all of his shame and disgust. The punch shattered Vinnie's nose and the table he fell across, sending the girl beside him, and the few others nearby, to different ends of the bar. Gino grabbed a white napkin from another table, tossed it to his son, and said, "Don't say a word. Just follow me home."

Despite all attempts to appease him in advance, Benito Bogardi lost all control when Vinnie walked into the meeting behind Gino. A small wiry man, he nevertheless looked like a wild boxer, his face approaching purple and the veins in his neck popping as he moved so determinedly across the room, having to be quickly restrained as he tried he tried to throw himself at his enemy. Once subdued by two of Gino's larger men, however, Benito noticed the blood-soaked towel held against Vinnie's widened nose and glanced at Gino Manzino with new respect.

The business was concluded swiftly. Gino would pay not only for the annulment and for the expenses involved in relocating the Bogardis to St. Louis, but would provide a generous cash settlement and offered "the profoundest sympathies of a family who would hope to be remembered for its basic sense of honor, whatever the transgressions committed in its name." Gino was very careful as he spoke in a voice touched with sorrow and dignity not to look at Rosanna, who was smiling at him shyly with appreciation. Then he left the room and began the process of pushing Vinnie from his mind, along with any remaining hope that his son might one day become someone he admired.

From then on, Vinnie slid even further into excess, especially in his sexual escapades. In fact, the only thing that ever slowed the abuse of his own body was abusing the bodies of others. In another irony that everyone would have preferred to miss, the only time Vinnie attempted to honor a woman was when Tessie became pregnant by Eddie Cordasco. The botched abortion by a fly-by-night Mott Street "doctor" almost cost Tessie her life, and the expensive doctor Gino brought in to save her said that Tessie would never again carry a child. Vinnie set out on a self-righteous rampage that ended with his putting a gun in Eddie's mouth in a crowded restaurant and making a show of his own manhood and strength. If he was expecting a hero's welcome, however, he was sorely disappointed. It was now Tessie's reputation, far more than Eddie Cordasco's, that was ruined.

Gino's disgust could scarcely grow stronger and though Vinnie would always be too arrogant to admit that his father was justified, he was at least perceptive enough to realize that Gino's image of him would now never change. In the face of so much disgrace, Vinnie finally surrendered his ambition. There was one occasion when he let his irresponsibility spill over the line while drinking at Sal's. Late into the evening, Vinnie launched into a tirade about women and his power over them that eventually led him to Rosanna. Too drunk to notice how silent the crowd became, Vinnie boasted about all the nights he had forced her to her knees to take him in her mouth, and the nights he would beat her when she fought to stay on her feet. He spoke of her clumsiness in bed and how he had used her body in so many ways that she would carry the scars for the rest of her life. By the time he left the bar an hour later, Vinnie was so clouded by alcohol and his own bitterness that he hardly noticed the man who stepped out of the shadows nor the huge fists that pounded him into unconsciousness. His drunkenness was the only thing that saved him. His assailant managed not only to break several ribs but to cause enough internal bleeding to place Vinnie in the hospital for a week. The doctors marveled at the damage done by one blow that had driven his cock and balls deep into his gut. It was several months before they descended again, and even longer before they healed enough for all the catheters to be removed.

Gino and Filomina were astonished at how one couple could have created children whose behavior functioned at such different extremes. No two could have been more opposite in temperament than Vinnie and Philly Manzino – one cruel, the other kind; one explosive, the other gentle. In their daughters as well, there were differences so dramatic that they scarcely seemed like sisters. Gino even began to wonder how many women in the world had been transformed into victims by men who had brutalized them in the name of male supremacy. In Sicily, the question might have never occurred to him, but in the open society of America, he found himself questioning the old values and arrangements. Although his own life, family, and community may have held on to many of the traditions of his ancestors, he could not fail to be touched by the change that was hovering in the air. However proud he might be of his own masculinity, Gino truly loved women. The idea of using physical force against them went against his entire being.

CHAPTER
TWENTY-THREE

ANGELA MANZINO SAW only what she wanted to see. In Rosa Manzino and Concetta LaRocca, she saw their contentment at family gatherings, their deep devotion at Mass, and the constant joy they seemed to draw from the simplicity of their lives. She never sensed the exhaustion and sadness beneath their placid surfaces, nor the hundreds of ways in which Giovanni Manzino and Vincenzo LaRocca dehumanized their wives under the mask of courtly manners and compliments to their cooking. Some failure of vision kept Angela from realizing how the world through which these women were permitted to move had been diminished. At the same time, she failed to appreciate her own mother's rebellious spirit and never truly comprehended Filomina's devotion to her father. She saw only the surrender and the man.

So it was not surprising that Angela's limited vision found its match in Jimmy Rossetto, a man of little talent and enormous ambition, who realized early in life that his best chance for prosperity would be to align himself with those who were already powerful and wealthy. From the moment he met Angela, his dreams for the future began to take form. He was well aware of Gino Manzino's reputation, and of the fact that Gino's uncle, Cesare Mulassano had recently left his organization in Gino's hands. Cesare had only been back in Sicily for a few months when a second stroke killed him and Gino, true to Cesare's words, had become his sole heir (after providing for Teresa, of course). Since then, Gino had been steadily assembling the elements that would one day form the basis of his own genuine empire. But his successes so far – in loan sharking, stolen goods, and gaining some control over the newly organized unions in the building trades – had yet to be brought together into any sort of network. There were many other challenges to overcome – and all in spite of Vinnie's depressing and manifold failures.

Jimmy Rossetto, however, had no doubts. He was one of those manipulators who could always sense the position of greatest advantage to himself. While others hedged their bets, Jimmy knew that if he hoped to gain a place for himself within Gino's organization, the time to move was now. In a few years, the Manzino family would be too well protected to approach.

Having heard about Vinnie's disastrous marriage and its effect on his father, Jimmy came to Angela full of honeyed sweetness. A more romantic courtship could not have been planned – and planned it was. Each moment was part of a carefully orchestrated campaign, each bouquet and gesture of affection chosen on strategic grounds, and Jimmy was infinitely patient in bringing about his desired effect. While both Gino and Filomina had their misgivings about the man who was slowly sweeping their daughter off her feet, they both underestimated him. They saw him as shallow, even comical, in his artificially elaborate pursuit. But they had no idea of how single-minded he could be: It never occurred to them that he could be dangerous until he became involved with Ferdulecci.

Pius Ferdulecci, nicknamed "the Pope," because his mother in a frenzy of religious fervor had named him for the newly-elected Pope, was much more than a thief and a bully, which in his world was considered praiseworthy. He subjected almost everyone he met to physical or psychological abuse and spent most of his time being unpleasant to no one in particular. It wasn't surprising, then, that he had no real friends. To most people, he was the obnoxious hustler with the enormous stomach and the strange, high-pitched

voice. Rumor had it that his voice was unnaturally high because
he had to squeeze its way out of so much fat to be heard. The other
rumor was that he maintained his weight by eating stray alley
cats. He wielded a considerable amount of influence in some of
the seedier houses of gambling and prostitution, but his relationships to those who had to deal with him were always marked by
mutual dislike and distrust. People gladly left him alone. As a
result, it was easy for Jimmy to ingratiate himself as an occasional
drinking companion. He simply had to tolerate with apparent
good nature the offensiveness that had driven so many others away.

When Jimmy first began to meet with Ferdulecci, he had no
plans beyond the immediate goal of making one more contact that
might be useful at some future date. But after the flare-up of hostility between the rotund Ferdulecci and some of Gino Manzino's
people, a scheme began to suggest itself.

The dispute was about territorial rights, or so Ferdulecci insisted. Although no overall authority was parceling out the neighborhood into separate territories, most operations respected one
another's spheres of power because the battles were too costly for
everyone. Half of the combatants in any street war would end up
dead, and the outside world might be forced to intervene, as they
had during the bloody drug wars further uptown. Ferdulecci, however, was one of the few who could never abide by any sanctions or
agreements. Jealous of the lucrative high-stakes *ziganet* operation
being run by the Manzino group in an apartment building just
outside Ferdulecci's domain, one night he impulsively crashed the
game. He roughed up the dealer and disappeared with all the cash
he could stuff in his pockets, somewhat drunkenly waving his antique Colt .45 at everyone who crossed his path.

Gino's people instigated a series of gradually escalating clashes
but hoped to end the affair with a simple act of retaliation. They
raided one of Ferdulecci's own games but stole only enough money
to cover their loss, throwing back the excess so that the message
would be crystal clear, even to a bullheaded man like Ferdulecci.
Then they bowed politely to the players and left. Ferdulecci responded with outrage, screaming to all who would listen that Gino

Manzino had initiated an unprovoked attempt to take over his territory. No one paid much attention to his ravings and Gino instructed his people to ignore him and his operations, which made it difficult for anyone to consider the takeover accusations seriously. Nevertheless, Ferdulecci persisted, conducting a street war all by himself. When his slander made little impact, he would wander out of his own perimeter to harass Gino's runners, disrupting dealings in the street for everyone. Gino had no desire to get into a major clash with a blustering fool, but pressure began to build for Gino to put an end to Ferdulecci's tantrums and restore business efficiency, if not tranquility, to the neighborhood.

Jimmy watched the events with a quiet smile. Somewhere within this chaos was the means to establish his position in Gino's organization. Jimmy had been in the lower echelon of the business, running numbers on the west side for a man well into his seventies. The courtship of Angela had been progressing at a careful pace, but the family still hesitated to accept him fully. Now, with a single gesture, Jimmy could finally move into the Manzino's inner circle.

He approached Gino one afternoon in his warehouse office with an offer to perform a special favor for him. He said that he was motivated only by the desire to restore peace between territories and, even more important, to demonstrate his respect for his beloved Angela's father. Ferdulecci was a notorious loner, Jimmy said, and almost impossible to approach on a rational basis; he was one of the only people Ferdulecci trusted.

Gino had little confidence in Jimmy, and the fawning way in which he presented his offer did little to alter his attitude. Still, the suggestion made sense. Gino knew of no one else who had maintained any lines of communication with Ferdulecci, so he gave his permission for a meeting on his behalf, cautioning Jimmy not to make any promises in exchange for Ferdulecci's cooperation. He was only to say that Gino would make no concessions to unfounded charges against him, but that he wanted to find some way to end a pointless campaign that could only undermine everyone's profits. Jimmy smiled and said that he understood, thanking Gino for the opportunity to be of service.

Jimmy found Ferdulecci in his usual hangout – a back room above Napolitano's Cafe on 96th Street. The room was one of several designed for card games and private encounters with the young girls who serviced the players, but Pius also conducted business there and a seemingly endless meal of pasta was brought up to him in stages from the kitchen below.

Ferdulecci invited Jimmy to sit down and join him in a glass of wine. A gallon jug stood in front of him, but there was little left. Pius must have finished most of it himself, Jimmy thought. Good, that will make the job even easier.

"Would you mind if I locked the door for a moment?" Jimmy asked before sitting down. "I have a business proposition for you."

Pius laughed. "Jimmy, when did you ever have any business worth my time? Sure, sure, lock the door." Ferdulecci began to struggle with the bulky jug in an attempt to get some wine into Jimmy's glass. His jacket was open and Jimmy could see the ornate .45 shoved into his belt. It amazed him how small the large pistol looked against the wide expense of Pius's belly. As Jimmy sat down opposite him, he eased his own revolver out of his waistline holster and flashed his sunniest smile. With his other hand, he reached into his jacket pocket and took out a sealed envelope filled with bill-sized pieces of newspaper. The envelope was a prop, and Jimmy tapped it rapidly on the edge of the table.

"Pius," he began, "I really need your help this time."

Flattered by Jimmy's reverent manner and deeply flushed with wine, Pius reached across the table with Jimmy's glass of wine and said, "Just tell me what you need, Jimmy."

Jimmy fumbled the thick envelope and it dropped off the edge of the table to the floor at his feet.

"Damn!" Jimmy muttered with a look intended to show embarrassment, then disappeared below Ferdulecci's line of sight. Without a moment's hesitation, Jimmy fired two bullets into Ferdulecci's huge gut at a slightly upward angle from beneath the table. His body jerked convulsively and he collapsed backward, chair and all. As the huge mass fell in what seemed like slow motion, Jimmy put a third bullet into him that cut a long gash into his upper chest and buried itself in the falling man's throat.

Ferdulecci's eyes widened in horror as he crashed to the floor. His arms and legs flopped grotesquely for a few seconds and his choirboy voice drowned in blood bubbles before they could form a sound. By this time, Jimmy had rushed around the table, snatched the .45 from the dying man's belt, and fired several rounds from it, splintering the table top and shattering the window just beyond where Jimmy had been sitting. Then he forced open the fingers of Ferdulecci's increasingly lifeless hand and jammed the Colt in place. He could hear feet pounding up the stairs, and soon several fists were beating on the locked door. Jimmy positioned himself on the floor just below the blown-out window, knees drawn up, arms pressed against the side of his head, his pistol a few feet away on the floor, and waited for the waiters to break down the flimsy door.

Gino was honestly shocked when the news reached him a short while later. According to the story that emerged, Ferdulecci had been drunker and wilder than anyone had anticipated, despite his one-man war these last weeks. Apparently he had gone berserk when Jimmy mentioned Gino's name, screamed out curses, and pulled out his gun. Because he was so drunk and clumsy, Jimmy had time to jump beneath the table before Ferdulecci fired, and then he pulled out his own gun and shot back blindly from beneath the table. One of the waiters who'd broken into the room right after hearing the shots said that in a room that size Pius was too big a target for anyone to miss. He was surprised that he hadn't shot himself.

When it was all over, no one mourned Ferdulecci's passing, one of the details Jimmy had counted on to guarantee that any investigation of the incident would be sketchy at best. Even Ferdulecci's mother had long since managed to forget him. Pius's more modest brothers and sisters had all found their way into religious orders, so she could afford to disavow herself from the one who had chosen the streets.

As the reality of what had happened sank in, Gino suddenly found that his relationship to Jimmy had shifted. Acting on his behalf, Jimmy had apparently come remarkably close to losing his life to a madman. He'd been forced to kill to defend himself. Already the neighborhood gossips were transforming Jimmy into a hero, and praising Gino for finding a husband for his daughter who was so courageous and loyal to the Manzinos. Angela was, of course, overwhelmed with pride and panicked that he had been in such danger. Gino would have to find him a position of honor at once, but one that would keep him out of the line of fire in any future conflicts. And perhaps it was time to fix a wedding date after all, she said.

Gino thought this all through before he spoke to Jimmy. But at the end of his ruminating, he felt a glimmer of something else, a nagging suspicion that wouldn't leave him alone. No one would mourn Ferdulecci and no one seemed to doubt that he'd behaved so irrationally and brought on his own destruction. And yet, Gino couldn't help feeling manipulated. Someone had killed a man for him, a favor he had never wanted, and now he was forced to shower that man with gratitude and sympathy. Gino could never be sure that he had been set up, but why the vague sense of guilt about Pius? He filled the funeral with anonymous gifts of flowers, but the fragrance couldn't really conceal the other scent in the room, the subtle stink of deceit. Little did he know that in Pius Ferdulecci's case, the failure to appreciate Jimmy's capacity for devious plots was what had actually proved fatal.

Nevertheless, Gino passed off his unsettled feelings as being traceable to his usual distaste for violence. Considering the dangerous nature of his daily life, he was remarkably free of bloodlust. Even though he controlled a complex organization whose members were frequently compelled to be violent, such force was always a lamented final resort; it was never the business itself. Gino interpreted any use of force as a signal that someone had failed to do his job properly. To keep the level of violence low, Gino insisted that his own people stay a few steps ahead of deadly confrontations. As long as they adhered to his instructions, he could keep them reasonably safe from attack and the need to strike back.

Instead, Gino depended upon intelligence, character, and honesty for his success. Honesty may have seemed to outsiders like an odd virtue in one now dealing so heavily in contraband goods. But blows struck against the outside world didn't count somehow. A man's honor was measured by his dealings within his own circle. Others had also begun their careers as benevolent chieftains, but when times became desperate, they were forced to abandon their ideals. Only Gino seemed resourceful enough to carry this concept as far as he did. He was like a quarterback who was so resourceful that he never had to worry if he was brutal enough for the scrimmages. And yet, when leaders did emerge who seemed half in love with brutality, they actually performed an indirect service for people like Gino. Like the strutting Mustache Petes and the self-styled nobles from the old days in Sicily, these butchers drew attention. Newspapers were sold and political careers launched by lurid descriptions of territorial combat, tribal battles, Black Hand vendettas, organization soldiers and button men, and Mafia dons. There was indeed a structure to the Black Hand. In New York five families each had a boss; and those five bosses met to form various agreements. But by imagining that all street crime could really be organized under a single system of bosses, the authorities could direct their efforts against obvious targets who attempted to control everything on a city, state, or even national basis. This left other true "professionals", as Gino preferred to think of himself, free to operate without interference. He knew that his own domain, enhanced by peaceful annexations over the years, could yield more than enough money and power if worked intelligently. It wasn't necessary to go after anyone else's business. Besides, as his reputation grew, it was only a matter of time before he would be asked to accept some position of authority in a corporate organization that would one day arise from the dozens of operations conducted on the streets. The one flaw that destroyed so many people around him was excessive ambition, and he had learned early on that you could win a great deal as soon as you stopped wasting time trying to win the whole pie. Gino was satisfied with just a large chunk.

Of course, there were times when bloodshed was inevitable. Early in his career a rival family had made an unexpected assault at one of his warehouses when they were loading trucks with contraband. When the smoke had cleared, Gino was one of only three left standing out of twenty-one men. His own gunfire had caught at least four of the fallen.

There was also the night he'd been caught unarmed in the street just two doors from Rosa's apartment building. Their old friend Gracia had finally given way beneath her excessive weight, and while scrubbing her floor on yet another steamy summer day, had quite literally dropped dead onto her glistening floor of a heart attack. As she had wished, Giovanni and Rosa moved into her ground floor apartment, which was not as large as theirs, but certainly easier to get to, and replete with Gracia's prized herb and vegetable garden. Gino had come to have dinner with Rosa on a night when Giovanni played cards down at MANZINOS. He remained talking with Rosa until late into the night as she was aging quickly, and he felt the need to spend as much time with her as possible. This evening, as he left, a man with immense shoulders and a short machete suddenly stepped from an alley, raising his arm to strike. Gino barely had time to block the hand with the blade when the man's other hand closed around Gino's neck. They were struggling on the deserted sidewalk when Gino realized that a parked car at the curb would have to be his weapon. With his back to it, he pushed with all his strength against his attacker. The man was obviously a "heavy," assigned to eliminate Gino, and he had the greater strength. Gino had to think swiftly. As the man began to counter balance Gino's energy, Gino suddenly reversed the direction of his thrust, getting the man off balance and momentarily out of control. In the same instant, Gino turned and smashed the man's head into the car's side window. Something in the angle of the blow, or the force of his body rushing at once, snapped the neck on impact. Gino couldn't just leave him to die on the sidewalk, but after with a quick phone call made sure that the thug would be rapidly disposed of.

Even though Gino's life was constantly at risk, Filomina's commitment to him was unshakable; she knew he was the best man these streets could produce. That didn't mean though that Filomina wouldn't oppose him if she felt the stakes were too high. They both remembered the first and perhaps clearest example of this devotion as "the night of the hidden shoes."

It was still early in his career, when Gino had begun work for the Testas and finances were at their most strained. One evening after work Gino told Filomina that he had been called to attend a meeting called by Alfredo "Big Al" Quartini and Mario Azzano. Filomina had heard of "Big Al," enough to know that despite his namesake, he was nothing but a small-time two-bit reckless schemer. But the more she urged Gino not to go, the more determined he was not to let her interfere in his business, and soon he was screaming and smashing dishes. Perhaps his own misgivings fueled his fury even more, especially as he was in new territory and wanted to make an impression. Filomina forced herself to drop the entire discussion so they could at least sit down for supper.

Afterward, however, the argument started up again. As he changed into a fresh suit, Filomina's sense of foreboding made him so nervous that he couldn't find his shoes. She sat silently as he stormed around, looking preposterous in his stockinged feet. Finally, he realized why Filomina was being so quiet. She had taken the shoes and hidden them.

Gino began an even louder torrent of screams and curses than before, but his roaring faltered almost as soon as it started. Filomina wasn't yelling back this time. She just sat there, silent and unmoving, and he knew that nothing he could say or do would break through to her. She obviously believed that she was acting on behalf of the angels, and Gino finally gave up the fight. He sat in a chair until he grew tired, and then undressed and went to bed.

The next morning, his shoes were shined and waiting for him outside the bedroom closet. But Gino just dressed quickly and left the apartment, refusing to kiss his wife goodbye for the first time in their marriage. All day, Filomina agonized and wept. Now that the danger had passed, she'd have to live with the consequences of her actions. When Gino did not return that evening, she was certain that he had left her. She fed the children and set Gino's portion aside, but she knew it was futile; Gino was not coming home for dinner. Unable to eat anything herself, she went to bed as soon as the children were asleep, crying for what seemed like hours.

She was awakened by hands, Gino's hands, slipping her nightgown from her body. Before she could awaken, his mouth was on hers and then all over her, and his lean, naked body began to enter her. As his fingers and tongue caressed her, she lost the desire to speak. Instead, she surrendered to the flow of his rising passion. When they were spent and she was certain that she was holding her husband and not some phantom of her imagination, he told her what had happened. Quartini and Azzano had reached the end of their violent careers. Someone had betrayed them, and the meeting had been a set-up. The police had moved in with no intention of going through the bother of a prosecution and killed every man present. Somehow, the angels had spoken the truth – and Filomina had used a pair of shoes to save his life.

GINO COULD NOT remember if it was bad or good things that came in threes. But when Rosa told him that Giovanni had placed himself in a hospital, the frailty in her own voice scared him as much as the news. Giovanni had not stepped inside a church for anything except a wedding, christening or funeral since his boyhood in Sicily. But when he realized he was dying, he instinctively wanted a Catholic hospital and the company of nuns rather than the faceless nurses in city hospitals. He didn't really believe that God was coming for his soul, or that the presence of nuns would make any difference if He did. He just felt that it was the way you were supposed to do things.

Giovanni had known that something dark and cruel was growing within him long before the doctors gave it a name, but it never occurred to him that something might be done about it. He only went to the hospital at Rosa's urging when the pain became unbearable. By then, the cancer had filled his body with horrendous rot, and his eyes and ears had already failed him. The sole images he carried with him were those of Rosa, Bianca, and the silver dancers on the hillside.

There were other visitors at the hospital – relatives and some old-timers from the neighborhood – but Giovanni became less and less aware of who they were, or whether they were there at all. Dreams and reality blurred as if cancer had finally penetrated the barrier between them. Besides Rosa, there was only one visitor he felt sure about – a young man who came to the hospital every day, although he never remembered his name. He wasn't even sure if he had ever known it. As far as he could tell, the man was there to see his own father somewhere else in the hospital but always found a moment to talk to Giovanni before leaving. Because his eyes only allowed him to see a penumbra of shadows, Giovanni had no idea what the young man looked like. He even questioned if the man was really as young as he imagined. The visitor would ask about Giovanni's condition and then seemed content to just sit and listen. Giovanni, who'd been so quiet for most of his life, suddenly felt the need to speak. In a hoarse, halting voice, he told stories about the old days, of his children when they were still small, of Sicily, Bianca, and – over and over – of Rosa. The young man listened to everything, no matter how difficult it was for the dying man to form the words, and only left after Giovanni drifted off to sleep.

Soon the days and nights became an endless battle with pain and the drugs that tried to muffle it. Eventually, Giovanni refused to swallow any of the medicine, more fearful of the darkness than the pain. The doctors found other ways to fill his veins, but his ability to hold himself back from death's tunnel began to erode at an increasing rate. The doctors' talk of the weeks remaining became a matter of hours.

On what turned out to be the last day of Giovanni's life, the young man appeared once more and listened to some strange story about silver dancers and Bianca dancing among them. When he was certain that Giovanni was gone, he kissed the old man's hand

and rose from his chair feeling drained and sad and left the room. One of the sisters called to him as he started down the corridor.

"I know," she said, in the whispery chapel-voice all nuns seemed to have, "your presence has made an enormous difference to him, despite all the pain and blackouts."

"It made it easier for me, too," the visitor said with a tired smile.

"Is it still the same?" the nun whispered as he turned to go. "I mean, has he ever realized who you are?"

Gino paused to smile at her. "No, I don't think so. But it doesn't really matter." Coming from a world as primitive and hard as the one he left in Sicily to face a country as strange and forbidding as this one – it was a miracle that Giovanni functioned at all, Gino thought. In the months that followed his father's death, Gino experienced the double-edged response of having stepped out of a shadow, however distant, to become the new patriarch. And yet, as determined as he was, Gino felt none of the driving force that might have characterized him at an earlier age. Somewhere along the way, he'd learned to believe in life's flow of events. It was this that softened the death of Rosa only a month after Giovanni. Blessedly, Rosa did not suffer as her husband had, but simply passed away in her sleep. Gino had brought Rosa home in the weeks of her mourning, but no one had thought she would die there. Only Filomina had her private suspicions.

Just as Bianca had told Rosa the secret of their family, that they rose not from the blood and body of a Corleone soldier, but from nobleman Luciano Santa Pietro, so did Rosa now pass on Bianca's legacy to the unsuspecting Filomina. Anyone who saw Rosa after Giovanni's death realized that grief had made her distant, yet also strangely calm, as if she was preparing herself once again to move on. Letting go of Bianca's secret meant entrusting it to the next generation, and when Filomina listened to Rosa in her shaded guest room one afternoon, she sensed the freedom that Rosa had now returned to, and the weight that had been shifted to her. Over time the secret would lose its power to hurt anyone living, and so be passed about freely. At this point though, it was still a sacred trust and Filomina, if not truly surprised, felt some measure of awe for Gino's ancestors.

The third tragedy to strike the Manzino's took Filomina's spirit and rattled it like a candle in a lantern on a stormy night. Angela had just married Jimmy and a new season begun to turn, when she received the call from Philly's college. Philly had been at the wedding, of course, and Filomina hadn't needed any special sensitivity to see that something was terribly wrong. Although everything he said was designed to communicate contentment, every gesture rang false. He was pale and thin, and frequently appeared to be on the verge of tears. He blended into the background as much as possible, refusing to be pressured into speaking seriously to anyone, including his mother.

"I'm just studying too hard, Mamma," he said, "and recovering from a bout with influenza."

The next morning he left as soon as he woke up.

The voice on the phone said that Philly was dead. Filomina sank into the first faint of her life. When she woke, she had a stillness that Gino had never seen before, as if she had simply shut down all her emotions to protect herself from the pain. Not even the funeral broke through her ghostlike composure. She is in the coffin with him, Gino thought, and with Giovanni dead only a month, he became aware of her mortality for perhaps the first time in his life.

School officials mumbled vaguely about a terrible accident, an unexpected reaction to a lingering illness, a tragic failure to fight off infection. But Gino knew lies when he heard them. The people at the university were sympathetic, but curiously closed mouthed when it came to discussing anything personal about Philly. After much thought and many conferences with a few close friends, Gino arranged for Matthew Fleming, a bright pre-law student from N.Y.U. and the son of the one of the few people Gino trusted, to transfer mid-semester to Philly's college and live in his dormitory. Matt was intelligent enough to discover what had really happened and discreet enough to bring anything he learned back to Gino without informing anyone else.

Matt had known Gino all his life; he was even reasonably sure that Gino was financing his college education. Blond and athletic, Matt had inherited his looks from his German-Irish father. He was the only boy among seven sisters, all of whom were dark like his mother, Francie, a lovely woman who always blushed when Gino visited. She had grown up in the basement apartment of the same building that Gino had lived in as a child. Matt's father died in a trucking accident while driving for the Manzinos when Matt was only ten years old. Since then, Matt often wondered if some hidden passion existed between Gino and his mother, but as Gino was one of the most decent men he knew, Matt was content to know that whatever gave his mother happiness was her private domain.

As soon as Matt arrived in Boston, he began hearing rumors about Philly. Perhaps because he refused to believe them at first, rejecting the image they presented of Gino Manzino's son, he took several weeks to conduct his undercover investigation. In the end, he understood why the college had been so evasive. He wasn't looking forward to breaking the news to Gino and thanked God that he'd be spared facing the grief-broken Filomina. When he finally met with Gino two months after leaving the city, Matt had trouble delivering his news. He began to speak several times, only to break off, apologizing and waving his hand in the air. Finally, Gino had to lean in and speak firmly. "Matthew," he said, "You have to tell me. I need to know the truth." Realizing that his own awkwardness only made the situation worse, Matt nodded solemnly and finally launched into his story.

"At first it was difficult to sort the rumor from the fact," he said, "but in the end everything seemed to stem from the fact that Philly had been having an affair with one of his instructors." Matthew took a breath. "His name was James Kilkenny. He is a well-respected instructor and had never been in any trouble. There was no coercion involved, and the two had a mutual attraction and relationship. The problems began when other instructors and the college administration became afraid of a scandal."

Matt looked at his hands and back to Gino, who simply nodded. "Even though the two were discreet, Kilkenny was brought under intense pressure to either end their friendship or look for work elsewhere. When he decided that a separation was best, Philly just couldn't handle the loss. He wouldn't eat and he stopped socializing. He started slipping in all of his studies and was alienated from other students, afraid that they and even Kilkenny were talking about him. Mostly though, he was simply broken-hearted, especially as Kilkenny had barred him from all of his classes and from his office. According to the medical examiner, and police records, he took an overdose of barbiturates before going to bed one night. His body was found when a dorm chief went to look for him the next afternoon. The school decided that it would be best to keep the matter private."

"Even from his parents," Gino said with a bitterness Matthew had never heard before. But if his face looked suddenly older, Gino asked no more questions and Matt was surprised at how calmly he accepted the truth. In a remarkably soft voice, Gino thanked Matt and hoped that his investigation hadn't disrupted his studies too seriously. Matt hesitated for a moment before pulling a folded piece of paper out of his pocket and handed it to Gino.

"I went through the stuff they'd taken from Philly's room, and this was tucked into one of his books. I thought you should have it." Gino thanked him again, waited until he had left, then slowly unfolded the paper.

In Philly's unmistakably tiny handwriting, Gino read the beginning of a poem:

In his breath, if not in his words,
I try to hear him call to me,
but the sound is only silence.

He read it over several times, feeling more for his son than he had in all the time they shared. Then he found himself remembering a story old Jesse Noli, his seventy-five year old former co-worker, once told him. In his younger days, Jesse had worked his way west with three friends and had finally crossed over the border into northern Mexico. They had some romantic notion of becoming cowboys, or vaqueros, and riding with Pancho Villa. They never reached Villa's army, of course, but they spent several months in local wars and far too many saloon brawls. Noli was the only one who came back alive.

On one particular evening, Jesse had been sitting in a tiny cantina in a dirty peasant town, watching two old men speaking earnestly to one another in Spanish while everyone around them listened intently. According to the bartender, the two men were local legends, two aging bandit chieftains who had spent their lives waging war against each other. The conversation between them seemed to be a solemn exchange of brief speeches that sounded somehow musical to Noli's ears. But he didn't speak Spanish well enough to follow the content, so he asked the bartender what they were saying.

"Each man is presenting the other with his best poems," the bartender whispered, "so that the other will know the measure of the man's soul."

Staring at the sheet of paper before him, Gino thought that he now had a measure of his son's soul. He wondered how many years it would be before he'd become an aging don, sitting down with his old enemies in a dusty cafe, talking the balance of his life away, writing poems about the son he barely knew. But the task before him was even more intimidating. It never occurred to Gino to keep the truth from Filomina. Ever since the call had come, she had experienced a death of her own that Gino feared would change her forever. She sat listlessly by herself, never crying, seldom speaking to anyone. And even though she never knew that Gino was conducting an investigation, she probably assumed as much, and yet had never ventured a guess as to exactly why Philly had died.

That evening they sat alone in the kitchen, the room that had always been the center of their home. Untouched glasses of port sat before them.

"Filomina," Gino began, "I have something to tell you. I sent someone to Boston to find out what happened. Philly . . . ."

"He did it to himself, didn't he?" she interrupted, staring at him blankly.

Gino was stunned, by her look as much as by her words. For a few moments they simply gazed at one another across the table. Then from somewhere within her, from the place beneath the ice where the woman still lived, a terrible sigh emerged.

"Oh Gino," she said and finally began to cry. "Why couldn't we save him?" She came into his arms and gave in to the grief locked inside her so long that the guilt had drawn off most of her spirit. And for the first time in his life Gino, having himself lost father, mother and son in one cold season, now cried with her.

CHAPTER
TWENTY-FOUR

CARLA'S "TROUBLE" WITH men began early in her life. While her sister Angela had the delicacy and vulnerability of character to match her fragile looks, Carla's lovely face and figure beamed with strength and intelligence. Angela would always wait to be noticed like some precious flower, but Carla saw no point in wasting time. When a man attracted her, she would aggressively pursue him, finding that most men were easily manipulated. She had enough self-regard not to throw herself at anyone – no man ever seemed to arouse that kind of desperation. Besides, her beauty was a powerful draw. She could single out a man and make him believe that he was choosing her, though she never remained interested in any of her conquests for long.

Women of wide sexual experiences and appetites were not exactly a rarity in the neighborhood. There were a dozen words in Italian which the Americans translated loosely as "tramp", and more than a dozen local girls fit the category. The only detail distinguishing them from actual whores was that they performed for free, but the distinction was minimal. They might have even picked up a few points of grudging respect if they had charged for the use of their bodies. At least then, the promiscuity would make some sense. Gratuitous availability had no redeeming value at all. Their careers were as brief as they were colorful. They spread their legs until their looks faded or until angry wives and mothers drove them from the neighborhood.

Although no one ever thought of Carla as cheap or weak-willed, something in her manner seemed to mock the conventions binding other young daughters of important and well-respected men. The rumors hovering around her, suggestions that she permitted sexual intimacies with more than one man, remained clouded. Some of the old women who wished to believe the worst and take some terrible tale to the parish priest, whispered that only Gino Manzino's power kept the full truth from being spoken.

But Carla was so sure of herself, and so much smarter than any of the women who wished to criticize her, that she intimidated them. She would return their stares with a look of amusement, as if daring them to voice what they could never prove. Eventually, the rumors would rise again, but with an important qualification: if Carla Manzino was sleeping with men, it was only with the men she chose. Her standards were high and she had a gift for discretion. In a world where young men bragged about real or imagined conquests, the few who had been seen with Carla were remarkably silent. When pressed about what happened when they were alone with her, they said that it was no one else's business, a completely alien concept to the neighborhood gossips. The only one who claimed to have slept with her was Joey Bellagio, but Joey insisted that he had slept with every woman on the block, whatever their age, race, or appearance. He even said he had spent an entire afternoon screwing Annette Zello, until Stevie Zello heard about it and broke his jaw and several teeth. Annette Zello was fifty-three years old and weighed two hundred and forty pounds, but Stevie wasn't taking any chances.

So while Carla's sexual exploits remained unconfirmed, an air of mystery clung to her, which was heightened by her style of dress, far more garish than anyone in her family or circle of friends. Her makeup was equally mysterious – splashes of color in a drab cityscape, never hard and trashy. She was like a tropical creature among duller and drearier species. Each time she made up her face, Filomina would ask, "Why do you want to cover the eyes and skin that God made so beautiful?" As she grew into her late teens, the tones of her dresses, skirts, and sweaters softened a little, but she had no gains in good taste, according to her mother's constant protests. Carla's clothes were skin-tight, emphasizing her firm body. Precariously balanced on platformed heels, she made certain that no one would miss her beautiful, long legs emerging from black silk hems far too high for local standards. When she walked along the block on warm evenings, her bounce and sway amounted to a kind of performance, igniting the passions of all the men she passed, as well as the condemnation of all the women. The older women would shout out curses or pray to the Virgin Mary. At those times, she would think of Mrs. Pietro's pink shutters.

All the houses on the block were identical, their windows framed with the same white or beige shutters. The people who lived there found security in this shared anonymity. But right in the middle of the block, Mrs. Pietro had decided one spring morning to paint her shutters the brightest pink she could buy.

"Why be the same as everyone else," she said when her neighbors complained, "when you have the chance to be different?" It was her one gesture of independence, her announcement to the world that she was unique even if everything else about her was ordinary.

As everyone suspected, sex was part of Carla's escape. On most nights she would wait for Angela to fall asleep, then climb out the window, and meet older men from other parts of the city. Eventually, her continued resistance to her parent's relentless advice that she "settle down and find a nice boy" drove her from the house. At barely seventeen, without a word to anyone, she drove to Maryland and married Peter Ruggerio, the one boyfriend Gino never respected. Pete had been at the center of one scandal or another ever since he was old enough to hold a knife. He was so arrogant that it would have taken a sledgehammer to break him. He stole wherever he could, but so erratically that he'd go for months without a making a profit. He was reluctant to use physical violence, so potential victims that sensed his essential weakness would refuse to play their part. The old Jewish widow who ran the delicatessen on Amsterdam Avenue, in front of a dozen delighted customers, had driven him off with a broom when he pulled out a switchblade and demanded money and beer.

"You're too young for beer," she screamed, ignoring his demands entirely.

In Pete, Carla had found the perfect reflection of her own irreverence. He was always rebelling, and yet fully accepted his own limitations. He had a rare ability to laugh at the many absurd situations he created for himself. Life was basically crazy, he would say, and not really worth the effort of worrying beyond the given day. Pete had a way of making her share in his laughter, and then extending the laughter to include all the things in her own life that had ever upset her. Besides, he was wonderful in bed.

When Carla announced her elopement, Gino said exactly the wrong thing. After screaming about betrayal and Carla's finally fulfilling the family's worst fears, Gino redirected his anger.

"At least we know you're not pregnant," he said. "You haven't known the bastard long enough. And of all the idiots you have dated how could you marry him? He's nothing but a petty thief!"

Her face flushed and the words were out before she realized what she was saying. "What makes you better than a petty thief? You've stolen more than a hundred Petes put together."

Gino looked as if the room had dissolved into ashes around him. Carla managed to catch herself before she said anymore; she was on the verge of giving voice to her father's need for other women as well, a suspicion that had always made it impossible for her to accept his disapproval of her lovers. Even so, she had said enough to shatter any hope that the crisis between them could be surmounted.

In a single outburst, Carla had stepped over a line that was more like stepping off a cliff. There was no way to step back. By contrast, marrying Pete was almost unimportant. Bad marriages could be dissolved or survived, but she had attacked the very center of the Manzino family. Everyone knew the nature of Gino's business, even Filomina. But this reality had never diminished his reputation as a man of honor. Even the most religious among his neighbors were unable to condemn him for the way he provided for his family. The need for immigrants to carve out a share of the wealth surrounding them was somehow unrelated to the moral principles endorsed by priests and catechisms. A man could be an outlaw by day and receive Holy Communion on Sunday without a glimmer of remorse, just as a wife calmly washed the blood from her husband's shirt knowing full well what it represented.

The silence that descended upon them was palpable. It was the first time that Carla had seen her father's anger cut off so completely, and she immediately understood what that meant: his pain was far too deep. As was usual, Filomina had been quiet throughout the confrontation, but her mood abruptly changed. Before it had been intense, the holding back of emotion. But now it was chilled. They each stood frozen in place, then gradually emerged from their solitudes and returned to the breakfast table, taking care not to look at one another. Nothing more was said.

Carla was the last to leave the table. She sipped the coffee that had grown cold in her cup with as much delicacy as possible. She was certain they could see her trembling, but they had chosen not to acknowledge its presence. She waited patiently for it to subside so that she could finally slip away. Tears fell soundlessly down her face until she glanced into the mirror dominating the foyer outside the dining room and saw the dark tracks of mascara bisecting her cheeks like clown's make-up. Her cheeks burned as if she'd been branded with the mark of an outsider, scarred by the mark of Cain that nuns and old women always warned her about.

From then on, Carla was hardly more than a stranger in her own home. On the days she would visit, Gino arranged his comings and goings so he wouldn't have to see her. If she showed up unexpectedly, he passed by her without a word. Filomina spoke to her, but with the same courtesy she reserved for distant relatives or neighbors for whom she had little affection. Yet Carla knew her entire life had been building toward this break. But she pretended for as long as possible that it wasn't really that serious; she was just going through one of those family quarrels that so many others had endured and eventually overcome. The little girl replaced the woman within her; she cried at night and would rush back to her Mamma time and again in hope of receiving forgiveness.

In time, however, her spirit began to reassert itself, and she felt like someone shaking off a long fever. She took stock of the new life she had created for herself and decided that she had done fairly well, all things considered. She and Peter shared a small apartment downtown above an olive oil distributor on Prince Street, in the heart of a section the local police called Little Italy. Most of the inhabitants were young, and the nearness to Chinatown and the tremendous bustle of Canal Street's commerce and crowds made her feel part of something revolutionary, a world of possibilities far beyond the scope of the narrow streets and alleys comprising Gino Manzino's kingdom. Little Italy wasn't exactly America; like so many others, she watched the movements of "real" Americans, those born into lives beyond the ghettoes, with a mixture of curiosity and fear. However sophisticated she became in dealing with life's demands, the vastness of the land beyond the neighborhoods she trusted was mystifying, like a great body of water too immense to cross.

As the months passed and her old independence returned, her marriage to Peter Ruggerio began to falter. The problem with any act of rebellion was that you sometimes had to live with its consequences, and Peter's many failings became increasingly obvious. He was never dishonest or cruel, and she enjoyed being with him, but he was in essence a child, and Carla had abandoned childhood long ago. She became restless with him and the gypsy life they shared, living from one misguided scheme to another and spending every penny irresponsibly. They had very little furniture in their small apartment and hardly any clothes, but he brought home dozens of radios. He loved radios. He intended to sell them uptown at an enormous profit, he insisted, but Carla soon realized that he would never part with any of them. He would turn on several at once, all tuned to the same popular music station and dance happily around their one room until the beating on walls by the neighbors became unbearable. Even the gun he carried and never fired was a toy – an oversized Colt .45 that he thought made him a cowboy. Carla longed to be on her own again, and felt the stirrings of the very rebellious spirit that had made her adolescence so tumultuous, but she had no desire to hurt Peter and kept most of her resentment locked within.

Meanwhile, Peter had encountered little success in robbing the couriers who criss-crossed Little Italy each day with the money they extorted from storekeepers. Some people were surprised that he hadn't been killed by now, but Carla figured he stayed alive because he was so clumsy the bosses must have thought he wasn't worth killing – as if anyone incompetent enough to be robbed by Peter Ruggerio had deserved it.

So Peter decided it was time to make a truly notable hit. A new plan came about when he sat hopelessly drunk one chilly afternoon, brooding over several whiskeys in a bar on lower Broadway. He'd been worried about Carla. She'd been tense lately, easily irritated, easily tired, and strangely unwilling to make love. Peter heard two men at a nearby table talking about the building they called "headquarters," the clearing house nearby where runners from various businesses – protection, numbers, loan-sharking – turned in their receipts and received their cuts. A few moments later, an old man sitting next to him brought up the "factory," a building in Chinatown where they manufactured explosives. Officially, the company manufactured fireworks, but the old man insisted that you could get anything there – bombs, dynamite, even nitroglycerin.

Nitroglycerin. It was a substance that had always fascinated Peter. He knew that the classiest safecrackers used it to blast their way through solid steel walls into massive safes. Somehow, in his alcoholic haze, he became convinced that he only had to steal some of the factory's nitroglycerin and he'd be able to help himself to the treasures stored at headquarters. Exactly how he intended to get through the army of guards that would be protecting the treasure was never clear in his mind. First he'd get the nitroglycerin, then he'd worry about what to do with it. Peter asked the old man if he could give him the address, expressing interest in buying some fireworks for himself. The man looked at him skeptically but then scribbled it down on a napkin.

The fireworks shop was on the ground floor of an old warehouse on the Hudson River, and had not yet closed for the afternoon. As soon as Peter was inside, he went through the door at the back of the shop and started up the narrow stairs despite the indecipherable protests of two Chinese clerks. When he reached the huge loft upstairs, he saw a number of Asian men and women working at several tables. By the back window, one man was wearing asbestos gloves and using tongs to pour something from a beaker into a small vial.

"The nitro," Peter mumbled, and smiled to himself as he drew his revolver and started toward the man.

At the sight of the gun, the other workers screamed and ran for the stairway. Peter paid little attention to them. The man with the tongs saw him approaching and almost fumbled his hold on the beaker. His eyes widened in horror, and Peter saw that the stuff he was handling frightened him far more than the gun coming toward him.

"Hey," said Peter, "is that the nitro?"

The man, too nervous to respond, slowly replaced the beaker on its iron stand. He was sweating profusely despite the coolness of the air and began whimpering softly. Once he replaced the beaker, he almost collapsed with relief, then looked at Peter's pistol as if seeing it for the first time.

"Nitro," Peter said slowly, "is that nitro? Is that nitroglycerin?" He gestured toward the vial with the gun.

"Nitro! Yes, yes, nitro!" the little man said excitedly.

"Good," said Peter, "that's what I want." He reached for the bottle and the little man threw himself back against the wall with a scream, covering his face with his hands. "Relax," said Peter, "I'll be careful." Just as Peter closed his fingers gently around the vial, he heard voices shouting behind him. He turned to see two men with guns who had come into the loft from the staircase and were staring at him with panic. The little man behind the table began screaming in Chinese.

With a carefulness that surprised even himself, Peter took the vial, pocketed the gun, and moved toward the window and the fire escape, saying "Shhhh, shhhh . . ." to the whimpering men, as if they were all rambunctious children who needed their naps. Holding the vial steady, he stepped through the window onto the fire escape and moved slowly down the ladder. Inside, he could hear the little man running to the other side of the room, shouting to the others.

Since the fire escape ladder was not lowered to the street, Peter did what veteran tenement kids had done for years. He stepped onto the ladder's lower rung and let his body weight carry it rustily to the ground. He held onto the descending ladder with his left hand and held the vial in his right, grinning blissfully at the thought of the power it contained. He wondered if he should walk directly over to headquarters and just throw it at anyone or anything there. On the other hand, he thought, maybe he should take it home first and wait until well after dark. He could hide the stuff in his medicine cabinet, maybe pour it into an old iodine bottle.

The ladder was rustier than he thought; when it finally came to a stop, he was still six feet from the ground. A few Chinese children stopped playing at the other end of the alley and watched him curiously. Peter thought hard for a moment, a puzzled expression replacing his simple smile and a few beads of perspiration appeared on his forehead. He decided that he couldn't risk climbing the ladder to re-enter the building and face the gunmen, so he released his hold on the bar and let his body drop from the rung.

The children, who were the only witnesses, said that the white man had disappeared entirely just as his feet touched the pavement. The blast had shattered every window on the alley, and near the spot where Peter had been, piles of garbage were blown into dust, and a hole was punched through the brick wall, causing the corner of the building to collapse slightly into the street. The children instinctively clapped their hands over their ears, but there was no further detonation. After a few minutes, they joined the men who had come out of the building and picked through the area, finding bits of Peter's clothing mixed in with the garbage debris and brick dust.

The only thing not completely evaporated was Peter's second-hand gun. It wasn't registered anywhere, of course, but it was easily identifiable on the street, and the police were at Carla's door the next morning. When they told her what had happened, she collapsed into her first dead faint. Filomina arrived with one of Gino's drivers and as soon as she saw Carla's ghostlike complexion, she sent for the family doctor. Later, when he emerged from his brief examination, he reassured Filomina that Carla would be fine in a few days, but she should drink fluids and rest to protect the baby.

"Baby!" Filomina gasped. "Lord have mercy."

Carla's sudden transformation into widowhood and mother-hood at once worked a small miracle in the Manzino family. The concept of honor would never permit her abandonment, no matter what the circumstances of her parting. Gino maintained his distance, but he allowed Filomina and the other family members to support her in her time of need. Since she insisted on remaining in her tiny apartment, Filomina and Angela came to care for her there.

At first, they came each week with small gifts and food, but as the pregnancy progressed, her mother stopped by everyday. She'd keep her company, cook her dinner, and laugh at all the radios. When the child arrived at last, another Manzino girl born with that special dark beauty, Carla's status in the family settled into a new definition. She would never again live at home, or even be fully acknowledged by her father, but no real bitterness would be directed against her, as long as she respected Gino from afar. She'd see him on special holidays and celebrations and though she was treated graciously, she was expected to make the center of her life elsewhere. Through this compromise, Gino felt that he had satisfied honor and responsibility. He just kept Carla far enough away so she wouldn't hurt him again. From Filomina's perspective, she was simply grateful that both Gino and Carla were safely in her life without conflict. All the rest was foolish pride, and not worth brooding about.

Carla was realistic enough to accept the help that was offered during the pregnancy, as well as some financial aid so the baby wouldn't starve. But soon it became necessary for her to reclaim her independence. When the baby was only a few months old, Carla found work in a small company on lower Broadway that manufactured and sold furniture. In a short time, she moved from the billing department to sales and from there to a supervisory position in interior design, all within a year. During the same period, the company that had hired her was busily transforming into one of the city's major businesses. Carla's natural charisma and aggressiveness were now combined with a talent for design that she never knew she possessed. Everything seemed to fall into place for her and the family was astounded. Filomina was certain that even Gino was proud of her, however unwilling he might be to admit it. For Gino, Carla's triumph awakened an old sorrow that she had inherited all the spirit, intelligence, and self-determination he had hoped to find in one of his sons. But for all her success, she was now guilty of another betrayal – she had become the first Manzino to cross over into America.

As THE LONG years passed, Gino and Filomina watched as all four of their children faded from view. Philly was gone and Vinnie lost in ways no less tragic. Angela seemed safe enough but Gino still thought of her marriage to Jimmy Rossetto with trepidation. And now Carla was completely on her own, achieving more recognition than any of her siblings. No matter how much the Manzinos had gained in wealth and power, when their thoughts were drawn back to their children, the day would be drained of color.

Filomina insisted that there was a balancing force in the universe. Although she would never be as dedicated to the sacraments as so many of the neighborhood women, she continued to believe that God eventually evened things out. She and Gino had been subjected to so much sadness and pain that something must be in store for them that would somehow give them their share of light.

"It's not that I don't see all our blessings," she said to Gino late one night as they lay in one another's arms. "The world is so poor and we have so much. And, despite everything, we have each other. But, Gino, we've tried so hard with our children. We've poured so much love into them for so long, and it never gave us the joy we expected. When does it start to change?"

And then, on January 5, 1952, the miracle arrived.

Although she would always be known as Sunni, their fifth child was christened Gina-Marie Manzino. Coming twenty-two years after the birth of Angela, and long after Filomina and Gino had abandoned any thoughts of additional children, the birth was pronounced miraculous. The fifth child, Sunni, was a remarkable combination of both parents. She had her mother's porcelain skin, but the angles of her face and her mouth's expressiveness reminded everyone of Gino. After so many disappointments in the past, Filomina was convinced that this child would, at last, be the long-awaited compensation. As much as Gino tried to protect them both from being hurt all over again, he soon found his hesitation melting away with each moment he spent with Sunni.

It wasn't just that she was beautiful. They had all been beautiful children. There was something magical about her, a glow that everyone sensed, beyond the usual brightness that all parents imagined their children to possess.

For Gino, the whispered promise that there were happy endings after all came into special focus one afternoon when Sunni was barely four. She had found her way into the office he maintained as a sanctuary for working quietly on the third floor of the large house they had bought in a quiet courtyard near Bryant Park. It amused Gino to remember how he had lived in this neighborhood with Rita Stewart almost thirty years ago. How much difference money and a few blocks could make – let alone the fact that it was a four-year-old, not a showgirl, who had Gino tied around her finger. No one ever disturbed Gino in his office, but Sunni had received a new green velvet dress, and Pappa had wanted to see her in it. It never occurred to her that she might be expected to wait until he had come downstairs to supper. When he looked up from the charts and papers on his desk and saw her there in front of him, spinning swiftly in place so that he could see the skirt and petticoats twirl, he had no choice but to smile. As she spun, she noticed the portrait that filled one wall of the room, and stopped to stare at it in wonder. The portrait was of Rosa, commissioned by Gino, and based on a faded tintype taken in her first year in this country. The artist had met with Rosa several times for additional sketches and had somehow incorporated the special grace and tranquility of the aging woman within the younger woman's face and form. The effect was astonishing.

When Sunni finally turned back from the portrait to face her father, she said "Pappa, that's me. That's me when I get all grown up like Mamma." As soon as she said it, Gino felt a sudden chill of recognition. There were differences in coloring and individual features, but he had never seen until this moment that Sunni was in some mysterious way a new Rosa. Had it been expressed through her mere physical presence, he would have realized it long ago. But it lay within the child's essence, some quality deep behind the eyes and the smile that flashed for him now. Gino wasn't sure what he found most overwhelming: the truth behind Sunni's glow, or the fact that Sunni herself had first seen it.

Born so late in the marriage, Sunni occupied a world all to herself. She had brothers and sisters to prevent her from ever feeling alone, but they were already young adults. Her childhood, therefore, belonged only to her, and she seemed to fully recognize how rich it was. By the time she was born, her parents had lost much of the anxiety that colored their relationships with their other children. Gino had no hidden plans for his last child, and Sunni knew only warmth and happiness from everyone in the family. Even Vinnie, who seemed beyond any genuine sentiment, became a doting brother each time he saw her. The effect, unfortunately, never spilled over into other areas of his life, but at least Sunni gave him one corner where he could go and be at peace.

In turn, Sunni became Gino's opportunity to make up for any of his failures with his other children. Even if Filomina was wrong in believing that God balanced things out evenly, Gino felt he'd been given a chance to do some of that for himself. He was no longer as obsessed with his empire as he once had been, and as Sunni grew up, detached himself more and more from the frenzy of the outside world. Sunni became the new center of his devotion.

For her part, Filomina was still astounded that she had conceived so late in her life. In fact, she had assumed that she was prematurely entering her change of life. How else could she explain the strange shiftings in her body's rhythms? She finally went to her doctor, hoping that he might be able to prescribe something to help her through the discomfort. When he told her she was pregnant, a little amazed himself, she just couldn't believe it. Angela had already presented Filomina with her first grandson and Sunni was a year younger than her own niece! Filomina found herself harboring her own superstitious thoughts. Perhaps, she thought, in telling Filomina her secret, Rosa had freed the spirits of the world to create this new child, a perfect manifestation of her father's true nobility.

With all this fuss surrounding her, it would not have been surprising if Sunni had become overwhelmed and possibly spoiled by the attention. But probably her greatest gift was her inability to respond to anything in a negative way. She loved the admiration, but gave the impression that her smile would have been just as wide if the world had offered her less.

Since Filomina's religious beliefs were more a matter of private devotion than public worship, it made her a little nervous to see Sunni so delighted at the sight of the Sisters at Saint Basco's during Mass or strolling through the neighborhood on late afternoons on some church errand. She even feared that she might lose her daughter to a convent. In fact, when Sunni was seven, Santa had granted her request for a very special doll: a beautiful china creation dressed in a nun's habit. The next morning, unbeknownst to anyone, she set off by herself with her new little sister to have it blessed at Saint Basco's. The nuns were charmed. They had Father Corderi pronounce the appropriate prayers, then the nuns warmed her with hot chocolate and hurried her home to the family that would be frantic if they knew she had left. Gino was mystified when he answered the early knocking on the door to find two elderly nuns and the beaming Sunni, proudly holding up her doll and saying, "Father Corderi made her a real nun, Pappa!"

Gino never missed any opportunity to be seen on the streets with Sunni. He carried her so often in her first years that friends teased him, saying that the child would grow into womanhood without ever discovering she had legs of her own. Many assumed that it was just his male pride, the delight of having produced a perfect child in his fifty-third year. But it soon became obvious that his joy was in the child herself and not in his own achievement. For her, Gino had even gone to the hospital to see her moments after the birth, something he hadn't been able to do for any of the others.

His desire to protect Sunni from any possible danger eventually inspired Gino to leave the city for the first time in his life. He and Filomina had lived in five different homes since their marriage, each one grander than the last, although almost anything would have been grander than the first flat they had shared. Gino knew other men who had prospered and who then became sentimental about the home that had marked their humble beginnings, speaking with nostalgia of their first household as if it was the only place where they were ever truly happy. But Gino had little patience with such sentimentality. Like any man, he missed many aspects of his youth – particularly the hardness that his body had then. He was still slim, still attractive to most of the women he met, but he was always conscious of his age. His one dread was that age would make him weak. But when he remembered the desperate world through which he had moved as a youth, he never had the slightest twinge of remorse that it was now all behind him. Nor did he fail to appreciate exactly how much he had accomplished. He could never walk through a room filled with the beautiful things he owned – carved woods, crystal, silver – without touching each of the things he loved the most.

Yet all of their homes had been deep within the city. Despite its many dangers, he trusted New York. He trusted his ability to

protect his loved ones there. It was a known territory. Except for
their luxurious Bryant Park townhouse, all of their homes had been
a fifteen-minute walk of where Gino grew up. And yet, even in the
townhouse, they lived with enough staff and security to insulate
themselves from the outside world. Sometimes the isolation disturbed Filomina, so she always kept the house filled with relatives
and friends.

"I don't know why we ever moved down here," Gino would
say to her. "You've brought the whole neighborhood with you."

So when Gino proposed moving to a farm in Connecticut,
Filomina was thunderstruck. He might as well have spoken of
moving to Japan. But as she thought of the beauty of the country
her heart expanded. She accepted his judgment, as she did in all
things, and from the day she saw it, loved her new home.

In some way Gino could never fully understand, every time
Filomina looked at him it was as if she were seeing him for the first
time and dedicating her life to him all over again. This sense of
constant discovery and wonder was never so clear as when they
came together in bed. No matter how many times his body entered hers, she always responded as if it were sweeter than she had
anticipated. She made him feel as though something was happening that had never happened before and would never happen the
same way again.

It was this capacity for a continual renewal of affection that
brought Gino back to Filomina in every sense. He had drifted to
other women many times during their marriage. But if Filomina
didn't know the exact nature of the betrayal, she was always aware
that he had never overcome his weakness for beautiful women.
And while she had far too much respect for herself to excuse her
husband's infidelity as easily as other women, neither would she
embrace the other extreme and drive Gino away. She could never
surrender him, and her childlike faith would come into play once
more. In the end, she'd win him back over and over by simply
being herself. She outlasted each of her rivals, and Gino finally
tired of his wanderings. Filomina was such a wonderful presence,
such a source of joy, that every other woman he'd ever known or

dreamed about just faded away. With each year they shared, his awareness of how greatly he was blessed grew stronger. In the time they had left, he pledged to preserve their gift and their new treasure, Sunni. Eventually, Filomina realized that moving to Connecticut was part of Gino's protective instinct and his need to find more time and space they could share.

There was a time when she might have suspected a hidden motive in Gino's desire to isolate his family in the countryside. It might have been a way of increasing his distance, of creating a totally independent life for himself in the city. With the family safely tucked away and cared for, he'd have the freedom to pursue any enterprise that interested him, no matter how dangerous – and, of course, to pursue women. But coming at this stage in their lives, Filomina knew that Gino's only purpose was to create a real home for their new family of three. Not even Rosa was alive to keep him tied to the city, and perhaps Gino also fancied living in a world reminiscent of Sicilian hillsides, with a quiet beauty to reflect the tranquility they had achieved within themselves.

Normally impatient with the details of setting any new plan in motion, Gino became completely absorbed in the process of finding the right house and location. While there were a number of factors to consider – size, seclusion, condition, and so on – first and foremost he was looking for a place that would enchant Filomina and Sunni each time they walked outside. The beauty and colors of the hills, trees, earth, and sky would be far more important than the furnishings and trinkets they might bring to the house. And animals. There must be animals. Enough horses to outnumber the people and enough birds to outnumber them all. After months of searching, Gino found the ideal place, a large parcel of land that formed a self-contained valley not far from the Massachusetts border, just above Mohawk Mountain. Relatives and friends grumbled that it would be difficult to reach, especially in winter, but that was the whole idea.

The house was more than adequate for their needs, even the kitchen exceeded Filomina's expectations. With its brick ovens, butcher blocks, and huge work area, it had obviously been used to feed the staff of a fully operating farm. And while he would never be so sentimental about his believed peasant roots as to consider becoming a true farmer, he appreciated the opportunity to grow enough vegetables to live off the land.

"And dogs, Daddy," Sunni said. "I want four dogs. And three cats." Exactly why she had settled on these numbers wasn't clear to anyone, least of all Sunni, but Gino intended to fill her order precisely.

Gino had never felt the need for constructing defensive strong-holds as had so many other men he knew, but the land provided enough security for him to feel safe. If anything, he felt that the men who built fortresses were being overdramatic, as they tended to be in other facets of their lives. In the ornate ways that they dressed and in their tendency to surround themselves with subor-dinates who served no useful purpose, these men had become the kind of feudal overlords they had crossed an ocean to escape. Be-yond being dangerously conspicuous, they were also, in Gino's estimation, pathetically vain.

So papers were signed, possessions were packed, and the Manzinos, feeling like pioneers, began their migration into the American countryside. It may not have been a wilderness they were entering, but it was still significant enough to qualify as an adventure. While Sunni would miss the nuns at Saint Basco's, she felt that the animals would be a fair exchange. Sorriest to see them go were Bennie, Sara and all the workers at MANZINOS. Now an institution in the neighborhood, the restaurant had the best cook, the grocery the finest vegetables, and seated the most dedicated clientele. Gino joked about transplanting the whole operation to the country – but instead had his own office and small apartment installed on MANZINOS top floor.

The year after they moved, Jimmy bought a parcel of land just down the road from the farm and had a relatively modern house built there for Angela and the children. In choosing the site, Jimmy echoed all of Gino's arguments for living in the country and cited the time-honored traditions that encouraged extended families to live and grow together. But no one was fooled. Along with the obvious advantages the cloying and all-ambitious Jimmy hoped to gain by setting up his household in such close proximity to his father-in-law's, Jimmy's real design was relatively easy to decipher. Everyone, with the possible exception of Angela, understood that the apartment he maintained in the heart of the city would serve the sexual intrigues that had, according to rumor, grown more extensive and bizarre in nature.

But this contrast in husbands could hardly provide much happiness for Filomina when the obvious victims were her own daughter and grandchildren. How much of Jimmy's true character was known to Angela was something Gino and Filomina could only guess, but Filomina felt that her daughter's eyes always held the haunted look of someone who lived in constant anguish, even if her suffering stemmed from a weakness of her own that she was not willing to face. Fortunately, Filomina and Gino had one full year in the country before Jimmy and Angela's move forced them to confront their old sorrows again. And that year was perhaps the happiest the two of them ever had.

Sunni's only real regret about moving, and it was serious enough to cause her first outpouring of tears, was her separation from Desiree, her niece. Desiree was Carla's daughter, so close in age to Sunni that the two felt like twins. They even looked alike, although Desiree was darker, slightly smaller during their early years and less light-hearted. Every weekend during the girls' second and third years, Carla had brought Desiree to play with Sunni in the New York townhouse and they had grown to love each other as true sisters.

When Carla first became a single parent, family speculation about the future of her motherhood took on two diametrically opposed positions. Some insisted that the experience would tame and ennoble her, finally transforming her into a respectful, domesticated woman, anxious to make amends for any past offenses to the family. Others predicted that she would abandon the child and run off with the first man she met. True to form, Carla did not pursue either extreme.

She loved Desiree devotedly and adapted quickly to the de-

mands of her new role with a calmness and efficiency usually found
in more experienced parents. She possessed a special blend of firmness and gentleness that was essential to the raising of children
with character. And yet Carla did not surrender her hard-won independence. With enough strength, she felt she could handle two
roles in life – one at home and one at the office.

So during the years in which she built her impressive career,
Carla raised a daughter of whom anyone might be proud. When
her work demanded her time, Desiree was left with Filomina or
one of the other Manzino women. When her work would take her
away from the city, sometimes even as far as England, Carla would
take Desiree with her, and the child seemed to flourish in the
richness of the new experience. In their early teens, Sunni would
tease Desiree about her sophistication and her unusual sense of
high style, and Desiree would tease her about her innocence. But
as much as he loved Desiree, Gino could never be convinced to
allow Sunni to accompany Desiree and Carla on one of her trips.

Carla never seemed to venture close to marriage again, but she
had a fully active social life with the wide variety of men she met as
business contacts. Still, there was no wildness or scandal being
flaunted in anyone's face. She never made the mistake of dating
someone from her old neighborhood. She was a mature woman,
moving through a world far more sophisticated than the one she
had left behind, and she behaved with discretion. Even Gino was
remarkably reluctant to criticize. Only the chorus of old women
whose only pleasure in life was the endless current of gossip were
willing to condemn her. But then, the Manzinos were a family in
whom they were constantly interested.

Desiree, then, had become the one part of Sunni's life that she
couldn't imagine leaving behind, but everyone had assured her
that Carla would find a way to get her to the Connecticut farm
just as surely as she had come to the New York townhouse. As it
happened, most of the relatives found their way to the country
with amazing regularity. Vinnie even maintained his uncharacteristically affectionate attitude, coming often with little gifts for
Sunni. It still saddened Gino that this single warm impulse in his

son changed nothing else about the man himself. Over the years, he managed to disappoint his father at a continual rate. It was impossible to imagine where or if it would ever end.

Not long after her twelfth birthday, a few years after the move to Connecticut, Sunni seemed to attract still another admirer. Jimmy, who never seemed to display any particular affection for even his own children, was always staring and smiling in Sunni's direction at family gatherings. He, too, would often present her with gifts, usually trinkets of some sort. And he frequently complimented her in a way that sounded surprisingly sincere. Sunni had become so beautiful that compliments were hardly rare, but it was somehow out of character for Jimmy. He had never seemed sensitive to delicate, innocent loveliness before. The uglier side of life always held the strongest appeal. But Sunni had charmed him as deeply as the others. She was fresh and new, like one of his unsmoked Cuban cigars.

Gino was not all impressed by Jimmy's overtures to his young daughter. Knowing the extent of the man's ambition, Gino assumed that this altered attitude was part of some new scheme to ingratiate himself. His marriage to Angela had not taken him as far as he had hoped, so he was probably searching for some other passage to the inner circle. Gino's anger flashed at the thought of Jimmy trying to use Sunni in some way, but he suppressed his distaste for the sake of Angela and her three children. Had Gino been aware of the dark thoughts that were forming in Jimmy's mind, he would have torn him to shreds.

Sunni's first indication of Jimmy's desires came one June afternoon not long after he had begun his campaign to become her most devoted relative, although her impressions of what actually happened that day would remain clouded for some time to come. He had shown up at the farm in a magnificent new car, a 1927 Pierce Arrow convertible that had been beautifully restored and painted a dazzling white. Angela was with him, and the children had come to spend the afternoon with Sunni and her growing collection of horses. The children, aged twelve, ten, and seven, always referred to Sunni as their "little aunt". Each had a share of

Angela's whiney nature and a suggestion of Jimmy's hardness, but Sunni could usually bring out their cheerful sides. She loved Jimmy's car, though, and he promised to take her for a ride after lunch.

They started out, just the two of them, down one of those untraveled lanes bordered on each side by farmland, orchards and paddocks. Jimmy insisted that Sunni was old enough to learn how to drive and, since the road was so deserted, he offered to give her a lesson. The simplest way to begin, he suggested, was for her to sit on his lap and help him with the steering. Sunni giggled excitedly at the idea of actually taking the wheel of such a beautiful machine, almost like getting on her first horse, so as soon as Jimmy pulled the car into the deep shade alongside the road and turned off the engine, she squeezed onto his lap, gripping the steering wheel tightly with both hands.

As she waited for something to happen with the car, a single guilty thought began to push its way into her mind. One of the oldest taboos she'd been told was to never sit on any man's lap – not uncles, grandfathers, or even fathers. It had to do with the dark, mysterious realm of adult sins. She remembered the warning: "The beast in any man is far too easily aroused." But what could that mean? Besides, it couldn't possibly refer to this situation. This was a driving lesson, and there was no other way she could reach the wheel and see out the windshield. Jimmy was just being kind. And hadn't her grandmother once issued a similar warning about riding horses, saying that a young lady should ride in a carriage or, if she must be on top of a horse, then only in a side-saddle position? Even Gino thought the idea was ridiculous. Wasn't this the same kind of thing?

Somehow she knew her arguments would never have convinced her grandmother. She wasn't even certain they convinced her. But she ignored the faint twinges of conscience and tried to concentrate on the car and all that Jimmy was saying. Still, Jimmy was taking a very long time explaining the machine's operation. She forced herself to listen politely as he pointed out various leather-encased knobs and instrument gauges rimmed in polished brass.

Then she sensed something else, a subtle change in Jimmy's breathing, the way it mixed in with his voice, and something to do with the warmth of his hand on her thigh as the other pointed out dials and levers. Some instinct told her that something wrong was happening, but the same instinct warned her not to say anything, so she remained on his lap, conscious of a faint trembling deep inside her and a fleeting impression that the shade surrounding them was growing darker.

Jimmy's warm, peppermint-scented breath touched her ear as he spoke, and she began to focus on a changed quality in his voice. In the next moment, Jimmy started the car, and they moved back into the ribbon of sunlight, finally reaching the road through the anchored walls of trees rising from both sides of the lane. Within the next few minutes, Sunni pushed the sense of danger from her mind, convinced that she had simply let her own imagination frighten her, as it sometimes did in her dreams. She was just being silly, she thought, and felt ashamed at her thoughts. After all, Jimmy was only trying to be nice. She soon lost herself in the motion of the car and the thrill of moving the wheel as it hurtled forward. Jimmy kept one hand on the wheel so that it couldn't wander too far off course, but he did allow the car to weave back and forth, much to the delight of Sunni who was laughing once more.

They reached the end of the lane, and Sunni surrendered control of the wheel to Jimmy so he could turn them around in the narrow space. As they headed back home, Sunni – still straddling his lap – was steering again and felt fully relaxed, the strange fear almost forgotten. But as they passed the stretch of road where they had paused earlier, she stared at the shaded spot and felt a distant chill. Jimmy kept one hand firmly on the wheel, and the other moved occasionally to shift gears. Yet his hand always returned to softly caress the skin just above her knee, slipping with seeming casualness beneath her short cotton skirt. Sunni was a naturally affectionate child, and relatives had caressed and hugged her all her life, but she knew that somehow this was different. As she concentrated on the wheel, her legs parted so that they could enclose his legs and allow her to hold her position. She suddenly became aware of a presence beneath her, a hardness pressing against her. It felt like a column of wood, filled with its own pulse.

At twelve, Sunni had not yet been given an explanation of sexuality. She lived in an environment of protected contentment where the realities of life had no opportunity to intrude. But she did have a sense of unresolved questions about the world around her. Fragments of conversations she had overheard within the family puzzled her. The suggestions of desires and emotions that motivated people were still beyond her understanding. And there were other elements, equally mysterious. She observed animals closely, noting the patterns in their behavior and wondering about their links to humanity. At nine, she had watched an Arabian stallion respond to the appearance of a mare in heat in a nearby paddock. It wasn't so much the desperation with which he flung himself against the fence; it was the instantaneous tensing of every muscle in his body, and the strange appendage that unfolded out of nowhere beneath him. The image stayed with her for a long time and occasionally haunted her dreams. There were also the strange stirrings within her own body, the heightened sensitivity to touch that came to her unbidden at night or during warm afternoons but which some instinct told her would displease the adults if they knew.

All of these isolated concerns troubled her deeply, but were usually overwhelmed by the more benign moments of her childhood. Then she became aware of Jimmy's physical arousal and all of these disconnected elements began to come together like shattered glass filmed in reverse. She felt a terrible fear, one she could not comprehend. She was certain that Jimmy meant to hurt her and equally certain that if he did so she would be lost to her family forever.

At that moment, Jimmy brought the car to a stop in the middle of the road and she felt both of his hands closing upon her waist. She closed her eyes, too frightened even to mumble the prayers that the nuns had taught her to say in times of peril. She thought of all the stories she had read where the heroines she hated always fainted in the face of danger, and she felt weak with dizziness.

Then Jimmy removed her from his lap, deposited her on the seat next to him, and restarted the engine without a word.

When they pulled into the driveway, she hurried from the car, but Jimmy held on to her arm and said, "Don't I get a kiss, Sunni?"

Sunni leaned over to plant a kiss on Jimmy's cheek, but he took her face in both hands and kissed her full on the mouth. She could almost swear that she felt his tongue on her clenched teeth.

A few minutes later, she ran into the hallway and Filomina saw she was upset. "What's wrong?" she asked, instantly concerned.

"Nothing, Mamma," she said hurriedly. "Jimmy just let me drive his car and it scared me a little. I'm okay." Then she rushed into her room.

As soon as she had locked the door behind her, Sunni buried herself deeply in her down-feathered bed, pulling the comforter around her in a vain attempt to ward off the shivering that had chilled her to the bone despite the warmth of the afternoon. At first what she felt was just fear, the aftermath of having escaped some unnamable, unknowable terror. Eventually, however, this was replaced with something even more oppressive. She began to experience a profound sense of shame.

She ran it over and over in her mind: what had she done that had left her feeling so unclean, so wicked? Was her sin imagining that Jimmy was doing something horrible? He had always been so kind to her, and Angela loved him so much. How could he be evil? She knew her father didn't like Jimmy; she could feel it whenever Jimmy came over. But that was something between men, about business, she thought. So if Jimmy wasn't really a bad man, what was wrong with her? If he had really come close to doing something dirty with her this afternoon, wasn't it somehow her fault? Suddenly she understood why she had always been told not to sit on any man's lap. Would she ever be forgiven? All of these feelings washed over her, wave after wave, as she lay huddled in her bed. She had heard so many whispered conversations in the family about the kind of girls Jimmy liked – trashy women, someone had said, women who lived in sin. Was she one of those girls?

Finally she fell into an exhausted sleep. Filomina checked on her from time to time, afraid that she had developed a sudden illness, but was pleased to see that Sunni was sleeping peacefully. She's just overtired, Filomina thought, and left her to her dreams.

In the morning, Sunni's memory of the previous afternoon had become somewhat blurred, but her stomach felt painfully knotted. At breakfast, however, no one seemed to notice any significant change in her, and everyone was cheerful. The day was beautiful and the horses were waiting to be exercised across the fields. Sunni forced herself to be a part of her childhood again.

When Jimmy's white car pulled in front of the house, Sunni felt that all her composure would vanish in an instant, but she was too weak to run away. What if he had come to touch her again? In another moment, Jimmy approached the house, smiling pleasantly as he crossed the porch to where she sat with Filomina, playing goldfish with oversized cards. He accepted Filomina's offer of a glass of sherry and waved briefly to Sunni as he followed Filomina into the house to find Gino. It was as if yesterday had never happened, Sunni thought, and she began to wonder if it really had, outside of her imagination. Still, there were some details she remembered that she could not have created herself. She could remember, for example, how it felt when Jimmy had lifted her from his lap and her leg had brushed against the tip of the swelling that had stretched the thin fabric of his trousers. But unless she dared to speak of it, the reality was hard to grasp, her sense of shame would never allow it, so perhaps it would be forgotten after all.

In the months to come, there was never the slightest hint that the secrets of that afternoon might ever be unlocked. Jimmy still came to the house, still brought her little gifts, but he made no attempt to be alone with her. As each day passed, Sunni became more and more uncertain as to what had actually occurred and felt increasingly safe in her life again. The only time that terrible anxiety would descend upon her was when some visit would draw to a close and the ritual of goodbye embraces would begin. Each time she approached Jimmy to exchange kisses, even with her parents standing close by, she felt the same gripping fear. The scent of peppermint when he kissed her was always the same as it had been that first afternoon. She always hurried through the gesture, hoping no one would notice and while he never seemed to hold onto her any longer or with any more intensity than seemed appropriate, there was always something beneath the surface that would never be visible to anyone else, the ghost of a longing known only to them, a suggestion of something unclean. But when the moment passed, the normal world would reassert itself and she would leave those dark forebodings behind.

By the time she was fourteen, the memory had faded in the rush of brighter, lovelier remembrances. While Jimmy continued to be a presence in her life, he seemed to have settled into the dual roles of family member and neighbor, giving her no more attention than any other adult. If she sometimes saw more in the glances that were coloring his face, she would simply move away.

On one occasion, however, even Gino had witnessed the flicker of panic in her eyes. She had come into the den late one evening and ran unexpectedly into Jimmy. She'd been sleeping and had lost track of time. In the few seconds it took for her to realize that Gino was there too, she looked as though she'd just been thrown into a snake pit. Gino interrupted his conversation with Jimmy – some tiresome business about hiring additional lawyers – and escorted his daughter to her room.

"You looked so frightened," he said to her. "What was the matter?"

"Oh," she said, still unwilling to give voice to the thoughts that had troubled her for so long. "I was having a terrible dream, and then I forgot where I was for a moment." Suspecting that this might not be enough to satisfy him, she added, "And then Jimmy was there. I've never really liked Jimmy very much, Pappa."

To her surprise, Gino laughed out loud and said, "None of us do, honey. Except perhaps poor Angela." Sunni's shock knocked out whatever residual fear she might have felt, and she found herself laughing with Gino. Neither of them had ever spoken openly about a family member in this way, and it felt wonderful to her. For one thing, she could stop pretending to care for Jimmy. For another, her father had actually shared a confidence with her. He had always treated her with kindness and affection, but this was the first time he had treated her as an adult.

"Whatever you do," he whispered as she got back into bed, "don't tell your mother what we said. She feels the same, but she'd never forgive us for actually saying it." Sunni was still smiling when she drifted off to sleep, feeling as if she had finally banished her deepest fear.

BECAUSE THE TWO families lived so close, Sunni was sometimes asked to come over on an afternoon or evening to watch Louis, the youngest of Angela's three children. He was eleven years old, but his reckless spirit made him seem even younger than his undersized appearance. He wasn't really a bad child, but he was certainly a handful, and attempts to leave him in the care of his older brother and sister usually ended in disaster.

Since Jimmy spent most of his weekday evenings in the city, Angela had created her own social life with the women she had met in Connecticut. Every so often, she would drive to New Milford to have dinner with two or three friends. At such times, Sunni would volunteer to keep Louis company if no other arrangements could be made. And so, one Wednesday night in late August, Sunni came to keep Louis company while the rest of the family was away for the night. The two older children were each in their last week at a youth camp in the Berkshires, Jimmy was God knows where, and Angela would not be home until very late.

Sunni had arrived early enough to cook Louis his dinner, even coaxing him to drink a reasonable amount of milk. Before the light failed, they shot baskets in the court behind the garage and she managed not to outscore him too badly. Her one concession for the evening was allowing him to watch two hours of professional wrestling on television before he went to bed. She even watched the matches with him, laughing at the silly antics and repetitiousness of it that even the costumes couldn't disguise. Louis could watch for hours, but she always found herself drifting off to sleep by the third or fourth match.

After a while, she was vaguely aware that the wrestling had

ended and Louis had turned off the set, mumbling goodnight to her as he disappeared down the hall to his room. She was stretched out on the large sofa, lost in the coolness that always followed warm days, her sense of time gently erased by her deepening sleep. She didn't hear the key that turned in the lock an hour or so later, the footsteps in the den, or the muted click of the room's one lamp being turned off.

The first thing she felt was a hand softly but insistently stroking her thigh. She was wearing shorts and a loose summer shirt and was lying on her back, her slim, tanned legs parted in sleep. At first, the touch seemed to be mixed in with the dream she'd been having. Then she became aware of the breathing, the scent of whiskey, and suddenly came fully awake. Frightened by the darkness, she sat up at once, the motion bringing her face close to someone else's. In the next instant, he was kissing her, his mouth pressed full on hers, his tongue forcing its way between her teeth.

Her mind was still fogged by sleep, but the hand holding her face was squeezing with too hard; the smell and now the taste of liquor overwhelmed her and she felt the raw panic and the beginnings of a scream rising within her.

"No!" she yelled, and she pushed him backward with enough strength to break his grip on her and tumble him onto the floor. She bolted from the couch and started blindly across the room, colliding with the copper floor lamp.

She fumbled for the switch as the voice across the room said, "Hush, hush. You'll wake the boy. Hush . . . ." Then the light clicked on and Jimmy stood before her. His eyes were blurred; he had drunk far too much, and he stared at her with a devilish gleam. There was a hardness in his body as well, and as she watched in disbelief, he stepped out of his pants, his swollen member protruding from the tails of his silk shirt.

"We have to be quiet, Sunni," he said hoarsely, "or we'll wake the boy. You can trust me, Sunni. I'll make you feel wonderful." Too stunned to move as Jimmy came toward her, she began to cry, sorriest of all that he had said her name, which meant she couldn't pretend that this wasn't happening.

"Hush, hush" he whispered again, although her crying was very soft, and before she understood what he was doing, he had yanked her shirt over her head and tossed it on the floor. Suddenly more ashamed at being seen than afraid of what he might do to her, she tried to cover her small breasts with her hands.

"Shhh," he kept saying, and then he pulled her hands away, bent and kissed each rosy tip quickly, and then he was on his knees, using both hands to pull at the buttons on the front of her shorts as his breathing became even more desperate. There was a ripping sound as he lost patience with the buttons and Sunni reached for the lamp, crashing it down on his head just as he was starting to climb to his feet.

He was caught off-balance, so the unexpected blow sent him sprawling backward and then over the oak chest that now served as the coffee table. Miraculously, the lamp didn't shatter, and in the oddly angled light, Sunni saw Jimmy do a complete backward roll and land heavily on the polished wood floor, calling out in a sharp cry of pain. She wasn't sure, but Sunni thought that his shaft had somehow taken the force of the impact. His fall had been so clumsy and so slow-motioned that for a moment she was before the television again, watching the wrestlers stumble through their mock battles.

Then Jimmy stood up slowly, a look of rage erasing every other emotion in his eyes. Sunni knew at once that the danger facing her had just deepened enormously. He was between her and the doorway leading outside. There was no hope of escaping him and finding her way home across the dark fields.

With a swiftness that surprised her, she ran into the hallway leading to the bedrooms, somehow managing to grab her shirt as she ran. She slipped into Louis' room and closed the door behind her. In another moment, she had hurried into her shirt and, suddenly shivering, lay down on one corner of Louis' large bed, drawing his extra quilt around her. Louis stirred slightly, but she whispered "shhh, shhh" and he didn't awaken. Sunni tried very hard not to cry, or even shiver, as she waited in the darkness.

After a space of several seconds, the door to the room opened slightly and the vague outline of Jimmy's body was blocked in the faint light drifting in from the overturned lamp in the den.

"Sunni," he whispered, the sound almost smothered by his struggle for control. "Sunni, please come out of there. Sunni, please."

Pulling the quilt over her eyes, she tried to blot him out completely. The whisper came again, more insistent this time, like a snake hissing in the doorway.

"Sunni," he said, and started to open the door wider. Louis stirred again, mumbling something that sounded like "wozzat" as his sleep broke apart and he raised his head from the pillow.

"Shhh, Louis, it's all right. Go back to sleep, honey." She spoke softly, pulling his blanket up against the night chill and gently caressing his back.

"G'night, Sunni," he sighed.

For another long minute, the figure of Jimmy stood in the doorway, then he backed away and closed the door.

When she was sure that he was really gone, Sunni let out a long breath. She was crying again, but the tears were silent and she let them come, sure that no amount of them could ever take away all her sorrow and disgust and shame. After a while, she heard the sounds of Jimmy prowling through the house – water running in the bathroom, an ice tray being opened and then thrown into the sink, footsteps heading toward the main bedroom at the far end of the hallway. Then silence. She lay unmoving in the bed, staring at the ceiling, trying not to think. She didn't sleep, but somehow the hours passed and, at long last, she heard Angela's car pull onto the gravel outside.

She hurried from the bedroom, grateful that her shirt hid the tear marks at the top of her shorts. She was at the door by the time Angela had unlocked it and rubbed her eyes as if wiping away sleep instead of tears. Angela seemed surprised to see her.

"Sunni," she said, "why didn't Jimmy take you home? I saw his car outside."

"He must have come in while I was sleeping," Sunni said, and they both glanced down the hall to the far bedroom. The door was ajar and a light was still on in the room. Jimmy was clearly visible, stretched out full across his bed in a semi-dressed state, clutching a Scotch bottle as if it were a teddy bear. Angela didn't notice the shudder that passed through Sunni.

"Well," she said at last, intent on suppressing her own dismay, "at least he's here. Let me run you home and then get him properly to bed." She flashed an embarrassed smile at Sunni as if Jimmy was just another mischievous child like Louis who could drive you a little crazy now and then, and then they both started out to the car.

As soon as she got home, Sunni showered in water as hot as she could stand in a vain attempt to wash away the dirtiness she felt. She scraped at her nipples until they were raw, certain that his obscene kiss would leave a scar. Finally, exhausted by her attempt to punish her body for what couldn't be undone, she emerged from the steam, wrapped her still-wet body in a terry cloth robe, and crawled under the covers of her bed, falling immediately into a deep sleep. When morning came, just a few hours later, Filomina was puzzled by the condensation clinging to the bathroom tile and hallway, but she didn't interrupt Sunni's obviously needed rest. She slept well into the afternoon and awoke feeling calm but almost unbearably sad.

In the weeks that followed, Sunni tried very hard to gain some perspective on the night. She was intelligent enough about human nature to realize that Jimmy was a sick and dangerous man and that it didn't make sense to blame herself for his attack. But she could not shake the fear that there was something about her, some wickedness inside that had triggered his madness. Did he sense some weakness in her? Is that why she had climbed onto his lap and set this nightmare in motion?

The few times she saw him at family gatherings, he showed no regret about anything he had done. All he had was the fear that Sunni might tell someone what had happened. But Sunni would do anything to avoid the explosion that would surely follow such a revelation. It wasn't just that Angela would be destroyed. Sunni knew that Gino's fury would be beyond measure, and, in avenging his daughter, might well usher the entire family into ruin. Still, each time she glanced at Jimmy and saw his eyes turn anxious, her feelings hardened into contempt, which was somehow easier to endure than all the guilt, and gave her the confidence to believe that she would rise above this.

CHAPTER
TWENTY-FIVE

OVER THE NEXT two years, Sunni's pain diminished to a dull ache, a kind of background hum in an otherwise peaceful existence. She hardly ever saw Jimmy, and so she was seldom forced to confront the memory directly. And yet it soon became clear that the episode continued to exert its influence in the way she responded to new situations, particularly the bizarre rituals performed by her mother and her mother's cousin, Beninia Marino, to cure the evil eye or what some people simply called "the eyes."

Beninia was well-known in Harlem for her healing powers and had become a fixture in the Manzino household. Each Christmas Eve, the only time when mystical talents could be taught, she would pass on her gifts to Filomina. Sunni would watch in silence as Beninia babbled on in an indecipherable dialect to all the nervous women who filled Filomina's kitchen with children supposedly afflicted with menace – babies with blank stares who'd been born under the wrong kind of moonlight, or cursed by the whispered prayer of some distant enemy – for "the eyes" only focused on the darkness in things and could lead the most innocent child into wickedness. When the babies were brought in for the cure, Filomina and Beninia would consent to the exorcism, "just as a precaution," and begin a ceremony involving chanting in Italian, a bath in cold tea, and the blessing of the child's eyes with an old crucifix fashioned from hemp rope. Afterward, the mothers were ecstatic, announcing a new clarity in the infants' sober looks. When modern mothers rejected such old-world beliefs, the grandmothers would take on the task of saving their grandchildren from lives of misery, swearing Filomina and Beninia to secrecy.

Sunni, like her Aunt Tessie many years before, enjoyed watching the special healings performed for every form of ailment. Her favorite was Beninia's cure for migraine headaches: freshly peeled potato skins bound to the forehead by tying a white cloth dipped in olive oil tightly at the back of the head. Beninia then placed both of her hands on the patient's head, closed her eyes, and recited words in an obscure Sicilian dialect, contorting her wide face in a wild succession of grimaces, yawning, and extravagant burping. It took all of Sunni's self-control not to burst out laughing.

Once healed, the faithful would inevitably want to give Beninia and Filomina some reward for providing the miracle, but Beninia insisted that it was sacrilegious to accept payment for a mystical gift. She was not opposed to accepting meat from the healed wife of a butcher, however, or cheese from the healed wife of a grocer. Filomina, of course, would not even accept these tokens. Gino would never tolerate any form of compensation for his wife's superstitious nonsense.

But the idea of warding off evil began to affect the way Sunni looked at the world. Gradually, she became aware of the strange nature of people's eyes at family gatherings, especially Jimmy's, whose penetrating gaze gave off an unnatural gleam. There was something inherently evil in those eyes, she thought, and she came to believe that Jimmy had been born with the evil eye intact, growing into manhood touched by the devil, his darkness too strong to be healed. At first, she pitied her sister Angela who was doomed to a life with this despicable man. But later she realized that Angela had freely accepted her fate and had settled into martyrdom, as if the suffering that was etched in her face had become a symbol of pride and endurance. Sunni feared most that she'd grow up to be like her, but as her vision of life matured, she swore that she would never become trapped in her sister's emptiness, and however much she loved her parents, she would create her own life apart from them as well.

Soon after the Manzinos moved to Connecticut, Sunni persuaded her parents – after a long campaign – to allow her to attend the local public school. In the city she may have needed the nuns' protection behind private school gates, but now they lived in a clean, healthy environment, and she wanted to become involved in the day-to-day lives of the other young people in the community. Their farm was too isolated for very much contact with neighbors; school was a way to make friends.

At sixteen, Sunni had grown into her full beauty imbued with the same warm spirit that had melted so many hearts in her childhood. She could barely get through one day without another boy falling in love with her. And though she enjoyed her popularity, she had little interest in committing herself to anyone. She dated often, but casually, and looked forward to the company of girlfriends as much as to that of any single boy. She had already kissed several young men in the moonlight and danced closely with them to the same romantic songs as other girls, but her unusual reserve held her back from any surrender to passion. Only one or two of the more persistent boys suspected something else was at stake and even noticed the glimmer of fear beneath her coolness. Still, they respected and cared for her too much to press any further. Sunni's self-discipline enabled her not only to survive the perils of personal contact, but to pretend that she could live her whole life without intimacy and never feel the loss. Matthew Bennett was the only exception.

The first time she met Matthew, he was hopelessly in love with Barbara Daniels, a girl who was slowly destroying both herself and him. She was very lovely – pale and delicate – and Sunni could easily understand his obsession with her. Physically, they could have been twins. With the same blue eyes, soft blonde curls, and slightness of build, they were often mistaken for brother and sister. This mirror image must have created much of the attraction that bound them, Sunni surmised. Perhaps it also explained why Barbara seemed so determined to hold onto Matthew even as she began to go down in a struggle of self-destructive impulses; it also explained why Matthew was powerless to resist her. Neither Sunni nor Matthew could fully account for Barbara's profound unhappiness. Her parents, prosperous dairy farmers who had alienated themselves from any contact with the community, had a coldness to them, a lifelessness that might have explained it. But instead, they figured that the greater problem was probably born inside of Barbara. Yet, Matthew loved her and his overwhelming sadness at the possibility of losing her had drawn him to the edge of an abyss.

Sunni first met Matthew in rehearsals for a school play, a fairly incompetent version of *I Remember Mamma* in which no one could get the Swedish accents right. Only Matthew's irreverent sense of humor eased Sunni's embarrassment throughout the performance, and their shared sense of how silly they sounded inspired them to work together on a second production the same year. With only minimal support from the faculty, they joined together with several other students and presented *Our Town*, surprising everyone with its sensitivity and polish; even Sunni and Matthew hadn't realized the extent of their own natural talents. He had played George and she had played Emily, and Sunni found herself feeling a genuine tenderness between them beyond what they imagined for the audience. Which was why she was so shocked when she saw the change that came over him whenever Barbara was near. Barbara radiated a strange tension and Matthew's optimism and sense of joy seemed to crumble in the face of it. At first, Sunni was only confused, but then she began to fear for his safety. Matthew had become a friend, her closest friend, and she felt a new sense of responsibility for his welfare. But his final separation from Barbara became a long and painful process. Since Sunni had no motivation beyond friendship, no desire to possess Matthew herself, her strength became the most positive force in his life. At times Sunni felt she was nursing him through an addiction like drugs or alcohol. She listened when he needed to talk. She pointed out, gently but clearly, the extent to which Barbara was slipping beyond anyone's help. And however gloomy the day, she discovered her own sense of humor and made him laugh. Touched by Sunni's selflessness, Matthew began to break away from Barbara's control over him. Sunni had given him another focus for his life – the world of acting – and slowly he reclaimed his identity. In turn, somewhere deep within her, Sunni's old coldness was melting away.

WHEN A BUNGLED suicide attempt finally led to Barbara's commitment to a private institution, Matthew was able to feel the full pain of his loss without surrendering to it. He would always love Barbara, but he would never again feel driven to join her suffering. Meanwhile, the friendship between Sunni and Matthew deepened as they worked constantly on one dramatic production after another. She would come to him for advice about the boys she dated and introduce him to happier girls who would help him forget about Barbara for a while. Sometimes they would go to a dance or party together, finding comfort in the ease true friends can share. If a family gathering required an escort, Sunni would frequently invite Matthew to accompany her – and soon her family grew to love him. Occasionally, a forgetful relative might ask when the beautiful young couple was getting engaged, but most of her family recognized that theirs was a special friendship, uncomplicated by romantic emotions.

Finally, when Sunni became a senior, her life moved swiftly away from the shadows that had been relentlessly holding her back. She gained a new confidence in herself that erased all memory of Jimmy's abuse. Jimmy had become more pathetic than frightening. Sunni could even remember the precise moment when she stopped being haunted by the shame that Jimmy had inflicted upon her. During a family celebration for her and Desiree – a double birthday party for their sixteenth year as friends – the two girls had been joking with a group of relatives about why they no longer wore matching dresses the way they did as children when Jimmy came up behind them, slipped an arm around each of their waists, and said something about his two "personal princesses." Sunni gave an involuntary shudder but suppressed it in the same instant. If it was visible at all, it could only be detected by the darkness in her eyes, so fleeting that almost anyone would have failed to notice it – anyone except Carla. Carla had been standing right next to her and saw with sudden clarity what Sunni was trying so hard to conceal. By the time the two girls had finished blushing and Jimmy had moved away, some mechanism in Carla's mind clicked like a camera lens fastening on a moment in time.

Carla stared at Jimmy across the room as he moved among the guests, oblivious to the conversation around her. Then she rose abruptly to her feet and gestured for Sunni to follow her. Carla led her upstairs to Sunni's bedroom, closed the door behind them, and told Sunni to sit on the bed. Puzzled and curious, Sunni smiled at her sister who remained at the door, leaning against it and crossing her arms. In a soft but iron-hard voice, Carla said, "Sunni, I want you to tell me exactly what Jimmy did to you."

For the first few moments, Sunni couldn't utter a sound. She knew from Carla's eyes and tone of voice that she would accept nothing less than the truth. Carla had always had an uncanny insight into human nature, which over time had grown into a worldly cynicism that seemed to dispel all of life's mysteries. And so, as the shock of being discovered began to soften, Sunni felt a rush of gratitude. She knew Carla was one person she could trust with her secret, someone who could help her sort out the jumble of feelings that still rattled her.

"Oh Carla," she said, instantly starting to cry, "was it my fault? He touched me and tore my clothes and . . . ."

When Sunni was finally able to describe all that had happened in a coherent sequence, Carla sat down beside her and drew Sunni into her arms, assuring her that she would preserve her secret.

"Sunni, you must never feel any guilt or shame over this. When a man is a predator," she said, "as Jimmy is, only the most innocent, only those of extraordinary goodness allow themselves to feel contaminated by the corruption. But once you confront and reject the evil, he will lose the power to hurt you, even in memory. He can only win if you take on the blame for his crimes. Jimmy is a monster, but he will never threaten you again. Eventually, he'll get the punishment he deserves, but now you have to push it all from your mind and get on with your life."

Sunni agreed, feeling the enormous release of having expelled some terrible poison from her system.

But even as Carla spoke her soothing words, her thoughts began to move in another direction — Jimmy had to be brought to justice. But how? She couldn't tell Gino. He'd tear Jimmy to shreds and tear apart the family in the process. I'll have to find my own vengeance, Carla thought.

From that day, Sunni's world seemed to brighten more each day. Matthew had conquered some phantom as well and took solace in the fact that Barbara was making steady progress in therapy. After several months, she was released from the hospital and returned to school to finish the year. But instead of slipping once more under her spell, Matthew simply rejoiced in her recovery. Both he and Barbara seemed to understand that their obsessive dependence on one another had to be put behind them — not that it could be done quite so easily. No matter how much distance had been created between them, to look at Barbara was to look at himself, at a past self, perhaps, but one that always saddened him. To escape, he turned with even more dedication to acting and directing the performances he shared with Sunni. Through artistry and concentration he came to no longer hide behind his rules but to approach them with a fuller understanding, raising his performances to an entirely new plane. Inspired by Matthew's breakthrough, Sunni also developed a reputation for excellence that stretched beyond the campus. Scouts arrived from Manhattan and only a few weeks before graduation Matthew received an offer to join a prestigious off-Broadway acting company. The director, a handsome young man named Tom Caruthers, promised to find an opportunity for Sunni to work and study with him, although she couldn't imagine how she'd convince her family that she was ready to leave her father's protected world for the brutal streets of New York.

And so, the last weeks of school became a lovely blur. Everything had clicked somehow — her studies, her social life, and, of course, her acting. At home, there was seldom any anxiety to darken the air. Whatever tensions Gino faced during his days in the city, he seemed to shed before reaching the farm; his smile was always warm and deeply felt.

Then came the night of the Senior Banquet, a ritual which took place the Saturday night before graduation, that had managed to surpass even the senior prom and the next day's commencement exercises as the focal point of the year. While Sunni and Matthew had been content to attend the prom with other dates, they had both decided to spend the evening of the banquet together. The prom, however beautiful, was only a dance; the banquet, on the other hand, celebrated their class, summing up the essence of a school experience that, for Sunni and Matthew, in large part centered on their friendship.

It was a night of nostalgia and silliness. Awards were concocted for almost every senior, slides were made from snapshots collected throughout the year, selected for their sentimentality or potential embarrassment, and projected on a screen in the cafeteria. Champagne was smuggled in and passed around in paper cups. There was singing, general rambunctiousness, and a great deal of crying.

As the evening approached the early hours of the morning, Sunni and Matthew found their way through the darkness to the stage in the small auditorium. Feeling like a couple of obsolete athletes returning to the playing fields, they came not so much to say goodbye to the theater as to one another. They were friends for life, of course, but they knew that one part of their shared life was ending.

The stage was still set for the last scene they had played in *The Importance of Being Earnest* – a few scarred pieces of furniture that were meant to represent a London parlor. Matthew remembered the floor plan from hours of blocking and was able to find his way to the small lamp on the end table without a single collision. Unaided by stage lighting, the lamp cast a feeble glow into the emptiness, and they sat in silence on the pillowy sofa, staring for a while at nothing. The door was locked behind them, but they could hear the distant voices of other seniors as they sang a song they had danced to as freshmen. The faint notes of the melody, snaking their way through the deserted corridors, added to the moment's ghostlike quality.

Then, before they were aware it, they began to kiss. At first, the kisses were gentle, whispery things. She stroked his hair softly as she kissed his cheek, his eyes. He kissed her cheek, her throat, and then the tempo began to shift. He found her lips with his own, and Sunni began to feel dizzy. Drawing deeply into his kiss, she wanted to hold on to this warm, wonderful night forever. She scarcely noticed her own murmuring, nor the way Matthew's hands were caressing her body. But at one point she was aware of his fingers touching the tip of her breast, her nipples hardening in response, and then felt herself shudder as he reached beneath her silk dress to touch the softness between her legs.

She threw one leg across his body and pushed herself against him, kissing him now with her tongue, her legs holding his body as tightly as the arms around his neck. His hands moved across the silk to her chest, the fingers spreading and strengthening to enclose each breast. He felt her body move with the same rising excitement of his own breathing, and reached behind her to slip his fingers downward into her panties. His hands moved across her skin, the fullness of his erection pressing hard through the layers of fabric still between them. Soon she felt herself drifting toward exquisite surrender.

Suddenly, something in Sunni detached itself. Her mind flooded with the memory of the dark mystery of the body's yearnings that had frightened her so much when Jimmy touched her. But desire, she now saw, was not evil. Desire could make you feel alive and take on whatever qualities you possessed. She wanted to give herself completely – to the man and to the moment – but as much as she loved Matthew she knew it was not the kind of love that would end in mutual fulfillment.

With a gentleness that saved both of them from an awkward, humiliating situation that could have damaged the trust between them, Sunni disengaged herself from their embrace. She slid from Matthew's lap, but stayed close to him, kissing his face with tenderness. She could see in his eyes that he understood why she was pulling away and that he'd been just as overwhelmed by their spontaneous attraction as she. Flushed with guilt, he was embarrassed that his body had slipped so far out of control, afraid that he had somehow spoiled all the time he had shared with her.

"Sunni, I'm so sorry . . . ." he began, but she hushed him by placing her fingertips to his lips and kissed him again, transforming her passion into the affection she had always felt for Matthew, together with the need to comfort him now.

"Don't be sorry," she whispered. "I'm the one who got us so . . . aroused." It was the first time she had used the word aroused and actually understood what it meant. "But if we don't stop now, we might go farther than we should." She kissed his cheek again and traced his face with her fingers. "It would be wrong for us, Matthew, and I don't ever want to risk losing you."

She sounds so calm, he thought. How does she understand so much? And yet, in her cool, reasoning tones, Sunni was explaining her feelings as much to herself as to him. She continued to caress him, soothing his mixed emotions, and became conscious again of the distant singing. Sunni picked up the melody and hummed softly, completely at peace within the small circle of lamplight. This was a night for farewells, she thought, and sensed a doorway opening in her future.

Matthew placed his head in Sunni's lap. Softly humming once more, she stroked his hair, turning the song into a lullaby. Within moments, Matthew was asleep.

The next day, the graduation ceremony moved slowly through the warm afternoon. When the time came for Sunni to be seated, Gino stopped her as she hurried from the crowd of family and faculty to join her classmates.

"I want you to have your present now," he said simply, handing her a small corsage and a gold trimmed envelope.

"Thank you Pappa," she said a little breathlessly, hoping he wouldn't hear the disappointment in her voice. She placed the envelope in the pocket of her graduation gown and rushed off, pinning her corsage on the way.

Gino had never been very successful at selecting the right present for Sunni. If Filomina wasn't able to pick out clothes or jewelry, he would usually give her a check to buy whatever she wanted. But this was different. She had hoped that for an occasion so special, he'd think of something more personal. Finally, when she became too restless to listen attentively to the pious drone of the principal's speech, she drew out the envelope and opened it. Even if it was just money, she thought, at least she could read the card.

"Oh my God!" she exclaimed out loud, breaking the polite if bored atmosphere and momentarily attracting the eyes of the students around her.

Sunni stared at the envelope's contents, trembling with joy. The card, embossed with gold, showed a steamboat sailing on a curlicue ocean. Inside were two tickets to Sicily and a message in Gino's careful hand: "Since neither of us have ever seen the land of our ancestors, I thought you'd be pleased if we saw it together."

She spun around in her seat, looking over the others toward the section where the parents and other spectators were sitting. She caught her father's eye, grinned and waved to him, just as one of the teachers whispered that she should turn to face the stage. She blushed and looked forward again, smiling through the balance of the program, so distracted in fact that when her name was called to receive her diploma, the girl sitting next to her had to nudge her from her seat.

Several rows behind her, Gino smiled back, equally transfixed. He'd been planning this moment for a long time. Exactly why he'd become so determined to cross the Atlantic with Sunni was something he only vaguely understood himself. He had never shared the sentimentality about "the old country" that seemed to obsess so many children of immigrants; for even though he was locked into the social fabric of Sicilian culture, he always thought of New York and now Connecticut as the appropriate contexts for whatever traditions he preserved. But lately he'd grown disenchanted with his business and longed for some adventure, some escape. The idea of sailing to Sicily had been born from a desire to find some treasure he could give his daughter and had grown into an experience he thought could change his life.

Gino had spent many hours trying to convince Filomina that she should be going with them, but she just smiled and held her ground. She had a variety of excuses to offer – the trip intimidated her, she didn't want to leave the farm completely unattended for so long, Angela needed her help – but none of these considerations had very much to do with her real reason for staying home. She wanted Gino to spend some time with Sunni alone. Also, some instinct told her that he needed this trip as a way of addressing his past, particularly Rosa and Giovanni, and sharing it with Sunni, who was crystallizing as a woman, would deepen its significance.

"You're just worried about knowing what to order in restaurants," Filomina teased.

Gino watched Sunni shake the principal's hand and proudly take her diploma, and in that moment, he saw his beloved child blossom into a sophisticated young woman right before his eyes.

THE SLOW DESPAIR that had been eroding Gino's spirit was centered, not surprisingly, on Vinnie, who'd grown bitterly resigned to his continued incapacities, and was turning more and more to the lurid excesses of his private life. At one point, in a last effort to salvage Vinnie's character, Gino had asked, John Molfetta, an old friend, to take Vinnie under his wing. John was a generation older than Vinnie, but like Vinnie, he was a wild man with an insatiable taste for wine and whores; unlike Vinnie, however, he never let his appetites spill over into his professional life, nor did life's underside make him cruel or dishonest with the people who loved and needed him.

Unfortunately, the experiment failed. After several weeks of trying to cope with Vinnie's petty outbursts, Big John came to Gino and said bluntly, "He's not worth it. He'll never be what you hope for, Gino. It's not just that he isn't enough of a son, or enough of a leader, or enough of a worker, he isn't enough of a human being."

Gino was quiet for a moment, then said softly, "You're right, of course. I'm sorry I subjected you to so great a burden. If he were not my son, I would have beaten the shit out of him years ago. As it is . . . ." He left the thought unfinished, and John, who had sons of his own, did not pursue it.

Gino could have shrugged away his son's failures if he didn't have an empire that needed a successor after he was gone. No matter how much his pride rejected the idea, Gino was approaching old age and though he didn't particularly care about extending his name beyond the grave and turning the organization into some kind of monument to himself, he was concerned about its future security. He couldn't stand by and watch it fall apart because he didn't have an heir. It was his life's work, something he alone had created. If it all came to nothing, what did that say about him? At this point, it didn't matter if it remained within the family as long as it remained. But the only men Gino trusted to run it were his contemporaries. The younger men, including the sons of his friends, had too little experience and too much ambition. They'd tear it to pieces.

THE SHIP WAS scheduled to sail for Italy a week after graduation and Sunni was in a frenzy. While any other eighteen-year-old might have filled the time with preparations – shopping for clothes, for example – Sunni spent the week sifting through photographs of Sicily in family albums and travel books, trying to determine in advance the places she most wanted to see. As a result, Filomina was up helping her pack at one a.m. on the day before their departure.

When it came, on a windy and sunny June day, Sunni and Gino were surprised by a Bon Voyage party that had gathered on the city dock that afternoon. Filomina and Angela had arranged it, and friends and family kept arriving to wish the two farewell. Matthew was there, and Bennie and Tina, as well as some of Gino's men and Filomina's entourage and even Carla with Sunni's niece Desiree. Champagne flowed and Sunni and Gino ascended the walkway with paper streamers flying after them. The two stood at the railing on the highest deck until Manhattan was a distant speck and the sun setting around them. Not used to the afternoon champagne, and exhausted with excitement, Sunni had to succumb to a delicious nap before she and Gino met again for dinner.

While their next weeks on board were delightful, providing Gino with his first real vacation in years, nothing compared to the beauty of Sicily. Sunni labored to explain the effect of its countryside in her letters and postcards to Filomina and Matthew, but felt that words were a poor imitation. None of the photographs or the few paintings she had studied had come close to suggesting the landscape she encountered. The colors overwhelmed her, especially the absolute vividness of the blues and greens and whites. Connecticut was so sedate, the colors seemed absorbed by objects. But in Sicily, the air was alive. It danced around her and even the lives of the people became part of her emotions and not her intellect. She didn't analyze or puzzle over anything. She simply took it all in and glowed in the sunlight.

But whatever else she may have found in Sicily, nothing moved her as profoundly as what she discovered in her father. Throughout their long days together, they grew closer than she would have dreamed possible. As much as she loved him, she was always conscious of the line defining the limits of their relationship. But now their new sense of sharing had formed an actual friendship. On a peaceful veranda in Palermo, watching the sun set over the soft hills and olive-scented valleys, Gino talked at length about Sunni's brothers and sisters, about his disenchantments and abandoned hopes for the future, and in the telling, his disappointments lost their bitter edge. He even spoke of finding the man who might one day take his place as if he could spin the man's presence out of the darkening air.

Sunni also spoke – of her awakening sense of life, of her indistinct but insistent yearning for some focus. Citing Matthew's almost immediate success, she tried to hint that she, too, might one day explore the possibility of working in the theater. She was still too nervous to ask Gino directly about a career in New York, wanting him instead to become gradually accustomed to the idea. But her discussion of acting led naturally into a deeper discussion of Matthew – what she did and did not feel for him, and her belief that their relationship would always be limited because of how it had evolved. And while she never spoke specifically about her sexual awakening, Gino was sensitive enough to infer such currents. He knew that Sunni was waiting for exactly the right man, someone who would embody all the qualities she demanded of life, someone who could appreciate, foster, and protect her.

The darkness was as warm as day, creating the sense that the sun was still there, concealed somewhere behind the trees, and together they talked on as the whispery breeze drifted in from the nearby sea.

PART
SIX

CHAPTER
TWENTY-SIX

ON AUGUST 2, 1943, a sweltering summer day in Little Italy, Gianni Ghianella was born and the doctors called it God's gift – a change-of-life baby. His father, a gentle and intelligent tailor named Carlo, was almost fifty at the time, while Christina, his even gentler mother, was forty-four. He was their only child, so instantly became the center of their lives; in fact, they were almost afraid to touch him, thinking he might shatter if they held him too tightly or disappear as mysteriously as he'd arrived.

And as though he were constantly trying to ease their fears, Gianni carried a sense of calm all through childhood. Even at twelve and thirteen, when the neighborhood boys were bashing each other around, he often assumed the role of peacemaker. He wasn't particularly afraid of fighting; he just felt that there were better ways to spend one's time and energy – making money, for example. Much like Gino in his youth, Gianni observed first hand how his father's long hours and thankless pay had worn down his spirit. Carlo Ghianella had spent his life trapped in the gloom of dingy sewing shops as his eyes and strength diminished, his back permanently hunched from endless hours over a sewing machine, trying to preserve the standards of his craft in a world that had ceased to care very much about the quality of a man's work. The other boys may be blind to the toll of a laborer's life, Gianni thought, because their own fathers are so much younger, but I know what lies ahead of them. He was determined to establish a better life for himself – in time for his parents to share in the rewards.

And so, by the time he turned fourteen, Gianni realized he didn't have time to build a prosperous career in traditional, law-abiding ways; he would have to find shortcuts, which soon included the robbing of liquor stores, candy stores, and fruit markets in neighborhoods outside his own so he'd remain unrecognized. It amazed Gianni how many boys were afraid to cross major thoroughfares to attack locations farther from home. Unlike the fledgling thieves who roamed the city, Gianni approached his enterprise seriously, with enough deliberation that he was always successful. In addition, though his parents were both under five feet four, and neither could find anything in their family history to account for it, Gianni had already grown to a height of six-one, which invariably led witnesses to overestimate his age. He was also extremely adept at sizing up potential dangers before committing himself to a situation. If he entered a store and felt the attempt might go against him, he left quietly to find a more promising opportunity.

So, while authorities combed the area for a young tough of nineteen or twenty, Gianni returned home and became the sweet, young Ghianella boy known and respected throughout the community. Neighbors knew him for his conscientiousness, working hard at any job he could find – stock boy in a shoe store, newspaper and delivery boy – and no one was the wiser. They couldn't imagine him stealing because he was so honest with the people he knew. Once, he spotted a thief fleeing Gambizzi's grocery store with a handful of money. Tackling him right in front of the store – and before a group of elderly spectators – he had his first true admirers and staunch advocates of his heroism. Gianni didn't think of himself as a hypocrite when he heard such praise; his actions elsewhere were a professional matter. And if there was anything shaky in his reasoning, he was far to busy to let it slow him down now.

But soon he grew impatient with the meager profits of even

his most successful thefts. Because he chose not to hurt or kill anyone, it was difficult to amass the amount of money needed to find a way out of Little Italy. Eventually, he began running favors for men with known ties to organized crime. Though many of the locals were involved in illegal operations, those who approached Gianni were linked to powerful councils and overlords, people who were gradually centralizing control over a wide range of activities. Gianni knew that a truly organized operation would be the surest, fastest way to gain access to the kind of money he needed, so he performed his assignments with quiet efficiency, no matter how tiresome or seemingly unimportant. He knew this was his testing period and if he showed genuine promise, they might groom him for better things.

Meanwhile, he continued to show his family respect and affection, and graduated from high school at the top of his class. Carlo was so proud, he persuaded Gianni to enroll at Hunter College, a challenge which Gianni took on easily enough at first, juggling his days in college and nights on the streets and still managing to do his homework. But then his long months of loyalty to the organization paid off. His duties and responsibilities increased, and he realized that the time had come to commit himself completely. So he left Hunter, mystifying his teachers and classmates, and hurting Carlo deeply. As hard as it was to see his father's disappointment, however, Gianni's ambition found new fuel. Since he couldn't explain his actions, he knew he'd have to transform himself rapidly if only to live up to his father's expectations.

The only possible concern – other than that he might end up in prison or a grave – was that the streets were littered with clumsy, stupid men who might inadvertently cause him trouble. But Gianni enjoyed some measure of danger, and was confident that he could find safety amidst the chaos. He was also becoming a more permanent member of the organization at precisely the right moment. Many gangs, large and small, scattered throughout the city, were slowly being consolidated into a single network. Their areas of activity would be allowed to exist as long as they did not intersect with the expanding circle of the organization – and their net profits were small enough to avoid takeover by hostile forces. The need to create a new order that could sustain and handle the threats of Federal investigators was being recognized by all men of real power. Even a proud loner like Gino Manzino eventually accepted his place in the council. According to street gossip, Gino would have preferred keeping his empire independent, but he knew it might lead to a full-scale war that could only destroy everything he had built. He elected instead to negotiate a position of great trust and authority.

Even the day-to-day business then had to be brought up-to-date. Those who still operated as old-world chieftains had to realize they were living in the twentieth century where new ways had been forged. There was a massive scramble for warriors and leaders who could not only ensure survival, but would carry them forward. Blood loyalties and tribal rivalries faded before the need to find the best men. For a man like Gianni, the son of a tailor with no family history of service to distinguish him, it might have been many years before he was granted a significant reward. But the spirit of renovation meant that his special qualities would not be wasted. No one could afford to waste the talent or the time.

And so, before he was thirty, Gianni was abruptly called from his modest loan sharking business to assume a new position, an appointment of great honor that was traditionally awarded to a family member of one of the bosses. Perhaps enhanced by his brief exposure to college, Gianni's intelligence had set him apart from his equally ambitious contemporaries. He had matured into an admired young man and was strengthened by a deliberate approach and simple self-confidence. Even in his private life, Gianni seemed immune to the excesses of other young hopefuls and avoided making their frequently disastrous mistakes on the job. He loved women, as well as the many luxuries of life he was finally able to afford, but he kept his pleasures in perspective. His goals may have been far grander than his father's, but they demanded the same dedication and patience as fine tailoring.

Nor did he forget his commitment to ease the burden on his parents. When he first quit college, he masked his true source of income with a respectable occupation – he began working at the local bank, both to soothe his parents' disappointment and to explain the money suddenly available to him. At first he worked in the mailroom, but soon was promoted to a teller's cage where he kept his customers happy with his charm, efficiency, and cleanly attractive appearance. When he resigned, once again, the people who worked with him were stunned. He had shown so much ability and had worked so hard. Still, he said goodbye without an explanation, giving the same easy smile in parting that he had offered each morning. Initially, one of the bank's officers, remembering vague rumors about Gianni's contacts in the neighborhood, thought he might have parted with bank funds. The officer checked and double-checked the books and receipts, but there were no discrepancies, and the man remained as puzzled as everyone else.

But all that Gianni intended to take with him was the experience of working with large amounts of money and a new insight into the intricacies of finance. He would never take a penny entrusted to his care, although he was perfectly capable of robbing a bank down the street on his lunch hour. In fact, when an old acquaintance approached him one afternoon and suggested that Gianni act as his inside man in a projected robbery, Gianni was shocked that anyone would consider asking him such a thing. To Gianni, even temporary commitments mattered.

Bringing the same spirit to his illegal operations was an easy enough transition. Gianni sincerely believed in the organization and his place within it – and no matter for whom – negotiating loans in one of the city's key territories at least seemed like a legitimate business. Loan-sharking gave Gianni the opportunity to put his bank skills to use. It also gave him an excellent understanding of the neighborhood's financial history – who needed money, who was unable to get it through legitimate channels, who owned property and holdings that might constitute worthwhile collateral, who was already overextended, and so on. Combined with his natural intuition, this information made him an unusually successful manager of street loans. He was so shrewd in selecting clients and setting reasonable demands that very little enforcement was necessary, which allowed him to keep his banker's image untarnished even longer. Wearing the same well-tailored suits and clean shirts in his street dealings that he had worn at the bank, the line separating the two spheres of activity often became blurred – for his customers and even for himself at times – as if he'd become a one-man branch of a real bank. Carlo and Christina could feel genuine pride in having a son of such stature in the community, he thought. Of course, no one was ever fooled by the facade of respectability, but Gianni always nourished the hope that his parents believed him and would be spared any possible shame.

Nevertheless, Gianni was unprepared for the morning he was summoned to the home of Generose Enboli, a man of considerable power in the organization's governing council who had supervised all the logistics involved in consolidating so many men and operations into one network. When Gianni was ushered into the dining room, Enboli was eating breakfast and motioned to a chair across from him. Emboli wiped his mouth with a napkin, then uttered calmly and dispassionately, "The council wants you to be Gino Manzino's personal driver."

The only visible sign of Gianni's feelings was a barely perceptible flush to his complexion, but he was completely stunned by the announcement. A promotion of this magnitude was almost unheard of for one so young. To be asked to drive for a man of importance was a gesture of profound trust since his life would be placed directly in the driver's hands, along with the knowledge of the man's comings and goings. The appointment was particularly unique because Gino Manzino was the last of the great loners, a man who in finally agreeing to join the council had somehow made it seem as if they were all joining him. He surrendered remarkably little of his independence and the other men, some of whom had directed far larger and more dangerous operations than his, welcomed Gino with an admiration, even reverence, that suggested the arrival of a noble from their homeland. He'd run his own empire with consummate skill and fairness, removing himself from meaningless conflicts that had destroyed so many others. In a world of force and intimidation, he had established his strength through respect instead of fear.

WHILE GIANNI'S RECORD was impeccable, he had been chosen partly because of the absence of family connections to the organization. This meant that he was also free of the corrupting influences of old alliances. In addition, Enboli sensed that Gino and Gianni were kindred spirits. However their working relationship evolved, Enboli expected Gino and Gianni to become friends. And, knowing the sorrows his family had brought him over the years, Enboli felt that Gino needed friendship more than anything else; Gianni was a gift for a man he respected.

On the first day they met, both Gianni and Gino were struck by their similarities. Gianni was taller, but both had the same physique – a leanness that suggested muscle, an elegance that set them apart from the dirty streets through which they moved. They shared the same intelligence, as well as a look that seemed to understand and to mock at once. This was so distinctive, in fact, that as they shook hands and their eyes locked for a moment, each saw himself in the reflection. They laughed a little in embarrassment at the sudden recognition, then quietly began their day.

Over the next months, the two men gradually became accustomed to one another. There was seldom any conversation beyond business – not because Gino wasn't being unfriendly or even superior – but simply because he concentrated intently when he worked. Besides, he was somewhat quiet by nature. But Gianni was also contemplative, so the silence was comfortable, and soon they felt like a team. Since neither Gino nor Gianni would have ever accepted the conceit of a uniformed chauffeur, they dressed in the same handsome dark suits and might have been any two business partners as they made their rounds of offices, warehouses, and alleyways in the city. Only an unusually astute observer would have noticed that the younger man always moved with the alertness and watchfulness of a bodyguard.

One cold afternoon in March, Gianni parked the car on a street gutted with warehouses on the lower west side. Gino was to attend a meeting requested by one of his shipping supervisors, an old man named Grzegorczyk who was in charge of a huge loft where contraband furs were inventoried and then redistributed to truckers who brought them to their customers. The call had been a little puzzling, a young voice identifying itself as Grzegorczyk's son saying that his father wanted to see Gino at the end of his rounds before he saw the council again. It had something to do with a suspected shortage, he said, a possible betrayal by the eastern European families. Gino had enough respect for Grzegorczyk's judgment to agree to the meeting and explained the general situation to Gianni as they arrived.

Because Gianni was so cautious in forming his opinions, and his judgments of people so perceptive, Gino occasionally used him as a sounding board for his ideas. Gianni was perhaps too gentle for some of the decisions that had to be made in a dangerous business, but Gino liked the younger man's rationality, the way it cut to the essence of a problem.

With his briefcase in hand, filled with the revenues collected from a dozen different operations throughout the afternoon, Gino took the freight elevator up to Grzegorczyk's tiny office on the second floor, high above the loading bays. How many office buildings, he wondered idly, how many warehouses, and factories in Manhattan had their most important business conducted in them long after the workers had gone home and the switchboards had shut down for the night. As dramatic as the word may have sounded, he always felt that the term "underworld" described the atmosphere perfectly. Theirs was an alternate world, one hidden behind the facade of hundreds of legitimate businesses. He was still musing about it when he knocked on the office door and a voice beckoned him to enter. Two young men sat at a cluttered desk with cups of coffee, and gestured to Gino to have a seat.

"An honor, Mr. Manzino, an honor," said one of the men with an oddly crooked smile. "This will only take a moment." He was a tall burly man with pale blue eyes that looked curiously childlike in such a hefty man. Something in them suddenly set off a sense of alarm as Gino began to sit. He was already expecting it when the crooked smile faded and the man drew a nickel-plated revolver from within his jacket. "Only a moment," he said again, as the other man, slighter and more sullen, also drew his pistol with a slight smirk. The pulse throbbing in Gino's temple was more from anger at himself than from his immediate hatred for these men. He had acted like an old man coming here like this, a briefcase full of money in his hand. Still, Gino displayed no emotion; only his eyes, jade colored in the fluorescent light, grew immediately colder.

The crooked smile reappeared as Gino's captor sat on the desk in front of Gino. Stupidly, thought Gino, the man seemed to be almost on the point of giggling. "I know what you're thinking," he said, "exactly how do we expect to get away with robbing Gino Manzino?" Gino didn't even need to think; he understood completely. His stupidity had made it possible.

"It will be easy enough, once we kill you," the man continued. "Your people will blame the dumb Pollacks who run this place and while everybody's blowing everyone else to hell, we'll be long gone."

Only an egomaniac would waste time this way, Gino thought, talking like some cowboy in a western movie. Cowboy! That was it. Now he remembered where he'd seen these two before – they were truckers who'd drifted in from the west and found work now and then driving fur shipments. Gianni had called them cowboys and they had obviously been planning this for some time. Then, somewhere in the distance, Gino heard the sound of a gunshot drifting up from the street.

"That would be your driver," said the cowboy. "We had someone take him out when you were safely up the elevator. Now we just have to wait for him to get the car into the loading bay and check it for any extra receipts. No sense doing things half-assed."

Crooked smile sipped at his coffee while the other man, suddenly looking a little less confident, walked over to the window and tried to see what was happening downstairs, though there wasn't much he could see from this angle. After another moment or so, the man on the desk began to talk again.

"The trouble with all you dagos" he said, "is that you take

yourselves so seriously with all this ritual shit, you actually believe you're something special, you know, like little kings or emperors or something, when all it's really about is taking what you want and getting the hell out."

"Why don't we do that," said the other man still staring out the window. "This is taking too long."

"Suits me," said the crooked-smiled cowboy. "We've got a lot of miles to cover." He extended the pistol toward Gino. "Nice meeting you, Mr. Manzino," he said.

All at once there was an explosion and Gino found himself staring at a small, dark hole in the man's forehead. But the strange smile didn't falter, and the man continued to grin as he slowly sank back beneath the desktop. The other man was raising his gun at the doorway when two holes appeared symmetrically below each eye, shattering his face as his body pitched backward.

"There was another one downstairs," said Gianni, "but I heard him coming long before he got to me. I didn't like the feel of this thing from the beginning."

Gianni's voice was as soft as if he were discussing traffic patterns, baseball scores, or possible restaurants for lunch.

"I dumped the other one in one of the trash cans downstairs," he said a little shyly as he unscrewed the silencer from the barrel of his Beretta. "I guess we can just leave these two here. It should be hours before anyone discovers them." Gianni paused for a moment, then smiled self-consciously and asked, "Ready to go, sir?" With his gun safely tucked away, he was once again the perfect image of a chauffeur, although he generally used "sir" only when others were present. Not knowing how else to respond, Gino returned the smile and nodded. He rose to leave and glanced briefly toward the dead men, shaking his head slightly in wonderment.

Gino still hadn't spoken as they started down in the elevator, but he noted how effortlessly Gianni had become the polite young man who seemed incapable of violence. Feeling the need to say something, Gino said simply, "Thank you, Gianni. That was very impressive."

Gianni grinned again, blushing slightly, and said, "Bottom of the ninth, dagos beat the cowboys." Both men laughed, and any lingering sense of danger slipped away. There would be other occasions when Gino would see this side of Gianni, how it emerged from the boyish charm to calmly take care of whatever needed to be done, and then disappear with an implied apology for having intruded. One occasion he would never forget occurred when "Crazy Eyes" Lorenzo finally went insane enough to justify his name.

Lorenzo was one of a dozen small-time hustlers who had been put out of business by the organization. But even at the peak of his influence, he was never much of a force. His "domain" barely covered a city block in a section of the lower East side hardly noted for its affluence. He made a modest income from the few operations available locally – kickbacks from merchants, cuts from whatever gambling or prostitution the neighborhood could support, the occasional resale of goods stolen elsewhere in the city. Although everything he did was on a petty scale, "Crazy Eyes" imagined himself to be some sort of power in organized crime. In fact, his nickname was probably inspired by Lorenzo's view of his place in the world and not just from the strange, unfocused look in his eyes. He was tolerated, despite his eccentricities, because nobody really cared too much about him.

In fact, he was considered so insignificant in the grand scheme of things that no one bothered to inform him when his tenure was over. All of a sudden, his collectors came back empty-handed, and after a few pompous speeches to his subordinates (mostly cousins of his wife, none of whom had mastered more than a few words of English) about the ingratitude of those in need of his protection, he set out to collect his compensation in person. This was when he first learned that men from the organization had informed the merchants that Lorenzo was no longer in charge. No one objected because, for one thing, the new people were offering slightly better terms. Lorenzo always had been a little greedy.

When he realized that his power had been usurped, "Crazy Eyes" ranted and raved, smashed a few store windows in fury, and swore vengeance. Meanwhile, Gino Manzino, who had nothing to do with the takeover, heard that there was trouble in one of the areas newly assigned to one of his lieutenants. Once he had pieced together what had happened, he decided that the organization had been guilty of an oversight in not providing Lorenzo with some share in the operation. As a gesture of goodwill, he sent someone to offer Lorenzo control of the loan business in his neighborhood. But the act of generosity had only one effect: it gave "Crazy Eyes" a target for his outrage.

"Who the hell is Gino Manzino," Lorenzo screamed at Gino's emissary, "and what makes him think he can take over my territory and give me crumbs? I'll kill the bastard!" Over his wife's wailing, he ran upstairs for his shotgun while the messenger wisely retreated.

When Gino received the report, he only shrugged, assuming that the man would eventually calm down when the blow to his pride had healed. But "Crazy Eyes" was not merely a colorful crackpot, an overdramatic "Mustache Pete" leftover from the twenties. He was genuinely insane, a desperate man whose self-delusions were being shattered. And so, after several days of brooding, with his wife and cousins milling about hopelessly in the background, "Crazy Eyes" Lorenzo became obsessed with murdering Gino Manzino.

Deciding on Friday morning that this would be the day, he set out to find Gino at his farm in Connecticut, the location of which he had somehow managed to find out, despite Gino's determination to keep it a secret. By mid-afternoon, Lorenzo and his shotgun were in a car racing across the Throgs Neck Bridge. There was, of course, an unwritten law that a man's family and private home were never to be touched, but "Crazy Eyes" was well beyond any laws, written or unwritten.

It was dusk when he reached the farm. Gino was in the barn, supervising the veterinarian's bathing of an open wound that Sunni's favorite horse had scraped into its stomach when it trotted through the rose bushes in front of the house. Filomina and Angela were in the kitchen, discovering still another way to cook veal and mushrooms, and Angela's son was somewhere upstairs, dragging out the electric trains usually saved for Christmas. Lorenzo hurried from the car as soon as he parked it, mumbling to himself and checking

the shells in the shotgun as he hurtled through the unlocked front
door.

Gino wanted to go back into the city later that night to prepare for a meeting the next morning, so Gianni was sleeping on a
leather couch in the den. But the sound of an unexpected car
crunching on the driveway gravel brought him awake. By the time
Lorenzo had stormed into the house, Gianni, gun in hand, was
waiting for him on the other side of the large front room.

As soon as his crazily-angled eyes focused on the young man
with the pistol, Lorenzo held the shotgun in front of him as if it
were some sort of club and bellowed, "I want Gino Manzino! Get
out of my way and let me have Gino Manzino!"

Gianni didn't know who Lorenzo was, but he recognized the
madness before him and answered in remarkably soft tones, "He
isn't here. But I want you to place the shotgun very carefully on
the floor in front of you, and back slowly out the door." He was so
gentle in his advice that Lorenzo faltered for a moment and began
to lower his arms. Then the rage returned, along with the need to
channel it before it all drained away.

"Get out of my way, asshole, or I'll blow you and your stupid
little gun out of the state!"

"You don't want to do this," Gianni said in the same careful
voice, fixing his pistol's aim on the man he had no desire to kill in
Gino's living room. "The moment will pass." With a more rational
man, Gianni's assurances might have had the intended effect. But
"Crazy Eyes" had abandoned all logic and with a snarl turned the
shotgun's barrel toward Gianni and jammed back the hammers
with his thick thumb.

"Oh shit," sighed Gianni, "he's going to make me do it." He
fired twice in rapid succession, the first bullet striking the center
of Lorenzo's chest, the second slightly higher, entering the base of
his throat. If Lorenzo had been a careful assassin and actually plot-
ted his assault, he probably wouldn't have gotten as far as he did.
But because he was nuttier than a fruitcake, no one had taken him
seriously. He'd moved haphazardly toward his target and had come
astonishingly close.

And yet, before the body had even struck the floor, Gianni was at the door making sure that no one was backing up the madman – although his erratic behavior certainly didn't indicate an organized hit. The only thing visible was Lorenzo's car, the door on the driver's side still open. In another moment, his gun holstered, Gianni recrossed the room to intercept Angela who was the first to arrive in response to the shots.

"Everything's under control," he said in his soft-spoken voice, smiling politely. "Would you mind going upstairs and keeping the children out of the front room for a while?"

"Of course," she said, surprised at how easily the young man could soothe her sudden panic, then quickly backed up the stairs to join the children.

Filomina had come in right behind her and Gianni immediately apologized for all the commotion, assuring her that there was nothing to worry about.

"I would appreciate it, though, if you stayed away from the front room for just a few more minutes. Of course, you should send your husband right through when he comes in. And could I trouble you for a bowl of ammonia and water and a few paper towels?" All this was said so quietly that Filomina, who'd been stricken with fear at the sound of the gunshots, simply went into the kitchen to get what he needed without asking questions.

Gino came hurrying through the back door, winded by the long run from the barn at the indistinct but obvious sound of gunshots. But before he had a chance to ask what happened, Filomina said, "It's all right, Gino. Gianni said that you should go into the front room." Mystified, and feeling a little vulnerable without a weapon, Gino found Gianni kneeling next to the body of a little man who he had never seen before, scrubbing at the wall with a dampened piece of toweling.

"Some of the blood spattered here," he said apologetically, choosing to explain the scrubbing rather than the body. "I wanted to get it off before it set. Bloodstains can be so hard to remove, and this room is always so clean."

Gino glanced down at the dead man and saw the small pile of

toweling under his head, absorbing most of the blood flow.

"Cleaning up the excess won't be any problem," Gianni added, characteristically relaxed. "Luckily he landed on the tile and not the rug. You might want to go through his pockets to see who he is."

Later that evening, Gianni and Gino returned "Crazy Eyes" and his car to his own neighborhood. Then Gino checked into a hotel and, giving Gianni the next day off, drove himself to his meeting the following morning. He had already decided on an amendment to the agenda: he wanted to propose that Gianni Ghianella be given greater recognition and responsibility within the organization, and that he be granted the opportunity to begin learning some of the tasks entrusted to Gino himself. It would all come about gradually; Gianni would continue to drive for Gino as the tutoring process progressed. Where it would all lead was purely speculative, but Gino was certain of one thing – however discreetly it was accomplished, Gino would start shifting his power to Gianni. Realizing that the time would come when Vinnie figured out what was happening and explode, Gino could only hope that Vinnie would have the wisdom to know his own limitations, a flimsy possibility at best. All of which left Gino in a somber mood when the meeting ended, so he turned to his favorite escape from gloom whenever he was in the city – he called Sunni and arranged to meet her for lunch.

Perhaps it was the possibility of a hundred such lunches that had finally persuaded Gino to permit Sunni to live in New York on her own – or almost. She shared an apartment in a safe neighborhood with two girls from families Gino had known all his life. He had resisted her pleas to study acting at N.Y.U. and enrolled her in the relatively secure environment of Mount Saint Vincents in Riverdale. Sunni had never really lost her affection for nuns, so she didn't object all that strenuously. Besides, she maintained constant contact with Matthew, which meant she could continue her involvement with the theater anyway, despite her father's attempts to limit it to only being a member of the audience on weekends.

That afternoon, however, she was especially effervescent, and halfway through the lunch she ventured the reason – Matthew had offered her a part in a play.

"Pappa, it won't interfere with my classes at all. Most of the people involved are students, and rehearsals have been arranged to accommodate class schedules. We'll work evenings and weekends, and then right through the mid-semester break. And here's the best part: we'll be opening in a real off-Broadway theater, with a chance to play into the summer if we're any good."

Gino had always been so uneasy about Sunni's dedication to acting, but took comfort in thinking that she was still young enough for it to be a fantasy that would fade in time. He also knew that Sunni was committed to her schooling and that acting was a full-time pursuit. Now she'd been given a miraculous opportunity to skip the dozens of steps usually necessary and become an actress overnight. It didn't matter that the odds against success were great. Precisely because he was hoping so hard for her not to succeed, he knew that she would. Her talent was real, and others would see the qualities in her that he had always cherished.

So distracted was he by the alarm growing within him that he scarcely heard her explanation of the details. The play had been written by an undergraduate at Columbia and had already won a prestigious literary award, which had generated funding for its first production, one of the stipulations for the financing being that all the participants had to be students currently enrolled in New York schools. Even a few high school students would be involved. Matthew had been chosen to direct, since his apprenticeship in the acting company, supplemented by a few part-time courses at N.Y.U., allowed him to maintain his student status. There was a lot of excitement surrounding the project, from politicians as well as theater people, and the cast had been promised all the pomp and ceremony of a real opening night. With the scarcity of good material on stage that season, there was every reason to hope (or, in Gino's case, to dread) that the show might have a decent run.

Whatever his fears, Gino fought back the impulse to forbid Sunni to participate. Her selection, however connected to Matthew's friendship, was an honor and would please Filomina and all the

family enormously. Sunni would still be able to meet her require-
ments at school and, since the production was supported by the
academic community, would even earn academic credits for the
performance. So Gino forced himself to smile, even ordering her a
glass of champagne so they could toast the occasion. She was pleased,
but she knew he was worried.

Although Gino had made remarkable progress in his acceptance of a changing world, there were some prejudices he would
not surrender. One was his conviction that show business was a
flashy, empty world, hopelessly corrupted and corrupting. Perhaps he had spent too much time in the audience, one of the men
at private tables who come to see both showgirls and actresses as
girls for hire. Gino never thought of his old flame Rita Stewart in
such a light, yet had he really treated her so differently? Gino
would never let his daughter be watched by so many crude eyes.
Whatever their pretensions, in the end, there was little difference
between legitimate theaters and sleazy nightclubs. And just as Gino
knew he couldn't stand in the way of Sunni marrying anyone she
wanted, that didn't mean he would allow her to marry scum.

As Sunni sat obliviously sipping her rose champagne, he tried
to push his misgivings at least temporarily out of mind. As for
Sunni, she never thought to confront him and say, "This is what
I'm going to do with my life, whether you like it or not," which
was something even Matthew couldn't understand. But he could
never know what it meant to live in a family like hers where respect was everything. She would never risk losing her family. She
loved her parents so much, her happiness was always secondary to
theirs.

OVER THE NEXT several months, as Gino busied himself with Gianni's
tutoring, he received frequent reports from Sunni about how wonderfully the play was going. Her part was much more significant
than she had first imagined and seemed to be growing steadily in
strength as they approached the premiere. The entire project was
beginning to attract attention from small newspapers and theater
publications. A number of important reviewers and producers were

attending the opening, and with so many newcomers being presented in such a creative setting, the papers were predicting that
careers would be born.

Careers would be born. Sunni's phrase began to eat away at
Gino. As much as he tried not to give in to his fears, he felt as if he
were watching some private nightmare develop like a photograph.
Each of his children had been lost to him in one way or another,
and now the one who made up for everything was being drawn
into something destructive. He often remembered Mrs. Nardone,
a woman in the old neighborhood who had lost a son in a tragic
accident. For years afterward, she told the story over and over –
how she watched him start up the street on his bicycle and knew
at once that something terrible was about to happen. She tried to
run after him, calling his name, but he was too far ahead to hear
her. Moments later she watched as a huge Mack truck turned on
to the street and his bicycle skidded out beneath him, sending
him sprawling under the truck's mammoth wheels. Gino had always been hesitant to accept the myth of a mother's intuition.
Perhaps Mrs. Nardone had created the horrifying scenario so often
in her dreams that she had come to confuse it with reality. Or
perhaps her cries of warning had caused the boy to stumble in the
truck's direction. But as Gino grew older, he had come to understand what Mrs. Nardone must have felt that day. Rosa had insisted that she had seen strange foreshadowing in Philly's eyes the
last time she had seen him. And now he was certain that forces
existed which could destroy Sunni's purity and sense of joy. Gino,
however, was not as powerless as Mrs. Nardone. He could see to it
that the truck never entered the street.

CHAPTER
TWENTY-SEVEN

THERE WAS ALWAYS a great debate as to who really controlled New York's newspapers – the politicians, the public, Wall Street, or even the journalists themselves. But the only consistent source of influence was far more immediate. Newspapers depended on circulation, which meant distribution, which meant delivery trucks, which meant the Teamsters. And the Teamsters listened to Gino Manzino.

The Teamsters, of course, did not have any real effect on the newsmakers' day-to-day decisions. They had no interest in them, as a rule, although pressure might occasionally be brought to bear on one sensitive political endorsement or another. They didn't even object to coverage of corruption within their own ranks since it often had the advantage of enhancing their reputation for muscle. The Teamsters were unique in that they never apologized for anything, no matter what their methods or associations. When evidence was published that showed how much union money had found its way into Jimmy Hoffa's private bank accounts, the response of the membership had been matter-of-fact: they were getting what they wanted, why shouldn't he? There was even a joke about the reason Frank Sinatra could never be a Teamster – he was much too shy about admitting who his real friends were. So when Gino asked Dave Scully, a high-ranking business manager at one of the daily newspapers, for a private conference with the newspaper's owner Scully knew well of Gino's power and only hoped that the favor would not be too costly.

It was Scully who escorted Gino to the owner's top-floor office one Thursday afternoon just after noon. He was not half as worried as the newspaper's owner George Lippman, however. Lippman had been mulling over what possible new monies or duties Gino Manzino was wanting to extract from him. A former newspaper editor himself, Lippman could not have been more unlike Gino. He looked like a harried city reporter, Gino thought: his jacket over his chair, his sleeves rolled up and a cigar burning in a ashtray. If it weren't for the unmistakable quality of that ashtray – a glass Steuben – of those white shirtsleeves, and of the diamond ring on his finger, Gino might have mistaken him for one. He and Gianni were quickly seated in two chairs before Mr. Lippman's desk – but as Scully began to sit in a third chair, Gino waved his hand and said, "If you don't mind, Mr. Scully, Mr. Ghianella, I should like to speak to Mr. Lippman alone."

Lippman raised his eyebrows, as did Scully and even Gianni, but the two men quickly left the room, Gianni planting himself at its door as Gino began to talk quietly.

"Do you have any children, Mr. Lippman?" Gino asked, unwittingly setting on end what was left of Mr. Lippman's thinning hair.

"Four," he said. All grown and out in the world."

"Any daughters?"

Lippman looked to his door, where Gianni's figure could be seen through cloudy glass. Was Gino Manzino going to threaten him?

"One," he said.

"I myself have a daughter, Mr. Lippman. And I am sure you can appreciate a father's feelings that his daughter's well-being should come before all else."

"Of course," Lippman said, having no idea what Gino was getting at.

"My daughter, Sunni Manzino, will be performing in a new

play, perhaps you have heard of it – *A Final Remembrance*. It is written and performed by all New York students and premieres next week.

"I know the one,' Mr. Lippman said.

"Your paper will be covering the event?"

With a rush of relief, Lippman suddenly realized what Mr. Manzino wanted. It wouldn't be the first time that someone without talent had been praised for her efforts.

"Yes of course, Mr. Manzino. And may I say what an achievement it is just for your daughter to have been chosen. I am sure she is wonderfully talented and I know my writers will think so also."

Gino smiled. "I'm afraid – "

"She will be an overnight sensation, Mr. Manzino. I'll have our drama critic start preparing now – perhaps a pre-performance interview with the lady is in order?"

But Gino was nodding his head.

"I'm afraid you've misunderstood, Mr. Lippman," Gino said and quickly told Lippman exactly what did want.

"Ah – ," Mr. Lippman said. "I see" – though he didn't at all. "I beg your pardon, Sir. Of course . . . it can be arranged."

"Thank you kindly," Gino said, standing and shaking Lippman's hand.

These crazy Italians, Lippman thought, shaking his head as Gino left.

AND YET, ONCE the plan was set into motion, Gino found himself haunted by an odd apprehension. He was always so sure of his position, even when it involved deception or violence, but this time he couldn't shake off the feeling that he had gone too far. A strange voice was whispering that perhaps Sunni's life wasn't his to control. Still, he pushed the thought from his mind; he was simply protecting Sunni from a threat she couldn't yet understand.

Sunni, meanwhile, was too caught up in the excitement of rehearsals, last-minute changes, and agonizing over whether they would make any sense to the audience, to notice any visible change in her father's behavior. The experience was becoming as frightening as it was exhilarating. The play was untested, not the usual known entity she had worked with in the past. All the plays she had been in with Matthew had been performed numerous times and were often analyzed in detail in drama classes. However original they may have been in their approach, (and Matthew was forever devising new variations on old themes), he had always had the basic structure to guide them. But this play was still taking shape. And as the actors moved through their lines and scenes, the uncertainty was unnerving to such young cast and crew. Reworking the script had brought more focus on Sunni's character and her feeling of responsibility toward Matthew and everyone else was growing stronger each day. And so, while she was an emotional wreck by the time the premiere arrived, another, deeper part of her felt strong enough to withstand the pressure and even longed for its challenge. This was the life she always wanted to lead.

On opening night, all the family bubbled around her in the theater lounge for the pre-curtain party, but Gino stood apart, seemingly distracted by some private doubt. She meant to ask him about it and would have if she could have found her way through all the kisses and flowers people kept pressing upon her. There was just too much happening at once. The moment passed, and she rushed away from the family to prepare for curtain call, stopped briefly by William Monroe, a local city councilman whom her family had known for years.

"Good luck, Sunni!" he called to her, his smile glittering, "At least with your father here the critics will be on your side." She just waved as she hurried by, paying little attention to his words.

During those two hours between the rise and fall of the curtain, Sunni felt as if she had lived an entire life. She had created a whole person for however short a time and even if no one had applauded, if no one had been there to see it, the night would have been just as wonderful. But the performance was sold-out, and the audience did applaud, and she never wanted it to end. Afterward, everyone was moved, Matthew crying even harder than she. They were sure now that all the difficult decisions they had made on the way to the stage had been right.

But they weren't exactly Broadway professionals, so there was no all-night party, with the director, actors, and producers waiting in some chic restaurant for the early editions to hit the streets, and they would have felt pretentious sitting around imagining that they were. Besides, the show had appeared off-Broadway with a late curtain and would only be picked up by the later city editions. So Sunni Manzino, brilliant performance notwithstanding, went home with her family as soon as the cast had shared a champagne toast. She was physically and emotionally drained and didn't mind being their little girl for at least one more night; she needed the sleep. The reviews would be waiting for her in the morning, and she was so confident of their accomplishment that it would be like waking up to Christmas.

She slept late, and when she finally awoke, the papers were waiting for her unread, as she had asked. But Gino was not there, which puzzled and disappointed her. She had wanted him to be there with her and had thought he would have wanted it also. But, too excited to wait any longer, she picked up the first paper, the *Daily News*, and turned to the arts section. The review was right in the center of the page, and she vowed to read it, calmly and analytically, all the way through, without allowing her emotional pitch to color her reaction to anything it said.

"On any given night in New York," the review began, "an audience can have the opportunity to witness a theater debut. But the audience gathered for last night's premiere of *A Final Remembrance* was presented with something truly unique. Except for the technical crew, everyone involved in the project was debuting simultaneously — the author, the director, and the entire cast of seventeen. There is an enormous risk in such a venture, and the good news is that, however mixed the results may be, it was a chance well worth taking. The play deals with . . . ."

Here, Sunni's determination to read the piece word for word dissolved and she skimmed ahead, looking for Matthew's name and her own. She only hoped that God would forgive her for not being more concerned with the play itself or the company as a whole, and promised to have the patience to read it slowly a second time.

"Despite his youth and inexperience," the review continued, "Matthew Bennett, the director, showed not only flashes of brilliance, but the discipline and sophistication to turn his theatrical insight into a profound interpretation." They loved Matthew, Sunni thought. I knew they would! Her eyes drifted down the column as the critic singled out one actor after another for special praise, and then spoke again of the play, which he said was exciting but flawed, and concluded with some congratulatory words for the school and public officials who had brought the production to the stage.

And that was it. Sunni stared at the page, unable or unwilling to absorb the simple fact: she was never mentioned. She read the review again, line by line this time, assuring herself that she must have missed her name in her nervousness. The critic spoke of her character's place in the narrative, but gave no assessment of the performance that had brought the character to life. If her name hadn't been listed in the cast along with everyone else's, Sunni thought, she might have wondered if she had been there at all.

With a growing sense of dread, she picked up *The New York Times*. Once more, the critic said kind things about the company (although he was somewhat harder on the playwright) and again it was as if Sunni hadn't been there. There was no direct reference to her acting at all. Telling herself not to cry, unaware of the tears already forming, Sunni turned to the *Daily Mirror* where at last someone spoke about her performance toward the end of the piece.

"Melinda," it read, "was played by Miss Sunni Manzino. While certainly lovely to look at, Miss Manzino didn't have the stage presence her part required. Somewhat tentative in her voice and manner, she was one of those members in the company for whom this play was simply a class exercise on her way to some other future. But for the others who view their performance as the beginning of a life in the theater, I can only wish them every success."

The paper slipped from her hands and she just sat there, unmoving, for what seemed like a very long time. If anyone in the house heard her crying, no one came to comfort her, and she had never felt so alone. That's why Pappa wasn't there, she thought. He must have read the reviews and knew she would be too upset to want company for a while. How could I have been so wrong? It felt so real to me and everyone there said . . ." She cried even harder, feeling utterly lost, and in another moment Filomina was holding her and hushing her sobs.

Matthew had to call her several times before she would come to the phone. He was outraged at the critics, everyone was, and he still wanted Sunni to join a new production he was preparing. It hurt her terribly to say no, but she had no choice. Everyone would assume that Matthew had found a place for her out of friendship, not respect. She knew he believed in her and was as mystified as she was about what had happened, but she couldn't let him risk being misunderstood. His own career was just beginning.

After speaking to Matthew, her despair lost some of its edge. At first she thought it was because she was so happy for him, and because he had tried so hard to make the reviews easier for her to bear. But she had been mourning more than her failure in one night's performance; she had been so sure of her instincts, and they had had been so wrong – how could she ever trust herself again? But her talk with Matthew allowed her to recreate the entire experience, and every element that went into it, and he'd been correct: the performance had been good, as right as it had felt to her on stage. For reasons she couldn't understand, the critics had been wrong. All at once, her mood shifted away from the darkness, and gradually she came to the conclusion that her performance had been exceptional after all – whatever the responses of others – and she felt a magical future emerging for her again. Even if the stage had been taken from her as a goal, she would never stop searching for another way of fulfilling her creative yearnings.

WHEN GINO RETURNED home that night, Sunni was waiting in a living room overlooking their lush gardens. "Tell me when Daddy gets home," she had said a little earlier, poking her head into Filomina's gorgeous kitchen. Filomina of course knew exactly what

Gino had done, but she too had no desire to have Sunni living in such a reckless world outside their own. When Gino had told her, long ago, that he could not allow Sunni to travel too long down such a path, Filomina knew exactly what he was saying. For once though, she told Gino not to tell her any more, to do what he had to do – but gently. So it was with sincerity that Filomina had finally gone up to Sunni's room that afternoon to ask what was wrong. And though she had immediately known that Gino was responsible for the reviews she only hushed her daughter and said her life was just beginning. When Gino finally arrived home, Filomina revealed nothing to him, only pointed Gino in Sunni's direction.

Gino knew, of course, that Sunni would be waiting for him, and was alarmed at his own nervousness. But he needn't have worried. "Pappa," Sunni said, standing up the moment he entered the room. A great rush of affection ran through her and she rushed to him for his protective hug. When she told him what had happened, he seemed as lost in sadness as she was. Everyone in the family would of course support her, but Gino shared her deep sense of suffering to an extent that surprised and touched her. How lucky she was to have such a father in a time of need, she thought.

A FEW MONTHS later, Sunni turned nineteen. Gino had planned a special lunch for her at a restaurant in the city and, impatient to get going, Sunni went to look for him in his study. He was still out on some business, so she waited for him, spinning around in his swivel chair the way she'd been doing ever since she was three. Looking up at Rosa's portrait, as always she imagined her grandmother's presence moving within her. Idly, she poked through the drawers in Gino's antique desk, wondering if her father had been sentimental enough to hide a piece of chocolate for her there, something he had done on her every birthday since she was a child.

In the drawer that normally held his personal correspondence, she was surprised to see a business letter. Suddenly, her curiosity was darkened by dread; the letterhead had the familiar crest and logo of the *Daily Mirror*. Quickly, Sunni picked it up. It was from one of the newspaper's editors, expressing "his hope" and "that of Mr. George Lippman" that the attached review capture the tone Mr. Manzino had wanted, "negating your daughter's performance in as gentle and courteous a manner as possible, so that no personal offense is rendered." Attached to the letter was a copy of the Mirror's review of her play.

Sunni placed the letter where she had found it, closed the drawer, rose from her father's chair, and sat in one of the dark green leather chairs on the other side of the desk. Her dark eyes opened wide, focusing on her inner concern. Only a slight trembling of her hands and the small pulse beating steadily at her temples betrayed her turmoil. As she sat there, thoughts and emotions drifted through her head in what seemed like a slow-motion accident. Soon, the jumble of impressions arranged themselves into a pattern she could recognize as the truth, and she blinked and shuddered slightly, then glanced around the office as if seeing it for the first time. In another moment, she stood up and started out of the room. At the door, she hesitated, then returned to the desk and retrieved the letter.

Gino was turning the corner at the end of the hallway as she emerged from the study, deep in conversation with the handsome young man working as his new driver. When he saw her, Gino broke into a full smile.

"My birthday girl," he said.

But Sunni said nothing, and wasn't at all sure that any sound would come out even if she tried. She simply handed the letter to her father, watching as a look of total shock washed over him.

"Sunni, I never," Gino said, reaching out to touch her shoulder.

He got no farther. Without a word, she stepped back from his touch, raising both palms in a gesture of self-protection. She stared into his eyes, silently telling him that nothing he could say could possibly make any difference, that it would be better if he said nothing at all. When a suggestion of tears tinged her eyes, she turned and walked away before they could fall. Gino stayed locked in place, afraid even to breathe, unconsciously letting the letter drop to the floor.

Off to the side, Gianni watched with strangely mixed emotions. He had no idea what the letter contained, and why it had triggered such a passionate confrontation. The only family problems Gino had ever confided in him concerned his constant frustration with Vinnie, but that tangentially involved Gianni whose position in the scheme of things was clearly related. Gino's other references to family life were relatively reserved, taking the form of a few stories about the old days, or an affectionate comment now and then about some special quality in Rosa, Filomina, or Sunni. Knowing how devoted Gino was to his daughter, Gianni understood the extent of his devastation at this moment, however mystified he might be at the cause, and was wise enough to stay silent. He simply picked up the fallen letter and handed it to Gino without glancing at it, then moved away, leaving the older man alone with his stunned sorrow. The scene had left Gianni somewhat stunned himself, but in an entirely different way. The image of Sunni, an incredibly beautiful girl, caught in a moment that combined great vulnerability and great strength had stirred something deep within him. Her intensity touched him in a way that her loveliness alone did not. If he had seen her in a casual situation – passing her on the street or watching her enter a crowded room – he might have smiled at her undeniable beauty, but he would have forgotten her the same way he forgot other beautiful women. But now the memory of her was indelible, and he needed some time to sort it out.

As the two men dispersed, each lost in his own thoughts, Sunni had already mastered her emotions. After stopping on the landing for several moments, taking a few deep breaths and clearing her eyes and mind, she suddenly climbed up to her room, hastily changed into riding clothes and left the house. Without a backward glance, she walked briskly to the stables where she asked the groomsman to prepare her favorite horse So No Wonder. In a few minutes, she had the reins in hand and quickly mounted, trotting off at an increasing pace until the groomsman was left scratching his head, watching her launch into a full gallop across the vast farmland. Sunni had no idea where she was going, her mind suddenly quiet during the headlong rush, but eventually she slowed down. It was then that she sensed the gradual return of the pain she had refused to absorb in Gino's presence. Dismounting by a cool stream that wound through the property, she allowed the horse to drink while she gazed into the clear rushing water. It wasn't long before a wave of shock and tears moved through her — but even as she wept, Sunni realized that she could not hate her father as she might have expected.

Had she really matured that much in so short a time? Could she actually understand an act of such massive arrogance? Perhaps loving her father as much as she did made it possible for her to see beyond the act. It would be easy to assume that he had manipulated her future for his own selfish ends and then dismiss him from her life and be done with it. But she knew he was miserable, and that in his pathetically misguided way, he must have thought he was protecting her from some terrible danger, which was his duty. He was wrong, of course, and his refusal to give her the freedom to choose her own risks hurt her deeply. But there was nothing hateful in him. She wasn't sure how this would affect their relationship, but she couldn't banish him from her life.

Oddly enough, the longer she stood beside the stream, the less horrifying it all became. She could even find solace in the fact that the critical response to her performance had been false. At least she wouldn't have to question her talent anymore. She may have lost an opportunity in the theater, but her faith that she could make a creative contribution to the world had suddenly been restored.

As Sunni once again mounted her horse and began to ride, she lost all awareness of time. Of course, she never had been especially sensitive to clocks, and for someone so intelligent, was amazingly out of touch with reality. Somewhere beyond the perimeter of her private life and its turmoil, mosaics were forming that would determine the fate of the world. Wars were forever renewing themselves, economies were crumbling on every continent, and people were being driven to increasingly desperate acts. If all this failed to intrude on Sunni's daily life, it was not a reflection of her lack of empathy. Her family was completely self-contained. Anything that happened outside it was just a series of important but probably irrelevant facts. In school, Sunni worked just as hard at analyzing Egyptian burial rites as she did on the Roman conquests, but when all was said and done, her formal education had no impact on anyone she cared about.

Uncle Bennie was the only family member she knew who paid attention to the news – and he was just about obsessed by it. He read the newspaper everyday, and was seldom out of the reach of a radio or television. His was the first car in the family to be equipped with a radio, and MANZINOS had a radio on every floor at the least. His was the first bar to have one going day and night – but to the frustration of all around him, he always preferred the news to music or a ball game. Since no one in the family would discuss these things with him, he maintained heated debates with customers, chefs, bartenders and even his more savvy suppliers.

The sun had lowered in the sky as Sunni once again drove herself and her horse over the wildest land of the farm. How proud her great-grandfather would of been to have seen this beautiful woman riding with such might. Filomina had even thought of naming her after him: Lucia for Count Luciano, but as only she knew the secret of Gino's lineage, she thought better of it. After galloping for what seemed like hours, both Sunni and the horse were damp with sweat and Sunni felt a ravenous hunger. Where had Gino planned to take her for lunch, she wondered. She could still see the stunned look in his eyes, and some part of her had also noted the flash of concern on Gianni's face. On the few occasions she had caught a glimpse of him before, he was usually dropping off Gino at the farm or picking him up. Though she'd always been aware of his dark good looks and the seriousness with which he carried himself, there must be something special in his strength, she thought, because according to Filomina, Gino placed an extraordinary amount of trust in him.

For the moment, however, she had something more immediate to think about. She would have to go home eventually – if only for her tiring horse – but what would she say to Gino? She couldn't pretend nothing had happened, and had no desire to play games with her father, submitting Gino to some arbitrary trial period in which he might regain her respect. Inevitably, she would forgive him, but he had to understand the gravity of his mistake. For the first time in her life, she had to teach her father a lesson.

When Sunni arrived home, giving So No Wonder some food and drink, then leaving her with the efficient groomsmen, she wandered back to the house with not only his eyes but those of Filomina watching from the kitchen. Gino's car was gone, Sunni noted, going to the kitchen for a glass of water, and asked Filomina if the cook could prepare her a late lunch.

"Of course, dear," Filomina said, greatly relieved after what Gino had told her. "A little pasta or salad?"

"Oh no," Sunni said, "Bacon and eggs and some bread and jam and butter, please."

After a shower, Sunni came down to a hearty meal and several cups of fresh coffee. By the time Gino returned home from business that evening, still visibly shaken by his guilt, Sunni was alone in the parlor, waiting for him. Instinctively, Filomina knew to leave them alone.

"Sunni," Gino began, "if you would just let me explain. It must seem awful to you, but . . . ."

"Pappa, it doesn't matter anymore," she said in calm, steady tones. "I know what you're going to say. The point is that you were wrong, terribly wrong. I will never let you impose your will on me again. I don't want to talk about it – not now, not ever. Words change nothing." Then she paused for a moment and said, "Shall we go in to dinner now, Pappa?"

Everything Gino had planned to say dissolved in an instant. He felt a day's worth of tension drain away and realized that his jaw was aching from sustained clenching. He glanced down at his lap and saw the birthday gift he had bought her – an elegant necklace wrapped in silver. Feeling absurdly shy, he extended the package toward her.

"No, Pappa, not this year," she said, finding the appropriate symbol. To soften the sting, she rose, walked over to him, and kissed his cheek, then led him into dinner. Holding onto his arm, she could feel his trembling. My father is aging, she thought.

Gino was also aware of his years that night and worried about his daughter's future now that time and circumstance were moving her away from him. Gino couldn't help but plan and care for her as best as he knew how. At some point, Sunni would be turning to someone else for support, and it was on this night that Gino determined to ensure that it was the proper person. By the time Filomina had brought out the cake with nineteen candles, Gino had already formulated a plan. Only this time, he thought, Sunni must never see his hand at work.

IT WAS A warm spring evening, and Vinnie Manzino was somewhere on the upper west side of Manhattan. Of course, he wasn't supposed to be on the upper west side. He was supposed to be in New Jersey, supervising a cigarette deal, and it took over an hour for Gianni to track him down. Although Gino had emphasized the importance of Vinnie's presence during the transaction, Vinnie had, as always, become impatient waiting around in a warehouse all afternoon. When he finally announced to the others that he had better things to do than baby-sit a fleet of trucks, no one was especially surprised. They'd been on assignments with Vinnie before, but they were nervous about this particular job, and wanted someone from the Manzino family to be with them.

Contraband cigarettes were a very deceptive business. Smuggling cigarettes into the city seemed so penny-ante, so harmless compared to drug sales and stolen cars, many of the crime bosses concentrated on flashier activities. But in its gradual, cumulative way, the cigarette business was enormously profitable, providing a consistent cash-flow that kept Gino's organization thoroughly solvent while other "investments" fluctuated wildly in value. It was complicated, however, because no matter how low in profile, the operation frequently attracted more than its share of government interference. Both Federal and state regulations were violated each time a pack of bootlegged cigarettes was bought, which meant that government agents had been brought into the field. These anonymous and usually unimaginative men (the "gray boys", Gino called them) were outsiders to whatever local systems of patronage and protection had evolved other the years. Therefore, these strangers were unpredictable and essentially incorruptible. They were simply passing through, performing their tasks with dispassionate efficiency before moving on to their next assignment. But whether out of frustration at all the criminal activity that seemed to flourish just beyond their reach or simply out of sheer vengeance, these agents often focused their energies on more modest operations they could contain with recurring raids, cigarette smuggling being one of them. It was like someone straightening books on a shelf while a storm destroyed the house, said Gianni one day when he and Gino were discussing the problem, and Gino had smiled in recognition.

So every large transaction was a touchy business, and Gino wanted Vinnie to be present whenever he couldn't be there himself. It was critical that no guns were impetuously drawn against the gray boys – far better to lose the entire shipment, and even the men for a while. The business would resume again and learn to flow around the government's sphere of influence. Violence, on the other hand, could bring the whole world down on top of them.

Vinnie had no desire to provoke open warfare with the government, but he lacked the foresight to approach each encounter as a potential disaster. He'd become restless and had convinced himself that his father was being overly cautious, so at dusk he headed up to the west side, leaving Augie in charge. Augie was like an old woman anyway, he thought, and would be much better at keeping the peace.

About the same time, Gino received a tip from one of his contacts in the police department – Federal and state agents had scheduled a raid within the hour. Government people acted independently, but the law required that they inform local authorities if they were operating in the area and normally they waited until the last minute to prevent any possible leaks.

The warehouse was abandoned and thus stripped of any phone lines, so someone would have to drive down and warn Vinnie. They would do what they had often done before: leave one unmanned, untraceable truck with a small supply of cigarette cartons for the raiders to find. This usually satisfied them for a while, giving them a sense that their time had been well spent and that their string of successes was still real.

Although he tried to minimize direct contact between Vinnie and Gianni in order to avoid (or perhaps just postpone) open conflict, Gino was forced by the timing and the seriousness of the situation to send Gianni across the river to the warehouse. He only hoped that Gianni could get there before the agents, and then get out again with the men and most of the equipment and goods. But traffic was a mess at this hour and, even with Gianni's prodigious driving skills, he was several minutes too late.

THERE WERE SIX agents in all, under the direction of a man named Frank Carmichael. Not as colorless as most of the gray men, Carmichael had a nastily aggressive personality, and took special pleasure in confronting Sicilians. He was also very good at what he did, and had taken complete control of everyone and everything in the warehouse before anyone had a chance to respond or to run. Believing in tried-and-true methods, Carmichael was old enough to remember what his predecessors had told him about raids on prohibition distilleries, he simply smashed through the building's ancient bay doors with his reinforced van (playing Elliot Ness, his men called it) and had everyone under the gun within moments. All of the trucks were there, those that had brought the stuff up from the Carolinas and those Gino had to send the shipment into New York, and thousands of cartons were caught in mid-transfer. It was a tremendous haul, but Carmichael was too cantankerous simply to take the prize and go home. He had Gino's men and the other drivers gathered in a knot in front of him, their guns and knives forming a small pile of hardware off to the side. Then he began to curse them out one by one, shouting occasionally and demanding answers to questions about their business. Everyone in the room except Carmichael seemed to understand that the questions were idiotic, and one of the agents and Augie even caught one another's glance at one point and exchanged a small shrug. Carmichael was a real pain in the ass.

Nevertheless, one driver was taking the agent's threats more seriously. Whatever intelligence or good judgment Louis Carlotta had ever possessed had long since been eroded by the cocaine he snorted to get him through his late night cargo runs. He was inching towards the back fender of his truck and the pistol that he kept taped just inside the rim, insurance in case he was ever stopped on a run. He had no particular plan in mind, but just a dim sense of how much fun it would be to blow the loud-mouthed agent away while he was still in the middle of a sentence. If no one noticed his movement, he might be able to get his chance.

Gianni, who had entered the warehouse through a window close to the roofline, was now on a catwalk just behind the agents and above all the men. When he had seen the smashed bay doors and the absence of police vehicles, some instinct, based perhaps in his distrust of Vinnie's ability to handle a real crisis, had convinced him to find a way in and assess what was happening. From his vantage point, he realized that it was only a matter of minutes before the situation exploded. He had to act quickly.

THE ONLY WEAPON he was carrying was his automatic, but two shots fired into a large metal barrel just behind the gents created a loud enough echoing in the cavernous room to jolt them practically off their feet. "Just freeze where you are!" Gianni shouted from above. "There's enough of us up here to blow you to hell several times over. Drop your weapons where you stand, kick them away from you, and then drop face-first to the floor. The rest of you men, get in your trucks and get the hell out of here." All of the agents, even Carmichael, complied instantly, although it would have been too much to hope for to expect his mouth to submit with the rest of his body. "GO AHEAD, YOU FUCKING WOPS!" he bellowed as the truck engines roared into life and, with the wrenching of gears and squealing of tires, the vehicles raced for the smashed opening. "RUN AS HARD AS YOU CAN, YOU'LL PROBABLY BE FUCKING DEAD IN A WEEK!" As he looked up from his prone position at the chaos before him, he was surprised to see Louis Carlotta walking towards him with a pistol in his hand and a manic grin on his face. "You won't even make it that far," said Louis, cocking the pistol just a few inches from Carmichael's face and bracing himself to fire.

GIANNI FIRED VERY quickly, and the two shells that struck Louis in the chest and forehead sent the little man sprawling several feet backward. "Stay where you are," Gianni called to the floored agents. "And keep it in mind that no one was allowed to touch you. And stay there even after the place clears out, because you have no idea how long we'll be staying up here." One of Gino's men tossed Louis' body into the back of his own truck and drove away, leaving the room empty except for the agents and a few scattered cartons of cigarettes. Even Carmichael had shut up, and Gianni slipped quietly away. He went back out the same window and returned to his car. As he sped away from the area, he wondered if the gray men would lie there all night, waiting for permission to leave.

BEFORE RETURNING TO Gino, Gianni thought he'd better make an attempt to find Vinnie. He had obviously not been at the warehouse during the raid, so he must have gone looking for whores and booze. Since Vinnie had a way of making himself unwelcome in so many places over the years, he was constantly forced to shift his center of social activity. Gianni finally found him in a filthy bar on 101st Street. He was already drunk and greeted Gianni with his usual silence and sardonic smile. The look was intended to communicate a venomous hatred but was always betrayed by a tiny movement at the corner of his eyes – the only visible sign of Vinnie's guilt for never being to his father what Gianni Ghianella had become – a confidant. But Vinnie had lived with the feeling so long that he'd almost forgotten it was there. Gianni, however, could see the tremor glimmering whenever Vinnie drew near.

Speaking in staccato sentences, Gianni told him what had happened at the warehouse and said that he had better get to Gino immediately to salvage whatever they could from the mess. There'd been no tragedy, he said, despite the screw-up, but he neglected to mention the role he had played in deflecting it. Word of that would reach Vinnie soon enough, Gianni thought, better if he didn't hear it directly from him. It would seem like an open challenge to Vinnie's position, and he didn't want a confrontation – not tonight, at any rate.

As soon as Gianni left, Vinnie brooded over his stirring resentment. Gino was grooming the man for something, he knew, but the only way he could handle it was by affecting disinterest and disdain for his father's plans. As long as he refused to acknowledge the existence of a competition, he would never risk the humiliation of losing.

Besides, Vinnie thought, Gino still believed in blood. No matter how displeased he might be in his son's performance, he would never allow his empire to pass out of the hands of the family. He was Gino's only son, and none of his sisters had presented son-in-laws who could possibly take his place. Look at Jimmy, for example. Gino would sooner give everything to the niggers than let that asshole inherit any power, Vinnie thought, so his position was secure.

Once he had gone through this process, which had almost become a ritual, and determined once again that Gianni wasn't really a threat, he turned his mind to the problem at hand. Gino had been very specific about Vinnie staying at the warehouse in case something went wrong and now something had. Well, fuck him. His being there wouldn't have helped anything. In fact, it might have made matters worse since he would have been identified as Gino Manzino's son. He'd have to invent some excuse for leaving. Maybe he could say that one of his people had told him about a possible raid, and he had left to check into the story himself. He'd think of something.

Reluctantly, he pushed himself away from the table and signaled to the two men who had come in with him that he had go. They still hadn't eaten, but the linguini and clams would have to wait. At least he had gotten in a half hour upstairs with that Spanish girl before they started drinking.

His two friends, who were almost as drunk, stumbled toward their sedan while Vinnie walked around the corner to where he had parked his Jaguar sports car. As he was searching through his pockets for keys, he suddenly became aware of a small group of young black boys swarming over his car. They had already removed most of the chrome – wheel rims, outside mirrors, hood ornament – and were struggling with a crowbar in an attempt to detach the wide, shiny bumpers.

The boys, none of them any older than twelve, spotted Vinnie as he began screaming, "SON OF A BITCH! THAT'S MY CAR! SON OF A BITCH!" The kids dropped the crowbar with a resounding crash and took off down the street while Vinnie, his reactions slowed in his alcoholic haze, stood there staring and cursing. Then he pulled out his pistol, an outsized Magnum, and started chasing after them, now a half-block away and widening the distance rapidly. A couple of the boys turned into a narrow alley, nearly crashing into a young child playing there by himself, and then vaulted a fence before Vinnie had reached the entrance.

The child, a chubby eight-year-old named Ronald Carter began trotting toward the wooden-slatted fence that he had seen two boys climb so unexpectedly and with such incredible speed. Despite his age, he was almost their height and wondered if the fence was really that easy to scale. He decided to try, and picked up speed as he approached the fence. Behind him in the shadows, peering into the gloom beyond the streetlight's glare, Vinnie pointed his gun at the running figure and shouted: "STOP RIGHT THERE, YOU SON OF A BITCH! STOP AND NOBODY GETS HURT!" But the boy kept running toward the fence, infuriating Vinnie still further. He fired a thunderous shot into the air and yet the boy ran, even faster. Then he lowered his gun and fired, just as Ronald reached the fence and leapt as high as he could to get over it. The bullet entered the back of his skull and spread its core over a sizeable area before the body fell back to the ground.

In the aftermath of neighborhood hysteria and keening police sirens, Vinnie felt the earth open beneath him and began a long, slow fall that he thought would never end. Somewhere in those first terrible minutes, just after he yielded his gun without comment to the first police officer who arrived on the scene, he heard that the black boy was only eight years old – and he was totally deaf. The news was astonishing, terrifying. The child had not heard his shouts or the first shot Vinnie fired. He played in the alley when he played outdoors because his mother wanted him to stay away from the street. Vinnie was lost in a cloud but still falling, a slow-motion descent into hell. He was vaguely aware of being in police custody, and that his lawyer had been unable to bring him home this time. The public outcry was overwhelming, he said. Their only option was to wait it out and maintain a posture of remorse and chastened dignity – no demands for release, no challenges to the accusers. Vinnie's only request was not to see his father.

Meanwhile, Gino was shrouded in a cloud of his own. He had lost all respect for his son long ago, but now he was in prison and there was nothing he could do to get him out. With his great influence and resourcefulness, Gino was able to free anyone from almost any tangled net. All crimes, even murder, were negotiable, as long as someone was willing to pay the price. But in a triumphant climax to his life-long obsession with self-destruction, Vinnie had managed to blunder into the only act that could place him beyond salvation. Over and over, Gino repeated to himself the simple, damning facts: Vinnie had killed an eight-year-old child, a black deaf-mute, by shooting him in the back of the head. Unbelievable. He might as well have tossed a bomb into a schoolyard, or a convent. The only defense Vinnie offered, uttered in a voice of profound weakness, was that the boy had looked older in the half-light, that he had been too drunk, that other boys had stolen trinkets from his car, and this boy had leapt into the bullet's path.

With every newspaper in the city calling for justice, the chorus of grief and outrage over the slaughter of Ronald Carter rose in a steady crescendo that transformed the shooting into a crisis. State and national figures petitioned the courts, and no one, no one whatsoever, was willing to offer Vinnie any gesture of clemency. The sum total of the Manzino influence could do nothing more than hasten the court hearing and spirit him away to serve his sentence in a small prison up north. The name of Ronald Carter was kept alive for some time as a kind of symbolic victim whose fate was linked to the many impoverished black martyrs in a city of hardening racial lines and tumultuous times. His murderer, however, having been disposed of so swiftly, was essentially forgotten in a few months. Vinnie Manzino was dismissed as just another low-life hood who got what he deserved.

Many weeks after his conviction, Vinnie finally agreed to see his father. Till then, all their communications had been through intermediaries – family, friends, and primarily lawyers. At first, Gino thought Vinnie was being uncharacteristically cautious, trying to keep his father away from the blizzard of public scrutiny. Or perhaps it was his anger at having failed to free him. But as soon as Gino saw him, he realized that the cause was much deeper. Vinnie had undergone a fundamental change in his personality, a collapse of the bravado that had always charged him with so much force. He had lost weight as well, so his physical deflation matched the loss of his human spirit.

They sat in the visiting room with two guards in attendance and one of Gino's lawyers fidgeting nervously in the corner. There was something hesitant, haunted, in the way Vinnie looked and spoke, Gino thought. He seems embarrassed, ashamed. Could the death of this pathetic child have stirred a conscience in him? There was no outpouring of bitterness, none of the anger he had expected to confront. Vinnie seemed drained and defeated, not outraged, and whatever resentment he felt toward Gino expressed itself only in his reluctance to look into his father's eyes. But as Gino began telling his son about the public's continued response to the tragedy, it soon became clear that Vinnie was not mourning the death of Ronald Carter. He didn't even seem especially upset that the boy was dead. So what had changed?

Gino had anticipated arrogance and blind self-righteousness, but Vinnie's reticence caused his comments to trickle to a close. He had no idea what his son was thinking or feeling. The silence between them stretched out for several minutes. Finally Vinnie looked up from his brooding, blinking away his private reverie, and spoke to his father gently.

"You know, Pappa, the bullet really went into me, not that little nigger. The minute it happened, my whole life was over. And you know what? Part of me is glad. I'm so tired of pushing for nothing. Now I can just let it all go."

With a small sigh, Vinnie stood up wearily and walked toward the doorway leading back to his cell. "Just do whatever you have to do, Pappa, you and the lawyers." His voice was so low that Gino could barely make out his words. "Tell Mamma I'm sorry." Then he was gone.

Faced unexpectedly with his son's odd sense of defeat, Gino felt a pain he hadn't experienced since Philly's death. Somewhere within the lost figure Vinnie Manzino was Gino's own failure. No matter how certain he was that he had done everything possible to enable Vinnie to become a man of character, his son's present despair, the flip side of his uncontrolled wildness, was clearly directed at him. Somehow Gino had turned Vinnie's life into a constant frenzy, a drive to achieve his approval and affection which had grown to be irrevocably out of reach. You can't just take away dark elements, Gino realized. You have to provide some light.

CHAPTER
TWENTY-EIGHT

Sunni was not far from hysteria – or so it felt. After her bout with her father and the theater, she had transferred to Pratt Institute and after months of preparation, was about to make her first formal presentation of a fashion layout. She'd won a national competition generally claimed by far more experienced designers, and with it the chance to create a full campaign for a major fashion house – something that, if the cards fell the right way – could lead directly into a position as assistant to the company's advertising director upon graduation. Normally Sunni thrived on a demanding pace. But making a solo presentation of her own designs to a potential client was giving her stage fright, something that she hadn't experienced since the premiere. When she thought of the hours and energy it took to transform her ideas into the finished product, she wasn't prepared for the criticism that everyone said she'd receive on a first attempt.

And now, with less than two hours to go before show time, Gino had called to say that he couldn't take her to the presentation as he had promised, but would send a car for her. Sunni wasn't sure which annoyed her more – not having Gino to give her strength during those last jittery moments, or having a car sent to take care of her. She hated the idea of being "taken care of" in any way; it reminded her of all the other young women in school, the daughters (or possibly girlfriends) of important executives who were always being chauffeured around in Daddy's limousine. She preferred her independence and counted on Gino only for moral support.

As the time drew near for her to be picked up for the drive cross-town, Sunni managed, with the help of her friend Amy, to bring her portfolio and easel downstairs and out to the sidewalk. As they struggled to keep everything from falling into the path of passersby, Amy looked up and said, "I think your ride is here, Sunni. Not bad."

Catching a glimpse of the limousine and becoming slightly embarrassed, Sunni said, "Yeah, I guess it's a nice car."

"I wasn't talking about the car," Amy said with a grin as she started back into the building. Turning, Sunni saw Gianni smiling at her as the design boards began slipping out of her hands; in another second, they fell to the ground, one of them opening to allow the sketches inside to get caught by a sudden breeze. Exasperated enough to scream, she lunged for the sheets and landed them all before they blew too far. By the time she lay them back in their carrier, Gianni had moved the rest of the materials onto the back seat, appearing as if he'd greatly enjoyed the entire spectacle. But he worked hard at keeping a neutral expression while the runaway sketches were safely stowed away.

Why does he see me in my most dramatic moments, Sunni thought, trying to bring her blush under control as she hurried into the front seat.

Gianni got in next to her, smiling politely, and said, "Hello, Miss Manzino. Good to see you again."

"Hello yourself, Mr. Ghianella," she answered, and added on impulse, "Are you mocking me?"

Surprised at her response, he laughed and said, "Maybe I was. I'll have to be more careful."

"About mocking or being caught?"

Still grinning, he said, "Okay, you win. I'll be good."

"It doesn't matter," she said. "I have a feeling I may not live through the afternoon anyway. This presentation scares me to death."

She really is beautiful, Gianni thought. And she does have the intensity I saw that day. No wonder Gino worries about her.

"Is there any way we can stop for some ice cream?" she said. "Please? It's really important. Ice cream calms my nerves."

"Sure," Gianni said. "But you'd better make it vanilla, just in case you spill something. This doesn't seem to be your day for holding onto things."

Glancing down at her white knit dress, she agreed that perhaps vanilla would be a good idea.

A short while later, Gianni double-parked on a side street which was, he assured Sunni several times as they walked up to a small frozen-custard stand on the corner, only five minutes from the appointment she had more than an hour to reach. It was early November and most of the concession stands were closed and shuttered, but Gianni said this one would be open even on the coldest day in winter. Today, however, the temperature was in the sixties, the sun was burning in a clear blue sky, and the stand was crowded with small children who seemed to be held over from some summer street game. The effect was so festive that Sunni forgot for a moment whatever tensions the presentation was creating in her.

As they returned to the car with ridiculously tall cones of soft vanilla, Sunni concentrated on not dripping hers all over her dress, now that the notion was firmly planted in her mind. The old man who owned the stand seemed to know Gianni very well and was so glad to see him, he'd given them each a triple portion.

"I can see why he has to stay open all year," Sunni said.

Gianni leaned against the fender as Sunni struggled with her cone. In the same gently teasing tone he used earlier, he said, "It isn't ice cream, though. It's frozen custard – an important distinction."

"That's just another name for soft ice cream," Sunni said, and Gianni watched her as she used her tongue to trace a circle above the cone's edge so that none of the custard could melt its way free.

"Not at all," he said, still watching her closely. "No one who's ever been to Coney Island would make that mistake. You've been living in the country too long. Frozen custard is custard, not cream. It has an entirely different base, a gelatin base, as a matter of fact."

Some subtle change in his voice caused Sunni to look up at him, and he dropped his eyes, just in time to sidestep a few falling drops of melted custard. "Whatever it is," she said, "it's wonderful."

Later, as he waited for her in the dress manufacturer's private parking lot (Sunni had insisted on carting everything inside by herself, saying that she'd look more "professional" that way) Gianni kept smiling at the thought of how she'd seen him staring. When he remembered the moment, he found himself focusing on her tongue and lips. No, Gianni warned himself. It's perfectly all right to like the girl, and to think that she's beautiful, but I'd better stop imagining things. Gino has entrusted me with his daughter's care and he might resent any romantic ideas. (Resent? Hell, Gino might shoot me. Living on a farm in Connecticut might have tamed him somewhat, but he was still a Sicilian.) Yet, there was something inherent in her character that he couldn't ignore, a quality that knowledge or experience could never touch, a kind of integrity, he thought, and he intended to treat it with the respect it deserved. Then he drew a deep breath, and his mind remained in check while he waited.

Upstairs, Sunni thought about his grace and the way his body moved, the vision so strong that the secretary had to call her name twice before she realized it was time to go in.

In another office across the city, Gino mused about the possibility of something stirring between his daughter and his surrogate son, but the reverie was cut short by an urgent phone call from Andy Holloway, one of several criminal lawyers he had used over the years.

"I thought you would want to know right away," Andy said as soon as Gino's secretary put him through. "Colatosti's out and back in New York."

A few hours later, Gianni was in a small uptown bar, nursing a bourbon and water, and trying to sort out his feelings. Sunni had, of course, scored a triumph with her designs and described every last detail to him at great length – what she said, what they said, how much they loved her ideas. Gianni had felt a surprising twinge of sadness in response to her contagious sense of joy. In one day, he'd become acutely aware of something rare in her, something worth preserving, and also had a glimpse of the fast-moving, glamorous world that might take her away. Fortunately, he realized how silly he was being and spent the rest of the drive enjoying Sunni's breathless recitation. When he dropped her at school, she gave him the most dazzling smile he'd ever seen.

As he sat alone with the one drink he allowed himself at the end of the day, a pretty young blonde took the vacant stool next to him, ordered a vodka martini, and watched Gianni out of the corner of her eye. She'd been sitting with a somewhat inebriated man who was hotly arguing a sports event with a few other men, but now she seemed to be switching allegiance to Gianni, who was much better-looking and far more sober than her original partner. In a move that tried but failed to look casual, she used a particularly loud uproar from the sports fanatics, causing Gianni to disengage from his private thoughts, as her opening.

"They'll just never grow up," she said. "Baseball season is barely over before they're screaming about football and basketball, even hockey. I mean, what's the point? Does it really matter who wins? It starts all over again the next season, anyway."

"Maybe that's the whole idea," Gianni said. "Sometimes you get so tired of things that really matter – jobs, families, relationships, money – it's good to be distracted by just a game. It's a kind of outlet." Gianni smiled at her and she smiled back, so pleased at having wedged out a response that she was sure a double meaning lurked behind his words. Perhaps the night had possibilities after all, she thought.

"I'm Terry Policik," she said, extending her hand and swiveling her stool in his direction, twisting her body so he would notice how it fit into her tight, low-cut black sheath.

"Nice move, Terry," her friend called from the other end of the bar. "You really know how to show it off." Apparently, there was nothing malicious in the remark because he and his buddies laughed benignly and then returned to their conversation, forgetting all about her again.

Terry colored slightly and said, "Sorry. I told you they'd never grow up." Gianni shrugged and smiled good-naturedly as she gazed into his large, dark eyes. "Did it work at least?" she asked. "Do you think I have a great body?"

Gianni gave her a conscientious appraisal, head to toe. Her skin was lightly tanned to complement her fluffy blonde hair, and her body was full and rounded in a way that any man would find sexy, although a softness about her suggested too many hours of sitting on bar stools. She was probably not very graceful, Gianni surmised.

"You have a very good body," he said at last.

Sensing a challenge in his qualified response, Terry said, "Thank you for the honest opinion. Now, exactly what has to happen before you say I have a great body?"

"Ask me again after two more drinks," he answered with a sting-softening smile.

She considered admonishing him for the put-down, but then decided that even his teasing was sexy and gave a what-the-hell shrug. "Well, tonight I'm in the mood to have a great body," she said and called to Paul, the solemn-faced bartender, "Two more drinks for the gentleman," which drew a spatter of applause from the boys.

The telephone rang before Paul had a chance to pour the drinks. "Gianni, it's for you," he said a moment later. "It's Gino."

"We have a problem," Gino said. Colatosti's back in town and he may try something."

"I'm on my way," Gianni answered.

Gianni returned to finish the dregs of his drink, pick up his jacket, and then leaned over to kiss Terry's cheek. "Thanks anyway," he said and left the bar to a chorus of boos that reflected the sudden look of disappointment on Terry's face.

Colatosti was one of the city's small operators who had managed to channel his brand of craziness into his power on the street.

He'd been considerably successful until three years ago when he blew it all in one stupid move. Like many other narrow-minded men, he resented that his territory had been limited to a few city blocks no one cared about, even though it was all he could do to handle that much efficiently, and like a hamster trying to break out of a cage where it lived quite comfortably, he had decided that his best chance for more control was to make a play for part of Gino's turf.

Beyond the fact that Gino's wealth always drew its share of predators, Gino's way of doing business inspired an extra ration of raiders. He treated everyone in a fair, even generous fashion, resorting to violence only on rare occasions. Gino had recognized long ago that a man could build a better organization by keeping people reasonably happy than by antagonizing them. The trick was to get them to deal with you rather than someone else, so that the chances of attracting unwanted attention were diminished. In the process, Gino had made himself almost invisible to the outside world. If it hadn't been for Vinnie's disasters, those who lived in the "other America" would have never known he existed.

But men like Tio Colatosti didn't understand this. To them, a quiet presence was interpreted as inattention or neglect. If a man didn't display his muscle and a willingness to use the "killing effect" that had become so popular in the black ghettoes of Harlem and the Bronx, then he must be vulnerable. So someone would make his move, never seeing Gino's invisible hand until it was too late. Usually Gino could cover up these skirmishes, but in Tio's case that had been impossible.

Lately, however, such raids had been happening at an alarming rate. Gino's age might have had something to do with it, as his enemies could interpret it as weakness. Vinnie's steady deterioration and disappearance into prison, had also left Gino with no recognized heir. Then too, the city had been carved and recarved so many times by generations of bosses that less was left for young and hungry newcomers. With no new areas to develop, it made sense for them to steal from someone else's. Gino, who had in recent years developed a passion for Hollywood westerns, felt like one of those pioneer cattlemen who endured great hardship and bloodshed to settle some wild territory, only to confront homesteaders, who'd taken no part in those early battles, suddenly moving in to conquer his range. When Gianni pointed out that the cattlemen were usually the villains, Gino simply replied that movies were made in the "other America" so they couldn't possibly reflect the principles involved.

Then, in a single afternoon, Colatosti's people had gunned down six of Gino's men and four innocent bystanders in a flurry of raids on storefront offices and a backroom gambling operation. While Gino's people swiftly isolated the raiding party and executed three of the men, two others panicked as they ran for their car and emptied their-shotguns into two policemen who'd come rushing toward them from the street.

In the days that followed, Gino stopped all his people from taking any further retaliatory action and made sure, through his elaborate system of contacts, that Colatosti's role in the double cop-killing became known. Colatosti's organization was completely destroyed, most of his men killed by overzealous police teams. Although the outraged district attorney's office couldn't implicate Colatosti in any of the actual killings, they strung together enough conspiracy and weapons charges to put him away for a while. He was sentenced to eighteen years in a Federal penitentiary.

"Obviously," Gino said a short while later, after Gianni had been ushered into his office, "the D.A. was a little sloppy. Colatosti's lawyers have been chipping away at the charges ever since he was convicted. They've finally managed to have everything thrown out except the time he's already served. In fact, I'm surprised they didn't force the state to pay him restitution for the two and a half years he was in."

"So he plans to take his restitution from you?" Gianni asked. "Or is he just planning to pick up where he left off?"

"He has no base, no allies. He'd never be able to put together a real threat. He'll throw his life away avenging his own stupidity," Gino said in a tired voice. "He's had a couple of years to twist everything around in his head so I come out responsible for all his problems – and time to plan what he intends to do about it. I have several people trying to find him before he can do any harm, but it may take a few days. In the meantime, I want to keep Filomina and Sunni safe. I'm sure Colatosti knows that the quickest way to hurt me is through them."

Here he paused and smiled for the first time since Gianni arrived. "You know, Gianni," he said, "I never really thanked you adequately for protecting me and my family from Crazy Eyes that afternoon. Filomina has praised you to the heavens ever since. Even Sunni said . . . ." He let the sentence end unfinished, and Gianni wanted to shout, "What did Sunni say?" but fought back the impulse and waited for Gino to continue. " . . . anyway, I'll never underestimate people's madness again. We have to assume that Colatosti might go after anyone close to me, and so we have to guard them accordingly."

"Do you want me to man the farm?" Gianni asked, careful not to show his disappointment that Gino hadn't returned to his reference to Sunni.

"No," Gino said, "I'll take care of that myself. Access to the farm is limited to one road, and it'll be sealed off from visitors. Angela and the kids will be there too, so I'll beef up security around the house."

"What about you?"

"I'll be armed and have Maggio with me to watch my back."

Gianni paused for a moment, then said, "So what do you want me to do?"

"I want you to take special charge of Sunni," Gino said flatly, taking care not to show any curiosity about Gianni's response. "I've already spoken to her and she's insisted on going to school for the rest of the week to finish some revisions on her project. She'll be safe enough in class – she works in crowded design and sewing rooms – but you'll have to drive her in from Connecticut and stay with her the rest of the time."

"Filomina must be terrified," Gianni said.

"No," Gino said. "Despite what happened last time, she's not that easily unnerved. She's mostly worried about Sunni spending her days in the city, but I said she'd be with you, which seemed to calm her. I also told her that Colatosti is obsessed with old honor and the unwritten code that forbids a man from touching the women and children of his enemy."

"And she believed you?"

"I'm not sure. People go on about this honor code all the time. And she reads a lot of fiction, which is full of that garbage. But she didn't grow up in Connecticut, you know. She's from the old school – that's why I married her, " he laughed. He remembered some of the stories Giovanni had told him when he was a boy, the way old timers romanticized the warrior chiefs in the old country, as if keeping the old days magical could make them somehow special. Gino had always been too much of a realist to take the legends seriously. Even where a code of honor did exist, he was certain that its origins were entirely pragmatic. In a small, isolated village, if anyone stepped over the line, a precedent was set that could wipe out the entire town in a matter of days, like the taboo that existed in farming communities against burning another man's barn. It had nothing to do with honor, only with the fact that no man could survive the loss of his barn, and so they had to avoid escalating the conflict to that point.

"In Sicily," Gino began once more, "the men wouldn't kill the women because they're too afraid of the priests who tell them that killing a woman is more of a sin than killing another man."

"Maybe it isn't the Sicilian priests they fear," Gianni teased. "They're just too afraid of the Sicilian women."

"You may be right," Gino said, laughing. "I know a few of them myself."

AS GINO AND Gianni pulled up in front of the school, Sunni came out of the building with two other girls and all three of them piled into the backseat, Amy and Debbie staring intently at Gianni in silence. They were both very pretty, in a bohemian, artsy sort of way, Gianni thought, which fit in with his idea of living downtown. He drove them home to their apartment in Greenwich Village, then headed for Connecticut.

"My friends checked you out pretty thoroughly, Gianni," Sunni said, teasing. "I'll get the final report tomorrow."

"Checked me out – for what?" Gianni asked.

"They always check out the men who pick anyone up," she said. "The rating system's fairly complicated."

"So why wasn't I checked out?" Gino asked.

"Well, Pappa," she said, "the system's just designed for men in general. It would never be adequate for someone like you."

Gino laughed and Gianni glanced at Sunni's face in the rear-view mirror. She caught and held his eyes briefly before turning her attention to the traffic rushing past them. None of them noticed the graffiti-painted pick-up truck driven by a man with sandy-colored hair who followed them discreetly all the way to the farm before disappearing from sight altogether.

Gianni stayed over that night, sleeping in the garage apartment with the other men serving as extra security. The night was so quiet; the clean autumn crispness to the air seemed to polish off any lingering concerns. As Gianni drifted off to sleep, he saw Sunni's gaze in the mirror once more, a look that appeared to acknowledge the current passing between them, and realized that something important was happening to him, and there was nothing he could do to stop it.

In the morning, Filomina insisted on making them breakfast before sending Gianni and Sunni on their way before eight. In what was quickly becoming a miraculous chain of events, Gino had an early meeting at home and wouldn't be coming into the city until lunchtime, so he and Sunni would be completely alone. I should say something to her, Gianni thought. But I'd feel like a fool if I'm imagining it. Locked in the silence of his thoughts, he started away from a stop sign before he saw a large truck bearing down on them. He braked sharply, causing Sunni to lurch forward, his arm instinctively reaching out to keep her from hitting the dashboard, then scooted the car backward as the truck went by, sounding its horn in a few angry bursts. Furiously embarrassed, he brought his attention to the duty at hand.

With a gently mocking smile, she said casually, "Your first

stop sign?"

Gianni laughed, his awkwardness evaporating. For the rest of the drive, they talked easily and spontaneously – about her family, her blossoming career as a designer, about his background and why he never finished college. Gianni regained his sense of control, and his driving was free of any further errors. He was also fully aware of the dark sedan that had been following them for several miles, then changed lanes to pass them on the left. The driver, a young man with sandy-colored hair, came abreast of the car and moved ahead swiftly as if the occupants didn't interest him. A short while later, Gianni saw the same car pulling out of a turnpike turn-around and returning the way he had come.

Midway through the afternoon, Gino called Gianni from a restaurant meeting with some lawyers and shipping people. Gianni had been waiting in the lobby of Sunni's school while she busied herself in the sewing room upstairs.

"Nothing positive to report," Gino said. "No one's picked him up yet, but he's definitely been seen in the city, asking about me and what I'm doing. By all reports, he hasn't changed much, although he may be a little balder and a little more demented. Stay close to Sunni." When Gino hung up the phone, he quickly surveyed the crowded dining room before sitting down with his colleagues once more. Meanwhile, a nondescript man with sandy hair ate alone at one of the smaller tables, apparently lost in his own thoughts.

By the second day of his guardianship, Gianni was beginning to have affectionate feelings for Tio Colatosti, who may have changed his whole life inadvertently, although neither he nor Sunni had expressed their growing attraction for each other in so many words. Instead, Sunni had a long break between classes that day, so Gianni took her for lunch at a small French restaurant on East 59th Street.

"Is this a date, Gianni?" Sunni asked as the maitre d' seated them.

"It can't be," he said. "You didn't buy me a corsage."

Sunni giggled, then ordered a glass of white wine.

It was a wonderful lunch, although Gianni couldn't concentrate on what he was eating. His sense of closeness to Sunni had reached a level of both ease and tension all its own. He still had no idea where it might lead, only that he had to preserve this newfound sense of communion. As the meal drew to a close, a waiter approached them who knew Gianni from previous visits and said that he had an important phone call from Gino Manzino. A miniature alarm sounded somewhere within him. How could Gino have known he was there? Gianni thought. He looked toward the public phones standing empty, with one of the receivers dangling off the hook, and then took careful inventory of the restaurant, but nothing seemed to pose any threat to Sunni. Their table was in the center of the room; at the other tables was a typically boisterous lunch crowd.

"Is something wrong, Gianni?" Sunni asked.

"I don't think so," he said, "but don't move until I come back. I'll only be a minute." With a final glance around the room, he started toward the phone.

As soon as he picked up the receiver, a balding middle-aged man in an oversized gray suit stepped out of the men's room and flashed a strange grin. His right hand was jammed into his jacket pocket, which seemed to hold a very large pistol.

"You do anything to make things difficult and I'll blow your face apart." Still smiling, Colatosti continued, "Now, I want you to step very slowly into the men's room. There's a guy in there washing his hands. We'll wait until he's finished before we settle our business. Otherwise, I shoot him and you and the Manzino girl. Remember: I don't have to kill her to get what I want."

Colatosti stepped aside to let Gianni enter first. The man inside was humming softly as he dried off his hands with a paper towel. Suddenly, one of the waiters opened the door and said, "Excuse me, is there someone here named Tio Colatosti?"

"He's Colatosti," Gianni said at once.

"You're wanted on the telephone," the waiter said, seemingly fixed to his place, wearing a perplexed expression with vague outlines of fear forming at his temples.

Fumbling with the weapon in his pocket, Colatosti gestured

for Gianni to go out ahead of him. Emerging into the corridor, the waiter hurried back to the restaurant floor while Colatosti approached the phones set into the wall below a darkened balcony, an additional dining area open only for dinner. There was no one nearby and no place for anyone to be concealed, so with a last look around, Colatosti picked up the receiver lying on its side on a lower shelf, pointing the pocketed pistol toward Gianni. It never occurred to him to glance upward, but Gianni did, just in time to see a heavy extinguisher hurtling down on Colatosti's skull.

The balcony wasn't very far above them, but the extinguisher was massive enough to strike him with considerable force and throw him to the ground. Before Colatosti hit the carpeting, Gianni had clamped his hand around the man's pistol, but by then Colatosti was unconscious and bleeding profusely. Gianni pulled the gun from the man's pocket, straightened up and turned as Sunni came rushing down the stairs and into Gianni's arms.

"My God, Gianni," she said, "are you all right?" She held him close and started to cry. As several waiters ran over to investigate, Gianni pushed the extinguisher under the coffee machine with his foot. Colatosti had slipped and struck his head, he told the maitre d'. As the thought of a lawsuit began to panic the personnel, Gianni assured them that he'd take him to the hospital in his car outside, then carried Colatosti out the back door and into the parking lot.

As Gianni and Sunni drove away from the restaurant, she explained what had happened in the same breathless tone she had used to describe her fashion presentation. When Gianni had left the table to use the phone, she had kept her eye on him and realized immediately what was happening as soon as the man who could have only been Colatosti appeared from nowhere and forced him into the men's room. She hurried after them, not knowing what she should do, then intercepted the waiter on his way to the kitchen and sent him into the bathroom with the message for Colatosti to come to the phone. She had noticed the balcony section during lunch and ran up the stairs, hoping she'd find something to throw down on him. She never expected to discover anything as effective as the fire extinguisher.

"I didn't kill him, did I?" she asked, turning to stare at his crumpled form in the backseat.

"No," Gianni said, "he'll be coming out of it pretty soon. I still can't believe any of this happened. I was supposed to be protecting you, not the other way around."

"Well," she said, smiling, "I can't help it if you were doing such a terrible job." If Gianni had any doubts that he had fallen in love with her, they faded away forever at that instant.

Sunni insisted that Gianni be a little vague about what happened when he spoke to Gino. She knew how humiliated Gianni would feel if he admitted his failure to Gino, and she knew that Gino would be horrified in retrospect if he knew too much about Sunni's involvement. While she grabbed a cab to get back to her remaining classes, Gianni carried Colatosti into the building through the underground garage and up the freight elevator. By the time he was in Gino's office, Colatosti had regained consciousness as well as his oddly lopsided grin. He seemed oblivious to the gash on his head and to everyone else in the room except Gino, whom he just kept glaring at and saying, "Here I am Manzino. I told you I'd get you. Your time is up."

Three armed men stood beside Gianni, but Colatosti took no notice of them. He was completely insane, Gianni thought.

"I'll have to kill you," Gino said in a soft, gentle voice appropriate for addressing someone so clearly incompetent, "for making such a desperate attempt to hurt my family. I never wanted this to happen, but you've made it so. The Manzinos are not responsible for everything that's gone wrong in your life, and I won't tolerate these attempts to seek revenge. You should have tried to rebuild your life in another city and forgotten all about us."

Colatosti suddenly stood up and, in an ear-splitting scream, bellowed, "MANZINO! YOUR TIME IS UP! MANZINO! YOUR TIME IS UP!" Then, before Gino or his bodyguards had a chance to respond, Colatosti hurled himself across the room with his outstretched fingers rushing toward Gino's throat. The fingers were less than an inch from their target when Gianni's bullet blasted through his left ear at an angle, leaving a large exit wound just below the right eye. The force of his momentum brought his body crashing into Gino, slamming him against the wall, but Colatosti was dead by the time his body touched the floor.

Now the problem was getting rid of the body. It would be relatively simple to get it out of the building, but then what? Gino thought. For some strange reason, he was reminded suddenly of his first dead body – that of Dominick Bazzano's partner, whose body he and Dominick had wrapped in a carpet from the dump before dragging it into an alley. He never had heard from Dominick again – he was probably long dead, or perhaps comfortably set up in another anonymous city.

Colatosti's corpse, however, could not be left about for anyone to find. Someone suggested a "cement overcoat," and Gino laughed the way he always did when someone used an expression from some Hollywood movie.

"We're not teamsters," he said. "We need something a little more subtle than that."

A short while later, he and Gianni were in one of two cars pulling out of the building and heading over the Queensboro Bridge to a dry cleaning plant in Brooklyn owned by one of Gianni's trusted cousins. They had driven into the bay used by the delivery trucks and had been inside for several minutes when a dark sedan drove up outside and a man with sandy hair entered the building.

Thomas Cashman was an assistant district attorney from the Manhattan District Attorney's office. He presented his card to the young woman who was alone in the plant's small office and struggling unsuccessfully with an ancient adding machine. After some moments of confusion, she ushered him into the main section of the plant, where Gino, Gianni, and a few other men were sitting on metal folding chairs drinking coffee, surrounded by pressing machines, sewing machines, and several large vats, one of which was bubbling softly.

"I'm looking for Tio Colatosti," Cashman said. "I thought perhaps you could help me, Mr. Manzino."

Gino and the others looked at one another and shrugged. "I know he's supposed to be in New York," Gino said, "but, frankly, I've been having a lot of trouble finding him myself. He's made several threats against my family, and I think I should talk to him."

Cashman glanced around the plant, unsure as to exactly what was going on. He'd been following Gino for the past few days, certain that Tio would make a run for him. Cashman knew about Colatosti's obsession with Gino Manzino; in fact, he had never understood why the Manzinos hadn't killed Tio in prison. Cashman wanted to find him before all the shooting started because Tio knew a great deal about people like the Manzinos and might be crazy enough to talk about it. An hour earlier, he'd gotten word of a scuffle in an east side restaurant involving Gianni Ghianella, Manzino's youngest daughter, Sunni, and an older man who might have been Colatosti. By the time he'd retraced their steps to Gino's office, Colatosti had disappeared again, but Cashman had trailed Gino here. They could have sneaked him in, alive or dead, in one of the cars, Cashman thought, but where was he now? No one but the hapless girl in the front office was working in the plant; everything was quiet except the distant drone of a venting system and the bubbling vat.

"Gentlemen," Cashman said in his polite, courtroom voice, "I don't have a warrant, but would you mind if I took a look around before I leave? It would ease my mind."

He seemed to be addressing Gino more than anyone else, so Gino turned to the man in overalls sitting on his right, and said, "Do you mind, Georgie?"

Georgie Cozza, who obviously ran the plant, shrugged and said, "Help yourself."

Cashman saw an unmistakable nervousness in his eyes, but it may not have been particularly significant. The whole situation just might be unnerving to him, he thought, and walked over to the two Mercedes sedans parked by the bay doors.

"Would you mind opening up these trunks?" he asked, courteously.

Gianni came over with a ring of keys and unlocked each trunk without hesitation. Inside were neatly folded blankets, tool kits, and spare tire paraphernalia, nothing more. The interiors of the two cars seemed equally innocent, so Cashman made a quick survey of the work area, poking into a couple of storage chests and barrels before deciding that his attempt to reveal anything was hopeless. It would take a full team of experts several hours to really search the place, he thought, but he had no probable cause for a court order. Then, as the others sat calmly sipping their coffee, Cashman noticed once more the erratic gurgling sounds coming from the large vat.

"What's that?" he asked. "It sounds like an upset stomach."

"It's a vat of commercial cleaning solvents," Gino said. "A combination of several powerful acids." Cashman was surprised that he hadn't let Georgie answer; after all, it was his plant.

"You soak clothes in it?" Cashman asked, taking note of the pulley system it required to open the heavy metal lid.

"No," Gino said, "clothes would dissolve instantly. It's a storage vat for used solvents from the cleaning machines. They do a huge business here, and the acid has to be stored until the waste disposal people can come in once a month and bring it in tanks to Jersey."

"Is that one of your businesses, Mr. Manzino? Waste disposal?"

"I own a few of the trucks they use," Gino said.

"Do you mind if I look inside?" Cashman said. "It sounds pretty volatile."

Georgie seemed to hesitate for a moment, but Gino nodded to him, thinking that Colatosti's bones would be dissolved by now. Georgie hurried forward to start the electric motor that unsealed the lid and pulled it open. It was a noisy process, and the harsh whining and clanking sounds echoed throughout the plant. Cashman and the others coughed and covered their eyes as a cloud of toxic vapor escaped. Then Cashman stepped up on the narrow platform and looked in at the steaming, bubbling liquid, not at all some witch's cauldron.

Well, he thought, at least I know where Tio ended up. After a few minutes, he climbed down, thanked the men for their cooperation, and left.

As soon as he was gone, Gianni said, "He knows, Gino."

Gino seemed thoughtful for a moment, and then said, "Yes, he does. It doesn't matter this time, but we may be seeing Mr. Cashman again."

CHAPTER
TWENTY-NINE

JEFF EGAN WAS the kind of detective whose easy grin masked a hard-edged nature. He'd been sitting in Cashman's office tossing crumpled paper balls into a wastebasket when Cashman returned to headquarters late that afternoon. Leaning back in a wooden chair against one corner of the room, Egan had more than a dozen paper balls in his lap, ready to be arced one at a time toward the high ceiling and into the wastebasket. He had yet to miss today, although the clutter in the room kept the target hidden. Two ancient metal desks stood back to back in the center, each topped with an old typewriter, along with two chairs, several file cabinets stuffed with books and folders and, oddly enough, a vertical stack of imported olive oil in cartons. The office, barely ten feet square, had sixteen-foot ceilings and Cashman was always complaining that he felt as if he were working at the bottom of someone's coffee canister. Jeff, on the other hand, liked the room's dimensions. It gave him more creative space for designing paper ball vectors. As he launched another one with sufficient force to bounce its way through the fluorescent fixture, ricochet off the ceiling, and rebound slightly before finding its home, Cashman entered the room in his usual distracted manner.

"You're really going to have to get a bigger office, counselor.

All the challenge has gone out of this one," Jeff said in a soft, mild drawl.

Cashman didn't bother to answer. He was puzzling over the boxes of olive oil, trying to figure out how to get rid of them before some smartass took them home as a bonus. More things disappeared from this building in a week than the average thief saw in a year, he thought.

"Did you find Tio?" Jeff asked, still smiling as he fired a shot that banged off two files before the balled-up trash dropped in with the rest.

"More or less," Cashman said, then focused his exasperation on Egan. "Did you open another pack of good paper?"

Jeff shrugged and widened his smile. "Don't worry. We've got tons of erasable bond, and Millie will give me anything I want as long as I give her a wink."

Cashman tried to imagine Egan having any effect on Millie in requisitions. She was at least fifty, two hundred pounds, and masculine enough to make even the roughest cop feel insecure.

"It seems to me you could find something more constructive to do than waste trees," Cashman said as he shuffled through the mess on his desk. He let his voice trail off as he found Colatosti's file, heavily thumbed and dog-eared, the product of too many hands over the years. "I think Gino Manzino melted Tio in a vat of acid," he said flatly, looking up at Egan once more. "Which form should I use for that?"

"Manzino again?" said Jeff, suddenly losing interest in the game. "The shadow man gets around pretty well for an old guy, doesn't he? Can you prove it?"

"Of course not," Cashman said, half-lost in his own thoughts. "You know how shadows are."

Cashman and Egan had been calling Gino Manzino "the shadow man" for over two years now. That was when they had first picked up traces of his presence while in the early stages of attempting to make sense out of the maze of alliances and activities in New York grouped loosely under the heading of "Organized Crime."

"Look for the forest, and not the trees," Cashman would say when he and Egan pored over the volumes of information continually passing through their offices. Egan, who hated aphorisms, would normally respond by belching.

Nevertheless, while most assistant district attorneys waited for the cops to bring them cases on a platter, Cashman initiated his own investigations, which often yielded arrests or convictions. Eventually he was chosen for "special duty" because of his unusual intelligence and flair for methodical research. "Special duty," in this case, meant studying the patterns of major crimes in the city in order to identify and build cases against the underground bosses behind them. The investigation had amassed comprehensive files, all cross-indexed with a system Cashman had devised himself. Much of the time, he simply served as a resource for the various teams appointed to chase after specific crimes or criminals, but now his status gave him a great deal of latitude. In a more arrogant man, this autonomy might have led to the sort of grandstanding and overreaching that could bring down the whole operation. But Cashman's quiet presence and unassuming nature allowed him to continue his private campaigns unimpeded. Soon he became that rarest of individuals: a man whose happiness was based on the knowledge that he was making a difference.

Although technically not his partner, Jeff Egan had been assigned to assist him once the scope of Cashman's investigations and his effectiveness had become clear to the upper echelons of the department. Cashman, however, wasn't particularly interested in questions of rank, so their working relationship had evolved into a natural sharing of responsibilities. No matter how different their personalities, they were equally dedicated to the job and had built an impressive reputation as a team. Egan's good looks and personal charm made Cashman seem even more nondescript than he already was, but Cashman had learned long ago that there was an advantage to appearing unremarkable, particularly when acting as an undercover officer, and their constantly expanding knowledge of who really ran the streets was beginning to pay off in concrete victories. Only a week earlier, Cashman had been wading through

a series of reports about the routes that were bringing fresh supplies to several known heroin distributors in the city. Several isolated links had been identified, but some maddening gaps still
made it unwise to bust the few they were sure of. The police were
reasonably certain that the Santucci family was the overseas sup-
plier – still as active in Sicily as they were in this country – but
how the drugs got from Sicily to America was the most frustrating
of the mysteries remaining. Even though the dealers were closely
watched and their contacts monitored, the powder seemed to appear out of nowhere. The Sicilian police had been useless in discovering how it was shipped – and so, it seemed, were the Federal
agents. One team, however, had been keeping track of the trucks
doing business in one quadrant, a section of lower Manhattan
known as Little Italy that was supposed to be controlled by the
Manzino family. Reading through the report, Cashman's eye had
been caught by an odd detail. A truck from Genoa Trucking had
been observed picking up several cartons of unspecified goods at a
small restaurant, La Dolce Vita, on Mott Street. He had almost
read past the item before a thought struck him – wasn't Genoa
Trucking owned by the Santucci family? What was one of their
trucks doing in Manzino's territory? Although there had never been
open warfare between the two factions, Manzino's people and the
Santuccis were said to be completely alienated from one another.
Manzino was known to abhor the drug trade – one of several idiosyncrasies that had enhanced his Robin Hood image in the community – but Cashman suspected that his anti-drug position was
more practical than noble. If you entered the narcotics trade – the
most brutally competitive criminal activity in the world – you
were forced to depend on outsiders. Gino had spent a lifetime
maintaining his independence, so his rejection of drug dealing
made sense. Then what exactly did this pick up mean? Had Manzino
finally made a deal with the Santucci scum – some late-life grab
for real money? Cashman's instincts said no, but anything was
possible.

Rather than jump to conclusions, Cashman had requested surveillance on the restaurant and waited to see if the truck showed

up again. Three days later, two men in a similar truck picked up six cases of olive oil and brought it to a warehouse deep in Santucci territory. It didn't take Cashman long to figure out what was happening. He ordered the stakeout team to watch for the next delivery of olive oil to the restaurant. Two mornings later, the truck appeared once more and Cashman convinced the brass to order a raid on the restaurant and then move in on the Santucci warehouse.

No time could be lost; Cashman wanted the shipment to be in the warehouse when his men came in. So he called for a team to act immediately. There was no time for a tip-off to La Dolce Vita; within the hour, a truck carrying a trained search party had pulled in and its men were routing through the olive shipment while the restaurant owner and his employees shouted out their innocence. Cashman, who was keeping a low profile with a vantage from inside the truck, actually believed the men. They were being used, as such people always are, even when they think they are receiving a piece of the pie.

The scheme had been simple. Shipments of olive oil arrived from Sicily and were stored in a waterfront warehouse until delivery trucks took them in ten-gallon cans, four to a carton, to legitimate restaurants throughout the five-state area. Federal agents had checked a few of these shipments, opening several cartons and cans at random, but found nothing amiss. But not all of the cartons were the same. Whenever a particular sequence of numbers was spotted in the identification code that had been stamped on the boxes in Sicily, the warehouse workers would make sure that they were stored separately and shipped directly to the restaurant in Manzino's territory. No one seemed to notice that this restaurant was getting more olive oil than it could possibly use in a year – a dozen cases every three or four days – probably because most of it disappeared a day or so after delivery. But as Cashman's men discovered while searching each case and can of olive oil, in one can out of each case of four (always the one in the upper left hand corner if you opened the carton with the I.D. number facing you) held only seven gallons of oil. At the bottom of the can, the heroin was sealed in heavy amber-colored plastic. The Santuccis owned the olive oil company and the cannery in Sicily and had affixed the special packaging codes themselves.

"It was really a terrific system," Cashman said when he first told Egan, who'd been working on another case at the time of the raid. Cashman's natural enthusiasm for careful planning made it impossible for him not to describe it without a certain amount of admiration. "There was virtually no chance that the Feds or customs officials would find just the right can from just the right box and think to drain away all of the oil to locate the heroin, certainly not in a routine inspection. They used legitimate trucks to and from an obscure, legitimate restaurant. From the time it arrived to the time of the pick-up was the only risky part."

"And Manzino?" Jeff asked. "Was he involved?"

"Apparently not," Cashman said. "We grilled Parisi, the old guy who owns the restaurant, and he poured out everything he knew in the first ten minutes. Business had been lousy. He said his wife was the only Sicilian woman who didn't know how to cook a decent meal. So when Santucci's people offered him a lot of money just to store some olive oil for a little while, the proposition was too good to pass up. His health was terrible, ulcers and bad lungs, and he needed money for retirement. But then I mentioned Gino Manzino's name and a look of terror came across his face.

"That's why I told you all this,' he practically shouted. 'If Gino finds out that I helped the Santuccis with their drugs, he'll kill me. He'll burn down my restaurant. And if he doesn't find me, the Santuccis will.' He began to wail and moan and then started hyperventilating so much, the arresting officers had to take him to the infirmary. Apparently, Gino's rejection of drugs was real. The Santuccis took brilliant advantage of this by burying the key link to their heroin operation in Manzino's territory because no one would think to look for drugs there."

All this was still running through Cashman's mind a week later, along with the thought of Tio Colatosti bubbling away in a dry-cleaning vat, as he stared at the unopened olive oil cartons and Jeff waited patiently for his partner to come back from wherever his thoughts had taken him again. Jeff knew that the shadow man had begun to consume more and more of Cashman's attention. Originally Manzino had been an interesting enigma, potentially more colorful than the usual run of butchers they encountered, but something about him had captured Cashman's imagination.

Finally deciding that it was up to him to break the silence, Jeff said, "One question, counselor."

Sure, go ahead," Cashman said, shaking off his reverie.

"Are you developing some sort of private grudge against Manzino?"

"Of course not," Cashman said a little defensively, shocked because Jeff should know by now that he had no interest in using personal vendettas – like some DAs and cops – to spice up his life. "Look," he continued, deciding that Jeff might need a fuller explanation, "if I thought I was becoming obsessed with someone like Manzino on a personal level, I'd disqualify myself from the case. I just have this thing about order, about putting all the pieces together. And I can't figure out how Manzino fits in to the larger picture. He's been getting away with god-knows-what for so long, maybe someone should take the time to find out. He's not like the other bosses – he has a gift for self-preservation, so he's liable to go on forever. He's even rid himself of the one weak mind in his organization – his idiot son, Vinnie. Sometimes I wonder if he didn't arrange the whole kid-killing episode just to get Vinnie out of town. Anyway, he's a mystery and you know how much I love to solve mysteries. Meanwhile," he said, gazing over at the cartons of olive oil and laughing. "I think we should make a gigantic batch of spaghetti sauce and invite the Santuccis and Manzinos over for dinner and let them split up old man Parisi for dessert."

Egan gave a small smile and tossed another ball into the basket.

In the weeks that followed, Cashman and Egan began concentrating their energies on bringing Gino Manzino out of the shadows – a nearly impossible task. Manzino had practically cut himself off from "America" proper, much less the lives of other Americans, and in so doing had formed his own self-contained world that no one had ever done so thoroughly. Most of the immigrants – criminal or otherwise – were either absorbed into the national mainstream or held on stubbornly to old country ways by creating pockets of Europe or Asia or Africa in their own backyards. Gino, on the other hand, had done neither. He never became truly American, nor had he clung to the Sicilian tradition of warring villages, wielding switchblades in the streets of lower Manhattan to avenge some macheted ancestor. He had no interest in blood feuds, the ancient struggles for power. His only interest was in constructing a life that assured his family an inheritance. But at least one other world did exist, Cashman thought. No matter how gifted Manzino might be at spinning webs, there was always the law. Gino Manzino's operation was so smooth, so controlled, there were very few instances in which an actual crime could be identified – only the fleeting suggestion of some guiding force behind a hundred different incidents, all taking place with a minimum of fuss while the rest of New York's underworld blew each other's heads off. Consequently, over the next several months in whatever time they could spare from court appearances for other erupting investigations, they made remarkable progress in coloring their shadow's outline. The more they learned, the more fascinated they became and soon found themselves running down leads on their own time, almost like professional football players who spent their free afternoons playing touch football in the neighborhood park.

Although there was never any clear-cut evidence to explain Tio Colatosti's disappearance, everyone on the street was aware of Gino's part in it. As various versions of Tio's final moments made their way through the city, Carlo Colatosti, Tio's alcoholic nephew who'd been raised on ridiculously distorted stories about the Manzinos, decided that it was his sacred duty to exact revenge. But since his resolve tended to fall apart on those rare occasions when he was sober, he was virtually incapable of formulating anything resembling a real strategy for stalking his quarry, and it might well have amounted to nothing if he hadn't stumbled into Gino and Gianni in Little Italy when his senses were somewhat blurred from wine and his ears were still ringing with one of his grandmother's end-less lectures on the lost glories of the Colatosti family.

Gino and Gianni had just left their Mercedes to attend a meet-ing to finalize the purchase of several warehouses uptown. As Gino waited on the sidewalk, watching a group of especially attractive secretaries hurrying by, Gianni walked up to a corner newsstand to pick up a paper. Carlo, suddenly realizing that the well-dressed man standing calmly on the sidewalk before him was Gino Manzino, stopped in his tracks and stared in disbelief. He'd been fantasizing about his vengeance for so long, he'd unconsciously abandoned all hope of it ever taking place. But now deep inside his haze some instinct told him that he'd better take out his gun and shoot before the vision faded. Gino didn't even notice Carlo stand-ing there until Carlo was using both hands to steady the barrel of the gun, and then he only had time for a single, flashing thought: Who the hell is this guy?

Gianni had already started back from the newsstand when two shots fired in rapid succession. He felt his blood chill, visibly jolted. Rushing forward at full speed, temples pounding, he knew the moment was over before he even had a chance to react. And so, amidst the sharp screams from passersby and the hundreds of feet running swiftly in several directions at once, Gianni found himself staring, bewildered, at the dead man on the pavement. Within minutes, the uproar subsided. The crowd circled the scene and waited with polite curiosity for the inevitable sound of sirens.

"Do you know who he is?" Gino asked as they looked down at Carlo's body.

Gianni shook his head in silence, the shock of the incident reeling through him. Carlo's eyes were still open, staring up in surprise, as if he were seeing the sky for the first time. Two stains grew steadily darker on his chest. His pistol rested a few inches from his right hand that had gone limp beside him.

"Good afternoon, Mr. Manzino, Mr. Ghianella. I'm Lieuten-ant Egan, D.A.'s office."

Gianni glanced up at the good-looking man, about his age, with light brown hair and a pleasant smile that seemed strangely out of context. In fact, everything about him seemed oddly out of place. His light sport jacket and open-collar plaid shirt made him look like a college student, or one of those guileless young men who filled Madison Square Garden to cheer on the Knicks. After replacing his revolver in his shoulder holster and giving instructions to the uniformed patrolman who had arrived on foot with his gun drawn, he'd approached Gino and Gianni and flipped open his gold shield.

It was supposed to be Egan's day off, but he had decided to wait for Gino outside the law office. He and Cashman had been tracking Gino's legitimate real estate deals through an insider, so they always knew when and where these meetings would take place. Egan used this information whenever he could to have yet another look at the shadow man and determine if there was anything of significance to add to the file. Since his face was unknown to Gino, Egan had been able to observe him in public places undetected. Usually, he learned very little.

Consequently, no one was more surprised than Egan when a crazy man suddenly appeared on the sidewalk, stared at Gino stupidly for several seconds, and then brought out a pistol. Egan had been just a few feet away, sitting by a nearby fountain pretending to be reading a newspaper beside a few office workers who were taking an early lunch. It all happened so fast that he didn't have time to shout a warning to Gino or the gunman or anyone else. He only had time to jump to his feet, pull out his gun and fire. His newspaper had barely touched the ground when the first bullet struck the assailant's chest. Egan's one regret was that he had spoiled any future opportunities to be an unknown agent of Gino's comings and goings.

While neither Gino nor Gianni were at all amazed that a New York detective knew them on sight, they wondered how he happened to be there at just the right time to save Gino's life.

Gino studied the young detective for a moment, then said, "You seemed to be waiting for him."

"Well," said Egan, "let's just say we had a tip that something might happen this morning, and we wanted to play it safe." That sounded plausible enough, Egan thought, doubting that Manzino would be anxious to explore the true nature of his business. "Do you have any idea who he is?"

"I was hoping that you could tell me," Gino said, surprising him then by smiling and extending his hand. "Let me thank you. Obviously, you saved my life. I'm lucky they sent someone who knew what he was doing."

Grinning in return, Egan said, "You're luckier than you think. I'm one of the worst shots in the New York police department. I was even suspended for two days last year when I failed to qualify on the pistol range. I'm surprised I hit him once, let alone twice."

"Not bad for a weak shooter," said Gianni as he stared down at the body once more. "One of your bullets apparently caught him in the heart."

"That figures," said Egan, momentarily concerned, "I was aiming for his arm."

Usually, Gino and Gianni would be out of sight long before any officials arrived to make out crime reports. But on this day the two of them visited a police station for the first time in many years. Cashman could barely contain his surprise when Egan led the two into his office.

"Mr. Manzino here suffered an assassination attempt," Egan said. "I managed to intercede but unfortunately the assailant was killed and is still unidentified."

Cashman nodded at the shadow and his assistant, wondering immediately if they recognized him from the warehouse. "Please," he said, gesturing towards a chair, "have a seat."

"Thank you," Gino said, who had of course recognized Cashman at first glance.

Cashman took down Gino and Gianni's statements personally, surprised at how soft-spoken both were – how patient and apparently grateful to Egan.

"Do you have any idea who might be trying to hurt you – this week," Cashman smiled.

Gino and Gianni had such an easy confidence, their insouciance had a strange way of rubbing off. And whereas the whole interview might have been tense and uncomfortable, Egan and Cashman soon found themselves in the uncanny position of being on Gino's side, with all four men anxious to remove Gino from danger.

Carlo Colatosti had been carrying mail indicating his home address and in half an hour a police officer had gone to the house and returned with Carlo Colatosti's sister. She was a large girl, and very pregnant, and Cashman feared she might deliver on the spot. Fortunately, a few minutes after identifying Carlo, she was wailing not about the Manzinos but about her brother's crazy ideas.

Cashman watched in disbelief as the girl – not yet twenty – came from the identifying room, saw Gino and Gianni in Cashman's office, and threw herself at Gino's feet. "Signor Manzino," she wept, "forgive my foolish brother. Our father drove him crazy with his talk. We are indebted to you, always."

Egan raised his eyebrows at Cashman, who was too struck to respond. "That's all right, dear," Gino said. "To all madness comes an end."

It was Gianni who gently lifted the girl from Gino's feet, handing her to Egan who himself handed her to an officer to drive her home.

"Well," Gino said, "we have disturbed enough of your day."

Of course Cashman would have liked to keep Gino in his office all day; there were a thousand questions he wanted to ask. But now was not the time, he thought. Gino slipped out of the station as quietly as he had come in – though not without thanking Egan again. Egan now had a set of entirely new impressions to supplement his understanding of the man. What had impressed him the most was Gino's quiet, especially when you considered how close he had come to death. There was none of the hardness or pomposity that Egan had come to associate with bosses of organized crime. He and Ghianella both seemed to be thoroughly likeable men. Even when Gino thanked Egan, there was nothing effusive about it, no foolish boasting about how he was a man who never forgot a favor or he would see to it that Egan received the proper reward for his vigilance, the kind of things that a man in his position might be expected to say. Gino simply thanked him sincerely for what he had done like any well-mannered citizen. Still, it didn't sway Egan's judgment at all – he was completely objective about his work and it only made his target more interesting. He was equally impressed with Gianni, who was rumored to be Gino's successor and already the subject of his own burgeoning file.

AFTER THE SHOOTING, Gianni became even more vigilant about acting as a bodyguard wherever Gino went. Gino, however, had taken it in stride and kept insisting that Gianni accompany Sunni instead. As a result, Gianni was falling deeper in love each day, so immersed in Sunni that she had grown into a full-blown obsession – not only because of the way he felt about her, or even his growing certainty that she felt the same way, but from the unspoken question of whether they should be feeling any of this. Whenever he was away from her, every moment seemed like another obstacle between them. Even when they were together – in the kitchen in Connecticut or riding back and forth from the city – he was always conscious of the tension, and going steadily mad with the fear that Gino would consider his feelings a betrayal of trust, which only made his awkwardness greater.

Sunni did, of course, feel the same intense longing, as well as a terrible panic that she would lose him, thanks to some unwritten law governing his place in her father's world. As Gino would not discuss business with Sunni, she couldn't know just what he had in mind for his driver. And though she suspected that their relationship was closer than any other Gino shared with a man, she didn't dare to inquire about it. Who knows, the wrong suggestion might lead to Gianni's being fired.

Still, her impatience was growing and finally, after a nerve-wracking afternoon when Sunni had waited all day to spend a few minutes with Gianni – only to watch him leave after some infuriatingly polite questions about her work and her health, she mounted one of her horses and rode him too hard down a narrow trail, almost colliding with an enormous tree branch that had fallen in the path. Realizing that she was taking out her frustration on the horse beneath her like some spoiled adolescent, she reigned to a stop and patted the horse's powerful neck while she soothingly apologized. The next afternoon, however, Gianni came to drive Gino into the city for a rare Saturday night meeting, a special courtesy for Peter Cantillo, an aging neighborhood chieftain who was returning to Sicily to live out his days in the mountain village where he was born. Apparently, Cantillo had forgotten that he bitterly hated his hometown. His memory seemed to distort even his own beliefs to fit whatever purpose he had in mind. When he asked Gino to attend his farewell celebration, for example, he cited forty years of friendship and a thousand imaginary favors, when in fact the only real favor Gino had ever done for him was not to kill him for having blundered into his territory again and again. But there was something likeable about the old fool, Gino thought, and by this time he was harmless enough. Even if his return to Sicily soured after a few weeks, at least he'll be out of my hair for a while.

Sunni had been waiting in the courtyard when Gianni arrived, ostensibly on her way to the stable, but hoping that somehow this day would be different and he would come forth and admit to her how he really felt. Instead, he seemed both happy and unhappy to see her at once. This time, however, she lost all patience and stormed away while he was in the middle of what was obviously his favorite sentence – seeing as he said it every time he came to the farm – about how the air there was so much better than the city's. Mounting her horse once more, Sunni started across the field at a full gallop while he stood speechless watching her go. Then easing the horse into a slow trot, she felt a calm come over her, and in that moment all her doubts and fears melted away. She saw the future as clearly as if it were projected on a screen, like a fuzzy image that clicked unexpectedly into focus. Like a heroine in a fairy tale, she felt magically transformed, emerging from her own enchanted woods. Smiling at the thought, she rode toward the blue Mercedes as it headed down the driveway.

"Quite a rider," Gino said with admiration as he and Gianni watched the horse and rider flow down the gentle rise. Gianni, still stinging from Sunni's sudden rage, was amazed at her effortless grace as she sailed over the high fence separating the road from the meadow, and then spun to a stop facing the approaching car. Gianni was so mesmerized by her performance – her face flushed and a half-smile on her lips – that it took him a few seconds to stop the car.

"Pappa," she said suddenly, "I want to talk to Gianni. Would you mind waiting for a minute?"

Stunned by her boldness, Gianni stepped out of the car, glancing back at Gino to make sure that he had his permission. Gino merely shrugged his shoulders as if to say he had no control over the matter.

Dismounting when he reached her, Sunni looked directly at Gianni, then spoke in a voice both warm and confident. "Gianni," she said, "this has to stop. We've both been acting like children for weeks. I know that I love you and I think that you love me. Let's just face it and forget the rest." Here she paused because the change that came over Gianni was so complete. His eyes gave up the inner struggle that had locked away their light, and his smile was so full that she couldn't remember ever seeing a face more beautiful. It took her a moment to catch her breath, and then he reached out to touch her cheek gently with one finger. When she spoke again her voice had grown softer and seemed to draw in the air around them, sealing out Gino, Connecticut, the whole world.

"Gianni," she continued, "I was going so crazy that I almost doubted my own feelings, let alone yours. And then everything cleared all at once. I had to tell you how I felt because . . . well, I just couldn't let it go on like this." Her soft hush drew him deeper into a circle that slowed time. "If I'm wrong . . ." she paused again, her brow wrinkling because the possibility had never occurred to her, "well, then I'm wrong about everything, and nothing matters anyway." She stopped then and gave him a wide smile, like a child who had recited her lesson perfectly and wanted to be congratulated. Finally, Gianni took a deep breath and said, "Yes. Yes, Sunni. Yes to everything." Suddenly the air cleared, and the rest of the world rearranged itself around them. Without another word and a shy, embarrassed smile passing between them, they stepped apart, and Sunni remounted. She guided the horse back across the fence and headed across the meadow while Gianni started the car and slowly pulled away, dazed but still smiling. He drove several miles before remembering that Gino was sitting patiently beside him. The old worry touched him again, but only for an instant. Then, to no one's surprise but his own, Gianni said, "I'd like to marry Sunni, Gino."

Gino stared at him with a look that was serious but free of alarm, as if Gianni had simply asked his opinion of some casual personal event. "Were your people Catholic, Gianni?" he then asked.

Gianni wasn't sure what he expected Gino to say, but it certainly wasn't this – Gino had never shown any interest in religion. "Yes, they were," he answered.

"Good," Gino said. "That was the question I was always taught to ask of men who intended to marry your daughters. She needs a strong man, Gianni. She's an unusual girl. I wish the best for you both." Then he settled down in his seat and closed his eyes, so full of good feelings that he honestly thought he'd miss Peter Cantillo after all.

As SUNNI AND Gianni opened themselves to one another, Gino saw the sweep of his life with a new understanding. Despite all the sorrow, he found far less remorse than he would have expected. There had been so many tragedies, but now their edges had softened and he had come to appreciate the direction of his fate. All those dark moments must have had a reason – for had they not existed, the final pattern would have been different, and would not have been his.

Strange thoughts for a man like me, Gino thought. The wisdom of age, I guess, or perhaps the foolish babble of an old man. One thing he never regretted was his decision to concentrate his power within clearly defined boundaries, to deepen rather than expand his influence and to serve those who served him. In the process he'd discovered the secret to survival: Keep your own kingdom small and solid, and let the giants slaughter themselves. Strike only in defense of what you cannot afford to surrender, and build loyalty by giving people a reason to trust you, instead of reasons to fear you, something Vinnie could never understand, Gino thought. The streets were littered with human wreckage brought about by too much ambition. Vinnie used whatever power he possessed to grab more, which inevitably destroyed him. He turned the people who depended on him into victims, until they rose against him or betrayed him to his enemies. Gianni, on the other hand, understood the need to conserve power. Perception and good judgment came naturally to him.

It was in one of these increasingly common contemplative moods that Gino, alone in his car one Sunday morning, did something entirely uncharacteristic. He'd been fiddling with the radio, trying to find some soft and unobtrusive music, when he drifted past and then returned to a weekly summary of news events. Listening with odd fascination and remembering fragments of other broadcasts he'd heard over the years – about Nixon, Korea, race riots in the South, the Kennedys, and the fall of Saigon – this "American" news seemed so strange to him, like the plot summary for some popular television show he never watched. He knew only the basic outline and a few of the major players by sight. There was a time when he thought that this profound distance made him part of a world that existed outside of reality, often thinking of the "other America" as a complicated and noisy engine hurtling along a track to some unknown destination. But lately he'd come to realize that, with very few exceptions, people's day-to-day lives had little or nothing to do with life as it was presented in news broadcasts. Gino was different only because he never felt any sense of loss about his alienation. All that mattered was your own life, and the lives of people you loved. All the rest was someone else's fairy tale.

LIKE GINO, FILOMINA had hoped that Gianni might be the man for Sunni long before Sunni herself did. But Filomina's heart had been broken so many times – by Carla, who had stepped irrevocably outside of Gino's world, by Philly, whose suicide had almost destroyed her, and of course by Vinnie, whose relentless hurtling toward doom had worn down the spirits of all those who had loved him – that she hardly dared hope too much, lest she be disappointed. As usual, however, Sunni came through where others had failed, not only forgiving Gino but doing so absolutely, and continuing on a stronger young woman. When Filomina first saw Gianni and Sunni walking toward the house arm in arm, the warmth and joy that rose up in her took her by surprise. Angela was the only one of their children still in a marriage, and it was such a facade, it was painful to behold. At last, though, Filomina could see a love like that between her and Gino, one with a life and energy and beauty all of its own.

"Mamma," Sunni said, Gianni and I have decided to marry." Behind them was Gino, whose beaming smile to Filomina was all she needed to be overcome with happiness.

SUNNI AND GIANNI wanted a wedding as private as decency would permit. They had no interest in the kind of traditional wedding that might be expected for Gino Manzino's youngest daughter. Theirs was a private passion and they wanted to preserve the circle that had drawn around them on the day that they had declared it by having a modest ceremony. For his part, Gino was perfectly willing to relinquish any plans he once might have had for turning his little girl's wedding into a pageant. The family raised a chorus of protests, of course, but Gino appointed himself arbitrator and set about soothing their disappointment.

Sunni and Gianni's one tribute to tradition was deciding not to make love until after they were married. But rather than bowing to old laws and beliefs, this was simply a statement of their faith in the future. They wanted the intimacy they would share on their wedding night to be a gift they would bestow to honor the union. So while not consciously following tradition, they reinvented it, returning to the original need for some gesture to mark the mingling of two lives. Besides, as Sunni kept telling Gianni each time she kissed him, this holding back until the moment was perfect would make the final surrender all the more fulfilling. Gianni accepted her approach, however reluctantly, but he did come up with an expression to sum up the situation, inscribing it on a card after a particularly restless night: "Anticipation may be wonderful, but waiting is absolute hell."

Then one April afternoon, deciding spontaneously to play truant from their various responsibilities, Gianni and Sunni packed a hastily assembled picnic lunch and drove to a quiet meadow a few miles from the farm. Perhaps it was the delicious infusion of warmth in the countryside mirroring their own growing heat, or perhaps the champagne was gently dissolving their restraint, but a moment came during the long afternoon, lying together on the lawn, when they heard a rushing in their ears that may have been the sound of their control fleeing from them.

Wanting Sunni had become as much a part of Gianni as breathing. It was something he constantly fantasized about – being with her far away from the world they both knew, becoming one. And here, in the soft, cool grass, she was his, gazing up at him now with a look of fire that spoke silently of her desire to be taken. For Sunni, it was the one time in her life that she had no second thoughts. She knew this was right and that she loved Gianni with a depth she had never experienced. And yet, as he hovered in the sunlight above her, she sensed his sudden hesitation, and wondered if she had somehow overestimated the measure of his longing by the extent of her own desire.

Gianni was thinking of Gino, who had so often trusted him with his own life, and now entrusted him with his greatest possession. Believing that taking her too soon would betray this honor, he pulled himself back, even though it meant denying what he wanted most in the world, and spoke with a gentle sadness, cupping her beautiful face in his hands.

"Sunni, when it happens for us, everything must be right. The moment must be perfect. This is not that moment."

Sunni tried to convince him otherwise, but her voice faded away when she realized that he had made his decision. Then she remembered all the talks her Mamma had given her about virginity. It didn't matter to Sunni that the notion was obsolete; the words had touched her nonetheless.

"Sunni," Filomina had said, "God's greatest gift to women is the custody of their bodies. Your virginity is your treasure, and not to be given lightly. It must be held in trust until you find the man who can match your dreams." As she thought over her mother's simple words, which she had not become sophisticated enough to dismiss, Sunni smiled at the knowledge that the treasure was still hers and hers alone.

CHAPTER
THIRTY

THE WAITING FINALLY ended on a crystal May morning at the Chapel of the Sacred Heart, a small stone building tucked into the low Connecticut hills just a few miles from the farm. If there was any disadvantage to having a country wedding so early in the spring, perhaps it was the chill that still clung to the air at sunrise, branding the emerging buds with a fragile frost. But the day's cool beginning only made the sunshine seem even brighter, gleaming like metal – as if you could actually touch the day.

As Gino stepped into the morning air, he could feel the presence of a warm spring growing beneath the sky's silver surface, and once again, he gave silent thanks to Giovanni and Rosa for breaking a cycle that would have offered so little to his children. But for all his seemingly casual acceptance of Gianni and Sunni's marriage, he still felt the last-minute uncertainties that might trouble any man on his daughter's wedding day. In a Manhattan bar filled with skylights and polished steel surfaces, his protective impulses had led him to have a talk with Gianni the previous day, echoing back to all the talks Sicilian fathers ever had with prospective sons-in-law. Perhaps Gino's words were softer than those of earlier generations – no threats of immediate dismemberment if Gianni's devotion ever faltered – but the significance was no less solemn. Gino spoke of the great joy that Sunni had brought into his and

Filomina's lives, of watching her grow into womanhood. He then asked Gianni to describe his vision of the future, what he wished for in the long years ahead. As gently as he could, Gianni broke into Gino's questions and began to describe what Sunni had become for him, speaking of the woman who bound them together as they sipped their brandy in the late afternoon. She was his center, the only thing worth living and dying for. He'd sacrifice anything for her happiness. Although Gianni had always thought of himself as a modern man, liberated from the cords of ethnic and family tradition that yoked so many people to a dead past, something in this moment touched him in a way that he hadn't expected. By the time the two men had finished their brandies, they felt a profound sense of shared understanding and trust.

Perhaps this accounted in part for the amazing serenity that pervaded the entire ceremony. Rather than a leap into some unknown state, Sunni and Gianni's exchange of vows seemed like a simple acknowledgement of something already known, though Sunni's beauty betrayed a rush of electricity. The grace of her movements, her face as delicate as a cameo, the full, sensuous mouth, her smile a full expression of her spirit, her deep green eyes and thick lashes set in a perfect oval of skin as fair as her mother's, and her hair, a deep auburn, reflecting every glint of light seemed to require the cool air just so the two of them wouldn't ignite.

Even Cashman and Egan felt the unusual peace and dignity. They had arrived at the chapel with a small contingent of local police personnel an hour before the ceremony, intending to maintain an unobtrusive surveillance from a distance. This moment of family celebration, they thought, might draw the presence of powerful people. There might even be an eruption of violence. Standard police procedure encouraged their attendance at weddings, christenings, and funerals for the families of men under investigation. In fact, they were instructed to make some attempt to photograph everyone attending, but there was nothing to distinguish this wedding from any one of a dozen small weddings held in this chapel over the last few weeks, except perhaps that the bride was especially lovely this time. Only members of the immediate family and several close friends and neighbors were in the congregation.

Two of the most moved were undoubtedly Gianni's parents. Unlike Gino's father, Carlo Ghianella did not pour shame onto Gianni because he had chosen a different way of life. Of course, Gianni had kept them believing that he was essentially a private bank manager for Gino, but Carlo was no fool and knew well of Gino's power in the underground. There wasn't enough time in life, however, for him and Christina to start judging their son. They had only hoped for him to be an honest and strong man, and in this he had succeeded. That Gianni had fixed up Carlo's tailor shop, hired an assistant for him and resettled his parents into a more comfortable apartment had seemed like good fortune for his parents, and seeing Gianni's joy at returning their help, was reward enough.

The wedding's simplicity was to them a pleasure. Nothing distracted from the true purpose: to unite two people in love and honor under God. How strange it was, Christina thought, that both Sunni and Gianni were change-of-life babies, two gifts from above that had brought so much joy to others.

Just before the church doors opened for Gino to escort Sunni down the aisle, Gino spotted Cashman and Egan in the small clan of undercover policemen hanging back under the trees. Smiling sincerely, Gino approached them and invited Cashman and Egan to join the service. Too stunned to refuse, they dismissed the other officers and ended up thoroughly enjoying themselves. So much for stereotypical Mafia weddings, Cashman thought. If he didn't know full well the legacy that Gianni was destined to inherit, he might easily have imagined that he was watching the wedding of some fledgling executive, and soon he found himself wishing the couple well with more feeling than he had for most of the weddings he attended in his own family. Upon leaving, Gino shook Egan's hand and thanked him again for making it possible for him to live long enough to see this blessed day.

GIANNI AND SUNNI reached a small inn over the Massachusetts border around midnight and hurried toward the first bed they would
share in their lives. All day they had been subdued, passing the
hours in calm contentment. But when the door to their suite finally locked behind them, they felt the spell of suspension dissolve and undressed one another as naturally as if they'd been doing it for years. In imagining this night, Sunni had anticipated
some shyness, but his kisses, his touch, the first brush of his lips
upon her skin as he slipped off her silk dressing gown, were so
familiar that when his hardness gently entered her, she surrendered her fears completely. Vaguely, she remembered the unclean
touch of Jimmy's hands, and the unbidden stirring that had frightened her so with Matthew. But those memories seemed to belong
to someone else, having nothing to do with the body coming alive
beneath Gianni's. Their passion left Sunni overwhelmed and almost embarrassed, the fire between them almost like a third presence in the bed. She had thought that she knew so little about sex,
which astonished Gianni who thought that he knew so much. In
each hour they shared, the ease with which they came together
grew dramatically. They found the wonder of moving ever slower
instead of ever faster and the magic offered by long stretches of
time between making love, time filled with gentle caresses and
shared laughter in the night, as well as the stunning realization
that all their glorious excitement could be rekindled to its peak
with the softest of touches. And then they fell asleep locked in one
another's arms until they woke the next morning to the subtle
stirrings of their bodies, and when their warmth melted away the
dust of sleep, they began again, following the crest of their desire.
For Gianni, Sunni's lovemaking took his breath away. She wanted
more than to simply accept his tender ministrations, however glorious; she wanted to initiate and give pleasure as well, exchange
roles of arouser and aroused. And yet, it was not only the act she
was giving in the blinding rush of communion. The act itself was
simply the best way to express all they felt. As he rose within her,
she relinquished herself, feeling none of the shame that her Mamma
had said she might feel, no sense whatsoever of being soiled. In

this one thing, her Mamma was wrong. Sunni did not even hear the little voice of warning from within, tiny and soft as a teardrop, the voice Mamma had buried deep inside her. Finding its way into her mind's miniature caverns, there it would remain, to whisper its cautions and protect her from any careless temptations. Now, however, the little voice was silent, and all she could hear were the sounds of peace, the distant chant of birdsong fading in the darkness, the faint hum of the village below, a life to which she belonged for the first time as Gianni's wife, now and forever.

SOMEWHERE DURING THE long months it took for Gino to transfer the reign of power to Gianni, Sunni began waking at night with an unexpected fear. She'd always known that her father's business existed outside the mainstream of American life, but she had never had any real reason to question Gino's basic decency – whatever his reputation beyond the household. Of course, she wasn't so naive as to think that he hadn't committed any crime or offense against society. She had heard the whispered scandal of her sister Carla calling Gino a thief and always wondered why the family's shame centered on the fact that Carla had spoken as she did and not on the incidents that might have inspired the outburst. Still, her faith in her father's sense of honor justified any instance in which he might have crossed the line. But when she thought of Gianni stepping into her father's role, she became more and more frightened about the nature of his work. At first, the fear only focused on the danger, though she knew that Gianni had moved through a violent world for most of his life and had demonstrated enough strength and courage to do so with ease. Now, she realized, he was in its very center, which meant that he'd be its most visible target. Raised with the concept of living in another America, she could understand and accept how someone might choose to be a kind of outlaw. But what if the family was responsible for acts that were far more than illegal? What if they were immoral as well, breaking laws more significant than the laws of an uncaring society? What then? What might that do to Gianni and to all of them? It wasn't the prospect of breaking God's law that made it so terrifying, although there were times when the image of the nuns came back to haunt her. Rather, it was an instinctive understanding that corrupt acts corrupted. And yet, whenever these feelings threatened to overwhelm her, Sunni would let her mind drift over the times she had confronted real evil, like Jimmy's drunken attack, and for a moment she'd actually breathe a sigh of relief.

LATER, WHEN GIANNI would speak to her about some of the situations he was forced to confront, he'd grow silent, and she'd tell him to look beyond the madness, at the individuals who moved at the heart of events and circumstances, and then form your judgments. Create your own pocket in the chaos and protect it. Their "other America" was a corrupt country, but one that would seek retribution from anyone who drew innocent blood. His actions, she said, would always be guided by character. And so history had repeated itself. As with Gino and Filomina, Gianni valued Sunni's opinion, yet whenever he tried to explain the enormous power she had over him, his normally agile mind lost all reason.

WHEN GIANNI FIRST started to appear without Gino in the neighborhood, acting as his emissary in certain key transactions, he never limited himself to matters of business. In keeping with Gino's philosophy, he was always concerned about the quality of life in the territory he controlled, walking among the people as a serious-minded community leader who not only shared their concerns, but would take decisive action to ensure their safety when necessary. On one insufferably hot summer night, when the concrete seemed in danger of melting in the humid air, he'd been waiting for one of his runners outside a broken-down apartment building, hoping to intercept some fugitive breeze that might miraculously find its way through the city steam. He'd just eased his body into the absolute stillness, the only possible defense against oppressive heat, when an agonized scream came from somewhere within the building.

In a few seconds, he was bounding up the decaying stairway until he reached a woman on the seventh-floor landing shouting in anguish, too hysterical to rise from the awkward sitting position into which she had apparently collapsed. As Gianni tried to determine what was happening, Salvatore Pinelli – the young runner he'd been waiting for – arrived, panting heavily, followed by a horror-stricken elderly woman who emerged from one of the apartments, talking and gesturing wildly.

"The baby, the baby!" she kept repeating. "He is stolen!"

"Who's stolen?" Gianni asked."

"My grandson. I left the door open so he could play with his trucks while we were sewing. Someone took him, a man. You must look upstairs. Please, please. He went up that way."

It was then that Gianni remembered talk of a dead, naked child found in a nearby alley a few weeks before – and that no one had been able to identify the murderer.

"Quick," he said to Salvatore, and the two reached the door to the roof a moment later. It was locked but the door was so feeble that a single kick splintered it open. On the dimly-lit rooftop, they found the man close to the edge, already ripping the yellowed underpants from the boy's body and fumbling with his zipper. The boy whimpered as the man bent toward him, dick in hand, so caught up in his frenzy that he didn't notice Gianni until his hand had closed around his throat.

The man froze in place, his erection withering, as Salvatore said, "Gianni. Let's push him over the edge before anyone gets here. That's what he would have done to the kid. Do it, Gianni. Jesus Christ, do it!"

"We're taking him with us," Gianni said in a hushed voice. "Hold him while I take the boy home."

Blanketing the still-whimpering child in his suit jacket, Gianni carried him down to his family and the other women who had gathered around them. With his gun drawn, Salvatore brought the man to the top of the stairs and waited while Gianni murmured words of comfort to the child on the floor below. The few people there assumed that they were the police, so Gianni and Salvatore walked the man calmly to the street where Gianni had parked his car an hour earlier. The prisoner, a shapeless man with dead-looking eyes, only spoke when Gianni had driven away from the area.

"There's nothing you can do to me," he said. "Children are everywhere, like maggots. No one misses them for long."

The fact that Gianni had prevented Salvatore from hurling the man over the rooftop had given him the courage to speak, but the silence that met his words stripped the last of his bravado. He sat morosely, breathing deeply in the stifling air, as the car turned into a dark corner of Central Park and pulled over to the side of a deserted pathway. Salvatore dragged him out of the car while Gianni paused to remove a large toolbox from the trunk before they pushed him forward into the woods. No one spoke until Gianni stopped the procession in a small clearing.

"Lie down and stretch out your arms," Gianni said gently, the barrel of his pistol buried in the man's soft neck. "Salvatore, I want you to pin him in that position."

As the man stretched out face-down in the dirt, Salvatore lowered his considerable weight on the man's back and used his feet to hold the man's arms to the ground. Quietly, Gianni lifted a small axe from the toolbox and in one throw swung it downward, severing the man's right hand at the wrist. By the time the man registered what was happening, Gianni had already brought the axe down on the other wrist. Before the pain kicked in, Salvatore had rolled off, cursing the blood spatters on his pant legs. Then Gianni worked meticulously with a sledge hammer, shattering every bone in the man's body before his final rush toward death.

In a single explosion of rage against the infliction of bestiality on children, Gianni had done something he could scarcely have imagined. But the thoroughness with which it was executed – the unswerving willingness to accept full responsibility for whatever had to be done – defined the man, and word spread along the hidden lines of communication that Gino's successor would be the deadliest of adversaries to any challenger. Still adhering to Gino's example, Gianni never promoted brutality for its own sake; violence was only utilized in response to a dire threat. Nonetheless, there was a clear escalation in the number of violent deaths once

Gianni assumed control. In some cases, they were simple retalia-
tions for new attacks upon the Manzino empire brought about by
greedy men anxious to test the new heir, but most instances
stemmed from the need for self-defense. Since the Manzino organization had no intention of joining the mad scramble for the control of drug-trafficking, the other organizations, desperate to secure as much of the city as possible so they could flourish without
interruption, were no longer happy to co-exist peacefully with local leaders like Gino. As a result, a new hardness and capacity for
cruelty had intensified, as well as the drive to eliminate indepen-
dents when the limitless potential for profit became evident. Their
best strategy for survival, Gianni thought, was to strike at the would-
be conquerors before they had the chance to act first. Consequently,
Gianni's cool assessment of the situation, as well as the nature of
crime itself, had undergone a metamorphosis. Even so, he was never
reckless in deciding how much force was necessary. There would
be no indiscriminate slaughters, no tests of strength, no killings
for convenience, no murders born of misdirected passion. Not only
did violence breed violence, but Gianni had no desire to kill, despite the image he'd created by the single episode in the park. In
order for Gianni to accept assassination as a solution, two conditions were required – all avenues of persuasion had to be exhausted,
and the man targeted must truly deserve to die – a man, for instance, like Frank Grillo.

The Grillo empire, founded almost entirely on narcotics, had
imposed itself on the city with astonishing speed and brutality.
Grillo was vicious when killing his enemies, real or imagined, and
he was also sloppy about it, often eliminating tens of innocent
bystanders in his zeal to destroy the opposition. When one of his
periodic rampages killed a Manzino runner while he was eating
lunch, as well as the ancient Sicilian who owned the luncheonette
and was serving coffee to the intended victim, Gianni decided that
enough was enough. Although it would be inaccurate to say that
the luncheonette was under Manzino's "protection" – during this
period the drug trade was cutting its way through all the old neighborhood divisions – it did occur just one block away from Gino's

offices at MANZINOS, close enough to be thought of as home ground.

Grillo's men had blasted away with sawed-off shotguns as soon as they entered the tiny luncheonette in their attempt to rub out a black heroin addict who'd tried to set up his own distribution system within an area of Harlem controlled by Grillo. The man would have never become a real rival; he was only interested in cutting his costs and impressing girls. But to Grillo, all offenses, no matter how small, provided an excuse to stage a massacre.

At the first sign of guns emerging from overcoats, the addict, whose sense of danger had been finely tuned by years of illicit drug selling, leapt over the counter with just enough speed to save his life. The runner's coffee cup was halfway to his mouth when the twin blast from the nearest gun cut through the side of his rib cage and blew him from the rickety stool like a gust of wind. The old man behind the counter hadn't even had time to absorb what was happening before another gun's barrel swung toward his face.

Atrocities like this had been traceable to Grillo's people for too long, Gianni thought, and all of his attempts, as well as those of many others to pressure Grillo into some semblance of restraint had only been met with hostility. In his capacity for bloodshed, Frank Grillo was a throwback to the Mustache Petes who once dominated the tenements. His taste in suits was flamboyant, at least a decade behind in fashion, and he favored wearing the wide fedora hats popular with pimps. Of course, Grillo thought of himself as modern and sophisticated – he even maintained a modest "business office" in a Long Island City warehouse and commuted to work every morning on the subway with a bodyguard – nevertheless, as much as he tried to pass for an executive, his true nature always revealed itself. After the luncheonette killings, Egan started trailing Grillo on the off chance that he might be spotted talking to someone who matched either of the descriptions they'd been given of the gunmen. No one on the police force doubted that the killing was ordered by Grillo, but they did doubt whether they could prove it. So the moment Egan recognized Gianni standing nonchalantly on the same subway platform as Grillo, looking just

as well-bred as he had at the wedding in his dark business suit –
particularly in contrast to Grillo's clownish figure – Egan knew
that something special was about to take place. But as little alarms
rang throughout his nervous system, he also realized that he wasn't
prepared for this. He had no back-up nor any time to call for one
– how could he keep two men under surveillance at once? Then,
the train arrived and he followed them through the closing doors,
trying to keep his face averted. Gianni seemed completely unaware
of either Egan's or Grillo's presence and took a seat at the far end of
the car, calmly reading his newspaper. Egan stood among a group
of people across from Grillo, wondering what in hell to do next.

When the train reached the next stop, Egan glanced back at
Gianni, who made no move to join the exiting riders, then returned his attention to Grillo, who was sitting quietly next to his
obviously bored bodyguard, smiling at some private thought. Probably something indescribably obscene, Egan figured. Just as the
doors were about to close, a young man he couldn't identify rushed
through them and shouted loud enough to disturb Grillo's reverie,
"Lieutenant! Lieutenant Egan! We need you on the platform fast!
The sergeant said it's an emergency!" Egan's instincts carried him
off the train, but he consoled himself over the loss of his double
quarry with the fact that his cover had been hopelessly blown anyway, and hurried down the platform after the man who had called
him.

"Down there! Cashman needs you!" the young man said in a
breathless voice, pointing to a small knot of people, including one
uniformed cop, gathered at the far end of the long platform. Egan
sprinted past him, outdistanced by the train as it thundered into
the tunnel, while the unfamiliar faces in the group ahead of him
merely turned to watch his running figure with curiosity. Some
corner of Egan's brain registered the information that the young
man had disappeared up the staircase to the crowded street, then
Egan broke his stride, suddenly realizing what had happened.

Gianni must have spotted Egan long before Egan had spotted
him, and the faceless young man must have boarded the train with
Gianni. When the train stopped, Gianni sent him out the door

with instructions to race through the other door up front and get Egan out by exposing his identity. The group on the platform had been just a convenient assembly. He had fallen for the entire ruse. Meanwhile, Egan knew that Frank Grillo was a dead man. Gianni had wanted him off the train for a reason, and there was absolutely nothing he could do about it.

"God fuck it!" he said, over and over.

The cop standing idly on the platform had approached him to see if he could be of any help, but then watched him with amusement when he embarked on a cursing tirade.

"What's the matter, fella?" the cop said. "Miss your train?"

A few miles away, the train reached Jackson Heights where Frank Grillo and his escort disembarked for the usual switch to the local on track five. As they stood in front of the small waiting crowd, watching the local roar toward them, neither man was aware of the pressure on their backs until they found themselves launched into the air, an act timed so perfectly that their feet never touched the cindered ground. The lead car caught them in mid-fall, carrying them for several yards before dropping them beneath the wheels. The *Daily News* was unable to get a cameraman there before the mangled bodies were cleared from the track, but they did get a terrific shot of a crushed fedora for the next edition's front page, which Egan tried to ignore for the week or so that Cashman had it tacked to the bulletin board behind his desk.

No one mourned Grillo, and the vacancy in the drug flow caused by his death was probably filled before the subway had screeched to a stop on top of him. His successor, anxious to hold onto his new power for a while, adopted a more conservative approach and the streets returned to relative calm. Cashman and Egan decided that there was no point in even questioning Gianni, and simply added another file folder to the drawer labeled "The shadow's shadow." Meanwhile, the growth of the narcotics trade had set off a feeding frenzy, in which those in power had decided that the Manzino territory was too valuable to remain self-contained and drug-free. Gianni had to be removed – but how? He had no identifiable weaknesses. He was not a womanizer or a gambler, he never touched drugs or drank excessively, and he never allowed his emotions to govern his head. Finally they realized that if he couldn't be reached through any vices, they'd have to reach him through his virtues instead.

GIANNI HAD ENORMOUS respect for his father, who still worked as a tailor after forty years, so he always felt a special affection for the craftsman and shopkeepers in the neighborhoods he visited – the old men who worked as upholsterers, cobblers, carpenters, and bakers. He was particularly fond of Ernesto Tetrazzini who'd been a friend of his father's ever since he could remember and who steadfastly refused to sweeten his pastries for American tastes. And yet, with the pride characteristic of his generation, Tetrazzini never asked a single favor of Gianni despite his dying business until one subzero evening he called with an embarrassed plea for a loan because his landlord had threatened to cut off the heat unless the back rent was paid, and he feared for the welfare of his bedridden wife.

Gianni reached the ancient building on 116th Street a little after eleven, amazed that the hallway felt even colder than the outside air. He hurried up the four flights of stairs and, after knocking twice, waited for Tetrazzini, who was lame in one leg, to answer the door. Suddenly the door flew open and Ernesto's frail body was hurled against Gianni in a hail of gunfire. It happened so quickly that Gianni was only aware of fleeting impressions, like a landscape glimpsed in the lightning flashes of a midnight storm. Gianni fired back instinctively and one man with a rifle pitched forward over the old man's body, the rifle slamming into Gianni's wrist and sending his revolver sliding across the polished linoleum as the man crumpled into a bloody heap. Gianni was knocked off balance, but managed to kick at a second gunman who'd come stumbling toward him from inside the apartment. The man fell to the floor but hung onto his weapon as he managed to grab Gianni's gun and throw it down the stairwell before aiming his own at Gianni once more. Slamming and locking the front door behind him, Gianni ran for the apartment's small bedroom, his arm stinging from the heavy rifle's blow, past the bed where Mrs. Tetrazzini lay in a lifeless mass, the white wall behind her splattered with blood.

All he needed was a few seconds to crash his way through the window, he thought, until he felt all the air escape from his lungs when he saw that the Tetrazzinis had installed iron bars. In the same second, the killer smashed through the flimsy door in a shower of wood and dust. Gianni threw himself away from the line of fire, looking desperately for something, anything, to use as a weapon.

"You're a dead man, Gianni!" the man yelled, as he reloaded his rifle.

Gianni headed for the bathroom and slammed the door, sliding its tiny bolt closed. He turned and tore open the medicine cabinet, hoping to find a straight razor, but all he found was a blade too rusted to threaten anyone. A pocket comb. A bottle of aspirin. Toothpaste. A worn toothbrush. Dental floss. A tube of liniment and another of mustache wax. He started to wrench the mirrored door off its hinges and the cabinet's contents spilled into the sink – comb, tubes, dental floss. Dental floss, he thought again. Gianni ripped open the container and the floss began to unravel. A single strand was almost impossible to snap with bare hands, he thought. Several strands would be truly unbreakable. Hurriedly, he twisted together a length of two feet, several strands thick, then turned on the shower to create a distraction and threw himself behind the door as it splintered open in response to the gunman's kicks. With the ends of the crude garrote wrapped around each hand, Gianni crossed his arms and held his breath.

The gunman entered the room, puzzled by the shower, and fired through the oilskin shower curtain. Gianni had just enough room to kick away the door and throw the loop over the man's head before he could turn. Luckily, the cramped space made it difficult for the man to move quickly with the rifle in front of him and so, in a single jolting motion, Gianni snapped his arms apart, raised his hands over his head, and spun his body around so that his back was against the back of the killer. Holding the twisted strands as tightly as possible, he bent sharply at the waist, pulling the gunman's bound neck with so much force that he could feel the shuddering crack through his own body. Gianni held his position for several seconds, body bent forward, the improvised strangle-knot rigidly taut. Finally satisfied that the man was dead, he let the body fall to the floor and then found his way out of the apartment, trying not to look too closely at what had become of the Tetrazzinis.

That night it took Sunni a long time to ease Gianni's mood. It wasn't his own nearness to death that had unnerved him, it was the fact that the Tetrazzinis had been murdered for his sake, as a way of reaching him. For the first time in his life, he was tortured by guilt, brutally aware of the price that his life had forced innocent people to pay. Sunni, who'd been holding his unyielding body for hours, knew precisely the moment when he needed her sense of balance and slipped off her nightgown as she moved her mouth across his flesh.

By the next morning, everyone from the old neighborhood was speculating on how Gianni would handle the massacre. Even now, they said, he was tracking down the animals who had ordered the butchering, planning the ways in which he would bring them special pain and degradation in their final minutes of life, and remembering the time when old Nicodemo Grande killed the man who had insulted his sister by having the skin on his face peeled off with straight razors, inch by inch, like a bloated apple.

But Gianni had no thoughts of vengeance filling his mind. This time the actual enemy was too nebulous to identify and any need for individual revenge had been purged in the sickening crack of the gunman's neck. The true source of the assassination attempt, he discovered, was far more complex than just another Frank Grillo.

CHAPTER
THIRTY-ONE

N O LONGER DID the streets that comprised Gino Manzino's world have a monopoly on crime. The sources of true wealth and power were now emerging from the unions of business and government. Their compromises, deliberately forged in the offices of the city's most powerful, would allow everyone to grow unchecked for years to come.

Instead of just a few bribed officials, a few corrupt unions extorting kickbacks from builders, a vast network of the city's leaders were seeming more and more like costumed rulers in a comic opera – the Teamsters who controlled anything moving into, out of, or within the city; the political operatives, especially those members of city committees who made actual officeholders irrelevant; the lawyers who could play with the mechanics of City Hall as if it were their private toy; the bankers and investors who manipulated money on a scale their legitimate clients could never approximate; the police and government agents who moved freely through their operations, easing friction before it had a chance to build. The system was astonishingly efficient – not so much a well-constructed machine as an organic being filled with its own longings and terrible gift for cruelty. It was this dark, amorphous soul of the city that had made the attempt on Gianni's life, ordered by some faceless, cost-effective committee as a way of testing his vulnerability.

Had it been successful, they would have found a new corner for expansion. As it was, certain business partners were willing to let the matter drop, at least for the time being. The men that were sent had been far too sloppy, drawing unnecessary attention, and were better off dead. When they really needed to eliminate Gianni, they would find a more appropriate solution.

In the meantime, however, Gianni had become the focus of another sort of pressure from the legitimate side of law enforcement. The spearheads for real corruption had become so insulated within the boardrooms of banks, corporations, and the chambers of government that alternate targets were needed to redirect the public's outrage. If the true criminals were too powerful to be touched, lesser villains had to be offered as compensation, along with a full-blown publicity campaign by the press to exaggerate their significance. At first, third-rate bookmakers with distant ties to Sicilian bosses were knocked over like lead soldiers and branded "major crime figures" and "Mafioso leaders." But then the "department" decided to take the plan a step further and choose a more visible character. The Manzino empire was the perfect scapegoat – large enough to fill headlines, independent enough to be completely destroyed – and Gianni Ghianella was heir to the throne.

As soon as word came down that someone in the department was finally taking their shadow men seriously, Cashman and Egan were flushed with pride. Suddenly, they had more manpower than they could manage. But Cashman began to get suspicious when all the new men assigned to him came from the same vague government "task force" and wore neatly pressed suits. Real cops, he thought, wore rumpled suits. Eventually, Egan turned to him and said, "They're using us, aren't they."

Cashman crumpled a sheet of paper in his hand. "Yes," he said, "they are."

While Cashman and Egan were expected to hand over all their hard earned information, they weren't considered part of the real team. Big egos were suddenly at stake, and Cashman and Egan were to be left behind in the wastebasket. Most galling to Cashman, was the fact that another chief, Detective Dick Orlin was brought in, apparently to work "in tandem" with Cashman. Once the stern Waspish Orlin had moved most of Cashman's files to his new office, however, Cashman hardly saw him – except at Orlin's staff meetings.

Cashman and Egan had long ago learned to accept corruption without participating in it, but this betrayal felt like a insult from the invisible powers above. They weren't about to allow their resentment to ripple the surface, but neither were they going to disappear into the woodwork.

"What do we do?" Egan asked Cashman.

"What we've always done," Cashman told him.

Aside from a few muttered obscenities here and there, the two continued on as before, hiding their feelings beneath the familiar cloaks of cynicism and indifference. However much they mistrusted the shape and direction of the Manzino investigation, and whatever its political end, they continued to search for evidence.

Then, one Monday morning, at eight a.m., Orlin leaned against the door of Cashman's office.

"We've got a raid going on this morning, Cashman," he said, as casually as if he were talking about the weather. "Nothing was moving, and it was time to shake things up. The boys are out now, pulling in some of the smaller men – a couple of runners, some warehouse workers and two-bit loan sharks. All Manzino men."

Cashman was incensed at being left out of such an important decision. But he wasn't about to let Orlin know. "I'd be interested in getting a list of the men," he managed to say as Egan came in, aware immediately that something had happened. "I'll have one of the boys bring that over," Orlin said, nodding to Egan.

"Thank you," Cashman said.

"What's going on?" Egan asked as Orlin walked off down the hall.

"Scare tactics," Cashman said. "Or maybe it's tear gas." He repeated what Orlin had told him,, shaking his head. "I guess they're trying to force some response, but if I know anything it's that the Manzinos don't react on demand."

"Or never the way you anticipate."

"Exactly."

SURE ENOUGH, WHEN Gianni heard how many of his men had been harassed, he knew he was being poked with a large hot stick. Of course he wanted to strike back immediately but the last group of people Gianni wanted to confront was the police. Any strike he made would give them just the excuse they wanted to end his reign in a bloody shootout.

Gianni met with Gino in Gino's fourth floor office at MANZINOS Bennie sent up espresso in the dumbwaiter, and Tina, Bennie's daughter, popped in a few fresh pastries. As the winter sky darkened outside the windows and a bodyguard shifted from foot to foot beyond the door, Gino listened closely to Gianni's concerns.

"The thing is that they're showing us their force," Gianni said. "They didn't pick anyone truly important. They didn't kill anyone – or even hurt anyone. But they got into areas we thought were undetectable, pulled in contacts we didn't think they knew about."

"What do they want?" Gino asked.

"For us to strike back."

"What do you want?"

Gino knew that Gianni would like nothing better than to strike back. His wasn't the temperament for game playing; he liked retribution, swift and sure. But Gino knew that the one thing he had helped to teach Gianni was wise patience.

"You're right," Gianni smiled. "I can't give them what they want."

"That's why you came to me."

"Yes."

Gianni stirred sugar into his espresso.

"I'm closing it down," he said, "all of it, every operation."

Gino smiled. "They'll be surveying themselves."

ONCE AGAIN, CASHMAN found himself impressed by Gianni's control. The legal Manzino enterprises went on as usual – the dry cleaners, funeral homes, trucks transporting suits, furs, and Italian food still being sold by old immigrant merchants – and Gianni's bodyguards and hit men were reduced to waxing their cars or playing stickball in the streets. As for Gianni, he relished the opportunity to spend more time with Sunni, knowing that a dozen members of a special anti-crime team were quietly going crazy.

"This is nuts," said Sanderson, the most easily rattled of the bunch. "If he doesn't start tending to things pretty soon, someone else is going to move in."

Then, Augie Donatella, a recent young immigrant from Italy trying to shoulder his way into the new world started a business of his own – some bookmaking, some bootlegged cigarettes, some loan-sharking – but no one took him seriously and even the squad had no interest in picking him up. In fact, they were annoyed that he was getting in the way of bigger fish and figured that Gianni would eventually take control of the matter. Gianni, meanwhile, seemed unconcerned, like an ex-pro who had lost all interest in the game he'd left behind, and as his weeks of uninvolvement stretched into months, Cashman's admiration turned to curiosity. Donatella was continuing to build a fairly profitable operation from the vacancy Gianni had provided. When would the Manzinos reassert their dominance?

Cashman was musing on this for about the thirtieth time when he suddenly arrived at the germ of the seed of his answer. He and Egan had one advantage over the new team: they had been watching them, in real life, for a long time now, and they knew both Gino and Gianni's circuit. While Donatella seemed merely a young man aping his temporarily retired predecessors, Cashman noticed that Donatella was moving in routes and eddies eerily similar to those of Gianni's. Watching this handsome young man stride into a store confident as a boy out to buy mozzarella for his mother, Cashman realized Donatella's one mistake – he wasn't making one. This guy wasn't picking up the slack for Gianni, Cashman suddenly thought; he was filling in for him.

"Oh my God," Cashman said, smacking his head with his hand. "How could I have missed it?"

"Talking to yourself again," Egan said, returning from a cigar store.

"Who does Donatella remind you of?" Cashman asked. "Take a good look at him when he comes out of that store."

"Nobody," Egan said, when the door opened and Donatella placed his hat on his polished hair. "Nobody and everybody around here."

"Does he look nervous to you?"

"No. Why should he?"

"Wouldn't you, taking over Manzino's territory?"

"He's just a kid."

"Maybe."

Donatella recognized the two government men as he always did – without seeming to – and moved from the store down the street without a backward glance.

"What are you saying?" Egan asked. "That he's actually involved in all of this?"

"How could I have been so stupid?"

"You don't think – "

"He's Gianni's man. He works for them."

AS IT HAPPENED, Cashman was right. Donatella had been brought in to keep services flowing while the stalemate stayed in place. But by the time Cashman could convince the other members of the team, he had disappeared, probably back to Italy after his extended American "vacation" – and the anti-crime unit was still stymied.

EDDIE "JELLY APPLES" Rizzuto was thinking once again about nicknames. All his life, he'd been surrounded by men with frequently mysterious but always colorful nicknames – Sammy, Bennie, Guido, and Frankie who grew up to be the Lip, the Weasel, Tonto, and the Barrel. Harry "the Hammer" Marillo was a carpenter's son who had driven his mother crazy by running around the apartment as a toddler banging everything in sight. "Chickie" Johnny Tess earned his first pennies at age three by making chicken sounds for all his relatives. Others earned their appellations by some characteristic criminal act. Two-Ton Triolo routinely stole large trucks, and Red Randazzo had never been known to stop for a single red light. Eddie also knew which of the names were bullshit. Joseph Colletti might train his subordinates to refer to him as "the Butcher," but everyone knew that Colletti was a pussy. Meanwhile, Eddie brooded, a truly tough man like himself had to go through life with a name like Jelly Apples, thanks to his mother.

Carlotta Rizzuto was possibly the worst cook in America. Her sauces were always burned just past the point of recognizing the ingredients, and the pasta was boiled until it achieved the look of a kind of stringy farina. So Eddie grew up with no interest whatsoever in traditional foods and developed an early passion for street fare, particularly sickeningly sweet candy apples, which he bought each day for his lunchbox. But the name was also appropriate because of his physical appearance: a short, round body, candy-apple cheeks, and bright red hair.

He'd been sitting on a wooden chair in the surprisingly lush backyard of his apartment building, a few feet from his half-harvested vegetable garden with the chair tipped back against the post supporting his little brother's backboard. This allowed him to angle his broad face toward a shaft of sunlight that had found its way through the fruit trees and tenement canyons on a sunny October morning still warm as midsummer. Then the sun disappeared behind a cloud, and as his eyes readjusted to the shade, he saw a slight figure alight on the third floor fire escape of the building opposite his. At first, he thought it was a child, but then he saw it was a small man trying to balance an oversized portable television on his narrow shoulder as he descended the iron ladder. The television looked like it weighed more than he did, and he was having some difficulty maintaining his grip on the metal with his one free hand. Instantly outraged that someone might be stealing from one of his neighbors, Eddie snapped out of his reverie and ran toward the building, shouting, "Hey you! Hey you!" As he got closer, sweating and panting a little harder with each fence negotiated, Eddie recognized Angelo Benfatto, a little punk he had known since grammar school. Stealing some old lady's television was exactly what he would have expected of him. He was probably taking it to his uncle's pawnshop on Northern Boulevard, Eddie thought.

Angelo Benfatto was so startled that he nearly dropped the television to the yard below. But when he reached the last rung and saw who was hurtling toward him, he relaxed a little, then jumped to the ground and hurried up the narrow path to the street. Eddie ran to his left along the row of buildings until he reached the alley that led directly to the boulevard. He emerged, puffing heavily, just as Angelo rounded the corner. They collided a moment later, and the television hit the ground with an enormous thud that blew out the screen. Eddie grabbed Angelo by the shoulders so hard that he picked him up off the ground.

"Angelo 'the Worm' Benfatto," he bellowed, "still a two-bit punk!"

Angelo poked his finger in Eddie's rotund form and said, "I see you're still a jelly apple."

In one motion, Eddie threw him toward the plate glass window of the corner deli and Angelo had just enough time to cover his face with both arms before shattering through it.

Carlo, the deli owner, was slicing bologna behind the counter when the splintering crash sent everyone out of the store screaming and he looked up in horror to see Angelo climbing to his feet, miraculously uncut, holding a twenty-pound salami from the ruins of his window display. Angelo rushed to stand out of sight by the open window until Eddie peered through, whereupon Angelo slammed him across the face with the salami. Eddie wrestled him back through the window, they both fell to the ground, and the fight was on. A crowd of delighted children quickly gathered to watch the skinny guy beat up the chubby one and kept up a chorus of cheers. They even applauded the cops who arrived a few minutes later to take the two of them away, pointing out the wreckage of the stolen television set in case the policemen hadn't seen it. They then managed to grab a few cheeses before Carlo nailed boards over the front of his shop, yelling at the kids to go home where they belonged.

Eddie and Angelo were brought into the nearest precinct house just as the shifts were changing on a relatively quiet afternoon, which meant that there were a lot of cops sitting around the station, drinking coffee, and looking for something to do – including Mahoney and Malreaux, partners for nine years who considered themselves to be the Laurel and Hardy of law enforcement, using their brand of mockery to help the battle-weary personnel survive the day. They even looked the part. In fact, Mahoney's appearance, with his ruddy complexion, heavy gut, disheveled hair, and the look of an athlete gone to seed, was such a cliché that he was often underestimated, an impression he used to full advantage on the street. He even insisted that his weight was an asset, that the presence of bulk, no matter how soft, tended to intimidate. Malreaux, on the other hand, was as trim and dapper as his buddy was unkempt. A French police officer was something of a rarity, so he did whatever he could to emphasize the image. He sported a trim mustache, dressed in distinctly continental clothes during his off-duty hours, and deepened his accent around pretty young women. Actually, his father's family had emigrated from Canada three generations earlier, so his accent was mostly based on late-night Louis Jourdan movies on television.

As soon as Eddie and Angelo entered the squad room, the other officers burst into catcalls and high-pitched hoots.

"Omigod! Mahoney! Look at what the cat dragged in," Malreaux intoned.

"Damn, Francis!" Mahoney called, "we might as well go home and rent out the squad cars. With these two busted at last, that's the end of crime in this city." Malreaux had been trying for years to get Mahoney to call him Françoise but with no success. Everyone else called him Frank.

Angelo made an attempt to look menacing, as if to suggest that harassing him was a fatal error, while Eddie tried a subtler approach – ignoring them all.

"It's Jelly Apples Rizzuto," Mahoney continued in a flat, deadpan voice, "and Angelo 'the Worm' Benfatto. I hope this news hasn't been leaked to the press."

"Imagine the secrets these two could share," Malreaux said, rubbing his hands together. "There's nothing about stolen appliances that Benfatto doesn't know," referring, of course, to the occasional blender that Angelo would steal for his uncle's two-bit store, though Malreaux was making it sound like a raid of manufacturing plants and hijacking truck convoys. "And then there's Jelly Apples," Malreaux continued, dropping his voice an octave for effect. "He's been in so many operations that we can only guess at what he knows."

Everyone nodded. Eddie's inability to establish any lasting connection with an organization in the area was legendary. He'd spent the last couple of years as a low-level errand boy for various local hoods and bosses, never truly penetrating their inner circles.

Just then a humorless young Fed from the "task force," who'd been filling his coffee mug at the other end of the squad room, joined the ring of cops watching the two hoods, taking the whole conversation very seriously.

"Why don't we try to break them?" he said.

Malreaux, Mahoney, and every other cop within earshot turned to look at him. Even the arresting officer paused in his attempt to line up the arrest report in the typewriter properly.

This was the first time Joey Toole had come up with an idea since he'd been hanging around. Rumors had it that he wasn't a cop at all, but some newspaper or government reporter, scribbling notes in one notebook after another. With his squinty brown eyes and pursed lips, he always looked as if he were in the middle of some complex philosophical or mathematical problem.

Malreaux and Mahoney glanced at one another, then read each other's minds: Toole might think he had everyone in the office pigeonholed, but it wasn't every day that they had a chance to make a fool out a three-piece suit. Compared to Cashman and Egan, Malreaux and Mahoney had limited involvement with gray men. But ever since the task force men had been floating in and out, they had gained more respect for those cops that had to deal with them regularly. Having a little fun with Toole would give every one a laugh.

"Shouldn't we split them up?" Toole continued.

"I believe you're right," Mahoney said solemnly, and then in a stage whisper: "We can play one against the other." The cops around him managed to stifle their smiles.

"Mind if I sit in?"

"Glad to have you," Malreaux told him, clapping him hard on the shoulder. "Call me Françoise."

"Toole."

"You know Detective Mahoney and Sergeant Smith. Smith – we'll be using interrogation rooms D and E." The desk sergeant nodded, keeping his head down and trying to keep a straight face. They had no such interrogation rooms, just two unused offices at the end of the hall, which they sometimes used for questioning. Malreaux, Mahoney, and Toole started down the corridor with Eddie and Angelo, and those they left behind slipped into muffled hysterics.

Before the "interrogations" began, Malreaux pulled Mahoney and Toole together for a quick consult. "Let's get this right," he said.

"Start gentle, build hard," Toole said.

"Right," Malreaux answered, wondering if Toole had read this in one of his textbooks.

"We'll begin with the television and the incident at the store, then expand to the neighborhood," Malreaux said.

"And don't forget the curveballs," Mahoney grinned and winked at Toole. "We get them so confused, they don't know what they're saying."

Toole was taking all of this in with a gravity that only increased Malreaux and Maloney's hidden amusement. When each settled in with their criminals, however, the real fun began. Malreaux joined Angelo in one room, where Angelo jumped up from his chair and shouted, "You'll never get nothing from me!" a line he had obviously been waiting to use all his life. Mahoney kicked back his feet in the second room with Jelly Apple while Toole shuttled back and forth with his notebooks, afraid to miss anything.

Mahoney's questioning moved from reason to nonsense relatively quickly.

"Tell me about the salami," he said, so Jelly Apples looked startled.

"What do you want to know?"

"I want to know why it was used as a weapon."

"I don't know. I guess cause it was there."

"You don't think it had a symbolic meaning?"

"Whadaya mean, symbolic?"

"Have you ever been to Nebraska, Eddie."

"No."

"How about Iowa?"

"No."

"Where have you been?"

"Nowhere."

"We had a report that someone in your house watches Bugs Bunny cartoons. Is that true Eddie?"

"One of my kids maybe."

"But you don't see the symbolism of the salami?"

"No."

"And you've never been to Florida?"

"I never said I'd never been to Florida."

"Is that right?"

"Yeah."

"So you have been to Florida."

"Yes."

"They grow good potted plants there too, don't they."

"What?"

"But you're got to know how to water them just right. You've got to know what you're doing, right Eddie?"

"I guess."

"Your wife likes potted plants doesn't she? She's got some in the house?"

"So what?"

"So your wife likes potted plants and you have spent time in Florida and maybe things aren't as simple as you're pretending."

Toole's eyes were going back and forth, back and forth, like in a tennis match. Taking a break, Mahoney leaned over and whispered to him that this was a particularly sophisticated means of inquiry designed to confuse the prisoners and trigger unexpected responses. Toole, as uncertain as Jelly Apples, nodded and made his way over to Malreaux and Angelo.

There, Malreaux was sitting on a bench, one leg dangling, with a jittery Angelo below him. Angelo was drinking coffee from a paper cup and at the same time saying "Can't I take a piss? Jesus. Jesus. I gotta go."

"In a minute," Malreaux said, as Toole looked on from behind him. Leaning to Toole, he said, "Talk quietly now Sir. Whisper something in my ear like you don't want Angelo here to hear you."

Toole, proudly keeping his eyes from Angelo, decided to participate in the act, nodding sternly and whispering, "The potted plant grows mostly in the Florida sun – as well as the salami."

"Right," Malreaux said, fingering his moustache.

"So Jelly Apples said that, did he?"

He stared at Angelo for a full minute, then laughed to himself as Angelo jiggled one foot up and down.

"Did you see the size of that salami?" he asked Angelo.

"Let me use the bathroom."

"I'm gonna do that Worm, I really am. But I just want to give you this opportunity to tell me something before your friend Jelly Apples does. Because whichever one of you gives us something first gets to go. And the other one we're keeping – do you understand?"

"Yeah."

"It's your choice."

BACK IN MAHONEY'S room, Jelly Apples was feeling overwhelmed.

"You're crazy," he suddenly screamed at Mahoney. "Florida and salami and growing green plants. What do you want from me?"

"First of all, don't call me crazy. Second of all, we know you've seen some things."

"So."

"So we're not asking you to put all the pieces together. We just want to see what you've seen."

"I've seen a few things."

"I know that, Eddie, and Mr. Joey Toole here knows it and so does your buddy Angelo across the hall there." Mahoney looked at Toole. "Just from one glance at my friend Mr. Toole here, I know from him that Angelo has given up a thing or two. Oh I know, you've both seen some things and you'd better hope that what you give me is better than what Angelo does."

Naturally, no one was more surprised than Mahoney when his technique began to work. Soon enough – and once Angelo had been to the bathroom and Eddie served half a sandwich – they were each told that whoever had the most interesting information would be given his freedom – and whoever lost would be responsible for the entire afternoon's fracas, including charges of grand theft and assault with a deadly weapon.

"Did you note the size of the salami?" Mahoney asked.

Eddie and Angelo thought they understood cops, but this sort of behavior was completely unknown. It made it painfully evident to both of them that once you were in the hands of the cops, you were powerless. None of the old rules applied and you could be convicted on some fanciful or spiteful whim. Finally, the two began to talk of anything and everything that might appease their interrogators. In no time, they were dredging up every miserable scrap of mob-related information they could. Angelo offered them his uncle, although the police already knew well of his hierarchy of petty thieves, stealing back some of his haul every now and then when complaints from the public grew too insistent. Eddie countered by offering an uncle of his own, a penny-ante loan shark in the garment district. With increasing desperation, Eddie and Angelo told everything they had ever observed about the neighborhood's underworld – and over the years, they had observed far more than they realized. Even so, they considered themselves too slick to be tricked into giving up anything truly useful, so the cops simply sighed a little when the bits and pieces formed familiar patterns.

After nearly three hours of questioning and cross-checking, however, new information was bound to surface, and to their own surprise, Malreaux and Mahoney found themselves to be the proud possessors of quite a few little leads on dozens of local operations – addresses for stolen goods warehouses, names of middle men and fences, timetables for projected operations – nothing as dramatic as a murder or a bank job, perhaps, but enough to keep them busy for a while.

Then, Mahoney threw out his final card and told Eddie that Angelo was giving them better quality information, so he'd better get used to the idea of sleeping on jailhouse cement.

Eddie wrinkled his brow and got very quiet, then said, "I can give you something on Jimmy Feet."

"Do you mean Jimmy Rossetto?" Mahoney asked, hoping that Eddie wouldn't notice his sudden interest.

"Yeah," Eddie said, "something personal that nobody knows."

"We know all about Jimmy Feet," Mahoney said with feigned indifference – at the same time, he gestured for one of the cops to fetch Malreaux from across the hall. "We know what a schmuck he is and how it's only his father-in-law's influence that stops anyone from putting a bullet in him. We also know that he's too careful these days to dirty his own hands. So what could you possibly know that we don't?"

Malreaux came into the room, and Eddie relaxed for the first time since leaving the shaft of sunlight in his backyard, sensing that he might have finally found something significant to offer them after all. Everyone waited for Eddie to speak.

"Jimmy Feet," he began, then paused, his brow knitted in concentration as he tried to figure out the right way to say it. "Jimmy Feet raped Sunni Manzino. When she was still a kid. Or at least he tried to."

"Sunni Manzino? You mean Gianni Ghianella's wife?"

Eddie looked up at Mahoney and nodded.

There was a long silence, then Mahoney said to one of the officers lingering in the doorway, "You'd better get Cashman and

Egan down here. We have a present for them they're not going to believe."

EDDIE HAD DRAWN one of his worst assignments in a career that had consisted exclusively of crummy assignments. He was hired to ride shotgun one night while Jimmy Feet went on a drinking and whoring spree. Eddie's job was to assist Tony Areleo, Jimmy's driver if Jimmy grew too wild and had to be carried out of some bar or brothel. Eddie hated it. Most of the time was spent waiting for the increasingly obnoxious Jimmy to wear out his welcome somewhere. After seeing a show on 42nd Street, Jimmy managed to ply one of the lesser showgirls with enough flowers and cash to buy himself dinner with her. Then it was off to a brothel in the east sixties, where Jimmy bought both he and Tony some time and then insisted on swapping partners. Some nights Jimmy followed the uptown brothel with a Harlem one, where he could get away with increasingly lewd and violent acts. That night, however, Jimmy settled on Spats, a strip joint on the lower east side, followed by a run-down tavern close to the river. There Jimmy liked to wind down with the boys before returning to Connecticut. There was always someone who would listen to his endless sexual achievements and that night, while Eddie and Tony nursed their beers at a corner table, Jimmy engaged all the drunks in a discussion of female body parts, particularly the size and shape of the perfect tit, which caused an argument so intense that it threatened to become violent. Tits were classified, criticized, and submitted to a crude rating system, with 1 to 10 marks on size, shape, firmness and weight. Most of the men had no compunction at all about comparing the tits of Marilyn Monroe to the tits of their wives, sisters, and real or imagined lovers. One faction maintained that size was all that mattered, another that firmness was the key, still another felt that roundness was the mark of perfection, while one guy at the end of the bar said over and over that unless they were perky enough to jut out on their own, a woman may as well not have them. Jimmy, however, who claimed to be a connoisseur, only cared about nipples – if they were large and dark, and how they swelled when you aroused her. Eddie just shook his head in disgust, wishing that he could go back to running bets or unloading trucks on the pier. It was past midnight when he and the driver pulled Jimmy away from the bar stool, saying it was time to leave. Somehow they managed to pour him into the backseat of the car, but Jimmy wouldn't leave the subject alone.

"Hey Jelly Apples! You like nipples?"

Eddie, who had touched maybe one female breast in his lifetime (Or was it two? He couldn't remember if Rosie had let him touch the other one, too) closed his eyes and groaned inwardly.

"You know who has the greatest nipples in the world? The best – full and rosy-red, and . . . . You know who, Jelly Apples?"

"Gee, no, Mr. Rossetto," Eddie mumbled. "I have no idea."

"Sunni Manzino," Jimmy said triumphantly, and for the first time all day, Tony Areleo showed some surprise. Eyes widening, he glanced quickly over at Eddie sitting beside Jimmy, and then stared in the rearview mirror at Jimmy's semi-sprawled figure. Eddie, who had been hugging the door, and watching for any sign that Jimmy might need to throw up, had a hard time keeping his shock off his face.

Jimmy really was crazy, Eddie thought, crazy for thinking such a thing, let alone saying it. Everyone knew Sunni Manzino – she was so beautiful and her reputation so unblemished that he couldn't imagine how any man could say a thing like that about her, much less someone in her own family.

When Eddie failed to comment, Jimmy continued, "Hey, you think I don't know what I'm talking about? I not only saw those nipples, I touched them, Jelly Apples, touched them when they were still young and ripe."

Eddie felt his stomach turn to stone. He didn't want to hear this.

"Not that she was particularly happy about it," Jimmy snickered, his voice thickening with an old resentment set free by too much liquor. "Not that snotty bitch. She was saving it for Daddy and his asshole driver. But I took it anyway. Ripped that fucking blouse right off her. If we hadn't been in my house . . . ." His voice trailed off into silence as he gazed ahead in a glassy-eyed fury. Eventually his body sagged lower in the seat, and he slipped into unconsciousness.

WHEN CASHMAN HAD been called in to see two tough policemen he knew little about, he knew right away that something important must have happened. But never could he have imagined what he was to hear. Mahoney delivered the basic news and Cashman was as incredulous as Eddie had been that night in the car. It wasn't so much the fact that such a thing could happen – every family knew some sexual predator – but that someone like Jimmy Feet could be bragging about it. Either this truly was the first time Feet had said anything, or the whole story was the fabrication of a sick mind.

Cashman took every precaution before hearing the story in full. He couldn't justify ousting Mahoney and Malreaux, but he did sit them down to take any traces of humor out of the day's procedure. No longer, he said, were there to be any games. The two had done excellent work, and they didn't want to blow it now.

While the four policemen intuitively knew the seriousness of Jimmy's words, Toole, coming from a different upbringing in suburban Maryland, could never grasp that the slander of a woman's purity could be a greater crime than the murder of a brother. Cashman, therefore, had little trouble getting Toole out of the interrogation room. Pretending to be greatly impressed at Toole's heavily scribbled notebooks, he sent him off to a typewriter to transcribe them immediately.

As Eddie told his story in all its pathetic details, Cashman's distrust gradually gave away to belief. A story such as this could get its teller killed – even if it wasn't true.

So why would Eddie make it up? Indeed, how could Eddie make it up? It was simply too wild and farfetched for someone of his limited imagination.

For Egan, it wasn't the bizarre story so much as the fear on Eddie's face that was the convincer. It became its most intense not when the story was being told but when it was over – when Eddie realized just what cat he had let out of the bag.

"Have you told anyone about this?" Cashman finally asked.

"No," Eddie said, in a barely audible voice. "How could I?"

Cashman and Egan nodded, while even Mahoney and Malreaux were silent.

Eddie was terrified of Gino Manzino and Gianni Ghianella. These armed cops would be terrified, too, he thought – if they'd been the ones to hear Jimmy. Eddie felt a hardening in his gut, certain that it was only a matter of time before he'd be dead.

"Do you think Jimmy has told anyone else?" Cashman asked.

Eddie shrugged. "When he was drunk, maybe."

"But no one's told the Manzinos," Mahoney suddenly pitched in.

"No," Cashman answered. "Or Feet would be dead."

AFTER MORE THAN four hours of "interrogation", Malreaux told Angelo he was free to go. No mention was made of Jimmy Feet and Malreaux said only that Angelo had won the contest for the best tip-off.

Eddie was taken into protective custody and never again, he thought, closing his eyes later that night, would he try to stop Angelo Benfatto – or anyone else for that matter – from stealing some crummy television.

If he had had his way, Cashman would have kept Eddie's story all to himself. It was simply too explosive to risk leaking. While he had managed to keep Toole away, however, he had to trust Mahoney and Malreaux. They had discovered the story, and knew everything, so there was nothing to be done but to work as a team.

The four men ordered in Chinese food and stayed talking until close to midnight. An incredible weapon had been dropped into their laps, Cashman said, and they needed to figure out the best way to use it. Cashman explained how Dick Orlin had attempted to shut them out of their own case – and that they weren't about to let it happen again. Orlin was greedy only for notches in his own belt, while Cashman and Egan had long ago became more interested in their shadow men than in bonus points for themselves.

At first, Mahoney suggested going to Gino or Gianni with the story, and threatening to make it public if the men didn't give them certain requested information.

"A good idea," Egan told him. "Only I can assure you Eddie would be dead by nightfall, at the very least."

"We've got to go to the one whom the news can hurt most," Cashman said.

"You mean Sunni Ghianella?" Malreaux asked.

Egan paused between mouthfuls of General Tsao's chicken. "Not Sunni – Jimmy Feet."

"Isn't that just tipping him off as to what's going on?" Malreaux asked.

"Not if he can't get away," Egan smiled.

Mahoney and Malreaux looked at each other. It had been a long day and the cleverness of their own little interviews earlier had left them tired of word games.

Cashman sat back in his chair, putting his napkin on the table.

"Jimmy has been part of Manzino's inner circle since the beginning. We give him a choice – he can share his knowledge with us under the government's witness protection program, or we can feed him to the Manzino people, piece by piece, with every sordid detail of what he did to Sunni Manzino." Cashman chuckled. "The very family bonds that usually protect him will become the garrote enclosing his throat."

"And what if he doesn't co-operate?" Mahoney asked.

"Oh he'll co-operate," Cashman said. "This guy is a double-crossing coward. The only one he always looks after is himself."

The real task was to work together and in secrecy until Jimmy was in custody. After that, the story could leak all it wanted to. By then, Eddie Jelly Apples Rizzuto would be living under a new identity in Atlanta and Jimmy would be talking.

JIMMY WOULD BE guarded, but Cashman had few illusions about guaranteeing anyone's safety for the length of time it took to bring a case as complicated as this one to court. Even keeping the story quiet was a near impossibility, given the corruption within the department. He'd just have to put it off as long as possible.

CHAPTER
THIRTY-TWO

JIMMY FEET HAD never been a subtle man. He had an avid look and eyes that darted about strangely, so that even the most brutal and dissolute could sense an ugliness in him. The only person who seemed blind to his darker side was Angela. To Jimmy, Angela had long become indistinct, holding little more significance than the toast he had for breakfast, or the color of the lining in his jacket. His indifference toward her was so profound that he was scarcely aware of her presence and similarly oblivious to their children, in whom he had never displayed more than a cursory interest. Boys would only grow up to threaten him, while Sunni Manzino had been the only girl to truly catch his eye.

Angela, however, learned to cope by imagining Jimmy's devotion. Jimmy was never at home, but Angela told herself and anyone else who listened that this was because he worked so hard for his family. She spoke of him as a wonderful provider, as if her situation was no lonelier than that of any woman married to an ambitious man. However thoroughly he managed to cut her off, her life was always centered round him. And yet, in the most private corner of her heart, she felt a certain measure of gratitude that Jimmy spent so much time in the city. He was not unlike Uncle Enzio, who had made his wife Maria's life so miserable that in the end she found life better without him at all. With Jimmy in town,

Angela didn't have to fear his violence, those terrible black moments when he would strike out at her or the children like an animal smashing at the bars of a cage. Meanwhile, her feelings for him were so numb that he could no longer hurt her. Only on certain gray afternoons would she sometimes succumb to episodes of true despair, in which their large and empty house felt occupied only by the ghosts of all she had hoped and failed to attain. Eventually, however, she reached the final stage of resignation: defining her happiness in terms of the absence of pain, and not the presence of joy.

When Jimmy suddenly appeared at the house with three Federal agents posing as bodyguards, Angela – along with everyone else – had a difficult time believing Jimmy's story that they were relatives from New Orleans protecting him from the crazy temper of a jealous husband. Firstly, Jimmy didn't have relatives in New Orleans, and secondly, why was it that no one ever saw a sign of this mysterious predator? Angela, as usual, managed to dismiss the inconsistency, but others were not so casual.

When Jimmy had been whisked off the street by Mahoney and Malreaux, he was sure he was only going to be asked a whole lot of questions about which he would say and mean nothing. When the two cops unhanded him to Cashman and Egan, however, Jimmy felt a slight queasiness his stomach. He was sure that he had seen one of these fellows at least once before. Could it even have been at Sunni's wedding? By now, Cashman and Egan knew exactly what they wanted, and Cashman was so sure that Jimmy was lily-livered he cut to the quick.

"Mr. Rossetto," he said. "I'm going to keep this short. We know something about you, something that, for your own well-being, should go no further than this room. But in return for this favor to you, in return for your life, I am going to ask you to use your position in the inner circle of the Manzino family to help us acquire some information that is most important to us."

Jimmy twisted his face in mock disdain. "You can't possibly have anything on me," he said. "And I'm not in any inner circle either. Those Manzinos are as snooty to me now as they were the day I married their daughter. Anyone would think they did me a favor – instead of me taking her of their hands."

Egan looked at Cashman, who nodded to him to proceed.

"I'm afraid this is beyond the usual, Mr. Rossetto," he said, "you see the information we have, and that Gino Manzino would no doubt like very much to share, concerns a certain young woman –. "

"Daniella! That bitch. I told that little whore I'd cut her dead if she mentioned my name."

"It wasn't Daniella that we were – "

"Oh no? Who was it then? Genevieve, or another of Ms. Manzino's loyal school friends," Jimmy laughed. "Women. There's no use getting upset over any of them. They've all got girlfriends that are just as good."

Cashman couldn't believe what he was hearing. From the sound of it, Jimmy truly had kept his obsession alive – to the point of seducing Sunni's friends. Still, what it covered up was the true ugliness.

"To tell the truth, I think you'll find that Mr. Gino Manzino will be extremely interested in – shall I say your "special relation-ship" with his daughter Miss Sunni Manzino, now wife of Gianni Ghianella."

Jimmy's face suddenly lost all of its color. How could this terrible secret have gotten out?"

"I'll be honest with you Mr. Rossetto," Cashman said, as if reading Jimmy's mind. "It is not Mrs. Ghianella who has handed out your death sentence, but a private source who some time ago overheard you bragging about Mrs. Ghianella's personal body parts, as well as an attempted rape."

"Attempted rape! You must be insane!" Jimmy said.

"Manzino might not think so."

"But – this is blackmail."

Cashman and Egan rolled their eyes. Jimmy could feign in-dignation, but everyone knew he was stalling. "All right, all right," Jimmy finally said, acting as if he were doing them a favor. "I ain't gonna be pulled down by any girl or rat. What do I have to do?"

LEAVING THE STATION that evening, Jimmy quelled his fear at the magnitude of what he was about to do by summoning up all the anger he had felt for the Manzinos over the years. By the next morning, he had worked himself up into such a state that he really did feel Gino had maliciously snubbed him over the years, that Vinnie had done nothing but use him, and that Gianni, even now, barely tolerated him. It wasn't hard, over the next days and weeks, for Jimmy to justify – as Cashman had predicted – becoming an informant. He socialized with his old friends with ease – consciously displaying great camaraderie while secretly passing on any useful information. His bodyguards accompanied him day and night, standing watch over his home. Over the weeks, the reason given for them became more and more absurd. Finally, the council considered that this was just another way for Jimmy to give himself a puffed-up sense of importance. It was inconceivable that he would go against the family – after all, he had nothing else – and in the end some people suspected that he was actually trying to con the government, exchanging useless information for money.

Whatever was going on, both Jimmy's behavior and certain other ominous events, began making everyone extremely uncomfortable. A raid came down on a Jackson Heights warehouse – a disastrous raid on the entire clearinghouse for goods currently being gathered in truck hijackings. Soon after came a flurry of arrests, seizures of contraband and one particularly violent crisis that brought things to a sudden head. At the scene of a liquor hijacking, several trigger-happy Federal agents left five men dead, including Louis Campo's nineteen-year old son, Joey. Put together with several other rapid, inexplicable crackdowns, it seemed painfully obvious that Jimmy was betraying the organization.

While Gianni tried at first to shield Gino from such rumors, Gino was no fool. In a way, he had been waiting for such an outcome since the first day Jimmy showed up to court Angela. Nevertheless, the day a grief-stricken Louis went to Gino demanding an emergency meeting of all seventeen council members, Gino felt his heart sink. He had never liked Jimmy, but Angela was his first child, and a betrayal so close to home was always devastating. He and Gianni organized the meeting for that very night, out in a secluded sub-basement of a warehouse in Long Island City. Campo and his second son, Gabriel, were both there, looking both exhausted and edgy. So, of course, were Gianni and Gino, as well as some of the most powerful men in the city's underground, from the patrician Alfonse Salieri to the boss of bootlegging Frank Mazzo. Somber and hushed, the men filled the room with enough Cuban cigar smoke to mask the stench of nearby Newtown Creek. For Campo, the business of the evening was to avenge his son and plan the death of Jimmy Feet – a task plagued with obstacles, the greatest one being Gino Manzino.

After listening to the detailed run-down of recent losses, Gino made his request. "The ties of blood and marriage are so much stronger than the hostilities between men," Gino said, in a voice that conveyed his recent sense of peace. "There is yet a chance that Jimmy is not responsible. How would we feel then, killing blood for blood? In all the years we have met together, you have never heard me ask for special consideration. Tonight I have a very simple favor. Give me one day to make sure that these suspicions are right. If they are, you have lost nothing and I turn over my son-in-law to you. But for now, let us go to our homes and meet again tomorrow night. Campo, especially, needs to be with his family."

At the end of the table, Alfonse Salieri nodded in silence. At this stage in his life, Salieri's presence was almost honorary, rather like a chaplain blessing the troops before battle. Tonight, however, he had work to do and only twenty-four hours in which to do it.

BUTTONING HIS OVERCOAT against the evening's chill and hurrying to his oversized Buick, Alfonse Salieri did not drive to his home in Sheepshead Bay that he'd been sharing with his sister ever since his wife had fallen to cancer eight years earlier. He headed into Manhattan to the small west side apartment where he spent several nights each month. Carla Manzino was waiting for him when he arrived, rushing into his arms as much for her own comfort as for his. She was almost half his age, but that never seemed to matter. He was the kindest, most loving man she had ever known. At seventy, his gentle nature was in part a discipline to calm an erratic heart, so what time they had together was precious and further limited by the need for secrecy. Unfortunately, the world they inhabited was far too traditional to tolerate a man of Salieri's age and position sleeping with the daughter of his oldest friend, especially when Gino had entrusted him to keep a protective eye on her. After a few minutes, she took his coat and then brought him a glass of sherry as he settled on the deep cushions of the couch.

"There is something I must ask you to do for me," Salieri said, softly.

There was a pause during which Carla watched him with her dark, beautiful eyes, waiting for him to continue.

"Actually," he said, "it isn't just for me. It's for everyone we love most in the world."

Another moment of silence passed while she waited, studying him.

"Carla, I want you to tell Gino what Jimmy tried to do to Sunni."

Carla felt a chill crawl up her spine. For years, this secret had been a hidden sorrow, a horror still capable of awakening her in the middle of the night and hovering around her in the darkness. So many loyalties pulled at her when she thought of it – her promise to Sunni to keep it from Gino, her impulse to protect Angela, as well, of course, as her recurring desire to see Jimmy punished. Soon after she and Alfonse had become lovers, her recurring nightmare invaded one of the nights they were sharing. She had awakened, as always, in a cold sweat, but this time, Alfonse was there to hold her, bringing her sudden terror under control. It was then that she told him what she had told no one else: how Jimmy had tried to rape her little sister, Sunni, when she was twelve years old – in his wife's house with his own son sleeping down the hall.

"Why?" she asked. "Why do you want me to tell him now? You know that would be betraying my promise to Sunni."

"I know," Alfonse said grimly. "But I promise you it's for the best."

"Something must have happened to make you ask this? Can't

you tell me what it is?"

"Let's just say that the time has come, Carla. Jimmy's time has come."

Carla understood then that some kind of reckoning was taking place, and that Salieri would never put her or anyone in her family in a position to be hurt. Instinctively, she realized that she had been waiting for this for many a year now. Pulling on her coat the next morning and descending into a car Gino had sent for her, she was actually glad that some terrible imbalance in the universe was perhaps about to be addressed.

GINO HAD RECEIVED Carla's urgent phone call at seven in the morning. He didn't connect it to his worry about Jimmy, however, until Carla was inside his study in Connecticut, taking a fresh coffee from Gianni. Carla hadn't expected Gianni to be there and raised her eyebrows questioningly at her father. "I think perhaps I need to speak to you alone father," she said. Perhaps it was innocent – or perhaps it was a residual anger from the long-ago day when Carla had overridden his authority – but Gino put aside his daughter's concern and said, "There is nothing I cannot hear that Gianni cannot."

"But father," Carla said softly, setting down her coffee cup and leaning into Gino's desk. "It concerns Sunni."

Perhaps if the moment had been any different – if a chair had squeaked or a door creaked – Gianni wouldn't have heard Carla whisper his wife's name. But he did hear her, and once he had, the effect was final.

"What is it?" Gianni asked. "Is something wrong?"

"Sit down," Gino said to Gianni. "Tell us what you must, Carla."

"All right, then," Carla said, obviously with some discomfort. "But first you must know that I cannot speak for anyone but myself. I can only say what I saw and heard many years ago – and how it has haunted me ever since." Carla then described the country day when she had seen how Jimmy's presence had terrified Sunni, how on instinct she had gone to Sunni and demanded to know why, and how Sunni had let out a terrible secret.

Gianni jumped from his chair saying "Son of a bitch! What did he do to her?"

Carla told them all she knew, of how Jimmy had often tried to touch and fondle Sunni, in ways that frightened the girl, and how, finally, one drunken night when Sunni was babysitting for Angela Jimmy had come home and tried to rape Sunni, stripping her shirt from her and kissing her body but Sunni had knocked him out with a lampshade.

At this part of the story, Carla saw how the pallor of Gino's face darkening, as if his blood were thickening with wrath. "Why did she not tell anyone?" he finally said.

"Because," Carla said, looking at the window beyond her father, "She was afraid of what might happen. She was afraid it would destroy the family."

Gianni, who had been sitting and rubbing his face with his hands, finally looked up, direct into Gino's eyes. He didn't need to speak. Gino recognized what lay behind his gaze.

"You have done right," Gino said to Carla. "This will go no further than this room. Even Sunni must not know what you have told us, at least not yet. Don't be afraid, Carla," Gino said, "Jimmy was always a bad seed."

Carla nodded.

"I blame myself."

Carla went to protest, but Gino only waved his hand. "Ignazio will drive you home."

Carla lowered her eyes and went to the door. "I'm terribly sorry," she murmured to Gianni, who opened it for her.

"You needn't be," he said. "Justice will be done."

When the door closed, Gino and Gianni returned to their seats. A few moments passed in complete silence before Gino said in a quiet even tone, "It must be a 'clean' hit."

Gianni, who had his hands in a prayer like position before his face, nodded in reply.

"The Federal people must remain untouched," Gino continued. "If we miss they'll take him into hiding."

Gianni's face was grimmer than Gino had ever seen. "We won't miss," he said.

A few days later, Cashman received a phone call just as he was leaving the office.

"We've lost Ghianella," Malreaux told him.

Cashman mumbled "shit" several times before asking, "Okay, okay, where did it happen?"

"Actually," he said, somewhat embarrassed, "it was in a church."

"A church," Cashman said flatly, feeling the tension rise in his neck.

Cashman had assigned Mahoney and Malreaux to keep Gianni under surveillance ever since Jimmy Feet had begun to talk. As Sunni's father, Gino was likely to order a hit on Jimmy Feet, but the police wouldn't imagine that the family patriarch would do the work himself. Besides an anonymous hitman, Gianni was the man who seemed to pose the greatest threat.

Gianni had walked alone from his office to St. Dominick's, an old church beside the stone residence of Monsignor Peter Daly, one of the city's most influential clerics. When Malreaux and Mahoney rushed inside, they saw Gianni light a votive candle, then circle the altar and vanish. It took the detectives a few seconds to realize that Gianni hadn't simply been swallowed up by the shadows; he'd actually disappeared. Racing after him, they found a doorway tucked into the alcove behind the side altar that led to the deserted courtyard outside. From there, they could see the monsignor's limousine beyond the iron fence leaving the rectory next door and merging into cross-town traffic.

"Something's up," Cashman said, hanging up the phone. "Call Reed and tell him Gianni's gone."

Reed was one of Jimmy's three full-time bodyguards, the smartest of the three – considering that guard work is generally filled by the lower ten percent of any academy's graduating class. Reed took the call in his car and stepped on the pedal to get to Cavallos on 57th Street.

Every Thursday, Jimmy shared pasta there with Reed and his two other bodyguards, the burly Timothy and Rick. Jimmy always acted as if he were doing the guards a great favor, though they were actually the only steady dining companions he could rely on each week. Reed found the three men at the bar and they soon made their way through a late dinner crowd to the large center table. Jimmy ordered the fettuccine alla Romano and enough Chianti to keep him talking non-stop. The bodyguards had already seen and dismissed the aged waiter with the shuffling walk, a waiter they recognized from lunch on Tuesday who'd been sent by the union to replace another waiter on vacation. He might have been wary if he had ever approached their table, but he was always busy in another section and never took any notice of Jimmy. At that moment, Gianni Ghianella walked into the restaurant with Monsignor Daly.

Jimmy was so surprised to see him that he was only vaguely aware of Timothy and Rick reaching inside their jackets to grip their revolvers. The owner was falling all over himself, trying to impress the Monsignor with his magnanimous hospitality. They were led to a secluded table on the other side of the room where Gianni accepted the special bottle of wine brought over by the owner and then settled down to dinner, apparently unaware of the restaurant's other occupants.

The scene was so calm that the guards eventually relaxed their holds on their weapons, although they kept their eyes fixed on Gianni. As for Jimmy, he soon concluded that Gianni's apparent disinterest in him proved his cleverness at successfully concealing his double-dealing. He then returned his attention to the food and wine, scolding his guardians for being such babies.

Another minor flurry occurred a few minutes later when three plainclothes policemen, including Cashman quietly walked through the entrance. Egan, who had been overexposed even more than Cashman, was waiting outside in a car. When Cashman saw Jimmy and Gianni dining at separate tables, innocently eating their pasta, it took him a moment to make sure he was seeing things clearly. Then he stood at the bar with the other cops and ordered some beer, watching both of them closely. At one point, Gianni glanced toward Jimmy's table as though he was surprised to see him there, caught Jimmy's eye and raised his wineglass in a gesture of salute. Jimmy confidently returned the greeting and then the two turned back to their meals.

With all the attention focused on Gianni, the old waiter became even more inconspicuous as he tidied up the unoccupied tables. He'd been in the restaurant since the shift began at ten, working adequately through a busy lunch. There had been plenty of time to sabotage the toilet in the second stall before the full crowd arrived when an early customer tried to use it, flooding his dropped trousers. The stall was locked behind an "Out of Order" sign.

The assassin told the cook it was time for his afternoon break and left the dining room by the back door. He then hurried along the alley way, climbed up the crates he had previously positioned, and lowered himself through the window into the locked stall. The metal screen in the window had been filed through the night before and pushed back into place. He removed the pistol, silencer in place, from the pocket sewn on the inside of his oversized trousers and crouched on the damaged toilet so that no part of him showed above or below the door. Then he waited for Jimmy, who could be counted on to make at least two trips to the men's room during any meal.

As if on cue, a bodyguard pushed open the bathroom door just a few minutes later and glanced quickly around the room. Muttering that all was clear, he went back out and Jimmy came in. The guard stood in the corridor, keeping a watch on Gianni in case he approached the bathroom. But Gianni and the Monsignor were sharing sherry and casual laughter, apparently oblivious to the fact that they were being studied. Meanwhile, Cashman and his cops were still nursing beers at the bar.

Jimmy went directly to the urinal, humming softly and rather tunelessly as he unzippered and began to relieve himself. He never heard the stall door swing open behind him, but he did hear a familiar voice.

"Hello, Jimmy."

Jimmy turned his head at the sound, cock in hand, and found himself staring into the eyes of the aged waiter. The impression blurred and Jimmy saw the makeup that had robbed the face of its distinctive features, saw the shapeless waiter's uniform and the deliberate slump in his posture, saw the facial expressions and gestures designed to resemble someone slow of thought, saw the walk meant to imitate the shuffle of aging Sicilians, common among men more accustomed to wearing sandals than shoes – and his look of horror became one of silent recognition.

The assassin fired the first silenced bullet between Jimmy's eyes, slamming his head into the sweating wall tile. Two more bullets were pumped into his chest, Jimmy's body slumped to the floor, and then he inserted the pistol into Jimmy's mouth at an upward angle, firing three times. He cursed him bitterly, then spit into the blasted remains.

By the time all three bodyguards had burst through the door, Gino had left the way he had come and was driving home, leaving the darkening city streets between himself and his final act as a warrior.

CASHMAN WAS STARING at Gianni Ghianella, who had joined the mob outside the bathroom.

"It's a good thing I came with the Monsignor," Gianni said. "At least he'll be able to give Jimmy last rites," then he gave a small smile and left the restaurant.

Cashman could never condone the violent way in which these people lived, especially the way they punished their own. Yet at the same time he had to respect a system that brought about so decisive a retaliation as that against the child-molesting Jimmy Feet. When he saw Jimmy's crumpled body, Cashman had to admit that he had heard of far worse tortures for a man who had done far less. One thing he knew: nothing would tie Gino Manzino or Gianni Ghianella to this crime – not a fingerprint or a hair, or even the blink of an eye. Cashman and Egan had done well in their work with Jimmy Feet; both would be awarded raises and citations. Eventually the task force would go away and they would still be there, watching and following, tracking their elusive prey from the darkness. At least, Cashman thought, some men managed to fashion a strange and rare art from their brief lives.

Two hours later Gianni slipped into bed beside Sunni, who woke up to welcome him, as always.

"You'll have to go over and stay with Angela in the morning," he whispered. "Jimmy was killed tonight."

For several moments she was absolutely still. When she could speak again, she said, "Gianni, did you . . . ."

"It wasn't me, Sunni. No one knows who's responsible. There's some talk on the street that the government people may have done it."

"But why would they do that?" she asked.

"Maybe to protect themselves."

Suddenly, Sunni bolted from the bed toward the phone, and Gianni could see that she was beginning to tremble.

As she dialed her father in Connecticut, Gianni rose from the bed and came to her, but she extended a hand in a silent plea to be left alone for a moment. Gianni sighed and held his place. As soon as Gino answered, Sunni blurted out, "Oh Pappa, have you heard about Jimmy?"

"Yes, Sunni," Gino said softly.

"Pappa, he was a terrible man," Sunni said, her voice quivering.

"I know." There was a pause and Sunni felt her father's rush of understanding. It was as close as they had ever come to addressing her dark secret. "He made your sister suffer for so long," he added.

All at once Sunni was crying, then sobbing so strongly that the tears seemed to be flowing from an inner pool. Gianni gently took the phone from her and told Gino that she would be all right, then quietly hung up the phone. He carried her back to bed and held her through her long surrender to grief, then brought her back to life with his hands and his body, melting into her again and again, restoring her vitality.

Alone in an unlighted room, Gino felt his fragile link with

Sunni's voice, and suddenly his mind skimmed over the surface of every moment they had shared, looking for some special place to rest. He thought of the days they had spent in Sicily, moving through the warm sunlight, searching for the valley of the silver dancers that Giovanni had told him about. The story of those ghostly figures in the mist had become the centerpiece of their family mythology, a tale rendered all the more believable because it originated with a man so unimaginative. Sunni had been somehow half-convinced that if they could find the right hillside, she could recreate the experience, as though she were mystically connected to her grandmother's world. But there were so many valleys that they could never be sure they had found the right one. Finally, they settled on one hollow and waited there for the sun to fall. But the evening chill chased them home before the moonlight could create its phantoms.

"Who do you think the dancers were?" she had asked him.

"No one really knows," said Gino. "Our ancestors, maybe."

Sunni was silent for a while as she tried to imagine their beauty and grace. "Pappa," she said, "couldn't they be from the future, a vision of happiness?"

Even Sunni's spontaneous innocence could never erase the sadness, the hard edges of reality that life had forced Gino to accept. But over the years, it was her childlike faith that had fulfilled the message of the sliver dancers. When you've lived long enough, Gino decided, and experienced more loss and pain than you ever thought you could handle, you earned the freedom of your own beliefs.

For most of the remaining night, Gino remained seated behind his scarred desk. No lamps were lit, but he was never in darkness. Above his head a large round window of beveled glass was filtering the moonlight through its facets, gathering the fragments of silver light and scattering them across the glimmering room like a thousand tiny dancers.